Praise for Lesley Lokko

'Be sure to add *A Private Affair* to the must-read pile too. A pacey read, it chronicles the lives of a cornucopia of complex characters . . . as they attempt to navigate the tricky waters of love and friendship' *Herald*

'A blockbuster with brains . . . the ultimate guilty pleasure'
Bella

'Perfect for a lengthy spot of tanning . . . immerse yourself in the lives of four women looking for love' *Grazia*

'A sexy, sophisticated page-turner' *Eve*

'Very exciting from start to finish. It's well-written, engaging and fast-paced, with a plot you'll be gripped by . . . I couldn't put it down' *Daily Mail*

'A delicious tale of power, revenge and true friendship'
Daily Express

'This is everything you'd expect of a blockbuster – glamorous locations, ambitious female protagonists and a singing, gliding narrative – but with a little more intelligence' *Glamour*

'A very 21st-century blockbuster . . . Much more than a coming-of-age tale, this creates a glamorous and exciting world that is so contemporary and convincing you'll feel like a special fifth member of their group' *Cosmopolitan*

'So engrossing, you'll want to read through your lunchbreak'
New Woman

After various careers from cocktail waitress to kibbutz worker, Lesley Lokko trained as an architect. Several novels later, Lesley now splits her time between Johannesburg and London. Find out more at www.lesleylokko.com

By Lesley Lokko

Sundowners
Saffron Skies
Bitter Chocolate
Rich Girl, Poor Girl
One Secret Summer
A Private Affair

A Private Affair

Lesley Lokko

An Orion paperback

First published in Great Britain in 2011
by Orion
This paperback edition published in 2012
by Orion Books Ltd,
Orion House, 5 Upper St Martin's Lane
London WC2H 9EA

An Hachette UK company

1 3 5 7 9 10 8 6 4 2

Copyright © Lesley Lokko 2011
ISBN 978-1-4091-0246-5

Typeset at The Spartan Press Ltd,
Lymington, Hants

Printed and bound in Great Britain by Clays Ltd,
St Ives plc

The Orion Publishing Group's policy is to use papers that
are natural, renewable and recyclable products and
made from wood grown in sustainable forests. The logging
and manufacturing processes are expected to conform to
the environmental regulations of the country of origin.

www.orionbooks.co.uk

Acknowledgements

Grateful thanks go to the website www.small-wars.com for their invaluable insights and considerable resources; to the book, *Sniper One*, by Sgt Dan Mills (Michael Joseph, London: 2007) and to the following websites: http://junglefighter.panamanow.net and www.worlddaily.net; and to the indomitable and incomparable Robert Fisk. As ever, friends and family have provided everything a writer could hope for by way of love and support. I would especially like to thank Sara Rowatt for her help and insights, and all the women of the e-bluey chatboard. Thank you enormously to Chrissie and Terry Farrell of Brisbane, Australia, who offered such kind words and thoughts during a particularly hellish month; to Patrick, Victor, EP and Sean in Accra; John, Rahesh, Jonathan, Yaw and Samir in London; the wonderful Biriwa boys and especially to Carsten Höller for his fabulous birthday bash in snowy Skeppsholmen; to the entire Jozi crowd, newcomers and old-timers alike, and to my agent, Kate Shaw – so nice to finally have you on board. I'd also like to thank Diane Banks, Jonathan Lloyd and Sarah Douglas for their generosity and insight in the early stages of this novel. Paris Pitsillides gave so generously of his time and translation efforts in the research around Cyprus; Kay Preston and Margie Wilson are, as ever, wonderful sources of insight and understanding and finally, and by no means lastly, I'd like to dedicate this book (as I said I would) to *all* those wonderful girls – Achieng, Ana, Audrey, Bärbel, Bridget, Carole, Caroline, Christina, Denise, Dee, Eva, Farhana, Frieda, Hannah, Heidi, Irene, Jutta, Kate M, Kate O, Kgomotso, Lisa, Liz, Mali, Marilí, Maz, Moky, Nana Amu, Nana P, Nane, Paula, Poem, Rawia, Rinnette, Rebs, Rootie, Sandy, Sharmini, Sonja, Spank, Tash,

Tselane, Veronica and Winnie – who picked me up, dusted me down and put me back together again. From the bottom of my heart, *thank you*.

Whilst some of the events depicted in the novel are based on historical fact, including the war in Sierra Leone, readers are advised to note that timings in some cases have been very slightly altered by the author. No offence is meant by these changes and the author sincerely hopes readers will forgive the occasional departure from historic accuracy in the interests of maintaining the pace and timing of the story.

This one's for Eva, pint-sized diva.

It worked!

'We have all become people according to the measure in which we have loved other people, and have had occasion for loving.'

Boris Pasternak

PART ONE

Prologue

Celle, Germany, 2009

It was snowing; flakes fell in light, feathery circles, whirling slowly through the air. She had forgotten to put on her gloves. She brought her hands up to try and protect her face but it was pointless. He brushed them aside as if they were nothing more than a distraction. He grabbed her hair, twisting her head around so that she was forced to look up at him. His pale blue eyes flickered over her face without expression. Nothing. She could feel herself saying something . . . a word or two, a plea . . . perhaps even in her own language, she couldn't tell. He took no notice. He slapped her lightly, almost teasingly and then he drew back his hand, correcting his aim. There was a moment's hesitation and then the weight of his fist made contact with her cheek. She felt the crack of her own jaw and then the sickening rush of inky black pain. She saw stars. Her mouth filled with blood. A second's pause, another awful wait, and then another punch, and another and another. Her mouth felt pulpy and warm. Suddenly there was ice on her teeth. It took her a moment to work out that the cold, sandy stuff in her mouth was grit, mixed with ice. She was on the ground. She was lying face down, brought there by the force of the blow. He was big, almost twice her size, and when he hauled her roughly to her feet again, she was as weightless as snow.

'Cunt.' The word hissed outwards, compressed between his lips and teeth. 'You fucking cunt.' He said it again and again, marking it with a blow, sometimes a kick. She could see his boots . . . polished black boots. She caught a glimpse of her own

3

face reflected in the shine. She felt the steel cap prod her before he kicked her, hard and fast. The poker-hot stab of pain went all the way up to the roots of her hair. He bent down, his face very near to hers as he pulled her coat from her shoulders and tossed it to one side. She was already cold – colder than she could ever have imagined but there was a chill on her bare skin that had nothing to do with the wind. He grabbed the material of her skirt, tearing it as he yanked it off her hips.

'No . . . please, no.'

'Cunt.'

'No, no.'

'Shut your fucking face.' The exchange lasted less than a second. Another slap to the side of her face and then he was on top of her, smothering her with his bulk and weight. He wrapped one thick, meaty hand around her neck and pushed her knees apart. She'd never felt anything like it. He was splitting her in two. The pain was overwhelming. She could feel herself sliding in and out of consciousness as his hand closed around her throat, choking her, cutting off her breath. The growl that came out of his throat seemed to have come from something else . . . an animal, perhaps. Human beings didn't make that sort of sound, she thought wildly to herself as she struggled desperately underneath him. Who could do this? No human being, surely. No one. Not even him.

She'd been with him once before – not like this, not out here in the open with the snow all around them and him tearing the clothes off her, choking her, but she'd known that first and only time that he was capable of anything. That was why she'd refused to go with him. 'Let one of the other girls take him,' she'd whispered to Birgit. 'I don't want to. I'm afraid of him.' Birgit nodded; she was a good worker, a good earner . . . she rarely made a fuss. If she really didn't want to go with him, she wouldn't be made to. It was one of the unspoken rules at Judy's, which was why she'd wound up staying there. It was safer there than anywhere else. Birgit had offered him someone else but he'd turned and walked out instead. They'd all breathed a sigh

4

of relief as they watched him go. They were a strange bunch, those British soldiers, even though bars like Judy's relied on them. No trouble, for the most part, but every once in a while an odd one would come along with an anger that was so raw and desperate and unknowable buried inside them that no number of visits could release it. Those were the ones to watch out for. Awful things could happen; the girls sensed it somehow and if they were smart, they walked away, turned the job down. Judith knew it; she made sure the bookers knew it too. If a girl felt the fear – it came off some of them like a sweat – then she wouldn't be made to go back. But he'd come after her anyway. That was the other thing she'd seen in him that time. He wasn't the sort to take 'no' for an answer. She should have known.

1

SAM
Notting Hill, London, 2009

7.01 a.m. Sam Maitland opened one bleary eye and glanced across the room. In the dark her alarm clock glowed a luminous, digital blue. *7.02 a.m.* In exactly three minutes she would push back her warm duvet and get out of bed. She closed her eyes, trying to claw back the last few minutes of her dream but it was gone. The clock slid soundlessly on. She burrowed her toes into the sheets . . . *7.04 a.m.* One last, blissful minute and then it went off, signalling the end of sleep. She sighed and reluctantly swung her legs out of bed. She stumbled across the bedroom floor to the bathroom and switched on the light, catching sight of her reflection on the way to the shower. Tangled hair, smudged mascara, a crease across her left cheek . . . thank God it was Friday. She'd been out drinking with two of her colleagues the night before. Fortunately not a heavy session, just a couple of glasses of red wine (and a single shot of whisky and a mouthful of someone's tequila) to finish off an unusually long and hard week.

She opened the glass door to the shower and switched it on. Within seconds, the room was filled with steam. She gave herself up gratefully to the hot, pummelling jets of water. Ten minutes later, her thick, blonde hair washed and combed, she was finally awake. She wrapped herself in her white robe and walked into the living room. She flicked on the TV, listening with half an ear to the news as she made herself a bowl of cereal. Her mind was already skipping several hours ahead to the meeting that Peter Linman, her boss, had scheduled with a

7

group of new clients – Americans, generally twice as demanding as everyone else with a keen eye for what they called 'the bottom line'. It was a line that always made her smile. She carried her cereal over to the couch and leaned across to her answering machine to play her messages.

'Hi, Sam. Peter here. Just a reminder that we're meeting Mark Silverman and his team at nine forty-five tomorrow, not ten. We'll have a quick coffee in the boardroom on the eleventh floor before we go in. Hope the view'll soften them up. See you tomorrow.'

'Hey, Sam . . . it's me. Give me a ring back when you can. This week, preferably. Oh, it's my birthday on Friday. In case you'd forgotten.'

'Good afternoon, Miss Maitland. It's the concierge from Chepstow Road. You've got two packages . . .'

'Hi, Sam . . . it's me again. Call me tonight when you get in, will you? I've got something to tell you. Doesn't matter how late.' She smiled as she erased the messages. Two were from Paula – best friend, extraordinary jewellery-maker and the most scatter-brained, hopelessly disorganised and yet brilliant person she'd ever met. *No, I haven't forgotten your birthday*, she mouthed silently at the phone. As *if*. Paula rang every year to remind her and at thirty-nine there'd been a fair few reminders. She finished her cereal and switched off the TV. It was 7.45 a.m. Time to get moving.

Fifteen minutes later, she was ready. She quickly checked her reflection in the mirror. Her hair was pulled back into a loose ponytail at the nape of her neck, held in place with a tortoise-shell comb. She was wearing her favourite black Armani suit with the knee-length skirt that flared just a little at the back and a fitted jacket. A stiff white shirt with a discreet ruffle at the collar, a thin gold chain and two large gold hoop earrings, killer heels (Blahnik, of course) and the heavy, antique gold ring she always wore on the third finger of her left hand – defiantly, her friends teased her – good to go.

She locked her front door and ran down the stairs. Her little silver sports car was parked outside. She pressed the alarm, opened the satisfyingly heavy door and slid inside. The smell of new leather never failed to thrill her. She loved her car. It had been a thirty-fifth birthday present to herself. A little expensive, granted, but definitely worth it. There was nothing quite like coming home in it after a long, tough day at work. She slung her briefcase onto the back seat, started the engine and pulled smartly into the thickening stream of traffic heading towards the Bayswater Road. Her offices were on North Row, just off Park Lane. On a good day, less than a five-minute drive. She really ought to walk to work or take the bus. But she'd worked so long and bloody hard to get to where she was that a short drive to and from the place she spent nearly every waking hour seemed a luxury definitely worth having.

'Morning, Miss Maitland.' Jim, the young, good-looking parking attendant turned up the full wattage of his smile as she opened her door. It was an open secret in the firm that his brightest, toothiest grins were reserved for her.

'Thanks.' She handed him the keys and quickly made her way to the lifts. She'd no desire to stop and flirt with Jim – or with anyone for that matter. Flirting made her uncomfortable. She'd never been any good at it, either. Too serious by half, according to most.

'Morning, Sam. Peter's already gone up.' Claire, her PA, looked up as she walked into her office. She handed her a large mug of black coffee and a stack of files. 'He said to let you know that Sue Walsh'll be joining you shortly.'

Sam's heart sank. Sue Walsh was the head of legal counsel in their New York office. Sue Walsh joining them could mean only one thing: the case would neither be as clear-cut or short as they'd all hoped. Well, everyone except Peter Linman, that was. He would be delighted. The longer the case, the more billable hours the firm could rack up. Having just spent the best part of the previous year on a similar case, Sam was praying for a quick end to this one. In three days' time she was going on holiday – her first proper holiday in almost five years. Six days at a luxury spa just outside Marrakech and there was no way she was giving it up or even postponing it, Sue Walsh or no.

She made her way towards the lift, her coffee and the stack of files in hand, her mind already on the meeting ahead. She hadn't had time to go through the files in as much detail as she normally did, or would have liked. From what she'd gathered, it seemed to be a pretty straightforward example of rights having been assigned to the wrong party – nothing unusual in that. The plaintiff – an English writer living in LA – had signed away an option on a screenplay at a ridiculously low rate. Now that the studio intended turning it into a film, they'd tried to muscle him off the job. It happened all the time. The firm Sam worked for – Bellitte, Hazelby, Forman, Lazards – was one of the top entertainment law firms in the world. If there was anyone who could sort out that sort of mess, it was them. She briefly wondered how an impoverished screenwriter could afford their legal fees but that was Peter's problem, not hers. She gulped down another scalding mouthful of coffee and pressed the lift button.

'See you later,' Claire called out as the lift doors opened. 'Don't forget . . . you've got dinner with Soltermann and Jim Burns later on. I've booked The American Grill at the Savoy.' She laughed at Sam's expression. 'Ah. I take it you forgot?' Sam nodded frantically. 'Don't worry. I'll nip out at lunchtime and get you a shirt. Pink?' she hazarded a guess, looking down at Sam's heels. Sam nodded again.

'Thanks, Claire, you're a star.' Claire's reply was lost as the doors closed and the lift moved smoothly upwards. Sam gulped down the rest of her coffee, made sure her hair was in place and turned her attention to the meeting ahead. If there was one thing Peter relied on her for, it was her ability to focus on the issues at hand. There were other lawyers in the firm who were either much quicker or able to think more laterally than her – but there were few with her diligence. She was rarely the one to put forward an argument that no one had thought of, or try an angle that others might view as risky – no, her skill lay in focusing on the details, seeing things that others in their haste might have forgotten. She was dogged and determined and there was little she missed. She'd been like that since school days – never the best or the brightest or even the one others thought most likely to succeed. That honour had always gone to her twin sister, Kate. Kate was quick off the mark, silver-tongued and flighty. Sam wasn't. A slow burner, everyone said, although she herself had her doubts. She wasn't one to burn full stop – *that* was the point. She was careful and considered and in her area of law those were the skills required. It was why she'd chosen it. She'd long ago come to the realisation that life was best lived according to one's skills, not one's weaknesses. It was the sole reason she'd been made a junior partner at BHFL ahead of her peers – she knew what she was good at and she stuck to it. In her teens, she'd tried desperately to be somebody she clearly wasn't and although it had been twenty years since then, the memory of the pain it caused her still stung. She wouldn't make *that* mistake again in a hurry. Once was quite enough, thank you very much.

'Ah, Sam . . . lovely. Glad you could make it a little early. Sue, you remember Sam Maitland? She worked with us on the Napster case.'

'Absolutely. Good to see you, Sam. Now, are we all here? Let me bring you up to speed . . .'

Sam quickly took her seat at the end of the table, pulled out her notebook and banished all thoughts of her unhappy teenage years *and* the thought of her upcoming holiday out of her mind.

2

Three days later, almost at the end of the day, she filed away the same stack of case notes, not quite as clear as she would have liked to be about their strategy, but for once in her professional life, she didn't care. It was almost four p.m. In approximately fifteen minutes her car would arrive and she'd be whisked away to Heathrow. Fifteen minutes; a quarter of an hour. It had been *years* since she'd watched the clock at work but today was an exception. She couldn't have picked a better day to leave London. It was raining, of course, a thin, watery drizzle that had lasted for almost a week and showed no signs whatsoever of abating, the sort of weather that made you want to weep in sympathy. Wasn't spring supposed to be on its way? She began organising her desk, tidying things away. There were a couple of loose sheets lying next to her keyboard – she glanced at them hesitantly.

'Come on.' Claire's voice broke into her thoughts. 'Put 'em away. Hand 'em over. Every last one.'

Sam looked up guiltily. Claire was standing in the doorway, grinning knowingly at her. 'But what if—' Sam began.

'No. No "what ifs". You're going on holiday, Sam. Come on . . . that one too.'

'But—'

'No "buts", either. If there's anything earth-shatteringly important, we'll call.'

'Promise?'

'Promise. Ah.' Claire glanced at the flashing phone. 'Looks like your car's here.'

Sam held up her hands in defeat. 'OK, you win. Call me if anything urgent crops up.'

'We will. Don't you worry. And for God's sake *enjoy* yourself!' Claire said sternly. 'You *do* know how, don't you?'

'Of course I do!' Sam protested, picking up her neat, compact little suitcase. 'I'll . . . I'll send you a postcard.'

'You do that. And here's hoping you find a nice young man whilst you're out there.' Claire laughed. 'Just for fun, nothing else,' she added hastily, seeing Sam's face. 'A fling, that's all. It'd do you good.'

Sam could feel her cheeks reddening. With one memorable exception, she was just about the last person on the planet to go on holiday and have a fling. In fact, she was just about the last person on earth with whom to have a fling in the first place. She was no good at flirting and she was most certainly no good at flings. Another area in which she was 'too serious by half', according to Philip, her best (and only) male friend. She mumbled a hasty reply, grabbed her coat and made her way out of the office before Claire could say anything further on the subject and embarrass her even more.

'Terminal Five, please,' she instructed the driver as she clambered into the back of the cab. She looked at her watch. Her flight to Marrakech was at seven p.m. – plenty of time. She would go upstairs to the plush business-class lounges, have a soothing glass of wine and get started on her holiday reads . . . perhaps stop off at duty-free on the way to the gate and get herself a pair of sunglasses? She looked out the window and gave a little shiver. The latest weather report had the temperature in Marrakech at 24°C. Given that it was currently 4°C in London, the thought of the warmth and sunlight to follow was nothing short of a relief. She looked down at her tickets. Claire, ever efficient, had organised everything. Business-class tickets on BA, *her* favourite airline, never mind the rest of the world; a week at a small, exquisite-looking boutique hotel, Dar les Cigognes, *and* drivers to pick her up from the airport on both legs of the journey. Dear Claire. She made a mental note to herself to get her something nice to say thank you.

She leaned back against the seats and closed her eyes. It had been a long, hard week. Peter had almost had a heart attack when she told him she was going on holiday. 'You're doing *what*?' He'd stared at her in disbelief. '*You're* going on holiday?' The emphasis wasn't lost on her. Although she was hardly the only lawyer at BHFL who wasn't either married, engaged or firmly partnered, she was probably the only one who'd *never* brought anyone other than a friend to any of the countless social events that the firm laid on. No one at BHFL had ever seen a 'significant other', as the spouses and partners of BHFL's employees were known. It was no secret that Sam Maitland, one of the firm's most successful and well-liked lawyers, had never had a 'significant other'. Neither, to Peter Linman's knowledge, had she ever gone on holiday. 'A holiday?' he repeated disbelievingly. 'You?'

She'd nodded firmly though she'd felt anything but firm. 'It's only a week, Peter,' she'd said, trying to sound more confident than she felt. 'I'll be back before you know it. Fighting fit, too.' He made no comment, simply twisted his lips in the manner that she knew only too well and stalked off.

Well, here she finally was, en route to Marrakech. It had better be worth it, she thought to herself as the taxi pulled up in the drop-off lane. She collected her bags from the boot, tipped the driver and carried her things through to check-in. Ten minutes later, she was on her way up the escalators to the lounges, trying somewhat unsuccessfully to banish all thoughts of Peter Linman and her current case load from her mind.

The flight to Marrakech was short and smooth. She accepted a glass of Sancerre from the friendly flight attendant and picked up one of her four holiday novels. After a few minutes she put it down, unable to concentrate. She was too excited. She couldn't remember the last time she'd had time to read anything other than a case file or one of the heavy legal tomes that sat on shelves around her office. She owned a share in a cottage in one of those gorgeous little French villages in the countryside of the kind that only exist in films or books until you actually go there and see it for yourself. She'd been talked into it by a group of colleagues at work and although they'd bought it almost two years earlier, aside from the initial trip to *see* it, she'd never actually spent a night there. There was something about the long drive from Paris or Avignon all on her own that was too depressing to contemplate. Staying in a luxury boutique hotel was different; there was always someone on hand to talk to, even if it was only the bellhop. Stop right there, she cautioned herself quickly. No need to go down *that* nasty little road, thank you very much. You're on holiday, Samantha Maitland. Nothing else mattered and certainly not any sort of reflection on the state of her lacklustre love-life. *Lack*lustre? She had to smile, in spite of herself. Non-existent would be nearer the mark. What was it Paula had said the night before when she'd finally found half an hour to call her back? 'Less isn't more, darling. *Some* would be good.'

'Don't *you* start,' she'd shot back. 'Just because it's been a bumper summer for you.' Paula was forever falling in and just as promptly out of love. No sooner had she phoned up with a blow-by-blow description of the man of her dreams whom she'd invariably only just met, than she rang a week later with a blow-by-blow description of his demise. Sam had long since lost count of the number of times Mr Right had made an appearance in Paula's life. The speed with which she moved – and moved on – was breathtaking. It was different for Sam. She couldn't remember the last time someone had asked her out on a second date. She didn't know what the problem was. She seemed to have no trouble attracting the initial glance – at five foot eight with a size-twelve figure and thick blonde hair she'd have to have been covered in warts, as Philip said, *not* to. But even though she got asked out on a regular enough basis, nothing ever seemed to come of it, or her attempts to take things further. 'Face it, Sam,' Philip told her earnestly. 'You frighten the pants off most men. You're smarter than most women I know, which makes you smarter than every single man I know. You *earn* more than most people I know. You're gorgeous, granted, but Christ, you scare me half the time and I've known you for ever. Don't forget I knew you way back when.'

'Don't remind me, please,' Sam said drily. It was true. She'd known Philip McGovern since she was eleven or twelve and the Sam Maitland who lived at 24 Georgiana Street in Camden bore absolutely no resemblance to the Sam Maitland who now lived at Flat 6, 16 Palace Court, Notting Hill. The Sam Maitland Philip referred to was hugely overweight, covered in spots, wore thick glasses *and* had a stammer to boot. That Sam Maitland lived almost exclusively in the shadow of her twin sister, Kate, who was not overweight, nor prone to spots, nor painfully shy. Kate Maitland was petite, slender, dark-haired and dark-eyed and was the object of almost every teenage boy's fantasy. Kate Maitland was the star; Sam wasn't. Simple as that. Everyone knew it and none more vociferously so than her mother.

It was only when Sam moved away to university in Bristol that things began to change. Kate went to University College Hospital, just down the road from home, and became a doctor. She met Grant, a fellow medical student, within days of starting her course. Within days of finishing it, they got married. Grant became a surgeon, Kate a GP. They moved to Surbiton and bought a big house and had two beautiful children in quick succession. Now, at thirty-nine, Kate had lost the sultry good looks for which she'd been so famous at school and had begun to 'spread around the middle', as she put it. When they met, which wasn't as often as Kate would have liked, there was a bitter tinge to her voice that hadn't been there before. It had taken Sam some time to realise that the balance of power between them had changed. According to Kate, Sam was now the one with the glamorous, fast-paced life, not her. Sam did Pilates and ate in restaurants Kate had never heard of. Sam earned pots of money and although Kate and Grant were hardly short of it, they had two daughters in private schools and an enormous mortgage to consider. Sam, in other words, had everything. Kate did not. 'But isn't that what you always wanted?' Sam enquired once, mildly irritated by her moaning. 'No, it bloody well isn't,' Kate snapped. And that was the end of *that* conversation.

'Ladies and gentlemen . . .' The captain's voice interrupted her; they were preparing for the descent into Marrakech. She folded away her table, stowed her belongings and looked out of the window. The night was like a thick, dense blanket over Marrakech. Far below, sparkling like a thousand solitary gems, she could just make out the city's glittering shoreline. There would be someone waiting for her in the arrivals hall, Claire had told her. She fervently hoped so. It was her first time to Morocco and if the hotel brochure was anything to go by, it promised nothing but peace, tranquillity and luxury, a winning combination if there ever was one.

Madame Sam Mattieland. The neatly if erroneously typed sign was held aloft by an anxious-looking young man as she came through the glass sliding doors. She waved at him. He sprang forward, collected her bags and shepherded her through the waiting throng to where a taxi was indeed waiting. He stowed everything away, made sure she was comfortably settled into the back seat and then jumped into the front. It was an old, extremely well-looked-after Mercedes. Sam leaned back against the leather seats, trying not to smile.

The hotel was located in the old Jewish quarter, he explained, as they wound their way slowly from the airport into the city. It was nearly eleven o'clock but the city was full of life. There were people everywhere – little stalls selling food on the edges of what should have been the pavement had it not been turned into a small market. He drove her around the edge of the famous Djemaa el Fna, full of tourists and locals, shopping, eating, being entertained. Sam watched everything through the window, already charmed. When he pulled up in front of an elegant townhouse in the middle of a winding little street, she gave a deep, heartfelt sigh of genuine satisfaction. It was everything the brochure promised, and more.

3

'And in here,' the girl said, pushing open a door to reveal an exquisitely decorated room in pastel shades with a soaring, vaulted ceiling, 'is your private sitting room.' Sam caught her breath. There were roses everywhere – stunning bunches of delicate pinks, whites, pale yellows – standing next to ornately decorated bowls of fruit and a couple of decanters of deep burgundy wine. A fireplace in one corner and an intricately carved bookcase full of interesting-looking titles completed the room.

'Thank you,' she murmured breathlessly. Her suitcase had already been brought up; the bed had been turned down . . . she could already feel herself beginning to unwind.

'Our pleasure. If there's anything at all you need, just dial zero. The reception desk is manned twenty-four hours. Enjoy your evening.' The girl smiled and closed the door soundlessly behind her, and Sam was alone. She crossed the room to the window and pushed open the wooden shutters, letting the cooler night air rush into the room. The Atlas mountains were somewhere in the distance; the roof terraces all around her were lit up with beautiful, soft twinkling lights. She stood for a moment, breathing in the scented night air, then she turned and looked at the room once more. She almost hugged herself in delight. She walked over to the foot of the bed and unzipped her suitcase. She took out the carefully folded kaftans, linen dresses and soft cashmere cardigans that she'd brought along and hung everything in the carved wooden wardrobe. Ten minutes later, her belongings neatly stowed away, she poured herself a large glass of wine and walked into the bathroom. She ran herself a bubble bath, slipped off her robe and stepped in. It was bliss. The water was hot but not scalding, the bubbles lightly perfumed. She took another sip of wine and slid down further into the scented water. The holiday stretched lazily out in front of her. Six days of nothing to do but read, eat and sleep.

Her skin was rosy and wrinkled by the time her wine was finished and she stepped out of the tub. She walked through into the bedroom, pulled her damp hair into a knot and drew back the sheets. She climbed in, luxuriating in the feel of crisp cool linen against her skin. She sank further into the bed, stretching her legs as far as they would go. She was tired. The following morning, she thought to herself drowsily, she would get up late, eat a leisurely breakfast on the terrace and begin reading one of the novels she'd brought with her. Which one? She tried to picture the covers but her mind began to cloud over, foggy with wine and an overwhelming sense of delicious lassitude. The soft pastel colours of the room ran together and her mind slipped free. She slept.

4

A morning can be passed in any number of ways, not just in the sense of time passing. Sam's first morning was spent in warm sunlight on her own private terrace overlooking the narrow street, the splendid white line of the Atlas mountains just visible somewhere far off in the distance. A sweet, weak perfume of baking and flowers drifted across from one of the adjacent roofs. She dipped her croissant in a bowl of milky coffee, brushing the flakes from her mouth and fighting the urge that came over her periodically to ring the office and check that things hadn't collapsed in her absence. She hadn't even been gone a day, she reminded herself sternly. And Claire would call. Her mobile lay silent on the glass-topped table in front of her. Below, in the street, the sound of women's voices carried up to her, drifting over her in a wave of unfamiliar, guttural sounds and the occasional volley of laughter. She turned her head slightly. A crack up the white wall revealed itself to be a line of tiny black ants; a flash of red was the pot of geraniums in the corner and the blue-green haze to her left was the olive trees that had been planted in giant terracotta urns in place of a screen. The noises from the street below shattered lightly against her. She sat with her legs pulled up underneath her, basking drowsily in the sun like the cat in one corner of the roof who watched her with one eye warily open for a sign of a titbit or a piece of fallen food.

She woke with a small start. Her hat had fallen off and was lying wedged between her head and her shoulder. She retrieved it, pushing it back into shape. She'd drifted off again. She squinted at her watch – how long had she slept for? Almost an hour – it was nearly noon. She looked around her almost guiltily but there was no one watching, no one wondering what she was doing or why. She picked up her book again, determined to read at least a chapter before lunch. Ah, lunch . . . where should she go for lunch? The hotel receptionist had handed her a list of local restaurants, bars, cafés and things to do. She picked it off the table and squinted down. They'd even drawn a helpful map. There was a little restaurant two doors down from the hotel – what better place to start?

Half an hour later after a quick, cool shower and a change of clothes, she walked out of the hotel and was immediately swallowed up by the crowd. She happily joined the throng of people moving down the street, stopping every now and then to chat, buy, sniff at food and prices, exchange gossip and small, crumpled bundles of notes. Small queues of people formed, broke apart and reformed again outside shops whose windows were stuffed with delicacies, breads, olives. Her nostrils widened as she took in the peppery-snuff scent of vegetables and meat grilled on small, open charcoal fires by men in long, billowing white djebellahs who squatted comfortably by the side of the road. Somewhere further up, someone was performing – she could hear the shouts and the sudden bursts of laughter. She walked in loose formation with the rest of the crowd, a group that moved as one, brought together by a mild curiosity and the desire to be entertained. She couldn't see above or around the shoulders and heads in front of her until they broke apart suddenly, revealing the source of the laughter and the shouts. A young boy and what appeared to be a blind, elderly man were speaking to the crowd. She understood nothing of it but it was amusing to watch. She stood for a few moments, letting the sounds of giggles and murmurs in the language she couldn't understand flow over and around her. She craned her neck with everyone else, momentarily pleased to be part of the crowd.

Suddenly, in the midst of bodies that were not aware of her, nor she of them, she felt a movement directed to her, alone. A hand, snaking past her hips to the flap of the bag she carried slung across her waist, stopped suddenly. She reacted instinctively and grabbed hold of the hand, seizing it tightly. Whoever it was couldn't jerk free; his body was jammed against hers, sandwiched between her and the man standing on the other side. To wrestle free would have been to draw attention to himself. He remained where he was, held fast. She turned her head. A young face, still carrying the pimple-marks of adolescence, expressionless, but she could read his fear in the tensely held stance of his body. She brought her other arm down to her bag – it was still there, untouched. She was about to let him go when she felt his whole body stiffen. Someone had grabbed hold of him on the other side. She bent her head forwards to see who it was. A tall, solidly built man was holding him fast. He said something in Arabic to the young pickpocket who appeared deaf with fear. Then he bent his head to Sam's and asked in a low, English-sounding voice. 'All there? Did he get anything?'

She shook her head. 'No, nothing. My bag's still here.' She patted the leather flap. He said something else to the young man and with a hard shove, pushed him away from them, releasing him back into the crowd. He watched him disappear and then turned to Sam.

'Are you all right?' he asked, looking down at her in concern.

Sam nodded slowly. The young man had disappeared. 'Gosh, I wasn't expecting that,' she said with a quick, shaky laugh. 'I felt his hand, but only just. He's good at his job.'

'Oh, they're just a bunch of opportunists, those kids. They go after the tourists, of course, and you . . . well, you stand out a bit.'

Sam put up a hand to her hair. She smiled self-consciously. 'I suppose I ought to cover it,' she said hesitantly.

'Wouldn't help. You'd still look foreign.' He smiled down at her. 'You're English, I take it?'

Sam nodded. She was suddenly having difficulty formulating her sentences. The man speaking to her was tall and broad with the imposing, protective presence of a statue. She was hardly small, but beside this man, who was easily six foot three, she felt dwarfed. It wasn't just his size; there was something wonderfully reassuring about the short grey hair, the tanned skin and twink-ling grey-blue eyes . . . she swallowed. What the hell had he just asked her? 'Yes, yes . . . I'm English. And you?' There was just the faintest hint of an accent in his voice that she couldn't quite place.

'Same.' He smiled at her.

'Oh.'

'Are you all right?' he asked again. 'You look a bit pale.'

'No, no . . . I'm fine. Just . . . just wasn't expecting it, that's all. Not on my first day, at least.' She gave another shaky laugh.

'How long are you here for?' He'd made a sort of passage through the crowd for her; she stepped into it ahead of him.

She turned her head back to look up at him. 'A week. It's . . . it's my first holiday in years.'

'Are you . . . did you come with your . . . with friends?'

She shook her head. She liked the way he'd stumbled over the question. 'No, I'm here on my own.' She felt her cheeks redden-ing and quickly turned away again.

He caught up with her easily, then stopped suddenly. They almost collided. Sam put out a hand to steady herself and then took it back as though she'd been scalded. He looked down at her, clearly amused. 'Look, it's nearly lunchtime. You look a little shaken up. How about grabbing a bite to eat? There's a really good restaurant just around the corner. I ate there on Thursday and the food's excellent.'

Sam hesitated for a second. There was a worn, rugged toughness to him that was suddenly utterly appealing. He looked safe. Strong. Dependable. *Just stop it right there, Sam Maitland.* She looked up at him, intending to thank him for his kindness in stopping the would-be thief and wound up hearing herself saying 'yes', instead. 'Yes, that sounds great.'

5

The glass in her hand was cool to the touch; there was the deliciously sharp feel of cold wine on her tongue as she took her first sip. Nick – Nick Beasdale, he'd introduced himself – looked on approvingly as she set it down again. 'Good?'

'Very.'

'Good,' he repeated, and smiled at her. 'Well, cheers.'

Sam's stomach gave one of those peculiar little lurches of the sort she hadn't felt in years. 'Cheers.' She lifted her glass. They were seated on the terrace of a tiny little restaurant overlooking the street, less than a hundred yards from where they'd met. He'd ordered a bottle of local white wine and a platter of cheeses, figs and the local flat breads as a starter in what sounded like fluent Arabic to her ears. Her head was swimming and she hadn't even taken the first sip! She leaned back in her chair and looked around with interest. The terrace was a shady patio of olive trees, potted roses and white and pale yellow awnings which made sunlight dance in wavering stripes. They sat next to the wrought-iron balustrade listening to the muted sounds of the street wafting up towards them and the drowsy buzz of oversized bees in black and yellow striped jerseys. 'So what brings *you* to Morocco?' Sam asked after the waiter had set down their plates.

'Holiday. Same as you, actually. I had a week's leave in between postings and decided at the last minute to come here.'

'Postings? Are you a diplomat?' she asked curiously.

He gave a short laugh. 'No, not exactly. I'm in the army. I'm an army officer.'

'An army officer?' She had no idea what to say. She'd never met an army officer before.

'And you?' he asked, smiling at her.

'Me?'

'What do you do?'

'Oh, I'm . . . I'm a lawyer. Entertainment law.' Sam was aware her cheeks had turned red.

He pulled a face. 'Impressive.'

'Oh, no . . . not at all.' Sam was quick to play her qualifications down. What was it Philip was always telling her? *You scare them off.*

'It is. I don't mean to be funny but you don't get much of a chance in the army to meet a beautiful, smart woman like you. Almost never, in fact.'

Sam's blush deepened. 'I . . . I don't think I've ever met a soldier before,' she said after a moment. 'Or an officer.'

'Well, always a first time, or so they say. I don't think I've ever met an entertainment lawyer either. So we're even.'

'Y-yes.' She took another large gulp of wine to cover her confusion. She didn't want to risk looking across the table into his face so she studied his arms instead. His shirt sleeves were rolled up; his tanned arms were covered in thick, dark brown hair – capable, tough-looking arms, the muscles moving faintly beneath the surface of his skin as he lifted and set down his wine glass. His hands were the same: strong, squared-off fingers, the nails clean and short, no wedding ring and no tell-tale pale band of skin where it would have been, either. She'd seen enough men who'd slipped it off for the evening to know. She liked his voice with its odd, flat quality and the way his smile brought out two faint dimples in his face.

As the food was brought to the table and the waiter topped up her wine, she could feel herself slowly dissolving in the lazy afternoon heat, basking in the pleasure of sitting on a terrace in the sun with a good-looking, interesting man. He was easygoing and good-natured with the staff but there was absolutely no mistaking who was in charge. There was a directness and a toughness to him, but also an unexpectedly boyish charm. He laughed easily and loudly; there was clearly a witty sense of humour lurking behind the grey-blue eyes that kept flickering back to her face. The waiters sensed it; they were all too eager to please, bringing an endless supply of delicious dishes to the table – long, charred tongues of grilled, shiny red peppers; beautifully decorated little saucers of thick, tangy pastes and carefully chopped vegetables glistening in olive oil and brine; thin, spicy sausages wrapped themselves around plates like languid snakes. They ate and drank and laughed. By the time Sam looked at her watch it was almost four and the sun was beginning to slide.

'Is that the time?' She looked up in exaggerated alarm.

His eyes twinkled. 'Is it?'

'I . . . I'd better get back,' she said. 'I've got some work to do.'

'Work? I thought you were on holiday.'

'I-I am. But . . . you know how it is . . .' her voice trailed off. She didn't want him to think she had nothing to do.

He shook his head. 'Not me. When I'm off, I'm off. We get little enough R & R as it is. Rest and recreation,' he added, smiling at her.

Sam laughed. 'It's like another language,' she said, tracing the wet outline of her glass on the table top with her finger. 'It seems quite an odd world.'

'You don't know the half of it,' he said drily. There was a moment's pause. 'Look, I don't want to seem too forward or anything but if you're here on your own for a week or so and I've got a couple of days, would you like to hang out together? Have dinner, visit the souk . . . maybe take a day trip some-where?'

Sam hesitated. There was no denying the attraction and it seemed to be mutual. He was charming and funny and articu-late. He'd been married before – too young, he said. The marriage hadn't lasted. No, no kids. An amicable split. No point fighting, eh? They both knew it was over. He smiled at her ruefully as he drained the last of his wine. He'd offered up the facts of his life easily, generously. He'd kept nothing back. Sam took a deep breath. Should she . . . ? Dare she . . . ? She'd never had a 'proper' holiday romance before, if that was what was on offer, and, despite her dismal track record when it came to flirtations, it was clear that he was interested. She could almost hear Paula. *Oh, for fuck's sake, Sam! Just do it! Who cares if you never hear from him again? You probably won't. He might be blown up next month for all you know!* She grimaced suddenly.

'That . . . that would be nice,' she said finally, a great knot of tension releasing itself inside her at her own words.

His pleasure was genuine. 'Great, that's great. Dinner tonight, then?'

'That would be nice,' she echoed faintly. She stood up giddily. What was she letting herself in for? 'I'm at Dar les Cigognes. The Palm Suite.'

He looked up at her, his expression faintly amused. 'A suite, no less. Well, Sam Maitland, entertainment lawyer *extraordinaire*, I'll pick you up at seven, shall I?'

'Er, yes.' She only just managed to stop herself saying 'that would be nice' for the third time. He stood up, peeled a few notes off a bundle and left them on the table. They walked back down into the crowded street in rather awkward silence. Within a minute they were back at her hotel.

'See you at seven, then,' she said, giving him a friendly wave of the fingers.

He looked down at her, a small, enigmatic smile playing around the corners of his mouth. 'See you at seven. Wear something nice.' And then he turned and disappeared into the throng.

She stood there for a moment, nonplussed. Wear something *nice*? Did that mean he didn't like what she was wearing? She looked down at her Boden turned-up jeans, her Jigsaw silk blouse and dark brown leather slingbacks from Toast. She'd thought she looked effortlessly chic. What did he mean? Something dressier? She tossed back her hair, fished her straw hat out of her bag (both from Joseph) and stuck it firmly on her head. Well, if Major Nick Beasdale wanted dressier, he'd get it. She had two options with her – the long, lime-green silk dress from Hobbs or the beautiful lemon dress from L.K. Bennett. Either way, she'd show him. Wear something nice indeed!

6

The lemon-yellow dress lay in a crumpled heap on the floor. There was a single lime-green stiletto caught by its slender heel on the bedspread and her delicate silk bra from La Perla had been tossed across one of the pillows. Through half-lowered lids she could see the thick curtain of her own hair spreading sideways and down the length of her body; somewhere near her thighs, she could see Nick's head as it slowly inched its way upwards. His tongue was a warm, wet flutter on her skin. Desire and disbelief battled within the warm, fuzzy confines of her head. A bottle of red wine and five shots of whisky between them had sealed the deal. In all likelihood, she would probably never see him again – what the hell was the harm? At dinner that evening, she'd lifted her head to look at him and suddenly found herself overwhelmed by the fact that less than twenty-four hours earlier, she'd listened to a couple on the neighbouring terrace, their heads bent towards each other in tender and close conversation, stirring up a longing in her for the same one day – *any* day – and now, less than a day later, here she was, doing just that.

To see the two of them together at dinner would have been to assume an entirely different set of circumstances. Nick was everything a dinner companion should be – warm, funny, attentive. He'd reached out once or twice to brush a strand of hair away from her face, claiming an intimacy that he probably didn't know was already his. That same hand was on her arm, now. There was a singing, lifting sensation in her chest, making it difficult to breathe normally. She hated it – the sense of shock that washed over her when a man reached out, touched her . . . claimed her. *Me?* She hated herself for even thinking it – why *shouldn't* he want her? She knew exactly why she found it almost impossible to believe but she couldn't seem to do a damn thing about it. But not tonight. Tonight she was lying in the same hotel bed she'd slept in alone the night before, her whole body pleasurably flushed with wine and an exquisite lust, watching the head of a man she'd met all of eight hours earlier moving gently and purposefully between her thighs. She closed her eyes at the shame of it all. And the pleasure, of course.

'D'you smoke?' She reached across and fished her emergency pack of cigarettes from the bedside table.

He shook his head. 'No, but go ahead. Doesn't bother me.'

'Just the one,' she promised, lighting up. 'I'm one of those idiots who smokes about a cigarette a week. I don't know why I don't just give it up,' she said with shrug.

'Gives you something to do with your hands in a bar and it keeps the weight off; isn't that what most women say?' Nick's voice was a disembodied rumble in the dark.

Sam felt her whole body blush. There it was again. A single comment whose meaning was ambiguous but still holding the capacity to stop her in her tracks. 'Er, no, actually,' she said, lighting up quickly to cover her embarrassment. She blew the smoke out through the corner of her mouth. 'A single cigarette a week wouldn't be much use, would it?' she said as lightly as she could.

He propped himself up on one elbow and ran a hand slowly down her body. She tried to see his expression in the faint light coming from underneath the living room door but his face was guarded. 'You're not the type,' he said quietly. His finger traced a line from her ribs to her navel. 'There's no weight to keep off. You're gorgeous. Just gorgeous.'

Sam's immediate intake of breath nearly choked her. She'd known him all of an evening – how could he possibly know exactly what to say? She leaned across him and stubbed out the cigarette carefully. She could feel something inside her beginning to crack open at the sound of his voice, after only a few hours, already strangely familiar to her. She reached out with one hand and touched his hair, feeling it prickle pleasurably through her fingertips. He caught her hand, brought it round, palm up, towards him and kissed her at the spot where the veins swelled, beginning their thick journey down the length of her forearm. His tongue moved lightly over the lines produced by the folds of skin at her wrist; if there was one line marginally thicker and rougher than the rest, he either didn't detect it, or didn't say. He pulled her hand impatiently towards his sex, already rising for the second time that night. Sam squirmed, half in embarrassment, half in haste. In her mind's eye she saw herself – a little drunk, bold, her body seeking only its own pleasure. She entered willingly into the unfamiliar image of herself, flushed with pride.

7

MEAGHAN
Celle, Germany, 2009

Meaghan Astor stepped gingerly through the doorway. Ahead of her, marching purposefully down the corridor, was the short, stocky figure of the estates manager, Warrant Officer Greaves. Tom, her husband, was outside, still piling suitcases and boxes onto the sidewalk. Alannah, their six-year-old daughter, was 'helping' him. She hadn't seen him for over a month and now clung to him like glue. She followed WO Greaves into the living room. The flat was uniformly dull in the way only army housing could ever be – magnolia-coloured walls, mottled green carpets in every room, standard, regulation-issue furniture – in this case a mismatched assortment of floral curtains, lopsided, bent-out-of-shape couches and cheap, plywood-faced furniture. Her heart sank. It was exactly as she'd feared. Awful. As ever.

'Two bedrooms, living room, dining room, kitchen . . . bathroom's down there, separate loo. You'll find the inventory on the kitchen counter. I'd advise you to go through it quick as you can and let us know if there's anything missing. Flat was painted six months ago – it won't be due for another coat for at least a year – but it looks pretty clean to me. You'll find all the regulations on the notice-board outside – rubbish collection days, garden waste and all of that. Right, if you've no further questions . . . ?' WO Greaves was in a hurry to leave.

'No, no . . . I think it's all pretty clear,' Meaghan said slowly, looking round in some dismay. It was dull. Dull and uninspiring. Just like the town. She felt the sharp tug of resentment rise in her throat. It was bad enough having to come back to Germany again without having to contend with a God-awful flat, too. Tom had just been promoted, for crying out loud!

'Righty-o.' WO Greaves spoke as though he were on the set of *Dad's Army*. 'Best let you get on with it then.' He shoved a clipboard at her. 'If you'd just sign here . . .' She did as he asked and handed back the pen. There was a movement in the door-way. She looked up. Tom was standing there, a suitcase in one hand and Alannah in the other. WO Greaves saluted smartly. 'Evening, sir. Everything seems to be in order, sir. Just said to the wife, you need anything, just give us a shout. We'll do our best.'

The wife, Meaghan thought to herself crossly. She hated the way they all said that. *The wife*.

'Thanks, Greaves.' Tom put the suitcase down. 'I'll see you in the morning.'

'Very good, sir.' He practically clicked his heels. He shut the door deferentially behind him and they were finally alone.

'Well, what d'you think?' Tom asked, peering into the first bedroom off the corridor. 'Not bad, eh?' He'd been living in the officers' mess hall for the past month whilst their accommodation was being sorted out.

Meaghan shrugged. 'Could be worse, I guess.'

'You said *that* about Shrivenham, remember?' Tom said to her with a faint smile.

'Have I got my own room?' Alannah asked, disentangling herself from her father's long legs. 'My very own room?'

'Yes, pet . . . it's at the end of the corridor, through that door. Go on, have a look.' Meaghan gave her a gentle nudge. She turned to Tom as soon as Alannah was out of earshot. 'It's *awful*,' she whispered crossly. 'It feels like a bloody prison. I thought Paderborn was the pits – this is worse.'

'Come on, love,' Tom said mildly. 'What did you expect? It's fine. You'll make something of it. You always do.'

Meaghan's mouth opened but she clamped it shut again. It was their first night together after almost four weeks apart and she was damned if she was going to spoil it arguing. Not tonight. She turned away from him and wandered into the living room. He was right; she'd make something of it, just as she always did. She would change the curtains, she thought to herself, paint the walls . . . once they'd settled in she'd pop along to Stores and see if she could change the blue sofas for something a little less decrepit and a little more neutral. She could hear Alannah bouncing on the bed in the room that would be hers. Alannah's room would be easy – some pretty stencils, a lick of pink paint, the antique chest of drawers that was at that moment winging its way from Shrivenham to Celle. By the end of the month, she'd have filled it with her stuffed animals and books and toys and it would no longer be the cold, dull room it currently was. In six weeks' time it would be full of the sound of the friends she would make at the primary school on the base and by Christmas, hopefully, she'd have forgotten she had three best friends in England, one of whom was already en route to Cyprus, and the cycle would begin all over again. Alannah was adaptable; you could plonk her down anywhere and within a couple of hours she'd have found something about her new setting to enthral and occupy her. Not like her mother.

Meaghan's stomach lurched at the thought of what awaited her. There was a coffee morning scheduled for the following day. As the wife of the battalion's second-in-command, she was duty-bound to attend. She knew the score; it was Tom's first posting after his promotion – the only other woman who outranked her on the base was Abigail Barclay, the commanding officer's wife. She felt another ripple of nerves in her stomach. She was now the wife of the 2/i/c, the second-in-command. She still couldn't get over it. She was the second-most-important wife on a British army base somewhere in the middle of Germany. How the hell had *that* happened? And to her? A beautician from Warra, for crying out loud! Abigail Barclay was a brigadier's daughter. She'd seen photos of Abigail – perfectly groomed, poised, elegant, impeccably dressed . . . the perfect officer's wife. Everything that she wasn't. She looked back towards the kitchen where Tom was dragging in a cardboard box. Celle was their sixth posting in sixteen years. How had she – a small-town girl from the middle of nowhere – wound up *here*?

'Mum!' Alannah's voice broke into her thoughts. 'Mum . . . come here! Look! Look what I found!'

Meaghan walked down the corridor towards her. She was sitting cross-legged on the unmade bed, triumphantly holding a rather dog-eared teddy bear by the scruff of its neck. 'Where d'you get that, angel?' Meaghan asked, looking at it rather dubiously.

'It was down there.' Alannah pointed to the narrow space between the bed and the wall. 'I saw its ears first. I think the little girl who lived here before left it for me.'

'Might've been a little boy,' Meaghan said mildly, gently disengaging the teddy from her daughter's hand. She quickly sniffed it – nothing that a quick spin in the washing machine wouldn't fix. 'Well, whoever it was, it was very nice of them, darling. I'm just going to give teddy a bath and then we can dry him on the radiator. He's been lying there for an awfully long time.'

'No, I want him now!' Alannah's face immediately crumpled.

'All right, all right.' For once, Meaghan gave in without protest. It had been a long journey from Stansted to Hanover and then an hour-long taxi ride from Hanover to Celle. They were both exhausted. The fight about the teddy bear could wait until morning. 'Right, time to get going. Dad's going to take us for pizza across the river and then it's bedtime for you.'

'Can I take Teddy with us?'

'All right. But just for tonight. Where's your coat?'

'Dunno.'

Meaghan sighed. She wandered back into the kitchen. Alannah's bright pink coat was lying on the counter. She picked it up and was just about to go back in search of her when Tom came in. 'You all right?' he asked, raising his arms above his head, leaning into the doorway.

She moved towards him suddenly and wrapped her arms around his waist. There was something so wonderfully reassuring about Tom. It wasn't just his size, the rugged good looks and the charm . . . all the things she'd fallen for all those years ago and which remained so startlingly fresh. No, there was something else about Tom, something almost noble. She'd long given up being embarrassed about it – it was true. She saw it; so did others. He *inspired* you; seemingly without trying, he brought out the best in everyone, including her. That, she knew, was the real reason for his promotion. That was why his soldiers loved him, why his superiors loved him – and it was why *she* loved him. He was a natural leader, able to command and take charge, yet full of grace. Even now, after all these years and everything they'd been through, he still had the capacity to surprise her, to make her catch her breath and wonder at just how lucky she was he'd picked her. He could have picked anyone, she often reminded herself. But he hadn't. He'd picked *her*. He'd singled her out from the dozens of girls who surrounded him, each hoping to be The One. There were days when she still couldn't believe her luck.

8

A fortnight later with the house still only half-unpacked, boxes scattered everywhere and no sign of the furniture she'd ordered as a replacement for the shoddy pieces they'd been given, she stepped out of the shower, shivering. The central heating wasn't working properly – another visit from WO Greaves – and although the days were slowly warming up, mornings and nights were still cold. She hurried across the room, plonked herself down in front of the mirror and took a quick anxious look at herself. Through the half-closed door she could hear the baby-sitter – the teenage daughter of one of Tom's officers – reading to Alannah. Of the three of them, Alannah seemed to have settled in quickest – of course. She'd already made two new best friends at school and could be seen every morning as Meaghan dropped her off marching confidently across the small yard, holding onto Sebastian Teddy as she took her place amongst the other five- and six-year-olds who'd also spent their short lives following their parents around the world. There were days when Meaghan felt younger than her daughter.

She looked at herself again. Her hair was lacklustre; it fell around her face in lank tendrils. There'd been no time after picking Alannah up from her friend's house and getting her home to wash and set it. She brushed it quickly, back-combed it where she could to give it a bit of bounce and finished off with a liberal dousing of hairspray. It would have to do. It wasn't her hair that was the major worry, though; it was the outfit. She looked over to the bed where she'd laid it out – a chiffon, leopard-print blouse and a pair of white jeans. They'd been invited to the CO's house for dinner, along with the other company commander, Mike Harding, who lived across the hallway. His wife, Sally, lived back in the UK with their two small daughters and, according to one of the wives she'd met on her second day, only came to Germany when she absolutely had to. It was quite a common arrangement – Meaghan had known a number of wives from their Paderborn posting who either couldn't stand the thought of leaving the UK or the thought of life in a small German town . . . and so they stayed whilst their husbands went, and saw each other once or twice a month. Privately she didn't know how they could bear it. She couldn't imagine living separately from Tom, no matter how miserable the base or remote the town. And it wasn't as if the bases in the UK were significantly better than those in Germany or Cyprus or Northern Ireland, the most likely overseas destinations for their battalion. Northern Ireland. She gave a little shudder at the thought of the two long years they'd spent on Massereene. No, Celle was definitely an improvement on Massereene. Mind you, she thought to herself grimly as she got up and fished a bra out of the cardboard box that still served as her chest of drawers, anywhere'd be better than Massereene.

Ten minutes later, she was almost ready. A final squirt of perfume, a final fluffing out of her hair with her fingers . . . she slipped her feet into her high-heeled pumps and picked up her bag. Tom was in the living room, doing something last-minute, as always, on his laptop. He was decidedly less bothered about what to wear – he was still wearing combat trousers although he'd pulled on a dark blue sweater and he'd combed his hair. At least. She sighed. What would Sally Harding be wearing? Or Abigail Barclay? Tom, of course, had no idea. He'd just shrugged. 'Wear whatever you like, love.' Tom's standard response to Questions of That Sort. Meaghan's stomach gave a nervous little flutter. She hadn't yet met Abigail, the CO's wife. She'd been on holiday in the UK when they arrived, though she'd heard plenty about her, of course. The perfect army wife, from what everyone said. Nice, not at all stuck-up, which she could so easily have been.

'Why?' Meaghan asked one of the wives at one of the many coffee mornings she'd been forced to attend since their arrival.

'Well, you know who her father is, don't you?'

Meaghan shook her head. 'No. Who?'

'Major General Hutton. Charlie Hutton. He was only the head of the SAS.'

It didn't mean much to Meaghan but it clearly meant a lot to the woman she was speaking to. 'Oh,' Meaghan said, which was her standard response when she didn't know what to say.

'Didn't hurt her husband's prospects any, did it?' The woman turned to her companion. Another wife of another officer – Meaghan hadn't yet managed to commit their names to memory.

The woman shook her head firmly. 'No, not in the slightest.' There was a slightly bitter envy in the way they spoke about

Abigail Barclay that Meaghan immediately recognised. She'd sighed and tried to turn the conversation elsewhere. Some of the wives she'd met in the sixteen years she and Tom had been married were even more ambitious than their husbands.

Tom, as ever, was reticent on the subject. 'Yeah, she's old Charlie Hutton's youngest daughter. So?'

'Er, nothing. Someone just mentioned it, that's all.' She said no more on the subject. Tom positively abhorred gossip.

Well, Charlie Hutton's daughter or not, she was probably also standing in front of her wardrobe wondering what to wear, Meaghan thought to herself quickly, trying to inject a little more confidence into her choice of outfit. She switched off the light and walked into the living room.

Tom looked up as she came through the door. He'd already switched off his computer. 'You ready?' he asked a touch impatiently.

'Yep.' She stood in front of him, hoping he'd say something nice about her outfit but he'd already turned away, looking for his own jacket. She hurried out after him. He was in a strange mood. He'd been preoccupied and withdrawn all week but she knew better than to press him. It was one of the rules she'd learned – the hard way, too. As he'd climbed up the ranking ladder, his ability to bottle things up had grown exponentially stronger. It had very little to do with her, she knew, although it was sometimes difficult to remember that. It was just the nature of the job – the Beast, as she only half-teasingly called it in the few letters and phone calls she made to her ever-decreasing circle of friends. The situation didn't help much, either. Although the British public could be forgiven for not noticing or caring that the country was at war. In less than six months' time the battalion would be in Afghanistan, facing an uncertain enemy in an ever-shifting political climate that made the job ten times more difficult than it would normally be. It was up to Colonel Barclay and Tom to make sure the men were ready for whatever would be thrown at them – and from the little Tom said these days, Meaghan gathered that they were in for one hell of a tour. He'd done postings in places he could hardly bring himself to remember, much less speak about – this was different, worse. For the first time in their marriage, there were now things he wasn't allowed to talk about. Now there were *real* reasons why he couldn't talk. And why she was afraid to ask.

'You look nice,' she said lightly as she got into the car, hoping for a similar response. Tom said nothing, just busied himself getting out of the tight parking space. 'Is it just the four of us?' she asked after a moment.

'Yeah. Mike and Sally left about ten minutes ago. They asked if we wanted a lift but I didn't think you'd be ready in time.'

'I would've been if you'd told me. Besides, it's not even eight o'clock. We're early.'

'Invite's for 19.45.'

'No, it's not. You said eight o'clock.'

'I didn't. I said 19.45.'

Meaghan sighed. She knew better than to argue over timing. 19.45. It was a small, hopelessly insignificant act of defiance on her part not to speak in the twenty-four-hour clock mode of all soldiers – and most of their wives. She'd grown up saying 'three o'clock' and 'half past five'. She hated the way they all said 'Oh-three-hundred hours', as if there were three hundred hours in a day. 'We'll be there in a minute,' she said soothingly. 'Do I look all right?' she couldn't help asking as he pulled up in front of the CO's house.

'Yeah. Fine. Did you bring the wine?'

'Wine? You didn't tell me to bring wine.'

'Meaghan . . . it's a dinner party. We always bring wine.'

'No, the last time I brought a bottle along you said—'

'Forget it.' Tom's tone was curt. 'Let's go. We're late enough as it is.'

'We're not—' Meaghan stopped herself just in time. She had no desire to argue, and certainly not now, just before they were about to meet the CO and his legendary wife. Her stomach gave yet another little nervous lurch. What would Abigail Barclay be wearing? She followed Tom up the steps wondering if she ought to have worn black. Safer. Classic. Suddenly leopard print seemed a little, well . . . cheap.

'Hello! Do come in. I know spring's supposed to be on its way but it's still freezing. Hello . . . you must be Meaghan. So nice to finally meet you. Welcome to Celle.'

Fuck, I should have worn black were Meaghan's first thoughts as soon as she set eyes on Abigail Barclay. She was wearing a simple light grey woollen dress with black tights and a pair of black suede boots. There were two small diamond studs in her ears and her blonde hair was pulled off her face in an elegant chignon at the nape of her neck. She was very pretty in the sort of English rose way that Meaghan had always admired – beautiful, looked-after skin, blue eyes, not too much make-up, discreet. She looked down at her own outfit with barely disguised dismay. She looked and felt like a hooker. 'Hi . . . er, hello,' she mumbled, holding out her hand, wondering if she ought to kiss her on the cheek instead. She never quite knew what to do – a permanent state of affairs. Abigail Barclay, she saw, was quick to sense her discomfort. She shook hands warmly, ushering them in.

'Mike and Sally have just arrived . . . do come through.'

As the battalion's commanding officer, Ralph Barclay's house was bigger than theirs, Meaghan noticed immediately as they walked down the short corridor to the living room. Better, too. The Barclays' home had none of the stark, regimental-issue look of any of the other houses. The walls were a mixture of soft, pleasing colours and thick drapes, a lovely, thick carpet, good furniture, vibrant paintings on every wall and an impressive collection of silver-framed photographs on the sideboards. There were fresh flowers everywhere and a silver tray with wine glasses and crystal decanters on the sideboard. Meaghan's heart, by now at the bottom of her stomach, sank even further. It would be her turn next, if not with dinner, then at least with a Kaffee-und-Küchen morning. She'd done her best to turn their little flat into something more hospitable than the cold, stark place they'd been given but it was nothing like this.

'Do have a seat.' Abigail smiled at her. 'And let me get you something to drink. Red or white? Or would you rather have something stronger? Do you know Sally?'

'No, no . . . we haven't met . . . er, red, please. Wine's lovely.' Meaghan struggled to keep up with the questions and shook hands with Sally Harding who, she was relieved to see, looked as gob-smackingly impressed as she was. She was a rather frumpy little woman with mousy brown hair, a permanently surprised expression and awful shoes. Sandals? In what was practically mid-winter? 'Hello,' she held out her hand. 'I'm Meaghan.'

'Sally. Pleased to meet you.' She didn't sound pleased at all, Meaghan noticed immediately. She sounded out of her depth and nervous. It made Meaghan feel marginally better. Don't be such a cow, she warned herself as she perched on the end of one of the sofas and accepted a glass of wine. The men, as usual, stood to one side, murmuring quietly amongst themselves. Shop talk, Tom called it. Meaghan found it boring. She'd met wives who hung onto their husband's every word, smiling when a joke had been made, nodding sagely even though they hadn't a clue what was going on. Not her. She hated that sort of pretence. So did Abigail Barclay, she noticed gratefully. It was only Sally Harding who sat upright in her seat, glancing every few seconds at her husband.

'Ralph tells me you're from Brisbane.' Abigail sat down in the chair next to her.

Meaghan nodded. She hesitated. 'Well, not quite Brisbane. I mean, that's where we met, but I'm from a bit further west. Practically the outback. You'd never have heard of it. Warra. It's tiny.'

'Warra? I have indeed. It's near a little town called Dalby, isn't it? Isn't there a flower festival or something every summer near there?'

Meaghan felt the blush of pleasure spread across her face. 'Yeah, there is. The Warra Rose Festival. My mum used to put in her roses when I was little. That's amazing, Mrs . . . er, Abigail. I don't think I've ever met anyone who's ever heard of it.'

'Oh, do call me Abby.' Abby smiled at her. 'Abigail sounds *so* old-fashioned. I've got two older sisters, Carmen and Natasha . . . I always curse my parents. No, my father was posted to Canberra for a year when I was about six and we drove up to Dalby one weekend for the festival. Is your mother a gardener? Mine too.' Abby chatted easily about flowers and gardening and Australia and being far away from home, and by the time they sat down at the table, Meaghan's earlier nervousness had all but vanished. She was very skilled at putting you at ease, Meaghan noticed. She wasn't *over*-friendly or prying. She just chatted away as if under the impression you were old friends. Sally Harding, in contrast, had no such grace. Meaghan knew no more about her than she had when she first walked in. She looked at the seating arrangement; the men were seated at one end of the table, the women at the other. That, too, was traditional. Another of the little things about the army she disliked. She took a quick gulp of red wine and tried not to think about her too-tight white jeans.

The food was delicious – coq au vin and tiny buttered potatoes tossed in caraway seeds and sprigs of parsley – but if it hadn't been for Abby, she noticed, conversation at one end of the table at least would have died. Sally Harding spoke when she was spoken to, not before. She seemed incapable of offering up an opinion or a comment without looking at her husband. Not that it did any good – Mike Harding barely registered her presence. By the time the first course was cleared, Meaghan actually felt sorry for her. She'd seen countless marriages like it – women whose very personalities had been eclipsed by the strain of following their men around, forever starting out again, making new friends, finding their feet . . . or perhaps it was just that

Sally Harding hadn't had much of a personality to begin with? Abby was the opposite – she chatted easily and smoothly, keeping the conversation between them at exactly the right pitch. At the other end of the table, the three men were engrossed in their own matters. It was only when Abby brought the dessert in that Ralph looked up and said, 'Oh, by the way, I've just had word in from London. Finally. The new company commander we've been waiting for – he's just been confirmed. Nick Beasdale. He did a tour in Northern Ireland . . . you might know him, as a matter of fact. He transferred around the same time as you, Tom—'

Meaghan nearly dropped her wine glass. She coughed violently. 'S-sorry,' she stammered, feeling herself turning bright red. 'J-just went down the wrong way.'

'Are you all right? Shall I fetch some water?' Abby quickly got up from the table.

'No, no . . . I'm fine,' Meaghan protested. From the other side of the table, Tom was frowning warningly at her. 'J-just something in my throat.' But she accepted the glass of water gratefully, gulping it down. She didn't dare look at Tom again. *Nick Beasdale?* The name leapt out of the past, knocking her off-balance. She fought to bring her blushing back under control before anyone noticed. She was aware of Tom's eyes on her. She accepted a small glass dish of poached pears in a red wine sauce and tried not to lift her head. Tom was silent. You'd be forgiven for thinking he'd never met the man, Meaghan thought to herself as the conversation began again, this time on something else. How long had it been since Nick Beasdale had disappeared out of their lives? Ten, fifteen years? She'd often wondered what had happened to him. She'd heard he'd been posted to Bosnia, then Iraq . . . someone had mentioned something once about West Africa. She personally didn't care if she never set eyes on him again. It was Edie she felt sorry for. His wife. *Ex*-wife, she corrected herself. No one knew what had happened to her. No one *wanted* to know. Just another army marriage that had fallen along the way. She picked up her wine glass and tried not to think about Eithne. Or Nick Beasdale for that matter.

'Why didn't you *say* something?' she asked Tom, as soon as they were safely out of earshot and in the car.

'Like what?' Tom busied himself reversing the car.

'Like . . . I don't know . . . that you *did* know him. That we *do* know him.'

'He knows I know him. That was just for Mike's benefit.'

'But what's he doing *here* if Barclay knows about him?'

'I didn't say that. I just said that Barclay knows we were together in Belfast, that's all.'

'But—'

'Drop it, Meaghan. I know you never liked him.'

'That's not it at all. What about—'

'Meaghan, just drop it, will you? He arrives next week. He's going to be one of our new company commanders and that's all there is to it. And I don't want you gossiping with any of the wives, either, d'you hear me?'

Meaghan gaped at him in the darkened interior of the car. She couldn't remember the last time Tom had spoken to her like that. The anger rose in her immediately. 'Don't be such a prick,' she said hotly. 'I never gossip, you know that. And don't talk to me as though I'm some stupid child.'

Tom was silent for a moment. Then he put out a hand and touched her arm. 'Sorry, love. I didn't mean it. We're all under a bit of strain at the moment. I'm sorry.'

Meaghan said nothing but the anger slowly went out of her. She looked out of the window at the street lights as they rounded the corner. Celle was tiny; the CO's house was barely a five-minute drive away. 'That's OK,' she said finally as they pulled up outside the flats that were now home. It was just past ten p.m. The new babysitter would be pleased. 'Well, maybe he's changed,' Meaghan said finally.

'It was a long time ago,' Tom said, switching off the engine and turning to look at her. 'And we don't know the whole story.'

I do, Meaghan longed to say, but she didn't. She held her tongue. She'd promised Eithne.

9

Abby Barclay picked up the last glass and set it back down on the polished silver tray. One of the glasses still had a small smudge; she hurriedly rubbed it off with the sleeve of her shirt. She refilled the elegant crystal decanter; everything was ready for the next set of guests. She took one last look at the now-empty dining room, bathed in soft, warm light. She'd swapped those horrid low-energy bulbs for normal ones as soon as they'd moved in. Ghastly things. She didn't care if they single-handedly saved the planet. She hated the cold, white light they cast. As a matter of fact, she'd replaced almost everything – furniture, lamps, paintings, rugs . . . the works. Over the years, she'd learned what to keep, what to throw, what to change . . . oh, yes, she knew the routine. No matter where they were sent – Aldershot, Innsworth, Leuchars, Dhekelia, Gibraltar, Belize – within a week of their arrival, she'd have transformed whatever accommodation they'd been given into a home. When the girls were still young and not at boarding school, they'd all laughed about it. 'Mum's been at work.' The girls would look at each other and roll their eyes. The house in Belize, a horrid little bungalow in Price Barracks, had been her toughest challenge – peeling paintwork, those horrible louvered windows that stuck fast in the closed position no matter how many gallons of WD-40 they sprayed over them, the cloying, clogging heat and the dirty, sagging mosquito nets at every window . . . horrid, horrid, horrid. But she'd done it – she'd marshalled the house-help into painting and cleaning, sweeping and polishing and finally, a fortnight after they'd arrived, the poky little bungalow was transformed.

'This looks just like Fulham,' eight-year-old Clara said, looking around. 'Really, Mum. It *really* does.'

'Well, not *quite*, darling,' Abby murmured, touched by the comment. Praise from Clara was praise indeed. Of their two children, Sadie and Clara, it was Clara who was the critical one, just like Ralph. Although *she* knew the bungalow looked nothing like the lovely house her parents had helped them buy in Evelyn Gardens, just off the Fulham Road, it was comforting to hear Clara say it. Home. Fulham. They'd only lived in it once, for a year, whilst Ralph was seconded to the MoD. Now it stood empty, as it had done for most of their marriage. She wondered if the girls still thought of it as home. She'd felt her heart give a sudden, unexpected lurch. She was surprised. It wasn't like her to feel homesick, certainly not for England. 'But it's lovely of you to say it.'

'No, *really*. If you close your eyes and you forget that it's so hot,' Clara said earnestly.

'And drown that bloody racket from next door . . .' Ralph came into the room, grinning. 'I don't know how you do it. Well done, darling.' He'd kissed the top of her head, making her blush even harder.

Now, standing in the living room of the almost-as-poky house they'd been given in Celle, she could still feel her cheeks warm with pleasure at the memory. Belize was seven years ago. Seven years and several postings since then and she knew there'd be a few more to go yet before they could even think about returning. She wondered what it would be like to go back to England. Back to ordinary little things like taking the bus, hearing English all around her, seeing her old friends again . . . silly little everyday things. It was unlikely to happen any time soon, though. After Germany, the battalion was heading out to Cyprus before they were shipped out to Afghanistan. It would be their second posting in Cyprus, though this time it looked as though they'd be down the coast on the other base. Akrotiri. Near Limassol. Not Dhekelia. She shivered suddenly. She had no desire to start thinking about Dhekelia now.

'Darling?' She heard Ralph's voice behind her. She gave a guilty start. He was standing in the doorway, looking quizzically at her. He yawned. 'Come to bed, darling. Why don't you leave all this till the morning?'

'Sorry,' she said, quickly collecting herself. 'What time is it?'

'Nearly midnight. It all went beautifully. Young Astor's just sent a thank you text.'

She grinned at Ralph. *Young* Astor indeed. Ralph was only a couple of years older than Lieutenant Colonel Astor, she imagined. At forty-six, Ralph was the battalion's youngest-ever commanding officer. He was born to the role. The eldest son of an officer who himself had been the eldest son of an officer, soldiering was in Ralph's blood. It was all he'd ever wanted to do, he'd told her within hours of meeting her. In that way, they were uncannily alike, though he hadn't known that, not that first night. Abby was herself an army brat, brought up on bases around the world. Her mother and grandmother had been army wives – and of the best sort, too. Her mother, Libby Hutton, had dedicated her entire life to one thing – furthering her husband's career, and she'd seen to it that when her youngest daughter married into the Firm, as they laughingly called it, she would do exactly the same. Abby had learned the rules the best way possible – by example. Ralph's career came first, before everything else, *above* everything else. The fact that her own father, Major General Charles 'Charlie' Hutton, had been Chief of the General Staff and then the Commandant Commander of the SAS didn't hurt. Daddy approved of Ralph; he'd said so the first day they met. 'He'll go far, Abby. Mark my words. Good man.' He was right. Ralph *was* a good man. They were an exceptionally good match – always had been, always would be. That was what *she* hoped for above all else.

She took one last quick look round. The lilies she'd bought that morning at the flower market were just opening; from the hallway you could just catch their soft fragrance. She sighed with pleasure. It was good to be back in Europe, somewhere nice and familiar where the water didn't have to be air-freighted in and there was no possibility of snakes under the bed. Best of all, it was only an hour's plane journey back to the UK to see Clara. She'd endured Belize, hadn't cared much for Cyprus at all and as for those dreary barracks in dreary towns and villages around the UK, no, she'd had quite enough of those, thank you. Compared to some of their postings, she thought to herself, Celle wasn't that bad. It was a pretty little town with a river, some fine old medieval buildings and a farmer's market that came in twice a week. The fact that she spoke reasonable German helped. In the two months that they'd been there, she'd managed to make some friends – well, hardly friends . . . just people to whom she said 'hello', exchanged a few words about the weather, their children, her children . . . the usual sort of stuff. It was the same every-where, she'd noticed. People appreciated the effort. It didn't take much. She'd studied German at school but in other places where she'd understood no more than a few words of the language, it always surprised and humbled her to see how delighted locals were by a little effort. There was something about the Eng-lish . . . the wives of the other officers rarely, if ever, bothered. She remembered Gillian Smith, the CO's wife on Dhekelia. She simply raised her voice when speaking to the 'natives', as she called them. 'I just don't understand it,' she used to complain to anyone within earshot. Possessed of an unnaturally loud voice, her complaints generally carried the distance. 'Why don't they bloody well learn English? We've been here long enough.' She smiled to herself as she wandered back through the flat into her study. Gillian Smith. No, she couldn't say she missed her.

She switched off the light and followed Ralph down the corridor to their bedroom.

'It went rather well, don't you think?' Ralph came to stand behind Abby as she pulled off her earrings and put them care-fully away in her jewellery box. 'Food was wonderful. As usual.'

Abby smiled. She looked at him in the mirror's reflection. He pulled off his shirt, folding it neatly and opening the wardrobe door. His back was to her; in the dim glow of the bedside lamps, his skin was golden-hued, the residue of the recent tan he'd acquired in Cyprus on a training exercise a few weeks earlier. He still had the lean, muscled physique she'd spotted all those years ago when he came into Henry J. Bean's on the King's Road and told her off for not having lemon with her G&T. She smiled at the memory. She'd noticed him straight away. It had taken him a week to get her phone number and a further week to get a kiss but she'd known the minute she set eyes on him that she would marry him. And that was exactly what happened, exactly as she'd pictured it. He took off his trousers and folded them neatly, slotting them into his drawer. She smiled to herself. It was one of the things she most liked about army life – and army men – she supposed. Neat, ordered, *practical*. Disciplined, above all else. Her father was exactly the same. As a child she'd never once come across a sweater thrown carelessly across a chair, or a pair of shoes that weren't neatly lined up, side by side, cleaned and polished to boot – a bit of a cliché, perhaps, but true. They'd had room inspections for almost as long as she could remember and when she married Ralph and the girls arrived she was amused to find he did the same. Sadie was naturally tidy; Clara was not. But she'd learned, and sometimes the hard way, too. Ralph wasn't a great believer in sparing the rod. Not many army men were.

She swivelled the chair around. 'I do like Tom Astor,' she said, peeling off her tights. 'And his wife's quite nice.'

'Terrible dress sense, if you ask me. Looked like something Sadie'd wear.'

'Oh. Well, she obviously wanted to look her best.'

Ralph gave a small laugh. 'At least she seemed to have something to say. I couldn't get a squeak out of Harding's wife.'

'Mmm. She *was* rather dull.' Abby stood up. She was wearing a lacy black bra and matching panties. It wasn't one of the lessons her mother or her grandmother had seen fit to pass down but it was a lesson Abby had somehow intuitively grasped.

Unlike many of the officers' wives she'd known, she had never let herself go. She'd always looked after herself – a careful, balanced diet, regular exercise, regular trips to the hairdresser and the beauty salon if they were in places where such things were to be had. She dressed carefully and conservatively, and always, *always* wore good underwear.

In the early days of their marriage, it was Ralph who'd opened up a whole world of sensuality for her. He was the experienced one; she was not. Aside from a couple of boyfriends she'd had as a teenager and the one young man who'd ardently pursued her whilst at Lucie Clayton's, only to see her lost as soon as Captain Ralph Barclay appeared, she was a complete novice when Ralph met her. She was a virgin; it was something they laughed over. He was the first, and the only. But Ralph's instruction served to open up another vein in her – the same artistic impulse that led her to draw and paint found another path, heating her sexually. It became a private source of wonder for them that somehow had never lost its edge. In bed, in the darkness and privacy of whatever home it was she'd managed to fashion, she made another home for him in ways that astonished and excited him beyond measure. Few would ever have guessed it – serene, polished, conservative Abby Barclay? But Abby was no fool. Over the years she'd seen army marriages come and go – mostly go. She knew only too well the sorts of pressures the army could – and usually did – bring to bear on even the most stable of relationships. To keep her family and her husband intact, another sort of bargain would have to be struck. Sex, and her inventiveness with it, was one part of an instinctive strategy that kept their marriage and their attraction for and to one another alive. For Ralph there would be no other, ever. Of that she was absolutely sure. From that private source of security, the generosity that was the hallmark of her nature was free to flow.

'Come here,' Ralph suddenly spoke out of the soft darkness. He'd turned off his bedside lamp; only hers remained. He shook his head as she tucked her arms behind her back to take off her bra. He liked to make love to her partially dressed, the more complicated her underwear the better. It amused her greatly. For a man so accustomed to the hardware of military life – guns, weapons, tanks, equipment – the delicate intricacies of lace, buttons, hooks and eyes was a welcome, secret distraction. He was equally adept at both.

She sat down on the edge of the bed next to him, turning her back to him so that he could unfasten her bra. She knelt astride him, bending down to take his penis into her mouth. It hardened immediately, filling her mouth. She could hear him groan softly, his whole body tensing with desire. It had been over a week since they'd made love; after a successful dinner party where the food, wine and conversation flowed, there was nothing better. She shifted herself downwards until her nipples lightly touched the inside of his thighs. His hands were in her hair, tightening as he thrust into her soft, warm mouth. Curiously, her last thought before he exploded in a rush of semen and muttered expletives was of Meaghan Astor. In her faux-sexy leopard-print shirt and her too-tight white jeans . . . would she do this for Tom?

Ralph slept deeply – the sleep of the dead and the sexually exhausted, every last drop of energy drained from him. Abby lay awake in the dark, unable to join him. Something about the dinner party was niggling at her. But what? She ran over the evening again in her mind's eye. The guests arriving one by one; her barely suppressed smile at the sight of Meaghan Astor; her attempts to get Sally Harding to answer in anything other than monosyllables; the conversation about Warra; the new company commander who was just about to arrive. Ah! That was it. It was his name. Nick Beasdale. Now, where had she heard it before? And the look that had passed between Tom Astor and his wife when his name came up. A 'barely there' look of the sort she would flash Ralph when something strange had been said. She frowned to herself. Nick Beasdale. She'd heard the name before, but where? What was it Ralph had said earlier in the evening, before the guests arrived? That Beasdale and Astor had served together in County Antrim, years ago. 'What's he like?' she'd asked curiously but he'd turned away, his mind already elsewhere. These days Ralph was forever beginning and abandoning conversations. In less than six months' time, the battalion was due to ship out to Afghanistan. Aside from the fact that the soldiers had to be trained to meet what would undoubtedly be their toughest challenge yet, they also had to face the reality that it was an increasingly unpopular war, both at home and abroad, and morale amongst the troops was at an all-time low. For a commanding officer like Ralph, accustomed to working within the prevailing morale, not against it, it was a particularly challenging time. He inspired and demanded absolute loyalty; now, for the first time ever, he couldn't guarantee it and the fact that it had absolutely nothing to do with him made it even harder to grasp. He was under pressure to deliver a tight, fighting-fit and battle-ready battalion – little wonder he couldn't always remember whether it was his turn to speak to the girls or what day the recycling truck came around. *Nick Beasdale. Tom Astor. Country Antrim.* A slow, drowsy circle of thoughts, each becoming heavier than the last until she succumbed and finally fell asleep.

In the morning there was little opportunity to talk. There'd been an 'incident' at one of the mess halls the previous night whilst they were at dinner. A soldier had jumped out of a window and it wasn't yet clear why. Ralph barely had time to down a coffee and snatch a bite out of her toast before he was out the door, picked up by one of his subalterns. She followed him into the hallway and watched him go, wondering how it was that he managed to stay so calm. She closed the front door and leaned against it for a moment, thinking through her list of things to do that morning. They'd been in Celle for two months and she'd only just managed to carve out a routine for herself. Today was Monday – she had a yoga class at nine thirty a.m., then a families committee meeting at noon. She'd go grocery shopping straight afterwards, stop off at the library on the way home and then spend the rest of the afternoon catching up on correspondence and painting until it was time to prepare supper. She no longer made the sorts of dishes that required a precise arrival time. These days, Ralph appeared anywhere between 5.30 p.m. and midnight. She hoped the arrival of the new company commander would ease the pressure on the others a little.

She looked forward to a glass of wine and a quick round-up of the day's events before bedtime. That was another of the lessons her mother had imparted with fervour. *Stay in touch with what's going on. Don't drift apart. Show an interest.* In the beginning, it wasn't so hard. Ralph's life *was* her life. There was the thrill of being newly married, of babies, the excitement of new postings and the joy in Ralph's rapid promotions. She'd had the houses to furnish and turn into homes, schools to worry about, homework to supervise and a household to run. She couldn't remember when she began to notice it wasn't quite as easy or as natural to enquire about his day. In the beginning he'd been away a lot so there was a lot to catch up on. There was the thrilling strangeness of being together again, of relearning what had been undone in the six-month tours that kept them apart.

It was only after his promotion to lieutenant colonel that they'd come full circle and he'd been at home again, every day, nine to five or thereabouts, and the routine of his day had become just that – a routine. Now it felt a little strange to see him off in the morning knowing he'd be back in eight or ten or twelve hours and that nothing out of the ordinary would happen to him in between. She enjoyed it. It was a relief to know he was safe and sound. She couldn't imagine sitting by the telephone every night, watching the news on TV and wondering if the next casualty would be hers, or the one after that. In six months' time that *would* be her. In six months' time he'd be in Helmand Province and she would be home alone and she was dreading it. But in the meantime, it was both weird and wonderful to take a walk or a bicycle ride across the road and down across the footbridge to the bustling town centre, to practise her German with the greengrocer and the florist, stop off at the chemist to buy shaving foam or the soap he liked . . . small domestic details that years of living outside Europe had all but curtailed.

She looked at her watch. It was almost nine. Time to get changed for her yoga class and get the day started. She passed her study and pushed open the door, glancing in at the painting she'd begun the other week. The large white canvas was set up on her easel, a few tentative pencil marks outlining the limits of sky, water, bridge . . . taken from her photographs of the view across the small river. A bank of weeping willows marked the bend in the river; on certain mornings, the empty sculls were lined up just below the bridge. It was a view that was picturesque in the artistic, tranquil sense of the word but full of life and movement too. She couldn't wait to start on the water. She'd spent an hour down there the other day, photographing and sketching, mulling over precisely the right technique for capturing the ebb and flow of the river as a boat pulled past or a line of ducks settled precariously on its surface. She shut the door gently, as though she feared disturbing the empty canvases before she'd even begun.

10

DANI
Freetown, Sierra Leone, 2009

The black Mercedes carrying Danielle Kingsley-Safo and her best friend and colleague, Sue Macalister, towards the Prime Minister's office was flanked by two outriders, one of whom wove dangerously in and out of the thickening traffic on Siaka Stevens Street. Dani leaned back against the stiff leather seats and watched the city slide past through the tinted windows. The air-conditioning was on full blast, periodically puffing small clouds of condensation through the vents. The driver, a taciturn man who had simply held open the door for them without a word of greeting, was doing his best to keep up with the dispatch riders, neither of whom paid the slightest bit of attention to passers-by. A sharp blast of the horn startled a lone goat, which darted across the street, narrowly avoiding its own death. The usual crust of hawkers and roadside kiosks wavered in and out of view; brightly painted steel shipping containers now bearing the colours and logos of the giant telecommunications companies had been cut open – inside, sweltering in the heat, market traders sat drinking warm, sugary Coca-Cola and gossiping amongst themselves. The car swept round the Cotton Tree, symbol of the founding of Freetown, and continued down Independence Avenue towards State House where half a dozen ministers, ambassadors, local dignitaries and photographers were waiting.

'God, I need a cigarette.' Sue's voice broke into her thoughts. 'I'm so nervous. D'you think the President will be there?'

Dani shook her head slowly. 'I don't know. Does it matter?'

'Jesus, Dani . . . how the hell did this ever happen to *us*?' Sue turned her head to look at Dani in stunned disbelief.

Dani shook her head again. 'Don't ask me. I still can't believe it. Fifty thousand dollars . . . it's a *fortune*!'

'It'll be in the papers tomorrow. We'll be inundated, you know.'

'I hope not. We can't take in anyone else.' Dani looked out of the window again. She wasn't joking – she had no idea how it had happened. One minute she and Sue were running Hopewell House, a temporary shelter for young, pregnant girls on Fisher Street, overlooking the white, sandy beaches of Susan's Bay, and the next minute a journalist from the BBC was on the phone telling them they'd been honoured with an award. The Bayard Rustin Award for Humanitarian Causes from the Washington-based A. Philip Randolph Institute, to be absolutely precise. She and Sue had simply stared at each other. Neither of them had ever heard of the A. Philip Randolph Institute or the Bayard Rustin Award. 'It comes with a cheque,' the journalist told her over the phone. 'Fifty thousand dollars. Yes, dollars. US dollars. You sound surprised.' Surprised wasn't the right word. She'd put down the phone and turned to Sue, astonishment written all over her face.

'Fifty thousand dollars?' Sue echoed faintly. 'For us? You're kidding. It's a mistake. It must be a mistake.'

But it wasn't. The phone calls that followed confirmed the award. A picture of the two of them appeared in the *New Citizen* the following morning and then all hell broke loose. Not only was it precisely the sort of African success story that every major news agency from Sierra Leone to Seoul was desperate to cover, there was the additional bonus of – as someone crudely put it – 'the most fucking gorgeous aid worker you've *ever* seen' – to boot. Dani Kingsley-Safo née Tsemo was twenty-four years old, her friend and business partner Sue Macalister a few years older. They'd met by chance a few years earlier. Sue Macalister was London born and bred, although her parents were from Sierra Leone. She'd come to Freetown in 2004, a couple of years after the war was officially declared over, with a degree in development studies from the LSE and a job as a housing coordinator for one of the hundreds of UN agencies. Danielle Kingsley-Safo was the receptionist for Oxfam next door. They'd met at a party one evening, struck up a conversation and, somewhat to Dani's surprise, they'd become friends. Soon afterwards, Sue had casually asked Dani if she fancied working together? Working together? Dani wasn't sure what she meant. It took Sue ten minutes to explain her idea and Dani less than a minute to make up her mind.

The idea was simple enough. Sue had inherited a house from her parents on Fisher Street – in a rather dilapidated condition, to be fair, but generously sized with a small garden in front and a cottage at the rear. Instead of sitting at a desk in an air-conditioned office with half a dozen expatriates, wringing their hands in sympathy at the conditions around them yet whiling away their weekends at parties and in bars, she said, her voice rising unintentionally, she wanted to do something on her own. After all, Sierra Leone was her country too. She couldn't just sit idly by, filling in a year or so 'out in Africa' whilst waiting for something better to come along back in London or New York. She took Dani down to see the house. They walked around it together, ignoring the curious glances of neighbours. 'I'd turn it into a refuge,' Sue said, climbing the stairs to the third floor. 'There's easily enough space. If we turned the living room into a reception area and cleared out the storerooms, there are about fifteen rooms in here. I mean, I work with these girls, Dani . . . some of them . . . you can't imagine what they've been through. It'd be somewhere for them to come whilst they make up their minds what to do.'

Dani was silent. It was a good idea – no, better than that. It was a brilliant idea. A *necessary* idea. Sue was right – some of the girls had been to hell and back during the war. They'd seen and done things that no other human beings had. To say they were traumatised was the understatement of the century. Sue had seen first-hand just how desperate some of them were. Barely in their teens, working the bars and beaches at night they fell prey to the worst kinds of men – from soldiers to shady businessmen – and often wound up pregnant. Alone, with no families or support to speak of other than each other, and the ever-present fear of hunger, a hurried visit to a backstreet abortionist usually followed and then what happened to them was anybody's guess.

She looked around her at the house which, although neglected and in need of some care and attention, could be the first step in changing a young girl's life – and promptly made up her mind. Sue was right about everything except one tiny detail. Dani *could* imagine what it was like. She knew because she'd been there herself. But Sue didn't know that – and never would. Dani had long since learned to keep certain things to herself. No one who walked through the doors of Hopewell House would ever have guessed that the line separating the poised, confident young woman who single-handedly browbeat donors into giving them the necessary funds and the desperate, wild-eyed girls who arrived every week on their doorstep was a thin one and one that had been breached before.

11

As was usually the way with functions of that sort, had either Dani or Sue been familiar with them, nothing began on time. They swept into the forecourt of the Prime Minister's office at noon. As soon as the car door opened they were swamped by photographers who'd been sent out to cover the human interest angle on two young women who'd done something extraordinary in the face of the most unimaginable suffering and deprivation, or so their editors said. Dani got out of the car, somehow remembering to keep her knees pressed together as she'd been taught at school, and turned to face them, hoping her smile would hide her inner nerves. The photographers were mostly men – she overhead someone whispering, 'Fuck, she's *gorgeous*. Get one of her . . . no, not the other one, you idiot. *Her.*' She turned away. It was the deal between them; she posed, Sue talked. She watched as the journalists came up to Sue. With her characteristic forthright manner, she deftly handled the questions. They thrust microphones in Sue's face like weapons, nodding enthusiastically as she delivered the sound bites they required. Within weeks Dani would take those same phrases into the boardrooms and executive offices in the city and extract cash and promises in return. Someone had told her once, 'Lust is the best fundraiser.' It seemed to work. She flirted; the cash came rolling in.

They were hustled past the assembled bodyguards, government officials, NGO representatives and general hangers-on who were milling around without direction on the front steps, waiting for something to happen. A harassed-looking official in a too-tight suit came tripping down the stairs to meet them. They were asked to wait in the lobby; the Prime Minister was on his way. He was *soo* sorry they'd been kept waiting. It was marginally cooler inside the vaulted entrance to the offices. Dani was uncomfortably aware of several small tributaries of sweat rolling down her back, gathering momentum until they met the river pooling gently at her waistband. As soon as they'd left the air-conditioned comfort of the government car, the heat had seeped through every pore. She half-wished she'd chosen to wear traditional dress – a loose-fitting *ka'aba* from Ghana, perhaps, or one of those long, swirling robes that Senegalese women wore with such aplomb. Instead she was trussed up like a turkey in a suit with a ruffled cream silk collar, high heels and a girdle that smoothed out the swell of her hips.

'Miss Kingsley-Safo?' A young man came running down the steps towards them on two-inch-heeled shoes, his black trouser suit obscenely tight around the crotch, suit jacket flapping open to reveal a light blue shirt stained with patches of sweat.

'*Mrs* Kingsley-Safo,' Dani corrected him lightly.

'Ah, of course, of course. It's just that you look so *young.' Jong.* He pronounced it the way a Nigerian or a Ghanaian might. He gave a queer, high-pitched giggle. 'And you must be Mrs Macalister.' He turned to Sue.

'*Miss* Macalister.'

'Oh. OK. So . . . anyway, ladies. Please come this way. The Prime Minister will be here any minute. Any minute. There will be a short speech and then the award. We would also like it if you could say a few words for national TV. It's a very big honour for Sierra Leone, as you know. A very big honour.'

He was fond of repeating himself, Dani noticed. 'Are you from here?' she asked as they climbed the short flight of stairs to the main hall. 'Are you Sierra Leonean?'

He nodded. 'But I grew up in Lagos. Here we are, ladies. This way. This way.' He led them through a series of small, crowded corridors until they reached the main hall. At least the fans were working, Dani noted as they were shepherded through the small crowd that had gathered to watch. There was a sudden burst of noise as the wail of a lone dispatch rider floated through the air. The Prime Minister had arrived. Heads turned in eager anticipation; the rumbling murmur of voices sounded through the hall. Dani could hear footsteps coming down the long, high-ceilinged corridor, echoing loudly until they stopped outside.

There was a sudden lull and then the doors at the far end were flung open. The babble of noise increased. 'Mrs Kingsley-Safo, Miss Macalister . . . this way, please. If you'll just put yourselves here . . . yes, like that. Just one moment.' The bum-waggling official fussed this way and that, selecting the right positions for the official photographs that would follow. Dani was dimly aware of being pushed forward in a line of people being presented; Sue reached the Prime Minister first. She shook hands, there was a brief exchange and then a dozen flashbulbs went off. Soon it was her turn. She looked up into his face; there was the customary faint widening of the eyes, the recognition that he found her attractive as most men did, the slightest pressure of his hand in hers and then she was being shepherded along.

She wondered briefly if her grandmother would see the news coverage that evening. As far as she remembered, there'd been no television in the rambling, falling-down house on Boyle Lane, overlooking White Man's Bay. And her mother? She tried to remember when she'd last seen her mother. She'd been how old . . . two, three? She had only the foggiest, dimmest memory of someone whose perfume impregnated the air and surfaces around her; a soft, warm presence with red lips. Little fragments remained – the sight of a pair of high-heeled, sequinned shoes; a powder puff left carelessly open; a tube of lipstick, half unscrewed. That was all. It wasn't much. She couldn't remember the whole of her, what she looked like or the colour of her eyes. Black, in all likelihood. Like her grandmother's. But not hers. Quite where Dani Tsemo got her lioness-yellow eyes from was anyone's guess, least of all her mother's. Sweetie Tsemo was a good-time girl, a prostitute or a whore, depending on who was doing the asking. Whether the man who'd fathered her daughter was British, French, German, Swiss, Lebanese or Italian, Sweetie didn't know, didn't care. It made no difference; he wasn't there, never had been.

'Is everything all right, miss?' A voice interrupted her thoughts. Dani blinked. She turned in the direction of the man who'd spoken. Slowly her eyes took in the image of someone whose face she had known before, in a different time and place. She stared at him incredulously.

'*Eric?*'

'*Dani?* Is that you? Fuck, it is, isn't it?'

The man she was facing was dressed in a suit, the tell-tale curled wire of a walkie-talkie trailing between the collar and his left ear. 'Wh . . . what are you doing here?' she asked, stunned. She was vaguely aware of Sue looking curiously at her.

He shrugged, his face reddening. 'It's a job, innit?'

'You're a *bodyguard*?'

'Yeah. Looking after the Old Man.' There was a moment's awkward silence. 'You're still here, then?'

Dani nodded, still too surprised to speak. 'Yes. Where else would I go?' She stared at him. 'Well, I've got to run, I'm afraid . . . they're waiting for me. Look after yourself, Eric.'

'You too, Dani. You look well, by the way.'

'Thanks.' She flashed a quick, nervous smile and turned to go. Her heart was hammering.

'Hey, Dani . . . did you ever see him again?' he called out suddenly as she made her way across the floor.

She shook her head and called out over her shoulder. 'No. Never.' She tried to make her voice as light and offhand as she could. She gave him a quick wave and then disappeared through the doorway, emerging a few seconds later into fierce, blinding sunlight. She slipped her sunglasses on, glad of the chance to hide her eyes. If anyone had looked, the film of tears that had suddenly appeared would have surprised them. The tears surprised her. It had been ten years – long enough for the pain to have disappeared. She gave herself a quick shake. It hadn't, though. It had just coiled itself around her heart, slumbering, dozing, just waiting for the opportunity to strike.

PART TWO

12

Camden Town, London, 1987

'Fatty Matty! Fatty Matty!' Sam Maitland walked out of the school gates with her head held high, ignoring the jeers. It was always the same ritual, day after day. Fat girls had names hurled after them, pretty ones got the compliments. Both sets of girls affected not to notice. But it was hard not to. 'Oi! Fatso! I'm talking to you, you stupid cow!' The ringleader was a tall, oafish idiot called Joel Crawford who had a crush on Kate, Sam's twin sister. As a result, he singled Sam out every bloody day for special attention. And because Kate had repeatedly rebuffed him, he'd intensified his attacks on Sam. She hurried out of the school gate, trying not to look in their direction. Joel Crawford had had a crush on Kate Maitland for years – not that there was anything unusual in that. Every boy she'd ever known had a crush on her twin sister.

Sam sometimes wondered if God had been having a particularly hard day on 11 April, 1971. Two girls, born within six minutes of each other – one dark-haired, the other blonde. One olive-skinned, the other red-faced. One slender and petite, the other large and chubby. Kate was the sort of baby everyone cooed over. Exotic, even then Sam was the sort of baby everyone pulled faces at, then sympathised secretly with her mother. She was loud, she cried, she was stubborn. Kate was sweet, angelic, contented. As they became toddlers and then children, the gulf between them widened. Kate, six minutes older but always a stone lighter – *au minimum* – became the darling child. Sam was

63

the difficult one. If it baffled their parents, Julie and Steven Maitland, they tried not to show it. The Maitlands were of the generation that read child-rearing books with ardent, assiduous attention and tried not to repeat the mistakes they believed their parents had made.

Steven Maitland was a dentist. His small, two-room practice was on the Camden Road, sandwiched between a fish and chip shop and an Indian takeaway. Sam loathed the smell of the waiting room with its potted plants, and posters exhorting parents to bring their children to the dentist at least every six months. His clients were mostly council estate residents and recently arrived refugees for whom the dentist was a last-minute, usually emergency situation. Unlike the sons and daughters of their friends, the Maitlands had made the decision to send the girls to a state school, not a private one, though they'd taken the added insurance of elocution lessons for both of them. Despite her impressively progressive credentials, Julie drew the line at the threat of common-sounding daughters. It was another reason why Joel Crawford tormented her so. He reckoned Sam thought herself posh. Kate, on the other hand, ever the mimic, had long since learned to adapt her accent to suit her circumstances. Sam's tongue was awkward. When she tried to talk like the girls around her she sounded false, earning her yet more contempt. At home she was usually quiet, always allowing Kate the privilege of speaking first. It was Kate who burst into the kitchen, sharing her news loudly with her mother before Sam could get a word in.

As teenagers, Kate was the one with the 'normal' teenage concerns – clothes, boys, music, what party to go to, when to come home. Sam mostly stayed in. She had a couple of close girlfriends, quiet, rather bookish girls like her. They were more interested in reading than raving, books rather than boys . . . it suited Kate perfectly – gave her all the more room to shine – and Sam supposed it suited her too. She'd grown so accustomed to deferring to Kate, seeing her as the brighter, funnier, more sparkling and definitely more beautiful side of herself, that it simply wouldn't have occurred to her to complain, or attempt to change things in any way. There was a part of her that seemed to recognise long before she could put it in words that the only way she would ever grow into the person she thought she *might* one day be was by moving away. Now that they were in sixth form with university choices only a year or so away, it seemed as though she might finally get her wish. She hadn't told anyone – least of all Kate – but she intended to read law . . . and in Bristol. Miles away. Kate wanted to be a doctor. It suited her perfectly. She was good at maths, good at biology, good at chemistry. She was diligent, not brilliant, and medicine was just the sort of crowd-pleasing, impressive-sounding career for a girl like her. Sam's choice – law – was a little harder for her parents to brag about. Law? What sort of law? She didn't know. No matter. She just wanted to get as far away as possible, as soon as she could.

She hurried up Camden Road towards the market. She'd seen a scarf in one of the stalls at the weekend – a red and white checked affair that Palestinian youths wore, but after seeing it wrapped tenderly around Madonna's neck in her latest video, she'd immediately longed for one. She couldn't admit the latter reason to anyone but there was a teeny little part of her that thought she looked a *little* like Madonna . . . if she lost a few stone, of course, and learned how to dance. They both had thick, blonde hair, dark eyebrows and eyes that sometimes looked blue, sometimes brown. Sam could neither sing nor dance but there was something about Madonna's 'fuck you' attitude towards the rest of the world that she secretly admired. Madonna was afraid of nothing. Sam wasn't *quite* afraid of nothing – Joel Crawford was a case in point – but she would love to be. To say 'to hell with you all' . . . what a relief that would be. She was tired of pretending to be someone else – *not* interested in politics or current affairs, *not* interested in going to law school, someone who *didn't* care that her sister was everything she'd ever wanted to be and, above all, someone who *didn't* go to bed each night praying she would wake up thin. The last was the bane of her life. She'd tried just about every diet going – crash, quick, fast, sensible. Nothing seemed to work. At dinner she watched Kate wolf down industrial-sized portions of whatever was going, plus dessert, whilst she studiously avoided whatever it was the latest research dictated – no bread, no starch, less meat, more meat, no meat, whatever it took. Except it seemed to take everything, and nothing ever worked. She'd slowly but steadily gained a stone a year since her early teens and now, at the age of almost seventeen, she was five foot eight and weighed a shocking 14.5 stone in her bare feet. She felt like a whale.

A car horn sounded suddenly, jolting her out of her reverie. She stepped back onto the kerb just in time to avoid being hit. A cold, wet slap of water broke over her – the driver had gone straight into the middle of the puddle. She gasped and swore, dirty water dripping down the front of her duffle coat, seeping into the tops of her boots. 'Fucker!' she yelled at the car as it sped up the road. She looked around her; there were people standing on either side. No one even looked her way. If it had been Kate, she thought to herself miserably, half a dozen young men would have sprung forward offering handkerchiefs and revenge. In her case, no one even noticed. Not even the old ladies slowly wheeling shopping carts up the street. She was of interest to absolutely no one. She hoisted her bag onto her still-wet shoulder. She was almost seventeen years old and weighed nearly the same in stones. Why should she be surprised?

'What on *earth* are you wearing round your neck, darling?' Her mother paused in the act of drying dishes as Sam came through the front door. 'And whatever happened to your eyes? Are you . . . is that *make-up* you've got on?' She couldn't keep the surprise from her voice.

Sam hurriedly unwound the scarf from around her neck and hung it up. She mumbled something about Siobhân having put it on her as a joke and disappeared up the stairs as quickly as she could. She had no desire to be on the receiving end of her mother's surprise or ridicule. She went into the bathroom and closed the door. Why had her mother made such a fuss? She'd only put on a little bit of mascara and the thinnest line of eyeliner à la Material Girl. She squinted at herself in the mirror. Oh. *That* was why. She'd taken off her glasses to do it and hadn't looked properly as a result. The eyeliner on one eye had gone off track . . . the line, now smudged, extended almost vertically upwards towards her eyebrow whilst the other was nearly horizontal. Her face burned with embarrassment. She'd spent a whole afternoon in school without realising how daft she looked. She hurriedly scrubbed at her left eye, succeeding only in making it worse. She turned on the tap and tried to wash it off. It was Kate's eyeliner – she'd borrowed it from her make-up bag. Now she'd have to go and borrow some proper make-up remover to boot. Oh, the humiliation of it! And now her eye was stinging – some of the bloody mascara had gone inside the soft, wet membrane, causing tears. She put up a hand to staunch the flow and opened the bathroom door. With any luck she could sneak into Kate's room, rifle through her make-up bag for something that would take the offending streaks off her face and—

'What've you done to your face?' Kate was coming up the stairs at exactly the same moment Sam was crossing the landing.

She blushed violently. 'N . . . nothing. I was just . . . just trying something out, that's all.'

'Make-up?' Kate's tone matched their mother's. 'Are you wearing *make-up*?'

'No, course not. Well . . . not really. Just . . . just a bit. It was Siobhân's idea and—'

'*Siobhân?*' Kate gave a derisive chuckle. 'Come off it. I've never even seen her wear lip-gloss! Is that *my* eyeliner, by the way? Have you been going through my make-up bag?'

'No, it bloody well isn't,' Sam said, stung by the little reminder that Kate and *her* best friends were the type who wore make-up to class and Sam and her friends weren't. She was just about to add something ruder when she heard the front door close and her father's voice in the hallway. Any second now he would hang up his coat and come upstairs. She had no desire to hear what *he* would surely have to say on the subject of her face so, for the second time that week, she held her chin as high as it would go and disappeared into her own room, banging the door firmly shut behind her. She lay down on her bed, her cheeks burning with a mixture of embarrassment and shame. It was her own bloody fault. What on earth had made her think she could look anything like Madonna?

13

'But *why* don't you want to have a party?' Julie looked at Sam, bewildered. 'Kate wants to have one.'

'Then let her have it,' Sam said sulkily.

'Oh, for goodness' sake, Sam! It's your seventeenth birthday – they don't come round every year, you know.'

'Yes, they do. Year after year, like clockwork. That's the whole point of birthdays,' Sam couldn't resist snapping back.

Her mother pointed the rolling pin. 'Don't be so bloody difficult, Sam. You're having a party and that's the end of it. Why can't you be a bit more like your sister? She's been looking forward to it all year. We're going to have special—'

'Oh, go to hell.' Sam got up from the table and left the room before anything further could be said. *Why can't you be more like your sister?* It was becoming the chorus of her life.

Upstairs, in the safety of her own bedroom, she dragged her chair across the room and opened the window. She kicked off her shoes and put her feet up against the window sill, fished in the flap of her school satchel and took out a packet of cigarettes. She stared at it. *Benson & Hedges. Extra Mild.* She'd told no one that she was either about to go into the newsagent to buy them, or that she'd done it. She'd never smoked a cigarette in her entire life. She wasn't even sure why she'd bought them. Don't lie, she admonished herself silently. She knew exactly why she'd bought them. It was *Frantic*, the film she'd seen the previous week. She'd fallen in love, not only with Harrison Ford as had every other woman in the cinema, but with everything – Paris, the whole rain-drenched, gritty atmosphere of the city and its warren-like streets, the stuttering *bicyclettes* that everyone drove around on and Emmanuelle Seigner herself, of course: effortlessly hip, chic, street-smart, kohl-eyed . . . and always, always smoking. She'd practised smoking in front of the bathroom mirror. She looked nothing like the dark-eyed, dark-haired beauty – but seeing herself in the mirror, her hair out of her pigtails, glasses off, waving a cigarette casually around in one hand, had given her the tiniest glimpse of what she might like to be and *might even one day become*. Emmanuelle Seigner lit one cigarette after another with the smooth, practised air of someone who'd been born smoking, inhaling with studied pleasure, exhaling out of the corner of her mouth . . . beautifully, in other words. She, on the other hand, couldn't even get the damn thing to light and when she did, her nose ran. She stubbed it out with a sigh. She longed to be thin, chic, French and a chain-smoker.

She walked over to her dressing-table mirror and sat down, contemplating her image miserably. There was another reason she'd suddenly discovered a passion for all things French. Well, *one* thing French. A French *person*, to be more precise. Loïc Malaquais. He was an exchange student who'd come to Camden Community High School for the spring term and for Sam, at least, school would never be the same. She'd fallen in love the minute he walked through the door. He wasn't like any of the other boys in class. He was tall, for one thing, with dirty blond hair, blue eyes and broad shoulders the likes of which she hadn't seen on *anyone*, in person, *ever*. He wore V-neck sweaters in muted, gorgeously sophisticated colours and grey flannel trousers that had a long crease in them extending all the way to his perfectly polished English brogues. She knew they were brogues because she'd seen a similar pair in a magazine. He was a *man*, not a boy, and there wasn't a single heart in the sixth form that didn't agree. Even Miss O'Connor, the history teacher, who was just about the fiercest person Sam had ever known, was completely bowled over. He was *gorgeous*. And he'd spoken to *her*. Once. "Ave you got a light?' She'd almost swooned, much to Siobhán's disgust.

'Stop making those silly moon eyes over him,' she'd hissed in English. 'And don't look at him. He knows you're looking at him.'

'So what?' Sam hissed back. 'He's gorgeous.'

'Yes, I know. We *all* know he's gorgeous. But if you want him to pay attention to *you*, you've got to stop looking at *him*. That's how it works. Look at your sister if you don't believe me.'

Sam hadn't wanted to look but Siobhán insisted. She was right. Kate sat at the front of the class and didn't once look round. Loïc, of course, was entranced. She saw him go up to her in recess but it was too painful to watch. No one could have been more surprised, therefore, when he fell into line with her one day walking into school. '*Salût*,' he said easily. 'You're Sam, right?'

'Me?' She'd looked up at him in shock. He was talking to her?

'Yes . . . you're Sam, *non*?' He repeated the question.

Sam thought her heart would burst, right there and then. 'Um, yeah,' she mumbled. 'Yeah. I'm Sam.'

'You're in my history class.' It was a statement, not a question.

Sam didn't know what to do with her hands, her legs, her heart. He'd noticed her. What did *that* mean? 'Yeah. Yeah, I am. Um, so're you. In history, I mean.' She could have kicked herself.

'See you around, Sam.' He looked down at her, gave her a wink and sauntered off. She stood absolutely rooted to the spot, watching him walk. He had his hands in his pockets, and his jacket flapped behind him in the most sexily casual way *ever*. A group of fifth-year girls were standing huddled in a corner, smoking. They looked up as he walked past, giggling. He walked on without acknowledging them but there was a confidence in his easy swagger that let everyone know he *knew*. He knew just how damn good-looking he was. She looked down at her feet and was overcome with a fierce, almost painful longing to have him near her again, just for the pleasure of looking up into those blue, half-serious, half-smiling eyes and to feel them looking down on her. *See you around, Sam.* In that wonderfully deep, unbelievably sexy French voice. Oh, yes . . . she was smitten.

Loïc. Loïc Malaquais. She mouthed his name silently in front of the mirror, devoutly, watching in fascination the way her lips fastened over the unfamiliar French syllables. Her face stared back impassively at her. All she could see were the pudgy folds around her chin and cheeks; her eyes were two brilliant blue dabs in the expanse of light pink skin. Even her eyebrows and eyelashes were vague, blurred. She felt suddenly sick. She'd seen the red silk dress Kate had bought for the party; she'd pranced around the living room the night before, drawing the usual admiring comments from her parents. 'What're you going to wear?' her father had asked her, looking up from his paper and trying to sound interested.

'A tent,' Kate snickered.

'Kate,' her mother said in a voice of mild rebuke.

Kate turned her enormous brown, black-fringed eyes on Sam. 'Sorry,' she muttered. 'But it's *true*. She never makes an effort. It's not my fault if—'

'Kate,' her father said warningly. He looked up at Sam. 'What about that pretty dress you wore at Christmas? When we went to— Where're you going, Sam?'

Sam didn't bother to reply. She left the room with as much dignity as she could muster, the thick, familiar taste of tears building in her throat. She could hear Kate's voice all the way up the stairs. 'It's not *my* fault. She just mooches around in those awful black trousers and—' She closed her bedroom door. There was a half-eaten chocolate bar on the bedside table. She picked it up, peeled back the silver wrapper and crammed it, whole, into her mouth. She waited a few minutes for the sweet, sugary rush of saliva to subside then she lay down on the bed and turned her face into the pillow.

Three weeks. She had three weeks until the dreaded party. How much weight could she lose in three weeks? If she ate practically nothing . . . a stone, maybe? Would it even make a difference? Would anything make a difference next to Kate? *Please don't let him like her*, she breathed silently to her own reflection. *Please.* Kate had so many admirers . . . aside from Joel Crawford, there was Michael Howarth, Kevin Doherty, Pete McMillan, Justin Mowyer, Gareth Johnston . . . the list was endless. Every single boy she knew wanted Kate. *Please don't let him like her.* She closed her eyes and folded her hands in a way she hadn't done since she was small. *Please God. Please. Just this once.*

'So, how many people've we got coming?' her mother asked her and Kate at breakfast a few days later.

''Bout thirty,' Kate said, not looking up from her bacon and eggs.

'That's nice. I'll make lots of little snacks, shall I? Those nibbly little things . . . doubt anyone'll want a proper meal, will they?'

'Mmm.' Kate was too engrossed in her magazine to pay her mother much attention. Sam didn't have the heart to tell her that most of the guests would be more worried about the quantities of wine and beer on hand, not the hors d'oeuvres, and that most of them would wind up in the bin.

'Di-did you invite that new French bloke . . . what's his name? Louis?' Sam suddenly heard her own voice.

Kate looked up from her plate. 'Loïc? Yeah . . . why?' Her eyes narrowed.

Sam's face was on fire. She bent her head. 'No, no reason . . . just wondered.'

'You? I didn't think you even knew him.' Kate's tone was dismissive.

'I . . . I don't. I-I just wondered, that's all.'

There was a second's silence. Sam could feel Kate looking at her.

'Who's Louis?' her mother asked.

'Loïc, not Louis. He's the exchange student I told you about,' Kate said impatiently. 'He's only here for a term.'

'Oh. Well, is he coming?'

'Yeah, course he is.' There was another silence. Sam didn't dare look up. 'You like him, don't you?' Kate said incredulously. 'You fancy him!'

'I . . . I do not,' Sam muttered. Her face was burning.

'Yes, you do. Mum . . . she *fancies* him!'

'Oh. Well, that's nice, darling,' her mother said, placating, looking from one to the other of her daughters helplessly.

'Nice? It's ridiculous, not nice,' Kate snorted. 'What on earth makes you think—'

'Just fuck off, Kate.' Sam pushed back her chair and stood up. She hadn't touched her own breakfast.

'Sam!' Julie looked at her, bewildered. 'There's no need—'

She left the kitchen before either of them could say another word. 'Oh, Kate,' she could hear her mother sighing as she ran upstairs to get her coat and bag. 'Why's she always so *angry* at everyone?' She slammed the door behind her, shutting them both out. She couldn't be bothered to listen to Kate's smug reply. She could have kicked herself for opening her mouth. Now Kate knew she had a crush on Loïc . . . she couldn't bear being the subject of her ridicule or, worse, her pity.

Exactly three weeks later and half a stone heavier, if anything, she stood in front of the same mirror, frowning as Siobhân tried to pin her hair behind her ears – she had to stand on the bed to do so – and told her off for being sulky. 'It's your birthday,' she kept repeating, as if that would somehow make Sam smile.

'I *know* it's my birthday but why do I have to have a party?'

'Because.' Siobhân could offer no better explanation. Downstairs she could hear the music beginning to thump its way up the stairs. Kate had invited half their year; aside from Siobhân and Cassie, Sam hadn't invited anyone else. There wasn't really any point – the invitation cards Kate had sent out included her name anyway, and Kate certainly hadn't consulted *her* about the guest list. She didn't actually care who was coming.

'I'm bad, I'm bad, you know it, I'm bad . . .' Michael Jackson's urgent voice boomed up the staircase. Her heart sank even further. Music. Dancing. In her black, far-too-tight jeans and the yellow and red striped sweater that some idiot shop assistant in Top Shop had persuaded her to buy, she looked like an over-sized bee. She pulled herself impatiently out of Siobhân's hands and glared at her. 'Come on, let's get it over and done with. I can't stand the waiting.' Siobhân and Cassie exchanged uneasy glances. Sam's heart sank. She was behaving badly and she knew it but she just couldn't help herself. She turned away from the window with a heavy, nervous trembling in her stomach that made her long for something to eat. Her parents, trusting as always, had gone to stay with friends who lived up the road and would be back in the morning. Her mother had cooked herself into a frenzy preparing the sorts of small snacks and savouries she thought seventeen-year-olds would like. She couldn't put it off any longer. She walked down the stairs, Siobhân and Cassie behind her, her heart thumping almost as loudly as the music.

The house was already full of people, some of whom she'd never seen before. Friends of friends . . . a few people made eye contact, mumbled introductions and turned away. The drinks were already flowing. She caught sight of Joel Crawford in one corner of the room, lifting a can of beer to his lips. His eyes roved over her and then he turned and said something to the friend he'd brought along. There was a quick snigger and they both turned away, convulsing with laughter. She could feel her chest tightening in shame. It wasn't hard to guess what he'd said. She pushed her way through the crowd to the kitchen. A glass of wine. She had to find something to do with her hands. Kate suddenly appeared in front of her with a group of her friends. Her long, dark red silk dress swished elegantly around her feet. Her dark hair was pinned up in much the same way Siobhân had tried to pin hers – a few loose tendrils had escaped the knot and trailed down her face. Her face was made up perfectly – smoky eyes, red lips, cheeks beautifully flushed. She felt a sudden wave of tender pride sweep over her. Kate was so beautiful; she flitted in and out of the group like a delicate, yet fiery butterfly. She felt a sudden longing for those rare moments growing up together when they'd been close, not at war as they usually were. She watched her gracefully accepting presents and compliments, smiling at this one, laughing with that one . . . a hand on someone's arm, an arm around someone's neck. She was completely secure in her role as the prettiest and most popular girl in school. Why wasn't she more like Kate? Sam thought miserably as she poured herself a large glass of red wine. Her mother was right. *It's your own bloody fault you've hardly got any friends. You walk around all day with a face as long as the month!* She ought to make more of an effort. She *had* to make more of an effort. It was her own fault no one liked her. She turned away from the sight of her sister and looked for Siobhân and Cassie instead.

An hour or so later she wandered into the kitchen, looking for something to eat. She'd just popped one of her mother's sausage-and-bacon tarts into her mouth when someone spoke. She turned round. Kate was standing in the kitchen doorway holding out an enormous bunch of flowers. 'Ooh, look at these. Look what Loïc brought me. Be a darling and find a vase, will you?' Kate asked her, looking at him admiringly.

'Actually, they're for both of you,' Loïc said, smiling at Sam.

She didn't know whether to laugh or cry. They were standing together; Kate had one slim, tanned arm on his leather jacket. They looked like a movie couple. The red roses perfectly matched her dress. She had turned her head up to look at him; she was almost half his size. They were perfect together, simply perfect. But Loïc had said the flowers were also for her? That was nice of him . . . and a sign, surely? He'd thought about her, too. She took the bunch from Kate and walked self-consciously across to the cupboards where her mother kept the vases. She was painfully, acutely aware of Loïc's eyes on her as she filled the vase with water, some of it spilling onto her hands, and then set it carefully to one side. 'Th-they're lovely,' she stammered, turning back to look at him. Kate had disappeared but her perfume hung heavily in the air.

'*Oui*, there was a shop still open near the station. I think I'm the only one bringing flowers . . . it's not very English, *non?*'

Her heart gave a painful contraction. She loved the way he spoke . . . that funny, endearing combination of French and English. '*Non*,' she said with a quick, nervous grin. '*Pas du tout.*'

He laughed delightedly. 'You have a nice accent. In French, I mean.'

Sam's heart gave another painful squeeze. 'Oh, I'm hopeless at French. I'm hopeless at most things, actually.' She stopped and swallowed nervously.

'*Je ne crois pas.*' He looked at her, still smiling, and then gave her a quick wave, just as he'd done in the school grounds a few weeks earlier, and disappeared through the doorway.

Sam stood rooted to the spot. What had he just said? *Je ne crois pas*. I don't think so? I don't believe so? Believe what . . . that she was hopeless? Or that she was hopeless at most things? Either way, it was a compliment. Or was it? She took the vase of roses from the sink and walked with them gingerly into the dining room. There was no sign of Loïc but the scent of the flowers curled itself pleasurably around her nostrils. It was a little like having him near.

Siobhân and Cassie both had to be home by midnight. Sam stood with them at the garden gate and said goodbye. The party hadn't been quite as dreadful as she'd feared – true, she hadn't been asked to dance but at least no one had laughed out loud at her. And the little exchange with Loïc in the kitchen had generated a warmth that stayed with her all evening. She hadn't seen him again – he must have left with a group of boys earlier in the evening. She didn't mind. It was so kind and thoughtful of him to have brought flowers that the fact he'd gone home early was almost irrelevant. At least he hadn't danced with Kate all night. She wondered where Kate was . . . the party was slowly beginning to wind down but she hadn't seen her for over an hour.

She waved to Siobhân and Cassie and went back inside. The slow dances had been going for almost an hour; the tightly knit couples moved together silently in the dark. She hesitated for a second, then walked past them into the dining room. The roses were still sitting in the centre of the table. She quickly plucked one stem out and then turned and made her way upstairs. It was nearly midnight; most of their friends had to be home by then. In half an hour or so, the house would be quiet. Let Kate say goodbye to everyone, she thought to herself as she walked down the corridor to her room. It was more or less her party anyway. The rose was wet and cold in her hand. She passed Kate's bedroom; the door was shut. There was the soft murmur of voices within. She hesitated for a moment – she could hear Kate giggling and the sound of the bed creaking. She swallowed. There was someone in the room with her. She hurried past; she had no desire to hear what was going on inside. She'd never even been kissed before, not unless you counted Jem, their cousin, at the childish age of ten. She opened the door to her own room and shut it firmly behind her. She tugged off her too-tight sweater and undid the buttons on her jeans. Her head was swimming lightly – too much wine, plus the shot of vodka that Siobhân had insisted she drink. She fished her pyjamas out from underneath her pillow and pulled them on. Drat . . . she'd forgotten to brush her teeth. She opened her door again and peered out into the darkened corridor. It was empty. She could hear the front door opening and closing as the last of the party-goers let themselves out. The music had been turned off. The gate creaked, someone yelled out something . . . the house was almost quiet.

She hurried down the corridor to the bathroom, hoping that

Kate and whoever it was she had in her room wouldn't come out. Her pink and white spotted pyjamas had definitely seen better days. She was almost at the bathroom door when Kate's door suddenly opened. She was just about to make a dash for it when she heard Kate's voice. 'Loïc . . . hang on a minute . . . where's my bra?'

She closed the bathroom door behind her just in time. It was dark inside but she made no move to switch on the light. She leaned against the door, too stunned to even think. She could feel her legs giving way underneath her as she slid slowly to the cold, tiled floor. She laid her head on her knees and pressed her hands against her ears. She could hear them moving outside, going down the stairs, Kate's high-pitched, girlish little laugh. He hadn't seen her; that was one thing to be thankful for. The only thing. She sat uncomfortably on the hard floor, wanting to die.

14

ABBY
King's Road, London, 1987

'Notorious, notorious . . .' Duran Duran thumped loudly in the background, waiters hurried to and fro with cappuccinos and cocktails, people walking past the café stopped to look inside . . . all was exactly as it should be at four o'clock on a Friday afternoon on the King's Road. The sun, for once, was out but it was still bloody cold. Nineteen-year-old Abby Barclay and her two best friends Lily Carmichaels and Nicola Pemberton-Jones were sitting at a small table on the pavement, shivering in their flimsy cardigans and skinny jeans which Lily claimed made their legs look twice as long, although privately Abby wasn't convinced. She didn't like her legs, never had. Long, certainly, but with a slight tendency to turn *in* at the knee instead of *out*. At school she'd been known as Bandy. No one at Lucie

Clayton's knew that, of course, but for Abby, the stigma had stuck.

Lily, who was also at Lucie Clayton's, lit a cigarette, blowing the smoke seductively out of the corner of her mouth. She looked so grown up and worldly, Abby thought to herself enviously. She was wearing a long black cashmere cardigan that fell almost to her knees, black skin-tight jeans and flat ballet pumps à la Kate Moss, the modelling world's newest sensation and the style icon for most of the girls at Clayton's. Underneath Lily's cardigan she had on a thin, silky little camisole against which her breasts stuck out like two ripe plums. She was incredibly pretty. Long blonde hair, baby-blue eyes and the sort of mouth that men were mesmerised by. Abby surreptitiously looked down at her own chest – flat. Almost perfectly flat. She sighed. Her two older sisters, Carmen and Natasha, appeared to have used up whatever curves their maternal genes might have provided; she, sadly, had none.

'So, where to tonight, gels?' Lily drawled, narrowing her eyes and looking at them both expectantly. 'It's Friday night. We're young, gorgeous and, er, broke. Any ideas?'

'How about Henry J's?' Nicola suggested. 'There'll always be someone we know at the bar. Who'll pay,' she added mischievously.

'Darling, unless you can *guarantee* Yves and Perry are going to be there, *I* don't fancy having to pick up the tab. Daddy's already cut my allowance twice this month – I don't know why. Bloody unfair, if you ask me.'

'Well, you did rack up a few hundred at Laura Ashley the other day,' Nicola said. 'I don't blame him. How many bloody boots did you buy? Here, gimme a fag.'

'Buy your own, you grubby little gypsy,' Lily said, quickly removing her packet. 'Why d'you never ask her?' she jerked her head in Abby's direction.

''Cos I don't smoke,' Abby said quickly. 'So . . . is it Henry J's, then?'

'God, you're eager.' Lily threw Abby a sly glance. 'Wonder why . . . ?'

Abby blushed scarlet. 'I don't know what you're talking about,' she said airily, looking anywhere but at Lily.

'Oh, *please*! Don't give me that. I *saw* you. We *both* saw you. Although he *is* dishy, it has to be said.'

'I've no idea if he'll be there again, anyway,' Abby said quickly.

'Of course he'll be there. They're always there. And don't tell me you haven't noticed.'

Abby was silent. Around her the chatter of the café receded; she saw out of the corner of her eye Lily pull another cigarette from the packet. A waiter hurriedly bent forward to give her a light. Cars came and went, slowing to take in the zebra crossing on the corner and disappearing quickly out of sight. The sun was shining but it was chilly; the shadows cast by the buildings around them made black canyons of cold. She shivered. She thought of Ralph Barclay. Captain Ralph Barclay, whom she'd met twice at Henry J. Bean's. She, Lily and Nicole had been regulars since first term. After an afternoon spent learning how to tell a poinsettia from a hyacinth or under what precise circumstances it was deemed acceptable to accept dinner from a wealthy sheik, the escape into the smoky, chatter-filled bar rooms of Henry J's was a welcome relief. That it was full of young men who either lived and worked or aspired to live and work in the leafy squares around Chelsea didn't hurt either. Captain Ralph Barclay, whom she'd met at the bar whilst she was trying to order a G&T – *ice, no lemon, please* – was an officer stationed at the Chelsea Barracks, around the corner from college.

'No lemon? But that's the best bit,' he'd said, lifting a brow in amusement. She'd looked up, taken in the thick, glossy brown hair, the twinkling blue eyes with paper-thin creases at the corners and the dashing uniform and promptly fell in love. Ridiculous, her older sister Carmen scoffed when she told her over breakfast the following morning. 'Absolutely ridiculous.

You're always falling in love, Abs. You've got to stop. It's dangerous.'

Carmen was probably right but she'd gone back to Henry J's the following night anyway and was crushed to find him absent. She'd thrown herself into the cocktails and conversation with the group that had gathered around Lily and Nicole but her eyes kept wandering to the door, hoping to see him again. She'd just about given up hope when someone coughed suddenly, behind her ear. She jumped and turned around . . . and there he was. It was nearly ten p.m. and she'd been on the verge of leaving.

'Hello again,' he said, smiling down at her.

She ignored Lily's knowing smile and stood up. She had to tilt her head. He was easily a foot taller than she was. She liked that. She was quite tall for a girl — five foot six. Next to him, she felt petite. Yes, she liked that very much. 'Hello,' she said happily. She saw no reason to pretend otherwise. Lily and Nicole were forever discussing ways in which they conspired *not* to let the various men who bought them drinks know that they were interested. Abby privately thought it an enormous waste of time and energy. Ralph Barclay wasn't like that; she could already tell. He led her away from the group, back to the bar.

'What're you drinking? No, let me guess. A G&T with ice *and* lemon.'

'All right.'

'Good. I like a girl who learns her lessons.' He smiled down at her. Without knowing why, a kind of ease was already established between them. They moved off towards one of the window booths. He was in uniform; she saw the way the other girls in the bar looked at him as he passed and smiled to herself. He was with her.

Over the next hour and a half she learned that he was from Wiltshire and had bucked the family trend by going to university rather than straight to Sandhurst. His father had been an officer, and his grandfather before him.

'Me, too,' Abby said eagerly. 'We're army brats. I think it's my father's greatest regret.'

'Your dad's in the army?' Ralph looked at her in surprise.

Abby blushed. 'Er, yes. Well, he was. He's retired now.'

'What's his rank?'

'Um, major general,' Abby mumbled.

'Major general?' Ralph couldn't hide the surprise in his voice. 'There aren't many of those. What's your last name?'

Abby hesitated. 'Hutton.' There. It was out.

Ralph put his glass down carefully on the bar. 'Hang on a minute. You're telling me your Major General *Hutton's* daughter?'

Abby nodded. Her cheeks were scarlet. 'Er, yeah. The youngest. Of three.'

'Jesus, Abby. Why didn't you say?'

'Well, it's hardly something you go around advertising, you know. I mean, what'm I supposed to say? "Oh, hullo . . . my dad's the head of the SAS, by the way." It'd frighten most people off.'

'Not me.' He was looking down at her with an expression of such pleasure that she had to look away.

'Well, that just goes to show you how many officers I've ever been out with,' she said primly.

'I'm glad. I don't like the thought of it.'

'The thought of what?'

'The thought of you with anyone else.'

There was a sudden silence between them. She looked up into his eyes and saw, for all the light-hearted banter and the teasing way he talked to her, that he was serious and that he'd risked something by showing it to be so. She put a hand on his arm. Both Lily and Nicole were forever lecturing Abby on her disturbing lack of guile. She knew herself to be pretty, at least in the way most people understood – long, fair hair, blue eyes, good skin that turned rosy in the sun, a nice smile, pearly white teeth and a slim, if slightly knock-kneed figure. No breasts or curves to speak of, but tall nonetheless. At school dances she'd been as sought after as anyone else; a few boyfriends, nothing remotely serious. There was one, Tim Jones, who'd been following her around like a puppy dog for the past few months. He sometimes appeared at the café on the King's Road, trying desperately to look as though he wasn't waiting for her to arrive. He melted as though he'd never been.

Ralph looked down at her hand on his arm and responded by putting his own over hers. Suddenly he leaned forward. His lips touched hers, briefly. The jolt of electricity that passed through her left her trembling. She was still holding onto his arm but it was to support herself, not to reassure him. She would have fallen off her seat if she'd let go. With that part of her brain that still dimly cared about such things, she wondered what Lily and Nicola would say. She'd met him twice. He'd already kissed her. *Slapper*. She smiled. Nothing could have been further from the truth.

'Can I see you again?' he asked.

'Yes, of course. I'd like that.' There was absolutely no need to pretend.

'So would I.'

15

She brought him home to tea the following weekend. He wore Number Two Service Dress, the same olive green tunic and trousers that her father wore on parades, and a khaki green beret with his regimental badge. The Royal Anglian Regiment. 2RAR. She opened the door to him and her heart nearly burst with pride.

'Mummy,' she said, pulling him in through the doorway. 'This is Ralph.' She turned and presented him to her sisters as though he were a prize she'd won somewhere along the King's Road.

'Hello, Ralph. Won't you come in?' Her mother stood in the doorway, smiling pleasantly. Like her own mother before her, Elizabeth 'Libby' Hutton was an army wife through and through. Her husband's career came before everything else. Neither of Abby's two older sisters had chosen officers for themselves. Now, in the form of her youngest daughter, salvation was at hand. Abby had made a choice that she could, at long last, whole-heartedly approve of. She beamed at Ralph. 'What can I get you, Captain? A cup of tea? Or something a little stronger, perhaps?'

'Tea would be lovely, ma'am.'

'Oh, call me Libby, please.' Her mother, Abby noticed, had gone quite pink. She squeezed his hand in pleasure. More than anything she wanted her parents to approve.

Her father made a brief appearance in the living room, looked him over with his quick, professional eye and stayed to ask a few pertinent questions. 'Cyprus, eh?' he said, when Ralph told him where he'd be posted next. 'Poachers. Excellent regiment. Who's the CO? Ah, McColl. Good man. Well, I'll leave you with the ladies. You're in good hands.' He nodded at Ralph, a sign that was about as close to a stamp of approval as he could give, and left the room. Abby breathed a sigh of relief. Her mother beamed at them both. It was clear he'd passed the test. She sat down next to Ralph on the sofa, aware her knees were trembling slightly. Her mother asked all the questions that would establish him in their minds as the right sort of candidate. Ralph was only too happy to oblige. He spoke of his childhood and his family with such warmth and affection that even Carmen, who was the cynic in the family, was charmed. 'He's lovely,' she whispered as she and Abby went into the kitchen to fill up the kettle for the third time. 'Where the hell did you find him? Look, if you get tired of him . . .'

'I won't,' Abby said firmly. She meant it, too. She'd seen something in Ralph that she couldn't quite put into words. When their eyes met, it seemed to her that it merely served to confirm a friendship that had existed all along; somehow it only needed them to meet to discover it.

16

It was a summer of discovery. Out of some old-fashioned sense of decorum, Ralph did not push her further than she was prepared to go. He was five years older than her and probably ten times as worldly. Abby's childhood and teenage years belonged to an almost bygone era. Apart from the time spent at boarding school, she'd lived most of her life abroad. Her childhood had been one weary succession of overseas military bases, from Basingstoke to Borneo. She'd lost count of the number of schools she'd been to and the number of countries they'd lived in where even the water had to be flown in. Boarding school – an austere, cold place on the wrong side of a Worcestershire hill – in some ways, was a relief. You always knew where you were, she explained earnestly to Ralph. You knew when tea was served, what time supper was and whether it was lacrosse this term or not. There was very little variation. Three times a year she and her sisters would make the journey from Hereford to Heathrow and six or eight or fifteen hours later, depending on where her father was posted, they'd be met by a staff sergeant and an army car and be driven to the bungalow or block of flats or large, rambling house that was temporarily called home. All that moving around, and the fact that the only England she really knew was the all-girls' boarding school that she and her sisters attended, meant that she had a curiously outdated notion of what it was like to be a teenager or a young woman in a city like London.

Now that her parents had retired to the beautiful townhouse in Chelsea that had been her grandparents' gift to her mother on her wedding day and in which the family had barely spent a weekend, she'd essentially been given the keys to the kind of lifestyle that half the young girls in England would have given their right arm for – except she neither wanted nor recognised it. She liked hanging out on the King's Road and she quite liked her friends and the weekend drives out to the countryside but she had the strong sensation of sitting waiting for her life – her proper life – to begin. She was marking time; the only problem was, she didn't quite know why. The only thing that mattered to her that summer was Ralph – and art. No one quite knew where the artistic streak had come from. It was the only subject she'd truly enjoyed at school and the only time she'd ever voiced an opinion about what she really wanted to do.

Her mother, in particular, was baffled. No one on *her* side of the family – as far as she was aware – had ever aspired to be anything other than a wife and mother. There were no hidden *artistes* amongst the aunts or great-aunts whom they met once a year at Christmas. And on Charlie's side? Well, yes, there *was* someone who'd run off to Australia to be a painter but that had happened three generations ago and she'd never been heard of or seen since. She looked at Abby's sketches and notebooks with bemusement. Libby was a patron of the arts. She was on the board of half a dozen museums and galleries as befitting someone in her position. She adored the National Portrait Gallery and there were at least two dozen fine oils hanging on the walls of their charming London home that she'd personally selected over the years. She just wasn't sure that what Abby referred to as 'art' was quite what she had in mind as such. After Abby's A-levels there'd been a little bit of fuss. She'd wanted to go to art school. Charlie, of course, wasn't having any of it. 'Art school?' he'd spluttered, looking at her as if she'd suggested a moon visit. 'Whatever for?'

And that, in a nutshell, was pretty much the end of it. A week later Abby followed her sisters' example and was duly enrolled at Clayton's for the following term. 'Damn fine place. She'll soon come round,' was Charlie's only comment when told of Abby's dramatic outburst: 'I'll kill myself if you don't let me go,' or something along those lines. She did come round. She'd very little choice. She'd spent the better part of the previous summer locked up in her bedroom, refusing to eat. At the end of it, she'd lost a stone, her skin had never looked better and the phone rang off the hook. In September she entered the hallowed grounds of

Lucie Clayton's, met Lily and Nicola on her first day and that seemed to be that. She took the requisite classes in shorthand and typing and did well at both. In the evenings and at night she went out. The fuss over art school seemed to have been forgotten. Everyone, and no one more so than Libby, breathed a sigh of relief.

With a career out of the question and the subject of art school closed, it seemed to Abby that the two-year course at Lucie Clayton's and the social events planned around it were simply preparation for what would surely be the biggest and most important event of her life – her marriage. It all seemed so straightforward. There would be two or three suitors over a two- or three-year period, none of whom would be The One but would nonetheless provide sufficient experience for her to actually recognise The One when he finally showed up. That seemed to be more or less the pattern that everyone recognised and, to a greater or lesser degree, followed. Carmen and Natasha had both enjoyed the same route – so too would she. In her case, however, the fact that he'd shown up sooner rather than later didn't seem to bother anyone, least of all Abby. Captain Ralph Barclay ticked every box and that was what mattered. If he recognised her lack of experience and the fact that, at the age of nineteen, there was a line in her that hadn't yet been crossed – and it wasn't just the matter of being a virgin, there were other, deeper, more intimate boundaries that had yet to be breached – he didn't push against it. He seemed to understand in those moments when they kissed or he held her, her eyes tightly shut, that she couldn't take the jump across the years that separated them in a single leap. He was content to enjoy her only as far as she was able to go. With a sense of wonderment that they both felt, she experienced with him a deep, sensual pleasure that until then had been reserved only for certain works of art or poetry. In a curious reversal of roles, she discovered she was the one to push the boundary a little further each and every time, not Ralph. She was the bolder one, not him.

The long, hot summer months slowly ticked by. June, July, August and then September rolled in, all blustery clouds and drizzle. In November, Ralph would begin his second tour, this time in west Belfast. On the last weekend in September, he invited her to visit his parents in their Wiltshire home. It would be the first time they'd spent the night together. He teased her a little; his younger sister's bedroom was available . . . she could have it, or the couch downstairs. 'What'll your parents think?' she asked, her cheeks reddening.

'Abs, you're hardly the first girl I've brought home.' He laughed, ruffling her hair. She leaned against him, her arms wrapped around his waist. Strangely, the thought of his previous lovers caused her no pain, only a lingering curiosity. Without anything having been said, she somehow understood that something was about to change; something big. Something that would set the seal of her life and send it on its course.

They drove down to Wiltshire in a car borrowed from a friend of his. An Alpha Romeo, he pointed out to her. Italian. It had a soft top; the weather, for once, was glorious. He picked her up outside the college; there was the gratifying moment when they roared around the corner, the top down, her long blonde hair blowing in the wind and they passed a group of her friends. She waved at them so warmly that they turned to see who she was with and she saw in their expressions a kind of curiosity and envy that made her lower her hand in embarrassment. She hated the thought of showing off or being seen as such.

Ralph threaded his way expertly out of the London traffic, heading for the M4. Abby leaned back in her seat and slipped her sunglasses on. She felt like a film star – somebody else, not Abby Hutton, nineteen years old with six O-levels, two A-levels and a nearly completed Certificate in Secretarial Studies. Ralph's hand lay on her knee when he could take it off the gear stick. He too was wearing sunglasses. His brown hair ruffled lightly in the wind. She sighed deeply, taking the late Indian summer air down into her body and exhaling slowly. A warmth came over her, sparking memories of other places, childhood homes, different kinds of heat – the steamy, tropical heat of Malaysia, the dry, desiccated heat of Oman and the soft, balmy heat of Malta. It was England she liked best, she realised, turning her head to look at the countryside as it slid past in a cornucopia of greens, yellows and golds. The trees were on the cusp of turning colour; another of the things she missed whenever she was away. In the Far and Middle East where she'd spent much of her childhood, the seasons barely registered.

'Isn't it beautiful?' she said, turning to Ralph. 'England, I mean.'

He turned his head briefly to smile at her. 'This fair and pleasant land,' he murmured.

'Won't you miss it?' she asked after a moment. 'Being away.'

He shrugged. 'Not if I take a little piece of it with me,' he said quietly. His hand was on her knee; his fingers tightened very slightly, just enough for her to know he was referring to her.

Abby blushed. Her sense of something momentous about to happen intensified all along the route so that by the time Ralph pulled into the driveway of his parents' home, her whole being was suffused with anticipatory joy that brought a delicate blush to her cheeks. She got out of the car. Ralph took their cases from the boot. A woman was standing in the doorway of an old, age-mellowed house, a trail of honeysuckle roses climbing the trellis that ran up one side. She was smiling – a broad, generous smile that was also her son's. Again Abby had the sense of entering into an image she already knew. She felt herself being enveloped in the woman's warm embrace, and, in a way she thought she would never be able to put into words, it was a homecoming of the sort she'd never previously experienced. In Ralph she'd already found a home. The rest, including the future, was simply the detail of how it would come about.

17

MEAGHAN
Warra, Queensland, Australia, 1989

She squatted in the shadow of the garage, fumbling for a cigarette. It was four o'clock in the afternoon, the shadows were already long and flat on the ground and in the distance, the hazy blue outline of the mountains would soon turn to milky, lilac infinity. She struck the match, felt it jump into flame and lit the first cigarette of the day. She drew on it deeply, feeling the inhalation becoming her own breath, taking it deep down into her lungs. When she blew out the smoke, the tension she'd been carrying all day disappeared with it. The first cigarette. How she looked forward to it. She smoked in silence, her own. Overhead, a floating pyramid of gullahs swooped on invisible currents of air, turning this way and that to some unseen, unheard command. Winter was approaching; there was a distinct chill in the air. She could hear the tractor growling its way up the hill; one or other of her brothers was already working, his day's work at school being the forerunner for this other, more important job: his life's work. Hers, too. The farm. God, how she hated it. She stubbed out the cigarette, finished now, right down to the yellowed butt, and stood up. She let her eyes follow the line of the hills closest to the house; they were shedding their autumn coats, turning bare. The blue-gums were parched and dry – amongst them stood several trees that had been burned, either by lightning in one of those late summer storms that swept across the landscape, or by fire, jumping selectively, destroying whole trees here and there, but never en masse.

'Meaghan?' she could hear her mother's voice calling from the kitchen. It was nearly four thirty – time to go in. There was a whole second shift waiting for her. If her four brothers had work above and beyond the algebra and history they struggled with every afternoon, she too had her own form of torment after school. By four thirty, her mother was barely able to stand, let alone conduct the orchestra of cooking and feeding five men – even Jimmy, the youngest, at thirteen was already a man. It was the farm. It sucked every drop of whatever they each had to give – blood, sweat, tears . . . it made no difference. They fought it at every turn, mucking, baling, clearing but it stubbornly refused to yield. Meaghan could hardly remember life before it. They'd lived in the town – well, you could hardly call it a town: a collection of houses, a post office, bottle store and a single supermarket – and then one day, just after her sixth birthday, her father had suddenly announced they were moving fourteen kilometres west of Dalby, to a farm. A *farm*? She'd looked from her mother to her father in alarm. Even at six she knew whatever little she and her brothers knew about farming was more than her parents put together. But her father was over the moon. One fight in the local bar too many, one hungover morning that had snapped his boss's patience . . . and he'd been sacked. Not that the loss of his job as a janitor at the local milk factory made much difference. The Conways were poor; always had been, always would be. The one bit of money they'd ever had – the payout from his compensation suit against the factory that had employed him for thirty years until his accident – was suddenly there for the taking. With it, he bought a farm. So there they were, the Conways from Dalby, now the proud owners of thirty-two acres of unfarmable farm land, sixteen cows which they struggled to keep alive and a vegetable patch. There were weeks when all they ate were potatoes, onions and cabbage. And the drink, of course. Of that there was always a regular supply.

'Meaghan?'

'Coming, Mum.' She ground the little stub into the dirt and slowly made her way back up to the house.

Her brothers trooped in, one after the other, still sweaty and covered in dust. 'What's for dinner, Meg?' Clive, the eldest, sniffed the air as he walked past.

'Same as yesterday,' she replied mildly, giving the stew one last stir. At sixteen she could already produce a meal out of nothing.

'Rabbit stew *again*?' Paul, second to youngest, pulled a face.

'It's that or beans on toast.'

'Oi! You complainin'?' Their father was sitting around the corner in the living room, his leg propped up on a footstool, the obligatory can of beer in his hand.

'No,' Paul said reluctantly.

'Good. Just as well. Or I'd up and give you a fuckin' hiding.'

Meaghan glanced quickly at her brothers. *Don't get him worked up*, she mouthed at them. Clive rolled his eyes but there was no fight in them. Meaghan was relieved. The last time he'd raised his fists to them, they'd all wound up in the fray. In the tight, terrible intimacy of those moments, all four of her brothers struggling and shouting to keep his blows off them, the two women in the family, Meaghan thought she might go mad. They were like wild creatures, a single, sweating, cursing mass of arms and fists and legs. Then, almost as suddenly as it had begun, it was over. One or other of her brothers would have delivered the punch that knocked Mike Conway out. Her mother would be led, weeping, to the bathroom to attend to whatever cut or bruise she'd sustained and the whole house would settle into a quivering, nervous quiet. Meaghan had long since learned how to duck and weave, avoiding being hurt. But her mother, reactions dulled by an afternoon of drink and the minor bickering that invariably led to the fight in the first place, wasn't always so lucky. Sometimes Meaghan thought she actually wore her scars with pride. There were many – one particularly nasty one above her left eyebrow. Meaghan could still remember the fight that had led to that. A burned piece of meat. A question and a lippy answer. More than anything, Mike hated what he called 'lip'.

'Oi!' Mike's voice brought her hurriedly back to herself. She blinked. He was sitting in his place at the head of the table, a knife and fork in either fist. She couldn't remember seeing him get up from his position in front of the television and walk over to the dining table. 'Oi!' he repeated. 'Get a move on, you stupid cow. I'm starving.'

'Sorry,' she muttered, hurriedly bringing over the pot. She looked around the table. Her brothers, faces and hands washed, hair combed back behind their ears, waited for her to start serving. In such moments, the hard, angry lump of pity would settle itself firmly in her throat and she'd be unable to speak. It was only thanks to her mother that there was any grace left in this graceless household. She ladled the stew out, choosing the best bits for Clive, her favourite, making sure the stringiest pieces of rabbit were reserved for her father, and then she served her mother and herself. They ate quickly and quietly; it was only when Mike was gone from the table, shuffling with his one crook leg over to his spot in front of the television, that the conversation started up. Mike wasn't a big man – how he had produced four such strapping lads was a mystery to everyone, Meaghan included – but the shadow he cast was long and deep.

She'd finished washing up the dishes and had just gone out the back door to have a cigarette when she heard the beginnings of an argument between her mother and father break out. She sighed. What the hell was it *this* time? *I can't stand a woman with a long fucking face. Nothing I fucking hate more.* And so on and so forth. She could hear her mother wheedling, pleading with him; it enraged her. Why didn't she just tell him to shut up? To take his anger and his drink and shove them up his arse? Sometimes she'd come in on them in the middle of one of their fights, he climbing into his anger like a suit, she half-dancing around him, sometimes even touching and kissing him, petting him into a better mood. Meaghan was a fighter; she desperately longed for her mother to be one too. But she would never be. Mary was a timid, careful woman who understood that she'd thrown her life away aged nineteen and no amount of drink, petting or wheedling would bring it back. *Don't do what I did,* she cautioned Meaghan over and over again. *No fucking chance*, Meaghan longed to shoot back, but she didn't.

She heard the first slap, then the second, and then the slow whimper that signalled defeat. She wasn't going to fight back. The boys were in their rooms, which was just as well. The last time Clive got involved she'd thought someone might actually die. She stubbed out her cigarette and walked back in. Perhaps the sight of her in the kitchen doing something ordinary, like making a cup of tea or feeding the parakeets that lived in the corner of the dining room, would calm things down. She gave a silent, mirthless laugh. Ordinary? There was nothing ordinary about anything in her life. Nothing at all. At school she had few friends – how could she, living fourteen kilometres away from the nearest classmate? At times she was grateful – she couldn't imagine bringing anyone back to this. There was no one to confide in. She was both fiercely ashamed of what went on at home and fiercely protective of it. She'd have slapped anyone who said anything about her family, and that, curiously, included her father. But she'd also sooner have died than bring anyone home.

'Cup of tea, anyone?' she enquired, walking into the kitchen. Her father was sitting in his chair, nursing a beer and a sullen mouth. Her mother was sitting next to him, an arm draped around his shoulders. She too was drunk. Her tipple of choice – Baileys – stood in a glass beside her, the thick, creamy liquid clinging to the ice cubes as they melted slowly. Meaghan felt sick.

'Oi. Shut your mouth, you. No one's talking to you.'

Meaghan felt the slow burn of resentment building up in her stomach, like bile. 'I was only asking . . .' she began, as mildly as she could.

'Yeah, well, no one's fucking listening, you dumb cunt.' Mike was truly in a rage.

'I only meant—'

'Will you shut the fuck up?' Mike turned his head to look at her. She lifted her head and looked him squarely in the eye. It

94

was her first mistake. She saw him set his beer carefully to one side and stand up. She ought to have walked out at that point; she knew it. Her mother knew it, too. She looked up at Meaghan and there was a strange, pleading look in her face. He walked slowly towards her but there was something in her that made her stand her ground. It was now or never. He'd hit her before, of course, but usually in the midst of some other, more urgent fight. She'd had a slap or two directed solely at her, but nothing like the menace she sensed coming towards her now. But still her legs refused to obey her brain; they remained where they were, rooted solidly in the kitchen tiles. Her chin, too, wouldn't budge. She stared him in the eye until he was so close she could smell his breath as her own.

'Mike . . .' It was her mother's voice. 'Mike . . . don't.'

The first slap caught her off-guard. It was so swift and aimed so squarely in the middle of her face that she thought she'd been shot. The shocking sting radiated outwards, like ripples on a pond. She should have gone down, put up her hands to protect herself, kicked him in the shin, the balls, anywhere. She didn't. The same stubborn pride that had prevented her from running brought her back to face him, upright and proud. 'Go on. Do it again.' The words came from her as if from someone else. The second slap was followed with a kick. Her mother leapt up, shouting. And then all hell broke loose. Clive burst through the dining room door, took one look at Meaghan's bleeding face and with an ugly roar, hurled himself at his father. Stevie and Paul weren't far behind. There was an awful lot of tussling; the boys easily had Mike pinned on the ground. Mary was screaming and crying; in the corner, Jimmy pressed his face against the wall, weeping. Meaghan was forgotten.

She stood in the doorway for a moment, breathing deeply. Her face was still singing from the slaps and there was a warm, wet trickle of blood still seeping from her nose. She put up a hand to touch it lightly; it was swollen, but not broken, she didn't think. She walked slowly down the corridor to her bedroom. The beast that was the fight she'd left behind was still shouting, struggling to give birth to *something*, she didn't know what. All she knew was that she couldn't be a part of it any longer. She closed her bedroom door behind her and leaned against it for a second. She wasn't sure what she was doing. She had to get away. The cold, hard hand of her future reached out to grab her and hold her fast but she shrugged it off. She didn't want it. A year or two more of useless, pointless schooling that would leave her fit for nothing other than marriage to someone like her father, or worse. Kids, a farm to run, nowhere to go, nothing to do with her life except that which her mother had done. Cook, clean, fuck, sleep . . . wake up the next day and do it all again, sometimes with the help and ease of a drink. She swallowed painfully. She wanted more. Of course she did. She wanted more and she wanted out. She walked over to the dresser, picked up a small bag and quickly began to pack.

She had no clear idea of where she was going. Away. Anywhere. She walked down the long, dusty track that led to the farm gate and from there the gravel road that ran into town. It was nearly seven o'clock in the evening and the colour was almost gone from the sky. No one would see her go; no one would miss her until the following morning when Jimmy came to knock on her door for school. It was Thursday. By supper the following evening, it would be clear to them that she was gone. She would phone her mother from wherever she landed up, and Jimmy, too. She thought of his little, earnest freckled face and the stars began to blur. She wiped her chin carefully; her face still ached. She hadn't even had time to wash it. She shouldered her bag, blew her nose as carefully as she could through her fingers and picked up her pace. Someone would come along at some point – if not, she'd walk. She wasn't afraid of the dark and she certainly wasn't afraid of a long walk. What she *was* afraid of she'd left behind.

18

It was almost dawn when the truck pulled into the parking lot behind the station. The driver, a taciturn older man who'd hardly talked on the two-hour journey in from Dalby, switched off the engine, readjusted his cap and looked at her. 'Well, here we are. Brisbane. D'you know where you're going, love?'

Meaghan shook her head. 'Not really. But I'll be fine. I . . . I'll find somewhere.' She turned her face away from him. She didn't want his pity. He'd stopped on the road just before Dalby, taken one look at her bloody face and opened the door. To his great credit, he hadn't asked her much. Not so far, at least.

He took off his cap and scratched his head. 'Look,' he said finally, settling it back again. 'If you're really stuck, give me sister a ring. Her name's Grace. She's out Woolowin way. You got any money on you?'

Meaghan shook her head. Her cheeks were burning. 'A bit,' she said softly. 'Not much. But don't worry about me, mate. I'll be fine. Thanks for the lift.'

'Here.' He stuck a hand into his pocket and pulled out a few notes. 'No, take it, go on. You look like a good kid. Dunno what's happened to you and I ain't gunna ask. Here.'

Meaghan hesitated, then took the notes from him. It was the unexpected kindness that brought tears to her eyes, not sadness at what she'd done or left behind. 'Thanks,' she said.

'Don't mention it. Here . . . here's Gracie's number. I'm Robbo, her brother. Robert King's the name.'

Meaghan took the scrap of paper from him. 'Thanks again, Robert,' she said, and slipped down from the cab to the ground. She walked away quickly, her back held very straight, looking ahead. She didn't want him to see her cry. She heard the great engine roar into life and the screech of the wheels as he pulled the truck around. He gave a single hoot and then swung out into the road. She waited a few moments, then turned round herself. The last she saw of him was his red tail lights disappearing into the dawn. She was alone. Properly alone. It was just past six o'clock in the morning. She was in Brisbane and she was utterly alone.

She walked down Chippendale Street towards the river. She had no clear idea where she was going, but the river seemed a good place to stop and gather her thoughts, think about what to do next. She was hungry, too. She looked down at the notes Robert had thrust at her – sixty bucks. She blinked in surprise. It was way more than she'd expected, and way more than she currently had. She opened her wallet. Thirty-odd dollars and a bit of change. She slipped the extra notes in carefully, zipped it up and stowed it back in her bag. She crossed the wide street that led to the banks of the Brisbane, now thickening to life in the hour or so before rush-hour traffic really began. The sun was up, glinting stonily off the cold blue surface of the river. She walked across the cycle path to the grass, feeling in the dampness underfoot the chill of the previous night. There were benches galore; on some of them, a few drunks were already sprawled, loose empty bottles lying where they'd rolled and come to a stop. She chose an empty bench and sat down. Her face was stiff but her nose no longer ached. She was hungry, too. Aside from a cup of coffee along the way, she'd eaten nothing since the previous evening. Down at the water's edge small metal kiosks were slowly opening up, setting up for the morning's trade. She could smell coffee and the scent of frying bacon. Her stomach rumbled alarmingly. She got up, hoisted her bag onto her shoulder and moved towards them. First, something to eat. Then a plan. Everything else could wait.

PART THREE

19

MEAGHAN
Brisbane, Australia, 1992

Trapped inside their second, steel crania, some of Brisbane's wealthiest ladies were soaking their nails in tepid oil or reading any one of the latest European magazines, unable to hear anything other than the hum of the dryer. Meaghan hurried past them with a bowl of hot water in her hands. Her client, Mrs Grace-Anne MacFarlane, wife of Jim 'Jonno' MacFarlane, the man widely tipped to be the city's next mayor, was waiting. Meaghan knew from past experience that Grace-Anne Mac-Farlane – *you must call me Gracie, my dear. All my friends do!* – didn't like to be kept waiting.

'*There* you are!' Grace-Anne looked up as Meaghan approached. 'I thought you'd popped out!'

'No, there was a queue at the back of the salon, Mrs MacFarlane. Everyone seems to have a party to go to.'

'Don't I know it,' Grace-Anne MacFarlane said with a deep sigh. 'I don't know *how* many of them I've had to attend. I tell you, if it wasn't for Jonno . . .' She trailed off significantly. Meaghan only just managed to suppress a smile. The salon had a chemical sweetness that attracted these women – wives of city politicians and businessmen – like bees. On Fridays and Saturdays they streamed in and out of the doors in twos and threes, cooing at each other, examining cut, tint and colour the way a jeweller might pick up a diamond and squint at it in the light, looking for flaws. These women wore their husbands' successes (and, occasionally, failures) like badges. Who was on his way up, who wasn't; who was tipped for a post; who'd just lost his. Meaghan scrubbed and polished and filed all the while affecting not to hear or see what wasn't hers to know.

'There we go,' she said half an hour later, adding the last few drops of hardener to Grace-Anne's red talons. 'All done.'

Grace-Anne held her hands out in front of her. '*Very* nice,' she said approvingly. 'I must say, you do a good job, my dear. A *very* good job. I've never been disappointed and that's saying something, isn't it, Jenny?' She turned to the woman sitting next to her. 'She's so good, our Meaghan. She *really* is.'

'Oh, I know. I'm always trying to get an appointment on Fridays but you ladies always take the best slots.' Jenny Gordon, the wife of a minor city official, was quick to defer to Grace-Anne's superior rank.

Grace-Anne took the comment as it was intended; a little flattery every now and then would do Mark Gordon's career no harm. No harm at all. 'Well, I've been coming here for years, haven't I, Meg?' Grace-Anne said archly.

Meaghan nodded. The faux-cheery chumminess that women like Grace-Anne affected with the girls who worked in the salon always made her laugh. *Call me Gracie! All my friends do!* For one thing, Meaghan was more than three decades Grace-Anne MacFarlane's junior. And for another, they came from opposite ends of the social spectrum. Grace-Anne MacFarlane was the closest thing Brisbane had to royalty. Still, if it amused and flattered her to make friends with a girl who'd run away from home and spent the better part of three months on the streets of Brisbane without a job or any idea where her next meal was coming from . . . well, who was she to deny her the experience? Not that Grace-Anne was to know any of that. No one knew. Certainly not the girls she worked with and for. No one would ever guess that three short years ago, she'd run away from a farm outside Warra with less than forty dollars in her pocket and no plan. No plan whatsoever.

She'd been lucky; there were some girls she'd shared a park

bench with over the course of those three months who hadn't been quite so fortunate. Two rapes, one knifing and one botched abduction attempt. True, some of the girls were junkies, so high they'd have done anything and gone with anyone for the money to score their next fix. But there'd been a couple like herself – teenagers who'd run away from home or fallen foul of a stepfather or the law and wound up on the streets. She'd found an unexpected kindness in some of those girls, one of whom, Marge, she still saw occasionally. Marge worked in a florist's shop, near the museum on the other side of the river. There was always a wariness in her eyes when they bumped into one another, as if she thought Meaghan might suddenly reveal to others what it was she hid from in herself. She needn't have worried. Meaghan had no more desire to remember those days than she did.

'You all sorted for tomorrow night, then, Grace-Anne?' she asked, getting up from the stool. 'Got your dress and everything?'

'Oh, yes, thank God.' Grace-Anne nodded and then leaned conspiratorially towards Jenny Gordon. 'I always have them bring the latest samples round to the house. Can't stand the crush in the changing rooms, if you know what I mean.'

'Oh, er, yes . . . yes, I do. I . . . I do the same.'

Grace-Anne's eyebrow twitched just a fraction, as if she saw through the little white lie. Meaghan picked up the basin and hurried through to the rear of the salon. Any moment now she'd burst out laughing.

'What's so funny, Meg?' Kylie, one of the senior beauticians, asked her as she squeezed past with a basin of her own.

'Nothing, really. They just make me laugh, that's all.' Meaghan jerked her head in Grace-Anne and Jenny's direction.

'Well, hold your laughter. Here comes your next appointment.'

Meaghan looked up. Her heart sank. It was Darya Zhuskova, the demanding, petulant girlfriend of one of the city's wealthiest property developers. She was Russian – or Turkish or Armenian or Lithuanian, depending on what gossip paper you read. She was fond of changing her mind at the very last minute. Just as you'd finished with the top coat and were preparing to clear up in time for your next client, there she'd be, standing in front of you with that ridiculous pout on those ridiculous lips. 'Darling, I don't like it. I must to change it.' And you'd have no choice. Sit down, take it all off, repaint.

'Hi, Darya . . . I won't be a moment,' Meaghan called out. 'Just have a seat.'

'Darling, I'm in hurry. Big hurry.'

Meaghan took no notice. Darya was always in Big Hurry. 'Just take a seat, love. I'll be right with you.' She went about calmly filling the basin with warm soapy water, adding a few drops of soothing oils. She wasn't about to jump through hoops for someone who'd take up all her own appointment and the next person's as well.

'Good on ye,' Kylie whispered as she filled her own basin alongside her. 'Silly cow.'

'Yeah, well, you never know,' Meaghan said and smiled, 'maybe today she'll drop a tip.' It wasn't likely. In the six months she'd been attending to Darya's hands and feet, she'd never so much as received a ten-dollar note for her troubles. A couple of bucks in change was more the norm, doled out with the largesse of the aristocracy. Still, she was a regular client – at least twice a week, sometimes more. Such clients, Sue, the salon owner, was forever telling them, were to be cherished. *Cherished.*

'Here we go,' she sang out as she set the basin down carefully in front of Darya. She carefully stowed Darya's many possessions to one side. The handbag alone would have paid the rent on the tiny flat she shared with two other girls, both beauticians but at different salons. It was Chanel – a large quilted and buckled affair, bristling with logos. Her matching keychain, keyring and wallet were equally expensive. The keyring alone would probably have paid for her car. Just thinking about her car brought an automatic smile and a flush of pride to Meaghan's face. It was old – exceedingly old – but it worked. A fifth-hand

Toyota of a number of different colours. She'd spotted it in the parking lot at the end of her road and gone in to enquire. Thirty minutes later she drove off in it, gears mashing noisily. It was the only thing she'd learned on the farm that had turned out to be of any use – how to drive. It was Clive who'd taught her. Dear Clive.

She busied herself putting out the various lotions and oils that Darya liked but let her mind drift for a second. Clive was in Warwick, about an hour and a half's drive south of Brisbane. He'd lasted another year after Meaghan and then he too had buggered off. He was the assistant floor manager in a large DIY warehouse. He had a girlfriend, Sal, with whom he shared a small house. Things had turned out OK for him. It was the others they worried about. Meaghan hadn't gone back since the night she'd left; through Clive, she sent messages home to her other brothers and her mum. She wanted nothing more to do with her father, ever. She couldn't have cared less if he lived or died. But it was her brothers she missed, especially Jimmy. He and Stevie more or less ran the farm. Meaghan phoned every month; somehow in the three years since she'd left, they hadn't once met. There was a tacit agreement on both sides that it would be too painful. Meaghan continued to phone; they continued to pretend in front of Mike that she no longer existed.

'So, what've you got lined up for the weekend?' Meaghan asked chattily as she lowered Darya's exquisitely manicured feet into the basin of soapy, scented water.

'Oh, you know . . . party, party, party. Boring. I hate parties.' Darya was busy thumbing through a copy of *Vogue*. Her tone was one of perfectly pitched dissatisfaction.

I'll bet you do, Meaghan thought to herself. She began to scrub Darya's already perfectly scrubbed foot.

Darya was still complaining. 'I ask Matt for car. Nice car. Jaguar. You know Jaguar? Black, with gold wheels. You know what he tell me?' Her voice rose in indignation. Meaghan shook her head. ' "Maybe for birthday, baby." You know when is my birthday?' Meaghan shook her head again. 'October!' Darya spat the word out. 'Two whole month. Why I must wait?' She pronounced it 'vait'.

'Well, October's only round the corner, love,' Meaghan said as mildly as she could. She tapped Darya's other foot. 'Just put this one up here for me . . . yeah, that's it.' She listened to Darya's petulant rants with half an ear – no, less. A quarter of an ear. She amused herself for a few moments thinking about various ways in which she could split her attention so that only the most minuscule, tiniest part of her brain was occupied with Jaguars and Chanel handbags. The other, larger side of it surged ahead to more pressing concerns. Like what to do with her life. She'd been working at Bliss, one of Brisbane's top spas, for almost two years. She'd been hired to sweep the floors and had wound up doing manicures and pedicures instead. Well, 'wound up' wasn't quite the right word. She'd passed by the salon on the way to her job as a checkout girl one day, seen an advert for a general cleaner and walked in, still wearing her Pick 'n' Pay apron – *Hi, I'm Meaghan. How may I help you?* She'd tossed the apron in the bin as soon as Sue uttered the magic words, 'Yeah, all right, you'll do. When can you start? Tomorrow? Great. See you then.'

That was two years ago. She'd started off cleaning up after everyone and finished with a City & Guilds Level Two Certificate in Manicures and Pedicures. OK, so it was hardly an MBA but it *was* a stepping stone, though she wasn't yet sure towards what. She knew she didn't want to work at Bliss for the rest of her life but a better, more ambitious alternative hadn't yet presented itself. It would, one day. Just not yet.

An hour later, Darya's hands and feet were set to dry under the new UV machine Sue had imported from the US and Meaghan had the luxury of a fifteen-minute break. She carefully carried over the several thousand dollars' worth of handbag and accessories to where Darya sat, her head still buried in *Vogue*, ticking off the items she wanted, and hurried out the back. Two other girls were leaning against the brick wall, cigarettes in hand.

Meaghan accepted a cigarette from one of the other girls and they smoked in companionable silence.

All too soon her short break was over. She popped a stick of gum in her mouth and pushed open the door again. The salon was even busier. There was a queue of women by the front door; Sue was running back and forth between, trying to squeeze clients in here and there where she could. It was chaotic but there'd be a nice fat bonus for all of them if they managed to see to everyone and turned no one away. Sue was good like that – she cared about her business and knew that the best way to make it grow was to care about the girls that ran it.

'Meg?' Sue caught Meaghan's arm as she rushed past. 'Do us a favour, will you, love? There's a bloke out in reception. Will you help him out for a sec? I've got two girls to see to right now. Oh, and when you're done, I've got Marjorie Heemens in the front. She wants a quick manicure. Won't take more than fifteen minutes, I promise. Just a change of colour. Thanks, Meg . . . I owe you one.' She disappeared down the corridor at a brisk trot.

Meaghan walked through to the reception area. It was her favourite part of the salon. An elegant old Victorian house in the middle of the city, it had been transformed by the architects into a series of slick, modern boxes with lush green plants, dark leather seats and gleaming white basins. White walls; aubergine, dark grey and mustard curtains and cushions; marble floors – it was easily the trendiest spa in Brisbane. The reception area was a light-filled, beautifully proportioned room with antique furniture and oriental rugs everywhere. Meaghan loved it; there was something so old-fashioned and soothing about the leather-topped desk where they took client bookings, the plush, velvet sofas where ladies sat and waited, a silver tray of coffee or sparkling water at their elbows, racks of the latest magazines spread out on the coffee tables in front of them. Today there were three women waiting for their turn to be called.

And in the corner, looking nervously out of place, a man stood, clearly wishing he were anywhere but there. Meaghan looked at him. Two things stood out. One, he was a soldier, dressed in uniform; two, he was tall and rather good-looking. The latter wasn't lost on the trio of women on the couch, who kept glancing coyly over in his direction, clearly adding to his already considerable discomfort.

'Hi, can I help you?' she asked in her friendliest, most unthreatening voice.

'Er, yeah . . . I was looking for a . . . a gift voucher, if you do that sort of thing . . . ?'

'Course we do,' she said warmly. 'Who's it for?'

'Er, my mum.' His cheeks were bright pink. Meaghan's heart almost melted right there and then. Just then the trio who'd been checking the poor man out were summoned through. Meaghan waited until they'd trooped out, still throwing him the sort of arch glances that would have any man running for cover. She smiled up at him reassuringly. 'Bit noisy in here today, sorry.'

'Yeah. You know, I . . . I wasn't sure I'd actually be brave enough to come in.' He laughed. He had a beautiful smile, she noticed. Wide and deep, with a spider's web of laughter lines around the eyes. Brown, like his hair.

'Wouldn't have thought a bunch of women would scare you,' she teased. 'You're in the army, aren't you?'

'Christ, nothing more terrifying than that lot,' he said, nodding his head in the direction of the salon behind them. 'I've been in some pretty tough places but I'd do Borneo any day over this.'

'Borneo? Wow . . . that's . . . that's tough,' Meaghan said, not sure what else to say.

'Na, not really. It's the jungle. There's always stuff to see, things you haven't seen before. It's the waiting around on base that's the real killer.'

Meaghan looked up at him uncertainly. 'Wh-what sort of thing did you have in mind?' she asked, blushing furiously as she spoke. 'For your mum, I mean.'

'Oh, yeah. Well, I dunno. Something nice for her birthday.

Maybe get her hair done? I don't really know what you women do in here, to be honest.'

'How about a half-day package that leaves it open? That way she can choose what she might like. Hair, nails, wax, er, massage,' she corrected herself quickly. Most husbands were squeamish about what went on behind the salon's closed doors; no reason to suppose a son would be any different.

'Yeah, that sounds good. She'd love it.'

'Great. D'you want to leave it to her to book?'

'Yeah, that'd be good too.'

'OK. A half-day package is sixty dollars. I'll give you a ten per cent discount which makes it fifty-four dollars. What's her name? I'll just put it here on the voucher.'

'Carole Astor. Yeah, Carole with an "e".'

'Great.' Meaghan finished writing, stamped the voucher and handed it over. There was a moment's awkwardness, then they both spoke at once.

'If you—'

'If she—'

They both laughed. 'Go on, what were you going to say?' he said, smiling.

Meaghan shook her head. 'No, you first.'

He looked down at her and her heart did a slow double flip. 'Look, I know it's a bit sudden . . . but, well, I was just going to ask you – if you're not doing anything else, that is – d'you fancy getting something to eat after work?'

Meaghan's heart did another back flip, and another. 'Tonight?'

'Yeah. It's really short notice, I know, but I've only got a couple of free days and well, I just thought . . .' He stopped suddenly. 'Oh, you're not married or anything like that, are you?' He looked down at her hand.

'No, no, I'm not.' Meaghan laughed. There was an endearing mixture of boyishness and cockiness in him that she liked. 'Something to eat? Um, yeah . . . sure,' she said slowly, wonderingly. 'Er, where?'

'How about the Queensland Art Gallery? Down by the river?'

'The art gallery?' A soldier who knew where the QAG was? 'OK. What time?'

'Seven thirty? We could go for a drink first.'

'That . . . that'd be nice,' Meaghan said faintly, her mind already racing ahead to what to wear.

'I'll see you then. Oh, what's your name, by the way?' He laughed suddenly.

'Meaghan.'

'Hi, Meaghan. I'm Tom.' He stuck out a hand.

'Hi, Tom.'

They shook hands and stood for a moment, smiling at each other. 'Well, I'll see you later, then, Meaghan,' Tom said, turning to go.

'Yeah.' Meaghan couldn't think of anything else to say. She watched him saunter out, his long, lean frame encased in some sort of camouflage uniform. There were a couple of stripes on one shoulder, she noticed. She tried to remember what she knew about the army. Next to nothing. She rang up the voucher in the till and went back into the salon, feeling quite dazed. Tom Astor. She liked him. Already.

20

'So, what're you drinking?' Tom looked across the table at her. Meaghan could feel the blush steal over her cheeks.

'I'll have a whisky and soda,' she said brightly. It was Sue's favourite drink. She'd watched her order it on the few occasions all the girls had been out together; it sounded so grown up and sophisticated.

Tom clearly thought so too. 'Whisky and soda? Sounds good. Make that two,' he said to the waiter. He turned back to her. 'So, where you from, Meaghan?'

Meaghan hesitated. 'Er, Dalby.' It was bigger than Warra. Dalby sounded better.

'Dalby, eh? Got a squaddie from Dalby in the unit. Mike Kinnear. D'you know him?'

Meaghan shook her head. Fortunately their drinks arrived before he could go through the list of people from Dalby she ought to know. 'Cheers,' she said, hastily raising her glass.

He smiled at her. 'Cheers.'

He had a lovely deep voice – educated, but not posh. Not like some of the ladies who came into the spa. He was easy to talk to, just as before. By the time he signalled to the waiter for a second drink, she'd learned he was the eldest of three brothers, that his father had been in the air force and that he'd grown up all over the South Pacific, including Fiji and Papua New Guinea. He'd studied art history at university – pointless degree for a soldier, he said, smiling ruefully. He hadn't wanted to join the army, not at first – didn't want to just follow blindly in his father's footsteps. But he'd joined the TA at university and enjoyed it. After graduation, with no clear idea of what he wanted to do, he'd finally signed up. He loved it. It wasn't what he expected.

'What did you expect?' Meaghan asked him, lazily stirring her drink.

He shrugged. 'Dunno. I thought it'd be all marching around, singing patriotic songs . . . schoolboy stuff, you know?'

'And it's not?'

He laughed. 'No, not at all. It's nothing like you imagine. It's professional, for one thing. I'm always learning new stuff . . . I like the responsibility, you know? I'm a unit leader. I've got thirty-odd squaddies under my command and it's my job to make sure they do theirs. I suppose that's what I like most about it – there's a structure. Everyone's got a role to play and if you do what you're supposed to do, then the next bloke's job is easy. Well, easier. And then you get to go places.'

Meaghan sat opposite him, stirring her drink as she listened. 'God, it sounds so exotic. I've never been anywhere. Not unless you count Brisbane.'

'Not even Sydney?' Tom looked surprised.

Meaghan shook her head. 'Nope. Warra, Dalby, Brisbane.

That's about it. Oh, and once I went to Coolangatta with a friend. Did you know Coolangatta has the longest waves in the world?'

It was Tom's turn to shake his head. 'No.' He laughed. 'I didn't know that.'

'It's true.'

'You want to know something?' He leaned forward suddenly. 'D'you know what I most like about you?'

Meaghan shook her head. She was blushing again. 'No, what?'

'You're so honest. You don't pretend about anything. I hardly know you but I know that about you already.'

Meaghan had no idea what to say. She let her hair fall in front of her face so that she wouldn't have to look at him. He was unlike anyone she'd ever met. He had a way of talking to you as if you were the only person in the room, all his attention focused on your response. His humour was light and easy and she responded to it warmly, perhaps because that too was her real nature. Years of living with her father, in the oppressive silence his moods brought on, had changed her. Yet here she was, barely a few hours after meeting him, and he already had the capacity to bring out the softer, easier side of her. She liked him for it.

He made light of the basic training he'd done at the start of his career and the two forays he'd made with his unit outside the country; once to Borneo where they'd lived in the thick of the jungle for eight weeks and the other to the OTC in Singapore. The Officer Training College. He described a world she'd only ever seen on television. There was a moment when their eyes met and she was struck by the same honesty he claimed he'd seen in her. He was off-hand about his achievements, though they impressed the hell out of her. 'Oh, that's nothing. I'm only doing my job.' She suddenly saw very clearly that he wasn't interested in her seeing those things that anyone else could see – he wanted something else of her, something deeper. He wanted her to see some other side of him that he kept hidden or allowed very few people to see. He wanted her to see *him*. It surprised and flattered her. That a captain in the Australian army, with all that had gone on in his life before he met her, should care what *she* thought.

TOM

She was special; he saw that from the start. She wanted to pay her share of the bill. Tom wouldn't hear of it — out of the question — but he liked it about her nonetheless. He was tired of taking girls out who simply looked the other way when the bill came, as if the price of a dinner or a drink was poor compensation for having to listen to him half the evening. Meaghan was different. He'd known that as soon as she came through the door at the spa that afternoon. It wasn't just the way she looked, all wispy blonde hair and those incredible blue-green eyes and that neat little figure that left you wondering what it would be like to hold her underneath the uniform she wore. He'd had to look elsewhere for fear of being caught out. But it was her attitude that caught his attention and held it. There was a kind of fearlessness about her — a boldness that was in her look, her walk, the way she held herself and the way her hands moved through the air when she described things. She was gutsy. She said very little about herself — she was clever that way. She asked all sorts of things about *you* but not as an excuse to download everything she'd ever thought, seen or felt about herself, the way some girls did. Once or twice during the evening, there'd been a pause . . . he'd waited, half-expecting some confession or revelation on her part that would say more about what she sought in you than anything else — but it never came. She matched his banter with a lightness and humour all of her own. Even the way she said she'd never been anywhere except Dalby and Brisbane — said without a trace of self-pity or coquetry. Just like that. She wasn't asking for anyone's sympathy, least of all his. Her attempt to pay her share was just that — she wanted to take care of herself.

He couldn't stop thinking about her after he'd dropped her off outside a small house which she said she shared with two other girls on the north side of town. She kissed him on the cheek; he could smell the faint trace of her perfume all the way home. She worked in a beauty salon. She'd barely finished high school, never even thought about university. In that way, she was very different from the girls he'd been out with – doctors, lawyers, an accountant, once. Professional girls from the same sort of background as he. Meaghan was different in every way and yet she was quicker, tougher, more ambitious and a hell of a lot smarter than any of the girls he'd known. He liked her. But – and it was a huge 'but' – his timing couldn't have been more wrong. In less than two months' time he was due to make his transfer into the British Army. It was the thing he'd been working towards for almost a year. He wanted it more than anything. He was fed up with the limitations of the Australian Army; tucked up safely within its ranks he would never go anywhere, see anything, do anything and he would certainly never see any action. His application for transfer had gone through smoothly, as everyone knew it would. If he was lucky, he'd be sent out to Northern Ireland almost as soon as he arrived. That side of his future beckoned brightly. So why was he making plans to see Meaghan again when he barely had eight weeks to go? He had no answer. There was something about her that made him want to see her again; that was all he knew.

21

ABBY
Colchester, England, 1992

She lumbered downstairs, holding onto the banister for support. It was almost midnight. The small house was quiet; there was an occasional creak of the floorboards or the walls – settling, her mother called it. *The house is settling.* For some reason, the phrase filled Abby with dread. She and Ralph had been married for nearly three years and the thought of settling in Colchester was enough to make her retch. Not that she needed any help in that department, she thought to herself miserably as she walked slowly into the kitchen and opened the fridge. She was eight months pregnant – anyone who said morning sickness always ended after three clearly hadn't come across her. She'd been sick almost every day for the duration of her pregnancy and it showed no sign of abating. *Hyperemesis gravidarum*, someone very helpfully called it. The medical term. Abby didn't give a damn *what* it was called. All she could think about was having the baby and having Ralph safely back home, not necessarily in that order, either. Ralph was in Bosnia, part of UNPROFOR, the protection force under UN command. He'd been gone four months already; with another two to go, it was likely he would miss the birth. She gave herself a small shake. She knew the score – her mother had given birth to all three of them without even a telex from her father. When Abby was born, Libby didn't even know where in the world her husband was. It was just part and parcel of being married to a man who would eventually lead the SAS. Ralph's position wasn't quite as illustrious but there was no telling when she'd next get a phone call.

The baby turned and kicked and Abby was again overcome with a longing to have Ralph near. She took out a bottle of cold milk and walked over to the cupboards to get a glass. She felt another sharp kick and a different, duller kind of pain. She put both hands on either side of her hard, high belly, trying to breathe normally. Her heart had suddenly started accelerating and she felt short of breath. She pulled out a chair and sat down heavily. She stayed that way for a few moments, telling herself to buck up and stop feeling sorry for herself. The clock above the cooker showed 12.13. It was too late to call her mother or her elder sisters. She would make herself a mug of warm milk and go back to bed. In the morning, everything would be fine.

She got up slowly and noticed that the hem of her nightdress was wet. She clutched her stomach again. Sharp waves of pain were radiating outwards, spreading from her lower abdomen up through her belly towards her chest. She put a hand between her legs and brought it back up. There was blood all over it. She stumbled out of the kitchen and felt her way along the hallway wall until she reached the phone. There was only one person in the world whose voice she wanted to hear but he was thousands of miles away. She dialled her mother's number with shaking fingers. She was thirty-four weeks pregnant. Her last scan, almost a fortnight earlier, confirmed that everything was fine. She was being silly. It was just a little leak, that's all. Another wave of pain hit her. She heard her mother's sleepy voice and then everything went blank.

The next hour was a blur. She dimly remembered someone coming to the door, hammering on it and then the splintering crash as it broke. She was lying on the floor in the hallway; her cheek hurt from where she'd hit it on the edge of the stair going down. Someone lifted her. His hands were gentle. Was it Ralph? She turned her face towards the jacket that was pressed against it – no, it wasn't Ralph. It wasn't his smell. She could hear voices floating around in the air above her head. *Prolapsed cord. ICU. Critical first few hours.* She put out a hand but grasped only the passing air. There were white lights above her – she was lying on something hard. There was running. She could hear the footsteps around her but she herself was curiously still. A sudden banging of doors; the sensation of being pushed through something into a room that was colder than anything she could have imagined. She slipped in and out of consciousness. Someone lifted her arm – there was a thin, sharp prick somewhere along its length. She opened her eyes and met the partially covered face of a man staring down at her. Her heart gave a sudden lurch. Was it Ralph? No, the hair at the sides was grey, not brown. Ralph's hair was brown. She was still focusing on trying to remember its precise feel and touch when the lights suddenly went out and she slid soundlessly into darkness.

22

RALPH
Vitez, Bosnia, 1992

Dawn threw up its usual dazzling display of colours – from inky, purple-tinged black to rosy yellow. The light spilled out slowly over the distant hills, illuminating the landscape just before the first rays of the sun appeared. Ralph squatted in the shadow of one of the burned-out buildings, his fingers lightly touching the cold steel casing of his gun. Ahead of him he could just make out the shapes of the four men with whom he'd been on patrol. Sergeant Keane, the sniper, was a few yards to the left, crouched down, eyes staring into the half-light, his whole body tense and poised for action. Next to him were the two privates, both new to the platoon. One was a South African, a nice, quiet lad called Jooste; the other was a Glaswegian thug named Jimmy, to whom he'd taken an almost instant dislike. A few yards away was the spotter, Corporal Kittering, whom they all called Kitty. Danny, the gunner, was still in the tank. Despite the Glaswegian they made a good team, the combination of brains and muscle that he liked. They'd been patrolling all night. In another fifteen minutes or so, their shift would end and another team would take over. There was tension in the air. A ceasefire had been announced – one of what seemed to be hundreds that were continually being broken – but a week before, eleven Malaysian peacekeeping soldiers had been killed in the very same spot. Everyone was tense; waiting for something – anything – to happen. It was the waiting and the silence that were the hardest to bear, Ralph thought to himself. The silences in Bosnia were never about peace and quiet, or tranquillity. Silences here were all about the lull before a storm. Sometimes the storm took the form of a blast – an entire house disappearing right before your eyes, killing anything and everything in its way; sometimes it was the singular whiz and crack of a bullet, aimed by a gunman, deadly accurate.

Danny signalled to him from the front of the tank. *All clear*. The five of them straightened up slowly, hands still on their weapons, and began to walk carefully towards the APC. A few yards, a few minutes more and they'd all be safely back at base. He was itching to get back. It had been almost a week since he'd managed to put a call through to Abby and the longing to hear her calm, measured voice was at times overwhelming. There was madness in the air in Bosnia. It seeped out of the men like sweat. *Ten yards to go*. The two white UN-painted APCs stood there, about a hundred yards apart, patiently waiting. The third vehicle, the Land Rover, was a few yards in front. His grip on his gun tightened involuntarily; his fingers twitched. And then something came hurtling over the wall. They all saw it at once. 'Grenade!' Everything went into slow motion. The small, hard object hit the ground and bounced once. The pin sprang off and landed elsewhere with a small, hard tinkle. He heard the two noises separately, every fibre of his being attuned to the tiny, tinny sounds that would call time on their lives. The grenade bounced again, slower this time, and rolled towards the Land Rover. There was a few seconds' wait whilst the men turned and dived in the opposite direction, then the blinding flash of light that, in the murky light of early dawn, illuminated everything within a hundred yards – pock-marked buildings, half walls, piles of rubbish, burned-out cars . . . everything. The pulsating shock wave detonated – there was a deafening boom and the Land Rover blew up, scattering shrapnel, metal, engine oil and dirt in every direction.

Ralph felt the first pieces rain down on him. Thanks to his body armour, the aftermath felt like a series of body blows, none piercing. There was a second and a third boom, followed by the sound of fire catching hold. He stayed where he was, face down, his arms cradling his weapon protectively, until the explosions had stopped. Then he was up, his whole body propelled by a rush of adrenalin that drove him forwards. He reached his men within seconds. No one hurt. Yet. He knew the grenade would have been thrown as the precursor to opening fire. He had to get them out immediately. The second APC was about two hundred yards away, parked beside the bridge. To get to it he would risk putting his men directly in the line of fire. The only way to get help was to radio it in – and the VHF was inside the vehicle. Either way, they were sitting ducks. He took a quick look around him – the closest APC was parked perpendicular to an alleyway of two chest-height walls. He made a split-second decision. 'Behind that alleyway wall. Now!' No one needed telling twice. Almost as one, with the first bullets beginning to ping around them, they upped and ran. Out of the corner of his eye he could see a lone gunman winding his way up the rickety emergency staircase of the building in front of them, presumably seeking height for a better shot. They had a few minutes, not more. Further down the alleyway was a series of smaller court-yards. His best bet was to get the men down there and for him to make a break for the first APC. He made the decision, firing out orders. 'Top cover!' he yelled, as he ran, zig-zag, towards it. He didn't know how many gunmen were in the building and how many of them had their sights trained on the five of them. Somehow, miraculously, the firing held.

He burst into the back of the vehicle, grabbed the receiver and made contact. Once their position had been established, it would be up to the Ops Room to organise help. He swivelled around, picked up his gun and searched for the gunman he'd seen a few minutes earlier. The light was good; it was almost full day, now. He lifted the Susat sight to his right eye, trained the weapon on the building, floor by floor until he'd found him. He tracked him for twenty seconds or so, knowing that every second wasted was potentially the time it would take the sniper to stop, train his own sights on one of Ralph's men . . . and pull the trigger. Now. He pulled his own trigger, taking the recoil directly into his own shoulder. The man went down like a sack. There was an answering burst of fire from within the building – but Keene and Kitty had them. Within minutes there was only silence, but he knew it wouldn't last. They had to get out of the area, and fast. He leapt out of the vehicle, sprinted down the alleyway to where the others were holed up and motioned to them to come forward. As quickly and as quietly as they could, they ran back to the vehicle just as the VHF erupted in a cackle of static. 'QRF's on its way, mate,' he heard the voice of Sergeant Pickering. 'Stay where you are.'

'No need. We're on our way back. No casualties.' A loud cheer went up behind him. An incredible surge of relief hit him, flushing straight through his veins. His men were alive; one vehicle down and one destroyed, the other busy tearing its way back through the streets towards base camp.

Ten minutes later they came through the camp gates. He'd never been so relieved to see it. The men inside swore viciously as they clambered down, still clutching their weapons as if they might be fired upon at any second. The adrenalin would take some time to dissipate. They were met by clusters of soldiers in combat fatigues, eager to hear first-hand what had happened, what it had been like. He recognised his CO, Lieutenant Colonel Grey, coming towards him. He nodded stiffly; it would take him some time to calm down, too, he realised. But Grey's face was all smiles. 'Welcome back, Barclay. Good job out there.'

'Thank you, sir.'

'Saved us a hell of a fire-fight. Good work. Oh, there's a message for you, by the way. Corporal Tidworth took it. From your mother-in-law.' There was just a fraction of emphasis on 'mother-in-law'. Libby Hutton. Major General Hutton's wife. It was no secret that he'd married into army royalty.

'Thank you, sir,' Ralph repeated. His ears were still ringing with the sound of the explosions and gunfire. He walked off in the direction of the makeshift mess hall. A message from Libby. He was too dazed to wonder if it was bad news. A measure of just how distant his other life had suddenly become.

23

ABBY
Chelsea, London, 1992

Across the floral patchwork quilt in her old bedroom at home, Abby could just make out the top of Clara's strawberry-blonde head cradled in her mother's arms. Libby was singing her to sleep. A lone tear slid out of the corner of her eye and rolled soundlessly down her cheek. Ever since Clara's discharge from hospital after a fortnight's stay in an incubator which Abby couldn't bear to look at, she'd done her best to hold her daughter normally, talk and laugh with her the way her mother did. She tried, but she was failing miserably. She was so terrified of dropping or squashing her that she became all thumbs and couldn't even hold her. Ralph hadn't seen her yet. He wouldn't be back from Bosnia for another six weeks and by that time the baby would bear no resemblance to the tiny, whimpering, blue-tinged creature they'd pulled from her by emergency C-section the night she blacked out. He wouldn't understand what she'd gone through; he'd missed it all. The terrible long, lonely nights standing outside the ICU, peering at Clara through the glass, willing her to make it through the night, for everything to be all right. The tests, the look of anxiety on the doctors' faces and the night she'd come upon one of the ICU nurses, crying. She backed away from the door, too scared to even ask. But some-how, miraculously, Clara had survived. After her first week in that awful machine whose memory still brought tears to Abby's eyes, she'd slowly begun to turn the corner. Her tiny, under-developed lungs had started to strengthen; day by day her breathing improved, her colour returned and she began to put on weight. Everyone cheered, no one louder than the nurse who'd cried. 'She'll be fine,' she reassured Abby. 'You'll see. She's a right little fighter.' And she was. Although she was born six weeks early, the doctors were satisfied there would be no permanent damage. Somehow, against Abby's worst fears, everything was as it should be. In a few months' time, the doctors said, they would all be hard-pressed to remember what the spine-tingling terror had been about.

It took Abby weeks to believe them. She still wasn't convinced. All she wanted was for Ralph to come home. She wanted him to see what he – they, together – had made. A perfectly healthy baby. If anything happened to Clara, he would never forgive her.

'Don't be ridiculous,' her mother said to her when she dared voice her fears. 'Absolute utter rubbish. I don't know what's got into your head these days, I really don't. You've got to pull yourself together, darling. Ralph'll be back before you know it but this is how it's going to be. You know that already.'

Abby *did* know. She wished desperately she had some of her mother's strength. She'd watched her soldier on alone without her husband for most of their childhood, doing everything that Abby knew would now be expected of her. She would be alone with Clara just as she would be alone with any other children they might have. She would bring them up alone, make homes around the world alone, worry about measles and scarlet fever and school results . . . all of it on her own. At best, she could hope for one posting in three or four when Ralph would be at home with her. She knew the score; she'd watched her mother take it all in her stride. Now it was her turn. 'I know, Mum,' she said tearfully. 'It's just . . . I just wish he was here, that's all.'

'Don't. Don't even think about it. That's all there is to it. You've got to focus on other things, Abby. If you sit here counting the days until he gets back you'll drive both of you crazy, not to mention this darling little child. You've got your own life to get on with—'

'But, Mum . . . that's just it! I *don't* have my own life. I wish you *had* let me go to art school, you know. At least *then* I'd feel as if I had something of my own—'

'Abby, stop this nonsense immediately.' Libby Hutton got up, still holding onto Clara. She walked round the side of the bed and put the sleeping baby back into Abby's arms. 'Just stop it. You've got a beautiful baby girl and that's all that matters. You're made of sterner stuff than this. This isn't the way we brought you up. You of all people should understand what needs doing.'

'But, Mum—'

'But *nothing*! Dry your face. Your sister'll be here any minute. I don't want to see any more tears, d'you hear me?'

Abby nodded miserably. Her mother was right; of course she was. She, of all people, knew just what it took. Ralph's career came first, above and before anything else, including her own happiness. Her mother and grandmother before her had been married twice over: once to their husbands and, at the same time, to the army. She had to put aside the childish notion that she, with a Certificate in Secretarial Studies, would have anything resembling a career. Her career was Ralph. End of story.

24

MEAGHAN
Brisbane, Australia, 1992

She applied the final top-coat to her client's nails, whipped out her fast-drying spray and finished them off. 'There,' she said brightly. 'All done.'

Her client, a notoriously difficult to please woman called Jean, lifted her hands up to inspect them. 'Yeah, they're good,' she pronounced reluctantly. A tiny sigh of relief escaped Meaghan's lips. She glanced at the clock – it was nearly five. She had half an hour to meet Tom down by the river. He'd bought theatre tickets for a show that evening; she could hardly wait.

'Sorry, Jean, I've got to dash. I'll see you next week,' she said, getting to her feet.

'You got a date or something?' Jean's sharp eyes missed nothing.

Meaghan blushed. 'Er, yeah.'

'Have a good time.' She carefully pulled five dollars from her purse, taking exaggerated care not to smudge her nails and bestowing it upon her with an air of benevolence as though it were a one-hundred-dollar note. 'Here, buy him a drink with this.'

'Thanks, Jean,' Meaghan said, slipping it into her pocket. 'I'll see you next week.' She hurried into the changing room at the back of the spa and took off her coat. Underneath she was wearing a white blouse, frilled at the waist and sleeves, and her favourite pair of jeans. She kicked off her rubber-soled salon shoes and opened her locker. The sandals she'd bought the previous day were waiting for her – gold, with thin straps and a cork wedge heel. They were all the rage ever since Kylie Minogue had been spotted at Sydney Airport wearing something similar. She slipped them on. One of the girls had done her feet for her the previous day – her red toenails added a lovely touch of glamour. She fluffed out her hair, added a touch of lip-gloss and she was ready. She picked up her handbag and made her way across the crowded floor. Sue looked up quizzically as she passed, much to her embarrassment. For the past couple of years she'd been one of the last to leave the salon every day – now she was usually the first. For almost a month now she'd seen Tom practically every day. He was on a course at Enoggera, just north of the city, and although he didn't say much about it or how long it would last, he never said goodbye without making another date. Crazy as it seemed, she felt as though she'd known him all her life. He was wonderfully uncomplicated. Right from the start there were no barriers in him that he made her feel she couldn't cross. She was so unused to a man whose face was as open as his heart seemed to be. Now, as she hurried down Alice Street towards the theatre, she could feel her heart beginning to race at the thought of seeing him again.

He was waiting for her on one of the park benches outside the Botanical Gardens. It was an early spring day. There was a freshness in the air but the sun was out and the river, for once, was sparkling. She came up to him, feeling the heat in her cheeks rise as they kissed.

'Hi,' he said, holding her tightly. He looked at her searchingly, and then quickly looked away again. He seemed nervous, which was unusual. She'd grown accustomed to his boyish pleasure in seeing her each and every time. She could feel an old, familiar sense of panic beginning to bubble inside her.

'What time's the performance?' she asked as lightly as she could, trying to calm herself down. It was probably nothing – perhaps he'd just had a hard day? He'd caught her completely off guard, just as she was beginning to relax.

'Eight. But there's something I need to talk to you about first.'

She glanced up at him nervously. 'What's that?' The panic she'd been trying to suppress rose in her again. She felt the sharp tug of tears in her throat. She couldn't help it. The sudden change in him produced all sorts of fears, none of which she felt capable of handling.

'Come on, let's get a drink. There's that bar on the corner. I've always wanted to go there. We've got loads of time.'

He brought two large glasses of white wine back to the table and slid one carefully across to her. She looked around her nervously. The bar was on the first floor of a building overlooking the river. On the terrace below, she could see people braving the still-chilly night air, pashminas and shawls wrapped around their necks. 'Cheers,' he said, lifting his glass. Her nervousness intensified. He'd brought her here to end things. Of course. The thought trembled inside her.

'Cheers,' she said, lifting her glass, fighting the disappointment that rose in her like the tide. She wasn't about to burst into tears even though the thought of not seeing him again sent a cold shiver of fear down her spine. If he'd had enough, he ought to just say it to her face and get it over and done with. Now that she thought about it, it was beginning to make sense. He'd said a couple of things . . . something about being overseas, but she hadn't wanted to seem as though she was prying. Perhaps he was about to be posted somewhere and he didn't have the guts to say it to her face and—

'Meaghan? Are you listening?'

'Huh?' She slowly became aware that his eyes were fixed on hers. 'Sorry . . . wh-what did you say?'

'Look, I know it's really early days and all that but the transfer's come through . . . well, it came through a while ago but I didn't know whether—' He stopped, agitated. 'I-I . . . I just didn't think it was the right time to bring it up but—'

Meaghan stared at him. She'd had enough. Her chin lifted defiantly. 'It's fine, Tom, honestly. You don't have to say any more.'

He appeared not to have heard her. 'I probably should've said something to you before but—'

He carried on stumbling over his words but she couldn't hear him. She was aware of a great build-up of tension in her neck and throat but she bit down on it, hard. She wasn't going to cry in front of him. No fucking way. She lifted her wine glass and swallowed the remains in one swift gulp. He stopped and looked at her with a puzzled look on his face. She banged the empty glass back down. Her eyes were stinging. Why was he looking at her like that? What the hell did he expect? For her to beg him? 'See you, Tom,' she said, praying her voice wouldn't crack. She slid off the bar stool and quickly turned away before he could see the pain and disappointment written all over her face. How could she have been so stupid? Why hadn't she seen it coming? She was almost halfway to the door when she felt a hand on her arm, pulling her back.

'Meaghan? What's wrong? What did . . . hang on a minute, what did you think I said back there?' He forced her round to face him.

The tears she'd been so careful to hide were flowing freely now. She tried to blink them back but it was pointless. She opened her mouth to speak but nothing came out. 'Will you?' he asked, his fingers gripping her arm tightly.

'W . . . will I wh . . . what?'

'Come with me.'

'Come with you?'

'Yes, you idiot. Come with me . . . to Britain.' His fingers tightened.

'To Britain?' she repeated, dazed.

'Yes, to Britain. Where else?'

'Tom . . . I don't understand. Wh . . . what are you asking me?' Meaghan's whole being was concentrated in her chest.

'I'm asking you to marry me, you idiot. To come with me.'

'*Marry* you?' Meaghan's eyes widened. 'Marry you? You're asking me to marry you?' She felt her knees begin to weaken. Her life began a slow kaleidoscope in front of her eyes. The farm; her father's long absences when the house was quiet and tranquil and her mother hadn't yet started to drink; sitting on the porch outside with her mother, shelling peas or sorting out the laundry, the special, quiet murmur of mother and daughter, bound by some trivial domestic task; and then the changes after her father's accident . . . the way the house turned in on itself, becoming meaner and more sullen the longer he was at home. By the time she was a teenager, she barely recognised it – now it had become a place of darkness and moods, of unexpected, unexplained violence and hurt. In Tom she'd seen someone who would *care* for her, protect her, just as he believed he protected others. She wasn't looking for a father figure; on the contrary, she'd fallen for a man who was in so many ways his polar opposite that he simply cancelled him out. Tom allowed her to bury the memory of the first man she'd ever known and replace him with another, kinder and more generous example in whom she could wholeheartedly trust.

'Oh, for God's sake, woman . . . say "yes", will you?' A stranger's voice broke in on their conversation. Both Tom and Meaghan turned round. The whole table was grinning at them. She looked up at him, still dazed. He was asking her to *marry* him. He wanted to take her away, overseas. He wanted to make a *life* with her. The thought made her dizzy. She'd worked so long and hard to manage what little she'd been able to make for herself – now he was asking her to give it up? All those months and years of scraping through, saving just enough for the next month, and the next, not knowing what would happen to her and when and how . . . would these now count for nothing? She'd managed; she'd survived – in fact, she'd done a heck of a lot more than just survive. She was living a life that was so far removed from what she'd come from that the thought of giving it up was terrifying. What if it didn't work out? What if she and Tom grew apart, fell out? What if . . . she swallowed nervously . . . what if something *happened* to him? She was no fool; he was a soldier. He would go to war, if he had to, and bad things could happen at any time in a war. What then?

'Well?' Tom's voice prompted her gently.

She looked up into those dark brown eyes that she'd come to know almost as well as her own. The expression of tenderness and care in them was so great it overwhelmed her. She couldn't speak so she nodded instead. Up, down; once, twice. Yes. Yes. Yes.

'Oh, thank God for that!' The stranger who'd spoken gave a satisfied yelp. A slow clapping began in the crowded bar as it dawned on everyone what had just happened. Meaghan's face was pressed against Tom's chest. She could scarcely breathe. The surge of happiness and relief had turned her legs to jelly. She breathed in the scent of him that had become so poignantly familiar to her and clung to him, ashamed of herself for jumping to a conclusion that was so far removed from the truth. He didn't want to end things – on the contrary. He was looking for a new beginning, one that included her. Britain . . . the images came at her, thick and fast: Buckingham Palace; the changing of the guard; the Houses of Parliament. And then those other images of Britain that she'd grown up with. Her father was English. At the age of fourteen, he'd run away to Australia. Aside from a single trip to bury his grandmother, he'd never been back. He hated it. He hated his whole family and the poverty he'd escaped from. Britain to him was nothing but deprivation and he'd done his best to transmit that hatred to his children. Now she was about to experience it for herself. She could feel Tom's heart beating against her cheek – slow, steady, secure, just like him. She would be safe with him, she knew, no matter what happened. All she had to do was hold on.

25

SAM
Bristol, England, 1992

Sam paused in her task of wiping down the bar and looked up at the clock. It was nearly eleven. In a few minutes Ollie, the manager, would ring the bell signalling the very last round and they would begin the slow process of clearing up in preparation for the next day. Well, not quite. Fortunately the next day was a Sunday, the only day on which Revolution, a trendy bar halfway down Whiteladies Road, was closed. She worked three nights a week and had done ever since her second year. She liked it. The crowd who came in every night – mostly well-heeled students and the younger staff at the BBC up the road, the odd doctor or group of nurses from the Bristol Royal Infirmary – were friendly and generally easy-going, unlike in some of the other pubs in the area.

'Come on, ladies and gents,' Ollie shouted, as he did every night. 'Go 'ome! We've 'ad your money, now drink up and piss off!' A few of the regulars around the bar laughed good-naturedly. She rinsed the sponge and gave the bar a final wipe-down. 11.15. In another fifteen minutes they'd close up, have a quick drink together and, with any luck, she'd catch the last bus home. It was March but it was still freezing and she certainly didn't relish the thought of either walking home or spending almost as much as she'd earned that night on a taxi. She was saving up for the holiday she and Paula were going to take – a nutty jewellery-designer whom she'd met in the first week at university and who had since become her closest friend. It was sometimes hard to believe four years had passed since she'd first arrived in Bristol, wide-eyed with nervous anticipation and the thrill of being away from home for the first time. Both her parents had been dead set against it. Bristol? 'But you'll be so far away!' her mother had exclaimed when she announced her decision. 'Why on earth would you want to go there? You won't be able to live at home.'

'That's the whole point,' Sam said defensively.

'But Kate's going to go to UCL.'

'So?'

'But why don't you want to be together?'

'We've been together for the past eighteen years. I just want to be on my own for a bit.' There was no way Sam could even bring herself to explain. The thought of seeing Kate every day for the next three or four years of her law degree was enough to make her feel ill. She'd never quite managed to swallow the humiliation of seeing her sister and Loïc swanning around the school yard together – or the look on Loïc's face when she casually dumped him a few weeks later. He'd never spoken to Sam again . . . within a couple of months he was gone.

'Yes, but *Bristol*?' Her mother looked at her with the expression she reserved especially for Sam – irritation mixed with incomprehension and a little bit of impatience thrown in.

Well, that was four years ago and moving away from home was the best thing she'd ever done. Within a year she'd lost nearly two stone, though she'd be hard-pressed to explain how. She'd simply been too busy to eat. Out from under Kate's shadow, she'd blossomed. For the first time in her life she felt free to do things exactly as she pleased. She discovered she was rarely hungry before noon. In the flat she shared with Tammy and Monique, two other law students, there was no one to chivvy her for not having eaten and no one standing over her with a second helping of eggs. She grabbed a sandwich along with everyone else on her way from lectures to the library and was too absorbed in her coursework to think about food. Paula persuaded her to cut off her thick, blonde ponytail and ditch the glasses for a pair of contact lenses. By the time the end of her first year rolled round and she went back to London, her old friends didn't recognise her. Kate, of course, didn't notice. She was so busy with her first-year courses and her romance with the impossibly handsome, impossibly boring Grant that she couldn't see beyond the end of her own nose. 'Don't you think I've lost weight?' Sam asked her one morning, shortly after she'd arrived.

'Have you? Oh, yeah, I suppose so. Listen, Grant wants to—' And that was the end of the subject. Sam had never brought it up again.

Now, at the thought of Kate and Grant, Sam's face fell. Grant was coming to Bristol to a conference the following day and, in a moment of misguided enthusiasm, Sam had offered to put them up.

'Ooh, super!' was Kate's response. 'Grant's always saying you don't like him. I keep telling him it's not true.'

Sam hadn't quite known what to say. She *didn't* like him, so why the hell had she offered to put them up for the weekend? She'd put down the phone and immediately rushed out to Habitat. A hundred-odd pounds later she had new bedding, new wine glasses, four new feather pillows and – dashing back to spend another thirty quid – two brand-new, large fluffy bath towels. She could have kicked herself. The cost of kitting out her room for the two of them (she would sleep in the sitting room) for the weekend was more than she earned in a fortnight – why on earth did she bother? She had no answer. She hadn't seen Kate since the previous summer yet time had done nothing to dull that peculiar mixture of resentment and longing that her sister always managed to inspire in her.

'You almost finished there, love?' Ollie looked up at her as she passed, a tray of glasses in her arms.

'Nearly. One more load for the dishwasher then we're done.'

'Lovely, lovely. Christ, what a night. Drink, fair one?' He held up a bottle of Jameson.

'Why not?'

'Good girl. Brian here'll run you home.' Brian was one of her fellow workers. He was from Belfast, doing a postgraduate degree in physics or something equally difficult. Sam immediately blushed. 'No, no, don't bother. It's fine, I can catch the bus. There's still one running—'

'No, it's no problem at all,' Brian said in his lovely, deep Irish brogue. 'It's practically on me way.'

'Well . . . only if you're sure?' Sam said hesitantly. The thought of forcing Brian to go out of his way for her was deeply unsettling.

'Course I'm sure.'

'Right . . . two wee glasses coming up.' Ollie poured with a flourish. At the other end of the bar Danuta, the Polish woman who came over to England every year to work for a few months, was polishing the bar. She came up, wiping her hands on her apron, and accepted a glass. Sam liked the Saturday night closing ritual; they all sat together over a glass or two of whisky, swapping their worst-customer stories and then dispersing home for the weekend. It struck her as she sipped her drink that in less than five months' time she'd be gone and a whole new phase of her life would start. She'd been offered a job in London with a big intellectual copyright law firm, Holman Kenton. She and Paula were planning to take a month's holiday somewhere warm and then they were both heading for London – Sam with a job in hand, Paula without. As usual. She was looking forward to it with a mixture of extreme joy and extreme trepidation.

'You ready?' Brian stood up and looked down at her.

'Oh, yes . . . sure.' Sam drained the last drop from her glass and got up. She wrapped her scarf tightly around her neck, said goodbye to the others and followed him out of the pub. His car, an ancient, nondescript banger of some unknown make, was parked just around the corner. It took a few attempts to bring the motor to life but Brian was unperturbed.

'She's a bit temperamental in the winter.' He grinned, pulling out into Whiteladies Road.

Sam settled herself down further in her seat, not sure whether an answer was expected of her or not. Despite the outward changes in her since she'd arrived in Bristol nearly four years ago, she somehow couldn't shake off the notion that if a man so much as talked to her, he was only being kind. Or that he felt sorry for her. It drove Paula – and a few of Sam's male friends too – round the bend. She'd dropped almost five stone in four years. She'd gone from being a size eighteen (on a good day) to a size twelve. She'd finished her undergraduate law degree with a first and was recognised by everyone as one of the top hundred law students nationwide. She could have gone anywhere to do her Master's – Oxford, Cambridge, London – but she'd always been loyal and she genuinely liked the faculty at Bristol . . . so she stayed. Everyone in the department was delighted. A student like Sam raised the bar for others. Aside from the fact that she was a pleasure to teach, she was the kind of person that everyone liked having around.

So, with all that going for her, why the hell should she be so uncertain when it came to men? Again, she had no answer. She had a handful of good male friends with whom she occasionally raised the subject. Their answer was always the same. 'You're a great mate, Sam, that's the problem.' She struggled to understand what they meant. She was a good and sympathetic listener and always full of practical advice about all sorts of things. Philip, her closest male friend, was the only one who'd known her before she came to Bristol. He lived a few streets down from the Maitlands in Camden and had known Sam since she was eleven or twelve. He didn't care much for Kate, never had. But even he couldn't put it into words – or at least words that Sam could understand. He'd said to her once, a few years earlier, when his heart had been broken yet again by one of the Arabellas or the Aramintas or Camillas who were the girls of his choice, 'Christ, if only I could find someone like *you*, Sam.' She'd been so surprised by the comment that, for once, she couldn't find anything to say. She'd gone home that night in a flurry of conflicting emotions. Did he like her? Did she like him? What did he mean by it? If he was so desperate to find someone like her, why didn't he just pick her? For about a week she'd been awkward around him, then the years of friendship re-asserted themselves, Phil found another Camilla and the moment passed. Except it never quite disappeared altogether. She wasn't a virgin – three one-night stands somewhere along the length of her course had taken care of *that*. But none of those encounters had resulted in anything other than a mumbled, embarrassed 'hello' when they met again in the street or in a bar, and a 'proper' relationship – such as Paula had every other month – seemed curiously out of her reach.

'Here we go. Home sweet home. She's never let me down yet.' Brian pulled up in front of Sam's flat. 'You got plans for tomorrow, Sam?' he asked suddenly.

Sam's stomach gave a lurch. If she was honest about it – which she tried very hard *not* to be – she fancied Brian. He was tall and strong with a great sense of humour and a lovely voice. She knew he'd broken up with his girlfriend a few months earlier but hadn't seen him with anyone since. So what was he asking? 'Er, no, not really. I mean I've got some revision to do which I thought I'd get on with tomorrow. I've got exams in a couple of months and . . .' She stopped suddenly, wondering if she ought to suggest doing something instead.

'Oh. Well, all right, then. Don't work too hard,' Brian said, reaching across to open the door for her. 'It's a bit stiff . . . there. See you next week.'

She unbuckled her seat belt and got out, bewildered. Should she have answered differently? Should she have jumped at the chance to do something with him? But it was true . . . she *did* have a lot of revision. She watched his car tail lights disappear down the hill. She pushed open the small garden gate and walked down the steps to the basement flat, wondering dispiritedly if she would ever get it right.

26

'Haven't you got any other towels?' The following evening, Kate's shrill voice floated along the corridor, setting Sam's teeth on edge. They'd only been in the flat a couple of hours and she was already counting the minutes until their departure. 'You know I'm allergic to these fluffy ones.' Sam winced. No, she bloody well didn't know. Since when?

'What sort d'you need?' she shouted back.

'Just a plain one. White, if you've got it.'

What difference did the colour of the towel make? Sam thought to herself crossly. She got up from the dining table and walked down the corridor towards Tammy's room. Tammy would have one of the plain white towels Kate so desired. She nipped into her room, pulled one out of the clean laundry pile and marched towards her bedroom. She knocked on the door. Kate was sprawled elegantly across her bed in her thick, terry towelling robe, the offending fluffy towel tossed across the floor, her freshly washed hair pulled up off her face with one of Sam's other, *non*-fluffy towels. Her skin was glowing and still faintly bronzed from the holiday she and Grant had taken in February to Sardinia – *just beautiful, darling, just beautiful. You can't possibly imagine.* Well, no, she couldn't. 'Here you are,' Sam said, a touch grumpily.

'Thanks.' Kate was busy flicking through one of Sam's many interiors magazines. 'Look at this.' She held the magazine aloft. 'What d'you think of those?'

Sam looked at the picture of an immaculately styled dining room. What was she supposed to be looking at? 'What? The cushions?'

'No, silly. The chairs. We're thinking of getting a new dining table. A long one . . . you know, for ten or twelve people.

Everyone's a couple these days . . . you invite four people over and you've already got eight.'

Sam was silent. It was exactly the sort of comment Kate liked to make. *Everyone's a couple these days.* Everyone except her, of course. She glared at her sister but the stare was lost on Kate. 'Lovely,' she said, with little enthusiasm.

'Grant wants to get something modern, you know, glass or something but I rather like wood. Did I tell you we're going to make an offer on a flat?'

'No, you didn't.'

'Mmm. It's in Primrose Hill. I'll be able to walk to work through the park. Fantastic, don't you think?'

'Mmm.'

'Shit, is that the time? I'd better get going. We're meeting some of Grant's colleagues at that new restaurant in Clifton . . . d'you know it? The little French one? I'm surprised you've never heard of it. It's been getting the most rave reviews.'

Sam shook her head. Two thoughts came to her immediately: one, that it wouldn't have occurred to either Kate or Grant to invite her along as a way of saying 'thank you' for having put them up for the whole weekend and two, how utterly typical it was of Kate to breeze into town, find out which were the best restaurants and bars around and then make Sam feel like an idiot for not knowing what restaurants had won plaudits in her own home town. 'Well, I hope the food's up to scratch,' she said, turning to go. 'It's only Bristol, you know. Not London.'

'I know, I know. Apparently the chef's from London, though.'

'Of course.'

'Oh, Sam . . . be a darling, won't you and iron this for me?'

Sam turned, speechless. Kate was holding out her dress. 'Iron it yourself,' she said indignantly.

'But I don't know where anything is,' Kate whined.

'I'll show you.'

*

Half an hour later, the door closed behind her and Sam breathed a sigh of relief. Two more days. The weekend stretched out tediously before her. She walked into the living room and plopped herself down on the couch. Monique was out with her boyfriend and Tammy had gone up to London to see her parents. The flat was quiet; with any luck Grant and Kate would be out until after midnight. She switched on the TV. There was nothing on save re-runs of eighties sitcoms. She put her feet up on the table and stared at the screen, pretending to herself that sitting at home alone on a Saturday night was what she really wanted to do. The next time Kate asked if she could stay for the weekend, she swore to herself, she'd say no. All it did was remind Sam of the shortcomings in her own life, most principally the lack of a suitable candidate to share it with. Well, a boyfriend's not *everything*, she reminded herself tartly. She had her exams to get through and then the holiday with Paula to look forward to. And then, of course, there was London and all the excitement of finding a flat. No, contrary to how Kate always made her feel, her life *was* full and exciting. Full and exciting, she muttered to herself, like a mantra. My life *is* full. It is. It *is*. She stared at the TV screen until it began to fuzz.

27

MEAGHAN
Brisbane, Australia, 1992

On Meaghan's side, there was only Clive and Sal and a couple of the girls from the salon. Clive and Sal stood awkwardly to one side at the reception Tom's parents had organised at their Murray Hills home, a Brisbane suburb that Meaghan hadn't even known existed. The hastily arranged marriage had been entirely franchised to Barbara, Tom's mother. They had a fort-night or so before Tom was due in London; she pursed her lips and said she would just have to do her best. Where they would get a church, a minister, flowers and caterers from . . . she let her voice trail off and Meaghan looked at the ground. But she'd managed, somehow. Presumably as the wife of a retired air force officer she had her contacts to call upon. The service was held in a small church just down the road from the house and the minister was a family friend. Afterwards everyone walked up the hill to the house where a group of laughing girls had transformed the garden with a profusion of gorgeously scented flowers. Young men in uniform stood around holding silver trays aloft and there was more booze on offer than Meaghan had ever seen at a gathering, wedding or no. Mrs Astor Senior obviously thought it would help.

She'd thought about inviting one or two of her clients – Grace-Anne MacFarlane or Darya, perhaps – just to bump the numbers up a bit but in the end she'd decided against it. She was nervous enough as it was. She'd met his parents a couple of times but Barbara walked around the whole afternoon with the dazed, slightly confused expression of someone for whom nothing makes sense. Dennis, Tom's father, didn't look quite as surprised but it was clear Tom's decision to marry her had come out of the blue. His friends were similarly surprised. She met many of them for the first time that hot afternoon. They shook her hand or hugged her but they too seemed baffled by his choice. There were a great many pretty, long-haired girls in pastel dresses with impeccable manners – the sort of girl she assumed his parents thought he would marry. They were pleasant enough but their eyes slid past her, widening ever so slightly. The Episcopalian minister who was also a family friend kept glancing at her stomach as if to confirm his own suspicions. She did her best to ignore them all. He'd chosen her; no further proof was needed.

'I like your dress,' Sal said shyly, taking tiny sips of champagne as though it would have to last her all afternoon. 'You look really nice.'

'Oh, thanks,' Meaghan said, blushing. She liked Sal, though

she hardly knew her. She and Clive clearly felt hopelessly out of their depth. She felt a pang of guilt for having dragged them all the way up from Warwick. She looked around her. She could see Tom's mother under the canopy that had been erected at the bottom of the garden. She was talking to someone, laughing and holding onto his arm. Every so often she threw a glance in Meaghan's direction . . . probably explaining to the man she was talking to how surprised she'd been . . . no, they'd had no idea. Some girl from the outback. She could feel the flush of embarrassment creeping up into her face. She looked past Clive and Sal to the neighbour's garden. The houses were large and expensive in this part of the city, on the ridge overlooking the river. She recognised a few of the trees – blue gums, stinkwood, ironbarks, a huge laurel tree. The gardens were a riot of colour: jasmine, hyacinth, azalea, rhododendron and trailing sweet peas. Her mother had been a keen gardener . . . back then. A rare memory of the time before the farm flashed before her. There'd been a back garden, filled with flowers and herbs. She could remember coming home from school to find her mother on her hands and knees, weeding the beds, a pair of pruning shears in one hand. She felt something. Something both familiar and near. She didn't want the feeling of sadness that had been with her all day under the throb of excitement and nerves to win out. She turned to Clive. 'D'you remember?' she asked, touching him lightly on the forearm. 'What did Mum used to call those scissors she had? In Dalby, when we lived in the town. She had a special name for them.'

Clive looked surprised for a moment. 'Secateurs,' he said quietly. 'That was it. Some French word for gardening scissors. We had to go look it up in the dictionary, d'you remember?'

Meaghan nodded slowly and swallowed. A single word float-ing up through the streams of memory; how long ago it seemed. Secateurs. It was exactly the sort of word her mother would know. *Had* known. A reminder of how far she'd come down in the world in her marriage to a man who'd taken everything that was curious and refined about her and beaten it down. At the same time she felt a sharp pain at the thought of what her mother had had to endure, and then an unexpected wave of happiness break over her in contradiction. What had happened to her mother would never happen to her. She only had to glance at Tom to confirm that. For a moment back there on the back porch, contemplating Tom's mother and the beautiful gardens all around her and the elegant house behind, the weight and pressure of a life that could never be hers, she'd felt a momentary panic, as if someone would suddenly step out in front of her and banish her back to where she'd come from: nowhere. But she saw Tom striding confidently up the hill towards her, his face breaking into the smile she'd come to depend on as he saw her and she knew it would never be so. In taking them both away, he'd unwittingly set them both free. She turned her face up to his as he drew level with them.

'G'day, mate,' he said to Clive, holding out a bottle of beer. 'You look like you could use one of these.'

Clive grinned sheepishly and took the bottle he'd offered. Sal too smiled timidly, and raised her own glass. There was a tenderness and a generosity in Tom, Meaghan saw, that spilled out of his own happiness and touched those around him. It wasn't the first time she'd seen it in him; it had been there that very first day when he'd come into the salon looking for something for his mother. But she saw it now again in the way he talked to Clive, seeking something in him that would put him at ease, bring out whatever was good and likeable in him. Under the release of beer and conversation, she saw how Clive grew expansive, losing the nervousness he'd arrived with when he and Sal pulled up in their decades-old ute with all the fishing rods still sticking out of the back. She'd seen the way everyone looked at them with such frank surprise but it was Tom who'd reached out and drawn them in, brought everyone round. By the time the wedding party broke up there were invitations to Clive and Sal to come back down to Brisbane and visit. Meaghan could hardly hold back her tears.

Later that night, when it was all over, she and Tom returned to Tom's flat on the other side of the quiet, almost deserted city. Tom drove fast under a smoky sky through which the moon bounced. Meaghan felt herself released, somehow, as if a great weight had been lifted off her. She'd managed to discard their awful, secret past. If she could do it, so could Clive. Under the surge of speed she felt herself weightless, as in space, or in a fleeting, pleasurable dream.

28

MEAGHAN
Hounslow, England, 1992

The flight to London was long and ought to have been excruciatingly boring, or so Tom warned her. Meaghan didn't find it so. After the initial excitement of getting her passport – Meaghan Claire Astor, not Conway – and the thrill of packing up, with the girls from the salon dropping by at all hours to wish her good luck and safe journey and *best-of-luck-when-you-get-there* and *don't-you-dare-forget-us* and all the things she'd never dreamed anyone would ever say to her . . . after all that had subsided and it was just her and Tom sitting in the back of his father's car on the way to the airport, holding hands, she discovered there was a whole other layer of excitement to be had. The airport was vast and gleaming. Tom had some sort of military pass that got them into a lounge with comfortable chairs and as much wine and orange juice as you could drink. She sat on the edge of her seat, too nervous to talk, let alone drink.

The flight stretched out languidly in front of them: eight hours to Singapore, a two-hour wait and then another eleven-hour flight to London. London Heathrow. She mouthed the words to herself. *London Heathrow*. In less than twenty-four hours they would be there. Barbara cried, of course, even when she turned to hug Meaghan. Meaghan was too excited to cry.

She'd shed a few tears in the days prior to their departure but once the day actually arrived, she felt nothing but relief.

They were amongst the first passengers to be called to the plane. Tom was in uniform; she saw already how people looked up to him, especially the older men. It was as if in him they saw something of the man they'd once been, or would have liked to have been. The flight attendants flirted harmlessly with him; they were conscious of Meaghan sitting next to him, the diamond and gold rings on her finger staking her evident claim.

At Singapore they disembarked into a terminal building packed with people and shops in which almost everything imaginable could be bought. Tom went off and came back with a camera, a bottle of whisky and a bottle of perfume, for her. He had an arm round her shoulders as they sat waiting for their next flight to be called. She snuggled into the circle of safety that was his chest and felt the rough scratch of his uniform against her cheek. She dozed on and off until it was time to leave again. They boarded for the second and final time. The plane began its by now familiar shunt down the runway, shuddering and gathering speed. Meaghan's face was pressed against the window, watching the earth rise up giddily as they swung in a graceful arc towards the sea, then fall away again as they straightened and climbed beyond the clouds. It was the last she saw of the earth until they came into Heathrow, landing at almost the same time they'd taken off – early in the morning, the city coming into view through the distorted lens of the aircraft window, an entire country under a blanket of grey.

They took a taxi from Heathrow to Hounslow, a suburb of London where they'd be staying for a couple of months, Tom explained, whilst his paperwork was sorted out and he was assigned his first posting – Camp Massereene in County Antrim, Northern Ireland. Meaghan looked out of the window at the identical-looking suburbs as they floated past, so different from anything she'd ever seen. She'd never encountered as many shades of grey – dark, light, gloomy, dreary, dirty, sharp, soft . . . every inch of the landscape from houses to fields seemed bathed in grey, shadowy light. It was October but even the people seemed grey. As they drove, the houses became alternately more closely packed, then sparser, leafier, and then denser again. It was hard to tell the difference between country-side and city. A high street full of traffic and shopping pedes-trians, a small river and a long, winding road and then all of a sudden they were in something that looked like an army barracks . . . and it was. The taxi stopped outside a house on Beavers Crescent. 'Number twelve, that's us.' Tom pointed out a house that was identical in every way to the houses on either side. Meaghan looked at it and swallowed nervously. Home. Twelve Beavers Crescent, Hounslow, England.

She opened the door and got out. There was a cold, blustery wind that swept off the stretch of open ground across the road, sending small whirlpools of dust and debris into the air. She wrapped her coat around her more tightly and followed Tom up the path. The driver obligingly brought round their suitcases. Tom gave him a large tip, put his arm round his wife and slid the key that had been left under the mat into the lock. The door creaked open. It was a little stiff. There was a pile of letters lying on the floor that blocked the doorway. 'I don't think anyone's been in for a while,' Tom said, kicking some of the junk mail out of the way. 'That's what the housing officer said. Well, dar-ling . . . here it is. Welcome to England.'

Meaghan peered eagerly into the hallway. The cold, late autumn air hadn't made it past the stiff front door. There was a smell of folded-away newspapers and ages-old cooking that still lingered, like smoke. She glanced around. There was a worn, dark blue carpet running the length of the corridor, disappearing under the glass doorway that led, she saw, to an open-plan dining/living room. The walls were a dull cream colour and there were patches where posters or paintings had once been hung. On the other side of the corridor was the kitchen and next to it a bedroom with a large, lumpy mattress and a lopsided chest of drawers. She followed Tom around, holding tightly onto his arm. This was her home. Their home. For six weeks or so, he'd said. Until the posting to County Antrim came through. She wondered if all army housing would be the same and then regretted the uncharitable thought. She would make it nice, somehow, she thought to herself as they inspected the bedroom together.

'It's lovely,' she said finally, loyally.

Tom snorted. 'No, it's not. But it's a lot better than the mess. It'll be fine.'

'Of course it will. I'll . . . I'll paint the walls and stuff . . . maybe get some new furniture and—'

'No point, darling. We'll be gone before you know it. Antrim'll be better, you'll see.'

Meaghan was quiet. Would she ever get used to the moving around? A couple of months here, a year or two there, never quite sure where you'd be and what it would be like. She'd only really lived in three places her entire life – Dalby, the farm just outside Warra and finally Brisbane. She couldn't imagine what it would be like to wake up the following morning and not see the river or the sea in the distance or hear the hum of traffic along the Expressway that ran behind the house. It came to her that she had no idea what living in England would be like. What would she do? She hadn't given much thought to anything other than the fact that she and Tom would be together. She looked around her again. There was a large dark wood table pushed up against the wall, a great sideboard with a forgotten lace doily covering its dusty surface. Out of the corner of her eye she could see the linoleum covering of the kitchen floor, skimming over the surface of the floorboards like a thin, shiny skin. The refrigerator hummed noisily. She would have to get used to the unfamiliar smells and sounds that would turn it from being a strange, uncared-for space into something she and Tom could call home. *That* would be her job for the first few weeks. That and getting used to the fact that the sun was a thing of the past.

29

'How do you do?' 'How d'you do?' It seemed less of a question than a statement. Meaghan was passed from one handshake to another.

'Um, fine, thanks. Yes, fine. Yes, really nice to meet you too. Oh, hello . . . yes, fine, thanks . . .' She murmured what she hoped was an appropriately enthusiastic set of responses. They'd been on the base almost three weeks and it was their first proper 'outing' – a welcome dinner at the officers' mess. Meaghan had gone into Hounslow to buy a dress, her stomach churning with nerves.

'Just arrived, have you?' A booming voice addressed her across the sea of uniforms. Meaghan looked up in fright. A large-bosomed woman dressed in a floral evening gown of the sort she assumed had long since vanished from the planet was bearing down on her. It was the commanding officer's wife. The CO's wife, as everyone called her. Tom had pointed her out earlier. Meaghan had had to hastily learn the army shorthand – the CO was the commanding officer. The 2/i/c was the second-in-command. WO was the warrant officer, and the OC was the officer commanding. It seemed endless. Meaghan smiled nervously. In her long, white strapless dress which kept slipping lower than she was entirely comfortable with, she felt like a fish out of water. All the other wives were wearing long, conservative-looking dresses of far duller material. Hers even had a sparkling band across the bust that served only to draw attention to the fact that it might slip off her at any moment. Tom thought it was lovely but, then again, Tom thought every-thing she wore was lovely, even her apron. The memory of just what he'd done with her apron the last time she wore it brought a violent blush to her cheeks at precisely the moment Marjory Dunn stuck out a hand. 'Welcome to England. Settled in all right, have you?'

'Yes, er, h . . . hello,' Meaghan stammered, trying to

remember simultaneously what it was Tom had said about greeting the wives of his superiors. What was she supposed to say? *Good evening, ma'am? How do you do?* Speaking of which, she suddenly remembered, the correct answer to 'How do you do?' wasn't 'Fine, thanks,' as she'd been muttering all evening. It was 'How do you do?' She had no idea why. Christ, the Brits. There didn't seem to be an end to the tiny, inconsequential niceties that seemed *so* important to them – and to the bloody army, of course. She pulled back her hand, wondering if she ought to risk a further 'How do you do?' 'Yes, th-thanks,' she stammered.

Marjory Dunn appeared to take no notice. 'I hear you've been assigned one of those grotty little places on Beavers Creek. Enjoying it, are you?' She seemed to tack on an 'are you?' to the end of every sentence but curiously didn't appear to expect a response. She rushed on. 'Weather's dreadful at the moment, though I must say, I prefer this to the heat any day. We were in Belize last year. *Dreadful* place. Malarial, third-rate staff, power cuts every five minutes. *Dreadful.* Ah, there's Eithne Beasdale . . . Captain Beasdale's wife. I think you'll both be sent to Northern Ireland around the same time. Come. Let me introduce you. You're from New Zealand, aren't you? I think she's Canadian, or something. I dare say you'll have a lot in common.'

'Actually, I'm from—' There was no time to correct her. Marjory Dunn turned on her considerable heel and marched purposefully off. Meaghan had no option but to hurry along behind her.

'Ah . . . Mrs Beasdale, *there* you are! I've found a fellow foreigner for you. May I present Mrs Astor . . . sorry, I didn't catch your first name, my dear. Ah, Meaghan. Quite. Well, I'll leave you two to get on with it then, shall I? Always good to have someone in the same boat, that's what I think.' She sailed off.

Meaghan stood with a drink in hand, watching the broad floral back disappear amongst the uniforms and then turned to the young woman whom she'd been abruptly thrust upon. She was small and dark-haired, with large, rather heavily made-up blue eyes. She was pretty, underneath all the make-up and was wearing a risqué green and black lace dress that showed off rather more of her cleavage than anyone else within a five-mile radius. It made Meaghan feel marginally better about her own dress. She had a tattoo on her left ankle, Meaghan noticed, and a silver ankle chain. 'I'm not actually from New Zealand,' Meaghan began apologetically. 'We're from Oz.'

'Oh, I know. Nick told me the other day that you'd be coming over. Aussies, Kiwis, Americans . . . it's all the same to them. I'm Eithne, by the way. But call me Edie. Everyone does.'

'Meaghan. How d'you do?' Meaghan couldn't help smiling.

Edie giggled. 'How d'you do? I know. I kept saying, "Fine, thanks," when we first got here until someone pointed it out. They're a funny bunch but you'll get used to them.'

'Where are you from?' Meaghan asked curiously. Her accent was hard to place.

'Oh, everywhere. My mum's Irish, but I grew up in Kenya, actually.'

'Oh.' It sounded very glamorous. 'How long have you been here?'

'Almost a year. Feels like for ever. The first month was awful. I've never been so cold in my life!'

Meaghan grimaced. 'I've forgotten what the sun feels like.'

'Well, don't hold your breath. Northern Ireland's even worse, so I hear.'

'The CO's wife was saying you're also going?' Meaghan asked hopefully.

Edie nodded. 'Yep. Same time as you, I think. We'll be there at least a year, that's what Nick said.' She looked around the crowded hall. 'D'you smoke?'

Meaghan hesitated. 'Well, yes, but I'm supposed to be giving it up.'

'Oh, come on. One won't kill you. Let's nip outside. It'll be cold but I'll get us a couple of glasses to warm us up.'

She beckoned to a passing waiter – a young, painfully earnest-looking private – and collected two large glasses of red wine. 'Come on.' She pointed the way to the door. Meaghan followed her. She looked around, hoping to catch sight of Tom, but he was lost to her in the sea of uniforms.

'Here,' Edie said, lighting one of the two cigarettes she held in her hand and passing it over. She pulled her wrap around her shoulders. 'God, what wouldn't I give for a bit of heat.'

'I . . . I didn't know there were any, you know, white people in Kenya,' Meaghan began shyly, taking a deep, luxurious drag.

'Oh, there's a handful of us left. Both me and Nick were lucky, I guess. His dad's English so we both had British passports. We don't really advertise it, to be honest. They all think I'm American or Canadian. Can't place my accent.' She blew out a mouthful of smoke. 'So where're you from?'

'Brisbane. Well, Tom's from Brisbane. I'm from a tiny place about three hours west. Warra. It's so small no one's ever heard of it. I'm a farm girl, really. Grew up on a farm.'

'A farm girl? Where d'you two meet? At university?'

'God, no.' Meaghan shook her head, laughing. 'I'm a beautician.'

'Thank Christ for that. I'm a barmaid, love. *Was* a barmaid. Now I'm an officer's wife. Nick's the clever one. We sort of grew up together but I didn't really know him back then. We bumped into each other here in London. I fancied his mate at first, but he got me instead.' She laughed and took another sip of wine. 'Well, here's to barmaids and beauticians.' Edie raised her glass. 'God knows what I'd be doing if I'd stayed in Kenya. Probably married to some no-hoper white farmer, clinging on. At least this way you get to see a bit of the world.' She lifted her glass. 'If nothing else.'

Meaghan nodded, not quite sure what she meant. She took another sip. The wine was warm and slightly sweet.

'Thought I'd find you out here,' a voice spoke behind them. They both turned round. There was a man standing in the shadow of the French doors. He was tall, almost as tall as Tom, but much broader, with the alert, aggressive stance of a rugby player. Meaghan found herself looking up into his face. In the dim light that spilled out from the hall behind them, she couldn't really see him properly. His eyes were cold and expressionless. There was a moment's pause whilst he stared at her. She felt herself blush under his gaze.

'Yeah, well, didn't wanna embarrass you by lighting up in there,' Edie broke in, sounding slightly defensive. 'This is Meaghan. Tom Astor's wife.' She made the introduction reluctantly.

Meaghan held out a hand. 'Hi,' she said, putting as much warmth into her voice as she could find. 'Um, nice to meet you.'

'Hi.' His tone was curt. He looked past her to his wife, who was busy finishing her cigarette. 'Ready?' he asked abruptly.

'Yeah, just a minute. We're having a chat.'

'I'm ready to go.'

'Just give us a sec, will you?' Edie's voice carried more than a hint of impatience. There was a second's wait as they stared at each other then Nick turned and walked back through the doorway. Meaghan was embarrassed. She wondered if they'd had an argument or something before coming out that evening. She couldn't quite imagine Tom behaving that way. 'D'you . . . shall we go inside?' she asked hesitantly.

'Sod him.' Edie's tone was defiant. But she finished her wine and stubbed out her cigarette. 'I . . . I'd better go,' she said after a minute. 'I'll catch you later.' She smoothed down her dress and, avoiding Meaghan's curious glance, disappeared after him. Meaghan stood in the doorway, watching her thread her way through the crowd. She stubbed out her half-finished cigarette under her heel and then went back inside.

'Oh, there you are,' Tom said, catching sight of her. He was standing next to a group of young soldiers. He stepped away from them and put out a hand to hold her, drawing her close. 'Wondered where you'd got to. You enjoying yourself?' he asked, smiling down at her.

'I was just outside, having a cigarette. I know, I know . . . I shouldn't have. But it was just the one. I met Nick Beasdale's wife. Edie.'

'She nice?'

'I think so. He . . . he's a bit creepy,' she said suddenly.

'Creepy?' Tom laughed. 'What on earth makes you say that?'

She laughed with him. A sudden sense of relief washed over her. 'I don't know . . . he's just a bit quiet, that's all.'

'I'd have thought you'd like that,' Tom teased her, pulling back a strand of her hair that had come loose from the combs and tucking it behind her ear. 'You talk enough for three people, at least.'

She smiled; it was a joke between them. *Haven't you run out of things to say? You mean there's more?* 'How long do we have to stay?' she whispered, looking around the hall.

'Ten minutes,' Tom promised. 'I've got to talk to the CO. Grab yourself another drink. I'll come back and find you. Ten minutes, no more.'

She watched him walk off in the direction she'd just come from. She looked around for Edie but she'd disappeared. She shrugged. Nothing so fascinating as other people's lives, she thought to herself. It was one of her mother's favourite sayings. And other people's lives are *their* business, she said to herself primly as she went off in search of the loos. Not mine.

30

She was standing at the sink the following morning, washing up the breakfast dishes, when she heard a knock at the front door. She dried her hands and hurried out. In the three weeks they'd been at twelve Beavers Crescent she'd had two visitors – three, if you counted the housing officer, which she didn't. She opened the door. It was Edie Beasdale. She held up a packet of cigarettes in one hand and a tin of coffee in the other.

'Hello. Thought you might like a cup. And a fag?'

Meaghan smiled broadly. 'No to the fag but *yes* to the coffee.'

She laughed. 'Come on in. It's a bit empty, sorry. Got enough chairs, though.'

'Oh, don't worry. We're still living out of cardboard boxes and we've been here a year. They keep telling us we'll be leaving next month.'

'Where were you before this?' Meaghan asked curiously as she put the kettle on.

'Sandhurst. That's where Nick did his commissioning course. Then bloody Cyprus.' Edie lit a cigarette. 'You?'

'Well, we only just got married. A month ago, actually.'

'Ah. Thought so.'

'What?'

'You look like newlyweds. Still polite to each other and all that.'

'How long've you been married?' Meaghan didn't know quite what to say to that.

'Nearly two years now. I was married before, mind you. Military policeman. Can't get enough of these blokes in uniforms.' She grinned.

'Oh.' Meaghan wondered how old Edie was. Twenty-five? Twenty-six?

'Twenty-four,' Edie said, reading her mind. She looked around the kitchen. 'I hear Antrim's a bit of a dump,' she said conversationally. 'A couple of the ladies at the NAAFI were talking about it the other day.'

'What's the NAAFI?'

'The army store. Didn't you get one of those welcome packs? Not that they tell you much, mind you. You've got to get out there and see stuff for yourself. You been into Kingston yet?'

Meaghan shook her head. 'No. I haven't really been any-where,' she said, pulling a face. 'We came here straight from Brisbane. I've never been to London. Apart from Heathrow, but I don't suppose that really counts.'

'You've never been to London?' Edie looked at her incredulously. 'Well, what're you waiting for? Let's go.'

'Go?'

'Into town. Into London.'

'What, now?'

'Why not?' Edie was grinning at her. 'What else've we got to do all day?'

Meaghan stared at her. Why not indeed? Tom wouldn't be back until late that evening. Edie was right. It wasn't as though she had a full day of work or anything ahead of her. Just the dishes . . . and dinner. She felt her heart lift suddenly. 'OK! Why not? I'll just have to get changed,' she said, pulling off the apron she'd donned to do the dishes. 'What should I wear?'

'Wear?' Edie started to laugh. 'We're only going into London, not the bloody theatre. Just pull on a pair of jeans. We'll take the bus to the station, then catch the train in. What d'you fancy doing?'

'I dunno . . . could we . . . could we go to Buckingham Palace?' Meaghan tried to think of what she knew about London. 'Or Big Ben?'

'God, you sound like a tourist!' Edie laughed. 'All right, we can stop by Big Ben if that's what you really want. But I was thinking more along the lines of Selfridges myself.'

'What's Selfridges?'

'Christ. You really *are* a small-town girl. I'll show you. You'll love it, I promise.'

They were like schoolgirls playing truant. Edie's laugh and her enthusiasm for the smallest, most insignificant things were infectious. She bought a bag of Liquorice Allsorts at the station – they sat in the carriage, chewing contentedly as the train pulled slowly out of Hounslow and began hurtling towards town. Meaghan sat back, her mouth pleasantly full, gathering in the sights of green fields and the shiny black strip of the motorway that ran alongside the track. Everything was smaller and more compact than Australia . . . even the cars were tiny. There was a low range of hills to the left of the train, punctuated every now and then by the upright form of a building or two, then the train suddenly plunged into a dark, airless tunnel. All down the sides were snatched glimpses of posters and greying, mildewed concrete. It was colder under the earth. The train shuddered to a halt, brakes screaming. The doors opened; people streamed in and out. Seconds later they took off again, the whole carriage thrusting forward as they sped towards the next stop, and the next. She sat opposite Edie, smiling at her when their eyes met, her cheek bulging with the slowly disintegrating sweets. Everything seemed to shear off into space, her mind was pleasantly clear. Then her thoughts began to trickle back to her – the previous night's dinner; meeting Edie's strange, taciturn husband; the floral dress of the CO's wife . . . the smooth, warm feeling of Tom's leg against hers in bed that night. She caught sight of her own face in the gloomy reflection of the train window: eager, a little nervous, lips parted breathlessly as if in some childish anticipation of something pleasurable yet to come.

It took almost half an hour to get from Paddington Station to Selfridges department store. The bus they'd jumped on inched its way slowly down Oxford Street, people getting on and off with a jaunty insouciance that Meaghan could only gape at. It wasn't as though she'd never seen a crowd before but Oxford Street on a Friday morning was something else. The pavements were six or seven deep, people streaming in and out of the shops laden with bags and parcels, hailing cabs, jumping on and off buses, cyclists weaving through the traffic. They were on the upper deck, peering down at the world surging past.

At Selfridges, Edie pulled her through the revolving doors after her. She stepped in and felt as though she'd passed through the looking glass into another world. Immaculately coiffed and made-up girls squirted perfume as they passed, handed out free vouchers and benevolent, knowing smiles. The downstairs beauty hall was a cornucopia of scents, products, creams, bottles, jars, pencils, brushes . . . she followed Edie to the elevators, already dazed. The salon in Brisbane had been well stocked and she had of course been in a department store before but this . . .

this was like nothing she'd ever seen. The air was saturated with wealth. In her jeans and denim jacket and thick woollen scarf she felt – and probably looked – like a hick. Wave after wave of beautiful, elegant women walked by, stopping to try this, sample that. An impossibly thin, carefully made-up older woman paused in front of the Chanel counter. Standing next to her were two identical-looking girls, perfect clones – clearly her daughters. They held out their hands dutifully as she dabbed their wrists with something – perfume, a lotion? One of them held up her hand to her nose. 'It's quite nice, Mummy. Here . . . *you* smell it.' Walking past, Meaghan experienced a sharp, painful pang. It was the sort of commonplace scene between a mother and daughter that she had never experienced, never would. She quickly averted her eyes.

Edie marched straight ahead, past the racks of designer clothes and fur coats until she came to the section she wanted. She clearly knew her way around. Meaghan could only follow obediently.

'So . . . what d'you think?' Edie asked, holding out one slinky dress after another. Meaghan eyed them doubtfully. They were mostly evening dresses, each a little more daring and gaudy than the last. Where on earth would Edie wear them? she wondered to herself. Aside from the officers' mess, she couldn't think of a place less suitable than the Hounslow barracks for a shiny black number slit to the thigh with a large diamante brooch on one shoulder.

'Dunno,' she said carefully. 'Where would you wear it?'

'Oh, there's loads of places to go. You just haven't been to any of them yet.' Edie seemed unperturbed.

'On the base?'

'No, not on the base, you dope.' Edie had the good-natured air of explaining something to a child. 'It'd be a waste of an outfit, wouldn't it?'

Well, where else would you wear it? Meaghan wanted to say, but didn't. She watched instead as Edie slipped into the changing room and emerged a few minutes later, her hair piled untidily on top of her head and her body encased in the dress as if it had been poured into it. 'Wow. It's . . . it's lovely,' she said as Edie slowly pirouetted in front of the mirror. 'You look really glam.'

'I do, don't I?' Edie seemed entranced by her own reflection. 'Yeah, I think I'll take it.'

'How much is it?' Meaghan ventured. She'd been too scared to look at the price tags.

Edie shrugged. 'Who cares?' She disappeared back into the changing room. Meaghan looked around her uncertainly. She and Tom were both careful with money, she out of a lifetime of necessity; he out of character. Now, with her future employment prospects severely limited, she was even more hesitant about spending any. She'd come to the UK with a modest amount of savings and whilst there seemed to be little need for her to dip into her own money, she couldn't imagine splurging on a cock-tail dress – or three – as Edie seemed to be doing.

Edie had no such doubts. Two hours later they emerged into the sunlight with more bright yellow bags than they could safely carry between them. At the last minute, Meaghan had suc-cumbed to one of the smiling salesgirls and bought a bottle of perfumed body lotion – about twenty pounds cheaper than the perfume itself. Edie looked exceedingly pleased with her pur-chases. Four dresses, two pairs of shoes, underwear, perfume, make-up and a designer handbag. Meaghan could only look on in a mixture of admiration and disbelief as Edie's credit card was whipped out again and again.

'Now, how about some lunch?' Edie looked up and down the crowded street. 'Fancy a glass of champagne?'

'Um . . . won't it be really expensive?' Meaghan asked doubt-fully.

'You're only young once,' Edie shouted cheerfully over her shoulder as she darted forward and hailed a cab. 'Come on. Next month we'll be in bloody County Antrim without a decent shop or a restaurant for miles around. You'll see. You've no idea how dreary those places are.'

Meaghan said nothing but clambered into the back of the black cab after her. Edie was right – she had absolutely no idea what Northern Ireland would be like but perhaps there'd be more of a social life than she thought. Why else would Edie have bought four evening dresses and a handbag the size of a sack?

It was almost nine p.m. by the time the taxi finally pulled up outside the house. The lights were on downstairs. Meaghan looked nervously up at the house. Tom would have been home for ages. She bid Edie a hasty farewell and hurried up the garden path. She pushed open the front door. Tom was standing in the kitchen. He turned as she walked in.

'Christ . . . there you are. I was getting worried.'

'I know, I'm sorry . . . I went to London . . . with Edie. I left you a note; did you get it?' Meaghan stammered, almost running up to him.

'Yeah, I saw the note but it's *late*, Meg. How d'you get back?'

'We took a taxi from the station. I didn't think we'd be out so late . . . I'm really sorry. Have you had something to eat? I didn't have time to make anything . . .'

'No, it's fine. I was just worried, that's all. Did you have a good time?' He smiled down at her and Meaghan felt her heart turn over with relief.

She nodded. 'I thought we were going to Buckingham Palace and Big Ben . . . see the sights, y'know? But Edie's seen it all before so we went shopping instead. Well, *she* went shopping. I just watched. It was fun, though.'

'Didn't you buy anything?'

'Just this.' She fished the bottle of lotion out of her handbag. 'But you should've seen Edie. She bought *loads* . . . evening dresses, shoes . . . a new bag.' She gave a quick, embarrassed laugh. 'She seems to have a lot of money.'

Tom was quiet for a second. He put a hand on the nape of her neck, his thumb slowly caressing her skin. 'Just be careful,' he said after a moment. 'I know it's nice to have a friend and everything, but there's something about her . . . I dunno. Just . . . just be careful around her.'

'What d'you mean?' Meaghan looked up at him in surprise. 'Don't you like her?'

'I don't know her. It's just . . . I overheard something, that's all.'

'What?'

'Nothing. Nothing important. Just a bit of gossip, that's all. Nothing for you to worry about.'

'Then why'd you mention it?'

His hand stopped its rhythmic stroking. They looked at each other for a moment. Meaghan was aware of something being held back but before she could ask any further, he turned away. 'There's some pizza in the oven. I ordered in,' he said mildly. He left her standing in the middle of the kitchen, her new lotion bottle in hand, unsure of what to say or do next. She thought back to the previous evening and to the vague discomfort she'd felt after meeting Nick Beasdale for the first time. She felt the same way about Nick as Tom appeared to feel about Edie. It was odd; there was an undercurrent to both of them that was so subtle she couldn't catch it. The events of the afternoon flowed over her, one after the other – the journey, Selfridges, the new clothes, lunch and the two glasses of champagne they'd each had, then the jaunt down Bond Street and the G & T they'd had at the station before running to catch the train – it all dissolved in her, like the peppermint sweet Edie had handed her just before getting out of the cab. 'Here,' she'd said, splitting open the wrapper. 'Stick this in your mouth. Worst thing, coming home stinking of booze. I've made that mistake one too many times, believe me.' She'd popped it in her mouth without thinking. She looked uncertainly after Tom. She'd suddenly lost her appetite. She had the strange feeling she'd done something wrong, overstepped some invisible mark or transgressed a boundary without knowing exactly what or where it was. She shook her head slowly as she took the half-eaten pizza out of the oven and wrapped it carefully in cling film. She could hear the

muted sounds of the television in the living room. She switched
off the light and walked upstairs, unable to shake the feeling that
something wasn't quite right.

31

She had little time to dwell on it, however. The next day, Tom
came home at lunchtime – a first in the weeks they'd been in the
UK – waving a letter at her. He was excited. His transfer had
come through. In less than a week, they were shipping out to
Northern Ireland. Meaghan was in the middle of preparing
dinner – a shoulder of lamb with vegetables – when he came
through the doorway.

'Next week?' she asked, half in alarm. 'God, that's soon.'

'Sooner the better,' Tom said, opening the fridge. 'Can't wait
to get stuck into things, I tell you. I'm going mad with all this
bloody paperwork.'

'How'll we get there?'

'RAF flight. Probably from Brize Norton. Your mate Edie's
leaving on Wednesday, I think, with the first transport. I've got
some more paperwork to sort out before we go but B Coy's ready
to roll.'

'Oh.' She hesitated for a second. 'Will we be on the same
base, d'you know?'

He nodded. 'Yep. There's only one. Look, about last
night . . . I didn't mean to upset you. I . . . I was just worried,
that's all. She seems like a nice person and it's great you've made
a friend. I shouldn't have said anything. You're perfectly capable
of making your own judgements about people. I'm sorry.'

Meaghan stared at him. Her heart lifted suddenly. That was
Tom all over. He surprised you, just when you least expected it.
Her throat was suddenly thick with tears. He was so different
from every man she'd ever met, including and especially her
father. 'You don't need to apologise,' she said softly, reaching up

a hand to ruffle the stubborn lick of hair that stood up on his forehead. 'But I do know what you mean. They're an odd couple.'

'They're probably saying the same thing about us.' He smiled. His arms tightened around her waist. 'I've got fifteen minutes, Mrs Astor, before I've got to get back. What can we do in fifteen minutes?'

Meaghan felt the blush travel from the roots of her hair to the soles of her feet. 'Fifteen minutes?' She giggled. 'A bloody lifetime.'

His reply was lost as her mouth swallowed his own.

The bell wasn't working. She pressed it twice before remembering Edie complaining about it the day before. She lifted a hand and rapped on the door. There was a bike propped against the outside wall and she could hear the faint hum of the television from within. She knocked again. She was just about to turn and walk back down the garden path when she heard Edie's laugh. Perhaps she was in the kitchen and couldn't hear the door? She walked around to the back of the house and climbed up the short flight of stairs to the back door. She heard Edie's laugh again, followed by a man's laugh. She hesitated; she didn't particularly want to bump into Nick. He might have come home early in the day, just as Tom had. She stood uncertainly for a second on the top step and then she heard the man saying, quite loudly and distinctly, 'Take 'em off. Dunno why you bother, honestly.' It wasn't Nick. *Dunno why you bovver*. If she wasn't mistaken, the accent belonged to one of the squaddies, not one of the officers. She heard Edie giggle. She couldn't help herself – she glanced through the kitchen window. Edie was standing with her back to her, clad only in a skimpy T-shirt, leaning into a man's embrace. The soldier in whose arms she stood was sitting on the kitchen counter; his camouflage-clad legs were wrapped around Edie's back. There was a moment's shocked awareness as he looked directly into Meaghan's eyes, then she turned and almost fell back down the steps. She ran around the side of the house and back down the road. It was a cold day but she'd been in such a hurry that she'd forgotten to take her coat. She wrapped her arms across her chest and ran all the way home.

She pushed open the front door and leaned against it, breathing hard. She could hardly believe what she'd just seen. Other people's business, she reminded herself, over and over again. But she liked Edie. She'd only just begun to think of her as a friend. Now what? She could hardly pretend she hadn't seen her. The soldier – whoever he was – would have described her shocked face and it wouldn't be difficult to put two and two together. What was she supposed to do now? What did people do in situations like these? And what, if anything, should she say to Tom? In a few days' time, they'd all be in Northern Ireland . . . should she just carry on as if nothing had happened? She stood leaning against the door as if she might otherwise fall, disappointment breaking over her in waves. She suddenly felt very young and very naïve. She walked into the kitchen and made herself a cup of tea. The shoulder of lamb she'd been in the middle of preparing when Tom came home stood marinating on the sideboard. She sat down at the Formica-topped table. From outside came the distant sounds of the base in the late afternoon. She could hear the telephone ringing in the neighbour's house – a sharp, shrill sound that stopped abruptly after a few minutes. The road had its usual muffled roar and, across the way, she could hear children's voices, rising in play. The sun made a brief, unexpected appearance through the living room curtains. She sat in the stiff-backed armchair, sipping her tea, feeling the uncomfortable space of silence hanging above the surge and fall of traffic.

32

SAM
London, England, 1992

'And in here's the bedroom. Yeah, it's a bit on the small side, I'll grant you, but it's cosy. And the bathroom's down the corridor.'

The estate agent opened the door briskly and closed it again. 'And that's about it.'

'When did you say I could move in?' Sam asked, making up her mind. It was her fifth viewing that morning and it was beginning to dawn on her that not only would she never find anything as remotely nice as her flat in Bristol, she'd better get used to the idea that she'd be paying three times as much for half the space – or less.

'Soon as you've paid the deposit,' he said cheerfully. 'But if you want it, you'd better put it down sharpish – you're the second person to see it and I've got a few more. It's a nice place. I'd take it, if I were you, frankly. You're not going to find anything nicer at this price, not round here.'

Sam nodded. The two-bedroom flat on Elgin Crescent was a five-minute walk from Portobello Road, a ten-minute walk to Ladbroke Grove Tube station and from there it was a short ride into the West End to work. 'OK. I'll take it. Shall I follow you to your offices?'

'Absolutely. Great.' The estate agent closed his file with a satisfied snap. 'I'll give you a lift.' She followed him out of the flat. There was a communal garden behind the house that ran the length of the street and the shared entrance was clean and freshly painted. She would be sharing it with a young woman named Lisa, a trainee barrister. 'The two of you can sue each other over the bills,' the estate agent had said, laughing appreciatively at his own wit. Sam didn't respond. He had a car waiting outside; he opened the door with a proud flourish. It was smart, in that flashy, newly qualified estate-agent kind of way. She folded her hands across her lap and tried to ignore his running commentary.

An hour later it was done. She handed over a cheque for the first two months and a letter from her employers and the keys were hers. She left the estate agents on Ladbroke Grove and hurried to the bus stop, an enormous smile plastered across her face. She had a new job, a new flat, a new flatmate and a whole new chapter in her life to look forward to. Plus, of course, a holiday with Paula. A week on a Greek island. It could hardly get better.

Exactly six days later, she peered at Paula from over her novel and pronounced, with a satisfied sigh, that no, it couldn't.

'Couldn't what?' Paula lifted her head sleepily.

They were both lying on brightly coloured beach towels slowly turning brown. Well, Paula was turning brown, Sam corrected herself. She, on the other hand, was turning pink, and pinker by the second. She slathered some more sun cream over her neck and arms. She set the lotion down again and distractedly grabbed a handful of sand, letting it trickle through her fingers. 'Get better. Life. It can't get better than this.'

Paula gave a derisive snort. 'That's where you're wrong, love. I could suddenly land a contract with Aspreys or Cartier, the most gorgeous man in the world could walk along the beach right now and sweep me off my feet *and* my bloody sisters would get off my case and come and live with Mum instead of badgering *me* to do it. But none of that's going to happen so, yeah, I guess life can't get much better than this. Though I wish it would.'

Sam had to laugh. She'd met Paula in the library a week after term started in her first year. Paula was studying to be a jewellery designer at the poly and she'd come into the library to search for books on medieval art. They'd bumped into one another in the stairwell, Paula carrying an armful of out-of-date books on Beowulf and Sam with her usual pile of dusty legal tomes. Neither could explain why but they'd stopped to chat for a second, then gone for a coffee together and then a drink . . . and that was that. Best friends by the end of the first term. They were about as different as was possible. Paula was petite and curvy with straight, dark brown hair that fell to her waist and large, hazel-green eyes. She was impulsive, wildly creative and completely scatterbrained, the most hopelessly disorganised person Sam had ever met. She was incapable of saying 'no' to anyone and anything and, according to Sam at least, she routinely allowed her entire family – two older sisters and an ailing, complaining mother – to walk all over her. She was the youngest and seemed perpetually doomed to that role. But she was also wickedly funny, unswervingly loyal and wildly talented. It was a real case of 'opposites attract', as everyone who met them said. Sam, organised, seemingly totally in control, calm and capable; Paula, the opposite, forever rushing around, hopelessly chaotic, falling in and out of love on a weekly basis.

'Why don't you just tell your sisters to take a hike?' Sam murmured, feeling the coarse texture of the sand prickle pleasurably against her fingertips.

'Oh, I couldn't. Mum needs me.' Paula's voice was muffled. She lay with her head turned sideways, her eyes closed against the dazzling brilliance of the sun.

Sam didn't reply. A reply would only open the door to the same old argument – if it could be called such. A one-way diatribe was closer to the mark. And it was hers, not Paula's. Paula almost seemed to accept the demands her family placed upon her. Sam was astounded at her reluctance to put her own needs forward, never mind first. Her mother lived in a one-bedroom council flat just off the Kingsland Road and seemed perpetually broke. Paula's father, whom she only saw sporadically, had remarried and moved to Belsize Park. He was an accountant; Paula's mother had been a housewife. When he left her for his secretary, she'd spent most of the divorce settlement out of rage and revenge and now lived alone, mostly off income support. It was the sort of lesson Sam paid attention to but Paula refused to see. Every so often she would make the journey up to Belsize Park from Hackney, sit with her father and his new wife and child and yet stubbornly decline to denounce him. 'His choice,' she'd say, shrugging her shoulders. 'Nothing to do with me.'

'But you're the one who's left behind to pick up the pieces,' Sam would argue with her. 'Why don't you say something to him? It's just not fair.'

'Life's not fair.'

'But why you? Why not Louise? Or Amanda? Why does it always have to be you?'

Paula shrugged, as she always did when the topic of her sisters came up, and closed the subject. Sam had long since given up arguing or even talking about it.

'Well, don't look now,' Sam murmured, lifting a hand to shade her eyes. 'But there *is* a man approaching. Not the most gorgeous-looking man I've ever seen, though.'

Paula raised her head, squinting. She gave a little groan and flopped back down again. 'It's that bloody waiter. The one from the restaurant next to the hotel. He's got a crush on you.'

Sam snorted derisively. 'On *you*, you mean. Watch out, he's making a beeline for us.' She picked up her book just as the waiter approached and pretended to be reading voraciously. She listened with half a smile on her face as Paula declined his offer of a drink, a sandwich, a ride on his motorbike or a moonlit rendezvous later that evening. In desperation, he turned to Sam. 'What about *you*?' he asked, making it clear Sam was very much a last resort.

'No. I'm busy,' Sam responded primly. He stood up, dusted the sand from his jeans and sauntered off, presumably looking for another sun-worshipper to harass.

Paula spoke out of the corner of her mouth, her head still turned away from Sam. 'Christ. D'you realise he's the only man we've managed to attract all week? No one else has even asked us for a drink. What's *wrong* with us? Sun, sea, sex . . . we've managed the first two, at least.'

Sam put down her book again. She sometimes couldn't get over how different she and Paula were. It hadn't even occurred to her that anyone would buy them a drink, or, perhaps more to the point, that if no one did, it automatically meant their holiday was a failure. She'd come to Mykonos for sun, sand and sea, in no particular order. Sex was certainly not on the menu. In fact, it was so far *off* the menu as to make the very thought of it ridiculous. She looked half-enviously at Paula's supine, almost-golden body. Paula was the sort of girl Sam had secretly envied in school – not bitchy; pretty, but not beautiful; clever, but not overly brainy. Normal, in other words. She wasn't a worrier, like Sam. She took life lightly, easily . . . it was part of her attraction, Sam often thought. Whereas she would spend hours thinking about doing something, weighing up the pros and cons, arguing herself alternately into or out of a hole, Paula simply 'did'. *Just do it*, was one of her favourite sayings. *Don't think too much or you won't.* It was true. There was a lightness to Paula that Sam admired. Yet for all Paula's lightness and her refreshingly casual take on men, she'd had no more luck in that department than Sam. A string of unsuitable boyfriends in college, a half-baked affair with a tutor who kept insisting he'd left his wife except he went home to her every night, and an unrequited crush on her bank manager had left her at twenty-three pretty much as she'd been when she and Sam met – single, in other words. Paula kept saying it was early days yet, but there were moments when Sam wondered if she'd be single for ever.

She murmured something to Paula but there was no reply. She looked at her more closely; lulled by the warmth of the morning sun and the faint muffle of the sea, yawning away, she'd fallen asleep. Sam sat upright, looking past the small cove where they lay to the dazzling blue canvas beyond. She got up, suddenly restless, and walked down to where the yellow, coarse sand gave way to whiter, finer bands of pale where the sea met the beach. The tide was coming in; the water, dazzling in its turquoise cleanness, spread itself over and over again, lapping endlessly at her feet. She walked slowly, enjoying the feel of the sun on her shoulders and back, lifting her gaze every now and then to meet the sharp, dizzying line of the horizon. Out there in the water, the simple story of the beach – every beach – played before her eyes. A young boy in a canoe was being taught to paddle by his father. At the same point each time, the canoe overturned slowly, he was brought to the surface, laughing and spluttering, and the performance repeated itself over and again. Down beside the blackened mass of the rocks that marked the end of the curved beach a lone fisherman stood, casting his line and reeling it in, empty each time. Her gaze slid past him. There was a couple lying in the shadow of the craggy cliff; she came upon them eventually, walked past them quietly but they were absorbed in each other. Out of the corner of her eye she saw him run a hand down the girl's back, a soothing, steady caress, whispering something in her ear. Sam looked away quickly, embarrassed. Displays of affection unsettled her.

She clambered over the first row of rocks, making for a perfect little crescent of white sand on the other side that appeared completely deserted. The rocks closest to the water bristled with barnacles and mussels; the back row was smooth and reddish, swirled into luxurious curves by the wind and water. She dropped down easily into the hollow on the other side. It was cool and shady where the shadows cast by the rocks lay on the still-wet sand. Her feet made sharp, shuddering indentations in the firm, packed ground. She turned her head towards the glittering sea again. The sun was almost directly overhead now; it was nearly lunchtime. In front of her the grassy-green outline of the cliff face cut off the dazzling brilliance of the sandy beach. She walked until she was almost upon it, then sat down. A thin film of water crept up to her toes, touching her. She lay back and closed her eyes. The sun puckered her skin; every now and then a shiver of cool, silky water flowed over her feet and legs. Like Paula, she gave herself up to the heat and the lassitude, losing that sense of herself in space – where was land? Where was the sea? Her own heartbeat in her ears was the same as the steady thump of waves breaking far out to sea, audible to her with her ears pressed close to the sand, but only just.

She opened her eyes on a bird that had settled itself almost within reach of her hand. She sat up, yawning. The bird's long tail tangled wildly as it took off in fright. She followed it with her eyes and saw a man sitting in the shadow of the rocks, his arms wrapped around his knees, his eyes fixed on the horizon in front of them. She saw his face move round towards her. She lifted a hand to her eyes; she recognised him from the hotel where she and Paula were staying. There were a group of young men – a few French, a couple of Spaniards and one or two Italians; she heard them in the mornings when they came down for breakfast. There was a moment's hesitation between them, then simultaneously, they both lifted a wary hand. He got up and began to walk towards her. Sam's stomach gave a little lurch. He was the good-looking one amongst the friends; Paula had noticed him immediately. As far as Sam could make out, he'd never so much as glanced in her direction.

'Ciao.' He squatted easily on the sand beside her. 'You're Sam, right?'

She looked up at him in surprise. 'How did you . . . yes, I'm Sam,' she stammered. Sunlight bounced off his dark brown hair, showing strands of gold, bleached by the sun. His skin was nut-brown, slick with oil. She swallowed nervously.

'I heard your friend call you the other morning. Sam . . . it's a boy's name, no?'

'Short for Samantha. But no one ever calls me that.'

'I'm Giancarlo. Pleased to meet you.' He held out a hand, oddly formal. 'You are English, no?'

Sam shook it, unnerved by his presence. She tried to look behind her, to see if there was anyone near. 'Yes, from London. And you?'

'Italian. From Milano.' He said it the Italian way. *Miláno.* His voice was a low, silky rumble. 'You're here on holiday?'

'Yes, with . . . with my friend. She's over there, on the other side of the rocks.' She turned her head in the direction from which she'd come. It was far, she realised suddenly. The little cove was easily half a mile or more from the beachfront at the hotel. They were quite alone on the strip of white sand. Not even the sound of jet-skis hurtling themselves through the waves in the distance could reach them.

'You want to swim?' Giancarlo stood up suddenly. Sam was forced to look up the length of his golden brown legs. She swallowed again. She felt practically naked. She looked down at the soft pink line of her own body, suddenly uncomfortably aware of its minute-but-all-too-visible flaws – the puckering of the skin where her thighs met; the short, bristly blonde hairs on her shins where she'd forgotten to shave; the silvery stretch marks around her knees. She had to suppress the urge to cover her stomach with her hands. He was looking down at her; she got to her feet awkwardly, unable to bear his gaze a second longer.

'Sure, why not?' she replied with an off-hand confidence that she certainly didn't feel.

They walked together into the peacock-toned sea. The water billowed gently about her legs as they waded in deeper. Then the ground underfoot fell away and suddenly they were neck-deep and had to swim. The sea and the sun, blackness and glare, the cold tongue of a wave as it crested and broke over the top of her head . . . the sensations came at her, one after the other. As if by some unspoken agreement, they turned together at the point where the cliff face plunged into the sea and rounded the bend to yet another perfect and perfectly isolated beach. They came ashore on a collection of small, smooth rocks, neither speaking. Giancarlo led the way ahead of her. She was conscious of the tight, muscular swell of his backside and thighs in his white swimmer's shorts as he picked out a path for her to follow.

'Ouch!' Something sharp and piercing suddenly shot through her foot. She stopped, hopping painfully on her left leg. Small threadworms of blood streamed out from the sole of her right foot. 'I cut myself,' she said, her face twisted into a grimace. There was an old sardine can lying nestled in a pool of water next to her; she'd cut herself on it.

'Here, let me see.' Giancarlo was beside her in a second, one hand holding onto her as he bent down. 'Your big toe . . . there, you see?' He held her foot in his hand. A huge blush of emotion rippled through her as they examined her foot together. She had to put out a hand on his shoulder to steady herself. 'We should tie it with something,' he said, squinting up at her.

'No, it's fine. I'll just put it in the water . . . it's cold, it'll stop the bleeding.'

'Does it hurt?' His thumb came to rest very lightly on the loose flap of skin that the can had torn away from her flesh.

She shook her head, though it hurt like hell. To her horror, she felt a second sting – tears behind her eyes. 'N-no, it's OK. It stings a little, that's all.'

'Here, sit down for a minute. Put your foot in the water.' He gestured to her to sit down beside him.

She lowered herself awkwardly into the small hollow of the rock and let her foot slide into the water. There was a moment's sharp pain as the cold water closed over the wound then the pain disappeared. His hand stayed where it was, halfway down her calf. She turned her head to look at him. The drops of water on his face as he emerged from the sea had already dried stiff in the sun. His eyes were the colour of aubergines, a dark liquidity that made it difficult to read his expression. The most suffocating feeling of both joy and terror took hold of her as he bent his head towards hers and she saw, with the numbing shock of recognition, that he was going to kiss her. She was still with fear as he took his hand from her leg and touched her on the shoulder, pulling her towards him. He gave a deep, curious sigh, as if submitting to something against his will, and all of a sudden, his warm, wet mouth was on hers, opening her tight, closed mouth with his tongue. All thoughts of her cut foot, the beach, the sea beyond, Paula, their hotel . . . everything fled before the surge of longing that rushed through her. Her whole body felt as though it had simply dissolved in a tidal wave of desire. The kiss was a kind of intoxication; when at last he released her, coming up for breath, she found herself nuzzling against him, the way a puppy might, following the hand that caressed it, not wanting him to stop.

33

MEAGHAN
Antrim, Northern Ireland, 1992

Together with three other wives and their assorted children from the Hounslow base, none of whom she'd met before, Meaghan flew into Aldergrove, just west of Belfast, on a wet, drizzling day in November. Edie wasn't on the flight; she'd taken a week's holiday with a friend of hers from her barmaid days in London. They'd gone to Lanzarote. She'd asked if Meaghan wanted to join them. Meaghan had looked at her as if she'd lost her mind. She couldn't imagine disappearing off to the sun whilst Tom flew to Northern Ireland on his own. 'Maybe later,' she'd offered apologetically, not wanting to sound as though she disapproved.

Edie simply shrugged. 'It's November, mate. It's a long way to summer. I'm desperate for a bit of sun.'

Now, as she followed the other wives off the RAF plane, she began to wonder if it might not have been a good idea after all. It was midday but the whole country looked as if the air and light had been sucked out of it. London was grey; Belfast, as someone said, was worse. There was a mini-bus waiting to take them to the new base. They collected their belongings and followed the young female soldier who briskly shepherded them on board with the weary air of someone who clearly has better things to do with her time. 'Meaghan Astor?' she called out. Meaghan had the sensation of being back in school.

'Yes, that's me,' she said, hauling her suitcase behind her.

'There's a message for you. Your husband's on patrol for the next three nights. Someone at the housing office will take you to your quarters. With luck he should be back by the weekend. Right, Susie Jenkins? Not on this flight? Fuck . . . can't they get *anything* right?'

They drove slowly out of the airport, turning onto a highway that led north, to Antrim, and the base that was soon to be home. Disappointment at the thought of not seeing Tom settled over her and, for a few moments, she was afraid she might actually cry. The other wives were clearly used to the routine and the 'cock-ups', as one woman put it, that the army seemed to make on a regular basis. 'Don't you worry, love . . . he'll be back before you know it. Make the most of it, I tell you. In a few months' time it's all you'll be looking forward to – a bit of peace and quiet when they're gone. It's a sodding place, I promise you. Makes them go a bit mad.'

What did she mean? Meaghan wondered, but was too timid to ask. 'Thanks,' she said, hoping her voice was steady. 'It's my – our – first tour.'

The woman smiled. 'You'll get used to it. Best keep yourself busy, that's the trick. No good sitting around waiting for them to come home. Keep yourself busy and the time'll fly. Least you're more or less in the same place. When Gary was in Iraq it was dreadful. Couldn't turn on the telly without me heart in me mouth.'

'Oh, I know. This is our third tour.' The other woman smiled sympathetically at Meaghan. 'I'm Gillian. Gillian McIlroy. And this here's Claire Gideon. What battalion's your husband with?'

'Poachers,' Meaghan replied. 'Royal Anglian.'

'Oh, so're we. What's his rank?'

'Captain. He's just transferred over from Australia.'

'Oh, he's an officer? Didn't think they put the officer's wives in this old cattle wagon,' Gillian laughed comfortably, but there was an edge to her voice that Meaghan caught immediately. In the month they'd been in Hounslow, she'd witnessed first-hand just how strict the lines separating the officers from the rest of the men were and how tightly they were enforced. The wives seemed to wear their husbands' ranks with even greater pride than the men.

'Made any friends yet?' Claire asked.

Meaghan nodded. 'One or two. Edie Beasdale. Her husband's also a captain.'

'Oh. Edie *Beasdale*.' Gillian and Claire exchanged a quick, knowing glance.

Meaghan felt her face reddening. 'She seems really nice,' she said quickly, wondering what the two women thought of Edie.

'Yeah. Lively girl,' Gillian commented drily. Claire muttered something that Meaghan couldn't quite catch. There was a short, uncomfortable silence, then the bus turned off the highway, heading towards what looked like the centre of town. Meaghan looked out of the window at the sodden streets wavering in front of her eyes under a curtain of rain. It looked impossibly dreary. Rows and rows of identical-looking houses as far as she could see. Brown brick, pitched roofs, no garden . . . she swallowed. Woodland Grove. Briarhill. Cunningham Way. Castle Manor. She read the street names as the bus turned down one, then the other in a labyrinth of grey. There was a short blast of open ground, then a barbed-wire perimeter fence emerged out of the drizzle.

'Here we go, kids.' Gillian turned round to look at her two children, who were quietly squabbling on the back seats. 'Home. Oi, Billy, stop that, will you? Leave her alone!'

They stopped at the base gates whilst more paperwork was exchanged, then moved slowly into the base itself. From the form she'd been given, Meaghan knew their new house was in the married quarters, on something called Site A. They drove past a main building of some sort; there were small army jeeps and large cumbersome tanks everywhere on the wide streets. A store, a series of small huts, some temporary-looking structures and a post office . . . and then the driver announced cheerfully that they'd arrived at Site A.

She was the first to be dropped off. 'Mrs Astor? You're in number sixteen. I think the housing officer's waiting for you. He'll have the keys.' She clambered down with her suitcase and carry-on and hurried up the short garden path. The front door was open. A soldier was standing in the hallway, clipboard in hand.

'Mrs Astor?' He stepped forward to help her with her suitcase. 'Welcome to Antrim. Did you get the message?'

Meaghan nodded. 'Yes, thanks.'

'Right. If you'll just sign here . . . that's it. Keys are in the front door. There's an inventory list in the kitchen on the counter. You're to go through it and hand it back into housing. They're over at the main camp. Your husband's stuff'll be brought up tomorrow or the day after, I should imagine.'

'Hasn't he seen the place yet?' Meaghan asked, surprised. Tom had been gone for almost a full week ahead of her.

The soldier shook his head. 'No. They were lucky. They were out on patrol as soon as they got here. Didn't even have time to unpack.'

'Oh. Where is he now?'

'Not at liberty to say, I'm afraid, ma'am. They're on patrol in the city, that's all I can tell you.'

Lucky? Meaghan signed the form as directed and closed the door behind him. She was alone in their new home. She looked around her. It wasn't much different from the house in Hounslow. The same furniture – what little there was – and the same peeling, magnolia paint. She pushed open the door to the kitchen. A few ill-matched cupboard doors, a cooker with a crooked grill, a washing machine and two small fridges. She opened one of the cupboards. Plates, a few glasses, some cups and saucers, and an old electric kettle, its cord wrapped tightly around its base. She put her hands up to her cheeks. It wasn't quite what she'd expected when she left Brisbane. She wasn't sure *what* she'd thought – aside from the day she and Edie had spent in London, England – and now, Northern Ireland – was nothing like the way she'd pictured it. She'd imagined herself and Tom in a nice, old house with a garden and honeysuckle roses climbing up the walls. She'd pictured the kitchen with its old-fashioned stove and a collection of copper-bottomed pans hanging from the ceiling. Tom would go out to work every day whilst she would stay at home cooking and preparing elaborate dinner parties for the other officers and their wives. She might take a course or two, perhaps get a part-time job doing something she enjoyed.

It was with a dawning sense of shock that she realised she hadn't actually had a clue what she would do. She hadn't thought it through at all. Yes, deep down she'd known there was always the possibility that Tom would actually go to war . . . that's what soldiers did, after all. She wasn't naïve. She knew it was what he'd spent the past few years training for and that it was what, in all likelihood, he would do for the rest of his life. But it simply hadn't occurred to her that she would spend the rest of *her* life on one dreary little base after another, stuck in the middle of nowhere with few friends and no family whatsoever. The latter wasn't a shock. Aside from Clive, she had no family. She was used to being alone. But in Brisbane she'd been at the centre of life in the salon; there'd been the girls she'd shared a flat with, the girls at work. She'd been popular, dammit! Here in the UK, without Tom, she was nothing. A nobody. An officer's wife without even a cat for company. She sat down at the rickety little table in the centre of the kitchen without even taking off her coat . . . and began to cry.

34

TOM
Ballymurphy, Northern Ireland, 1992

'Fuck a duck. Look who's here. Look lively, lads. IRA heard you were coming and they're pissing themselves laughing. Patrol's in an hour. Astor, come with me.'

Tom looked around him, bewildered. Their headquarters for the week-long patrol assignment was a school. A primary school. The tables, chairs, toilets and makeshift beds were designed for people under ten years of age and under five foot.

None of his soldiers even remotely fitted that description. It looked like being an uncomfortable week ahead. He followed the regiment's 2/i/c, Major Doug Henderson, out of the door. It was his first tour as a company commander; the pressure was on from all sides to make sure he – and his men – performed.

'How's things?' he asked as Doug kicked out a chair and they sat down.

'Worse than you'd think. The regiment before your lot lost five men on a single night. It's Beirut out there, I promise you.' Doug drew deeply on his cigarette.

Tom was quiet. On the way over in the truck he'd been shocked to hear some of the conversations. He was Australian, not British; as he listened to their 'it's us or fucking them' talk, it dawned on him that he hadn't grown up with as clear and defined a sense of 'the enemy' as the British clearly had. He'd been on the verge of telling a few of them to cool it, quieten down, but some instinct had warned him to hold back. There was no telling what sort of trouble they would find themselves in over the next few weeks and months; as one of the officers in charge, he had to win their respect and their trust, not their suspicion. 'What are you saying, Doug? That we won't win?'

'Course we'll win. We're just not always going to be comfortable about how we do it, that's what I'm saying. The last lot just strolled around, handing out sweets and shit, trying to chat up the locals. All that bullshit about hearts and minds. These kids out there'll put a rock through your head today and a bullet tomorrow. We're not here to be target practice. I want you to keep the lads moving, keep their eyes open all the time and when we get a contact, we take it as it comes. You follow me?'

Tom nodded. 'I'll get the lads ready.'

'Good man. We'll do a quick round just to familiarise them with the area and then you and I can roster them up for the next couple of days.' He stood up. 'Welcome to Belfast. With any luck we'll make it out of here in six months' time without a single casualty. That's my aim and it should be yours, too.'

'Good as gold.' It was one of his mother's favourite sayings and it brought a sudden smile to his face. It seemed strange to be thinking about her in this place, he thought to himself as he walked back down the corridor to where the rest of the company were waiting. Or Meaghan. He found it hard to picture her. She'd have arrived by now on one of those VC10 flights from Brize Norton. He was sorry he couldn't be on hand to meet her but, if he were honest about it, she'd hardly been on his mind since he arrived. She'd figure things out, find her way around. She was tough, Meaghan. She could handle pretty much anything. He pushed open the door; all the men looked up expectantly. He felt a sudden rush of warmth for them. Charlie, Bozo, Ginge, Ronnie, Garcy, Don the only trained sniper in the group, Kevin, Martin . . . he had fifty-three men under his command, though they were split into smaller sub-groups, each with a leading lieutenant. In the coming months, he knew, he would rely on them – and they on him – in ways that few people outside the army would ever experience. Closer than brothers, yet aware at all times of the hierarchies between them. It was his job to make sure the unit came out of the tour alive, with as few casualties of any description as possible. He was an outsider on a number of counts – an Aussie commanding British men; a transfer from outside the battalion and an officer to boot, but he relished the challenge of knitting them together and showing his superiors that their decision to give him company command was well placed.

'Right, lads. Here's the situation.' Every eye in the room was trained on him. He looked at them all, one by one, for the duration of the fifteen-minute speech. When it was over, he knew he had their undivided attention and the beginnings of their respect. It was up to him now to keep it.

35

MEAGHAN
Antrim, Northern Ireland, 1992

She looked around the small dining room for the last time, anxiously wondering if there was anything she'd missed. It did look lovely. Well, 'lovely' was perhaps stretching it a bit – it *was* Massereene Base, after all – but it looked nice. The table was set with the new plates and the crockery she'd bought on her last trip into Belfast. White, oval plates with a gold trim and terribly fancy-looking wine glasses. She didn't care much for the knives and forks – a bit too elaborate for her taste but Tom thought they were OK. 'Only OK?' she'd asked nervously. It was her first Christmas dinner as an army wife and Tom had invited his commanding officer, Major Clifford, and his wife Janet. Edie and Nick were also coming. She'd taken the news of the invitation in her stride but now, half an hour before the guests were due to arrive, she was beginning to panic. She picked up the vase of lilies that she'd bought the previous day from the florist on Church Street and moved them to the centre of the table. No, they'd get in the way, she thought, putting them back on the sideboard instead. But the table looked a little bare . . . it needed something in the centre. A sprig of holly? Something festive? She'd placed Christmas crackers on each side plate but now, looking at them, she wondered if they didn't look a little . . . tacky?

'Looks great, darling.' Tom came into the dining room, his hair still wet from the shower.

She looked up at him. He'd lost weight since their arrival in Northern Ireland. He rarely spoke about what they did on patrols but she knew from Edie that it wasn't always plain sailing. Only the other day Edie had told her about the two gunmen they'd killed on the streets of one of the worst estates. The exchange of fire had gone on for almost an hour. She'd listened to her half-enviously. Nick obviously had no qualms about letting her in on the grisliest details of their job. Tom, on the other hand, made it clear that what went on outside the base stayed there. Home, Tom made it clear to her, had to be a place he could escape to, somewhere he could forget about the dangers they faced every day. It was not his way to bring the madness of the outside world into their home. Meaghan wasn't sure which was better. It irked her sometimes that Edie seemed so much more in touch with what went on in the men's lives, but it was Tom's decision, his way of coping, and she had to respect it.

'You sure?' she asked now, eyeing the table dubiously. 'You're not just saying it?'

Tom grinned. 'Why would I just say it? No, you've done a grand job.'

'Grand? Listen to you . . . you sound like the postman,' Meaghan laughed, relieved. 'Shall we have a quick drink before they get here? I'm nervous as hell.'

'Why? You've met the CO's wife before, haven't you?'

'Yeah, but that was in the butcher's and she hardly said a word. They scare me, you know.'

'Who do?'

'Them. The wives. They're all . . . I don't know . . . they all seem so much more *accomplished*, you know? Me, I'm just a beautician from the outback. Didn't you say she was a teacher or something?'

'Don't think so. I can't remember. But you'll have Edie for company. Dunno what *she* did before she met Beasdale but I can't imagine she'd have been up to much.' Tom went over to the sideboard and opened a bottle of red wine. He poured two small glasses. 'Haven't we got any beer?'

'Tom! It's Christmas. You can't drink a beer at Christmas lunch,' Meaghan smiled. 'Even *I* know that.'

He pulled a face, then laughed. 'Yeah, you're right. OK, Mrs Astor. Wine it is, just for today.' He brought a glass over. 'Cheers.'

The wine was warm and slightly rough-tasting. Meaghan

knew next to nothing about wine but it had been Edie's idea to serve what she called 'New World' wines at the lunch. She'd had to take the train into Belfast to get them; the man at the local off-licence had simply looked at her blankly. 'New World, ye say? What world would that be, now?' She took another sip then set the glass down carefully and moved towards him for a kiss. 'Merry Christmas,' she whispered against the stiff, starchy feel of his uniform. Since they'd arrived in Northern Ireland she could count on the fingers of one hand the number of times she'd seen Tom out of uniform. He sometimes slept in it. Once or twice they'd come in from a week's patrol and he'd been too exhausted to even speak. He would lie on the couch, his eyes closed but his lips moving occasionally, as if he were giving orders or explaining a point. She knew better than to disturb him. He needed the time and space to decompress before attempting to enter back into the life that existed beyond his daily routine. Sex, which until that point had been marked by tenderness and a delicacy that had surprised and then enthralled her, changed. Each time he came back from patrols it was no longer the first thing he thought of. Sometimes it took a day or two for the normal balance of their lives to reassert itself. At first she worried about it. Why didn't he want her? Why did he no longer make the first moves? She lay beside him at night, listening to the sound of his exhausted breathing, herself too rigid with doubts to be able to sleep. As usual, it was Edie who had the answer. 'It's the tension,' she said knowingly. 'It gets to them. They can't relax, even if they want to. He's probably afraid he'll hurt you.'

'Hurt me? What d'you mean?' Meaghan looked at her, puzzled.

'You know . . . he might get a little rough.'

'Why? That's not . . . he's not usually like that. With me, I mean,' she added, blushing.

'Oh, forget about what he's usually like. This place changes everything. You can't expect them to go out every night, kill a few bastards and then come home as if nothing's happened.'

Meaghan was silent for a few moments. 'D'you think . . . he might have killed someone?' she asked timidly.

Edie laughed. 'Of course he has. Didn't you hear about the fire-fight they got into on Sunday night? I think they got three of them. Went on for half the night, that's what Nick said. One of them hit that eighteen-year-old in the platoon. What's his name . . . Marty. The kid from Liverpool. You know the one . . . short black hair, blue eyes. Bit of a looker.' Meaghan shook her head. She hadn't noticed. 'Well, he took a bullet in the thigh. Your Tom went after the gunman. Got him, too. Clean shot, apparently. Then he told the priest who was giving him the last rites to fuck off. I nearly wet myself.'

Meaghan stared at her. It seemed so unlikely she couldn't quite believe her. '*Tom?* Are you sure it was Tom?'

'Course I'm sure. Just about kills Nick to admit it but he's a good company commander. The lads all really like him.'

'Oh.' Meaghan hadn't known what to say.

Now, looking up at his clean-shaven face, his familiar blue eyes twinkling down at her, she was suddenly overcome with a wave of tender longing and admiration for him. He was so far removed from her but the distance she felt in him, instead of scaring her, suddenly made him overwhelmingly attractive. She felt the strong pull of desire flood through her body. He felt it too. His hand tightened at the nape of her neck. He set his glass down beside hers and took her properly into his arms. They stayed like that for a few moments, delighting in the pure, simple sensation of holding one another. He was hard; she could feel it through the baggy fabric of his combat fatigues. She slid a hand down his front, touching him lightly as if in promise. He gave a light shudder, then moved away from her, breaking the embrace. He put up a hand to his face, which was warm and pink. 'If they weren't coming round in five minutes,' he said, his voice thick with need, 'it'd be a whole different story.'

She giggled, a wave of relief and pleasure and longing

breaking over her. Tom had always had that effect on her. As long as things between them were fine, she had the feeling she could take on the world. She understood why the 'lads', as Edie called them, liked him. He inspired confidence; it was that simple. He took what was best in him and made it yours. She picked up her glass again, her spirits lightened. The Christmas lunch would be fine. *They* would be fine, she and Tom. In the end, that was all that mattered.

'D'you think I should go over? See if she's all right?' Meaghan paused in the act of drying the plates Tom handed over, carefully rinsed. The lunch was finally over.

Tom shrugged. 'He said she was fine.'

'I don't know. It's . . . it's odd, though, don't you think? I mean, a headache's not the end of the world. She could have rung. I saw her this morning and she seemed fine to me.'

'Well, these things come on suddenly. Anyhow, it all went well. Food was great.'

It hadn't and it wasn't – the turkey had been completely over-cooked and the atmosphere at the table had been strained – but it was typical of Tom not to say so. She set down the dishtowel and turned to him. 'I'm going to go over. Just to see how she is. It's Christmas, after all. I'll take her a piece of cake.'

Tom looked at her and shook his head. 'I can see you're going to go, no matter what I say. Don't be too long, will you? We've got a bit of unfinished business to attend to, remember?'

She smiled up at him as she slipped off her apron. 'I won't. I'll just nip in for a few minutes. She's practically my only friend here . . . I just feel I should.'

Tom waved a soapy spoon at her as she pulled on her coat. 'Half an hour, no more.'

She blew him a kiss and opened the front door. It was cold and damp outside. She pulled her coat more closely around her and hurried down the street. Most of the houses were lit up with Christmas lights and small decorations – a bough of holly, a wreath, one or two Christmas trees glimpsed through the net curtains. The wives had made an effort where they could, she thought to herself as she crossed the street and took a short cut through the small park to Blairgowrie Crescent, where Edie and Nick lived. She pushed open the small gate and walked up the short path to the front door. The Beasdales' house was a little different from theirs: smaller, with only one bedroom, but there was a tiny front and back garden. The house was in darkness. She pressed the bell, wondering if they'd gone out. Perhaps Edie's headache had suddenly got better? There was no answer. She was just about to turn and walk away when the inside hall light switched on. She stopped and waited. All of a sudden, she felt rather foolish. Nick had only just left their house, after all . . . what explanation would she give, standing there on the doorstep with a piece of cake wrapped in foil?

But it wasn't Nick. The door opened a crack and Edie's face appeared. She felt the cold hand of shock travel up and down her spine. 'Edie?' she said, staring at her. 'Edie? Wh-what the hell happened to you?'

Edie closed her eyes briefly. She tried to speak but her lip was cut and swollen. 'It's . . . it's nothing,' she croaked, still holding onto the door.

'Edie. Let me in. What happened? Is . . . is Nick here?'

Edie shook her head. 'No, he's gone out. Go away,' she whispered. 'Please. I'm fine. I . . . I just tripped . . .'

Meaghan put out a hand and stopped her from closing the door. 'Bullshit. You're hurt . . . you're *bleeding*.' She looked at Edie's face in alarm. 'Let me in. You need to get that seen to.'

Edie hesitated for a moment, closing her eyes. Then she seemed to give in, and allowed the door to open wide. Meaghan stepped inside. The two women stared at each other. Meaghan felt her eyes go wide with shock. Edie's face was bruised and bleeding. Her lip was split almost down the middle and there was a nasty gash above her left eye. The eye was almost completely closed. 'Edie? Who . . . who did this?' She was almost too frightened to ask.

Edie shook her head again. 'It's nothing, I swear. I tripped. I fell down the stairs. I must've caught my head on the banister.'

Meaghan didn't reply. She took Edie by the arm and led her through into the kitchen. She switched on the light and pulled out a chair. She'd seen her mother in exactly the same state too many times to remember. There would be no fooling her. Expertly, she ripped off a length of kitchen towel, ran it under the hot water for a few minutes and began wiping the semi-dried blood from Edie's face. Neither spoke; Meaghan continued her gentle, soothing strokes, removing the worst crusts, asking no further questions. When it was done and she could see the extent of the damage, she put down the blood-soaked tissue and said, quite firmly, 'You need to get to a hospital. That looks as if it needs a stitch or two.'

'I . . . I can't,' Edie stammered. 'Nick . . . I don't know where he's gone. I don't know when he'll be back.'

'Then I'm taking you. Come on. I'll call a cab. It's too cold to walk over to the clinic.'

'Meg . . .' Edie began to cry silently.

'Shh. It's all right. You'll be fine. They'll pop a couple of stitches in there, clean you up and give you some painkillers. You'll be fine by tomorrow. Bit of bruising, but that's about it. Don't worry, Edie. It's fine.' She didn't add what she was thinking. *Until he hits you again. You might not be so lucky the next time.* She picked up the phone in the kitchen and rang the mini-cab service that operated on the base. 'Two minutes,' the driver promised. She hung up and rang Tom at home. 'Edie's had a small accident,' she said quickly. 'I'm taking her down to the clinic. No, I don't know where he is . . . I won't be too long. No, you don't need to come round. It's fine. It's nothing serious. I'll see you later.' She hung up before he could ask any further questions and helped Edie into her coat. Her arm was also badly bruised. As she lifted it gently into the coat sleeves she could see, quite clearly, the imprint of a man's fingers against the pale, bruised skin. A silly, giveaway detail. Even her father, drunk and stupid as he was, had had the sense not to do *that*.

A sharp toot of a car horn announced the arrival of the cab. 'Come on, love,' she coaxed Edie. 'Cab's here. No, don't leave a note . . . let's just go. You can explain later.' *If you need to*, she mouthed silently to herself as she helped Edie down the path. *I wouldn't. I'd leave now before it gets any worse.*

36

ABBY
Dhekelia, Cyprus, 1993

'*Dhekelia is located in the Eastern Sovereign Base (ESBA) on the south-east side of the island. The closest major town is Larnaca, which hosts the main commercial airport for Cyprus. Dhekelia Garrison is split into several sites . . .*' Abby put down her copy of the *Cyprus Factsheet* that someone in Housing had helpfully left for her. She could hear Clara crying upstairs; she'd only just put her down to sleep. She got up stiffly and made her way up the narrow staircase. It was probably the heat. Clara just wasn't used to it. The cot, a rather gaudily painted wooden affair, stood in the centre of the room. She leaned over it, forcing a smile to her face. 'What's the matter, my angel?' she cooed. 'What's wrong?' Clara's whimpers subsided as soon as she heard her mother's voice. She gave a little hiccup and clutched at Abby's hand. Her face was bright red. 'What is it?' Abby murmured soothingly, though she herself felt anything but soothed. It was her third night in their new home, a simple two-storey, semi-detached house slap bang in the middle of the base, rather incongruously named Mount Pleasant. The nearest mountains were a distant line on the horizon and the base was anything but pleasant. Ralph had been in Cyprus for almost six weeks but, by the looks of things, he'd hardly done anything in their new place other than snatch a few hours' sleep whenever he could. There were still cardboard boxes in every room and the kitchen looked practically untouched. The battalion was preparing for Ex

Grand Prix, a two-month training exercise which took place every year somewhere in the wilds of Kenya. In a few weeks' time she'd be on her own again. She was dreading it.

She stroked Clara's warm little hand until she felt her relax. Sure enough, within minutes she'd dropped off to sleep again. She stayed for a few more minutes, making sure Clara's breathing was nice and steady, and then she gently disengaged her hand and went back downstairs. The clock on the living room wall showed it was nearly seven. She wondered what time Ralph would be home. On her first day he'd come in at five p.m. The following day it was six thirty. Tonight . . . well, she hoped he'd be back before eight p.m., otherwise the carefully timed roast chicken would be a charred heap. Silly of her to cook a roast chicken, she thought to herself ruefully as she went into the tiny kitchen. She ought to know better. Another of her mother's famous instructions. Stews, soups, casseroles . . . things that wouldn't overcook.

She turned down the gas oven. There was a bottle of red wine left over from yesterday's supper sitting on the counter. She looked at it hesitantly, then poured herself a glass. She didn't like drinking alone but it had been a very long day and she needed something to soothe her nerves. She took the glass into the living room and sat down on the hard, faux-leather couch. Who had bought it? She wondered. She took a cautious sip, feeling somewhat uncomfortable. What if Ralph came back at that very moment and found her drinking alone in the half-darkness? She got up and switched on the lights. It was too bright, of course, but she felt a little better. She looked around the living room and began making a mental list of the things she would do to change it. Paint the walls, get in a new sofa and a nicer dining table. She had a generous enough income of her own, though the subject of money always made Ralph a little tetchy. She didn't care. She wasn't about to spend the next eighteen months in squalor, especially if she was going to spend them mostly on her own. Some new curtains, a rug for the dining room and another one for the living room. Something nice and warm – a Persian, perhaps. Her mind drifted on. She would be hard-pressed to find decent furniture in Dhekelia, but she could always go back to the UK for a week or so.

Her mother had said something about making sure she was there for her father's sixty-fifth, which was in about six weeks' time. In fact, she thought suddenly, it made perfect sense. Ralph would be away again by then. It would be the perfect time to take Clara back to London, do some shopping, spend some time with her parents and her sisters. She felt immediately cheered. She took another sip of wine and tried to get comfortable on the hopelessly uncomfortable sofa. She ought to go along to the local HIVE in the next few days and find out what sort of activities went on in the garrison. There would be committees and clubs she could join. Clara was still far too young for a playgroup but there would be a library and a café and a hairdresser's where she'd meet other officers' wives and their children. She knew from experience that the sooner she made an effort to join in and start to make a routine for herself, the better. She'd watched too many of her mother's friends make the mistake of sitting at home alone in foreign postings, waiting for their husbands to come home and give some sort of shape to their days. Her mother had always been active – the first to set up a book club, a swimming club, an amateur dramatic society. She smiled when she thought of some of the performances she and her sisters had been drafted into playing. No, there was lots to do. And then there was the beach, of course. She'd take Clara down there the following day. If nothing else, the weather in Cyprus promised to be lovely. If nothing else.

A sudden knock on the door interrupted her thoughts. She glanced at the clock again. It was seven fifteen. She opened the front door, wondering who it was. A young squaddie stood stiffly to attention in front of her. His face was pained, as if he were struggling to keep in some emotion that would otherwise slip out. She felt her own heart contract in fear. Ralph? Had something happened to Ralph?

'Evening, Mrs Barclay. Sorry to disturb you. I've just been

asked to come down and let you know Major Barclay'll be back late tonight. Pretty late, I should imagine.'

'What's the matter? Has something happened?' Abby put a hand to her throat.

'No. Yes.' He shifted uncomfortably from one foot to the other. 'Well, not to Major Barclay, ma'am. No, there's been an, er, incident.'

'An incident? What sort of incident?'

'I'm not at liberty to say, ma'am.' The young man's face was rigid, flushed with embarrassment.

Abby knew better than to pry. She read his name badge. *Pte Simmons.* 'All right. Thank you, Simmons. Thanks for letting me know.'

'Very good, ma'am.' He was so young and inexperienced and she saw he had no idea how to take his leave.

'Well, goodnight, then,' she said, starting to close the door. He saluted smartly, relieved, and turned on his heel. She listened to the sound of his footsteps fall away as he walked down the path, then the sound of an engine starting. She wandered back into the living room. An incident? What could that mean?

It was pitch dark in the bedroom when she heard Ralph finally come in. She lay in bed, not moving. She listened to him moving softly about the room, undressing quietly and putting away his clothes in the dark. When he finally slid into bed beside her, taking care not to pull the thin sheet away from her, she put out her hand as though she were still asleep, letting it fall where it landed, on his stomach. He too lay for a moment, breathing deeply, not speaking.

'Are you all right?' she whispered.

He made a small sound, followed by a deep sigh. 'It'll be in the papers tomorrow.' His voice was tinged with exhaustion.

'What will? What happened?'

He swallowed, as if trying to find the right words. 'Ayia Napa. At the resort. A woman. They found her early this morning.'

Abby sat upright. She held the sheet to her chest. 'A woman?

What woman?' She turned and switched on the small bedside lamp. The room was instantly flooded with light. She looked at Ralph. His eyes were closed; there was a faint twitch at the corner of his left temple. She knew it from moments of extreme agitation.

'Polish or Russian, they're not sure. She worked as a barmaid. The police arrested three of our boys this afternoon. They—' He stopped suddenly. He couldn't speak.

'What did they do to her?' Abby's heart turned over.

It took him a few minutes to continue. 'She's dead. They killed her. Raped and killed her. Battered her head in with a spade. She was nineteen, Abby. She'd been at the bar for three months. They'd been drinking at the same bar, apparently . . . they followed her and her boyfriend to a petrol station and abducted her.' He stopped. 'It happened last night. I saw the lads before they went into town. Purcell, Gardiner, Crowther. C Company. Dunn's boys. Only he's not here. He's on compassionate leave. His 2/i/c was supposed to be in charge but no one knows where the hell he disappeared to last night.'

Abby felt a wild, awful stab of relief. They weren't *his* squaddies. In the inquiry that would surely follow, Ralph wouldn't be named. She suppressed the thought, ashamed of herself for even daring to think it. 'Wh . . . where are they? Did the MP come for them?'

Ralph shook his head. 'No, it's a civvie affair, at least for now. They're in custody at the police station outside the base. It's a mess, Abby. It's a fucking mess.'

His eyes were still closed. Abby winced at the swear word. It wasn't like Ralph to swear. 'Darling, it's nothing to do with you,' she said quietly. 'They were Gregory Dunn's men, not yours.'

'Makes no difference. They could've been. God, it's going to be all over the papers tomorrow. She was nineteen. I saw a photograph of her. Beautiful girl. She was nineteen, Abby. Her boyfriend was beside himself. He ran away when they grabbed her. They threatened to kill him. He didn't think—' He stopped again.

Abby switched off the light. She couldn't bear to see the look on his face. 'Shh,' she said, in the same voice she used to soothe Clara. 'Shh. Don't think about anything right now. Go to sleep. You'll need the rest. You know what tomorrow's going to be like. Go to sleep, darling.'

There was no answer from him. They lay together in silence until Ralph finally turned to her, putting his hand around her waist and laying the length of his body along her back, as he'd always done. She felt him press his face into her hair, felt the tense shuddering of his breath as he held her, like a talisman or a shield against an unspecified fear.

In the morning there was no time to talk. A military jeep came for Ralph just before seven. Abby was upstairs feeding Clara when it roared up. He called out to her as he pulled on his beret and hurried out. 'I'll probably be back late tonight, darling. Don't wait up for me.' She stood at the top of the stairs with Clara in her arms and watched as he climbed into the front seat alongside the same young private who'd come round the night before. There was another soldier in the back seat. They exchanged a few words and then the jeep screeched off down the road. The sunlight through the blinds was dark and saffron, almost malarial. Already the heat was thundering. She thought again of the girl they'd found, of the way she'd died and her throat closed up with sudden, choking tears.

37

The courtroom in Larnaca was packed. Almost a fortnight after the body of the young girl had been found, the three soldiers who stood accused of murdering her were being brought in to face the charges. Abby slipped into the hall, unnoticed. She was breathing fast. She'd left Clara at home in the care of the girl they'd hired to look after her. It was the first time she'd left the house without her and she was nervous. She stood at the back and watched as the men were brought in, unsmiling and unshaven, to stand and hear the charges being read against them. The local policemen, in blue shirts and black trousers, stood between the soldiers and the crowd of men, women and even children who pressed against the wooden balustrade. She'd been in Cyprus less than a month and had got no further with her Greek than a 'hello' and 'thank you', but it wasn't hard to guess the meaning of the words being tossed about in the air. There were several military observers present in the bright courtroom; she recognised them by their expressions. One of them, dressed in slacks and a striped shirt, made notes as the names were read out. The policeman stumbled over the names. Private Alan Purcell. Private James Gardiner. Private Mark Crowther. Purcell grinned; Abby felt the awful pull of shame in the pit of her stomach. Three British soldiers. *Soldiers.* The thought of what they'd done was so far removed from her understanding of the word 'soldier' that she was having difficulty grasping hold of the situation. She'd told no one she was coming, not even Ralph. He would be appalled to know where she'd gone.

There was an answering murmur of disgust from the crowd as the charges were read out in Greek. Crowther and Gardiner studied their fingernails as the prosecutor repeated the accusations and the details of the young girl's abduction, assault and death. Abby listened to the words; alongside her, the crowd gasped. 'Seventeen blows to the head', 'her face was split in two', 'beaten with her hands tied behind her back.' One by one the witnesses were brought forward. The mechanic who'd towed away the soldiers' blood-splattered jeep; the bouncer from the bar whose voice broke as he described the girl whom they were still legally unable to name. Apparently her next-of-kin had yet to be contacted, but the barman couldn't help himself. *Magda.* The name slipped out. The last witness to be brought forward was a young man – almost a boy. Michaelis Angelenous. The dead girl's boyfriend. He too was unable to speak; he silently identified the three soldiers and was led from the courtroom, distraught beyond belief. Abby overheard someone say, in English, 'Poor fucker. Dunno how he'll live with himself after this.'

It took almost an hour before the parade of witnesses was over. As the last man was brought forward, Abby turned to leave before the stampede to get out of the courtroom began. She walked dazedly outside into the blinding sunlight. Across the road was the beach and beyond it the shimmering outline of the mountains. She stumbled as she crossed the road and made her way back to the bus stop. Above her, the silvery outline of an aeroplane cut across the sky, diminishing to a dot in the intense blue expanse. A British military jeep stopped at the lights in front of her. The men were close enough to speak to but she said nothing. No one from the base knew she was coming. She'd walked out of the main gates and waited for the bus alongside the Cypriot workers who came into the base each day. She'd sat at the back, squashed alongside two young women whom she recognised as cashiers at the NAAFI store but who either didn't recognise her, or chose not to.

She caught a glimpse of a uniformed soldier sitting in the back of the jeep, whom she hadn't seen in the courtroom. He turned his head briefly just before the lights changed and the vehicle moved off. A burly, broad-chested soldier in camouflage. His light blue, almost grey eyes moved over her without expression. Three stars on his epaulette gave away his rank: captain. The jeep gave a sudden lurch and they were gone. She wondered who he was. At the mess dinner the day after their arrival, she'd been introduced to all the other officers and their wives and she didn't recall seeing him. But before she could think about it any further, the bus arrived, belching smoke. She knew from the timetable that it would be another hour before the next one arrived. She hurriedly fished out her return ticket and climbed on board.

38

Ralph was right about one thing: it *was* a mess. An unholy mess. Within hours of the men's arraignment, the tabloid press had descended on the island. Hordes of them could be seen outside the base gates, pointing long lenses through the barbed wire. 'For Shame!' 'A Disgrace to the Nation.' 'Sex, Sand and Shame.'

Her mother rang from their country home in Wiltshire. 'Thank God they weren't Ralph's men,' she said briskly. 'That sort of thing can wreck a man's career.'

'Mother, what about the poor girl?' Abby said indignantly.

'Oh, yes, of course. The girl. Have they located her family yet?'

Abby shook Clara gently from side to side. 'No. No one's come forward from her family. It's unbelievable. The press got hold of her name, of course. Magda Evgeni. She's Ukrainian, apparently. She'd only been in Ayia Napa a few months. Can you imagine?'

'No, quite frankly, darling, I can't. Well, I'm just relieved Ralph's not mixed up in it any further than he has to be. That's the problem, these days, you know, darling. The army's just taking *anyone* in.'

Abby was silent. There were times when her mother's old-fashioned snobbery appalled her. She listened for a few minutes more then made her excuses and hung up. For the second or third time that day she felt herself close to tears. She couldn't say why the fact that no one had yet come forward to claim the girl had upset her so. She looked at Clara's little face and tried to imagine a world without her, or Ralph. She couldn't. She'd gone along for a second time to the preliminary hearing at the same courtroom – again leaving Clara in the care of their new helper – but she'd left after an hour or so. She couldn't stomach the details. The girl's boyfriend had described in a voice almost completely devoid of emotion how one of the soldiers had chased him around the back of the petrol station where they'd stopped, threatening him with his gun. He'd stumbled into the bushes, thinking that at worst they would assault or rape his girlfriend, but certainly not kill her. Abby felt the fear and horror rise in her throat again; she'd stood up and stumbled outside, unable to hear any more. She'd gone home, her mind unable to settle, to comprehend what she'd heard. And again, just as the last time, she'd said nothing to Ralph. It was enough to try and draw out of him each evening the details of how the murder had affected the battalion. She had an intuition, deep down, that her visits to the courthouse would only upset him further. So she said nothing. No one would know.

39

'They're going to bury her in the local cemetery,' Ralph said a week later, coming into the kitchen where she stood with Clara on her hip, ladling out soup into two bowls. 'Chief of MP decided they couldn't wait any longer.'

'What? Without a funeral?'

'No, there'll be a small service. We're not allowed to attend, of course. It'll be her boyfriend and his family . . . a few of the people she worked with, I suppose. It's been a month; no one's come forward.'

'But . . . what d'you mean you're not allowed to go?'

'Abby, it's a civilian affair.'

'No, it's not. She was murdered by our soldiers. *Our* soldiers. I know they haven't been convicted yet but that's just a technicality. Of course they did it.'

Ralph sighed. 'I don't make up the rules, Abby.'

'No, but you follow them. It's not right. We should be there.'

'Well, we won't be. And that's all there is to it.'

Abby bit down on the urge to respond. It wasn't Ralph's fault. He was only following protocol, as he should. But she didn't have to. She turned back to the soup, her mouth set in an obstinate line. If he wasn't going to go, she would. As far as she knew, there were no such restrictions on civilians. It was a fine point but *she* wasn't in the army. She was just married to it. There was a difference.

40

She held a bunch of white roses in her hand and walked awkwardly to the grave, bending down to place them carefully on the mound of freshly turned earth. There were only a handful of people in the cemetery. The Orthodox priest read out a few words in Greek that she didn't understand. The boyfriend whom she'd seen in the courtroom was there, supported by a woman who looked to be his mother, along with a few girls – blondes, mostly – whom she presumed were the dead girl's co-workers at the resort. No one spoke. There wasn't a single army representative present. If anyone wondered at her presence or wondered who she was, it didn't show. No one spoke to her. The funeral was over in thirty minutes. Local council officials lowered the coffin, a plain, unadorned wooden box, into the ground at the rear of the cemetery – the pauper's corner, she understood – and that was it. The boyfriend's mother held onto her son for support. As they walked out in front of the few mourners, Abby noticed that she was the only one crying. It was a strangely comforting thought. At least one person had shed tears for the girl. As she walked through the cemetery gates, holding onto her handbag with her sunglasses in place, she passed the figure of a man standing to one side, not quite in the small garden, but definitely, in a quiet, purposeful kind of way, part of the group of silent mourners. She looked up at him; recognition dawned slowly. It was the man she'd seen at the traffic lights on the day of the arraignment. She wondered who he was and why he was there. But she could hardly ask Ralph. It was the third time in almost as many weeks that she'd done something she would have to conceal.

She walked down the road to the beach head, weak sunlight glinting off the bonnets of cars as they passed. The sound of the sea blew over the sand: a muffled, heavy whisper, in and out, in and out. There were dark clouds hanging onto the horizon, heavy and angry-looking, thick with rain. It hadn't rained once since they'd been on the island but every day she heard the ladies at the mess hall or in the supermarket or the post office discussing it, as the British do, wherever in the world they are. The bus shelter was empty; she took a seat on the bench, still holding tightly onto her handbag. Behind her, the wind rose. The pine trees that followed the curve of the bay were bent this way and that as the late summer storm rolled in. The first few fat drops of rain began to fall, landing on the tin roof of the shelter with a surprised smack. She'd forgotten to bring an umbrella. Leaving the house that morning the sky had been perfectly blue and still, just another clear, sunny day of the sort she'd come to expect. There was a sudden, brief flash of lightning, and the sun disappeared. All along the beach the waves had turned dark, crested with white foam where they crashed into one another, rolling round and round. From air to water and back again . . . the whole sea heaved.

She looked back across the road and up the small hill to the cemetery where they'd just buried Magda Evgeni. The road leading up to it was deserted; not a single car or a passer-by. She wondered with a wave of sadness if anyone would ever visit the grave again. Then the bus suddenly rumbled into view. A huge gust of wind blew her skirt up behind her as she hurried to catch it; in her haste to pull it down and board at the same time, she lost her train of thought. As they pulled away and she turned to look back in the direction from which she'd come, she was marginally comforted by the thought that someone from the community that had so casually forgotten about Magda had come. Two people, as a matter of fact – her and the army officer she hadn't yet met. She wondered who he was and why he had chosen to come to the funeral. The bus trundled along the seafront until it turned into the lay-by just in front of the base.

She got down and hurriedly crossed the road, wind and rain whipping at her feet and face. Two squaddies were scrubbing the perimeter fence as she passed. *Yamisu re mal* . . . the words were wiped away. She didn't have to understand Greek to have some sense of what it meant. The anger in the graffiti was palpable. She shivered suddenly, despite the heat. Army life had become more complicated than she ever remembered it as a child. In all the places and bases they'd lived in, she'd couldn't recall a single incident in which the very nature of what the army did had ever been called into question. Honour, discipline, fair play . . . those were the qualities she'd always associated with the army and with her father in particular. Just thinking about him now brought a lump to her throat. He'd seemed to her to embody the very best of everything, including Britain. The moral compass by which he set his life seemed so clear . . . now, with Ralph unable to talk about his job and what he was being asked to do, the murder of that poor young girl by their very own soldiers and a war in Bosnia that no one seemed to understand or be able to explain, her unshakeable belief in the *rightness* of what they were doing suddenly felt misplaced. She forced herself to stop. She knew Ralph had doubts; there were nights when he lay beside her, unable to sleep. She could read it in the faint lines of worry on his forehead and the frown he wore when he thought she wasn't looking. But if he had doubts, she also knew that she couldn't afford to. That was part of the deal. As an officer's wife, *she* had to be strong – if not for herself, then for him. She simply couldn't afford to voice what she felt and neither could he.

PART FOUR

41

DANI
Freetown, Sierra Leone, 2000

'Dani? Dani!' Her grandmother's voice reached a shriek. 'Where you tink you goin', girl? Come back here! I talkin' to you! I ain't playin', girl! Just you come back here!'

Dani ignored her and ran down the stairs. The front door slammed satisfyingly shut behind her. She swept past the disapproving looks of the two women who sat outside on the street, day in, day out, gossiping and occasionally selling the odd packet of cigarettes or box of juice from the dripping cool-box which was their excuse for sitting out there in the first place. She didn't give a damn what they thought of her. She crossed Boyle Lane, took a short cut through the houses until she reached the gas station and then made her way down Wilkinson Road. At the corner she caught a taxi heading towards Aberdeen and the bars along Lumley Beach. It was a cool night; it had rained that afternoon, huge gusts of wind that swept the dust off everything, turning it into mud. Her room at home was leaking. She'd sat on the edge of her bed, watching the drops come through the peeling plasterboard ceiling and fall, one after the other, into a muddy, reddish puddle on the floor. She'd shoved her narrow bed out of the way. She didn't fancy getting wet. Or muddy, for that matter.

'Paddies Bar?' The driver didn't bother turning his head. One of the other passengers looked her slowly up and down, contempt written all over his face. Dani couldn't have cared less.

'Yeah.'

Ten minutes later he pulled up outside the bar and she got out. She shoved a handful of leone through the window and he sped off. She looked down at her feet. The sandals she'd found in the room that used to be her mother's were already splattered with the reddish laterite mud that was everywhere in the rainy season. She made a small 'tsk' of annoyance. It was Friday night; the bars would be full of soldiers and expats, a few Lebanese and the odd hapless tourist or two. Arriving with mud on her shoes would mark her out as a local, a *kolonko*, which she most certainly wasn't. She and her new friends Dixie and Lorraine weren't prostitutes. They'd never done it for money, not as far as she knew, anyway. As a matter of fact, Dani hadn't done 'it' at all. Not that she'd tell either of them *that* little fact. They already thought she was young and naïve. She'd met them both a few months earlier, hanging out at Taverna, one of the bars across the road from her school. Dani sometimes skipped classes and hung around the bar instead. Lorraine was a couple of years older than her and had long since left school. Tall and well built with skin the colour of shiny coal and long fake hair extensions, Lorraine was the sort of girl everyone looked at twice. Sometimes thrice. At seventeen, nothing scared her, and certainly not the soldiers who'd come with Operation Palliser, who made up the majority of the customers in the bars and clubs. Thanks to them, Freetown was slowly coming back to life. In addition to the UNAMSIL combat soldiers who came out of operations exhausted and looking for action, there were also several hundred other IMATT soldiers, the training team the British had sent out to work with the Sierra Leonean army. Lorraine and Dixie preferred the IMATT group, which meant Dani preferred them too. They lived in town, not in the jungle. They were a bit older, had manners – some of them, at least – and they knew how to order a drink and a meal for a girl and not immediately demand a blow-job in return. Lorraine had been going out with one of them, a stocky, middle-aged man named Eric who lived in a block of flats on Cockle Bay Road. Eric was kind enough. He always bought Dani and Dixie a drink and the odd meal or two. She was hoping he'd be there tonight. She hadn't eaten all day.

The place was crowded as usual. She walked up the gravel driveway to the front door, painted yellow and green in honour of St Patrick, or so they said. It was the only Irish bar in town. She pushed open the door and walked straight into a wall of sound. There were several TV screens hanging from the ceiling – football matches, mostly . . . motor car racing on one, snooker on another. The bar – a long, wooden affair that snaked around the corner – was packed with soldiers in and out of uniform, a few local businessmen she recognised and dozens of girls, the real *kolokos* whose sole aim was to relieve as many men as was humanly possible of most, if not all, of their cash. She ignored their hostile looks. At fifteen, Dani Tsemo was prettier than most of the girls in Freetown put together. They knew it, she knew it. From her mother she'd inherited her figure – long, lean legs, a flat stomach and full, wide-set breasts – the sort of figure that made other girls envious and turned men's heads, even the old ones. From her father – so the story went – she got her thick, wavy hair, dark brown, not black; yellow-green eyes and wide, generous mouth. She had a smattering of freckles across her nose – *kissed by the sun*, Eric had told her once, touching her lightly on the cheeks, which earned him an immediate, quick slap from Lorraine. Her skin was the colour of molasses – burned brown where the sun caught her, milk chocolate where it hadn't. She couldn't walk down the street without someone calling out *something* to her and, since she'd started hanging out with Dixie and Lorraine, not a single night went by without someone putting a drink in her hand or the offer of a meal. Three months had gone by since Lorraine had first persuaded her to come with her for the evening and in that time, not once had she paid for her own rum and Coke *and* she'd been given two watches, a bracelet, three pairs of earrings and, somewhat incongruously, a Walkman. Brand new. All for free. She hadn't even so much as kissed anyone.

'Dani!' She looked down the length of the bar. Dixie and Lorraine were already there, Lorraine practically sitting on Eric's lap. She waved at her. 'Here, girl. Over here!'

Dani threaded her way past the soldiers and the hookers, avoiding the stares of both. 'Hi,' she said, sliding a leg up onto the free stool beside Dixie. 'Hi, Eric.'

' 'Ello, love.' Eric smiled at her. 'Look lovely, you do.' He nodded approvingly at her pink-and-white-striped sun-dress with the thin straps. She'd found it in a pile of second-hand clothing in one of the market stalls. It had cost her almost all her savings.

'How come you never say nuttin' nice 'bout me?' Lorraine did her best impression of a pout.

Eric laughed and smacked her lightly on the bottom. 'That's 'cos I don't need to, love. You always look nice.'

The three girls giggled. The bartender, a surly man with dreadlocks that resembled nothing so much as a nest of snakes, slid two rum and Cokes in their direction. Eric peeled off a wad of notes and passed them across the bar. Dani eyed the bundle curiously. There was easily more money in Eric's pale, pudgy hand that evening than she'd seen all year. She wasn't envious, just curious. The inequalities that made up her daily existence were a source of fascination to her, not sorrow. Take Eric, for example, she often thought to herself. A nice enough man. Short, a bit bald and a little overweight. Not the best-looking man in town. Not much education, either, at least not as far as Dani could make out. His knowledge of Sierra Leone and Africa in general was shaky. He could only just point out Freetown on the map and he'd seemed nonplussed when Lorraine explained to him that the Nigerian and Ghanaian peacekeepers with whom he worked were actually from two separate countries. He was a staff sergeant, whatever that was. Not an officer, but not one of the young, trigger-happy and generally uncouth squaddies who came from the fighting areas with another, more urgent kind of need. Eric worked in 'logistics' at the IMATT base, a little further up the road. Lorraine, Dixie and

Dani had no idea what 'logistics' meant, but whatever it was, it was clear that Eric earned in a day what most people they knew earned in a month, maybe more. He was married; he proudly showed off the picture of his two sons which he kept in his wallet, now firmly stuck to the plastic sleeve with the heat. Lorraine didn't mind. Eric was here, in Freetown, and his wife was not. A simple enough equation and one that seemed to work for all concerned.

'Cheers, love.' Eric raised his own sweating glass of beer. They clinked glasses. Dani swivelled round on her bar stool to look at the rest of the room. Paddies had once been a house – a large, rambling, ramshackle house, much like the one she'd lived in on Boyle Lane all her life. Her house had belonged to her grandfather, a Mende trader who'd made his money doing business with the Lebanese and Europeans who'd filled the streets of Freetown back then. The money was long since gone . . . nothing of his earlier fortune remained except the house, which was now home to half a dozen relatives, most of whom Dani didn't speak to, and her grandmother who, in the absence of Dani's own mother, was her closest living relative. Something of the old man's pride remained, however, and Dani had been sent to a private school – the Methodist Girls' High School on College Road. Somehow – Dani had no idea how or why – her grandmother had kept enough to pay the fees and not much else. Since she'd started hanging out with Lorraine and Dixie, however, school had lost much of its attraction. What the hell was the point of studying when all around you there was nothing but death and destruction? No one she knew had a job, much less a job that required algebra or a working knowledge of the French Revolution. It was hard to keep your head buried in textbooks when there were kids with guns roaming the streets outside. Freetown was all hustle, nothing but. You hustled morning, noon and night just to keep the basics covered and a roof over your head. Not that sitting in a bar on Lumley Beach of a cool evening was exactly a basic need, she thought to herself, sipping her ice-cold rum and Coke. But in the absence of anything else for a teenager to do . . . well, it certainly beat sitting in a leaking room watching a pool of muddy water collect on the floor. There was no television to watch, no books to read, no films to see . . . the cinema had long since shut down and the only clothes available to someone with her means were in the market stalls on Andrew Street, second-hand clothes from Europe that had been stolen from Oxfam and strung up on wires.

A new group of soldiers had just come into the bar. She watched them walk in, eyes quickly darting around, establishing the tenor of the place before committing themselves to a seat. She smiled to herself. She'd learned quite a lot about people in the last three months, information that she could already tell would be far more useful to her than knowing when Stalin was born and the precise number of deaths he'd caused. She'd learned to tell whether a man was genuinely friendly, just looking for a bit of company in a town that was far, far from home or whether he'd buy you a drink and expect something more than a bit of conversation in return. She'd learned not to walk past the prostitutes in the bathrooms if she didn't want to hear something nasty said about her and, perhaps most importantly, she'd learned that offering without giving was also a form of power.

'That's the new boss,' Eric said suddenly, giving a nod to someone who'd come into the bar area.

Dani turned her head to look. He was standing a few feet away from them, still scanning the place. Her stomach gave a sudden lurch. She stared at him. He was tall, extremely well built, with dark brown hair cut short in the manner of most of the soldiers. He had a square, determined jaw, a tight line of a mouth, but it was his eyes that caught and held hers. They were light blue, almost grey – steely eyes that flickered over her and everyone else, giving nothing away. A strange tremor of something akin to recognition flowed over her. She knew nothing of her father – or the man her mother *claimed* was her father – other than a single faded photograph that she'd found one day in one of the upstairs bedrooms, years after her mother had disappeared. 'Who dat?' she'd asked her grandmother one day, showing it to her.

'Dat? Oh dat's your father, girl.'

'Where is he?'

Her grandmother just shrugged. 'Don' know. Can' say.' And that was about as much information as she could get out of her. Dani had carried the photograph back to her bedroom, tucking it carefully under her pillow. It was old and faded and creased but that didn't stop her taking it out every night and staring at the features to see where hers might have come from. There was a faint bracket-sign at the corner of his mouth, as if he'd just smiled or spoken before the camera clicked – it gave him a faintly mocking, sardonic air.

That same expression, together with the cold, grey-blue eyes, was in the face of the man standing a few yards away from her, ordering a beer. She couldn't stop staring at him. She was drawn to him in a way she couldn't explain. She slipped off the bar stool, ignoring Lorraine's questioning glance, and walked up to him.

'Got a light, mister?' She looked up at him flirtatiously.

'Nope. And you don't have a cigarette.' He looked down at her, his expression determinedly neutral. He held her gaze for a second, then turned away dismissively.

Dani blinked. She'd forgotten to take a cigarette along. She felt the blush of embarrassment travel slowly up her face. 'No, but don't you have one for me anyway?' she asked, lifting her chin just a fraction as his face came back to meet hers.

He looked her up and down. 'You're too bloody young to smoke.' His voice wasn't quite English to her ears – there was something rather flattened about the words. Was he American? But Americans didn't use the word 'bloody', that much she knew.

'I'm old enough,' she countered, still looking up at him.

He snorted. 'How old are you, then?'

'Eighteen.'

He snorted again, derisively. 'Fourteen's more like it. Go on, scram.' He lifted his bottle of beer to his mouth and turned his back. She was dismissed. Again. She could feel Lorraine and Dixie's eyes boring into the back of her skull. She collected herself as best she could and slunk back to her stool.

'What the hell you go talk to *him* for?' Lorraine hissed as soon as she'd seated herself again. Eric's attention was momentarily claimed by a young squaddie who'd come up to talk to him.

'Why not? I just thought . . . I just thought I'd seen him somewhere before, that's all.'

'You stay away from him, I warnin' you.' There was a strange, tight look in Lorraine's face.

'Why? Who is he?'

'He the new boss.' She jerked her head in Eric's direction. 'Can' remember what dey call 'im. Nick, Dick . . . something like that. He dangerous.'

'What are you talking about?' Dani felt a quick thrill of excitement run up and down her body. 'How d'you know, anyway?'

'I know. I hear tings. You think 'cos I didn't go to no fancy school like you I *stupid*?' Lorraine sucked her teeth impatiently. She tossed her braids back. 'I know shit 'bout him.'

'Like *what*?' Dani was getting impatient. She looked over to where he was standing with a couple of other soldiers. The resemblance to the man in her photograph was uncanny. She felt again a pull of some emotion she couldn't identify, other than the fact that it began in her belly and was slowly working its hot, teasing way up the rest of her body.

'He's crazy. That's what de girls say. He likes it, you know, *rough*,' Dixie hissed finally. Her fingers were curled around her almost empty glass. Her fake nails stood out blood-red against her blue-black skin.

'What d'you mean, rough?' Dani was puzzled.

Lorraine and Dixie exchanged glances. Then Lorraine laughed. 'Don' you worry 'bout that, Dani. Jus' stay away from him, that's all.'

Eric turned back to the three of them. 'Who're you talking

206

about?' he asked, signalling to the bartender for another round of drinks.

'Caught her tryin' to chat up your boss.' Lorraine laughed delightedly.

'Wouldn't do that, if I were you, love,' Eric said solemnly. 'He's a right odd one.'

'Is he English?' Dani asked, trying not to sound too curious.

Eric nodded. 'Yep. Nick Beasdale. But 'e's *Major* Beasdale to you an' me. Don't know much about him, to be honest. He doesn't live with us . . . he's got 'is own place up on Damba Road, 'bout a mile away from the rest of us.'

'Why's that?'

'Dunno.' Eric shrugged. 'He keeps to himself pretty much. He's all right. He's only just got 'ere, to be honest . . . dunno how long he'll last.'

Dani said nothing. She watched Major Beasdale pick up a second bottle of beer and move away from the bar. There was something about the tight, controlled set of his shoulders and his wary, watchful stance that made her want to come closer. He looked capable of anything, as if nothing could shake him, catch him off-guard, bring him down. His strength radiated, like electricity, from within. It seemed to her as if she'd never seen anyone stronger. She, on the other hand, often felt like a piece of jetsam, drifting this way and that, in free fall, occasionally snagging herself on something or someone – like Lorraine and Dixie, whom she'd just bumped into by chance. She'd be taken in, made part of something, made whole but then, when it suited them no longer, she'd be cast off, left to her own devices to find another snare or someone else to take her in. She didn't feel sorry for herself, or put upon. It was simply the way she'd lived her life until now. And it wasn't that she'd never experienced love. On the contrary, her grandmother's love threatened to stifle her. She couldn't and wouldn't let go. But it was a strange kind of love – a possessiveness that had everything to do with the disappearance of Sweetie, her mother, and the fear that Dani too would go. It seemed to have nothing to do with her. No one knew the *real* Danielle Christelle Tsemo. No one knew because no one really cared. But when she looked across the bar at the tense, wide shoulders of the man Eric called his boss, she suddenly felt calm and commanding, even adventurous. Here was someone who would *want* to know her, she was sure of it. Here he was. At long last.

42

NICK
Freetown, Sierra Leone, 2000

He'd noticed her hanging around the bars along Lumley Beach – who hadn't? Gorgeous, fucking gorgeous. Tall, lithe, skin the colour of smooth, clear molasses, thick wavy hair, none of that braided and fake shit that half the population of Sierra Leone seemed to glue to their heads. And those eyes. Lioness eyes . . . tawny, feline, the lashes naturally thick and curled, lips like honey . . . the line of the song came back to him, suddenly, catching him out. He shook his head, half in amusement, half in irritation. There'd been no one who even remotely looked like Dani in Gachege, where he grew up. Nothing but the fuck-ugly Masai girls with their blue-black skin and hair that looked like rat tails, or the short, fat Kikuyu maids who worked in the house. No, not a single Dani amongst them.

He looked at the mountain of paperwork in front of him, spread across the makeshift, already peeling Formica-topped desk. Piles of paperwork. It was never-fucking-ending. He'd come out to Sierra Leone to train soldiers, not write reports. But that was the British Army for you. He'd signed up almost ten years ago, receiving his commission from the Queen in the process. He'd been so bloody keen. Three years of a sodding useless degree and the slow realisation that Kenya was finished for people like him, and his parents. They'd finally sold up and moved to Bournemouth. Bournemouth? He'd spent a weekend in their cramped little bungalow and on his return to London the following day, he'd signed up. He wanted action, for his life to have more meaning and purpose than a retirement cottage in Bournemouth could ever provide. So he'd signed, much to his father's disgust. But he was long past caring what his father thought. He'd done his six months' training at Sandhurst and was immediately shipped out. He'd done two tours in Northern Ireland, followed by one in Bosnia and a few weeks in Cyprus, but the action he'd so hoped for hadn't quite materialised. Bosnia had been the hairiest – there'd been some moments there when bullets whistled over his head and he fancied he could smell the enemy not fifty yards away . . . but in almost ten years he hadn't once fired his rifle in combat or engaged the enemy in any way other than through writing fucking reports. And now here he was, back in the middle of tropical, malarial Africa, training a bunch of hooligans who hadn't a hope in hell of turning themselves into anything that even remotely resembled a modern army . . . and it looked as though he'd be here for another five months. Five months! It was enough to make you fucking weep.

He looked down at his desk. It was covered in ants. Small, red ants that were practically invisible on your skin until they bit. *Then* they were visible all right. The angry pink welts they left behind put you in no doubt as to who was in charge. There was an empty can of Coke to his left – the trail led straight to it. He picked it up and hurled it across the floor. Africa. Couldn't even leave a cigarette butt out for fear of some unspeakable, unknowable insect getting its teeth into it. It was home but of course it wasn't. Kenya wasn't Sierra Leone, thank God.

'Sah.'

He looked up, interrupted and irritated. One of said idiots was standing in the doorway, grinning at him. 'What is it?' he asked wearily.

'Sah.' The man hesitated. 'Sah . . . about the housing you promised us . . .' The man launched into a complicated story about a relative who'd moved into the temporary barracks and was now claiming the place as his own. Nick listened with half an ear. It was always the same story. They – the British – thought they'd come out to sharpen skills, impart knowledge, train soldiers up to be better, fitter, tighter, faster. The Sierra Leoneans, on the other hand, on whose behalf they'd come, seemed to view them as walking banks, dispensers of cash, credit and counsel, none of which had much to do with fighting and everything to do with getting ahead. There were days when Nick didn't blame them; he couldn't. Fuck, he'd never *seen* a place like Freetown before and Christ, he'd seen some shitty places. Garbage everywhere, filthy open streams in the middle of the road, craters where the tarmac should have been and buildings pock-marked with mortars and death. The fighting had officially stopped some six months before he got there but the minute he'd landed at Lunghi, he'd have been forgiven for thinking it was still going on. There were more guns roaming the streets than cars, and that was saying something given the number of taxis he'd seen. Guns, gangs, *kolokos* and garbage . . . *that* was Freetown. A shit hole, in other words. One he would never return to once his tour was over.

He got rid of the soldier who'd come whining about housing with the sort of vague promise that seemed to work wonders in these parts and turned back to his computer. He forced himself to concentrate. It was the heat; that was the problem. Heat and boredom. When he closed up the office at five every day there was nothing else to fucking do other than wander down to Paddies or across to Lumley Beach and then the chances of running into the most gorgeous fucking girl he'd ever seen were very high indeed. There was a sudden soft bang and the air-conditioner stopped. A power cut. He gave a short, mirthless laugh. A generator cut, not a *power* cut. They hadn't had mains power since he got here. The whole country was running on diesel fumes. No wonder it stank. He felt a revulsion crawling over his skin, like the ants. Africa. Try as he might, he couldn't get away.

43

DANI
Freetown, Sierra Leone, 2000

'So how old are you anyway?' He looked down at her with those cool light blue eyes that made her head swim and her mouth suddenly run dry.

'I told you. Old enough.' She traced the sweating, wet outline of her glass on the bar counter.

'Cut the crap, Dani. You're still a kid.'

She liked the way he said her name. *Deeh-ni*. Not *Daah-ni*, the way Eric and the other soldiers did. It made her feel special. 'I'm not. I'm sixteen,' she lied. 'Nearly seventeen.'

He pulled the corners of his mouth downwards and then took a swig of beer. 'Sweet sixteen and never been kissed.'

'Of course I've been kissed.' She pouted in mock-indignation, the way she'd seen Lorraine do.

'I'll bet.' His tone was sardonic. He turned his head away from her, looking down the length of the darkened beach. There were canoes out in the water; their lanterns bobbed up and down, marking the horizon. 'So what d'you do when you're not kissing, Dani?'

'I'm in sch . . . I work,' she said quickly.

'Ah. In school.' He ignored her obvious lie. 'What d'you want to be when you grow up?'

'I *am* grown up.' She paused. 'A lawyer.'

He didn't laugh the way most people did. 'A lawyer? You need brains for that.'

'I have brains. I'm pretty clever, you know.'

'I can tell.'

She liked the way he talked to her. His dry, off-hand comments were decoys, tiny signs that were designed to throw you off-track, away from what he really thought. She liked the way she had to work out what he meant, see beneath the surface of things. He was . . . engaging . . . that was the right word. She'd read it in some book the other day and liked it. He *engaged* her. 'Good,' she said, smiling prettily. 'That's good that you can tell. It means you like me.'

His eyes narrowed as he appraised her. 'Oh, I like you all right, Dani. But don't let it go to your head.'

'Wh . . . what d'you mean?' All of a sudden she was uncertain again. He was like that – one minute you were on sure ground, the next he'd pulled it out from under you.

'I'm not the sort you can fleece, not like some of these poor bastards around here.' He gave a jerk with his head. 'Idiots. The girls run fucking rings round them. They've spent their pay before they've earned it.'

Dani frowned. She'd been hanging out with Major Nick Beasdale for almost a week and in that time he'd bought her dinner once and three drinks, not that she'd asked for them. It hardly qualified as a fleecing. She drew herself up huffily. 'You don't have to buy me anything.'

'I know.'

She looked at him warily again, unsure as to how to respond. To cover her embarrassment, she picked up her drink. 'Lots of *kolokos* here tonight,' she said, looking round them at the others in the bar. 'You ever go with them, major?'

'Don't be stupid.'

'Why not? Some of them are pretty.'

'Pretty's not everything.'

'No? What about me? D'you think *I'm* pretty?'

'Yeah, Dani, you're very pretty. Too pretty for your own good, if you ask me.' He drained his beer and slid the empty bottle across the counter. 'Look, I've got to run. See you around.' He stood up, ready to leave. Dani looked up at him, suddenly upset and unsure of herself again.

'Where're you going?' she asked, sliding off her bar stool to join him.

'Home.'

'Can I come?'

'What the hell for?'

She struggled to keep up with his long strides. 'I don't know . . . I . . . I like being with you.' She was astonished at herself. She'd never heard herself speak that way. She'd never *felt* that way about anyone, before. She didn't want him to leave her alone.

He pushed open the door and then stopped, just before the road. He turned round. She was still there. His face in the darkness was a blur. 'Look, Dani . . . you're a nice kid and all but—'

'I'm not a *kid*,' she said, all but stamping her foot in childish anger. She stopped herself just in time. 'Can't I come with you?' she pleaded. 'Please? I won't be a nuisance, I promise.'

He sighed and looked away. When he brought his face back towards her, the expression in it had changed. 'All right. But just for a bit. I've got work to do.' He turned without waiting for her and crossed the road. She had to run just to keep up.

His flat was on the sixth floor of an old block overlooking the bay, up on Damba Road. There was no lift. She was panting by the time they reached the front door though he was scarcely out of breath. He pushed it open and walked in ahead of her, switching on the light. It was almost totally bare – a couch, two chairs and a couple of side tables. There were no pictures on the walls, no cushions, no rugs, no books or magazines . . . nothing, in other words, to indicate anyone actually lived there. 'Have a seat,' he said shortly and walked past her into the kitchen. She watched his back; there was the tell-tale bulk of a gun hidden underneath his T-shirt and the muscles rippled as he reached up to open a cupboard door. She felt something turn inside her, not in her stomach, but lower down, where the monthly dull ache of her period pains began, only this time the sensation was one of pleasure, not pain. He took two glasses and bent down to open one of the lower cupboards. He produced a bottle of whisky and, from the fridge, a small ice-tray. She watched him crack it open, fishing out the cubes and slipping them into the glasses. He poured a small measure in each and then brought them both over to where she sat.

'Here,' he said, setting one of the glasses down on the small side table to her left. He sat down opposite her in one of the upholstered chairs. 'Have a drink.'

She took it, feeling the shock of the ice-cold glass against her fingertips. She lifted it to her lips and took a cautious sip. The cold, sour liquid flooded her mouth, a combination of fire and ice. She looked up at him. There was a curious expression on his face, a combination of intense scrutiny, as if he were weighing up something, and a look of regret, of reluctance. It puzzled her, but she was suddenly afraid to show it. He already thought of her as a child, a kid – she didn't want to do anything that would confirm it for him. She smiled timidly at him as if in under-standing, but there must have been something about the smile – too bright, too quick – for he shook his head slowly. A sense of distress flowed over her. She took another gulp of the fiery liquid, feeling hopelessly out of her depth. Something was happening in that bare living room overlooking the sea that she could only dimly grasp, an understanding that came out of her own intuition, though she'd never experienced anything like it that would even hint at how she ought to respond or behave.

'Come here.'

She looked at him uncertainly. Then, very carefully, she set the tumbler of whisky and ice down on the worn carpet and got to her feet. She walked across to him and stood in front of him, her arms hanging limply by her sides. It was his turn to look up at her. His eyes were still cold but there was a warmth emanating from deep within him that spread its way up through his chest and neck and into his face. As she watched, the molecules of his face rearranged themselves slowly, another image coming into play. The face he presented to her just before his mouth came down on hers was one she knew she would remember for the rest of her life. Lust, anger, sorrow . . . it was all there, held in that still, single moment when his face blotted out the light. She held her mouth very slightly open; he took the whole of it into the warm, wet membrane of his own, his tongue pushing hard against her teeth, looking for something, seeking some strange reassurance. She was afraid but she didn't want him to stop. She clung to his shoulder, her nails digging into the skin as his tongue plundered her mouth and his hands began the business of removing what clothing she had. She could feel the heat in him, coming from some unknown centre between his thighs.

He dragged her down beside him onto the couch. Swiftly and deftly so that she couldn't remember quite how she'd got there, he manoeuvred her into the right position underneath him. She felt his hand slide up the length of her thighs, fingers going impatiently underneath the elastic of her underwear, pulling it aside. His fingers were suddenly inside her; she gave a gasp, then another, her knees pulling themselves upwards of their own protesting accord. He shoved them down again, hard. One hand cupped the heavy weight of her breast, stroking the dark nipple to its own blind, unseeing hardness. The other was busy at his trousers, unbuckling, unzipping. She gasped again as the full realisation of what was about to happen came at her but again, it was too late. She could no more have stopped him than she could have stopped herself.

She arched her body towards him; there was nothing she wanted more. That same mouth that she watched in fascination as he spoke was nuzzling the soft damp skin of her neck. The creak of the fan overhead came to her, its slow rhythm matching perfectly the rhythm of his thrusts. It hurt a little – a sharp, stabbing pain that was almost immediately obscured by the wonderfully heavy fullness with which he seemed to swell inside her. She caught a glimpse of his face, teeth bared in a dreadful concentrated grimace of pain. She shook her head in wonderment. He was gone from her, taken off by some unseeing force to some other place where she could neither reach him nor follow. His whole body seemed to be caught in some terrible concentration that drowned everything out, even her own breath. He thrust inside her again and again and again . . . his hands grasping at her flesh, pulling her, twisting, gathering her into handfuls and releasing her again, grabbing her hair, her neck, fingers raking her back, twisting and pulling. She cried out but he would not hear. His elbow had somehow jammed up against her throat. Now the pleasure was all gone; now she struggled to breathe. Terror blocked her throat. She tried to prise him off, to push his arm away but her strength was no match for his. She began to cough and choke; the room was spinning around her, her legs were pinned on either side of him . . . one, two, three . . . she was beginning to slide, to lose sense of place. A terrible blackness was falling on her, cutting her off. She closed her eyes and ears.

She felt rather than heard his voice. It vibrated harshly against her skull. 'Dani. Dani . . . wake up. Come on, get up.' She struggled to open her eyes. There was a searing pain in the lower part of her body and her throat felt as though it were on fire. 'Come on, open your eyes.' She felt something cold and soothing being pressed against her cheeks. 'That's it. Open them . . . come on.'

'I . . . it . . . hurts,' she whimpered, trying to work out where the pain was coming from.

'I know. Sorry . . . got a bit carried away there. That's it, up you come.' He half-pulled, half-tugged her into an upright sitting position.

'My throat—' She put up a hand to it.

'Here, press this against it; it'll dull the pain. I'll go get some more ice.' He handed her a sopping, ice-cold tea towel. 'Back in a sec.'

She did as he instructed. He was right. It did help. She looked around her, trying to remember what had happened, the sequence of events. Her half-finished tumbler of whisky was still on the table, the ice long since melted. The rumble of the air-conditioner drowned out the tinny screech coming from the radio behind her. Some well-known jingle . . . washing powder, or soap, she couldn't remember which.

'Here you go.' He crouched down beside her and put another

cold towel between her legs. 'Bit of blood, not much. You're fine.'

She looked down at her thighs in shame. It was all beginning to come back to her. The bar, the walk back to his flat, the drink . . . watching him fetch ice and glasses and the shock of desire . . . the way he'd kissed her and touched her. Her cheeks began to burn. What would her grandmother say? He finished wiping away the blood with a gentle, careful tenderness that made her eyes sting and water. She couldn't remember anyone touching her that way, ever. 'I . . .' She tried to speak again, to express something of what she was feeling. 'It was nice . . . the first bit, I mean.'

'Course it was. It'll get better, too. I dunno what happened . . . lost my head there for a moment. Sorry about that.' His tone was brisk but his touch was still thoughtful. 'Why don't you take a shower? That'll make you feel better. Here, come on . . . you can stand, can't you?'

She tried but her legs were still wobbly underneath her. He put an arm round her waist and helped her to stand. They hobbled together to the bathroom where he fussed with the taps and the showerhead whilst she took off what was left of her clothing. Curiously, she wasn't embarrassed standing naked in front of him like that. It was hard to explain, even to herself, how she felt. He'd hurt her but he hadn't meant to. It was her fault, he explained as he brought forth a bar of soap and hunted around for a clean towel. She was too fucking beautiful for words. He'd just lost his head. He hadn't realised . . . a virgin? He didn't think there were any left in this godforsaken country of hers. He was so used to the tarts and hookers who lined the streets . . . it just hadn't occurred to him that there'd be someone like her . . . young, fresh, *clean*. She was beautiful. So fucking beautiful. That was what he said.

She listened to him, entranced, as she soaped herself down, including the sore parts between her legs. He was leaning against the wall smoking as she washed. Smoking and talking. She'd never felt so grown-up and important in her entire life.

He wrapped her almost tenderly in the rough towel he'd fished out from one of the cupboards and helped her back into the living room. He brought her another drink whilst she dressed – it was sweet, not alcoholic. A fizzy drink of some sort. He watched as she fixed her hair, brushing it until the curls were out and then tying it behind her ears. He seemed on the verge of saying something but didn't. She drank the rest of her drink in silence, the pain in her throat slowly subsiding.

'You'd better get home,' he said, when she'd finished. She felt a wave of disappointment break over her. She wanted to stay, to be held by him, to feel his arms around her and his lips pressed into her hair, but he seemed in a hurry to see her go. She turned a confused face towards him. 'You need a good night's sleep. It's better if you go home. I don't trust myself not to start something up again.' He grinned suddenly and she felt her heart turn over in relief.

'Shall I come back tomorrow? After school, I mean?' she asked, hoping against hope that he'd say yes.

'Yeah, why not? I finish at the base around six. I'll take you out to eat.'

She looked at him. In that moment, she'd have done anything he asked. He wanted her. He wanted to see her again, to take her out to dinner . . . to make love to her. Properly, this time. In her mind's eye, she saw herself in the restaurant, her hair straightened and blow-dried, lipstick and eye-shadow carefully applied, lifting a glass of red wine to her lips. She didn't like the taste of it at all but it always looked so sophisticated. Nick would be in uniform, watching her closely, the way he did. Everyone in the restaurant would know. She was his. She belonged to him. She *belonged* to someone. At last.

44

SAM
London, England, 2000

'Your own flat?' Paula's voice rose on a surprised note. 'What d'you mean? You want to *buy* a flat?'

'Mmm. I've seen a place just off the Fulham Road. It's a studio . . . it's quite big, though. It's in this little artists' colony, just next to Stamford Bridge.'

'But won't it be awfully expensive? You'll wind up with a huge mortgage round your neck. You're only thirty, Sam. There's plenty of time.'

'No, there isn't. House prices are going up every bloody week. I reckon I'm just throwing money down the drain. If I'm going to pay this much in rent, I might as well own a place.'

Paula was still dubious but Sam was unmoved. She'd been in London nearly eight years and in that time had spent almost a quarter of the price of the flat she'd just seen on rent. She had just been made a junior partner in the firm where she'd been working for the past two years and she'd nearly finished her course in intellectual property law . . . *now* was the right time to scrape together every spare penny she could find and put down a deposit, despite everyone's misgivings. Plus, she was fed up sharing. She couldn't have said why but suddenly owning her own place had become the most important thing in the world. It was already painfully clear that the road to joint ownership that everyone else seemed to be taking wasn't on offer – at least not to her. There would be no boyfriend to share the highs and lows of house-hunting, no husband to come home to . . . that sort of future wouldn't be hers. If she was to make a home for herself in the world, it would be up to her to do it. And she would, no matter what it cost.

She hung up the phone after Paula had managed to extract a promise from her that she wouldn't actually sign on the dotted line before Paula had seen it. 'I don't trust you,' Paula said, mock-sternly. 'Let me see it first.' She'd agreed readily but only just managed to stop herself from wondering out loud why Paula felt herself qualified to judge. She still lived in a bedsit with four other girls somewhere in the less salubrious part of Kilburn . . . it took Sam an hour and a half to reach it from her offices in Covent Garden and most nights when she'd braved the journey, she had to take a mini-cab home because the buses weren't running. With five girls crammed into a four-bedroom house, there wasn't a spare inch, let alone a couch, to sleep on.

She hummed to herself under her breath as she quickly finished dressing for work. As she applied her mascara and a quick dash of lipstick, she thought for the umpteenth time how wonderful it would be *not* to have to share a bathroom with anyone else. She'd been sharing the large, airy flat in Bayswater with two other girls for over a year but there was only one bathroom. With three sets of make-up, half a dozen different bottles of hair products, lotions, creams, anti-ageing remedies and assorted bits and pieces, the bathroom was always full to overflowing. She thought back to the place she'd seen the other day. It was only of average size, but the setting was beautiful and more than made up for the lack of space. The small, hidden complex of studios had once been an iron-forge, or so the estate agent told her, incongruously plonked down in the middle of Fulham. An Italian painter had bought the property in the 1970s and turned it into an artist's colony with a small garden that led onto the street and a fountain that still bubbled away gently in the central courtyard. It was charming and the sort of place you'd never expect to find in London. There were six studios in the main building, each with a mezzanine floor, a tiny fitted kitchen and an open-plan living/dining area. She would have to fit a bathroom and shower herself, but there was just enough space at the end of the mezzanine to manage it. She'd fallen in love with it as soon as she walked through the door. The question was: could she afford it? Her answer was simple: she would have to.

A week later, she and Paula stood in the centre of the room. Sam couldn't stop grinning. 'Bloody hell, Sam . . . it's *gorgeous*! How on earth did you find it?' Paula looked up, open-mouthed, at the soaring cathedral roof and the skylights that had been cleverly fitted by the previous owner.

Sam shrugged, pleased that she wasn't the only one to see its potential. It was grubby; the last tenant, an artist, had used it as his painting studio and the floor and most of the walls were covered in spatters of oil paint and grime. It would need a thorough scrubbing, fresh paint, new floors and a much-improved kitchen, but it was charming, perfectly formed and, best of all, it would be *hers*. No one else's. She dangled the keys jauntily from her little finger. She would drop them off at the estate agent's on the way to her parents for Sunday lunch. So far, Paula was the only person who supported her decision to buy it. She was rather hoping that her parents would offer to help her with the deposit. She had just enough savings of her own to make it but a little extra certainly wouldn't go amiss. 'Come on, then,' she said to Paula, taking one last look around the place. 'Glad you approve. And thanks for coming with me.'

'I'm *so* envious,' Paula sighed as they locked the door behind them and made their way through the garden to the front gate. 'I wish *I* could afford something on my own. It's beautiful, Sam . . . just beautiful. Tell you what, I'll help with the painting!'

Sam tucked an arm through Paula's. It was absolutely typical of her. Not a shred of jealousy or resentment in her voice. She was genuinely pleased that Sam had found a place she liked and her offer of help was heartfelt. Sam knew from past experience that Paula would work longer and harder than anyone else to help a friend get things done. It was one of her best qualities. It almost made up for her scatterbrained approach to everything else, Sam thought to herself with a smile. 'You're an angel,' she said to her as they walked down Fulham Road together, arm in arm. 'And you can stay over whenever you like. I know how crazy your place can get.'

'Might not be there for much longer,' Paula said with a sigh. 'My sisters think I should move in with Mum.'

'I'm not even going to answer that,' Sam said primly. 'You already know what I think.'

'Yeah, I know. But there's no one else.'

'Oh, yes there is. But don't let me get started. OK, I've got to drop off the keys and then I'm going back up to Camden. Where're you headed?'

'I'm meeting someone . . . some guy I met at the gallery. We're having brunch down by the river. He's lovely.'

Sam snorted. It was only the third time in as many weeks that she'd met 'some guy' who was invariably 'lovely' or 'great', or even 'gorgeous' . . . until the second or third date, by which time she'd either declared him a total creep or he'd fled the scene. Not that she could claim to be anything of an expert in that area, she reminded herself hastily. She'd been out on a total of seven dates in seven years and none of them – not *one!* – had progressed beyond the initial encounter. She told herself over and again that it meant nothing and that it was most certainly not her fault. She'd been as charming and witty and fun as she knew how to be. Philip, as usual, wasn't much help. No, correct that – he wasn't *any* help. He simply shrugged when Sam complained and made the sort of comment he always made – 'Clearly not good enough for you, darling.' Or, even less helpfully, 'You probably scared him off.' How? Sam couldn't understand it. She'd done her best. She'd sat and tilted her head to one side as Paula suggested. She'd refrained from talking too much about herself, and certainly not about her job. She'd listened with as much interest as she could muster to them talk about their jobs, their careers, their challenges, their problems. One of the men who'd asked her out, a broker whom she'd met through a colleague at work, talked for nearly four hours straight about his recent divorce. It was only when she got home that evening and replayed the conversation in her head before dropping off to sleep that she realised he hadn't asked her a single question about herself . . . no, not one. He knew she was a lawyer. That, in itself, seemed to be as much as he needed to know. The focus of the evening was on him and him alone. In truth, she wasn't disappointed when he didn't ring as he'd promised but she still couldn't work it out. She couldn't possibly have been nicer, could she? 'It's not about being nice,' Philip said reluctantly when she pressed him.

'Well, what's it about, then?'

He shrugged. 'Dunno, really. I mean, you either click or you don't.'

'But why? What makes people click?'

He sighed. 'Um . . . God, I don't know. Men like to feel they're in control, I suppose. Yeah, control . . . that's it.'

'And how'm I supposed to make a man feel in control?' Sam asked, even more bewildered. Surely listening to him talk all night long with her head tilted uncomfortably to one side would do just that?

Philip scratched his head. 'I don't know,' he repeated. 'Some women are . . . just better at it, I suppose.'

Sam shook her head in a mixture of disgust and despair. She didn't get it; she never would. It was a mystery to her. After her week-long holiday in Greece and the humiliation she'd experienced at the hands of the handsome Italian tourist whose name she could scarcely bring herself to mention, she'd sworn never to put herself in a position where there was even the faintest, most remote possibility that she could be snubbed or ignored. Even now, eight years later, the memory still rankled.

She'd spent the night with him, to Paula's complete astonishment, discovering in him a whole world of sensual, erotic pleasures that she'd never even imagined existed. For three days they were inseparable. He seemed to delight in her Englishness, her foreign, reserved ways. He made gentle fun of her attempts to speak Italian, was impressed that she was a lawyer and liked foreign films. They talked almost non-stop. He told her about his childhood in a small town outside Milan, about his family and his disabled younger brother, whom he adored. He was in his last year of university studying economics and harboured ambitions to be a politician. He was a skilled, thoughtful lover, more affectionate and passionate than anyone she'd ever known, or could have imagined. Each morning, she awoke in his arms to the feel and touch of his lips all over her. She'd closed her eyes and surrendered entirely to the sheer pleasure of it all.

On their fourth morning together he woke up early, without kissing her awake, and went to take a shower. He showered for longer than usual and when he'd finished, he came back into the bedroom and told her it was time she left. He'd shooed her out of his room with a haste that bordered on indecency. Bewildered, she crept back along the empty corridor to her own room and to Paula's accusing stare. She'd hardly seen her for four bloody days! She hadn't come on holiday to sit on her own at every meal. Red-faced, Sam apologised profusely. They went down to breakfast together and that was when she saw her. Sitting next to Giancarlo, holding his hand. A pretty, dark-haired, dark-eyed girl who chatted away to him in Italian. She avoided Paula's incredulous stare and managed to swallow a cup of coffee and a single piece of toast. From snatches of the conversation that wafted over, she understood that the girl, whose name was Francesca, was his girlfriend. She'd been in Athens for the week, visiting friends. Giancarlo didn't even acknowledge Sam's presence. For the rest of the day she sat on the beach alone, too stunned to think. How could he have held her with such tenderness, listened to her stories with such amusement, sympathised and empathised and all of those other things he'd said and done that made her feel so special? It was a sham; it had been a sham from the very first moment and what made it especially hard to bear was that she'd failed to spot the signs. She who was normally so careful, so suspicious, so cautious . . . he'd completely and totally disarmed her, breaking past her barriers, and then he'd snubbed her. She was so humiliated that she couldn't think straight. She couldn't even bring herself to look at him. Fortunately she and Paula only had two more days at the hotel. She'd cried herself silently to sleep every night, avoided Paula's questioning glances and decided there and then never to allow it to happen again. Never, ever, *ever* again.

Well, it hadn't happened again and the way things were going, it wouldn't, either. Seven dates in seven years and not a single follow-up phone call. In that way she and Paula were more alike than they might care to admit. Paula gave everything; Sam gave nothing but the end result was the same.

'Have a good time.' Sam turned to Paula and hugged her. 'Phone me later and let me know how it goes.'

'I will. And thanks for letting me see the place. You're right, you've *got* to buy it. It's perfect for you.' Paula grinned at her as she turned up the collar of her coat. 'And I know you will. You'd have bought it even if I'd hated it.' She gave her a wave and then disappeared down the steps of the Underground. Sam walked on, pushed the keys through the estate agent's letterbox and continued on her way up the road towards Earls Court. She needed some time to work out how to phrase her request for help to her parents.

'A flat? On your own?' Her mother pulled a surprised face and looked at her father.

'What's wrong with that?'

'Nothing . . . it's just . . . well, don't you want to wait?'

'For what?'

'Until . . . well, you might find somebody . . .' her mother said cautiously.

'Find somebody? Why, is someone lost?' Sam asked sarcastically.

'Oh, don't be like that, dear. We're just concerned that it's a rather large undertaking on your own, that's all. I mean, Kate and Grant have bought a place but at least—'

'Can we leave Kate and Grant out of this? Just for once?' Sam

225

said, her temper already rising fast. 'I don't *care* what Kate-and-Grant have done. This is about me, not them.'

'All right, all right.' Her father puffed on his pipe, no doubt sensing an argument. 'If you're absolutely sure, darling . . . ?'

'I am,' Sam said firmly. 'I want a place of my own.'

'Well, can we at least see it?' Her mother's tone was sulky.

Sam's heart sank. Persuading Paula of the little studio's charms was one thing. Persuading her parents would be something else altogether. She'd redone her calculations; she was roughly four thousand pounds short of the deposit she needed. Would her parents step forward and help her out? She fervently hoped so. The house Kate-and-Grant had bought in Richmond was almost triple the price of her little flat and neither set of parents had baulked. Clearly Kate-and-Grant's trajectory was one they all understood and approved of. Unlike hers.

Christ, she reflected bitterly to herself on her way back home to Ladbroke Grove later that afternoon, no matter what everyone said, at the end of the day convention still won out. She couldn't recall ever having had a conversation with her mother about marriage or a boyfriend. She'd never had a 'proper' one; it had just seemed out of reach. Kate was the pretty, popular one who'd always had one boy or another in tow. Sam was fat and shy. Within a week of arriving at university, Kate and Grant had found each other. Sam went off to Bristol and found no one. True, she'd lost all that weight, her mother was forced to concede, and these days, aside from the rather severe clothes she wore to work, she looked every bit as attractive as anyone else, including her beautiful sister. But she still hadn't introduced them to a single boyfriend and her mother was almost afraid to bring the subject up.

It was always so much easier with Kate. *Everything* was easier where Kate was concerned. Grant was a wonderful man. They looked upon him as a son. Kate-and-Grant. Grant-and-Kate. They'd moved in together at the end of first year and married soon after graduating. Then they'd bought a house together.

They'd both qualified as doctors, although Grant had gone on to specialise in surgery. Kate was staying at home in the leafy suburb where they'd settled to look after their baby daughter and make everyone happy. Sam, on the other hand, had never so much as mentioned a man, much less brought one home. She worked all hours of the day and night, took holidays in strange places with her equally strange best friend – *all that red hair and those jangling bangles, darling!* – and was now buying the most odd little flat in the not-so-nice part of Fulham. Most odd. She could practically hear her mother's voice.

A week later, looking up into the dusty rafters with her mouth set in the tight, bewildered line that Sam knew only too well, her mother gave her verdict. 'Most odd, Sam, I must say. Most odd. But . . . if your heart's set on it . . . ?' She looked at her husband and shrugged. 'If it'll make you happy, darling. Maybe then . . . ?' She left the rest of the meaningful sentence unsaid.

Sam resisted the temptation to snap at her and concentrated instead on the feeling of warmth and relief that swept through her. Her father had already promised her some help with the deposit and the legal fees. The flat would be hers. She'd already begun planning what she would do to it, how she'd furnish and decorate it and make it truly hers. She couldn't have said how or why the realisation had come to her but she'd somehow grasped the importance of making a place for herself that was hers, no one else's. Whatever happened, from now on she would always have a place in the world that belonged to her in the fullest, most meaningful sense of the word. She followed her parents and the estate agent out the door, filled with relief and a sense of wonderment. It would take just about every penny she earned but she knew, deep down, it was worth it.

45

ABBY
Airport Camp, Ladyville, Belize, 2000

'Is this it, Mum?' Clara's face was pressed flat against the window pane as the car swept into the barracks. A uniformed guard saluted and then grinned as he recognised the driver.

Abby did her best to sound cheerful. 'Yes, darling, it is.' Sadie was fast asleep in her arms, utterly exhausted by their eighteen-hour journey from London to Belize. It hadn't changed much, she thought to herself as they drove alongside the dusty pitch where a group of soldiers were being put through their paces. She'd been ten years old when her father was stationed here, although she'd actually only come out twice during the school holidays. In fact, it hadn't changed at all. Smaller than she remembered, but that was only to be expected. From the perspective of a ten-year-old's eye, the swimming pool had seemed endless and the line of corrugated roofs stretched all the way to the horizon. Now, stepping out of the car into the balmy heat that her skin immediately remembered, the pool was half the size and she could clearly see where the jungle reasserted itself at the edge of the camp.

'Mum! Look! There's a swimming pool!'

'Mmm. We'll go down after lunch and have a swim, shall we? But let's get all our things together first.' She looked at the bungalow in front of them. Price Barracks, Airport Camp, Ladyville, Belize. Home for the foreseeable future. 'Oh, thank you, Mills.' She surrendered her shoulder bag gratefully to the young corporal who was waiting. 'Come on, darling . . . let's go.' With Sadie in one arm and holding tightly onto Clara with the other, she walked along the short path and up onto the veranda. It was immediately cooler. She pushed open the front door and stood in the darkened doorway.

'Mum, it's smelly.'

'I know, darling. It probably just needs a good clean.'

'Um, where would you like your things to go, Mrs Barclay?' Corporal Mills hovered uncertainly behind them.

'Let's put everything in the living room for now,' Abby said decisively. She would set about finding a maid and someone to help wash down the walls the following morning. Ralph wouldn't be back until the weekend. At that very moment, or so Mills had informed her, he was with his company deep in the jungle, some sixty or so miles to the west of the camp. She remembered what those training exercises meant – sleep deprivation, mental and physical exhaustion, irritability and short-temperedness when the men got back. At least for the first few days. Then they'd settle back into the more relaxed, on-base training regime . . . until it was time to don the camouflage paint and fatigues and head back out again. She sighed. Twelve more months of this, maybe even more. Could she cope? She had to.

The housing officer, a cheerful man named Peabody, helpfully supplied her with an LEC, a locally employed civilian, called Rosie, and two big, burly privates, Danny and Jethro, whom everyone called Tully, for reasons that escaped her. Sadie slept most of the way through the clean-up. Their new next-door neighbour, Harriet Maclean, who popped round almost as soon as the jeep pulled up, pronounced both Clara and Sadie the most trouble-free children she'd ever encountered. Harriet was a large, pleasant-looking woman in her early thirties with three small children under the age of five. There were more than a dozen officers' wives with young children, Abby was pleased to see – and at least four little girls Clara's age, which would make life so much easier. Harriet's kids, three tearaway boys whose names all began with 'J' – Jonathan, Julian and Jem – were struck dumb by the sight of Clara and Sadie. The elder two, Jonathan and Julian, spent long hours staring at blonde, angelic Sadie as she slept in her pram, her skin already turning golden brown in the sun. Harriet was from Norwich; her husband, Tim, was

Ralph's 2/i/c and she'd already done her homework on the new couple coming to live next door. 'Heard your dad was head of the SAS,' she said cheerfully over a cup of tea the following day. 'Expect this is all rather familiar. Wasn't he posted here once?' Abby nodded reluctantly. She certainly didn't go around advertising the fact; it always surprised her when others did.

'I was only ten,' she said quickly. 'Don't remember much, to be honest. Just the heat.'

Harriet shrugged. 'God, give me the heat any day. We were in Germany before this. Nearly froze to death. I do miss the seasons, though. You know, the colours changing and everything.'

'How long will you be here?'

'God knows. You know what the army's like. One minute they say six months, the next it's two years. Tim enjoys it. Suppose that's the main thing. I'd rather he were here than out in Kosovo, to be honest.'

Abby nodded absently. They were sitting on the veranda at Harriet's house, having tea. Abby was taking a break from supervising her three charges. They'd soaped and scrubbed the bungalow to within an inch of its life – walls, floors, ceilings, cupboards . . . everywhere. She'd commandeered several cans of white paint from the army store – in a week's time, the place would be spotless, and fresh. She'd had a note from the housing officer to say that their boxes of possessions had also arrived. She thought briefly of the lovely, colourful rugs and curtains and bedspreads she and her mother had bought just before they left England. By the time Ralph came out of the jungle, the place would be unrecognisable. She felt a sudden wave of longing to see him again. It had been nearly three weeks.

46

RALPH
17° 15′ 0″ N, 88° 46′ 0″ W, Belize, 2000

The thick curtain of trees suddenly ended; as they pushed and hacked their way through the last wall of green, the ground fell away before them and there was a sudden opening out of thick, long-stemmed grass and, in the distance, the glint of silver that marked an expanse of water, pushing the horizon even further away. Sweat was running off his face and body in streams. The soft, shape-shifting buzz of flying insects that had accompanied them everywhere for the past ten days abated abruptly, carried away by the breeze that the end of the forest had brought about.

'Fuckin' 'ell.' One of the lads behind him spoke, echoing the sentiments of most of the platoon.

Ralph grinned to himself. He took off his glasses and the shimmering, wavering world receded even further in front of him. They were on the edge of a ridge, high in the central plateau of the country. The names on the map he consulted from time to time were quaint – Crossing Landing Bank, Dry Creek Bank, Cotton Tree, Roaring Creek . . . there was even a little village named Meditation. But there'd been nothing quaint about the fortnight he'd just spent with his first platoon of twenty-four squaddies. In his new post as the CO of Panther Cub, the British Army's jungle-training programme, it was his job to take the men of his regiment out into the dense, almost impenetrable rainforest surrounding the capital. After his own, week-long induction, he'd spent ten days on base preparing for the expedition and then they were ready. They'd flown in one of the new Gazelle helicopters along the Macal River, glinting steel as it snaked through the dense, dark green carpet of trees. They'd landed at the Guacamalo Bridge after one of the most turbulent flights he'd ever taken. Several of the lads were already green around the gills by the time they had their faces streaked with camouflage paint.

Now, after nearly a week in the semi-darkness of the jungle, to be standing on a ridge overlooking a grassy steppe was to feel relief permeate their bodies as well as their minds, to take in the sense of space and light and freedom as a physical release. As they emerged out of the jungle one after the other, the men fell silent. In another month or so, they would be shipped out to the Balkans for an operational tour that would last four to six months, depending. Their ability to survive it depended on their ability to survive what he had just put them through, and would continue to for the next few weeks. They were a good bunch; morale was high and the way they looked out for and after one another was exemplary. He couldn't have asked for a better platoon on his first trip out. God knew they would need each other in the coming months. He knew from his own tour in Bosnia a couple of years earlier that it would be tough. Their rules of engagement for the theatre they were about to enter were murky. What worked on the streets of Belfast wouldn't necessarily work in Pristina, yet the army was a slow, ponderous machine and it took time for changes to work their way up the operational chain, and then back down again. He was proud of the company and knew from the way they addressed and listened to him that he'd already won their respect. He'd learned from his father that a strict hierarchy lends itself to a better command situation. He never addressed his men by their first names and they were only ever to address him as 'sir'. Respect was more valuable than popularity. He knew from experience that nothing could bring down the morale of a unit faster than a commanding officer who didn't declare where he stood. His men knew exactly where he stood and that in itself was half the battle won.

'Right, lads,' he turned around. Twenty-four blacked-up faces looked expectantly at him. He glanced at his watch. It was nearly five o'clock in the afternoon; in just under an hour, the sun would begin its rapid descent towards the horizon and the blanket of darkness would fall. He grinned. 'Tea time.'

47

MEAGHAN
Paderborn, Germany, 2000

The Christmas market in the town square was quite possibly the prettiest thing she'd ever seen. Meaghan walked along, her body encased in several layers of clothing – a woollen hat, gloves and Gore-Tex lined boots – stopping every now and then to admire the hand-made decorations, home-made cakes and biscuits and toys on display all around the square. The whole town had turned out for the afternoon. She recognised a few faces – the checkout girl at the supermarket and the woman who ran the pharmacy, which was just about the extent of the places she went to on a daily basis. They'd been in Paderborn for nearly three months. After the misery that had been Belfast and then Shrivenham and Aldershot, before their departure to Germany, it was a relief to be away from the dull grey skies and accents that she'd never quite managed to penetrate. Not that she understood a word of German. She'd yet to get beyond '*Guten Morgen*' and '*Danke schön*' but most Germans spoke outstanding English and always seemed keen to practise . . . why bother? Why bother indeed? Why bother with anything?

She turned away from a collection of beautifully carved and decorated little dolls, hunching her shoulders against both the cold and the sudden wave of despair that flooded her at the sight of all the children's toys and books and clothes. She took a deep breath and tried to steady herself. It had only been two months since the last miscarriage and the doctors had warned her that the lingering sadness would rise up from time to time, often when she least expected it. They'd been wrong, though. The sadness didn't flare up. On the contrary. It had never died down. It had all started in Belfast, about a year or so after they'd arrived. Edie was still around then. Despite everything, Edie had turned out to be the only person Meaghan could turn to. At first she'd thought nothing of it. They were both young, she and Tom; it would happen naturally, as a matter of course. All the women she met on Massereene were full of helpful advice. *Get pregnant. Quickly. If you don't, you'll go mad.* She didn't have a career to speak of, and her husband was more often away than not. It seemed the logical step to take. Having a family would give her a sense of purpose, it would bind her and Tom together but, most importantly, she sensed, it would bring some kind of order and meaning to her days. At first she wasn't keen on the idea. She felt as though she'd only just arrived at adult life – did she really want to give up her independence now, when she was only in her twenties? She'd barely seen anything of the world . . . she wanted to travel, to see different places, experience other ways of life. Edie had just looked at her blankly. 'Other ways of life? You'd better leave the army now if that's what you're looking for. Let me tell you, life on a base in Belize is the same as life on a base in Gibraltar. There's no difference. I promise you. It's all the fucking same.'

By then, Meaghan understood enough of what went on behind the closed front door of the Beasdale home to know that Edie was speaking from bitter experience. 'But a child?' she said hesitantly, trying to imagine herself pregnant, or, harder, as a mother.

'I agree with them,' Edie said, lighting a cigarette. 'You'll go potty if you don't.'

'So why haven't *you*?'

Edie was uncharacteristically quiet for a few minutes. 'I . . . I can't,' she said eventually, blowing cigarette smoke carefully across the kitchen table. 'I had . . . there's a bit of damage . . .' Her voice trailed off. She smoked for a few minutes, then said with a short, bitter laugh, 'The doctor said it'd be a fucking miracle. And there's been no miracle yet.'

Meaghan only just managed to hold herself back from asking, 'What sort of damage?' She'd picked Edie up one too many times after a so-called fall to be under any kind of illusion about the nature of her relationship with Nick. 'Well,' she said carefully, 'I'll . . . I'll have to think about it.'

She paused in front of a table selling the sweet, cinnamon-scented Christmas cakes that Tom liked. That conversation with Edie had taken place years ago, six months before the whole camp had woken up one morning to the news that Edie Beasdale had run off with Captain Dale Flanagan, who'd left his wife and a two-year-old baby behind. They'd apparently gone to South Africa. Dale Flanagan was immediately dismissed from his commission *in absentia* and aside from a Christmas card the first year after her disappearance, Meaghan had heard nothing further from Edie since then. Nick Beasdale received the usual acknowledgements of loss that follow a scandal of that sort, but he'd never been a popular officer and it seemed as though most people were relieved when he was transferred out of the battalion and sent somewhere on secondment to the UN. Massereene was a flutter with gossip for a month. People talked of little else. But such things happened, perhaps more often than everyone cared to admit – it took a while but the fuss eventually died down and Nick and Edie Beasdale, along with Dale Flanagan and his abandoned wife, Catriona, and the little two-year-old whose name she couldn't remember, were forgotten.

At first Tom was all for the idea of having a child. Meaghan came off the pill, just as her doctor directed. She was young and healthy – it shouldn't take long, the doctor promised. After six months of trying, made more difficult by the fact that Tom was away more often than not, she'd gone along to the medical centre, only mildly concerned. 'Give it a few more months,' the same doctor advised. Three more months passed, then another couple . . . and then she decided to go along herself to be tested. The results came back; there appeared to be nothing wrong with her. Would her husband come in as well? It took a further month for Tom to find the time and inclination but again, there appeared to be nothing wrong. 'The more you worry about it, the less it's likely to happen,' Dr Morland told her kindly.

'Relax. There doesn't seem to be anything wrong with either of you. It'll happen when you least expect it, that's been my experience. Don't underestimate what your husband's going through out there, either. It's hard on them, you know.'

It's hard on me, too, Meaghan wanted to yell, but of course she didn't. She knew the score. Good army wives didn't complain, especially not when their husbands were operational. Tom had promised her a holiday in Australia when his tour was over. Perhaps it would happen then?

In the event, neither happened. Tom went straight from Northern Ireland to Paderborn with a week's R & R in Portugal in between. His transfer coincided with a promotion – he was now a major and a company commander. If he did well in Germany, everyone seemed to think he'd be the battalion 2/i/c before too long. At the age of thirty-four it was almost unheard of. Young and an outsider to boot. No wonder he thought it a waste of time to fly to Australia for a month. He wanted to get stuck into his new role in Paderborn as quickly as possible. Meaghan bit back her disappointment – she hadn't been 'home' in nearly eight years – and did her best to smile. The week's holiday in the Algarve was nice. It was sunny and warm and there was little else to do but relax. Only Tom couldn't. He was edgy and irritable and snapped at her all the time. On their third day, it struck her that she and Tom had all but forgotten how to enjoy each other's company. It frightened her and made her more determined than ever to conceive. Without a child, she thought to herself miserably as they sat avoiding each other's eyes over dinner, what on earth was the point in staying together?

'What's the matter?' Tom had asked her, frowning. 'You look as though someone's died.'

'Nothing,' she said automatically. 'I'm fine.'

'Then cheer up, will you? It's like sitting next to a corpse.'

Meaghan looked at him, stung by the impatience in his voice. To her dismay, she felt the sudden, unmistakable surge of tears. She looked down at her plate but they'd already begun to slide down her face. They sat for a moment or two in silence, then

Tom reached out across the table and took her hand. 'Meg . . . I'm sorry. I shouldn't have snapped at you. I'm sorry.' The slide became an avalanche; Tom was mortified and angry with himself. He cancelled the rest of their dinner and took her upstairs to their hotel room, his hand stroking her hair the way he hadn't done in months. They talked for the rest of the night and by the time the short holiday was over, the damage to the marriage seemed repaired. It had given them both a fright, she realised, and whilst there was still a part of her that was angry with Tom for bottling everything up, she knew it would be down to her to draw those things out of him that caused him so much pain.

And then, of course, the miracle that they'd all been waiting for happened. She fell pregnant. Everyone was delighted, especially Tom. 'See?' the army doctor at the base in Shrivenham told her, reading her notes. 'Exactly as Dr Morland said. Congratulations, Mrs Astor. I'm very pleased for you.'

Six weeks later, she miscarried. A week after that they moved to Germany.

She walked round to the back of the block of flats, shook the snow off her boots and hung up her coat in the hallway before opening her own front door. There were four officers in the block – three single men and her and Tom. Soon there'd be only her. In just under a fortnight's time, Tom was being sent out to Kosovo as part of KFOR, the NATO-backed stabilising force they hoped would bring some sort of peace to the troubled region. She'd yet to understand the logic behind sending him there. 'Who *cares* about Kosovo?' she'd raged at him the evening he came home to tell her he'd be going.

'It's my job to go where I'm told, Meg,' he said as mildly as he could. 'I don't have a choice.'

She'd no choice but to swallow the tears and the frustration. Mindful of what had happened the last time they'd drifted apart, she set herself to understanding why he was being sent there in the first place, and to try and have some clue as to what he'd face. She bought or borrowed as many books as she could find and,

much to Tom's amusement, ploughed through them determinedly night after night whilst he watched TV or dozed in
front of it. It was sobering, complex stuff and after a week, she
had all but given up. 'But *why*?' was her favourite question,
usually directed at Tom but mostly left unanswered.

'I keep telling you, it's not my job to ask why.'

'But surely . . . I mean, I've just been reading all this stuff
about Kosovo and—'

'Meg, that's all it is, love. Just words and books and crap that
no one reads anyway. It's the shit on the ground that matters,
not words. People are dying every day; *that's* why we're going in.
Serbs out, peacekeepers in, refugees back. That's our job. Leave
the other stuff to the politicians.'

'But that's exactly the reason why everything's such a mess,'
Meaghan said earnestly. 'It's because the politicians have—'

'Meg, leave it alone, will you? You've got no idea what's going
on. I've got a job to do, I'm going out there to do it and that's all
there is to it.'

And that was the end of the discussion – if it could be called
such. He'd turned back to the TV and Meaghan was left alone
with a pile of books whose very language she struggled to read.

She walked into the living room. The same pile was still standing
next to the sideboard, almost knee-high. The titles on the spines
leapt out at her. *Death of Yugoslavia. The Tito Years: 1943–1972.
War in the Balkans.* She eyed them curiously, half nervously.
She'd never been much of a reader; in school, she'd enjoyed
English and art and the little bits of history that the Warra
School Board deemed necessary for the students of the territory,
but there'd been no one at home to encourage her in any way
other than to hurry up and finish high school . . . and then what?
Marry a local boy and set about reproducing the scenario of
family life from which she'd fled. But, she suddenly thought to
herself as she absent-mindedly picked up a cushion and plumped
it back into shape, what the hell had she done with her life that
could give her such a lofty position from which to criticise

everyone else, including and especially her mother? She stood for a long moment clutching the cushion to her stomach. What was her mother doing at that very minute? Was she dead or alive? Happy or still miserable, beaten down by everything and everyone around her? An image of her bending down to carefully tend the basil and rosemary herbs that she grew in the galvanised steel buckets at the back of the house came to her without warning. She pressed the cushion to her chest, trying to contain the sadness that rose in her like the tide.

48

SAM
London, England, New Year's Eve, 2001

Everyone raised their glasses and joined in the countdown. 'Six, five, four, three, two, one . . . Happy New Year!' There was a thundering crack and the whole of the London skyline lit up. They all looked up – through the dormer windows the night glowed green and gold and red. Sam looked back down the length of her new dining table. Five of her closest friends were gathered in her living room to celebrate the New Year. They were in her new flat, which she'd decorated with great care, toasting one another with glasses of champagne and enjoying the last remnants of the meal that her mother had cooked. Cooking, Sam declared happily, was not her forte. Philip agreed wholeheartedly. 'D'you remember the time you made us scrambled eggs for breakfast?' he grinned at her.

'Smashed eggs? Yeah, hard to forget. We tried to feed them to the cat, remember? Look, can we leave the subject of cooking alone for a minute? I can do lots of other things.'

'We know.' Philip laughed. 'But it's nice to be able to bring you back down to earth every once in a while.'

'Down to *earth*? What are you talking about? I'm not full of myself, am I?' she turned anxiously to Paula.

'Course you're not,' Paula said loyally. 'But you've got to admit, you do do most things rather well.'

'I'll say.' Martin, one of Sam's colleagues at her law firm, piped up. 'She's scarily efficient. I've never seen her go into anything unprepared. Makes the rest of us look like amateurs.'

'Such rubbish,' Sam scoffed, her cheeks turning pink. 'Now, who's for more champagne? There's loads.' She wanted to deflect the conversation away from her as rapidly as possible.

'We're only teasing.' Paula smiled at her. She handed Sam her empty glass. 'Here's hoping the next few years'll bring us all untold happiness and fabulous wealth.'

'I'll drink to that,' Sam echoed, topping everyone up.

'Yeah, well . . . you're already halfway there.' Martin smiled. 'Great flat, Sam. Congratulations.' Everyone raised their glasses. Sam turned an even deeper shade of pink and, just for a second, felt her eyes mist over. She looked at her friends again. Philip, Paula, Martin, Cassie – another lawyer at Holman Kenton – and Christopher, who'd been with her at Bristol and was now up in London. The six of them made a good, tightly knit group. The fact that they were all single helped. Paula and Martin were the ones who were always falling in and out of love; the other four were much like Sam . . . cautious, level-headed and, above all, practical. Philip had had his heart broken a few times, usually by the sort of girl who looked from the outset as if she'd break it. Paula had often wondered why Sam and Philip just didn't get on with it and go out with each other but Sam could no more think of Philip as a boyfriend than she could her own brother, not that she had one. 'But you know what I mean,' she'd said hastily.

'No, I don't. He's good-looking, kind, funny . . . *and* he's employed. More than I can say for half the blokes I go out with. What more d'you want?'

Sam shook her head firmly. 'No, he's a mate. That's it. I couldn't . . . I just couldn't.'

'Oh, well. Just thought I'd bring it to your attention, that's all.' Paula smiled ruefully.

Now, looking at the table, Sam felt a sudden surge of warmth for everyone. Kate was at home in Richmond with Grant, the perfect husband, and Louise, their nearly two-year-old daughter, with another one on the way. As adorable as Louise was, and as happy as Kate and Grant seemed to be, Sam knew already that the path Kate had chosen wasn't for her. She couldn't bear the smug possessiveness with which Kate and Grant treated each other or the way they both seemed to think her life was so much less meaningful for want of a husband or a child. She couldn't stand the way Kate no longer spoke of 'I' but always of 'we', even when talking about things Grant had no connection to – which was rare. Sam's ambitions lay in another direction altogether. Surely it was possible to do both?

49

DANI
Freetown, Sierra Leone, 2001

'Happy New Year, kiddo.' Nick lifted his sweating glass of beer to her.

Seated across the table from him in the crowded restaurant, Dani positively glowed. She raised her glass of champagne, copying him. 'Happy New Year,' she said shyly. She looked around her, eyes wide with excitement. She'd never been in La Chaumière before. Not only did it look forbiddingly expensive but the clientele who ate there were enough to put ordinary Sierra Leoneans off. It was frequented mostly by wealthy Lebanese businessmen, government ministers and their mistresses, and soldiers, but not the sort of soldiers who hung out at the bars on the beach. Officers, not 'squaddies', as Nick called them. 'Who's that?' she whispered, turning her head a fraction.

'Who?'

'Over there, in the corner. Sitting with that white woman.'

Nick's eyes flickered past her and back again. 'That's Colonel Brown. My boss.'

'Oh. Isn't he the one who said you shouldn't sleep with local girls?'

Nick's head came up from his plate. He looked at her with a strange expression on his face. 'Yeah. That's him. Although—' He seemed about to say something, then stopped himself. 'Whatever.' He bent back down to his food, feigning a lack of interest.

Dani smiled to herself. He was pleased she'd remembered something he told her, she could see that. He was funny; they were *all* funny, these soldiers. They pretended to be so tough, to assume that nothing could touch them; they'd seen and done everything. Nothing could surprise them. In fact, it was the smallest, littlest things that did. She and Lorraine often talked about it. Some of the men who came down to the beach only wanted one thing – a quick, mindless fuck and they didn't care how much it cost or who they got it from. They were the ones who, after a week or a month in the bush had all but forgotten how to make conversation, to have a laugh, give a compliment or receive one in return. Some of the girls preferred that sort. Less complicated, they said, and easier to manage. Dani and Lorraine watched them, night after night, each time with a different man, some of them so rough and crude that it shocked them to watch. Some of them were barely house-trained. They didn't know how to eat properly or hold a knife and fork; they drank beer as though it were water and burped and farted as if they were alone. Lorraine wondered what sort of homes could produce men like these. 'No, not a home. More like a pig-sty, if you axe me. An' dem say *we* de animals?' She often laughed scornfully.

But there were others, like Eric, who wanted a little extra. A bit of conversation, someone to laugh with, share a joke or two. They'd been keeping some other dream of a woman alive back there in the jungle and once they were out, it wasn't enough to take a girl behind the bar and have a quick poke in the sand – they wanted more. Not a *whole* lot more, mind you. Most of them had wives and girlfriends back wherever they came from, but still . . . both Lorraine and Dixie were happy to be taken to a restaurant every once in a while or to be asked to come over to where they lived when they were in the city and cook, or wash their clothes. Small, domestic things that reminded them of what waited for them back home. Or what they *hoped* was waiting for them. Dani had listened to a few of them talking and even she, young as she was, recognised the talk for what it was – a pipe dream. There was no one waiting, or if there was, the threat that she might up and disappear with someone else was as real to these men as if it had already happened.

That was what had happened to Nick, she knew from a conversation she'd overheard, though he'd sooner have cut out his tongue than admit it, especially to her. He was just about the loneliest man she'd ever met. He had few friends back in England, other than his parents. His phone – a large, complicated mobile that seemed to be permanently attached to his hip – seldom rang. Or if it did, it was Colonel Brown, or Eric. Someone wanting him to do something. No one ever rang to ask him how he was, or just to have a chat. She'd noticed that immediately. She didn't think she'd ever heard him utter the words 'Fine, thanks,' at least not whilst she was around.

It had been almost three months since she'd gone back to his flat with him and while he was very particular about the fact that it was his, he seemed to tolerate and even enjoy her presence in it in ways that surprised her. He wouldn't let her leave any of her clothes there but he did like the sight of her perfume in the bathroom, or a bottle of her shampoo on the ledge beside the shower. He'd bought her both. In his own, rather surly way, he was generous. He seemed to have enough cash – and wasn't shy about spending it, though she noticed he only spent it on her. He rarely bought anything for himself, other than food and drink. On the odd occasion they'd been to one of the beach bars and met up with Lorraine and Eric, or Dixie and whichever soldier she'd shacked up with for a few days, he would always carefully pay for his share – which included her – but never for the others. 'Got to keep a distance,' he would say to her whenever she brought it up, however obliquely. 'Eric's my subordinate. Can't let him forget that.' Privately Dani thought it came from some other source – the spoilt, rather selfish behaviour of an only child, maybe – but she never voiced her opinion.

Twice a month, around four o'clock on a Sunday afternoon when the stinging heat was beginning to seep out of the sky, he went into the spare bedroom and called his mother. She was his closest friend, he'd told her once. Dani didn't know what to say. She didn't know whether to feel sorry for him or envious. Lorraine and Dixie were her best friends. Could she even consider her grandmother a friend? She thought not. But her grandmother cared for her in a way that no one else did, or would. Despite her brusque tetchiness, she knew that the only person who cared whether she'd eaten a square meal once a day or followed her progress in school was her grandmother. But as far as giving her a hug or a pat on the shoulder was concerned, she'd have dropped down dead in surprise if her grandmother had ever lifted a hand to her in any other way than to punish her. No wonder she liked it so much when Nick touched her or stroked her hair. No one else did it or had ever done it, not as far as she could remember.

It was during one of those conversations one Sunday afternoon that she overheard him telling his mother that he'd had a letter from his ex-wife, the woman who'd left him for someone else. 'I can't believe she's got the nerve to write to me now,' she'd heard him say, his voice rising with indignation. She'd been reading a magazine, which she put down. 'After all this bloody time.' She held her breath. There was silence for a few minutes. Then, 'You've got to be joking. I'll never forgive her. Never. She can rot in hell for all I care. The fucking *bitch*. Sorry, Mum.' Then his voice had gone quiet and she'd been unable to catch the rest. He'd come back into the living room a few minutes later, his face still red with anger. 'Time for you to go home, Dani,' he'd said, catching sight of her. 'I've got work to do.' She knew better than to argue. He was like that; she'd never met anyone who could go from hot to cold quicker than he could. His moods were like rainy season storms, bewildering in their speed and intensity, seemingly coming out of nowhere and ending abruptly before she could even begin to work out the cause. There was no way of knowing beforehand which way a conversation or a gesture might turn.

'So who's he with?' Dani asked, her eyes straying to the back of the room where Colonel Brown was sitting with the woman whose floral dress drowned out everything else in its vicinity.

'His wife.'

Dani's eyebrows shot up. She'd seen him on more than one occasion with any number of girls on the beach. 'So why does he say *you* can't go with local girls when he does?'

'He can do what he likes. He's the boss.'

'He's a hypocrite,' Dani said tartly.

Nick gave a short, mirthless laugh. 'Yeah, well, like I said, he can do what he likes. He could molest kids for all I care.'

'Don't say that,' she said sharply.

'Why not?' He seemed surprised.

'Because it's . . . it's not nice,' she said after a minute.

He snorted. 'What's nice got to do with anything? We're not here to be nice, Dani. Even you can't be that naïve.'

'I . . . I'm not naïve. It's just . . . I don't like it when you talk about people like that. Of course it matters what sort of person he is. He's your boss.'

He put down his knife and fork and took a long draught of beer. He looked at her and she caught sight of it again – that strange, almost animal look of fear in his eyes that made her drop her own. Something was gnawing away at him, far from the surface of his pale, freckled skin. Not so much a secret as a secret wound, some sort of failure of spirit, or act, that he kept tightly to himself. She was afraid of it herself. She sometimes wondered if the fear in him might be catching and some deeply buried instinct told her to keep clear. But she didn't know how. How could she be with him and stay away at the same time? He was a man, in the fullest sense of the word . . . how could he have been through so much, seen so much and not know how to deal with it? As she got to know him better, mostly against his will, she began to see that the trouble inside him wasn't only a mental thing – it expressed itself through his big, capable body. Sometimes he woke from a dream shouting at her and the only thing that seemed to push the fear to one side was sex. Then he was rough, as he had been the first time, pushing and thrashing against her as if he might drive it off by driving it into *her*. In those moments she was truly terrified but she'd learned to hold on, to hold still and wait it out until he collapsed on top of her, lapsing immediately into unconsciousness and the weight on her body was the weight and feel of a dead man, one who had pushed and shoved himself through her right to the other side.

She reached across the table impulsively and laid her hand on his arm. It stayed there for a second, her chocolate-brown, sunburned skin against his lightly freckled forearm. There was a scar just below the elbow, which shone with a mother-of-pearl whiteness. She stared at it, suddenly choked with pity. His body was dotted with delicate, almost feminine blemishes that reminded her how vulnerable he was in spite of the heavy combat gear and the guns and the air of invincibility. Behind the mask was someone who was as helpless and soft as anyone else, though he would sooner have died than face the fact that she, little more than a silly schoolgirl, had seen through him.

He shook her hand off irritably, but not before she'd seen the momentary flicker of gratitude in his eyes. She sighed, and took another mouthful of champagne. The warm, fizzy buzz was beginning to go to her head. She looked around the restaurant again, suddenly filled with awe at herself, at what, in the short space of a few months, she had learned. She felt older than anyone she knew, including Nick. She felt as though she were the oldest, wisest person alive.

50

She walked up Garrison Street towards the market around Victoria Park, on her way to Lorraine's. It was the third week in a row that a lesson had been cancelled because a teacher had walked out and no replacement could be found. The Mother Superior reluctantly released the girls early. At the foot of the hill, just before the food market began, a whole cluster of traders had set up kiosks bursting at the seams with second-hand clothing. Some of the owners recognised her as she passed and threw out light, teasing compliments as an enticement. 'Come, come, sweetie . . . come look. Lookin' don' cost you nuttin'.' She stopped in front of a brightly painted wooden kiosk selling underwear and swimsuits. A yellow polka-dot bikini hung on an elaborate contraption of wires and broken coat-hangers. She eyed it enviously. 'See . . . it gon' fit you, baby,' the woman who owned the stall came forward eagerly. 'Yeah . . . it gon' fit you *right*.' She pulled it off the hanger and handed it to Dani. She turned it over in her hands. *D&G*. Dolce & Gabbana. She'd heard of the name. She saw it sometimes in the months-old magazines that occasionally found their way into the classrooms. Expensive, even second-hand – but the stall owner wouldn't have known that.

'How much?' Dani asked, her heart racing a little faster as she imagined herself in it, walking slowly down to the water's edge, Nick's eyes on her as she walked.

'For you, baby . . . gimme three dollars.'

'Two,' Dani said firmly.

There was a peal of laughter from the stall owners. They enjoyed a good bargain. 'Na, man . . . three. You gon' look so good in it, darling. You can pay three dollars, rich girl like you.'

Dani smiled to herself. If only they knew. Green eyes and tawny skin meant nothing. If anything, her circumstances were even more humble than theirs. At least they had the luxury of belonging. She did not. Her white father had unwittingly made sure of that. Wherever she went in the only country she'd ever known, she stood out. Her skin colour carried with it an assumption of wealth that couldn't have been further from the truth, though she'd long since learned it was pointless to protest. 'Two fifty,' she said, 'mi money done finish,' her pidgin every bit as good as theirs. The women laughed again.

'Two seven' five.'

'OK.' She fished a couple of crumpled notes out of her pocket and some coins and handed them over. The bikini was shoved into a black plastic bag which she stowed away in her school satchel. No good letting her grandmother see what she'd been up to on the way home from school.

Lorraine lived in an old, ramshackle house on West Street, further up the hill. Dani had never been able to ascertain exactly how many people lived there. Like most of her friends, there'd never been a male figure in Lorraine's life. The house was ruled by the formidable trinity of females – Lorraine's mother, Beauty, and her two aunts, Gloria and Prayer, the latter aptly named since she was a pastor in one of the local Pentecostal churches. Dani had never had much time for church, especially not the sort that seemed to be springing up on every street corner in Freetown since the end of the war. The Miracle Moment Church. The Church of the Living God. Action Church. Heavenly Justice Church. She was sixteen but she was no fool. She was six when the war broke out, too young to understand its causes but not so young that she didn't see the effects. She'd grown immune to the sight of amputees and child soldiers, to the prostitutes, drugged-out youths and broken, hopeless adults who'd poured into Freetown in the last decade. She couldn't tell the difference between the RUF and the APC, between the SLPP, the NPRC and the AFRC. In Sierra Leone over the past decade, there had been so many 'Revolutionary Councils', 'Supreme Military Leaders' and 'People's Parties' that she'd lost count. Who cared, anyway? Perhaps it really was just as Nick often said. Fighting and squabbling was in their blood; you only had to walk around the marketplace listening to the arguments to see *that*. When you tossed in the world's richest diamond mines, a weakened army and a practically non-existent government, well, it was no bloody wonder they'd had to call in the UN. And those strange, silent South African soldiers who never took their sunglasses off, even at night. 'That's 'cos their future's so fucking bright,' Eric was fond of saying, chuckling into his beer. It took him several attempts to explain the reference.

She reached Lorraine's front gate – not that there was much of a gate left. The house, like so many others in the street, had once been grand. If you looked hard enough, traces of the original lemon paint could be seen here and there. There was even a stained-glass window left more or less intact in one of the stairwells. But it had been decades since the house was painted or repaired. Now it stood, like all the others around it, in a street of rotten, decayed splendour, all the wood, windows, flowers and trees having either been hacked down or carted away for sale. Lorraine and her younger sister lived in a warren of rooms at the back, separated from the main house by a row of rooms that contained half a dozen cousins and half-siblings whose arrivals and departures were scarcely noticed. At times Dani envied them the close-knit camaraderie and the laughter that always seemed part and parcel of the house. There was never a dull moment. Everything was conducted with the maximum fanfare and drama. No one in Lorraine's house was ever sad, as far as Dani could tell. There were plenty of fights, but there was also plenty of laughter. The same couldn't be said for her home. No wonder she escaped here whenever she could.

'Lorraine dey?' she asked one of the aunts as she walked through the hallway to the kitchen.

'Dey for back. Why? No school today?' Aunt Gloria looked up from where she was washing a large pan of rice.

Dani shook her head. 'Teacher no come.'

Aunt Gloria made a sound of exasperation. 'You see now? All dem school fees your mamma done pay . . . waste of time.

249

Everytin' be waste of time. This place . . . ?' She shook her head sorrowfully. Dani didn't wait for the rest of the sermon. Lamentations amongst the older generation at the state of affairs in the country was a familiar – and beloved – topic. Privately Dani thought the lamentations were a waste of time. God, how Sierra Leoneans liked to talk! If they spent a fraction of the same energy on *doing* something other than talking, perhaps things wouldn't be quite as disorganised or corrupt or whatever it was they complained about.

She sloped past the kitchen as unobtrusively as she could. There were a few other girls there – helpers, servants or relatives . . . let *them* listen to her. She pushed open the door to Lorraine's room. Lorraine was lying sprawled on the mattress whilst her cousin, Barbie, braided her hair. 'Don't you know how to knock?' Lorraine asked, not looking up from her magazine.

'Why? What thing you go do for here?' Dani flopped down into the only chair in the room and lifted a magazine to fan her face. It was boiling hot and the only fan in the room was trained right on Lorraine's head. She pulled her satchel to her and drew out the black plastic bag. 'Look what I bought,' she said, tugging the yellow and white polka-dot bikini out.

Lorraine looked up and gave a low whistle. 'He buy it for you?' she asked, eyeing it enviously. Lorraine was a good two sizes bigger than Dani; there was no way she would be able to squeeze herself into it.

Dani shook her head crossly. 'No, I bought it myself. Don't have to ask him for everything, you know.'

Lorraine shrugged, unperturbed. 'You should. Him get *plenty* money.'

'I don't care. One day *I'm* going to have plenty of money of my own,' Dani said primly.

Lorraine snorted. 'Yeah. Him goin' *give* it to you.'

Dani shook her head. 'No, you're wrong. I'm going to be rich on my own. You'll see.'

'Sure. That's the day you goin' marry whatsisname? Prince William? Jes' don' forget invite me to the wedding.' Lorraine slapped Barbie's hand away from her ear. 'Be *careful*,' she snapped. 'How many times I for tell you? Don't do it so *tight*. You givin' me headache.'

'Sorry,' Barbie murmured mildly, rolling her eyes at Dani.

Dani smiled to herself. It was a typical Friday afternoon at Lorraine's. There was an ease and softness about the place that she'd been drawn to from the very first time she came there. In Lorraine's house there was none of the hard, angry air of resentment that seemed to permeate the walls of her own home. Disappointment hung in the air at her house. It was expressed in the walls and floors, in the way her grandmother insisted on polishing and repolishing those old, ugly bits of furniture that had somehow survived the passing of years and the selling off of whatever luxuries her grandfather's wealth had secured; in the way the servants were relegated to the back of the house and never allowed into the stuffy, over-baked rooms at the front that no one ever entered. At home there was none of the easy, noisy laughter that there was at Lorraine's. There was none of the fun.

'So what you doin' tonight?' Lorraine looked up from the bed. 'You wan' come with us? We're goin' to dat new bar down by White Man's Bay.'

Dani shook her head. 'I . . . I think I'll go over to Nick's,' she said, as nonchalantly as she could. It was no secret that Lorraine disliked Nick, though she remained surprisingly tight-lipped about the specific reasons why.

Lorraine rolled her eyes. 'You don' listen to me, girl, do you? I tell you stay away from dat man.'

Dani shrugged. 'What*ever*.' It was currently her favourite saying. It was also Nick's.

'Well, don' you come cryin' to *me* when he blackout dem pretty green eyes of yours,' Lorraine said derisively.

'I won't.' Dani too could be stubborn.

'Good.'

'Good.'

They glowered at each other for a second. Then Lorraine smiled her usual lovely, easy-going smile and yawned. 'OK. If you change your mind, we goin' be there at ten. Now, help me find somethin' to wear. An' help me get *into* it.'

Half an hour later, Dani left Lorraine's and wandered back down the road towards the beach. Her grandmother would be wondering where she was but she didn't care. It was her favourite time of day. The heat was out of it and the sinking sun was just beginning to throw its evening colours up to the sky. The market traders were busy locking up their kiosks and trunks; the air was full of the sound of goodbyes and exchanges, women commenting on the returns of the day; children, released from the confines of the school yard and sometimes their uniforms, darted in and out, picking up the leftover, unsold fruit that the market women handed out like sweets. The few Lebanese traders who'd stayed on through the war stood in the doorways of their concessions stores, idly scratching an arm, watching with feigned indifference as the street began to wind down for the day. She wandered past upturned crates that had once held Coca-Cola bottles and now supported towering pyramids of tomatoes, onions, garden-eggs, their waxy, pale yellow skins gleaming in the dying light. By the time she reached the bottom of the hill, the air was full of the scent of kerosene as a thousand small lanterns were lit and the night-time traders moved in. They began to set up steel pans of burning palm oil for frying plantain and small coal fires for grilling the tiny roadside kebabs that people from all over the city came to eat. She pushed her way through the gathering crowds, dodged a splash of dirty water as a car came too close to the gutter and then cut across the main road, looking for a taxi that would take her towards Damba Road where Nick lived.

She noticed the car as she walked up Aberdeen Road towards the block of flats. It was white, very shiny, with blacked-out windows. It was also empty. She wondered who was fool enough to leave such a car anywhere in Freetown, then she noticed the man standing with his back against the wall, smoking. His cigarette glowed orange in the near-dark. She walked quickly past him. There was something in his tense, watchful manner that made her avert her eyes. As she drew level she could see the outline of his gun. She crossed the street and hurried up Macaulay Road. He hadn't said a word to her or even glanced in her direction, but she felt threatened by him nonetheless.

She pushed open the chicken-wire gate at the front of the block of flats and walked up to the front door. There was no bell, of course. She climbed the stairs to the sixth floor, pausing outside his door to catch her breath. She was just about to tap on the door when she heard raised voices inside.

'Yes, but only if you can guarantee—'

Nick's voice, tetchy with the impatience she already knew well. 'Course I can. That's what I'm here for.'

'And the others?'

'Leave the others to me. Everyone'll get his due, don't you worry about that. There's plenty to go around.'

'What about the Nigerians? Won't they want a share?'

She heard Nick snort derisively. 'I'm not interested in what the Nigerians want. This is a closed deal. They're not party to it and that's the end of it.'

'If you're sure . . . ?' She could hear the hesitation in the man's voice.

'Of course I'm sure.'

There was the sound of glasses being chinked gently, and the lower, softer murmur of congratulations going around the room. She stood outside the door, her hand still resting lightly on the handle, wondering whether to go back down the stairs again and come back later, or whether to knock and pretend she hadn't heard a thing. She was still debating what to do when the door was suddenly flung open. Nick stood there, an unwelcome scowl on his face. 'What do you want?' he ground out, his voice low and menacing.

'I . . . I just . . .'

'Get lost. Go on, scram.'

'But . . .'

'I said, *get lost!*' He raised his voice. Behind him, she could hear someone coming into the hallway.

'Who is it?' She caught a glimpse of someone in a dark suit before Nick reached across the threshold and gave her a shove.

'No one. Just one of the fucking prostitutes from the street. Looking for a john.' The door was slammed shut in her stunned face.

She stood there, aware of a sharp stinging behind her eyes. *One of the fucking prostitutes?* Was that what he thought of her? She swallowed nervously. She'd better disappear before he opened the door a second time and said something even worse. She turned and ran all the way back down the stairs again. Her heart was racing and her breath came in short, angry bursts. A *prostitute?* She walked back down Damba Road, tears streaming down her face, but she didn't care. It was almost six thirty. Out at sea, in that stretch of inky, infinite blackness, she could just make out a line of fishing canoes disappearing beyond the horizon, identifiable only by the tiny kerosene lanterns that the fishermen brought on board. They twinkled and dipped like stars. She stopped for a moment, watching them enviously. She too longed to disappear, to get into a vessel that would take her somewhere far away from the dirt and heat and chaos of Freetown and the endless buffeting around from school to home and back again without any clear sense of why. What was it all for? She could no more hope to get a job or have a *career* – that elusive, promise-filled word that the nuns and teachers dropped from their lips every other minute without once stopping to ask themselves how it might be achieved – than she could imagine herself on one of those canoes, heading for the horizon.

She'd never really stopped to think about it properly before but it suddenly seemed crystal clear. Whenever she thought about her future – the one that existed beyond the run-down house and skipping boring classes and running down to the beach with Lorraine and Dixie – that future took place elsewhere. England. London. New York. Paris. Anywhere but here. She dreamed of becoming a lawyer, like the women in the

American TV series someone had shown her, long ago . . . *LA Law*. That was it. She loved the way they talked, those women . . . all so sure of themselves, words coming out of their mouths like bullets, sharp and sure. Their clothes, too . . . beautiful suits and blouses and high heels and jewellery that sparkled and shone. They were so pretty and smart and smiling. They didn't have to hang around bars listening to stupid, uneducated men like Eric pretending they knew all about the world and the way everything worked in order to get a decent meal or buy a shirt that hadn't belonged to ten other people before.

That was what she liked about Nick. When he wasn't moody or irritable and withdrawn, he *talked* to her. Properly. About places he'd been, things he'd seen, *interesting* things, little bits and pieces about himself. She was entranced. She'd never been anywhere, not even to Bo, the second-largest city in Sierra Leone. He talked to her of the farm he'd grown up on in Kenya, just outside Nairobi. She didn't even know there were white people in Kenya, never mind white people who lived on a remote farm, miles from anywhere, struggling to grow tea or whatever it was they'd farmed. He said little about his parents. 'Didn't work out,' was all he would say. 'We left.' She ran the words over on her tongue, tasting them. Nairobi. London. Belfast. He'd told her things about her own country that she heard for the first time. Like the real reason they'd been at war almost as long as she could remember, or what her father might be doing at that very moment back in England. 'Probably driving a Ford Escort and living in a two-up, two-down, struggling to make ends meet, like most people,' he said off-handedly. 'Most of the guys who come out here have never had it so good. Look at you. D'you think I'd ever get anyone like you back in Belfast? Or Eric someone like Lorraine? Not a chance.' Dani thrilled to hear him say it. 'Get someone like you?' So did that mean he 'had' her? Her father had had 'the time of his fucking life' in Sierra Leone, or so Nick said. That too helped. Whatever he'd left behind or forgotten about and abandoned, he'd had a good time.

By the time she reached Aberdeen Street, she was calmer and the tears on her cheeks had dried. He hadn't meant it. Not really. She'd surprised him, that was all. She should have rung first, not that the telephones ever worked, but she shouldn't have just turned up like that. He was in a meeting and she'd surprised him. As a matter of fact, his boss was probably in the room . . . the one who'd said they weren't allowed to sleep with local girls. He didn't understand that Dani wasn't like most of the local girls. He wouldn't understand. She was Nick's girlfriend, wasn't she? Wasn't that what he'd said? Why else would he have said it – *d'you think I'd ever get anyone like you back in Belfast?* She was here, in Freetown. She was his girlfriend. That was all that mattered.

51

MEAGHAN
Paderborn, Germany, 2001

Meaghan looked at the growing pile of stuff in the centre of the living room and tried not to burst into tears. Tom was leaving. In less than twenty-four hours' time he'd be gone. She would be alone in Paderborn, a town even smaller than Warra, with no one to talk to, no one to turn to and no one to help her get through the long four months that lay ahead. He'd been on tour before, but never quite so far away and never in a place whose very name she struggled to pronounce. Racak, Rambouillet, Rugova . . . she tried to keep up with events and names, if only to give herself some kind of picture of what he might be going into, but she usually wound up lost in a sea of dates and unpronounceable names and Tom himself wasn't much help. Although it pained her to see it, he was excited at the prospect of seeing action. Kosovo, he seemed to be saying, was a 'proper' war. He'd very quickly grown disillusioned with Northern Ireland. Although they'd been fired upon constantly, the rules of engagement, he complained endlessly to Meaghan, meant that they couldn't simply go in and clear out the rot. He was tired of being chanted at by schoolchildren, spat at by housewives and shot at by terrorists who were little more than kids. He wasn't British; the animosity felt by some of his soldiers towards the Irish was something he couldn't fully comprehend. Kosovo was different. He would be part of a UN-backed peacekeeping force charged with establishing order, saving lives. This would be an honourable war, not a dirty one. He couldn't wait to go.

Meaghan helped him pack his kit in near-silence. He would be gone for sixteen long, lonely weeks. Four months. She watched the neat pile of khaki socks and combat trousers on the living room floor grow. By the following week there would only be her plates in the sink and breakfast every morning would be made for one. How did the other wives cope? Hounslow and Northern Ireland had been different; Edie was there, and the other wives she'd been friendly with, Sue and Carmen. Here in Paderborn there was no one.

She carried the last of the breakfast dishes through to the tiny kitchen and turned on the taps. She stood by the sink, washing the plates, her mind racing to the months ahead. How would she fill the time? She ought to take up a course, or something . . . maybe even find a job. Tom hadn't wanted her to work whilst they were in Northern Ireland. There'd been no hairdressers or beauty salon on the base and after there'd been that attack on a florist's just outside, in which two soldiers' wives had been killed, he'd deemed it safer for her to stay in the barracks. But Germany was different, she thought to herself, still rinsing suds off the plates. She couldn't speak a word of German, mind you, and Paderborn was definitely too small to have a salon on the base, but perhaps there'd be something in Peine, which was only a few kilometres away. She could get a bike and cycle in to work. Anything to get her out of the house and keep her mind off what he might be going through. The news coming out of that corner of the world was hardly encouraging. She knew little of the politics behind the Kosovo conflict but what little she managed to glean didn't look good. Each night brought a new round of uncovered atrocities and reports of ethnic cleansing, violence, killing. What did it have to do with *them*, she felt like asking, but managed – only just – to keep her mouth shut. It was his job to go where he was sent, not question the wisdom of sending him there in the first place. She knew the lines off by heart.

She dried her hands and took off her apron, then walked into the living room. His kit bag was standing against the door. One of his many camouflage jackets was hanging on the handle. She picked it up and began to fold it, then suddenly brought the stiff material up to her face. She buried her nose in it, breathing in the mixture of soap, sweat and aftershave that was so dear to her. She tried to imagine what it would be like to be one of those women whom she saw on TV from time to time whose husbands and boyfriends would never return. She tried to imagine what it would be like to open the door and see the military police whose job it was to dispense such news . . . she couldn't. She breathed in Tom's scent over and over again as if the very smell of him might ward off such an image or prevent it from ever taking place.

She said nothing to Tom about her plans to find a job whilst he was gone. His mind was elsewhere, in any case. They were due to fly from Hanover at 0700 hours the following morning and, as always, there were a thousand and one details that required his attention. She cooked one of his favourite dishes for supper that night: chicken in white wine and tarragon sauce and even managed to make him laugh as she recounted her difficulties asking the vegetable lady in the market for fresh tarragon.

Later that evening, when the dishes were cleared away and Tom was on the phone to the CO, she took a shower and trickled perfume between her breasts. Whether or not they actually made love that night would depend on him, not her, but she couldn't have forgiven herself for not trying. Sometimes, in Belfast, on nights before leaving on patrol, he would make love to her two or three times as if trying to bury fear of what might happen deep inside her, between them. This was different. In Belfast, she'd said goodbye knowing he'd be back in a week or, at worst, a fortnight. Now, he'd be gone for four months . . . maybe even for ever. She shoved the thought fiercely aside and turned to him as he finally climbed into bed beside her. His hand lay slackly on her hip for a while, his thumb absently stroking the gentle swell of soft flesh. Neither spoke.

'You'll be OK, won't you?' she whispered after a while.

It took him a few seconds to respond. 'Course I will. I'll be back before you know it, Meg. You'll see.'

She turned to him, her lips desperately seeking his. She hoped against hope he was right.

52

The salon owner, a brisk, capable-looking woman in her mid-fifties quickly looked Meaghan up and down. 'And you've worked with acrylics and gels?'

Meaghan nodded confidently. 'Yes.'

'But you don't speak any German?'

Meaghan shook her head. 'No, not yet. Unfortunately,' she added quickly.

The woman pulled the corners of her mouth downwards. 'Well, it's not always so necessary. Most of you English don't. And most of my clients are English. So—'

'I'm hoping to learn, though,' Meaghan said, smiling timidly. 'There are classes on the base.'

'And your husband's an officer, you said?' The woman looked at Meaghan curiously.

'Yes. He's one of the company commanders. They're, um, away at the moment.' She had no idea how much information she was supposed or allowed to give away.

'OK, Meaghan. It's a nice name, by the way. That's a very English name, no?'

'Um, actually, I'm Australian.'

'Ah. Well, Meaghan . . . *ja*, why don't we try it out for a couple of weeks? I'm Hedwig. I'm the owner. Let's see how it goes.'

'Oh, *thank* you,' Meaghan said with some relief. 'I wasn't sure how easy it would be . . . if my qualifications and everything would be OK.'

'Let's just see how you get on. We can just do it between us, if you know what I mean. Someone with your qualifications . . . *ja*, that sounds about right.' She quickly pencilled in a figure on the notepad she was holding and passed it across the desk. Meaghan took a look but she couldn't have cared less. Fifteen DM an hour sounded fine to her. Hedwig was quite happy to 'bypass all the paperwork', as she put it, and just pay her cash under the table at the end of every week. Meaghan shrugged happily; fine by her.

By the time she left the little salon half an hour later, she'd decided she liked Hedwig very much indeed. She was divorced, with two grown-up sons. She was stylish and trim. Short, bright red hair, piercing blue eyes that were half-hidden by her blue, mannish glasses that hung with a multi-coloured chain like a necklace around her neck, and a trim, lean figure in black leather jeans, a crisp white shirt and a dark green jacket with purple and red piping. Her nails were purple, presumably to match the jacket, and her skin was lightly tanned. There was a sun-bed in the back of the salon; one of the perks was a fifty per cent discount on its use. Meaghan had never used a sun-bed in her life but looking at Hedwig's olive-toned skin next to her pale, white forearm, she was almost persuaded to start. She'd grown so used to her new non-colour that she'd forgotten the golden brown skin that had been hers for the first twenty-odd years of her life back home in Australia.

She cycled back to Paderborn along the river. It was a cold afternoon and as she rode along, the wind lifted her hair, curling in around the back of her neck and producing a cold shiver that made a pleasurable contrast to the heat rising up from the rest of her body. It had been ages since she'd been on a bicycle. She'd bought it the day after Tom left. She'd walked into the cycle shop on Höhnstrasse just by the railway station, picked it out and bought it, just like that. It was red, with large, white-rimmed wheels and straight, upright handlebars. It even had a wicker basket. It was exactly the sort of bicycle she'd always wanted as a child. Well, now she had one. She clattered over the wooden bridge that led to the old part of town and turned left towards the barracks. She had a job, a bicycle and at least one person to talk to. All in all, it wasn't a bad start to the first week of sixteen of her new, quasi-single life.

Her first day at the salon passed quickly. She was given a quick introduction to the rest of the team – four hairstylists, a podiatrist and Lotte, the young student whose job it was to sweep the floor and make endless trips to the café. She reminded Meaghan of herself when she'd started out – keen, friendly, eager to please. The other girls were pleasant enough – she repeated their names carefully, one after the other. Heidi, Simone, Kirsten and Gretha. Dina, the podiatrist, was originally from Turkey. Hedwig was on first-name terms with everyone except Lotte, who seemed too young and too shy to call her anything other than Frau Riedesal.

Her first appointment was with an older woman whose English was as good – or bad – as Meaghan's German. But with a lot of smiles and hand gestures, Meaghan managed to grasp what she wanted done and when she left forty-five minutes later, she pronounced the manicure one of the best she'd ever had. Clearly, she was off to a good start. She'd forgotten just how much she enjoyed the banter and buzz of a salon. Even though she couldn't understand a word of what passed between the girls and their clients, the atmosphere was remarkably similar to what she'd known. The smells were almost identical – that sweet, chemical scent that mingled with the lilies only just opening on the reception counter and the faint trace of perfume as clients traipsed in and out. Lunch was a salad from one of the many cafés along the main street. She ate it with Hedwig in the small kitchenette at the rear of the salon; they smoked a cigarette in the doorway afterwards.

'They like you,' Hedwig noted, as two of the stylists walked out together to get their own lunch. 'You're not like the other English women here.'

Meaghan smiled. 'Well, I'm not English.'

'Ach, *ja* . . . you said. Well, whatever you are, I think you'll fit in well.'

'Thanks,' Meaghan said simply, with feeling. It was a relief to know her skills hadn't completely deserted her. Strange, she thought to herself, stubbing out her cigarette before turning back inside . . . work had once been such a huge part of her life. Funny to think she'd given it up so readily, without a backwards glance.

'Right, let's get back to it. You've got two English girls coming in after lunch. They're from Fallingbostel – that's the other British garrison. It's about twenty kilometres from here.'

'It'll be nice to be able to talk to my clients,' Meaghan laughed. 'I felt a little silly with poor old Mrs Schobb, or whatever her name was.'

'Oh, you won't be saying that this evening, trust me. The things you hear! Sometimes you wish they'd shut up. We're halfway between being priests and psychologists, I promise you.'

'Don't I know it,' she grinned, and followed Hedwig back into the salon.

'How long have you lived here?' Meaghan asked one of the girls, a rather sour-faced, pasty-looking English girl whose fingernails were too badly bitten to be able to do much with them.

'Too fuckin' long if you ask me,' came the surly response. 'You sure you can't put them false ones over mine?'

'There's not enough nail bed,' Meaghan said mildly, inspecting her hands. 'They'll just come straight off.'

'I don't care. It's only for that fuckin' dance on Saturday.'

Sa-i-day. She marvelled at how some English people managed to almost completely swallow their words. Saturday was only two days away. 'Well, I can't promise they'll stay on until then,' Meaghan said slowly. 'But let's give it a try, shall we?' She smiled at the girl and was rewarded with another scowl.

'How comes you speaks English?' the girl's friend asked suddenly.

'I'm Australian.'

'Oh. What're you doing here?' her client asked, her expression clearly one of disbelief. Why would anyone – never mind an Australian – choose to come to Hohne?

'My husband's in the army. We're stationed in Paderborn.'

'Oh, is he? What battalion's he in?'

'Royal Anglian.'

'Oh. What's it like in Paderborn? Falling's a right fuckin' dump.'

'Oh, it's not so bad. It's quite pretty.'

'When's your lot shippin' out, then?'

'My husband's already gone, actually. He's with KFOR.'

The two girls exchanged a glance. 'What's he do?'

'He's the company commander.'

'Oh. He's an officer, then, is he?' Something else had crept into their voices. Meaghan could feel it; she remembered it from Massereene. The old barrier between soldiers and officers, never so present as in their wives.

'Yes.' The less she said about Tom, the better. 'There . . . how does that look?' She held up her client's left hand. The acrylic nails were about as close as she'd ever get to having real ones.

'Yeah, they're all right. S'only 'til Saturday anyway.'

'What's happening on Saturday?' Meaghan asked, relieved to have the conversation turn away from Tom.

The girls exchanged glances again. 'Squaddies' ball. Last one before we ship out to Cyprus.'

'Cyprus'll be nice, won't it?' Meaghan asked, starting on the other hand.

The girls shrugged. 'Dunno. Least it'll be hot. Can't wait to get a fuckin' tan.'

Meaghan only just managed to hide her smile. Why did so many English girls use the word 'fucking' the way someone else might use a punctuation mark? Fucking. Fooking. Fuckin'. The variations seemed endless. She was glad it was one habit she hadn't picked up. It didn't sound . . . well, nice.

At quarter to five, she was finally done with her last client. She pocketed the tip gratefully and opened the door. '*Danke*,' she called after her as her client made her way down the steps. She cleared away her work station, carefully cleaning and sterilising all her tools before giving the counter top one last wipe. Heidi and Kirsten were putting on their coats as she walked into the back office to get hers. 'You talk very nicely with the clients,' Simone said, with a kind smile as she reached for her scarf. 'They like you.'

'They're mostly nice clients,' Meaghan said. 'That helps.'

'Sometimes the army ones aren't so nice. They don't even bother to say hello. Not all of them, just some.'

'Well, I suppose they're like people anywhere.' Meaghan shrugged. 'Some nice, some not.'

'I prefer the officers' wives. They are much more polite. Tomorrow is Mrs Cleave-Smith's day,' Kirsten said, pronouncing the unfamiliar name with some difficulty.

'Mrs Cleave-Smith?' Meaghan paused. 'Oh, that must be the CO's wife. C Company.' She'd heard Tom mention him several times.

Kirsten nodded. 'Yes, they've been here for about a year. She's quite nice. She speaks a little German.'

'I haven't met her yet,' Meaghan said. 'We only just got here.'

'What does your husband do?' Simone asked curiously.

'He's a company commander. He's not here at the moment. He's on secondment.' She only just stopped herself saying 'Kosovo' in time. She hadn't really given it much thought but perhaps it was best not to say too much about where Tom had gone and what he was up to. Best to err on the side of caution, particularly as she hadn't told him – or anyone for that matter – that she'd taken a job.

'That must be hard,' Simone said. 'When they're away, I mean. There was one girl . . . d'you remember, Kirsten? The little blonde girl who used to come in and get her highlights done. Her husband was killed . . . I don't remember where . . . Bosnia, wasn't it?'

A cold chill suddenly went through Meaghan. She pulled hold of herself. Nothing like that was about to happen to Tom. 'Have you got far to go?' she asked them, hoping to change the subject.

They both shook their heads. 'No. Not so far. We both live in Hohne.'

'Well, I'm cycling back home so I'd better get a move on,' Meaghan said, pulling on her gloves. All three stepped out into the cold air.

'Be careful,' Kirsten said, as they parted company at the end of the road.

'Yes,' Simone agreed. 'Here we are worrying about your husband but you'd better not have an accident!'

'I won't.' Meaghan mounted the bike, wobbling as she went along. 'See you tomorrow,' she called out, but her words were quickly whipped away by the wind.

Tom rang whilst she was making herself supper that evening. His voice was a disembodied growl on the other end of the line. There was an echo, too. Every time she said something her own voice came back to her, overlaying his.

'Everything OK?' he asked, the words ricocheting down the miles between them.

'I'm fine,' she said, then had to press the receiver hard against her ear to hear what he said next. There was the distant hum of some other noise in the background – a steady, thumping kind of drone. 'What's that noise?' she asked, but her own question drowned out his reply. It didn't seem either possible or right to tell him she'd started a job . . . she decided to leave it for the time being. Although she was thoroughly enjoying herself, there was no telling whether she'd still be there in a week's time, or a month. Best leave it for now, she told herself. He's got other things to worry about. 'Are *you* OK?' she shouted, twice.

'We're all fine.' He started to say something else but the line chose that moment to fizz and crackle . . . two seconds later, it was dead. He'd warned her about that. 'Just because the line goes dead doesn't necessarily mean I am,' he'd grinned at her. 'Lines go dead for all sorts of reasons.' She stared at the silent receiver, willing it to ring again. She waited for a further few minutes but there was nothing. A few seconds later the smell of burned onions reached her nose. Her dinner. She dashed back to the kitchen and only just managed to avoid a fire.

'Australian? My, you're a long way from home. Our new second-in-command's from Australia. Brisbane, I think. I haven't yet met him. He's *very* nice, or so everyone says. Dashing, that's what all the girls say. Haven't met his wife yet, come to think of it, though I dare say I will soon enough. Ooh, that's lovely. I *do* like pink, don't you? What do you think? Too strong? Shall we try something softer . . . ooh, what about that? Now, a dark plum . . . I know, I know, there I was looking for something softer but I do rather like the look of *that* one . . . mmm. What do you think? *I* think it's rather nice.'

It was impossible to get a word in edgewise. Mrs Cleave-Smith kept up a running commentary, barely pausing to draw breath. The moment at which Meaghan ought to have inter-rupted her and introduced herself as the new 2/i/c's wife passed and for the next thirty minutes, all she could manage to do was nod. 'Absolutely lovely,' Mrs Cleave-Smith pronounced, look-ing down at her hands in glee. '*Absolutely* lovely. Now, where's dear Hedwig? Oh, she's gone out? Well, I'll just have to stop and say hello to her next time. Goodbye, girls, thank you, thank you. Thank you *so* much, dear . . . Moira, wasn't it? Yes, thank you, Moira.' The door opened and she was gone.

'You should see your face,' Simone laughed, pointing at Meaghan in the mirror with her hairdryer. She said something in German to her client, who laughed indulgently with her. 'She's always like that. You can't even say "good afternoon". She talks . . . how do you say it? Non-stop?'

Meaghan nodded, smiling. 'Non-stop pretty much covers it.'

'I'm surprised you haven't met her yet. She knows everybody.'

'Well, we're new. I'll meet her soon enough, I suppose.' Meaghan picked up the bottles of nail polish she'd used and screwed the caps on tightly. She'd spilled a few too many bottles in her time. She smiled happily to herself as she began to run over in her mind how she'd tell Tom the story of the day she polished the CO's wife's hands and how *nice* she said he was. And dashing. She giggled.

53

She was in the NAAFI, the army store, the following week when she heard, rather than saw, Mrs Cleave-Smith coming down one of the narrow aisles. There was no mistaking the voice. Meaghan paused in the act of choosing a chocolate bar. She was coming towards her, talking at the top of her voice. She was with a friend, a tall, very pale-haired woman whom Meaghan vaguely recognised. She was the CMO's wife, the Chief Medical Officer. She couldn't remember the woman's name. They'd been introduced once, immediately after Meaghan's arrival. Rosemary? Rosalind? The two women drew level, Mrs Cleave-Smith still talking, and then stopped suddenly. Mrs Cleave-Smith's eye was arrested. She beamed at Meaghan, frowning slightly at the same time, giving her face a rather comical expression. She seemed to be trying to place her. The penny finally dropped. 'Oh, hel-*lo*. It's Moira, isn't it? The manicurist. This is the Australian girl I was telling you about.' She held her plum-coloured hands up in front of her face, showing them off. 'She's the girl who persuaded me to—'

'No, you're Meaghan Astor, aren't you?' The other woman was frowning at her. She turned to Mrs Cleave-Smith. 'No, silly, that's Tom Astor's wife. You've got your Australians mixed up.'

'No, you're the new girl at Hedwig's.' Mrs Cleave-Smith shook her head firmly at her friend and smiled chummily at Meaghan. 'But what on earth are you doing here?'

'She's the second-in-command's wife, Cynthia, I *told* you. We met the other week, didn't we? How is Tom?'

'I . . . er, yes, no . . . it's not Moira, actually, it's Meaghan . . . I wanted to . . . I just didn't—'

Both women looked at her, Mrs Cleave-Smith's eyes narrowing immediately. 'What d'you mean you're the second-in-command's wife?' she asked incredulously. 'But what on earth were you doing in Hedwig's salon?'

'I'm . . . I'm a manicurist. By training, I mean. I . . . that's what I used to do . . . back home. I . . . I just started working there. I mean, Tom's away at the moment and—'

'Listen here.' Mrs Cleave-Smith's voice suddenly dropped an octave although there was no mistaking the note of surprised outrage contained in it. 'You're not *allowed* to work outside of the base. What on *earth* do you think you're doing? Does your husband know?'

Meaghan blinked, stunned. It had simply never occurred to her. She hadn't told Tom not because she was trying to hide anything from him, but just because it hadn't seemed like the right time. What did she mean she wasn't 'allowed' to work? 'I . . . I just didn't . . . no, Tom doesn't know . . . I didn't know that I wasn't allowed—'

'You're an officer's *wife*, for God's sake! This is the *British* Army.'

'She didn't know,' the pale-haired woman suddenly sprang to Meaghan's defence. 'She just made a mistake, that's all.'

'A *mistake*?' Mrs Cleave-Smith's tone implied it wasn't the sort of mistake that anyone would ever be forgiven for making. 'A *mistake*?'

'Honestly, I didn't know,' Meaghan stammered. Her cheeks were on fire and she felt herself dangerously close to tears. She blinked them back furiously. She couldn't possibly allow herself the luxury of bursting into tears in front of Mrs Cleave-Smith and her friend, however sympathetic she might turn out to be. 'I just thought, whilst he's away—' She stopped herself short.

'I don't know what Michael's going to make of all this,' Mrs Cleave-Smith muttered crossly. 'I really don't. And what on earth's got into Hedwig? She ought to know better!'

'I—' Meaghan's voice suddenly failed her. A cold feeling of dread was slowly making its way up her spine. She'd made a mistake – a silly, stupid mistake of the sort that wouldn't easily be forgiven, or viewed with anything other than scorn. She'd seen enough of the way the tight, closed world of the military worked. She'd seen what had happened to Edie and how they continued to gossip, months after she'd gone. She knew how the mistakes of wives followed their husbands around even more viciously than the errors they might make for themselves. She knew the score. She'd fucked up. *More* than fucked up. She'd made a goddamn dreadful mess of things and the worst thing was, poor Tom didn't know anything about it. He was out there in Kosovo, doing his job, doing them all proud and what had *she* done? She dropped her basket of toilet rolls, tea, baked beans and chocolate bars right there on the ground and turned and pushed her way past the two women, the tears forming thick and fast in her throat so that she couldn't speak. Not that she'd have wanted to. There was nothing she could say.

54

SAM
London, England, 2001

'Samantha?' Someone stuck a head round the door. Sam looked up from her desk. It was Michael Chilters, one of the senior partners at the firm. 'Ah. There you are. D'you have a minute?'

'Of course.' She wondered what would bring Michael Chilters to her office at nine thirty in the morning.

'Would you mind coming up to the boardroom?'

She felt a flutter of nerves in her stomach. The boardroom? What had she done? 'Er, yes, of course. Right now?'

'Yes. We just wanted to have a word, that's all.'

We? Now she was really alarmed. She got to her feet, hoping that her tights hadn't laddered and that her skirt wasn't too creased. She'd been in her office since eight going through her notes on her latest copyright infringement case – a writer who claimed a recently released film was based on a previously published poem of his. She was acting for the defence, New Cinemas, Inc., who were becoming increasingly impatient with what she suspected they perceived as her inability to bring the case to a close. But it was a complex case and the lawyers working on behalf of the writer were very good indeed. So damned good, in fact, that she was reluctantly impressed. 'Do I need to bring anything?' she asked, hoping her voice was steady.

'No, nothing. Just as you are, that's fine.' He held the door open for her. They walked to the lifts in silence, Sam's heartbeat rapidly increasing as they ascended to the ninth floor.

The view from the floor-to-ceiling windows never failed to impress her. Holman Kenton's offices on North Row looked out across Hyde Park to Kensington and beyond. It was a clear winter's morning and a faint mist still hung over the park. She had just enough time to take it in and sit down in the seat

Michael indicated when the door at the far end of the room opened and three of the firm's most senior partners entered. Sam's mouth suddenly went dry. Aside from Michael, she'd never actually spoken to any of the senior counsel. The firm's founders, Gordon Holman and Sigmund Kenton, were long since retired. Walking towards her were the three men who'd taken over the reins – Dudley Fayden, Lawrence Cullingham and Richard Turner-Balthorpe. She got to her feet, her heart now racing.

'Ah, Samantha.' Lawrence Cullingham reached her first. He extended a hand. His grip was firm and his smile warm. 'Good to see you.'

She shook it nervously. The three men took seats opposite her and Michael at the far end of the immensely long, polished table. Lawrence cleared his throat.

'Nothing to worry about,' Richard Turner-Balthorpe interjected, obviously picking up on Sam's unease.

'No, not in the slightest. Tell me,' Lawrence began, leaning back in his chair and bringing his laced fingers up towards his chin. 'How far along are we in the Stromback case?'

Sam blinked. 'Um, well, it's taking a bit of time,' she began hesitantly. 'We're just about to go to court for the second time. I'm not sure if you've been following it—'

'Oh, yes. We follow such cases quite closely,' Dudley Fayden murmured. 'Do go on.'

'The judge upheld the decision not to bring in expert witnesses. My – our – argument was that there weren't any technical or complex questions at issue. The themes that Alan Stromback listed as similarities are common themes and therefore not protectable under the copyright act. Stromback's defence tried to bring in the Lanham Act but we've argued that if there's no substantial similarity that would result in a copyright claim, there can't be a Lanham Act claim.' She stopped and looked hesitantly at the three men.

'Quite right.'

'Well argued.'

'In other words,' Richard Turner-Balthorpe said thoughtfully, 'there's every likelihood that the preliminary judgement will be upheld.'

Sam nodded. 'We'd like to think so. It's quite a complex case but the law's very clear. I don't think Alan Stromback's going to win.'

'Excellent.'

'How much do you know about the visual arts?' Dudley Fayden asked suddenly, leaning back in his chair.

Sam looked at him, now truly bewildered. 'The visual arts?' she repeated.

He nodded. 'Yes. What would you classify as visual art?'

All four men were looking at her. She felt her palms beginning to itch. Art had been one of her favourite subjects at school but aside from the odd trip to a gallery and the occasional discussion with Paula over the inspiration for her latest piece or collection, she hadn't given the arts much thought over the past ten years. She glanced quickly at Michael but he seemed to be studying his shoes. She swallowed nervously.

'Well, if we're talking about the definition in usage since the Arts and Crafts Movement, then it includes fine art as well as applied art and craft. I suppose you could call it any art work that is primarily visual in nature.' The definition suddenly rolled off her tongue. 'We could include painting, drawing, sculpture and architecture, I suppose, but also more modern practices like photography, video and film. Then there's industrial design, graphic design . . . even fashion and interiors. It's quite a broad category.' She paused for breath. She'd no idea how she'd managed to summon her high school art teacher, Mrs Jones, but she had. She could practically hear her voice. The men sitting opposite her were listening intently.

'Nicely put.'

'Indeed.'

'Let me put you in the picture, Sam,' Dudley began, leaning forward. 'Holman Kenton has been involved in the business of intellectual property for nearly three-quarters of a century.

We've an outstanding reputation and we've always prided ourselves on hiring the very best talent coming out of the law schools and universities and so on. We're also committed to innovation and making sure we're not only abreast with market developments but, particularly in our sector, making sure we're ahead of new trends and fields of endeavour.' He paused and looked straight at Sam. 'One such field that we're beginning to identify is in the area of the visual arts. We've a marvellous team in almost every other department of entertainment law, bar this one. I happened across your resume the other day and saw that you'd done art and art history at A-level. What do you think?'

Sam blinked. What did she think of what? 'Er, I'm not sure I follow you . . . .' she said hesitantly. 'D'you mean, do I think it's a good idea?'

'No. I'm asking if you're interested in the challenge.'

'The challenge?' Now she was even more confused.

'Yes.' Richard's voice was beginning to sound slightly tetchy. 'We've six areas of outstanding performance – film, music, television and radio, theatre, multi-media and publishing. We're asking if you'd like to head up the seventh, the visual arts.'

'Me?' Sam couldn't keep the surprise from her voice.

'Well, there's no one else in the room,' Dudley remarked drily.

Sam recovered her composure in a flash. In an instant, she grasped the importance of what was being offered. The conversation wasn't just about opening up new avenues within the firm; it was about *her*. She looked at the three men opposite her and suddenly, there it was. An image of herself as she would like to be seen. Cool, confident, capable. Someone who could handle things, push something through . . . this wasn't about winning or losing cases, this was about *building* something from the ground up. Something new, even experimental, possibly risky. She was being offered the chance to prove their opinions of her and put them to the test. How she answered them right here, today, in the boardroom, would be the yardstick by which everything else she did at the firm would be judged. It was a solemn moment. She brought her hands up from her lap and placed them firmly on the polished surface of the table, palms down. She drew her lower lip into her mouth, catching it on her teeth for a second, then she raised her eyes. 'I think,' she said carefully, her voice as measured as she could make it, 'That you're absolutely right. It's the right direction for the firm and I'd like to think I'm the right person for the job.'

There were nods of assent and quiet murmurs of approval around her. Michael was smiling broadly, as if to say, 'See? What did I tell you?' 'Excellent,' he said, looking at the others for confirmation. 'Excellent.'

Sam listened to the rest of the discussions with a dazed expression on her face. Her mind was racing ahead. The position and responsibility they had just offered her was way beyond anything she could ever have dreamed of. She was thirty-one years old. She would be the youngest junior partner in the firm's history. She would move from her current, cramped offices on the second floor to a spacious office of her own on the sixth. She would have her own assistant and her own team of young lawyers to lead. Everything about her working life was about to change.

She got up suddenly, aware that four pairs of eyes were on her. She mumbled something incoherent about having to go to the bathroom and walked quickly from the boardroom before anyone could see the tell-tale rise of colour in her cheeks and an unusual brightness in her eyes. She hurried down the corridor and pushed open the door to the toilets. She shut it and leaned against it, closing her eyes. She was more touched than she cared to admit by their unexpected estimation of her. As she struggled with her conflicting emotions of pride and pleasure, it dawned on her that she had no one to tell. Aside from her friends, there was no one special whom she could ring and say, 'Guess what . . . ?' Her parents would be pleased, of course, in the rather distant, uninvolved way they followed her career progress and Kate would no doubt send a bright, breezy card . . . but there was no one whose opinion counted in the special, intimate way she sometimes overheard her colleagues talking to their significant others. There would be no one to take her out for a celebratory dinner, no one to hug her and say 'well done', or 'I knew you'd do it.' She felt a sudden wave of longing for something she'd never really known. Don't be silly, she whispered to herself fiercely. At least you won't have to hear Allegra talking to her boyfriend or Greg whispering sweet nothings to his wife. You'll be in your own office with no one around you. No more exchanged glances when everyone's off to the pub to meet girlfriends and boyfriends and husbands and wives. No more asking if you did anything special at the weekend. There'd be no one to witness the fact that outside of office functions and the occasional meal or film with Paula or Philip, her life was pretty much all about work. She took a deep breath, blew her nose and cursed herself for being so silly and weak. Her life was exactly the way she wanted it. After all, she'd chosen it, hadn't she? She dabbed her eyes one more time, fluffed out her hair with her fingers and opened the door. Michael Chilters was walking towards her.

'Ah, Sam . . . was wondering where you'd got to. We'll make the announcement at Friday's staff meeting. Well done. Thoroughly deserved.'

Sam looked at him in surprise. She'd never heard him address her as 'Sam' before. It was always 'Samantha', occasionally even 'Ms Maitland'. 'Thanks,' she said, feeling a sudden rush of warmth for him. She'd never had much to do with Michael Chilters – he was one of four partners who specialised in intellectual property rights. He was in his mid-fifties and had been at the firm most of his legal career. Aside from her interview and the odd occasion they'd spoken about one case or another, she'd never had very much to do with him. But he was beaming at her in a way that made it clear he'd taken an interest in her work and was of the opinion that the promotion was merited. The lift door opened and he stood aside for her to enter. 'Second floor?' he enquired, pressing the button. 'Well, won't be long before you're up on the sixth floor with the rest of us.' He smiled again. 'Oh, and you'll be eligible for a parking space, too. Very handy. D'you drive in? Or does the boyfriend drop you off each morning?'

Sam's face turned bright pink. 'Er, no . . . no I don't have one,' she stammered.

'Which one?' Michael chuckled. 'Boyfriend or car?'

'Er, neither,' she stammered again, blushing even deeper. She'd never managed the art of light, carefree banter, especially not with colleagues.

'No boyfriend?' Michael murmured, lifting a quizzical eyebrow. 'I'm surprised.'

Fortunately Sam was spared having to reply by their arrival on the sixth floor. The bell went, the lift doors opened and Michael stepped out. The touch on her shoulder as he passed was so light and fleeting that it barely registered. He disappeared around the corner and she was left standing with her back pressed against the mirrored wall, her hand going automatically to her shoulder, as if seeking some sort of confirmation that she hadn't imagined it, that she wasn't dreaming. She shuddered suddenly, confusion breaking over her skin. She got out on the second floor and walked quickly to her office, trying to rid herself of the strange mixture of embarrassment and shame surging through her veins. By the time she was seated back at her desk with her computer screen blinking dully back at her and the familiar aspect of Allegra's head somewhere to her left, a sense of disbelief returned to her. Of course she'd imagined it. Michael Chilters was old enough to be her father. What on earth had possessed her to think otherwise?

55

The only person at Holman Kenton who was surprised at Sam Maitland's sudden promotion to junior partner was Sam herself. After it was announced at their twice-monthly staff meeting, literally scores of people came up to her to offer their con-gratulations – even people she couldn't recall ever meeting had something kind to say. She was thoroughly disarmed.

'Hasn't it ever occurred to you that you might just be good at your job?' Paula asked over the phone later that night. 'And that people genuinely like you? I don't know why you're so surprised.'

Sam blushed and laughed. 'I . . . I suppose so,' she said reluctantly. 'I just wasn't expecting it.'

'Well, get used to it, darling,' Paula said drily. 'I've a feeling we'll be celebrating many more promotions before long.'

'Paula,' Sam said suddenly, hesitantly. 'I . . . can I ask you something?'

'Of course. What?'

'It's nothing. No, well, I think I might be imagining it, to be honest, but . . . there's this guy at work. He's one of the senior partners. He's old . . . he's got to be fifty at least—'

'That's not old,' Paula interjected quickly.

'Well, he is to me. Anyhow, he was one of the partners who interviewed me when I first started and—'

'Don't tell me . . . he made a pass at you?' Paula's voice was high with surprise.

'No, no . . . nothing like that. Well, maybe. No, look, the thing is, I don't know if I'm imagining the whole thing. Nothing's happened. I mean, nothing real . . . it's just I keep catching him looking at me and there was this one time in the lift, I thought he touched my shoulder . . . oh, I don't know. I'm probably making it all up.'

'Don't be silly. You're the *last* bloody person on the planet to make that sort of stuff up. Christ, I can't imagine what it would take a bloke to get into your knickers, Sam Maitland . . . you've got them sewn up so tight—'

'Yeah, whatever,' Sam said hurriedly. She didn't need any reminder of just how wrong Paula was. 'But I just don't know what to do.'

'Well, he hasn't actually done anything, has he?'

Sam shook her head. 'No, not really. I mean, he just looks at me in a weird way and he calls me Sam. Everyone else calls me Samantha.'

'Oh, I wouldn't worry about it. Just some old bloke who's taken a shine to you. Happens all the time.'

'Not to me, it doesn't.'

'Well, sit back and enjoy it. Is he married?'

'I've no idea.'

'Don't panic. Just brush him off, nicely if you can.'

'How?'

'I don't know. Depends on what he does. If he asks you out, just say you've got a jealous boyfriend, something like that. Make a joke of it.'

'But he already knows I don't have a boyfriend.'

'How?'

'Because I told him,' Sam sighed, knowing before she opened her mouth how silly it would sound.

'You *told* him? What sort of conversation were you having?'

'It . . . it was just . . .' Sam hesitated. 'It was nothing, really. He asked if I had a car or a boyfriend and I said neither.'

'Well, just wait and see what happens,' Paula advised after a moment. 'But for God's sake don't just assume he's coming onto you. That'd be too embarrassing for words.'

Sam nodded glumly. She found the whole conversation hideously embarrassing already. She shoved all thoughts of Michael Chilters to the back of her mind and tried to think of something else.

A week later, standing at the windows of her new office on the sixth floor overlooking the park, she decided she'd imagined the whole thing. Aside from a single cheery 'good morning' as she'd passed him in the corridor one day, Michael Chilters hadn't so much as stopped by her office. She was relieved. From somewhere deep inside her, an old memory surfaced as she stood watching the early afternoon traffic surge past on Park Lane. She'd been called upon to read one of her poems at school assembly one morning. Neil Roberts was a temporary replacement teacher who'd taken over from Mrs Higgott whilst she was on maternity leave. He was young, hip and good-looking and the object of much adolescent desire. He'd found one of her notebooks that she'd left behind in class one day and had read a few. 'These are really good, Sam,' he'd said, handing her back the notebook. 'Why don't you read one out next week? That one there, the one about beauty being only skin deep. It's beautiful.'

Sam snatched the notebook from him, her cheeks ablaze. 'No, they're nothing . . . just silly stuff.'

'Not at all. I'm going to ask Mrs Strathairn to arrange for you to read one of them out in assembly. You're very talented.'

Sam shook her head furiously but Mr Roberts refused to listen. The following Monday, with her heart in her mouth, she'd climbed up onto the stage, her hands shaking so much that she'd almost dropped her notebook. When the moment came, she opened it to the last page and slowly began to read. 'On my wall hangs a Japanese carving/mask of an evil demon, decorated with gold/sympathetically I observe/the swollen veins on its forehead, indicating/what a strain it is to be evil.'

There was a moment's silence when she finished, then the assembly burst into applause. Mrs Strathairn turned to her with an enormous smile. 'Thank you, Samantha. That was marvellous. Very profound.'

She walked off the stage with the school still applauding. Mr Roberts was sitting in the front row with a puzzled expression on his face. She avoided his eye and walked quickly back to her seat. When the assembly was over, he sought her out.

'Why did you do that?' he asked.

'Do what?' Sam mumbled, still unable to look him in the face.

'That wasn't your poem. That's a Bertolt Brecht poem.'

Sam looked at the ground. 'No, it's not. It's mine.'

There was silence for a few seconds then Mr Roberts walked off. It was the last time he'd spoken to her. She had no idea why she'd done it, or why she'd lied. Every time she saw him, she wanted to explain that she hadn't actually *intended* to read the

Brecht poem. It was just that she'd opened the notebook to the back by mistake and the poem was there, right in front of her. She'd always liked it. She didn't know who it was by. She ought to have said something when she'd finished reading but she'd looked up and seen everyone looking at her, including him, and then she just froze.

But she didn't get the chance to tell him. He walked away from her that morning, his assignment at the school ended a few weeks later and she never saw him again.

She turned away from the window, aware that her cheeks were burning. That incident had happened fifteen years earlier and it had the power to embarrass her as if it were yesterday. The lingering sense of guilt she felt whenever anyone complimented her on anything would never quite disappear. She looked around her office, trying to steer her mind clear of the past. Cream walls, a thick dark grey carpet and a solid, beautifully polished desk – it was a far cry from the communal office she'd been sharing for the past couple of years. Down on the second floor, the desks were of shiny grey moulded plastic and there were flimsy screens separating the lawyers from each other. There was a single PA tucked away in the corner of the large, open-plan room and a small boardroom for them to use should the need arise. Up here, she thought to herself, things were different. *Very* different. It was her first taste of the trappings that seemed to accompany power – from the framed pictures (which she would change) to the view (which she wouldn't) – and she was shocked and rather surprised to find she quite liked it. She ran a forefinger across the surface of the desk . . . not a speck of dirt. Clearly the cleaners came round on the sixth floor rather more often than on the second.

'Sam?'

She looked up with a start. It was Michael Chilters. 'Oh . . . sorry, I was just—'

'How're you settling in?' he asked, advancing into the room. He was a stocky man, not much taller than her, but with a solidly barrelled chest and the tell-tale beginnings of an impressive paunch. She swallowed nervously. There was something about his presence that was both menacing and comforting at the same time, as difficult as that was to comprehend.

'Um, fine, thanks,' she said, hoping her voice was confident and breezy, just as Paula had instructed. 'It's very nice,' she added, gesturing around the office.

'Isn't it?' he murmured. He walked over to the windows and stood looking out, his hands shoved into his trouser pockets. 'We've a client dinner tomorrow evening,' he announced suddenly. 'At The Ivy. Ivana Wetherly-Blazcik. She's the new curator at the Tate Modern. Good opportunity for you to meet some of the more important figures in the art world. Seven thirty for eight. Shall we meet in the bar beforehand for a drink? You've no plans, I take it?'

Sam blinked. 'Er, no, none.'

'Good. Well, see you there.' He turned from the window, flashed her a dazzling smile and then strode off. She was left standing in the middle of the room, unsure as to whether the dinner would be something to look forward to . . . or dread.

56

She took one last look at herself in the mirror. Stylish, but not excessively so. Elegant, but with a slight edge. Not too classic. Ivana Wetherly-Blazcik was almost as famous for her outfits as she was for her taste in contemporary art. Sam still couldn't quite get over the change in her working circumstances. A fortnight ago she'd been stuck behind a computer screen, endlessly reading and re-reading briefs, judgements, closing arguments, remarks and opinions in an attempt to close the case against an opportunist writer, now she was getting ready to have dinner with at least one of the senior partners and the art world's most famous and controversial head. She pulled her hair back off her face – yes, better. She looked a little older, a little less the blonde ingénue. She pulled out a pair of her favourite black pumps and slid them on. She was now at least a few inches taller than Michael, although she'd be towering over Ivana. She'd never actually met the woman, of course, but from TV programmes and magazine articles she'd seen, she appeared tiny. She pulled a long, black coat out of her wardrobe, touched up her lipstick and picked up her bag. She'd dashed home at six fifteen – the first time she'd been home before eight in almost two months – taken a quick shower and changed into what she hoped would pass muster at The Ivy. There was a cab waiting for her downstairs . . . she grabbed her keys and was out the door in a flash.

'The Ivy, please,' she said as she clambered into the back seat.

'Right you are,' the driver said, glancing at her in his rearview mirror. 'Meeting someone special, are you?'

Sam shook her head. 'No, it's for work.'

'Oh, that's a shame. Girl like you ought to be meeting someone special.'

Sam had no ready answer. She turned beetroot, as ever, and looked out of the window.

The doorman at The Ivy looked her up and down briefly and broke into a smile. Clearly her outfit had passed muster. She was led through the crowded room to the bar where Michael Chilters was already waiting, a large drink in hand. 'Ah, Sam. Good to see you.' He leaned forward as she approached. For a brief second she thought he might kiss her, but he waved a glass in front of her instead. 'What'll you have?' he asked, and there was already the unmistakable whiff of alcohol on his breath. Sam's heart sank. She hoped Ivana Wetherly-Blazcik would arrive soon.

'Er, I'll have a white wine, please. Dry.'

'Very good, ma'am.' The bartender was unctuous in the way only bartenders in expensive bars can be. A second later a large glass was placed in front of her.

'Cheers,' Michael said, lifting his own and taking an unnaturally large gulp. 'Good day?'

'Er, yes,' Sam stammered. 'Yes.'

'Good. That's what we like to hear.' He took another gulp and looked at her cleavage.

Sam could feel the heat beginning to rise through her chest. She resisted the urge to fold her arms across it and concentrated instead on staring at the menu. Where the hell was Ms Wetherly-Blazcik?

Forty minutes later, with no sign of the woman, she followed Michael into the dining room, inwardly seething. He seemed curiously unperturbed. 'Probably got held up somewhere,' he said blithely. 'Busy woman.'

Sam sat down in the chair the waiter had pulled out for her and to her dismay, instead of sitting opposite her, Michael pulled out the chair next to her and eased his frame into it with a satisfied sigh. His knee touched hers. She pulled back slightly, but he inched his way forward. She looked around the room, hoping there might be someone else from Holman Kenton present – anything to break up the cosy diner à deux that Michael had somehow engineered – but there was no one she recognised. She looked down miserably at the menu. She was stuck with him for the rest of the evening – unless Ms Wetherly-Blazcik suddenly showed up, which she was beginning to doubt – and there wasn't a damn thing she could do about it. She felt an old, stubborn resentment begin to rise in her stomach. She was trapped, as much a prisoner of her own unwillingness to cause a scene as she was his dinner guest. He was her boss; he'd singled her out and promoted her – and now he wanted his due. She suddenly felt nauseous. 'Excuse me . . . I'm not feeling very well,' she stammered, getting to her feet. 'I'll be back in a second.' She rushed towards the toilets before he could even get to his feet. She slammed the door behind her, sat down hard on the toilet seat and put her hands up to her burning face. What now? And what next?

57

DANI
Freetown, Sierra Leone, 2001

There was a certain rhythm to her life with Nick, Dani noticed after a few months had gone by. A certain rhythm and a certain pattern. A week or so of closeness, sometimes two, if she was lucky. Then a few days of brooding, as if building for a storm, then an argument, a fight, followed quickly by the eventual rupture. If she was unlucky and happened to be around him at the time, she usually bore the brunt of it. She'd learned to recognise the signs. He was short with his men; he lost his temper with the bar staff down at the beach; he became surlier by the minute and then the explosion. He would never hit her – at least she didn't think he would – but his demands became stranger and more volatile as the weeks and months wore on. It wasn't her; his moods were caused by his job. She had no idea what the British Army thought they were going to achieve in Sierra Leone but from the smatters of conversation that she picked up between Nick and his men, and from the bits and pieces she overheard Eric telling Lorraine and Dixie, all clearly was not well. Things weren't going quite according to plan, whatever the plan was. 'There *is* no fucking plan, that's the problem,' she heard him say to someone over the phone. 'No one has a fucking clue.'

It appeared to be true. After nearly a decade of brutal fighting, the RUF were holed up in the east of the country; the UN sent in yet more troops to boost the British presence and rout the rebels but it was slow, painstaking and often murderous work. People talked of a ceasefire but it seemed a distant, far-off prospect. The streets were choked with people who'd been to hell and back. Dani saw the drugged young women and children who lay around the streets, too stunned by what they'd been through to rouse themselves beyond their day-to-day survival.

The stories were horrendous; sometimes Lorraine and Dixie would whisper details of what they'd heard the soldiers talking about. Dani put her hands to her ears. She didn't want to know. The bars were full of soldiers – as well as the mostly British UNAMSIL soldiers there were Nigerians, Guineans and South Africans. Business, for some, was good. When she saw one of the bar-owners she knew from the streets around her house – a rather dim, uninteresting fellow whose name she couldn't even remember – driving a brand-new Mercedes through the clogged and dirty streets, it dawned on her that there was more to the whole messy business of war than death and destruction. A whole lot more. There was money to be made – and lots of it. She wondered if that was the reason behind Nick's unexplained disappearances and the presence of the men in dark glasses and suits that she occasionally saw waiting outside his flat. He would never talk to her about them; he'd made it clear that there were subjects that were strictly off-limits – his ex-wife, the men in suits, where he might be posted next . . . what he felt about *her*. The list was long and strictly observed.

Once, when they'd come back from an evening out and she was sitting perched on the edge of the bath, soaping his shoulders and neck whilst he lay half-submerged in the cooling water, she blurted out, 'I think I love you.' It was her only means of expressing what she felt – an overwhelming gratitude, not just for the meal and the promise of spending the night together, but for what she saw, however clumsily, as his assurance that life would be different for her. Her future would be different from the only one that seemed to be on offer. She would not wind up like Dixie and Lorraine; not like the thousands of other pretty girls who bounced from soldier to soldier, man to man, their bodies their only currency. No, she was different. By singling her out and allowing her, however hesitantly, into his life, Nick was unwittingly holding out a card that was both an incentive *and* a guarantee. She had lost faith in all the other assurances – the promises of the nuns at school that, despite the chaos around them, if only the girls worked hard and paid attention to their studies, things would be different. How? Dani's scornful gaze forced even Mother Superior to lower her eyes. It was a lie and they all knew it.

Nick offered no such promises and yet their relationship was all the assurance she needed. He could have chosen anyone but he hadn't. He'd chosen her and that in itself was reason enough. One day she would leave all of this behind. She would go with him wherever he was sent. She'd heard him talk about it to others – Cyprus, Britain, Germany. Anywhere, he said to someone over the phone, except Northern Ireland. He wasn't going back into that fucking hell-hole. She tried to picture herself in some of those places – in the cold and snow of Germany, walking along the streets of London. She knew where Cyprus was but had no mental image to summon up. No matter. She would be away from here and that was what counted. Away. Gone. Gone to a place with a future. Anywhere but here.

'I love you,' she repeated dreamily, reaching for the shampoo.

He caught her hand and held it. 'Don't say that,' he said sharply. 'Don't ever say that. I hate that fucking word.'

She was surprised and a little embarrassed. Love? What was wrong with love? 'OK . . . I won't. I . . . I just—'

'I've got a problem with that word,' he said, interrupting her, but not looking at her. 'I hate hearing it. It doesn't mean anything anyway.'

Dani didn't know what to say. She continued to wash his hair, trying to work out the real meaning behind his words. As was often the case with Nick, there was a deeper truth lurking. *I hate that fucking word.* No, he didn't. He feared it. Fear and hate were not the same thing. Even *she* knew that.

58

NICK
Lunsar, Sierra Leone, 2001

The jungle was so thick it was a curtain pulled across his eyes.
Up there, 'up-country', as they called it, though to him there was
nothing of the ascendant about it – plunging into the dense
jungle after the chaos and endless horizontal spread of Freetown
was more like a descent. Into darkness. Green, fecund darkness.
Africa. The heart of darkness. And here he was, right back in the
middle of it, a darkness so profound it had nothing to do with
light, or its absence. There was a darkness gnawing at him and
his men and occasionally, like yesterday, it burst to the surface,
clawing wildly at something – anything. Even the body of a
young girl. His skin shuddered, pulling back from him. His
cigarette was almost finished; as it glowed to an end, the colour
shrank away into the black surrounding them. He felt something crawl over his foot – one of those blundering, large ants,
no doubt, following some ancient, unmarked trail up the massive
tree beside which they'd set up camp. The huge, gnarled roots
that swelled together to form a trunk as wide as a house were
useful seats. In the daytime, it was cool under the canopy of
leaves and branches.

They'd been at Lunsar almost a week; in another few days
they would dismantle the makeshift camp and move on. The last
remaining stragglers of RUF fighters were holed up some two
or three kilometres away. In the morning, he and his soldiers
would attempt to finish them off. With the sort of weaponry at
their disposal, it would be easy enough to blast what was left of
them into sorry oblivion. Killing them wasn't the problem;
finding them sometimes was. He'd never been anywhere like
'up-country' Sierra Leone. He'd never known there to be quite
so many shades of green. That was what he dreamed about when
he closed his eyes at night – green . . . dark, light, dissolving,

coalescing, thickening. Green that moved; the green of slithering, toxic mambas, of poisonous chameleons, deadly grasshoppers, crickets, birds, slugs as thick as your arm and insects he couldn't even name. The whole jungle of green was alive with danger and at the end of it, somewhere, like the pot of gold, were the men his own men had been sent to kill. Only, sometimes, when you found them . . . a motley assortment of characters wearing sunglasses, oversized T-shirts with the oddest slogans: 'Beckham', 'Hollywood', 'New York Marathon' . . . the other day they'd killed three fighters on one of their sorties into the jungle, one of whom died with his arms flung wide open, as if in surprise or salvation, revealing the words 'It's Good To Talk' emblazoned on a British Telecom T-shirt across his bloodied chest. They weren't even men. Most of them were boys. Children. Like the girl the men had brought with them. He fished into his pocket for another cigarette.

He knew whose idea it had been. That fucking goon Martins. 'Duffy', was what the men called him. One of those silent, mean types who barely talked but who could be counted on to do anything. Anything at all. He'd seen him let his hair down once or twice in the bars . . . wild, uncontrollable. He would drink himself into a stupor and then, almost like a dying man gasping for breath, he would grab the nearest girl and head onto the crowded dance floor, flinging himself about, thrashing, shaking, clutching onto whichever poor *kolonko* he'd grabbed as if she would be the pillar that would save him. He'd seen the girls shrink from him and that in itself was saying something. Most of the girls he knew would do close to anything for cash. The girl they'd brought along was different, but only because she was so high most of the time she had difficulty focusing on anything. Desirée, something like that. Pretty but ruined. He'd heard someone say her father was one of those Lebanese traders who seemed to be behind everything that went on in Sierra Leone these days. Behind, not in front. He'd never met a culture so comfortable with secrecy. Her father had never acknowledged her, or so the story went. He'd met a few like that.

Come to think of it, Dani wasn't all that different. There was a hunger in her that he'd recognised almost as soon as he met her. He shrank from it – he couldn't bear the thought of being responsible for anything, let alone her happiness, but at the same time it was so raw and powerful it was hard to resist. She was that strange, haunting combination of strength and weakness; she was tougher than anyone he'd ever met. Fearless, too. She could look you in the eye and see straight through you to some truth you'd rather conceal, even to yourself. Not Dani. She looked life straight in the eye, faced it down, came out on top. He'd never met anyone so determined. But the other side of her, that awful, desperate longing to belong to something, someone, somewhere . . . it floored him because he knew exactly what it was she sought. It was what he'd sought too, when he first arrived in England, aged eighteen, with his strange, Kenyan accent and his memories of home that had nothing to do with the cold and damp. Seeing it in Dani unnerved him and he struggled to be free of it.

It was in that girl Desirée too. She'd come along with them, smuggled in the back of the last jeep in the convoy, huddled down amongst the sleeping bags and the supplies with a bottle of her own supply to keep her happy. That, and a couple of joints. They'd brought her out the night they set up camp for the first time. She emerged out of the dark greenness into the light of the fire, that fucking Martins grinning like a Cheshire cat. 'Look who's here!' he'd crowed, making out as though she'd popped along for the ride. Ludicrous. There were eighteen men in the unit he'd brought with him. Seventeen of them cheered. She'd tipped a bottle of brandy to her lips and practically swallowed it whole. The platoon cheered her on. She began to dance, that lithe little body swaying to the sound of their clapping. He'd had no option but to endure it. What else could he do? Send her back? How? A few metres away from the circle they'd cleared in order to light the fire and pitch tents was the jungle, so thick you couldn't see through it, let alone walk. Sending her into that would be sending her straight to a savage, painful death. He'd sat to one side, nursing a beer and his cigarettes, not saying anything.

He couldn't tell exactly when the mood had changed; it was inevitable. He'd known it the minute she'd emerged from the jeep. He thought they would have fun with her . . . she'd known it, of course. Why else would she have agreed to come along? Quite how a twenty-something-year-old girl would have fun with seventeen soldiers was beyond him, but in his time in Sierra Leone, he'd learned not to question things too much. What seemed normal and sane 'out there', wherever that was, became distorted and ugly in here. He sat to one side of the clearing, watching them out of the corner of his eye. Martins first, of course. He'd brought her along . . . it was his right. She seemed OK. Then Patterson, Royds, Brendon . . . they lined up silently, each waiting his turn. He couldn't remember when it got ugly. Was it the sixth, or seventh? He'd seen it happen before. Some line so faint you couldn't tell it was there before it had been crossed. Giggles, a bit of laughter, a light slap or two . . . a pause and then something harder, animal-like. Grunts, swear words, the pack of men breathing as one. He got up from his position on the trunk and approached them. Carefully, not wanting to startle or frighten anyone. He had seventeen men under his command, armed to the teeth. Nervous, excitable, aroused. All of a sudden there was a madness in the air; he could smell it. They were thrown into a place where the blood thundered in their throats and lungs and in a collective, animal fury, they pounded into the creature lying splayed out before them, as helpless as a beast brought down by the weight of the pack. He stood for a moment, watching them and then he turned and melted back into the dark. There would be no stopping them. It was a dance of sorts, a mad, crying, ecstatic dance and the sound of it rang in his ears as he found himself gasping for his own breath. He sat down on the trunk, forcing himself to look away. Behind him was an incomprehensible, crazy fury. All he could do was wait it out. The girl was probably already dead. No sense in anyone else dying too, least of all him.

59

Freetown, Sierra Leone, 2001

DDR. Disarmament, Demobilisation and Reintegration. The papers and airwaves were full of it. What had they talked about before DDR? Dani sometimes wondered. A second ceasefire was announced in Abuja and suddenly it, too, was in the air. The Abuja Agreement. It was all everyone talked about. The end of the war. The *proper* end. Nick was often gone from Freetown for days at a time. He didn't speak about where he'd been or why. He would not allow her to stay in the flat whilst he was gone. 'Too dangerous,' he'd say brusquely, packing yet another kit bag with the camouflage trousers and shirts she took great care to launder and iron. 'See you when I get back.'

'But when will that be?' she'd ask, trying not to sulk. 'And how will I know when you're back?'

'Dunno. I'll find you.' And that would be it.

He'd been gone now for almost a week and she was bored. On Friday evening she took a taxi down to Paddies. She'd been hoping he would be back for the weekend but there was no message from the women who'd set up shop on the pavement outside the house. They were usually the ones to tell her he was back in town. She passed them on her way back from school that afternoon, hoping one of them would call out, 'He back now, girl.' But there was nothing. Only silence and the usual suspicious, mildly accusatory glances as she walked past, her satchel banging awkwardly against her legs.

She got out and paid the driver, tsking in annoyance as he called for another dollar to the fare. Since the announcement of the ceasefire, prices had gone up. War was as much about profit as it was about fighting. She'd learned that much over the past few months and she didn't need one of the nuns to spell it out for her. She crossed the road and pushed open the door to the bar. As soon as she stepped inside, she realised something was amiss. Instead of the blaringly loud music and raucous shouts from everyone, including the bar staff and Paddy, the owner, tonight it was quiet. There was a TV in one corner of the room showing re-runs of some football match or other and the men grouped around the bar nursed their drinks in silence. She spotted Lorraine and Dixie in one corner, but no Eric.

'What's going on?' she asked as she pulled out a stool and climbed up. 'Why's everyone so glum?'

Lorraine's face was a carefully held mask of tight control. 'You no hear?' she asked, dragging furiously on a cigarette.

Dani shook her head. A tremor of disquiet rippled up her spine. 'Hear what?'

Dixie lowered her voice. 'You know Desirée, that half-Lebanese girl from Foulah Town . . . the one that used to go with the South African fella?'

Dani nodded. 'The one with the fake blond hair?'

'Yeah. That's her. She dead.'

Dani stared at her. 'What d'you mean she's dead? I saw her on Saturday.'

Dixie nodded solemnly. 'She dead.' She looked around the bar nervously. 'An' dey say some soldier-man kill her.'

Dani's eyes widened. 'A soldier? Which soldier?'

Lorraine leaned over, stubbing out her cigarette with sharp, vicious jabs. 'A whole group of soldiers. What dem call it? Platoon? They was having . . .' She paused and then said, with some difficulty, 'Fun. They was having fun. That's what de major say.'

'Which major?' Dani became aware of a pulse beating rapidly at her temple.

'*Your* major.' There was just enough emphasis on the 'your' to let Dani know exactly what Lorraine thought. 'Him tell de police so. They was just havin' fun.'

'Wh . . . when did it happen?'

'Sunday night. That's when they found her. Some villager-man found her by de roadside.'

Dani thought back rapidly to the previous Sunday. She hadn't seen Nick in over a week. She had no idea where he was. 'How you hear all this?' she asked, reaching for a cigarette herself. She wasn't much of a smoker but she needed something to do with her hands.

Lorraine tossed her braids over her shoulder. 'Eric. Your major tell dem say nobody leave the base.' She made a small sound of exasperation. 'Dunno why he keep all dem inside. *He* the one gone up-country.'

'What d'you mean?' Dani's heart was beating fast. Why hadn't she been told? And how come Lorraine knew more about Nick's whereabouts than she did?

'That's where dem find her. Up-country. Near Lunsar.'

'Wh . . . what are you saying?'

Lorraine shrugged. 'Me not saying nuttin'.' She took a long drag on her cigarette. 'Eric don't got nuttin' to do with Desirée. So why your major punish everybody?'

Dani didn't know what to say. She was aware the other two were looking at her half-accusingly, as if she had any influence over Nick's decisions. It was embarrassing to admit that they knew more than she did. She didn't even know Nick had been up-country. She puffed on her cigarette and tried not to cough. 'Poor Desirée,' she said after a moment. She hadn't known her well – hardly at all, in fact. Just another one of the pretty, light-skinned girls who'd found an appreciative audience in the foreigners who now more or less ran the show. A wave of sadness began to wash over her. She looked around her at the bar, at the girls sitting perched on stools waiting for soldiers, mercenaries, shady businessmen and losers to buy them drinks, airtime for their mobile phones, a meal, a new pair of shoes . . . anything. She was suddenly sickened by it. She stubbed out the remainder of the cigarette and slid off the stool. She couldn't bear it any longer. Ignoring Dixie and Lorraine's questions, she picked up her bag and walked out into the warm, sultry night.

Nick, Eric, Lorraine, Dixie . . . and Desirée. She didn't want to know the details of what had happened to her. Just thinking about it would make it more real and if there was one thing she had learned over the past few months, it was better and safer not to dwell too much on the way things were. Far better to dream and ignore the reality of her life. And that, she muttered to herself as she made her way across the road and stuck out her hand for a taxi, included everything to do with Nick. Better not to ask, or to probe. She might not like what she found.

PART FIVE

60

MEAGHAN
Paderborn, Germany, 2002

Meaghan looked up at the arrivals board for the hundredth time in less than fifteen minutes. *AB094 from Istanbul. Landed.* There it was! She grabbed her bag from the empty seat next to her and ran towards the gate. She knew Tom; he would be one of the first off the plane. He would stride through with those impossibly long legs of his, his kitbag tossed casually over one shoulder and his eyes impatiently scanning the small knot of people, waiting to catch his first glimpse of her. He'd told her once, a long time ago, that the first moment of eye contact was the best. She'd had her hair washed and styled; it hung around her face in long, soft wavy curls. She was wearing one of his favourite outfits – tight-fitting jeans and a flowery, summery top that showed off the tanned and lightly freckled skin of her shoulders. She'd spent the past week getting herself and the house ready. Both were waxed, polished, buffed and carefully groomed. There were fresh flowers in the sitting room and candles in the bedroom; she'd done her nails, her bikini wax, her toenails . . . everything she could think of to welcome him home. He'd been gone for almost six months. The tour had been extended from sixteen weeks to twenty, then twenty-four. Now it was twenty-seven weeks and four days since she'd last set eyes on her husband and the thought of seeing him walk through the arrivals gate in a few minutes' time was enough to make her heart stop beating.

She stood to one side, her fingers clutching at the strap of her handbag and her stomach in knots. Six months . . . would she even recognise him? She shook herself; she was being silly. Of course she'd recognise him! She would know Tom anywhere. She craned her neck to look. The first passengers were beginning to make their way across the polished floor towards the sliding glass doors that separated them. A woman holding two small children, one of them crying silent tears of some childish mutiny; an elderly man, carefully pulling his wheeled suitcase behind him. A couple of teenage girls, giggling conspiratorially as the doors flew open and shut again behind them. Her heart was pounding. Someone else approached; no, it wasn't him. And then she saw him. Head and shoulders above most of the others. He strode quickly towards the doors. It was exactly as she'd imagined it over and over again, almost daily for the past three months. His eyes darted from left to right, skimming over the heads of the small crowd and then finally catching, and locking, with hers. She put up a hand to her mouth. He'd lost weight. His uniform hung off him in a way she didn't recognise. She turned and began to walk towards him, her whole body suffused with a sense of unreality. How long had she waited for this moment? Everything seemed to slow to a standstill as she reached the end of the barrier separating them and stopped, waiting for him to catch hold of her. Five seconds, four . . . three, two, one. There was a muffled pause and then all of a sudden she was pressed against his chest and the old, familiar scent of him came rushing back. She began to cry.

All the way back to Paderborn in the train she held onto him tightly, unable to say much other than ask the usual question. *Are you OK?* It seemed such a meaningless, trivial phrase. She could no more imagine what he'd been through in the past six months than he could imagine the sheer boredom of hers. She'd spent it waiting for him; that was the truth. After the disastrous attempt at finding work which, thankfully, seemed not to have reached his ears, she'd pretty much kept to herself. She'd made a casual acquaintance out of a couple of the wives but some instinct in her had stopped her from going any further. In the first couple of weeks following her dressing-down in the NAAFI by the CO's wife, she'd been too embarrassed to go out or join any of the other officers' wives in their daily activities in and around the town. She'd stayed at home, wondering how and when to break the news of her transgression to Tom.

But the moment never came. From Kosovo reports of violence that the troops hadn't expected to find began to trickle in. Mass graves, war crimes, genocide. Suddenly the ground had shifted. Tom was no longer fighting a straightforward, clearly defined 'enemy', whomever that might turn out to be. Suddenly there were no 'good' and 'bad' guys, simply shades of each. In the patchy telephone calls he managed to make to her, she could sense his bewilderment at this new theatre of war, as he called it. He was part of the UN, now, not just the British Army. Even more puzzlingly, they seemed to be as much a part of the problem as the solution he'd been called in to provide.

Home at last. She unlocked and opened the front door. She couldn't remember what she'd changed since he'd last been there. Was the kitchen painted before or after he left? The new dining table and six chairs that she'd badgered the housing officer into giving her? What about the rug in the living room? She watched him walk from room to room, nodding very faintly to himself, as if trying to reassure himself of his place in the flat that he'd never properly known.

'D'you want something?' she asked shyly. 'A cup of tea, maybe?'

He came back into the living room and raised his arms above his head, holding onto the door frame. He shook his head, still looking around. 'You've made it nice, Meg,' he said softly. 'Forgotten what a home looks like, y'know?'

She nodded slowly. She was overwhelmed and felt herself close to tears, more upset than she could admit. She turned away. It was too difficult to put into words what the sight of his tall, rangy body moving around the flat meant to her. The scenario was one she'd played over and over in her head in the long, lonely weeks of winter and the sudden arrival of spring. She'd lost count of the number of nights she'd gone to bed in tears after watching the news – a bomb explosion here, a sniper's bullet there, dreading the sound of the ringing telephone – only to wake up in the morning half in relief, half in dread. Not today, but maybe tomorrow? The fear of not having him home again had become so much part and parcel of her normal, waking life that now that he was here, in the flesh, splendidly alive and tanned, despite being thinner, it was so unreal as to make her wonder whether she'd dreamed it. Was it really Tom? Was he really here?

She went to him suddenly. He stood just inside the door, his body at once compact and tense. She stood in front of him and reached her hands up to his face, touching him lightly. She looked past his face to one that she'd never known in him; he was too deep inside himself to try to conceal what might be written all over it. She was tense, but suddenly the sense of panic and shyness she'd felt when he first walked out of the airport with her on his arm was gone. She traced the outline of his lips and nose with her fingertips. She felt his whole body shudder. There was the trace of a smile around his mouth. He sighed, a long, soft expiration of all the tension that was stored up inside him and she was filled with a sudden lightness. He took her hand, very gently at first, then he tightened his grip. She was filled with a longing for him, not just his body and the feel of the weight of it on hers, but for his words, sentences, stories . . . whatever there was inside him that was waiting to exhale. Six months, she thought to herself in wonderment as he began to unbutton her shirt, slowly, button by button, in between the light, teasing kisses she remembered from the days of their first meetings. In six months Tom had become a stranger again. But it was a pleasurable strangeness, erotic and sensual all at once. His hand moved underneath her top, urging it over her head. Behind her, the gauzy curtains rose and fell like a veil in the summer breeze. Her skin tingled at his touch. He was gentle with her, just as he had been in the beginning. His fingers slipped underneath her bra, pushing it aside, teasing her nipples, first one and then the other, into hardness. She opened her mouth to draw in his tongue; she'd forgotten its warm, heavy wetness. He peeled her jeans away from her hips and sank his fingers into the soft, firm flesh, pulling her closer to him, and closer still. It took him a few seconds to unbutton his own trousers and even less time to push her against the dresser, hastily clearing away the assortment of photographs and knick-knacks she'd spent the whole morning artfully arranging and rearranging. The frames clattered to the ground; he lifted her with one hand, the other guiding himself into her as fast as he could. His eyes were shut tightly as he began to make love to her right there in the living room with the windows wide open and the curtains billowing wildly to and fro. She lay backwards, crushed between his thrusts and the wall, but she couldn't have cared less. Tom was back. He was home and he was whole and undamaged and things would go back to the way they'd always been. Nothing else mattered. His body began to race away from him and his thrusts became faster and harder. His hand slid from the dresser to the tangled strands of her hair. He pulled hard, once, twice . . . grabbing onto her as if he couldn't bring her closer or push himself deeper inside her. 'Meaghan,' he gasped, as if her name was the last word he could bring himself to utter. Two things happened at once – she conceived, right at that very moment. Her whole body was flooded with the most intense passion she'd ever experienced and in the same moment she knew, beyond a shadow of doubt, that hers was not the last body her husband had entered.

61

ABBY
Airport Camp, Ladyville, Belize, 2002

A shadow fell across the page she was reading. Abby shielded her eyes against the fierce sun and looked up. It was Nuñes, their Venezuelan batman. Or houseboy. Or house-help, whichever term you preferred. She personally disliked all of them, almost as much as she disliked the very idea of having someone around the house. But it was Ralph's idea – although 'idea' was stretching it. An edict. A command. *I'm not having you and the girls out here on your own whilst I'm away.* And that was it. A week after Ralph left for training at an 'undisclosed location', Nuñes moved in. To be fair, the houses were designed for it. Nuñes had his own 'quarters' as he called it, to the rear of the property, tucked out of sight. He'd been an army batman for almost ten years, he told her, though he barely looked old enough and quite how he'd come to Belize from Venezuela was anyone's guess. He spoke passable English with an accent that veered from ridiculously pompous upper-crust English to the Spanish-inflected intonation that came with his mother tongue. He'd spent two years with Lieutenant Colonel Price, from whom he'd learned how to make an omelette, iron a shirt so that the crease would never fade and, somewhat incongruously, tunelessly whistle the theme tune from *Blue Peter.* She found it endearing. After Price, he'd worked for eighteen months for the Henderson family where his English had improved dramatically alongside his culinary skills. Now, at the age of twenty-seven, he knew all about making Yorkshire pudding in the tropics and how to live a life of utmost discretion. It unnerved her slightly, his creeping up soundlessly on bare feet whilst in the house and his habit of anticipating practically everything she said to him. It came, she supposed, from a professional life spent being spoken to, never speaking, and occupying the strange, half intimate, half at a distance life of a live-in servant. She'd grown up with servants of one sort or another on her father's overseas postings, but as far as she could remember, they'd been almost exclusively female and the only men she could recall being in the house were the army drivers and the occasional gardener who came up to the back door looking for a glass of water. Where had that been? she wondered to herself. Probably here, in Belize, half a mile from where she now lived. Funny how some things come full circle, she thought suddenly. Here she was, back where she'd started, in a sense.

'What is it, Nuñes?' she asked, suddenly uncomfortably aware of her bikini-clad body as she lay by the pool. It was a Thursday morning; the girls were both in their respective schools. In an hour, she would walk across the football pitch to collect them but, for now, she had the whole swimming pool gloriously to herself.

'Mrs Kendall she ring the house. She say she comin' in twenty minutes.' Nuñes had the authoritative air of having something of great importance to say.

Abby sighed. Mrs Kendall was the insufferable wife of Brigadier Kendall, one of the regional commanders who regularly came out to Belize. She'd singled Abby out on her last trip and it looked like being a repeat and regular performance. 'Thanks, Nuñes,' she said, sitting up and reaching for her sarong. 'I'll be home in a minute.'

'Yes, sir.' It was another of Nuñes's idiosyncrasies. No matter how often she corrected him, he seemed unable to call her anything other than 'sir'. He seemed on the verge of saluting but changed his mind at the last moment and loped off. She waited until he'd crossed the road and was out of sight before standing up and pulling her sarong tightly around her. She picked up her bag, slipped her sunglasses on her face and followed in his trail.

The house was quiet and cool. The fans were blowing in the sitting room and in her bedroom. She kicked off her sandals and walked into the bathroom, unwrapping her sarong as she went. A visit from Daphne Kendall was enough to make anyone break out into a cold sweat. She truly was awful. She was in her late fifties with two grown-up daughters who somehow made their way into every single conversation on any given subject, along with the typically small-minded views of a small-town woman thrust into the international spotlight of her husband's career. Abby couldn't stand her. Why she was coming to visit was anyone's guess. She had an inkling that Daphne Kendall knew how tiresome Abby found her, though she was at pains to conceal it. She turned on the shower and stepped gratefully under the stream of cool water.

Ten minutes later, sitting in front of her dressing table in a pretty summer frock, her hair swept up off her neck and pinned loosely on top of her head, she surveyed her reflection in the mirror. As hot as Belize was, she had to admit the climate suited her. The humidity and sun had done wonders for her skin. She was lightly tanned with that healthy red glow around her cheeks and cleavage that came from spending hours by the pool. She'd taken up tennis and yoga, which had improved her figure. Not bad for a thirty-four-year-old broad, she grinned lightly at herself. She applied a light coat of lipstick, brushed her face hurriedly with powder and stood up. She walked over to the windows; the master bedroom looked out into the courtyard at the back of the house. The bougainvillea that normally shaded Nuñes's quarters from the rest of the house had been pruned, rather too vigorously, she noticed. She would have to speak to the gardener about using a lighter touch. She'd never understood the enthusiasm the locals had for chopping down almost every shrub, hedge, bush or plant. If Oliver, the gardener, had his way, they'd be living in a clearing absolutely devoid of plants or flowers. Less work for him, she supposed, suppressing a sigh. She'd worked hard as soon as they arrived to make the garden something pleasant and soothing to look at. It was too hot for the sort of flowers she knew and understood – there were no roses, dahlias or sweet peas here . . . instead they had huge, waxy bird-of-paradise flowers and the glorious riot of colour that was the bougainvillea.

She was just about to turn away when something caught her eye. It was Nuñes, walking towards the outside shower. He had a small bucket in his hand and a sponge. No doubt, like her, he was about to shower before coming in to serve Mrs Kendall her requisite G&T. She ought to turn away. But she didn't. She watched in curious fascination as he filled the pail with water and then balanced it on top of the wall next to the drain. Clearly the showerhead wasn't working. She gave an almost inaudible gasp as he loosened his towel and stood naked before her, barely ten yards away. He sang softly in Spanish as he began to soap himself, oblivious to the fact that his employer was watching him. He had a rather beautiful body – of average height but compact and muscular. His skin was a dark coppery colour, burnished by the sun. She'd never given it – or him – much thought but he was clearly a *mestizo*, a mixture of Spanish, Negro and European blood, like many of the locals. He reached up and tipped the pail over his body, obviously enjoying the feel of cold water on his skin. She felt the familiar pull of desire in her abdomen as she watched him rinse himself, his muscles gleaming wetly in the sunlight. She found herself unable to look away. She ought to; she *had* to. She had no business standing in her bedroom watching the servant in the house as he bathed. It wasn't right. More than that, it was downright dangerous. She put a hand up to her face. A blast of heat settled over her, confusion mixed with anxiety. She was sweating again, but this time the heat was generated from within. A long-dormant memory surfaced and could not be suppressed; it blundered, blindly, into the present.

Mother is sitting at the dressing table that is the source of everything that is beautiful, sweet-smelling and feminine to the six-year-old's gaze. She loves watching her powder her face, her expression one of dreamy self-contemplation. She is standing half-hidden by the door. Her parents are going out – one of the many dinners to which they are always invited, her father resplendent in uniform, her mother beautiful in the way of film stars and actresses she and her sisters watch on TV. Her hair is swept up into something she calls a chignon – Abby stumbles over the word. Her dress is midnight-blue, with tiny sparkling diamonds. Abby thinks she's never seen anything so beautiful. It has a long, shiny zipper down the back, a thousand tiny steel teeth, and it's open; she hasn't yet done it up. She, Abby, wants to do it for her, even though she can't quite reach the top. She is just about to step forward, out of the darkness and into the soft light that comes from the lamp next to the bed when her mother calls out to someone. Not her. It can't be her father; he's not yet home. She freezes. 'Junior?' her mother calls softly. The batman, whom they all call Junior, comes forward. He's in her parents' bedroom. She watches, frowning in incomprehension as he puts his hands on her mother's waist in the way her father sometimes does, and slowly zips her up. His hands rest for a moment on her shoulders in a gesture of intimacy that even she understands is wholly inappropriate. There's a flash of understanding that slips away from her almost as immediately as it surfaces. She steals away, unseen and unheard. She's stumbled upon something she cannot name.

62

DANI
Freetown, Sierra Leone, 2002

Sweat was pouring down her back as she made her way up Wilberforce Road, two large plastic bags full of groceries in either hand. Somewhat unusually, Nick had left her a large wad of cash before leaving for Bo, almost a fortnight earlier. Also unusual of him, he'd told her when he would be back – two weeks on Saturday, he'd said. Was it a sign he was slowly – *finally!* – getting used to the idea of her being around?

She turned up Damba Road, shifting the bags around to give her arms a break. She'd gone to Koala, the Lebanese-owned supermarket on Kissy Road, and spent most of what Nick had given her. Prawns, a large red snapper, some spinach leaves, tomatoes, onions. She would make one of her grandmother's famous spinach and palm oil stews – only hers would have fish *and* prawns, and rice. She knew he liked rice. She lugged the bags up the short pathway to the front door and surveyed the lift. Out of order, of course. She sighed and began the slow climb to the sixth floor. She stopped, halfway up, already out of breath. She frowned. It seemed to her of late that she was always out of breath. She put the bags down and put a hand on her waist, which hurt. There was a small roll of fat just above the waist-band of her skirt; she looked down at herself in annoyance. She'd put on weight in the past couple of months. It was all the good food and wine at the restaurants he took her to. She would have to watch what she ate; she didn't want to wind up like Dixie. Dixie had gone from being a slim, elegant girl to being almost matronly in less than a year. She was solid now, not slender, and by the looks of things would never be slender again. No, thank you very much, Dani didn't want to look like *that*.

She climbed the last few stairs and walked down the corridor to Nick's front door. It was open, she noticed in surprise as she reached out a hand to knock. The door swung open easily. 'Hi,' she called out, her heart lifting in anticipation as it always did at the thought of seeing him again. 'It's only me. The door was open.'

There was silence from within. She frowned and set the plastic bags down carefully on the ground. The hallway was empty. Usually his duffel bag and kit-bag stood propped up against the wall on one side and on the top of the counter there'd be all his paraphernalia – keys, wallet, box of matches, sometimes his mobile phone. There was nothing. The counter was empty, swept clean. She pushed open the door to the kitchen. It was completely bare. He'd never had much; a kettle, toaster and one of those counter-top fridges that hummed loudly day and night. The fridge was there but everything else was gone. She became aware of her heartbeat, a loud, rhythmic thumping in her ears. She turned and walked into the living room. It too was empty. She tried to take hold of the sudden panic that swept through her. No, he hadn't disappeared. There was an explanation. He'd been moved somewhere else, another flat. He'd mentioned something about needing a bigger, better place once . . . that was it. He'd moved, that was all. She walked back into the hallway, all thoughts of the meal she had been planning to cook gone from her. She had to find someone – anyone. Eric. Eric would know where he was.

*

Eric rubbed the back of his head, the folds of fat settling themselves around the soft collar of his terry-towelling robe. He was barefoot. Lorraine had gone to the market. They were in the outdoor corridor, Dani on one side of the front door, Eric on the other.

'Thing is,' he said, clearly uncomfortable, 'it was sudden, like. He shipped out on Monday.'

'Shipped out?'

'Yeah. He was . . . he was transferred.'

'Transferred? What d'you mean? Transferred where?'

'Dunno, love. Nobody tells us anything.'

Dani stared at him. His words came at her in a language that her brain didn't have the shape to receive. Shipped out. Transferred. Gone. She couldn't help herself; she reached out and gripped his arm as if he would bodily bring Nick back. He caught hold of her hand. There was a sympathetic tremor in the way he held her. 'No,' she said, shaking her head. 'No, it can't be. He wouldn't just . . . he would have told me. Something's happened to him, hasn't it?'

'No, love . . . he was transferred. Nothing's happened to him. He's just gone, that's all.' Eric's face had reddened uncomfortably.

'But he *can't*—' Dani's voice rose hysterically.

'He has. That's . . . that's just the way it is, love. I'm sorry, really I am.' Eric looked even more embarrassed.

Dani felt the ground shifting dangerously beneath her feet. She was dimly aware she was still holding Eric's arm. Her heart was hammering. Her fingers were so tightly knuckled she felt she would never get them unstuck. She looked into Eric's blushing, sympathetic face and felt something inside her snap. 'He *can't*,' she repeated, her voice catching on a sob. 'He can't just disappear.' There was an agonising pause as they stared at each other and then Dani opened her mouth and the words just slipped straight out. 'Eric, I'm . . . I'm pregnant.'

63

SAM
London, England, 2002

To whom could she turn? She lay in bed on Monday mornings, the knot of tension slowly curdling deep inside her stomach, exhausted from a night through which she hadn't slept, dreading the day ahead. It was like that each and every week. On Fridays she no longer went with her colleagues to the pub across the road from the American Embassy, just around the corner from the office. The thought of being trapped in a conversation with Michael Chilters was too much to bear. He was clever. Oh, yes, he was clever. He made no direct claims, no direct threats; there was nothing she could put a finger on or point accusingly at. On the surface, he was charming, professionally courteous, avuncular almost. In group meetings or when there were other lawyers present, he could be brusque, almost dismissive. No one would ever have suspected him of anything other than the most perfunctory professional interest. But beneath the suit and the expensive ties and the air of collegial camaraderie, another Michael Chilters lurked, one whom she loathed. He would come upon her in the corridor, and, seeing they were alone, flash her the sort of special smile that indicated there was more he would like to do, should the opportunity arise. Nothing overt; a hand on her shoulder, on her arm and once – the memory of it made her skin crawl – he laid a thick index finger on her cheek, ostensibly brushing a lock of hair that had escaped the severe bun she'd taken to wearing. The legal, rational part of her brain took over, dissecting and analysing the facts. It was harassment – no other word for it – and by her silence, she was both accomplice and victim. Who could she turn to? Philip? She shrank from the suggestion, even to herself. What was wrong with her? She could put an odious little creep like Chilters in his place, surely? She was tough; *everyone* said so. Why was she allowing him to get to her like that?

The alarm clock sounded uselessly. She glanced at it through eyes thick with tears. She'd been awake for hours. She reached across and turned it off wearily. It was Monday. Another week to be got through, endured. She pushed aside the covers and got out of bed. The week could not be put off any longer.

After the weekly staff meeting was over, she escaped to her office as quickly as she could. She had only just sat down and turned on her computer when there was a tap at the door. She looked up anxiously but it was only Martin. He too had been promoted from the ground floor but now worked on copyright law, mostly in music, which suited him down to the ground.

'Can I come in?' he asked, hovering uncertainly at the door.

'Course you can.' Sam looked at him, relieved.

'Is—' He hesitated for a second. 'Is everything all right, Sam?' he asked, the words coming out rather hurriedly. He closed her door behind him.

For an absurd moment, Sam felt she might burst into tears. She swallowed. 'Yes, of course,' she said, hoping her voice was steady. 'Of course it is.'

'You're not . . . you sure you're OK?'

'Yes. Yes, I'm fine. Why?'

'It's just . . . you don't seem yourself these days. Oh, I know everyone's busy and we're all overworked and all that but it's been ages since you've been out with any of us and . . . well, Cassie and I were just wondering—' He stopped, clearly embarrassed. There was a note of some other emotion in his voice. Sam frowned at him; his tone wasn't one she'd heard before.

'What?'

He cleared his throat. 'It's not . . . it's not because you've been promoted, is it? I mean, I didn't think you were like that. Cassie neither,' he added hastily. 'But we were discussing it with—'

'Me?' Sam stared at him incredulously. 'You think I'm being a snob?'

Martin's cheeks immediately reddened. It was clear that the topic had come up between him and Cassie, and whomever else they'd spoken to. 'No, of course not. But it's just . . . it's not like you, Sam. We've hardly seen you since you got your new job up here. You never come out for drinks any more. We've had three dinner parties in the last month and you haven't come to a single one. We're just worried, that's all.'

Sam was speechless. It was true she didn't feel much like socialising these days. In fact, she couldn't recall the last time she'd been out for a coffee or a drink with anyone. Yes, she was overworked – there was a lot to learn in her new role and she'd taken the challenge her associates had thrown at her seriously – but the thought that her closest friends thought she was being snobbish was enough to undo her completely. She stood trans-fixed by his concerned gaze, blinking hard so that she wouldn't cry. 'I . . . I'm fine,' she said finally, making a great effort to control herself, and her voice. 'I'm just a bit . . . I'm new to a lot of this,' she said, waving her hand around the small office. 'There's an awful lot to learn, that's all. I'm not being snobbish, I promise you.'

There was relief in Martin's face. 'Of course you're not . . . I didn't – we didn't – really think that for a minute. But you haven't been yourself lately. I don't know. Clutching at straws, I suppose. Any old explanation.' He smiled at her, clearly relieved.

She smiled back, for a second able to act as if nothing had happened, nothing had changed. The moment of danger had passed. She felt the sudden urge to be amongst them again, those friends for whom she was a concern. 'Let's go out on Friday night,' she said lightly. 'Like we used to.'

'Done.' He grinned. 'So you're sure there's absolutely noth-ing?'

She nodded firmly. 'Absolutely. Nothing at all.'

The door closed behind him and she was able to breathe again. There was a tightness in her chest that came from the knowledge that she mattered – at least to her friends. She was unexpectedly touched by it, and by their estimation of her. She turned back to her computer screen and to the complex intricacies of the case she'd been handling, her mind momentarily taken off the unpleasantness surrounding Michael Chilters and what to do about him.

Her relief was short-lived. She had just come back from lunch later that afternoon and was settling back into the rhythm of checking and cross-checking references in the preparation of her latest brief when her office door opened again. This time, there was no knock.

'Ah, Sam.' Michael advanced into the room uninvited. 'Got something for you,' he said, holding out a file.

She got up quickly from her desk. She didn't like being forced to look up at him; there was something almost threatening about it. She held out her hand. 'What is it?' she asked, her voice as steady as she could manage it.

'It's a new case.' He came to stand very close to her, still holding onto the file. 'Thought it'd be right up your street.' He cleared his throat. 'Right up *our* street, in fact. Thought we ought to work on it together.'

Sam's heart sank. 'Wh . . . what sort of case?' she asked, moving fractionally backwards. Her bottom touched her own desk. He had her cornered.

'An interesting one,' he murmured. He was very close to her now. She swallowed nervously. The soft, slack folds of skin around his jaw were almost touching her cheek. She could smell his aftershave and the scent of some kind of cream – a thick, cloying scent. She felt her whole body shrink in revulsion. There was a smile on his mouth as he brought the file up with one hand; in horror, and in slow motion, she felt the other slide around her back, touching her lightly between the shoulder blades before trailing down the length of her spine, coming to rest on her bottom. His fingers flexed, exerting just enough pressure to let her know he'd fondled her, right there in her own office, against her own desk. She'd been promoted on his recommendation. This, then, was the price.

64

DANI
Freetown, Sierra Leone, 2002

The clinic on Benjamin Lane to which he'd brought her was
new; she'd never heard of Marie Stopes, never had the occasion
to. Eric's face was red and sweating; he bundled her out of the
car as quickly as he could and was in through the front door
before she'd even managed to catch her breath. He'd borrowed
the car from a friend of Lorraine's. He didn't want to be seen in
an army vehicle in this part of town. 'Come on,' he chided her,
waiting at the top of the stairs. He held the door open, and
ushered her through, solicitous now, as if to make up for his
impatience. 'You just sit yourself down over there an' I'll take
care of the rest.'

Dani moved over to where he'd indicated and sank down
into one of the plastic chairs. She felt sick. She'd woken up
each morning for the past three weeks retching into the
chipped white enamel basin as she waited for Eric's call.
'Leave it to me,' he'd said firmly. 'I'll sort you out.' Well, he
had. Here she was, sitting nervously on a white plastic chair in
the waiting room of a clinic of sorts. He'd 'arranged' things, he
promised. It would all be 'taken care of'. She understood only
too well what the words meant. She was about to have an
abortion. Get rid of the only thing Nick Beasdale had left
behind. Everything else was gone. The flat had been swept
clean; nothing remained, not even a toothpick. She'd been
through it a dozen times, looking for something – anything –
that would give some hint as to where he'd gone, and why. Eric
was no help in that department at all. He'd shrugged his shoulders. There was nothing to be said. He'd buggered off, gone.
End of story. But that was before she'd told him her own. Then,
as now, he'd gone bright red with embarrassment and promised
to do everything he could. So here she was. Here *he* was. At the

Marie Stopes Clinic in Foulah Town, waiting for whatever would happen next.

'No, no . . . she's not . . . it's not mine, like. She's a friend. A friend of my . . . my wife's.' If the smooth-faced receptionist who stared out at them both from under her canopy of dreadlocks didn't believe him, it wasn't apparent. With brisk efficiency, she handed him a form attached to a clipboard and a pen.

'Get her to fill it out,' she said, 'and bring it back to me.' Her accent was English and she chewed loudly and incessantly on a wad of bright pink gum. One of the many who'd returned after the civil war, no doubt. Dani took the clipboard from him and busied herself with the task. *Name. Address. Date of birth. Occupation.* She glanced further down the form. *Procedure. TOP.* What was a TOP? *Medical* or *Surgical*? She had no idea. It didn't take long to find out. A TOP was a Termination of Pregnancy. A fancy way of saying what it was she'd come for. Ms Dreadlocks-With-a-Snappy-English-Accent glanced at her form, took the payment envelope from Eric and summoned her through to the ward.

The corridor was bright and white under the glare of fluorescent tubes and the petroleum smell of fresh paint still hung in the air. Dani followed the receptionist to the end and into a small room where a nurse in a dark blue uniform with a hat pinned haphazardly on her head was waiting. 'Danielle Tsemo?' she enquired as Dani entered. Dani nodded. 'Good. If you'll just put your things there . . . that's it.' She pointed to the empty chair. 'When last you ate, child?'

Dani swallowed. It had been in the small instruction booklet Eric had brought back for her. *No solid food for 12 hours before your procedure.* Why couldn't they just call it an abortion? she'd wondered, reading the leaflet. 'Yesterday,' she whispered.

'Good, good. Now, just step up here.' She indicated the bed. The mattress was thin, but covered in a clean, white plastic sheet. Everything was just as Eric said. *I'll make sure you get in somewhere nice, love. Least I can do.* He was a decent man, she thought to herself as she waited for the nurse to begin her examination. It was more than could be said for Nick. At the thought of him, her eyes began to fill with easy tears. How was it possible to simply walk out? With no word, no explanation, no warning – nothing. One minute there, the next he was gone. She loved him; she'd told him so, many times, despite his not wanting to hear it. But she'd proved it, hadn't she? She'd taken care of him in her own young, inexperienced way. She'd cooked and cleaned and washed his clothes, made sure there was food in the house for him to come home to, company when he wanted it, silence when he didn't . . . and as for the other stuff . . . he'd used her body in ways she didn't always understand, or like . . . but she'd never refused him. Not once. Not even when Lorraine and Dixie advised her to. Mustn't give it *all*, they murmured, instructing her as older sisters or even a mother might. Hold back a little. Keep a little for yourself. What, she wondered miserably, would have been the point of *that*? Who was she keeping it for? What use was it to her? She turned her face to the wall as the nurse slipped a gloved hand inside her, feeling for the thing she didn't want to have. Nick's thing. The thing he'd left behind. The thing she didn't want, and wanted no reminder of. Ever.

She woke to the slow, rhythmic buzz of voices around her and the glare of light over her head. 'Come on now, child. That's it . . . open your eyes. All over. It's all over.' Coming into consciousness was like swimming to the surface of a thick, soupy pool. She floated for a second, treading water, then broke through. 'There we go . . . that's it. Careful, now . . . you may feel a little sick. You wan' vomit?'

Dani shook her head. There was a sharp pain in her right hand. Looking down, she could see the faint trail of blood where the anaesthetic needle had gone in. Someone had already removed it. There were two nurses in the room. They both bustled around her, helping her to her feet. She felt a little dizzy, the result of not having had anything to eat for almost a day. 'Here,' one of them said to her, handing her a tumbler full of Coke. 'Drink this; it'll settle your stomach. We gonna take you through to the ward for 'bout an hour or so. Doctor'll need to see you before he can send you home.'

'Is . . . what about the man . . . the one I came with?' Dani stammered.

'Told him to come back 'bout five . . . plenty of time. You need to rest up for a bit. You're fine . . . you just lost a lot of blood.' The nurse took the empty tumbler from her. 'Come on now, that's it. Easy, now. You're still bleeding a little. Careful . . . there we go. Just sit yourself down there. Doctor'll be in in a minute.'

'Miss Tsemo?' Dani's eyes flew open. She struggled upright. Standing in front of her in a spotless white coat with a stethoscope slung loosely around his neck was a young man – late twenties, early thirties, perhaps – with a worried look on his face. 'Miss Tsemo?' he repeated.

'Y . . . yes,' she stammered. The pain in her lower abdomen was increasing.

'Hi, I'm Dr Kingsley-Safo.' He held out a hand.

Dani took it. It was warm and wonderfully enveloping. He held it for a second, the fingers pressing strongly against hers. 'Hi,' she said warily.

'You're fine, nothing to worry about,' he said, noticing her frown. 'You bled rather a lot, which is why we've asked you to wait here for about an hour or so. We just want to make sure everything's as it should be before we release you to go home. How're you feeling?'

'It hurts a little,' Dani admitted, suddenly terrified she was going to cry. It had been a while since anyone had spoken to her in quite such a kindly tone. He was young but his professional manner was both calming and reassuring. She looked up at him. He was good-looking, too, she noticed. His skin was the same colour as hers, perhaps a little darker. His eyes behind the glasses he wore were dark brown, fringed with thick, curly lashes. His accent was English – decidedly so. 'Actually, it hurts quite a lot.'

'We'll give you something for that,' he said, making a quick note. 'And is there someone to take you home and stay with you?'

Dani hesitated. Eric would take her back to her grandmother's but she'd told no one of her condition, or the fact that she'd asked Eric for help. Not even Lorraine knew. 'Yes, a . . . a friend will take me home but I haven't told anyone. I . . . I live with my grandmother. She wouldn't . . . well, she wouldn't understand.'

'I see.' He regarded her gravely. 'Well, in that case, it might be better for you to stay overnight,' he said. 'I'm a little concerned about the risk of infection.'

'Stay here?'

'Yes, we do have a ward, a small one. Is someone covering the, er, cost of this?'

Dani nodded, swallowing nervously. Asking Eric to pay for the abortion was one thing; asking him to pay for an overnight stay was another altogether. 'Yes, but . . . I don't know if . . . if that would be OK. With him.'

'Is he the father?' Dr Kingsley-Safo asked gently.

Dani shook her head. This time, she couldn't hold them back. The tears started to fall. There was silence in the room for a few minutes. Dr Kingsley-Safo simply let her cry. She looked at the ground and the great welling up inside her chest would not subside. It was hard to get a handle on what was worse – the knowledge that Nick had disappeared, leaving her without so much as a goodbye, or the fact of what she'd just done . . . or what her grandmother would say; what the teachers at school would say if they ever found out. She was seventeen and already her world felt as though it had fallen apart.

'Here,' a voice broke through her sobs. A white, starched handkerchief was pushed gently into her hands. 'You'll be fine. In a month's time, you'll have forgotten all about this.'

She shook her head. 'N . . . no,' she sobbed. 'I w . . . won't. I c . . . can't.'

'You will.' His voice was gentle, like his hands. She felt as though her heart might break at the sound of it. She couldn't remember anyone ever talking to her that way. He was a complete stranger yet he'd shown her more kindness in five minutes than she'd received most of her life. He stood in front of her; she could just make out the white hem of his coat and the workaday khaki trousers underneath it.

He let her cry until the tears had dried up and then he led her outside. She was utterly spent. She heard him give instructions to the nurse to tell Eric she'd been admitted for the night – not to worry, he would take care of the expenses himself – and then she was led away. The nurses too were kind. They undressed her, bathed her and helped her into bed. The last thing she heard was his voice as he popped his head around the door. 'Goodnight, Dani. Sleep well. I'll check up on you in the morning.' The door closed behind him but before she even heard it click shut, she was asleep.

65

His name was Julian Kingsley-Safo. His great-grandfather was the renowned Ghanaian pan-African politician who'd received part of his education at Fourah Bay College in Freetown, almost a century earlier. The family were wealthy. Julian's mother was a well-known children's writer; his father, like him, was a doctor. He'd been educated in Britain and had decided to spend a year or so in Sierra Leone, following in the footsteps of his famous relative, giving, in his own words, 'something back'. Dani had never met anyone like him. He was half-English, like her, but unlike her, the English side of his family was completely known to him, and knowable. There was no mystery. His mother was from Cheltenham. He showed her exactly where it was. In his living room one Saturday afternoon, shortly afterwards, he pulled out a photo album. She sat next to him on the couch and pored over the photographs of a family that in another time and place might have been hers. There was his father, a stern expression on his face, so dark he was almost obliterated by the

318

camera's automatic exposure . . . his mother the polar opposite, fair-haired, pale, smiling. His brothers and sisters – six of them – *six?* – ranged around the garden table. And there, in the corner . . . he pointed out his grandmother, an Englishwoman of the sort Dani had only ever read about, in a tweed jacket and pearls, her legs tucked neatly underneath her swathed in a blanket that hid the wheelchair. It looked easy. Comfortable. A family at peace in a way families rarely are. She flicked through the pages, the sepia-tinted photographs producing a longing in her that she could scarcely suppress.

He seemed to want nothing from her other than a friendship and in this, too, she was perplexed. He was intrigued by her, but there was nothing predatory or sexual about his interest. He was content to observe her, always at a safe and comfortable distance and always with the utmost kindness. She supposed, wrongly, that it came from his medical training. He'd spent six months at the end of the civil war in a rural clinic in Bo, treating the devastated, mutilated and scarred survivors of a war that no one could bring themselves to describe. What he'd seen in Bo, he told her one afternoon, had so profoundly altered his view of the world and the lengths of both kindness and savagery to which people could go that he'd had to go back to London, temporarily, to return himself to his customary sanity.

'What d'you mean?' Dani asked, struggling to follow him.

He pursed his lips in a gesture that she'd come to recognise, a mixture of helplessness and acute observation. He shrugged. 'I'm an optimist. By nature, I mean. But the time I spent in Bo . . . what human beings are capable of . . . I saw stuff that I couldn't get out of my head for months afterwards. Terrible things. But it wasn't all bad. There were other things, too . . . generosity like you can't imagine. Complete strangers taking in orphans, raising them as their own, protecting them. Kids walking along a dusty road, their parents being shot in front of them and then villagers coming out to hide them, protect them, even at the expense of their own safety. It's a kind of madness, Dani . . . both ways. Good *and* bad.'

She wasn't sure she understood him but it didn't seem to matter. His experience of her country was so different from Nick's. There was none of the anger rumbling just below the surface, waiting for any old opportunity to erupt. Julian was one of the calmest people she'd ever encountered; just being around him calmed her too. He had a way of talking that was both a conversation with the person he was speaking to and an inner dialogue with himself. He could talk about anything. In some senses, she realised, after a month or so had passed, he was the closest thing she'd ever had to a friend – a *real* friend, in the deepest sense of the word. Here was someone she could say anything to. Anything at all. Any little nonsense that came into her head or, like now, with whom she could talk about the world and the things that had happened to her and to it. Big things, big ideas. Places she would like to visit, the sort of person she wanted to be, the sort of life she might one day like to have. Julian wasn't like Lorraine or Dixie or even Eric. Or the girls with whom she'd been at school. He treated her as an equal, no better or worse than he. He didn't ask her about Nick or the circumstances that had led to her being brought to the clinic by a British soldier. He wanted nothing to do with them, or the small, cloistered world of the expatriates in Sierra Leone. He was an African, but of a kind she'd never before encountered. Worldly, wealthy, immensely wise. She found herself emulating him without even thinking. She took greater care over her appearance on the days she went to his small house on the hill overlooking the Methodist College. With Nick she'd worn the sort of clothes that showed off her body and the smooth lines of her legs. With Julian, it was the opposite. He would compliment her on her choice of colour, or the cut and shape of her skirt . . . it was never about the amount of flesh she showed. He had taste. She looked around his neat, tidy flat and for the first time in her life was encouraged to explore what he called her 'innate style'. 'You've got style, Dani . . . bags of it. I don't know quite where you got it from, but it's there. The way you put things together. I don't know. I like it.' She *glowed*.

He was right about one thing. She did forget. By the time the
rains came in September, almost three months after she'd first
met him, her memory of the clinic and the abortion had faded
almost to the point where she had difficulty connecting herself
to the events of that terrible month. It seemed to her to have
happened to someone else. But she hadn't forgotten Nick. The
wound was buried deep inside her, so deep she sometimes had
difficulty getting at it herself. But it was at night, alone in her bed
at home with the sound of traffic rolling down the hill and the
human chatter on the street outside, that the wound came
floating back up to the surface and she would grimace, her face
contracting in pain. It was just another in a long line of abandon-
ments – her father, her mother, even her grandmother, whose
interest in her at times appeared to the teenager as being only
surface deep – but somehow, Nick's betrayal was worse. She'd
never known either her mother or her father. At best, the idea of
a family to her was a distant, abstract *thing* she sometimes
returned to when she felt especially lonely or sad. She'd *known*
Nick. Intimately. As he'd known her. Somehow his rejection of
her was worse. At least neither of her parents had ever got to
know her or understand the type of person she'd become. Nick
did. He knew she liked American pop bands like Blondie and
that she preferred strawberry jam to raspberry, on the odd occasion there was any in town. He *knew* her. And despite it – and
maybe even because of it – he'd thrown her away.

She told Julian none of this but with his doctor's divining
instinct for what often lies beneath, in time, small bits of it
began to escape. She hadn't known a friendship could be like
this. Through him, she began to meet different sorts of people.
Rochelle, the dreadlocked receptionist at the clinic where Julian
worked two days a week, was a revelation to her. Like him, she
was young, educated overseas and could have done anything,
gone anywhere but had chosen to come back here, to the country
of her parents' birth which she'd never known. In all likelihood

321

she wouldn't stay, at least not for ever. With a British passport she wasn't trapped like everyone else around her, but it was her choice to be here, for now. She was perhaps ten years older than Dani but the age difference didn't seem to matter. She lived with two other girls – a Danish girl called Mette and an American nurse called Barb – in a large, spacious flat overlooking the sea. It was decorated in a way Dani hadn't seen before, like Julian's place. African masks hung side by side with the prints she vaguely recognised from the years when there'd been an art teacher at her school. Colourful woven cloths from Ghana; low-slung furniture that Julian told her were copies of Scandinavian designs that had been popular in the country in the sixties and seventies. And books. They all seemed to have arrived in Sierra Leone with more books than anything else. Julian's flat was crammed with books of all kinds: novels, medical texts, crime thrillers, books so heavy she could barely lift them with one hand. She soon discovered her favourite thing to do on a Saturday afternoon when the heat outside was too intense to do anything other than stay indoors was to lie on his large, slip-covered couch and read. She began to read the sorts of books she would have read at school, or at home, if the war hadn't interrupted them and made books a resource more precious than life. Austen, Dickens, Thackeray . . . the classics of the English life she imagined her father belonged to. But he gave her other books, too. Harold Robbins, James Michener, Leon Uris. She devoured them, whole. He was delighted. 'Where on earth did they get you from?' he asked, squatting down beside her one afternoon, examining the cover of the novel she'd picked out. 'Dostoyevsky? At sixteen?'

'It's very good,' she said solemnly. 'It's about two brothers . . .'

He'd surely read it before but he good-naturedly allowed her to finish, nodding gravely as she talked. 'Where did they get you from?' he repeated.

'What d'you mean? From here. You've seen where my house is.'

He looked at her and there was a strange, faraway expression in his face. 'No, I know where you live. I know how you live, too. I just mean . . . you're different. From anyone I've ever met, especially here. You're an enigma, Danielle Tsemo, d'you realise that? An enigma.'

Dani could feel the heat rising in her face. 'No, I'm not,' she mumbled, embarrassed. It made her feel awkward to hear him describe her that way. The truth was, she just didn't know how to behave around him, or what to expect. The idea of a male friend who didn't seem to desire her the way other men did, or want anything from her other than her laughter and chatter, was completely baffling to her. There were times when she caught him looking at her in a way she thought she understood – and then there'd be nothing. No follow-up, no attempt, no pass. It unnerved her, and yet she'd come to value his attention more than she could put into words.

'Oh, but you are.' He grinned at her. 'I've never met anyone like you. You're a proper little survivor, you know. Smart as hell, too. You'll go far, Ms Tsemo. You'll go as far as you want to.'

Dani didn't know what to say. Pride and embarrassment burned simultaneously within her. She let the hand holding the book drop; it lay between them on the couch. Slowly, very gently, he picked up her hand and brought it to his own cheek. There was absolute silence in the room as he laid the back of her hand across his mouth in a gesture of such tenderness that the tears sprang to her eyes. Everything happened in silence, in complete trust. The couch was big enough for both of them. He lay his long, rangy body alongside hers and kissed her, on the cheek at first, but she turned her face towards his so that she received him as a woman, on the mouth. The first kiss was slow and long and deep and she felt herself dissolving in the exquisite sensation of tongue against tongue, his mouth nuzzling along the ridge of her lips, producing rills of feeling that washed over her again and again and again.

Later, much later, when the streets outside were plunged into darkness by yet another power cut and the familiar hum of generators competed with the chirrup of crickets, a particular feature of nights in the tropics, he got up from the couch and went to light a candle. A bird cried out somewhere, an owl perhaps. There was an answering volley of barks from the neighbourhood dogs, then it went quiet again. He brought it back, placing it carefully on the floor. The blinds in the living room were open; outside, beyond the line of the roof, the stars showed up a dazzling encrustation of quartz across the night sky. The smallest sounds rang out – women still selling newspaper twists of fried plantains and peanuts, beers plucked dripping and sweating from battered cool boxes, themselves swimming in melted ice and murky water. The light from the candle threw dancing patterns across the ceiling and across their bodies. Dani looked down the length of the couch, a faint sheen of sweat covering them both like a shiny film. She caught her lower lip between her teeth as she stared. His legs were intertwined with hers – impossible to tell where his began and hers left off. He was like her, and he was not. Different and yet the same. She experienced a powerful surge of some unidentifiable emotion – a sense of belonging? Acceptance? She reached out a tentative hand, wanting to express something of what she was feeling. Julian, more in tune with her than she could ever guess, stirred and caught it, holding it tightly against his chest, right there where people thought the heart was, the organ most capable of love.

66

ABBY
Ladyville, Belize, 2002

The children sang songs in the back of the car. Abby drove, her whole being concentrating fiercely on the road ahead. Behind her, two cars drove in slow, steady succession – Harriet and her three boys and, behind her, Nuñes and Shakespeare, Harriet's cook, the pick-up truck packed with the supplies they would need for the weekend. They were going to the beach, to Faber's Lagoon where the army kept a bungalow especially for family use. It was one of those hot, steamy days when the sun rose almost vertically in the sky and remained there, dangling oppressively, white-hot and sultry. The sea was to their left; as she drove, its blue vastness tilted at her this way and that as the car followed the long, slow bends in the Western Highway that led south. Time seemed to stand still in Belize. She'd made the same journey with her parents, twice, she thought, out on holiday from school in England. Everything looked exactly as it had done all those years ago. The sea to one side, all flat, shiny, shifting planes and the dark green bush on the other, thickening to jungle as it raced towards the hills. In Europe, if you'd been away for twenty, ten, even five years, everything would have changed – vast housing estates where there'd once been fields, new cars, new styles of clothing, new buildings . . . here, nothing changed. It was as it always had been and there was a measure of safety in that. Except something had changed.

The dirt track leading to the army bungalow threw up clouds of reddish dust as they thundered down, the only vehicles to have come this way in months, she thought to herself as she manoeuvred the car in between ruts and potholes the size of craters. Here and there around her a clearing appeared – neat little rows of corn, or maize, some cassava . . . there were farmers eking out a living in the dense cover that represented nothing so much as danger for her, for them. There was a little hill, just as she remembered it, then the dirt gave way to a coarse kind of sand and then suddenly, there it was, below and in front of them: a vast, dark blue lake that was so big it was the sea.

The children burst out of the cars like caged birds suddenly released; their excited chatter punctured the soft stillness, sending the real-life birds whose habitat was all around them shrieking into the air. For a moment all was noise and light. Sunlight bounced off the bonnets of the cars. The air, coming off the surface of the lake, was surprisingly cool. The lake was a climate all of its own. She stood with her sandalled feet sinking into the soft sand, instantly calmed. Ralph was overseas; she alone knew where. She couldn't tell anyone, least of all Harriet. Harriet's husband, Greg, was out in the jungle somewhere to the north of Belize City with the new platoon that would soon be shipped out to the barren, wasteland deserts of western Iraq. It wasn't in her nature to question things, certainly not where the army was concerned, but there were days when it suddenly came upon her without warning . . . an impatience for this business of war to be over so that their life together could begin. She had two small children; she'd spent most of her life trotting backwards and forwards between school and distant army camps and now, she realised, she'd consigned her girls to the same. They were young enough now to view the different places they lived in as adventures. Both of them had the same, slightly disinterested air in other children's games and excitement that she recognised from her own childhood – some stubborn, innate reluctance to get too involved in the world of those around them. After all, tomorrow they'd be gone. She turned away from the car in impatience. She didn't *want* this; she didn't *want* theirs to become her own life, all over again. And, more than anything, she thought to herself, catching sight of Nuñes and Shakespeare unloading the pick-up, she didn't want to do what her mother had done. A cold sweat broke out over her, despite the heat.

The two young men had swept and cleaned the bungalow in preparation for lunch. There was a small dead cockroach lying in one corner of the area that was the dining room. Abby kicked it away with her foot – Clara was the sort to be put off her food by the sight of it. The table was set: a clean white cloth, plastic plates, cups, a couple of wine glasses for her and Harriet. In a metal bucket in the centre of the table, a bottle of chilled white was already perspiring. They were grilling fish in the yard out-side. She always marvelled at how easily and with such little fuss men like Nuñes and Shakespeare could rustle up a four-course meal with almost nothing at hand. They had a little barbecue going, the portable generator had been hooked up and started . . . tomorrow there would be a full English breakfast . . . marvellous, really. She supposed it was something the army taught them – how to make something out of nothing.

She wandered over to the table and lifted the dripping bottle of wine out of the bucket. Harriet was already splayed out on one of the brightly striped deckchairs facing the lake. She poured two glasses of wine and carried them outside. The children were at the water's edge, absorbed in some game in the way only children can ever be, all claim of the outside world shoved impatiently away as they concentrated on whatever it was that held them.

'Cheers,' she said, settling herself down in the chair beside Harriet.

'Cheers.' Harriet lifted her glass appreciatively. 'Gorgeous out here, isn't it?' Abby nodded distractedly, her gaze taken up by the tilting, shimmering triangle of the lake as it spread itself towards infinity. Now and then the blackened, silhouetted shape of a pirogue slid silently past, becoming a shape that slipped in and out of the dazzle that was heat and light out there on the water. Harriet sat upright, drawing her knees up to her chin so that her big thighs almost covered her torso entirely. She was wearing an old-fashioned bathing suit that cut into her soft, jiggling flesh. She was the sort of girl Abby had always secretly been afraid of at school – large, jolly, frighteningly competent. The sort who did well, but not too well. The sort who had friends, but not too many; doubts, sometimes, perhaps, but few. 'Hot, though,' Harriet murmured, taking a large gulp of wine. She pulled a T-shirt over her head, tugging it down past her pendulous breasts. 'I burn so bloody easily, I'm afraid. Wish I was a bit more like you,' she said, casting an envious glance at Abby. 'You look bloody amazing, if you don't mind me saying.'

'Me?' Abby turned to look at her in surprise. It had been a while since anyone had complimented her on anything, let alone her body.

'Oh, come on . . . you must've noticed the way the soldiers ogle you.' Harriet laughed. 'I see them stop practice every time you walk across the pitch to the pool. You stop them dead in their tracks, I promise you.'

Abby blushed scarlet. 'They do not,' she mumbled.

'Oh, but they do. I say,' Harriet said suddenly, looking past Abby to something or someone beyond. 'He's awfully good-looking, you know.'

'Who?'

'Your batman. What's his name? Muñez?'

'Nuñes,' Abby replied automatically. She was careful not to turn her head.

'Mmm. Gorgeous, if you ask me. God, if I were a couple of years younger. And a couple of stone lighter . . .' She looked significantly at Abby and swallowed another mouthful of wine. 'Have you ever . . . ?'

'Have I ever what?'

'You know . . . done it with anyone else? Had a bit of a fling?'

'Of course not!' Abby was genuinely shocked. 'I . . . I love Ralph.'

'Of course you do. That's not what I was asking.' Harriet's eyes suddenly narrowed and Abby saw that she was really asking a question of herself. 'Christ, if I really were a couple of stone lighter, I'd be tempted.'

'By whom?'

'Oh, anyone, actually!' Harriet gave a short laugh. 'Greg and I . . . well, it's been a bit difficult. Ever since he came back from Bosnia.' She gave another laugh and drained the last of her wine. 'Post-traumatic stress, they call it. Impotence, in other words.'

Abby didn't know what to say. Both women looked out across the water to where a lone fisherman moved his boat close to the bank, tilting dangerously under his load. The sun beat down on their words and the awkwardness they had generated in Abby. 'I'm sorry,' she said presently, unable to think of anything else.

'Oh, don't be. I just have to do what thousands of other army wives do.'

'What's that?' Abby asked, although she knew the answer before it was said.

'Find something else. Some*one* else. Preferably someone like Nuñes.' This last was said with an embarrassed shrug. 'Someone who won't rock the boat. No good having an affair with one of the other officers. Or a squaddie, come to that. No, a good, old-fashioned fuck from time to time would sort me out.'

Abby winced at the crudity of her words. 'Would . . . would it be enough?' she asked, almost timidly.

Harriet grinned. 'Better than nothing. D'you know how long it's been?'

Abby shook her head. 'You don't have to tell me,' she said, wondering how to ward off the sudden onslaught of confidences.

Harriet leaned back and reached for her packet of cigarettes. 'Got to tell *some*one,' she said good-naturedly. 'And you're probably more discreet than most.'

'How d'you know?' Abby was curious, in spite of herself.

'Oh, I can tell.' Harriet drew the blue smoke into her lungs with a sigh of satisfaction. 'You're the sort who sees all sorts of things, but you keep them to yourself. It's an admirable trait, you know. Especially for a CO's wife. Ralph picked right.'

'You make it sound as if I were a vegetable at some country fair.' Abby laughed suddenly. 'Oh, I'll have that one, please. It wasn't like that at all.'

'Well, however it was, you both seem happy. Can't say that about many of these army marriages. Disasters, most of them. Not surprising, either.'

Abby was silent again. She knew just how close to the truth Harriet was, on both counts. She and Ralph were happy together. She heard a sound behind them. Nuñes was standing there, waiting patiently. She tried to suppress the sudden irritation she felt whenever he came upon her without warning, but failed. 'What is it?' she snapped.

'Lunch, sir. Lunch is ready.'

Harriet stubbed out her cigarette. 'Fetch the children, will you?' she said imperiously.

'Yes, sir.' If he noted the tone in her voice, he made no sign but turned and walked down to the water's edge with the easy, graceful gait that held their joint gaze. Abby was the first to tear her eyes away. She got up impatiently, unnerved by the conversation and by the sneaking suspicion that Harriet was about to put into practice something she'd only subliminally dared dream about. Was she jealous? She couldn't bring herself to answer.

She woke with a start in the middle of the night. Something – a sound, a movement – had crossed the boundary between dream and waking and she sat up in bed, half in fright. The girls were asleep on a mattress on the floor. Clara had her arm hooked possessively around one of the Maclean boys – she couldn't tell in the dark which one. She was alone in the house; the thought flooded through her, then she relaxed. No, she wasn't alone. Harriet was asleep with her other children next door. Outside, on the veranda, two men slept. They were perfectly safe. She listened intently; there was nothing beyond the endless muffled yawn of the lake as it lapped against the shores. No, there it was again. A whimper, something . . . someone . . . in pain. She clutched the sheet to her and fumbled for the little torch that she kept beside her bed. She switched it on carefully, swept it around the room. *All* the children were in there with her, lying in flung-out positions on the ground, limbs and arms entangled. She slid her legs out of bed and crept towards the door, the torch firmly in her hand. She opened the bedroom door. The living room was empty but the kitchen door at the far end of the room was half ajar. Someone – Nuñes or Shakespeare – had left a candle burning inside it. She frowned in annoyance. What would happen if the place caught fire? she thought to herself crossly. What then?

She made her way carefully across the living room floor and pushed open the kitchen door. She stopped dead in her tracks. They both had their backs to her; Harriet was bent over the kitchen table. The very same table on which they'd prepared salads together that evening, chatting over a bottle of wine as

Nuñes and Shakespeare grilled steaks and pork chops outside and she and Harriet sliced cucumbers and thin, transparent slivers of onion. He – Nuñes – was entering her from behind. His muscles gleamed wetly in the candlelight, his body thrusting in an almost obscene parody of lust into the shaking, quivering mound of spread thighs and arms and breasts that was Harriet. The stifled cries that had woken Abby up came from her. He had a hand buried in the sweaty, tangled mass of her dark curly hair, tugging on it as he jerked and thrashed inside her. Her head was turned to one side; her pink tongue was sticking out between parted lips, almost like a dog. Abby swallowed and closed her eyes. She didn't want to see any more. She backed away as quietly and carefully as she could. Only when she was in the middle of the living room did she turn around and walk quickly back to bed.

She slept late; when she woke, the room was hot and the children were gone. She pulled back the curtains and a dead moth flopped to the ground. The lake was all dazzling surfaces, shifting this way and that in response to some unseen wind. The children were already at the water's edge; Shakespeare was with them. She watched as he allowed them to clamber all over him, half-burying his dark limbs in the sand. She pushed the damp hair away from her forehead and went into the bathroom to shower. Afterwards she walked into the living room, not sure what to expect. But Harriet was sitting on the veranda alone, smoking calmly. Nuñes was nowhere to be seen.

'Morning,' Harriet said brightly, as Abby appeared. 'Sleep well?'

Abby nodded, not quite trusting herself to speak. Harriet smiled, a private, secretive smile that forced Abby to look away. Other people's happiness, like sorrow, is an embarrassment to watch. She continued to look out towards the shore and the water, the heat already coming off the blurry shine of the lake in waves. She had a moment of violent dismay, her whole being shrinking from the memory of what she'd seen in the kitchen.

But as Harriet stubbed out her cigarette and rose languidly from the chair, asking if she fancied a coffee or some toast, she began to wonder if she'd dreamed it. Not Harriet, surely not? And not Nuñes. No, not him.

67

SAM
London, England, 2002

Michael Chilters had his shirt sleeves rolled up. He had got up from his chair and was leaning on his desk, his white, fleshy forearms cutting across her line of vision to the windows and the leafy green trees that fringed the park beyond. His arms were freckled, she noticed, a blotchy combination of mottled pink and white skin dotted randomly with what looked like liver spots of darker tan and brown. His fingers were thick, the nails short and clean, although there was one ragged nail . . . the little finger. She'd noticed every once in a while that he stuck it in his mouth, chewing absently. She swallowed down on the sudden surge of revulsion sweeping through her. She *loathed* Michael Chilters. Absolutely loathed him. Ever since the incident in her office where he'd made it abundantly clear that not only did she owe him for her promotion, he fully intended at some point to collect on it. Collection, moreover, would be on *his* terms, in *his* time, at *his* leisure, not hers. In the meantime, he was content to toy with her. Nothing overt, nothing she could put a finger or a hand on and lay claim. It was a game at which he clearly excelled, and was probably experienced in. Now that she'd understood exactly what he was up to, it made things even worse.

'I think,' he was saying pompously, 'that you really ought to contact the dealer on his behalf. Sounds suspiciously like theft to me.'

'Er, that's the conclusion I came to,' Sam pointed out, as respectfully as she could manage. It was another of his tricks. He was fond of reading her reports, then claiming ownership of the legal arguments she presented.

He ignored her completely. 'If I were you,' he began again, his voice rising peremptorily.

'You're not me.' The words slipped out before Sam could stop herself. It was the first time she'd stood up to him and it surprised them both. He lifted his head, his eyes narrowing as he looked at her. She ought to look down, look away. But she didn't. Something inside her had finally snapped. She stared him down. She'd had enough.

'My, my,' he murmured, an unmistakable sneer in his voice and eyes. 'We're a little touchy this morning, I see. Time of the month, perhaps?'

Sam said nothing. She collected her notebook and files that were spread out on his desk in front of her and walked out of his office. She ignored his call of 'Excuse me, just where d'you think you're going?' and walked down the corridor to her own office. She opened the door and locked it firmly behind her. Her heart was hammering inside her chest but her mind was clear. She'd had enough. She was no fool. There was no evidence or clear proof that he'd done anything untoward. There'd been no witnesses to any of his more aggressive remarks or approaches. In public and in the presence of her other colleagues, all was as it should be. She was a junior lawyer, just starting out in her career. He was a member of the board, a senior partner, an apparently well-established and well-respected member of the profession. She couldn't hope to take him on and win. But she couldn't stay on, either. Today's little exchange, as mild and short-lived as it had been, had clearly drawn the battle lines between them and if there was anything she understood about Michael Chilters in the short time she'd worked for him, it was that, from now on, he would make her life hell.

The tears were in her throat as she packed up her bags and her books. Walking out of her job would be the riskiest, most foolhardy thing she'd ever done – and Sam Maitland wasn't in the habit of making rash moves. But something inside her had finally given way. She'd sat back and watched too many people take everything they could from her, including her self-respect – the pattern had started with Kate, back in school; it had followed with Giancarlo, on holiday in Greece and now, in her professional life, with Michael Chilters. Like the others, he'd backed her into a corner, confident she would never have the courage to lash out. Walking away was hardly lashing out, but she was a pragmatist, above all else. She would walk out and she would find another job; she *had* to. For now, she wanted nothing more to do with Holman Kenton and the whole miserably corrupt world they dealt in. She'd had enough.

She switched off her computer, picked up her bag and her briefcase and walked out. She walked down the corridor to the lifts, her heart lifting with every step. She hadn't realised the extent of the stress she'd been under. As she descended to the ground floor, she felt as though an enormous weight had been taken from her. She would phone Martin and Cassie later and do her best to explain. For now, it was enough to be free – and to *feel* it, too, at long last.

68

MEAGHAN
Paderborn, Germany, 2002

Like many women, she supposed, her initial reaction was to doubt her own intuition. No, not Tom. He'd never so much as shown a passing interest in anyone. He was one of those men for whom other women – in the sense of them being potentially 'other' to Meaghan – just didn't exist. She'd known that about him right from the start. It was as if, for him, the possibility simply wasn't there. He loved her – always had, always would. But now there was doubt. She had no one to share her misgivings with. She couldn't imagine talking to any one of the other army wives with whom she'd – albeit reluctantly – struck up an acquaintance over the long months of his absence. Delia, Corinne, Susannah . . . she listed them, one by one, and, one by one, she dismissed the idea. What would she say? *Oh, by the way, I think my husband's having an affair?* Except she'd no proof it was an affair. So what was it? *He's slept with someone else.* In all likelihood they'd laugh at her. *Of course he is. Of course he has.* She knew the statistics. One in two, or one in three . . . she couldn't quite remember. What difference did it make? She was now a statistic, just as their marriage was. What was the divorce rate for the army? *Stop it,* she cautioned herself sternly, talking to herself in the mirror. Just stop. It might be nothing. Just the once. Some random girl he'd met somewhere in Kosovo. One of those meaningless encounters . . . she looked at her reflection. The problem was, once she'd admitted the thought, she couldn't get rid of it. She found herself staring at him for signs – what would those be? She listened to him talk, trying to divine in his conversation the slightest, tiniest slip that would give her a clue as to who it might have been, when, how often . . . she was beginning to drive herself crazy.

He would be home for a month and a half. Enough time to rest, catch up on the paperwork that his tour had generated . . . and gear up for the next one. He broke the news to Meaghan on their last weekend. They were eating dinner at Tortellini d'Oro, the little Italian restaurant across the bridge, in the older part of Paderborn. Meaghan's fork was halfway to her mouth when she heard him say, 'I'll be going back, Meg.'

'Back?' She lowered her fork. 'Back where?'

'Back to Kosovo.'

'No.'

'Meg . . . be reasonable.'

'Reasonable? You've been gone for almost the whole year, Tom,' Meaghan said, aware that a lump the size of an egg had suddenly formed in her throat. That was the problem these days – she was always close to tears.

'Hardly,' Tom said drily, attacking his linguine. 'A few months. The job's not done, love.'

'But . . . what about me?' Meaghan said, by now properly tearful. 'What am I supposed to do?'

Tom put down his fork and sighed. 'Meg . . . I'm in the army, love. This is what I do. You knew that before we got married.'

'I didn't know it was going to be like this,' she said, trying to staunch the flow of tears with her napkin. She was aware of a few of the other diners turning their heads to look at them. She didn't care. Let them stare.

'You'll be fine. You are fine. Look at you . . . you've done up the house, you've made a few friends—'

'Friends? You call those numbskulls *friends*?' she retorted angrily. 'They're not friends. They're just people I've got to put up with because there aren't any others.'

'Look—'

'No, *you* look, Tom. Take a good look around you. How many bloody marriages make it through this . . . this shit?' She was properly angry now and the words just kept tumbling out. 'You're gone half the bloody year, I'm stuck here with nothing to do and no one to talk to. You're out there God-knows-where, fucking everything that moves and I—' She stopped suddenly. Tom's face was white.

'You're what?' he asked icily.

'I'm pregnant.' The words dropped like stones into the widening pool of silence between them. She swallowed, her anger and hurt suddenly vanishing before her.

PART SIX

69

DANI
Cheltenham, England, 2008

It was cold; her breath scrolled out before her in a long, misty tongue, snatching up what few words she could muster, dissolving in the weak winter light. Less than eight hours after leaving Freetown in the middle of December, the hottest month of the year, she was deep in the English countryside, now covered in snow. She stood by the graveside, too stunned to cry. She stood there, flanked on both sides by his family and people she'd never met, struggling to take it in. His mother was on her right, holding her fast in case she fell. To her left were his siblings – all five of them. She'd heard all about them in the course of the six years they'd been together. Bella, Clementine, Veronica, Joseph and Daryl. They had other names, Ghanaian names, he told her. Afua, Abena, Ama, Kwesi and Kweku. Customary names that were handed out according to the day of the week on which they were born. He was Yaw. Thursday's child. Julian Yaw Kingsley-Safo. Born on Thursday, died on the same. Hit by a stray bullet as he drove home from the clinic – the very same clinic in which they'd met. No one knew how or why. It had come in through the open passenger window and hit the soft, pulsating artery that sometimes stood out when he played soccer in the dusty park at the bottom of the hill, or when he made love to her. He'd come to Sierra Leone intending to work for a few months, perhaps a year. He'd met a girl, Danielle Tsemo, and stayed. And then he died. Killed on the road, his body tumbling from the car when a passer-by, noticing that something was wrong, had opened the door. By the time they called her and she'd rushed down the hill, her own blood thundering in her veins and heart, he was dead, his life blood ebbing away into the gutter. Those were the facts.

'Dani . . . it's over. Come, now.' His mother held her arm and led her carefully away from the grave. He was buried beside his English grandmother in the grounds of the family home just outside Cheltenham. She'd never been inside a house like that before. Of pale stone, with lintels and sills worn smooth as soap, tall, imposing columns with cherubs and angels adorning the ceilings and sides and a garden that seemed to stretch for ever, she'd fallen silent as soon as she saw it, awed by its aged, handsome presence. *This* was Julian's home? She'd walked gingerly up the steps to the huge front door, keeping her eyes firmly on the ground. His mother had been waiting for her in the hallway, her eyes and voice dimmed with grief. They could not have been kinder – there was a generosity amongst them that simply enveloped her and took her in, no questions asked. It seemed Julian had told them more about her than she guessed. She was humbled by their regard.

They were a formidable family. It didn't seem to matter to them that she and Julian had never married properly. They'd announced their engagement in Freetown in the traditional, local way. 'Knocking', was what her people called it. Her grandmother and aunts had come to the house, beaming with pride and relief. *What a nice man! And a doctor, to boot. Fancy that. Well done, Dani. Well done!* After the small ceremony – more like a drinks party, really – they'd made plans to do it 'properly', in England, with all his family present. Except, of course, his father. His father had died long before Julian came out to West Africa. It was a great pity; he was sure Dani would have liked him, and vice versa. They would go to England, perhaps even stay. Julian was full of plans for her. He'd encouraged her to apply for a university course. History or politics – yes, she nodded gravely. She thought she'd like that. She hadn't given up on her dream of becoming a lawyer and, just like Nick –

340

although for different reasons – he hadn't laughed at her. He'd
dug out old prospectuses and had gone online, looking for ways
to encourage her, make it possible. The University of Sussex was
a good place, he'd told her, or the LSE. The London School
of Economics. She'd looked over the printouts he brought home
with awe. That might be *her* one day? Walking onto a platform
with a funny hat on her head to shake the hand of a man in a
long, Cinderella-like gown? He smiled at her doubts, encouraged her to dream.

And now he was dead. Just like her dreams.

70

'I know you weren't *legally* married,' his mother said to her, her
grieving voice tinged with earnestness, which was simply her
way of coping, Dani saw immediately. 'And unfortunately he
didn't leave a will. Who does, at that age? He – we – just didn't
think . . . no one does. But we'd like you to have something,
Dani. At the very least.'

Dani looked at her in genuine distress. 'No . . . no. I don't
want . . . I don't need anything.'

'Of course you must have *something*. We'll set up a trust fund.
You were my son's partner. There's no question of leaving you
out.'

Dani shook her head emphatically. 'Please, Mrs Kingsley-
Safo. I don't need anything. You've been kind enough . . .
getting me a visa and the plane ticket and everything. I
didn't . . . I wasn't with Julian for his money,' she stammered,
her whole body burning with embarrassment. Was that what
they all thought?

'Of course you weren't,' Jessie Kingsley-Safo said firmly. 'Of
course not. But the fact of the matter is, he would have inherited
a considerable sum from us – from my side of the family at least.
It's only fair that you should have some of it.'

'No. No. I don't want anything.' Dani shook her head

stubbornly. 'I couldn't. I just couldn't. You've done more than enough.' She got up from the breakfast table, afraid she would burst into tears.

Jessie Kingsley-Safo made no move to stop her, but watched her go, her hand going thoughtfully to the pendant she wore around her neck. She twisted the looped gold chain around and around, seemingly lost in thought.

At dinner that evening, the matter was decided. The family had conferred and in Dani's absence had come up with a plan. There would be a trust fund, just as his mother had said. For now the money would be held in an account in London; there would be three signatories – Dani, Jessie and Julian's eldest sister, Bella, who shared her brother's passion for giving something back. There was no immediate hurry to decide what to do with the money. Dani didn't have to know the details if she chose not to. But, at some point in the future, when she was ready, she was free to approach them again to talk about how best to honour Julian's memory. It was what he would have wanted, of that they were sure. She listened to them, tears streaming down her face. This was a different kind of family all right. One in which decency, commitment and responsibility reigned supreme. Julian had come from such a place; it was up to her now to make sure she too belonged there.

She flew back to Sierra Leone in the first week of January, still numb with sorrow, but humbled by her first experience of being overseas.

Lunghi Airport was the usual mass of thronging, chaotic crowds, impatiently pushing past the security cordon to get to the first clutch of passengers trooping wearily across the tarmac. After the quiet of the English countryside, the noise and din was a shock, just like the blast of heat that hit them as soon as the doors were open. But, in a sense, she was also relieved to be back. In some ways, her trip overseas had only served to remind her just how much she actually belonged in Sierra Leone. It wasn't

342

surprising – she didn't know anywhere else, had never had the opportunity to call anywhere other than Freetown 'home'. As she retrieved her small, battered second-hand suitcase and pushed past the thronging crowd, none of whom were there for her, the realisation not just of Julian's death but of a way of life that might have gone with it hit her suddenly. She was alone. Properly, utterly alone. She would go back to his flat – his mother had insisted on paying out the rent for the remainder of the year – but the question of what to do with the rest of her life had surfaced again with an urgency she couldn't have predicted.

Grief, she soon found out, is a state to be avoided. People whom she'd assumed were *her* friends as much as they'd been Julian's, vanished. Where was Mette? Or Douglas? Or Famke, the Dutch aid worker who'd been so taken by the two of them . . . or Faisal or Hassan, the two Anglo-Lebanese young men who'd been at the same school in England as Julian and who'd spent weekend after weekend on the balcony outside the living room, smoking, talking, laughing, arguing. Suddenly they were no longer there. When she bumped into them on occasion at the supermarket or in the street, they stopped, enquired how she was but their eyes slid past her in a mixture of embarrassment and guilt that she found hard to take. What were they afraid of? she wondered to herself alone in the big double bed that she and Julian had shared. His things were still in the flat – in the large, ungainly wardrobe that stood in one corner of the room, his clothes still hung, neatly pressed, lined up . . . as if waiting for him to open the door one day and select a jacket or a shirt. His books, papers, even his laptop . . . all around her was the evidence of a life they'd shared and would never share again. She ought to get rid of the stuff. Send it to his mother, to charity . . . anywhere but here. But she couldn't. Weeks ticked by; she did very little. She went to the market in the mornings but bought less and less. She'd lost her appetite, and not just for food. She stopped by her grandmother's occasionally but soon tired of hearing the same questions. When you gonna move on, child?

When you comin' back home? *This isn't my home*, she wanted to scream, looking around at the peeling, chipped paint, the chairs in their plastic covers and the leaking rooms full of children whom she didn't recognise. *My life is somewhere else*. But where? She returned to the empty flat, each time slightly more empty and bewildered than when she'd left. Something would have to change, and soon. But what?

It was Lorraine, of all people, who provided the shove. They passed each other on Macaulay Street, about six weeks after her return. It was Dani's turn to look away, embarrassed. It had been over a year since she'd last seen Lorraine and the memory of it made her cheeks burn. In a sense, it had been a long time coming. Since moving in with Julian and finding a whole new circle of friends, she'd dropped Lorraine and Dixie, despite her guilty protestations to the contrary whenever they met. The truth was that they'd embarrassed her; in front of Julian and his erudite, urbane crowd, Dixie and Lorraine were out of place, and they knew it. After the first few visits to the flat where they sat awkwardly perched at the edge of their seats, she'd stopped inviting them. She no longer went down to the beach or to the bars. There'd been some fuss, a couple of years back, when Eric's wife showed up unexpectedly one day from Birmingham or Manchester, or wherever it was that he had a home, and children . . . she'd overheard the story from a couple of the vendors outside her grandmother's house. She'd gone home to Julian that night with a shameful sense of glee. It wouldn't happen to her. She'd moved on in the world; she'd moved up. Eric and Lorraine and Dixie had been side tracks to her life, not the main road. Julian, and all that he'd offered, was it.

'Dani?' A voice rang out from amidst the small crowd walking along the pavement.

Dani stopped. Standing in front of her, holding a black plastic bag full of oranges, was Lorraine. 'Lorraine?' Her voice was barely a whisper.

'Girl . . . how de body now?' Lorraine's smile was generous. 'Heard 'bout your man. I sorry, girl. I sorry.'

Dani's eyes flooded immediately with hot, heavy tears. It had been weeks since she'd cried, she realised, standing there in the middle of the road, her shoulders shaking, ignoring the curious glances of passers-by. She opened her mouth to say something but the words kept getting stuck. 'I . . . I'm sor . . . sorry,' she mumbled, the salty tears streaming into her open mouth. 'N . . . no, it's me . . . I'm . . . I'm the—'

'Tcha, don' you worry 'bout dat, girl,' Lorraine said, quickly tucking an arm into Dani's. 'How de body? You keepin' you head up?'

Dani shook her head slowly. 'I . . .' She started to say something but was unable to finish.

'Here.' Lorraine took hold of her arm. 'Come wit' me, now. You not lookin' so good, girl. When last you eat something?'

Dani couldn't answer. She allowed Lorraine to take her by the arm and lead her back down the road towards the flat. Lorraine said very little, just murmured encouraging words as they crossed the street and walked up the short flight of stairs. She fished for the key in Dani's bag and opened the door. When she saw the state of the flat, she crossed herself quickly and led Dani into the kitchen. 'Jus' you sit down here, girl. I'll bring you some water. You can't be livin' like this, girl. It ain't right. You jus' sit tight. I'm coming now, now.' She placed a glass of cold water from the fridge in front of her, touched her lightly on the shoulder and left. Dani was unable to move. She sat at the small kitchen table, the glass slowly condensing in front of her into a small puddle. She heard the front door open and close but still she was unable to move.

Half an hour later, she was still sitting there when the door opened again. Behind Lorraine was Dixie. Hot tears of shame smarted behind her eyes but Dixie, like Lorraine, had no time for them. She hugged Dani briefly, ignoring the year or more that had slipped between them, and turned to Lorraine. 'Come on,' she said, jerking her head towards the sitting room. 'Let's get this done. No, don' you move, girl. Leave everythin' to us.'

It took them just over two hours to clear the flat of every scrap that had been Julian's. They left no corner untouched. Dani remained where she was as they moved briskly and efficiently around her. When it was done, his belongings were neatly packed into two gigantic candy-striped bags – the sort the market women used to lug second-hand clothes up the hill from the port – and the place was polished and gleaming. The fans were going; plates that had been left for weeks were washed and shining; the stove and sink sparkled . . . the very air inside the flat had been changed. Dani could hear them sweeping up the last of the dust and dirt in the corridor. She got up from her chair and walked through.

'Attach herself to some man, that's de problem,' Dixie was saying to Lorraine as she bent down to brush the dust off the broom. 'Dat's what she always done. Attach herself to some man. Poor Dani.'

Dani stopped. Shame flooded through her. They were right. She'd attached herself, first to Nick, then to Julian . . . and look where it had got her. She'd been so proud of herself – living up there on the crest of the hill with Julian, reading his books, chatting to his friends, spending his money . . . looking down on everyone, including the two women who'd pulled her back from the brink only that same afternoon. How dare she look down on them? How dare she even *think* she was better than anyone else? If there was one thing she ought to have learned from Julian, it was humility. He was the most humble and yet most intelligent person she'd ever met . . . yes, he was gone and yes, it was a tragedy, not just for her, but for all his family, his colleagues and his friends. And what had she done in the weeks since his death? She'd sat around moping, unable to cope. She turned away from the conversation as quietly as she could and walked back into the now-sparkling clean kitchen. She had somewhere to live, free of charge, at least for now. She had the beginnings of a pretty decent education, which was a lot more than either Dixie or Lorraine had. She had the support of Julian's family back in England, never mind that she'd met them only once. There was enough of him in each of them to make her understand that their offer of help was genuine. She had her grandmother to fall back on, if everything else failed. And she had ambition, or at least she'd *had* it. All the pieces were there. It was up to her now to put the rest of her life in motion.

71

ABBY
Hereford, England/Celle, Germany, 2008

'She'll be fine.' Ralph patted her arm awkwardly as they drove away from the school. 'She'll settle in like lightning. You'll see. You did, didn't you, darling?'

Abby couldn't bring herself to speak. She turned her head carefully towards the scenery, not trusting her voice. Of course Clara would be fine. She was that sort of girl. She'd always known that about her, always. But then again, she'd had to be. She shivered suddenly. It was September and the weather was still lovely and warm, yet she was cold. What was that expression? she wondered to herself. *My blood runs cold.* Yes, that certainly explained the shiver. She pulled a scarf from her handbag and wound it carefully around her neck. They'd been in England for almost a week. In a few days' time, she would return to Celle with Sadie and Ralph would be gone, this time on a month-long training exercise in Kenya. 'When do you leave again?' she murmured, more as a distraction to herself and the dangerously wayward direction of her own thoughts than a genuine desire to know. No, of course she wanted to know, she chided herself.

'Sunday. I'll fly back to Celle ahead of you and then ship out with the rest of the battalion. We've got three glorious days, darling. All to ourselves. What would you like to do?'

She didn't answer for a moment. Sadie was with her parents; after all the fuss surrounding her elder sister's departure for boarding school, Abby's mother had stepped in firmly. 'That's what we did with each of you,' she said, in that tone of voice that brooked no argument. 'Works wonders. She needs a little bit of spoiling, poor little thing.' Abby gave in gratefully. The truth was, she was overwhelmed – not by the fact of her daughter going off to boarding school, but by guilt. She forced herself to concentrate. As a child she'd harboured the sneaking suspicion that her father could sometimes read her mind. Now, sitting next to her husband, the same childish fear arose. Ridiculous. And what, she wondered to herself briefly before answering, would have happened then? What if Ralph could read her mind? 'How about the seaside?' she said carefully, the idea only just occurring to her. Long walks along the cliffs, the endless tug and sway of the sea, blustering winds and sand beneath her feet – she was suddenly gripped with a longing for the seaside holidays of her childhood. 'The weather's glorious. We could go to Ferring. It's near Worthing . . . not so far. We used to go there when I was young.'

'Good idea. Where shall we stay?'

'Oh, let's just see when we get there, shall we? It's not that far . . . from here.'

'What? Now? You mean, go right now?' Ralph took his eyes away from the road briefly to look at her.

A kind of urgent giddiness took hold of her. 'Why not?' she said gaily. 'Why not?'

'Well, we haven't really planned it . . .' Ralph's voice was hesitant.

'Oh, for goodness' sake! Not everything in life has to be planned, Ralph,' Abby said, more tetchily than she intended. He turned his gaze back to the road. She could see from the sudden hunching of his shoulders that he was hurt. 'Sorry, darling,' she murmured. 'I'm just a little . . . upset.'

'I know. No, you're right. Why don't we just go now . . . there's nothing stopping us, is there?' He glanced at her again, as if for confirmation. Abby didn't know whether to laugh or cry. He was the CO of the Royal Anglian battalion. He'd been everywhere – Kosovo, Bosnia, Afghanistan, Iraq . . . and now here he was, more or less asking her permission to turn off the M4 to London and head for Brighton and the beach instead.

'Nothing at all,' she said soothingly. 'And it's not even lunchtime. We'll be there before tea . . . it'll be easy to find a place, you'll see. I'm trying to remember where we stayed with my parents . . . don't suppose it'll still be there, though.'

'You never know. Some places don't change much,' Ralph commented mildly, his good humour restored.

No, Abby thought to herself, turning to look out of the window again. Some places don't change much. But other places change us.

The tiny hotel she half-remembered wasn't there any more, but others had sprung up in its place, including a charming little guesthouse facing the sea with an inside courtyard and one free room. Abby looked around her in scarcely contained delight. The owner, a recently divorced, middle-aged woman from Wimbledon, of all places, bustled around them with ease and efficiency. 'I'll just pop an extra duvet on top of the bed,' she said, her eyes sweeping over the room to make sure everything was just so. 'It's warm now, but there's a strong wind that sometimes blows in off the sea. If you don't need it, just toss it aside.'

'Thank you,' Abby murmured, already taken by the place with its charming blue-and-white décor and evidence of its owner's good taste. Linen sheets, thick, beautifully embroidered counterpanes, fresh flowers everywhere you looked . . . it was charming. Just what she needed. For almost the first time in a year, she was overcome with a warm tenderness towards Ralph. She was able, quite naturally, to go up to him when the owner had left the room and put her arms round him, just as she used to. If he was surprised, he didn't show it. They stood in the middle of the room for a few minutes, not speaking. Just as it used to be.

'Everything all right?' Ralph asked, his arm tightening around her waist. She could feel his lips against her hair.

She nodded but couldn't speak. The carefully held mask of composure was firmly upon her face. She swallowed almost imperceptibly, as if swallowing down on her words. How many times had it been on the tip of her tongue to blurt it out? 'Everything's fine,' she whispered eventually, after the wave of guilt had passed.

'Good. That's what we like to hear.' Ralph used an old phrase that had once been something of a joke between them, but there was something in his voice that gave her to understand he knew more than he was letting on, or was prepared to say.

The wet, wrinkled sands stretched as far as the eye could see. Late afternoon sunlight glinted off the beach, catching the eye here and there as the water advanced and retreated, a long, drawn-out sigh. Somewhere up ahead a dog bounded along, stopping every now and then to pick up and then race after a stick that its owner had flung. The wind whipped at their faces; Abby had forgotten to bring along a comb or a band and the strands of blonde scored her vision as she looked out to sea. They walked along in comfortable silence, neither feeling the need to break it just yet. The sun was a yellow orb dangling just above the horizon. She loved its slow, ponderous descent during those last days of summer when the shadows on the ground were long and wavering and night seemed to take for ever to come. She thought of Clara, and for a moment a guilty flash rippled through her for having forgotten her in the time it had taken them to clamber down the slope and gain the smooth, damp sands. *Clara's fine*, she mouthed to herself. *Clara's fine. It's me who's in trouble.*

'Ralph.' She stopped suddenly. The need to unburden herself came over her suddenly, like a blast of heat.

'What is it?' He stopped, turned and looked at her, a frown between his eyebrows.

'I . . . Ralph, there's something I have to tell you.' She was blushing from head to toe; she could feel the competing tugs of guilt and relief pulling at her as she spoke. She couldn't stop herself, even if she'd wanted to. 'It's about . . . when we went back to Belize. I should have told you, I know . . . but I . . . I just couldn't . . . I couldn't bring myself to . . . I . . .'

'I know, Abby.' Ralph's voice was quiet. 'I know all about it. I've known almost since it started.'

A cold horror gripped her. She stood absolutely still. It was fear coursing through her now, not guilt or relief. He knew? He knew and he'd said *nothing*? 'Wh . . . what d'you mean?' she stammered. 'Who told you?'

Ralph moved away so that his profile was turned towards her. She stared up at him. It took him a while to answer. Her heart was thudding uncontrollably by the time he finally opened his mouth. 'I didn't need anyone to tell me, Abby. It was written all over your face. I *know* you, Abby. Better than you think.'

There was a lump in her throat that constricted her speech. She could feel the blood in her veins cooling again, turning icy. She put up a hand to her face, which was already wet. Suddenly a hundred and one disparate images began to crowd her brain – half remembered, half understood, images that did not connect: Ralph's mouth opening to say something that she'd already forgotten . . . his face, his arms, his warm, lovely body . . . the things she'd so taken for granted that she'd almost thrown them away. She choked back a sob and started to walk ahead, very fast, wanting only to rid herself of the disgust that had come over her at the thought of where she'd been and what she'd done – and who she'd done it with. Ralph *knew*. And he'd said nothing; he'd simply tried to ride it out. *I know you, Abby. Better than you think*. It was absolutely true. She felt the vibrations in the sand before his arm reached out and grabbed hers, pulling her around.

'Don't,' he said, forcing her to a stop. He looked down at her. His hand came up, between them, and he brushed the strands of hair out of her face. 'I know it hasn't been easy, Abby. I'm gone most of the time . . . I know you're all on your own with the girls . . . don't think I don't know how hard it is for you.'

'But . . .' She started to speak but he held up his hand.

'No, listen to me. The army's tough on marriage, you know that. How many of our friends are divorced? D'you want that?'

She stared at him. 'No . . . no, of course not! Of course I don't . . . why . . . I'm sorry, Ralph . . . I'm so sorry. I don't know why I did it. It was stupid of me, it meant nothing . . .' She was crying in earnest now.

'Shh. Abs, come here . . .' He pulled her into his arms, cradling her head against his. 'I know. I know . . . I should've said something . . . maybe this is as much my fault. I just kept thinking it would go away. *He* would go away.'

Abby couldn't speak. Her throat and mouth were full of brine. Her mind was a kaleidoscope of images and emotions. She clung to him, weeping as though she would never stop. And all the while Ralph simply stood there, solid as a rock. He wasn't going anywhere, least of all without her.

72

SAM
LA, USA, 2008

Sam drove down Hollywood Boulevard, the wind in her hair, sun on her face and the endless blue skies overhead, thinking that life couldn't possibly get any better – professionally speaking, at least. She was thirty-eight years old, a partner in one of the world's largest entertainment law firms, Bellitte, Hazelby, Forman, Lazards, she'd paid off her Notting Hill flat, owned a sleek little sports car that was at that very moment languishing in the garage at BHFL's London HQ, and was just about to buy a share in a charming little cottage in the hills outside Avignon. She was just coming to the end of her second six-month stint at their Hollywood offices – an absolute necessity for anyone connected to entertainment law – and in a couple of days' time, she'd be on a business-class flight back home.

LA was great – the sun shone almost every single day, people were friendly (perhaps a little too friendly for her English sensibilities but hey, she wasn't complaining) and she'd never done as much socialising in her life. There was always an event to go to – an opening, a launch, a premiere . . . anything. Some of the people Sam worked with would go to the opening of an envelope if it came with free wine and the chance to Meet Somebody. It took her a couple of weeks to work out that Meet Somebody didn't just mean *any* old Somebody. Somebody Famous. Somebody Rich. Somebody Powerful. Somebody Pre-ferably-All-Three. Well, she'd been in LA for six months – a year, if you counted her first trip, two years earlier – and she'd met plenty of rich, famous and powerful people, but none whom she'd have given up a Saturday night sitting at home watching a good film for. Famous people were the same the world over, she told Lori, her colleague and closest friend (if you could call anyone in LA a 'close' friend): arrogant for the most part and generally quite insecure. Lori begged to differ. She was a forty-one-year-old divorced lawyer with two young children, both of whom were in expensive private schools – what was the point of being an entertainment lawyer if you didn't get the chance to meet famous people and possibly run off with one? Sam just laughed and shook her head. It was about as unlikely a scenario as getting stuck in an earthquake.

She turned left on Sunset Boulevard and brought the car to a stop at the lights. Above her, the dark green line of the Hollywood Hills rose in splendid formation. It had rained the previous day and the city was at its best. Light sparkled and bounced off the crisp white buildings, the billboards were satur-ated with colour, there were convertibles full of gorgeous, happy people . . . could it actually get any better? Yes, it could, a small, niggling voice inside her head said. You could have someone to share all this bloody gorgeousness with. Well, she didn't. She shoved the gearstick firmly into first and shot off at the light.

She drove along Sunset and then turned right to head into the canyons. It was her last Saturday in California and she intended to make the most of it. The following afternoon there'd be a farewell barbecue for her at one of the partners' Encino home and then early on Monday morning, she'd be on her way back across the Atlantic to London – and the inevitable rain and drizzle that would await her. It was September – glorious sunshine in LA, doom and gloom in London. She gunned the little engine, whipped round one bend and then another, savouring the view. Yet for all its outstanding beauty, she thought to herself, pulling over by the side of the road just outside Malibu and gazing down on the ocean below, she missed London. She missed her flat, her office, which was only half a block from her old office – Holman Kenton – and overlooking the same park.

At the thought of Holman Kenton she gave a small shudder. She couldn't believe she'd put up with that awful Michael Chilters for so long. Five minutes ought to have been enough to see straight through him. Odious little creep! She'd seen enough sexual harassment cases in the intervening six years to know she could have hauled his sorry arse over the coals, and *then* some. She'd been young, then, and so inexperienced. Not any more. There was no way *any*one – senior partner, founder, God himself – could pull that one again and expect to live. Six years in the corporate jungle of American lawsuits had taught her one thing – take no prisoners. Absolutely none. It was a lesson she'd learned particularly well. She took one last lingering look at the hazy blue horizon and started the engine again. Time for a quick stop, a glass of wine and the last few pages of the spare novel she always carried along with her. She'd long ago grown accustomed to eating on her own – and now she rather enjoyed it. She nudged the car towards the main road, looking for somewhere nice to stop and have a bite.

73

Brisbane, Australia, 2008

'Alannah! Stop that!' Meaghan reached across the table and took the open jar of marmalade away from her five-year-old daughter, whose face was quickly settling into its habitual mask of mutiny. Alannah turned two sticky orange palms up towards her. She'd been drawing, in marmalade, on the table.

'God, I don't know where she gets it from, I really don't,' Meaghan apologised hurriedly. 'She's ever so stubborn.'

'Probably from you,' Sal smiled shyly.

'Me?' Meaghan was genuinely surprised. She tried to mop up Alannah's hands and the table top at the same time.

'Yeah. That's all I remember about you from the wedding. That and your dress. I thought to myself, crikey . . . how'd someone like you manage to come out of *that* house?'

Meaghan smiled, touched by Sal's comment. She looked around the living room of their small, tidy house, not fifty miles from where she'd grown up and had never returned. Clive was the only one of her brothers she kept in touch with. The rest were gone, scattered around the country. *He* kept in touch; that was just like him. A phone call every month to their mother and the odd call or postcard to one or other of the brothers when he knew where to find them. From him she knew her mother's drinking had got worse and that her father rarely left the house; all the fight had gone out of him, or so Clive said. 'You ought to stop by, Meg. Mum'd be thrilled to see you.' But she couldn't. It was a side of her life she didn't want to remember. More than that, now, she didn't want Alannah to ever know.

'It was a long time ago,' Meaghan said, smiling faintly at the memory.

'Yeah, it was. You've been all round the world but we're just here, y'know. Nothing's changed.'

It wasn't quite true. Clive and Sal, even though they hadn't yet got around to tying the knot, had certainly moved up in the world. Clive was now the floor manager of a builder's warehouse and Sal was newly qualified as a primary school teacher. They'd bought a small Victorian worker's cottage and slowly done it up. Now, sitting at the dining table looking across the living room to the garden beyond, Meaghan felt a surge of pride in her brother who, like her, had beaten the odds and survived. 'So when are you two gonna have one?' she asked, looking across the table at Alannah.

Sal blushed. 'Oh, maybe next year? With my course and all . . .'

'I can't wait to be an aunt.' Meaghan grinned at her. 'And she needs a cousin.'

'What's it like?' Sal asked suddenly. 'Living overseas and everything. Isn't it lonely, though . . . I mean, when Tom's away?'

Meaghan nodded slowly. 'Yeah, it is. But that's just the way it is, y'know? It'd be different if I could work. But it's hard when you're moving around all the time. We're due for another posting when we get back but I don't know where. It could be anywhere, really. South America, Cyprus . . . back in England, I don't know. And now there's Alannah. It's fine. I'll . . . I'll find something to do.'

'What're the other wives like?' Sal asked curiously.

Meaghan shrugged. 'They're OK, I guess. I don't know . . . when we were in Belfast, there was one – Edie. She was nice. But she ran off with someone and I never saw her again.'

Sal nodded sympathetically. 'Yeah . . . I suppose from here it all seems so glamorous . . . different country every couple of years, travelling the world . . . I dunno, I wouldn't mind getting out of here for a bit.'

Meaghan smiled. 'There's no glamour, believe me. Most of the wives are a right dowdy bunch. I remember turning up at some dinner dance in a dress with a slit down the back – Christ, you should've seen their faces! Only reason *I* get away with it is because we're not Brits. They think we've got no taste. Or class. I don't care . . . now that Alannah's here, I'm sure I'll meet other young mums wherever we go. It'll be fine.' She was aware, as she finished, that the little buck-yourself-up speech was probably as much for her own benefit as Sal's.

Sal got up from the table and brought over the pot of freshly brewed coffee. 'Well, wherever it is, you'll make the most of it. That's what Clive always says.'

Meaghan was silent. She hadn't realised how much she missed family – *any* family – and hearing Sal's words brought it suddenly back home to her. She picked up her coffee cup, blinking slowly and carefully. She was overcome with a wave of love and tenderness for them both. In a week's time she and Alannah would be gone and God knows when they'd be back in Australia again. It was different for Tom. He spoke to his parents every other week – they were involved in his life in a way hers had never been, and never would be. She looked across the table at her daughter and, not for the first time, offered up a quick prayer of thanks that things would be different for her. And for the next one. She hadn't said anything to anyone yet but she was desperate to have another child. Girl or boy, it didn't matter. She wanted more children . . . a large, happy brood, to replace what she'd never had. She'd decided to stop taking the pill a couple of years after Alannah was born but nothing had happened in the three years since then. Not that it was likely to, either. She was suddenly acutely aware of her own body and its mysterious rhythms – with Tom gone for such long periods, and so often, it was hard to plan things. She hoped it would happen soon. It was beginning to look as though she'd never work again; she desperately needed something else in life. A large, happy family, with herself at the head, holding it and everyone together: *that* was what she longed for.

'Germany? *Again*?' Meaghan couldn't keep the disappointment from her voice. Tom's own voice came down the line mingled with the inevitable static. He'd been in London for a fortnight at a series of high-level meetings at the Ministry of Defence. Something was up; she could feel it, but it would have to wait. In the meantime, she had to swallow the news that they were returning to Germany.

'It's only for about eighteen months,' Tom said, trying to sound cheerful. 'And then it'll be somewhere stable, probably in the UK, for a couple of years.'

'I don't care if it's for eighteen days. I don't want to go back to Germany, Tom.'

'I haven't got a choice. I'm the battalion 2/i/c and that's where the battalion's stationed. I'll be hopping back and forth for a bit . . . we'll talk about it when you get here. You'll be here for another couple of months whilst I'm in Iraq then when I get back, I'll go ahead of you and get the new place sorted out.'

Meaghan was silent for a moment. She knew only too well that not only would the new place *not* be ready, but she'd have another two months – possibly even three – on her own before the move. 'Whereabouts in Germany?' she asked after a moment. 'Don't tell me it's Paderborn again. Please.'

'No.' She could hear him give a low chuckle. 'No, it's not Paderborn. Celle. You remember it? It's nice. It's much bigger . . . we've been there a couple of times. We've got a house . . . well, it's actually a flat but it's huge, apparently. It's in the centre of town, right by the river. There's a nursery just around the corner . . . it'll be fine, Meg.'

Meaghan sighed. The truth of the matter, of course, was that it had to be fine. She had no choice.

Exactly as it had been the first time, the flight back to Europe was long and tedious, made more difficult by the fact of a five-year-old child. She woke up somewhere over the Andaman Sea, Alannah weighing heavily on her lap. In front of her on the small screen she was able to watch their progress, a slow-moving line across the outline of the continents, impossibly slow. She slid open the blind; outside it was bright daylight. The sun streamed into the cabin. She gazed down. The outline of India below appeared like a picture taken from a school atlas. A sandy-coloured ridge of mountains fell sharply to the sea; the sea itself was a swirling mass of thousands of shades of blue. She stared at it for a few minutes longer, her eyes glazing over with the imprint of the light below, then she shut the blind, still temporarily dazzled.

Alannah stirred briefly, but luckily fell straight back to sleep. She touched her smooth, perfectly unblemished brow and tucked a strand of hair that had come away from her Alice band behind her ears. She had Tom's eyes and mouth, but Meaghan's colouring – blue eyes, blonde hair, pale, lightly freckled skin. Was Alannah pretty? She liked to think so – after all, which mother wouldn't – but there was more to her face than prettiness. She was interesting. Yes, that was the right word. She had a way of looking at you squarely, her jaw set in the same obstinate line she recognised in Tom. She was fearless, Alannah. The usual childhood anxieties washed straight over her. She wasn't afraid of the dark, of spiders, of bogeymen . . . none of that scared her. What did scare her was grown-up stuff. Would Daddy come back from the war? The first time she'd asked Meaghan that her heart nearly stopped. Where had she heard it? 'Who told you that?' she asked. Alannah regarded her mother calmly, then pointed to the television. Mortified, Meaghan hurriedly bent down so that she was on eye-level with her. 'Of course Daddy's going to come back, darling. What a silly idea. He'll be back before you know it.'

'Is he fighting the bad men?' Alannah asked, her face set in an expression Meaghan knew only too well. *Don't lie to me.*

'Yes, darling. That's exactly what he's doing.'

'Is it dangerous?'

'No, of course not. He's not running around with a gun, poppet. Soldiers do that. Daddy's an officer. It . . . it means he's in . . . in an office.'

Alannah nodded. 'I hope they kill them all,' she said darkly after a moment. 'All the bad men.'

Meaghan had no idea what to say. 'Er, I'm sure they will,' she murmured, watching Alannah pick up her favourite teddy bear and walk off, more or less satisfied with Meaghan's response.

Now, looking at her peaceful, relaxed face – the face of five-year-old innocence – she felt her heart contract with fear. Would Tom come back?

He was waiting for them at Heathrow. Alannah gave a shout of recognition and tore herself away from Meaghan's hand. As she watched the crowd give way to the little girl rushing towards her father – a soldier, too – she felt her fears dissolve. Tom was the sort of man who would always be all right. She was reminded of an article she'd read a long time ago in one of those weekly glossies you find in dentists' waiting rooms and salons all over the world. Nicole Kidman had been talking about her then-husband, another dare-devil of a man named Tom. 'Tom's the sort of man you'll want to be in a plane with. It'll never crash. He's the man you want by your side.' Nicole could have been talking about *her* Tom. It had to have been an old issue, she thought to herself with a wry smile. Tom and Nicole were no longer together, unlike Meaghan and Tom.

'Hello, mate.' Tom gently disentangled himself from Alannah's possessive embrace and turned towards her. She grinned up at him, suddenly shy. One or two older men looked at Tom with a faint flicker of pride, a barely lifted eyebrow, as if to say, 'Good on you, son.' She'd forgotten that aspect of stepping out with a soldier. 'Car's just outside,' he said. 'Got one of the staff sergeants to drive me down.'

They collected their luggage and made their way outside. As always, when she'd been away from him for a while, Meaghan found herself anxiously looking him over, as if to make sure everything really was there, in its rightful place. He caught her at it; there was a faint smile of mutual acknowledgement between them and then Alannah demanded his attention again. Meaghan let the childish babble wash over her as she got into the car and turned her head to the window. Tom was sitting up front. He interrupted Alannah to take a call on his mobile, barking out a few terse commands to whoever was on the other end of the line. The driver, a silent, red-haired young squaddie whom she didn't recall ever meeting before, met her eyes for a second in the rear-view mirror. There was some expression in them that she couldn't quite grasp. She'd seen it in Tom sometimes – a kind of wary pride at the things *they* had to deal with, the sort of life *they* led that bore almost no resemblance to the lives of the millions of others amongst whom they set themselves down, momentarily, before taking up the guns and tanks and hardware that set them so far apart. As Tom rose up through the ranks, becoming more and more embedded in the command structure of an organisation that she could never fully be a part of, the recognition was slowly dawning on her that the more successful he became, the further removed he would be, not just from her, but from any kind of ordinary life she might attempt to build between them, to bind him. He would not be bound. For him, the army wasn't just a job, the way she'd seen and heard other women describe their husbands' attitudes towards it. She supposed it was what set him apart; the reason, perhaps, for his swift promotions. He lived and breathed it. He got it, in a way that many men didn't. It was a tribe, in the deepest sense of the word, and Tom would live to become one of its elders.

But she also saw that if there was a sense of belonging and security in it, there was also a terrible price to be paid. When he came back from wherever it was he'd been sent, the fact that there were no visible wounds or that his body had returned intact was no insurance whatsoever against another kind of damage that festered, unseen. She couldn't pinpoint exactly when the first signs had surfaced. Bosnia? There was a missing period of nearly eight weeks in between the end of the Massereene posting and being sent off to Bosnia that he was not allowed to talk about or disclose where he'd been. Perhaps it was then. He'd come back changed in some unspecific, intangible way. She didn't like to think about what he might have seen or done and, for the first time, a kind of wariness had come between them. She wondered at what he'd been through; he saw her nervous curiosity but could offer neither reassurance nor explanation. Since he couldn't, she had to make up for herself some kind of story about his experiences that she'd culled from television or the news. She could tell her account fell short in some way she couldn't bring herself to think about but there was nothing she could do. When he wasn't home with her – and now, with Alannah – he lived in another world of actions and consequences where the smallest gesture might have ramifications beyond anything she could imagine. It had been years since they'd been out amongst people who were not, in some way or the other, connected to the army. The month-long holiday she and Alannah had just taken had been spent entirely outside it and she was shocked to discover just how alien the outside world had become. She was now an army wife, a paid-up member of the tribe. As the car swept through the suburbs towards Shrivenham, she found herself struggling to put into words that would make sense to her, what this next separation and a return to Germany would mean for her. For him, for Alannah. For the image of the large, smiling family that she'd always assumed would be theirs.

74

DANI
Freetown, Sierra Leone, 2009

The woman sitting across the table was perhaps ten years older than her. Her name was Malin Nielsen, from Stockholm, and she was Oxfam's station chief in Sierra Leone. She was fair in the way only Scandinavians can be: a kind of bleached-out, ethereal paleness that had nothing to do with the sun or lack of it – she was actually quite tanned. But the near-whiteness of her hair, eyebrows and eyelashes was a source of fascination. Dani had never seen anyone quite so blonde before. She stared at her, at the same time trying *not* to, so that when Malin looked up, Dani was caught out.

'Have you ever worked in the NGO sector before?' Malin repeated the question.

'N . . . no. Sorry, I was just . . . no, I haven't.'

'You speak beautiful English. I'm sorry, I don't mean to be rude. It's just . . . well, you don't often hear . . . have you lived overseas?'

Dani shook her head. She wondered where the interview was headed. She'd seen an advert in the *Daily Standard* for a receptionist at the Oxfam HQ in Freetown . . . why not? She might as well start somewhere. There was no possibility of going to university or leaving to go overseas. Those dreams were finished. She had to start somewhere and an NGO was as good a place as any. Better, in fact . . . the pay was almost double what she'd earn anywhere else and there was no way in hell she was going back to her old life before Julian. As kind as Lorraine and Dixie had been, she wanted more out of life than they had ever dreamed of, particularly as she didn't intend making some random man pay for it. Julian had taught her that much.

'Kingsley-Safo?' Malin said suddenly, looking at her application form. 'Wasn't there someone . . . what was his name? Julian? He was killed, I think. Did you know him? Were you related?'

Dani swallowed. It had been Lorraine's idea. 'Take his name, girl. You all was married, everybody know dat. Don't matter if you never go inside de church. And people gonna respect you more if you say you is "missus". Trust me. I know.' So she had. 'Yes,' she said quietly. 'He was my husband.'

'Oh. Oh, my God. I'm so sorry.' Malin looked genuinely distressed. 'I never knew him but I heard all about him. Actually, now that I come to think of it . . . I think I've heard your name too. I'm so sorry. When can you start?'

And that was it.

*

The job itself was undemanding. Answer the phone, take messages, keep the stationery cupboard stocked . . . make sure the generator had enough petrol, that the fridge in the back office was functioning . . . she could have done it with her eyes closed. But she liked the people she worked with and the atmosphere in the office, and Lorraine was right about one thing – she did have their respect. Julian had known many of the people who worked in the NGO sector and whilst he'd never been particularly friendly with any of them, he'd been liked and respected in spite – or perhaps because – of it, she saw. For the foreigners who'd flocked to Sierra Leone after the end of the war, he represented a contradiction that many of them could not resolve. African, yes, but not of the starving, cup-holding variety and this drew them to him, in search of answers that they did not realise he could not provide. They liked him, had genuinely sought to be his friend but he had a wisdom and subtlety about his own behaviour that Dani was only now beginning to see. He kept them at arm's length, preferring it that way, which in turn made them all the hungrier for his company . . . now that he was gone, it was Dani to whom they turned, charmed by her looks, her association with Julian and the fact that she might, if they worked hard enough at it, be able to open windows onto the Africa that they'd come out in their droves to save.

In this, Dani was both comforted and strengthened by Julian's memory. In the weeks that followed her appointment at Oxfam, she found herself talking to Julian almost every day. What would *you* have done? She saw that the six years they'd been together had served as a kind of apprenticeship about the world in general that would stand her in better stead than anything she'd ever learned in school, or from anyone else. She did her job, was quick to learn and eager to get things right . . . but no more. She was not to be found with the others on the beach after the office had shut down for the evening, drinking away the stress of providing – or attempting to provide – for people who had so little it made every beer you drank taste different out of the knowledge that its price alone could have made the difference between life and death. She watched from the sidelines as they struggled to balance the fragmented pieces of a life that included a genuine desire to help but an equally genuine reluctance to give up the small luxuries of their own lives that made their situations tolerable, worth living. They looked to Dani to provide some answers, just as they'd looked to Julian. And just as he had, she turned away. Her status as his widow, however young she was, afforded her the luxury of being able to do so without being ostracised. They were compassionate; after all, who amongst them had suffered the way she surely had?

By the end of her third month, a routine had settled itself over her life. She was slowly beginning to become more involved in the writing of reports that made up the bulk of Malin's working day. Malin's background was in gender development, a term that Dani had heard, but never fully understood. Now, as Malin's reports began to stack up in her in-tray for typing or filing, she began reading them in an attempt to understand more fully exactly what it was that Oxfam did. *You're more likely to be poor if you're a woman. That's a fact.* She picked up one of the leaflets that had been sent out by Oxfam UK and slipped it into her bag. She read it at home that night, lying on the couch overlooking the city, her hand going occasionally to the bag of freshly roasted peanuts that would replace dinner. It wasn't long – four typed pages – but by the time she put it down, she was filled with a new respect for the organisation she now worked for, and for Malin herself.

Over the course of the next few weeks she began to read in earnest, her interest sparked not only by the hundreds of reports stacked neatly along the office's bookcases, but also by a deeper understanding of the powerlessness of women that came from her own experience, however deeply buried. She had no illusions. The women of the Oxfam reports were not like her; she had had an education, a roof over her head, food on the table, no matter how scarce or difficult it had been for her grandmother to find. She hadn't been raped or been forced to watch her children die in front of her. None of that had happened to her and the more she read, the more thankful she was.

But despite the differences in experience, there was something about the helplessness of these women that struck a chord in her. She understood what it was like to be at the utter whim and mercy of a man. She'd been unlucky; Nick's irrational, sometimes violent outbursts had cowed her. Instead of standing up to him, she'd shrunk from confrontation, seeking only to placate him, even as she knew, deep down, that what he asked of her was not only unreasonable, but often downright cruel. His abuse – and she was only now learning to recognise it as such – was emotional, not always physical, but she'd suffered nonetheless. In the face of the suffering she read about, it was nothing. A bruise here, a shout there, occasionally a hand around her throat during sex. But he'd imposed his will on her nonetheless and although she had neither the experience nor the insight to recognise what it was in her, not him, that allowed it to take place, there was something about the reading she was doing on a nightly basis that gave her a certain kind of strength. Julian would have been able to place it – he would have told her exactly what was happening to her, and why. But Julian wasn't there, never would be again and so she had to figure it out for herself.

One evening, about four months after she'd started at Oxfam, one of her colleagues had persuaded her to come along to a party at the next-door offices. She'd seen the sign outside – just another of the many welfare organisations that had sprung up like mushrooms in the past few years. She couldn't even recall the name. Housing for All; Housing for Everyone . . . something along those lines. She looked up at the person who'd asked her – a thin, rangy English guy called Dave who'd been in Sierra Leone for about a month but had been with Oxfam in Sudan and was fond of telling everyone that Freetown, in comparison, was a tropical paradise. Privately Dani couldn't see how. She'd never been to Khartoum – or anywhere else other than Cheltenham, for that matter – but how could anything be worse than Freetown?

'Go on. You *never* come out,' Dave complained. 'It's only next door. We'll get you back home before you turn into a pumpkin, I promise.'

Dani smiled. 'No, it's not that . . .'

'So what is it? I put on a clean shirt today *and* I'm wearing deodorant. Special effort. Come on. One drink.'

Dani hesitated. What was she in a hurry to return home to? An empty flat, clean as it might be, and a small portion of fried plantain or some plain rice and gravy for dinner? 'Oh, all right. But one drink, that's all.'

'Excellent. Come on. Get your bag. Malin's waiting downstairs.'

She switched off her computer, picked up her handbag and followed him half-reluctantly down the narrow flight of stairs. He was right; he *was* wearing deodorant. She could smell it behind him. She suppressed a small smile.

'Oh, you're coming with us,' Malin said, unable to hide her surprise. 'That's nice. Do you know anyone there?'

Dani shook her head. 'No, I've never met them.'

'They're a nice bunch. Mostly Brits, I think, but still—' Malin smiled impishly at Dave.

'Nothing wrong with Brits,' he said staunchly. 'As a matter of fact, if it hadn't been for us, we wouldn't be here today.'

'*You* might not be,' Dani said tartly, then immediately regretted it. She saw the look of surprise on both their faces. She busied herself looking for something in her bag. She oughtn't to snap at them; they were only doing their best. As had sometimes happened with Nick, she felt herself to be so much older than those around her, in spite of the real difference in their ages. At thirty, Dave was six years older than her, but occasionally it felt as though it was the other way round. 'Ready?' she asked, as lightly as she could.

'Absolutely.' It was one of Dave's better qualities – he never bore a grudge.

The party was on the third floor of the building next door. It had been so long since she'd been so high up, overlooking the city. As she accepted a glass of wine from someone and wandered out onto the balcony, she was suddenly reminded of Nick's flat, on the sixth floor, overlooking the bay. The city spread out horizontally, bounded almost directly in front of her by the immense blackness of the sea. As always in Freetown, huge swathes of the town were plunged in darkness, blank spots on the night-time map where the power had failed. She could hear the hum of generators that seemed to be as much a part of the night music as the crickets and the stuttering farts of motorcycles, interspersed with occasional horn blasts from the taxis down below. The minivan drivers who went up and down certain main streets tooted for custom, the faint 'tap-tap-tap' of their horns another layer to the symphony.

'You were Julian's girlfriend.' Someone spoke to her out of the darkness.

She turned around. It was a woman. Tall, slim, with long twisted dreadlocks that fell to her shoulders, glasses that glinted in the light thrown out by the hurricane lamp. An English-sounding voice. 'Yes.' Dani was unsure whether it was actually a question.

'I'm Sue. I knew him in London. I'm so sorry.'

Dani looked more closely at her. Had they met before? She didn't think so. 'Thanks,' she said carefully, as she had learned to do. 'Are you English?'

She shook her head. 'No, actually I'm from here. Well, my parents are. I'm the programme manager for Housing Relief.'

Housing Relief. That was it. 'Oh. Well, I'm Dani.'

'Yes, I know. He spoke about you often.'

Dani was surprised. Julian had been back to the UK a couple of times in the years they'd been together but she didn't think he'd mentioned anyone called Sue. She was reminded yet again how vast his networks had been, how many people he'd known and touched. 'Did you know him well?' she asked, curious.

Sue nodded. 'Sort of. We were at uni together. At SOAS. He was a couple of years ahead of me but we used to meet at the African Students' Union. When I last saw him . . . must've been a couple of years ago, I told him I was thinking of coming back here. He thought it was a great idea . . . especially since I've never actually lived here. Not as an adult, anyway. And working here is very different from being on holiday.'

'How d'you find it?' Dani asked. There was something warm and open about Sue's voice that she liked. She was somehow different from the other aid workers she'd met.

Sue smiled. In the dark her teeth flashed very white. 'Oh, I don't know. I don't find the stuff everyone complains about that hard. I mean, it doesn't really bother me if there's no electricity or water. You can work around that. It's the other stuff . . .'

'Like what?' Dani really was curious.

Sue smiled again. 'It's the way money corrupts everything. Everyone's on the make, all the time. You can't smile at someone without some sort of expectation that you're going to give them something. That's the stuff I find hard.'

Dani nodded slowly. It was true. The war had done that. Before it, everything was normal, the way it was everywhere else, she imagined. If people went out of their way to help each other, a reward wasn't always necessary. Now, if someone did something as small as help you carry your bags to your car, or flag down a taxi, a hand would quickly be stuck out. If you refused, a torrent of abuse would quickly follow. They'd lost their basic humanity towards one another. It wasn't that people were malicious, it was poverty, pure and simple. Poverty and powerlessness. She didn't need Julian to teach her just how lethal a combination it was. 'Yeah, I know what you mean. It wasn't always like this, though.'

'So I hear,' Sue said drily. 'D'you smoke?' She pulled a packet of cigarettes out of her back pocket.

Dani shook her head. 'No. How long d'you think you'll stay?' she asked, emboldened by the turn the conversation had suddenly taken.

Sue shrugged. She drew deeply on her cigarette. 'I don't know. I enjoy what I'm doing, but it seems so . . . I don't know . . . pointless, in a way. I mean, as quickly as we manage to secure one set of agreements to build more shelters, something goes wrong and we're back to the drawing board. I probably wouldn't say this publicly – at least not yet – but we've only managed to rehouse about one hundred and fifty refugees out of the thousands that are sitting around in camps. I keep thinking I ought to be doing something else. Something more direct. I don't know.' She gave a short laugh. 'It's probably better than nothing,' she said, gesturing at the offices behind her. 'But it's not enough, that's the problem. Not nearly enough.'

Dani didn't know what to say. They chatted for a few minutes about people they knew in common, mostly people who worked for Oxfam, then Sue ground out her cigarette under her heel, gave Dani a quick smile, and headed back indoors. Half an hour later, she collected her bag and made her way downstairs as well. It was the first time since Julian's death that she'd met someone with whom she would have liked to have a further conversation. She wondered if she would ever see her again.

'Hi, is that Dani?' The phone rang almost as soon as she got into the office the following morning.

Dani fumbled with the receiver. It was Sue. 'Hello? Yes, this is Dani. Hi . . . hi, Sue.' She hadn't expected to hear from her, and certainly not so soon.

'Hi. Just wondered . . . d'you fancy having a drink after work?'

Dani was surprised, but pleased. 'Yeah . . . that would be nice,' she said shyly. They arranged to meet on the steps outside Sue's office at five. She put down the receiver, slightly bemused. Since meeting Julian she'd lost the brash, cocky confidence with which she'd approached life in her teens. In showing her a different world in Freetown, made up mostly of people who were worldly and accomplished, he'd also unwittingly placed her out of her depth. She'd understood immediately that his friends were of a different order altogether; the sorts of conversations she'd had with Nick and Eric and the few friends she had were woefully ignorant and inadequate. She'd just about summoned up enough confidence to begin to take part in Julian's circle when he was killed. Now, after his death, she shrank from them again. Sue's phone call and her apparent friendliness had taken her by surprise. Why would someone like Sue want to be friends with *her*?

That evening, sitting in one of the new bars along Siaka Stevens Street, sipping a glass of wine, she felt some of her anxieties begin to disappear. Sue was amusing and droll and had a healthily cynical view of what the hundreds of so-called returnees like herself were doing in the country. 'Truth is, we live better here than we'd ever live in London or New York,' she said, waving her cigarette smoke out of Dani's face. 'Even with all the bloody power cuts.' Just then the bar door opened and a group of army officers strolled in. Sue looked up. 'God, I can't stand that lot.'

'Which lot?' Dani glanced over at them and was relieved to see she knew none of them.

'Those IMATT guys. They make me sick. Ever since that fuss over the prostitute they took out into the bush. You must have heard about it . . . happened about six or seven years ago.'

Dani felt a shadow of fear fall over her. 'What prostitute?' she asked, though she knew exactly who Sue was talking about.

'I don't remember her name. She was a local girl . . . half Lebanese or something. They raped her to death and then just tossed the body in the back of the truck and dumped her by the side of the road. Villagers found her. Apparently the officer in charge just sat back and watched the whole thing happen. Some hunters from the village were hiding in the bushes and they saw it all. It makes you sick. They're out here supposedly training our local army and they behave worse than anyone else. The whole thing was completely hushed up. They didn't even reprimand the soldiers who'd taken part.'

Dani looked into her half-empty glass. Some strange, buried emotion broke over her. Whenever she thought about Nick, it was as if she couldn't quite piece things together. There was some part of her brain – or her heart – that refused to believe what her intuition told her. He was capable of anything; she'd seen that in him almost immediately. He reminded her of a character in a novel she'd once read, and had seen again on Julian's bookshelf, *East of Eden*. Cathy . . . that was it. A girl without a conscience. That was Nick. He was without a conscience, and therefore capable of anything. It wasn't that he'd been evil – on the contrary, there was a vulnerability to him that she'd sensed from the first time she saw him. But he was incapable of empathy. He simply couldn't put himself in anyone else's shoes or experience what someone else might be feeling. She'd talked about it from time to time with Julian. He recognised the condition; he'd often said to her that the real, lasting problem in Sierra Leone was that the trauma of the war had produced similar human beings – capable of anything. It was as if the shock of what they'd been through had robbed them of the capacity to feel. She'd often wondered to herself what on earth Nick – who appeared to have nothing in common with the rebels and child soldiers Julian came into contact with – could have gone through to be so immune to suffering. He'd said very little about his childhood but to her eyes, at least, he had everything. A home, parents, an education . . . what had gone wrong? And now, here was Sue, telling her something she already knew. She was shamed. *The officer in charge just sat back and watched the whole thing happen.* She'd seen that sort of detachment in Nick over and over again. Not only *could* she believe it, she did. 'I . . . I remember something about it,' she lied, her face on fire. 'Poor girl.'

'That's the problem with the sorts of soldiers that come out here, though,' Sue said, watching the group of surly-looking men who'd taken a table at the end of the room and were busy shouting out orders to the harried-looking waitresses. Opposite

them, a group of local girls were preening themselves, in preparation.

Dani suddenly felt ill. That had been her, once. *Attached
herself to some man. Poor thing*. She shoved the glass away from
her and stood up. 'I . . . I'm sorry. I just remembered . . . I've
got to do something . . . my grandmother.' She fished in her
bag for some money but Sue put out a hand.

'It's on me. I'm sorry. I didn't mean to upset you. I . . . I
know a little about you . . . Julian did mention you'd been out
with a soldier before him. I'm sorry. It was insensitive of me.'

Dani swallowed. There was a lump in her throat that stopped
her from speaking. She nodded and turned away, not wanting to
cry in front of Sue. She pushed her way past the small crowd that
had come into the bar, ignoring the comments from the soldiers
who were looking at her, and shoved open the door. The night
air outside was warm and soft, a relief from the chilly, air-
conditioned interior. She flagged down a cab, her heart heavy
with embarrassment and fear. She'd lost the chance of a friendship with Sue, just as she'd lost Julian and Nick. What was
wrong with her? She got into the back of an ancient, creaking
cab that smelled of cigarettes and sweat and shut her eyes.
Everyone with whom she came into contact left her, pushed
out either by her or circumstances beyond her control. Either
way, it made no difference. In the end it all boiled down to the
same thing: she was alone. At the age of twenty-four, she had no
one. Chances were, it would always be this way.

75

ABBY
Celle, Germany, 2009

'*Guten Morgen, haben Sie Spärgel, vielleicht?*' Abby greeted the
greengrocer warmly.

The woman, plump, dark-haired and always smiling, pointed

them out. '*Ja, klar. Die sind gerade heute angekommen,*' she said, selecting the biggest bunch. *Just came in today.* They chatted for a moment about the best vegetables of the season, where to get the best fish and why the flowers at the farmer's market the previous day had been so disappointing. Abby slid the brown paper parcel of asparagus – so light and white the stems were almost translucent – into her wicker pannier and pushed her bicycle slowly along the cobbled stones. By the time she'd moved along the little street, stopping to compare prices, accepting a slice of home-made apple tart from one of the other vendors with whom she'd struck up an acquaintance, it was nearly lunchtime.

She wheeled her bicycle across the old wooden bridge and stopped for a moment to watch the children playing in the park next to the river. Someone had rigged up a volleyball net and brought in a few wheelbarrows of sand – it wasn't quite beach volleyball but the intention was there. The weather was lovely and warm. She rested her forearms on the handlebars, taking in the scent of freshly cut grass and the giggling, high-pitched sound of girls laughing. She thought again of Clara and her heart gave a little lurch. She'd settled in beautifully at school in England. In her weekly letters and the phone call they made on Sunday mornings, she seemed to be having the time of her life. It would be different with Sadie. She was enrolled at the German-speaking school just down the road from where they lived on Halkettstrasse, close to the Allgemeines Krankenhaus, a name which, for some reason, always made Sadie laugh when she heard it. A woman was cycling slowly and sedately towards her. She drew level with Abby, then smiled in recognition, her chin settling into the flesh of her neck as she greeted her. '*Guten Morgen.*' It was the vet's receptionist from the clinic across the road. They'd bought Sadie a kitten to replace her sister, or at least that's how Sadie saw it. The previous week the poor thing had been sickly . . . nothing to worry about, the vet assured the distraught Sadie. 'She's just missing her mama and her brothers and sisters, that's all.'

'Like me,' Sadie said earnestly, pleased at the parallels between her pet's life and her own. They'd prescribed some sort of tonic to be added to the kitten's water and within a few days, she'd perked up.

They chatted for a few minutes in German and then the lady rode off. Abby had forgotten to ask her name. She mounted her own bike and cycled off in the opposite direction, towards home. Yes, it was already beginning to feel like home.

The house was quiet. The cleaning lady, a friendly blonde named Heidi who also cleaned the officers' mess at the barracks where Ralph worked every day, hadn't yet arrived. Abby stowed the morning's purchases into the fridge and freezer, made herself a cup of tea and wandered into the study that doubled as her studio. She closed the door behind her. Heidi would arrive at any moment and the twice-weekly hurricane of cleaning, vacuuming, sweeping and polishing would take place. Like the cleaning lady Abby remembered from when her father had been posted to Fallingbostel, just up the road, Heidi took her job seriously, and the dirt and dust that accumulated in between her visits personally. She'd watched her the other day beating the curtains to within an inch of their lives and had to shut herself up in the study to stop herself from laughing out loud. *Furchtbar, furchtbar*, Heidi muttered angrily to herself, slapping them together and then hitting them hard with the flat-handled brush. *Terrible, terrible.* Abby, who was certainly no slouch herself when it came to cleaning, was clearly out of her league.

She picked up the photographs she'd taken the previous week of a bowl of fruit. She held them in her hands, admiring the different angles and light conditions that brought out different qualities in each. The peaches were particularly beautiful, their skins waxy and furry at the same time, a particularly tricky quality to capture. But she loved a challenge and the colours would look stunning in an oil painting above the fireplace in the living room. She slipped on the splattered overalls she used when painting and tied her hair back into a ponytail. The canvas had been set up the night before; it stood by the window, capturing the steady, northern light. She took a deep breath, picked up her pencils and began making the first, tentative strokes across its surface that marked the beginning stages of a piece of work. Her strokes became progressively bolder as the picture began to take shape – a line here, an area of shading there . . . slowly the bowl of fruit emerged out of what had been blankness only an hour or so before. Peaches, plums, apples, apricots and a bunch of those dark purple grapes that you could only find in German markets, each so perfectly rounded and plump that the fruit seemed to shine through the skin. The bowl containing the fruit was copper; it too shone out of the picture with a dull, metallic glow. She traced the outline of the table, a corner of pale, waxy oak just visible, and the frame of the window beyond. She'd taken it in the kitchen but the angle and manner suggested an old country home, not the semi-detached, rather poky house on a suburban street in Celle that was now their home.

She painted for half an hour, perfectly and steadily absorbed in the task of bringing the scene to life. At twelve thirty she stopped, packed away her brushes and paints, taking care to clean them thoroughly. She untied her overalls and slipped them onto a hanger. She would have a cup of coffee and a biscuit with Heidi and then walk down the road to fetch Sadie from school. There'd been a little bit of an argument over where to send her; Ralph didn't see what was wrong with the school at Trenchard Barracks but Abby was adamant. 'What's the point of all this travel and upheaval if they don't at least learn another language?' she asked. Ralph, who couldn't speak a word of anything other than English and a smattering of schoolboy French, was forced to admit she was right. He'd seen the admiring looks on his colleagues' faces every time they'd gone out to eat and Abby ordered for everyone in fluent, almost accent-free German. She'd picked it up as a result of her father's postings; let Sadie do the same. Sadie had been in school for almost a month and she was already beginning to swap English words for German ones. Abby watched her with a sense of pride and amazement.

'The new second-in-command's just been confirmed,' Ralph told her over dinner that evening. Sadie was fast asleep in bed, her kitten tucked up somewhere between her chin and her neck as she had been every night since they'd got her. The dishes were stacked in the dishwasher, the table was cleared and she and Ralph were having a rare, after-dinner drink in the living room.

Abby looked up. 'Who is he? Don't tell me it's Ian Harding.'

Ralph smiled and shook his head. 'No, someone new. He's Australian, actually. Transferred over about sixteen years ago. Tom Astor. Major Tom Astor. Got the memo this morning. He's been all over the show . . . Bosnia, Kosovo, Iraq. He was in Paderborn a couple of years ago, actually. Seems like a sound bloke. He arrives on Friday.'

'Married?'

Ralph nodded. 'Yep. His wife's also Australian, I think. They've got one daughter. A bit younger than Sadie.'

'That's nice.' Abby was pleased. Although she herself rarely made close friends amongst the officers' wives, it would be good for Sadie to have an English-speaking friend on the base . . . particularly as most of her immediate friends were from the town, not army kids. 'I'll have to organise a welcome party for them.'

'Mmm.' Ralph's interest in Major Tom Astor wasn't really centred around his or his family's social life. 'You do that, darling.'

'When do they arrive?'

'Not sure. Probably in a month or so. They're in the UK at the moment. Shrivenham, or something.'

Abby gave a light, theatrical shudder. 'Shrivenham. God, well . . . Celle'll be a welcome change for them then. Did you say they were in Paderborn before?'

Ralph nodded. 'Mmm. Think so.' He was already lost in the paperwork he'd brought home with him.

'D'you want some coffee, darling?' Abby got up. There would be little more to be got from him now. He shook his head. 'I'm going to turn in,' she said, picking up the two empty glasses. 'You sure you don't want anything else?'

There was no reply. He was properly gone. She closed the door gently behind her and took the glasses through to the kitchen. She was suddenly very tired; strange, considering she'd done so little all day. She remembered something her mother had said once, uncharacteristically tart. *You'd be surprised just how exhausting it is, always putting someone else's needs before yours.* She remembered looking anxiously at her mother, wondering if the criticism were somehow obliquely directed at her. She frowned suddenly. She'd been such an anxious little girl, nothing like her own daughters. It came to her suddenly that it had been a while since she'd felt nervous or out of her depth. When had it stopped, that sinking feeling that everything that *didn't* go right was somehow her fault? She stood by the kitchen window for a moment, looking out onto the garden beyond. It was April and the clocks had gone forward the week before. Evenings were long and light-filled as the seasons shifted from darkness to sun. It was nearly nine o'clock and night was beginning to close in. There was an apple tree just outside the back door; she could see the beginnings of round, hard little fruits dotted along its branches. In a few months' time, as the summer/winter reversal was about to begin, the tree would be ready to shed its ripe load. By then Ralph would be in Afghanistan. She felt a shiver of fear ripple across her skin, like wind over the surface of a lake.

76

SAM
London, England, 2009

It had been almost six weeks since her return from LA and to say she'd hit the ground running was an understatement. There were mornings when she woke up feeling as though she hadn't been to sleep. It was most unfair, she thought to herself morning after morning as she got ready for work. The case she'd been working on in LA was long and tediously complex, yet no sooner had they managed an out-of-court settlement which had finally brought the whole thing to a desperately needed close and she'd returned to London than she was landed with another one. D&B Records vs Apster, a spin-off of the original Napster file-sharing company who'd been forced into liquidation a few years earlier. Even the sound of the case was enough to make her break out into a sweat. As soon as it had been assigned, she'd had to take a crash course in music industry terminology. She owned an iPod herself, like most other people she knew, but she was embarrassed to admit she'd never got much further than turning it on. She still had no idea how to download her CDs onto the blasted thing, something she generally left for Philip to do whenever he came round for dinner. Now she was being asked to enter the as yet completely mysterious and murky world of digital music sharing and it terrified her.

But, as she grimly reminded both Philip and Paula, she hadn't got to where she was in the law firm by shrinking from those things she didn't understand. She took her laptop home with her dutifully each night and attacked the problem with the same diligence that had got her a First in Bristol, years earlier. MP3 files, peer-to-peer file sharing, vicarious infringements, wholesale copying . . . the list of terms and concepts seemed endless. BHFL were acting for D&B, who'd brought the suit, though she had to admit to harbouring a secret admiration for the computer nerds who spent their lives inventing ways to fleece the large record companies of their even larger profits. Shawn Fanning, the original inventor of Napster, had walked away with a considerable fortune himself – not bad for someone barely out of high school, she noted, whilst grimly surfing the internet for as much information on how the damned thing worked as she could possibly find.

She had almost – *almost* – managed to get her head around the basic concept of peer-to-peer file sharing when Peter Linman stuck his head around the door one Thursday evening, just before she was getting ready to leave for the day, and said, in the breezy manner that her boss always adopted when he had bad news to deliver, 'Oh, by the way . . . you're off the D&B case. We've got another one on its way in that I think you should handle. Are you free this evening? I'm having dinner with Bradley Feinstein, who brought us the case. I'll brief you in the taxi. We go to trial in a couple of weeks' time.'

She looked up at him, aghast. 'But . . . but I *can't*. I've spent six weeks on—'

'I know, I know. But I'm going to pass it down the chain. Clive can take it over. Or Lionel. I need you on this one, Sam. I'll have the taxi waiting.'

And that was it. She was now the lead counsel on a new case that she hadn't even had time to read before meeting the client the following morning. They went out to Peter's favourite restaurant, Tortellini d'Oro, a small, family-run Italian restaurant in Mayfair where she wound up having two glasses of red wine, a single shot of whisky and a mouthful of Bradley's tequila – not a helpful combination. She got home at midnight feeling decidedly blurry and sorry for herself. She was about to go on holiday – her first in almost eighteen months and there was no way in hell she was going to cancel it. It was typical of Peter. Giving her a brand-new case would mean he could go on holiday safe in the knowledge that she would either cancel hers, or take her files with her. It was the one major drawback of being the youngest partner at the firm. Not only was she expected to put her job before *every*thing else, the fact that she was single and didn't even have the excuse of a social life to speak of made it twice as easy to be dumped on. Still, the new case seemed relatively straightforward, she thought to herself as she tumbled gratefully into bed. Claire, her PA, would have the details for her in the morning. Through the semi-open bedroom door she could see the red, blinking light of her answering machine. Sod it, she thought defiantly, as she closed her eyes. Whatever it was could wait.

PART SEVEN

77
A fortnight later

SAM
Marrakech, Morocco, 2009

There was the wholly unfamiliar feel and weight of someone else in the bed. Sam's eyes flew open. Light was filtering in through the wrought-iron shutters, falling onto the bed in a shifting kaleidoscope of patterns and shapes. Nick slept as though he were dead. His left arm was raised above his head, almost cradling it; the other was buried somewhere in the sheets below. She pushed the covers cautiously aside, looking incredulously at the body of a man she'd only just met. What had she been thinking? Or drinking?

She was just sliding her legs as quietly as possible out of the bed when he stirred. She lay still, hoping he would settle back into sleep again. She had so little experience of waking up next to a man when there was even the remote possibility she might see him again that she wasn't sure what was more important – brush her teeth, go to the loo, take a shower, repair her make-up . . . which? She heard him give a little grunt, then a sigh . . . was he awake? She held her breath for a few minutes . . . no, he was still slumbering. She slid her legs all the way out and was just about to touch the floor when his hand snaked out and caught hold of her arm.

'Where to?' he mumbled, his voice thick with sleep.

'Um . . . just thought I'd go to the bathroom,' she whispered, though why she felt the need to whisper wasn't clear.

He turned to look at her. She was struck again by his eyes:

neither grey nor blue, so light they were almost invisible in the tanned, rugged face. 'Sheepish?' he asked, grinning.

She shook her head, her face breaking into a smile. He'd made it easy. For them both. 'No, not at all,' she said lightly. 'I'll be back in a minute.'

'A minute. Any more and I'll come looking for you.' There was a smile in his voice.

She hopped awkwardly out of bed, wondering how to cover her naked body as she walked across the room to the bathroom. At least it was a separate room; she couldn't have borne the thought of taking a pee in front of him. She looked around quickly for something to cover herself. 'Don't bother,' he drawled. She turned her head to look at him, embarrassed. 'No, go on . . . you look good from where I'm sitting. Better than good, actually.' Her whole body burning with embarrassment and pleasure, she practically ran across the room and shut the door firmly behind her. She rushed to the mirror. Hair a bit messy, smudged mascara, a faint scratch on her neck, just below her chin . . . she looked no better or worse than she did after a night out with her colleagues. Except for the blush that was staining her breasts and face, she looked . . . well, normal. As usual. But she wasn't. Sam Maitland, thirty-nine years old, on holiday for the first time in nearly five years and she'd wound up in bed with a complete stranger. A British Army officer. You couldn't make it up. She began to giggle and had to stuff her fist in her mouth to stop herself from laughing out loud. She hurriedly turned on the shower, went to the loo and began brushing her teeth under the noise of the water.

Five minutes later, smelling sweetly of her favourite perfume and body lotion, her mouth tasting of peppermint and her hair and face carefully washed and brushed, she opened the bathroom door in a cloud of steam and walked across the room, this time wearing the silk bathrobe that the hotel management had thoughtfully hung on the back of the door. She stepped out of it as gracefully as she could and slid back into bed. She was rewarded with a grin, a kiss and a hard-on. This cannot – *cannot*

– be happening to me, she thought to herself wildly as Nick pulled her impatiently back into his arms. She was still dreaming, surely. There was a moment's sudden discomfort as he thrust into her without waiting or warning but his impatience was all the more thrilling for being totally unexpected. When had a man ever been impatient – never mind *too* impatient – to be inside her? Never, was the answer. She turned to him willingly and eagerly, suddenly excited beyond belief. This was what she'd waited her whole life for, she thought to herself as he exploded inside her, minutes after entering. This was it, surely? *This* was what she'd been missing.

'Where's Celle?' she asked, half an hour later as they lay together, limbs and arms loosely entwined, still half drowsy but talking softly. She had the sudden urge for a cigarette but thought it rather rude.

'Near Hanover. I'm their new company commander.'

'What does that mean?'

'I'm responsible for about a hundred-odd soldiers. The battalion's being prepped for Afghanistan in about nine months' time. From Germany we'll go to Cyprus for a couple of months' training . . . and then we'll be deployed, probably Helmand.'

'Gosh.' Sam didn't know what to say. Her knowledge of the army was about as extensive as her knowledge of Germany or Afghanistan . . . non-existent, in other words. She doubted she'd ever met a soldier before, let alone an officer. 'How . . . how long will you be out there?'

He shrugged. 'Dunno. Tours are normally about six months. Could be extended . . . we never know.'

'D'you enjoy it?' she asked curiously.

'Course I do. It's all I've ever wanted.'

'Oh.'

'D'you enjoy what you do?' he asked.

'Yes, of course. I love it. Can't imagine doing anything else, to be honest.'

'Well, same here.'

'But it's not, is it? I mean . . . I just get up every morning and go to work. There's nothing even remotely dangerous about what I do. But you . . . I can't imagine you in uniform, with all those guns and things . . .' She stopped, wondering if she'd gone too far.

'It's exactly the same. It's a job, no different from yours. It works because everybody knows their place and that's all you focus on. You can't afford to think about the bigger picture. Your responsibility's to your mates, your company, your battalion . . . that's it.'

Sam was silent, awed by the enormity of what he described. She tried to picture him in the places he'd just described – on the base in Celle, in Cyprus, in Basra, where he'd been stationed for two years . . . and couldn't. Before meeting him – that was to say up until the day before – she'd never paid much attention to the news about the war. Like everyone else on the planet, she'd been caught up in the drama around the September 11 attacks . . . in fact, she could remember precisely where she'd been and what she'd been doing the moment the news filtered through – but ask her what the link between Iraq, Afghanistan and September 11 was and she would surely falter. She had no clear understanding of why Nick had been in Basra, nor did she understand what he would be doing in Helmand. Not only was the army another world, light years removed from her own, it had its own language, too. A tour of duty; the theatre of war; a company commander . . . she was suddenly fascinated. 'C-could I come and visit you?' she said suddenly, the words almost forming of their own accord.

'My thoughts exactly,' Nick said, his hand lazily caressing her hair.

The relief that flooded through her nearly made her weep. 'You sure?'

'Course I'm sure. You took the words right out of my mouth.'

'When?'

'Whenever. When d'you want to come?'

Sam did a rapid calculation. She had less than a week to

prepare herself for the trial that was about to start . . . once it was under way, she wouldn't even have a weekend off . . . but with any luck, they'd be finished in a fortnight. 'How about three weeks from now? It'll give you time to settle in and everything.'

'Sounds good. It's easy, from London. Air Berlin flies from Stansted to Hanover and I'll pick you up from there.'

Sam's eyes closed of their own accord. *I'll pick you up*. When had she ever heard those words uttered by a man? So he *did* want to see her again, even though she'd slightly jumped the gun and asked him, rather than the other way round. But he seemed as keen as she was. And he did say she'd taken the words right out of his mouth. She could see herself replaying the entire conversation and scene for Paula's benefit. 'So . . . three weeks, then?' she said, hoping she didn't sound anxious.

'Three weeks.' He muttered the words against her ear. 'And in the meantime, there's something I'd like you to do for me. Something that'll keep me going until the three weeks are up.'

Sam felt his fingers tighten across her scalp as he pushed her head gently but firmly downwards. She could smell her own perfume on his body as she slid down his chest, the light blotted out by the covers. She was half excited, half nervous . . . she'd never done anything like this before. She'd never met anyone like him before. 'Like this?' she mumbled a few minutes later, lifting her head slightly. She was rewarded with a groan.

'Yes. Exactly like that. Damn, you're good.'

78

'You did *what*?'

Sam had to hold the phone away from her ear. 'Shhh!' she whispered excitedly. 'I'm at work, Paula. I'll call you tonight—'

'You bloody well won't. You'll tell me right now. Every little detail, d'you hear me? Every tiny scrap. I'm not hanging up the phone until I've heard it all.'

389

'I *can't* . . . I'm at *work*.'

'Should've thought about that before you picked up the phone, my girl. Who is he? How'd you meet him?'

Sam recounted it as quickly as she could, finishing with an 'I'll call you later, I promise,' before hanging up the phone. Not a moment too soon, either. Peter Linman's head appeared round her door.

'Ready?'

'Absolutely.' She got up, smoothed down her skirt and prayed her cheeks weren't too red.

'Enjoy the holiday?' he asked as they rode upwards in the lift.

'Er, yes. It was . . . lovely.'

'Glad to hear it. Nothing like a spot of sun.'

'Er, no.' She had to bite down on her tongue to stop herself smiling.

It was nearly ten o'clock by the time she got home that evening. She opened her front door, dumped her briefcase and handbag and practically ran into the living room. Her answering machine glowed reassuringly. Six messages. She played each one, her stomach going round and round in knots of anticipation . . . two from Paula, a missed call, another one from Paula, one from her mother and . . . she held her breath. *Yes!* 'Hi, it's Nick. Just called to make sure you got back OK. I'm at Stansted now. I'll call tomorrow.' She all but collapsed on the sofa. She played it back twice more. She got up, unwound her scarf and slipped out of her jacket and heels. She padded across the living room to the kitchen and opened the fridge. The chilled bottle of Sancerre stared back at her. She opened it, poured herself a glass and walked back to the phone. Eleven minutes past ten . . . too late to call Paula? Just as her hand reached out, the phone rang again.

'Hello?'

'Hi, it's Nick. You're not asleep, are you?'

Her heart contracted so painfully she nearly yelped out loud. 'Asleep? No . . . no, I just got home from work.'

'Ah. You work too hard, I remember.'

Her heart gave another squeeze. 'What time d'you get back to Celle?' she asked, looking at her watch.

'Oh, it'll be a couple of hours yet. The flight's delayed. As usual. But I've just seen a couple of squaddies . . . we'll get a cab back to Celle together. Should be home by one.'

'And up at six?' Sam teased. 'What do you call it? First reveille?'

'Clever girl. Although I don't live on the base, so no . . . just the alarm clock for me. Anyway, better run. I think they're calling the flight. I'll call tomorrow.'

'OK. Well . . . bye?' Sam said, not sure what else to say. I miss you? It had only been a day. It hardly seemed appropriate. But he was gone. She sat on the edge of the couch, staring at the phone, unable to believe her luck. Not only had he called, but he'd called twice! Suddenly it rang again. She picked it up, her heart accelerating. It was Paula.

'So . . . you were going to call?' Paula's voice was dripping with as much sarcasm as she could pack into it.

'I was . . . I only just got home. And, Paula . . . guess what?'

'Don't tell me. He called.'

'Yes, he called.'

'All right, all right . . . keep your knickers on. Or is it too late for that?'

Sam had to smile. Paula definitely had a way with words. 'Yeah, sadly. Anyhow, the point is . . . I'm going to see him in Germany in three weeks' time.'

'Germany? OK, that's enough. I need to know every fucking detail. Start.'

She lay in bed after the hour-long conversation, during which time Paula had wormed every 'fucking' detail, just as she'd threatened, out of an ecstatically happy Sam. She lay back against the pillows, her head swimming in a manner that was alarmingly uncharacteristic. She who was normally so cautious, expecting and anticipating the worst in almost every single situation . . . how had she ended up with a goofy grin on her face, daydreaming wildly about a man she'd only just met? Not only was it not *like* her, it just wasn't her. She'd never felt this way about anyone before, ever. Nick. Nick Beasdale. She whispered his name into her pillow. Just thinking about him produced the most alarming response throughout her whole body. 'You've got it bad,' was Paula's final pronouncement. 'Just be careful. You don't really know him yet.'

'But I do,' Sam protested. 'That's the funny thing. I feel as though I've known him all my life.'

'Oh, Sam. He's practically the first boyfriend you've ever had.'

'I know. I can't explain it . . . but it's true. I feel . . . I feel so safe around him.'

'Safe? Why? Are you in danger or something?'

'No, of course not. It's just—'

'He's a *soldier*. Of course you feel *safe*, you dope. That's what they're trained to do . . . make us feel safe. Haven't you been watching the news?' Paula interrupted her with a laugh.

'No, well, yes . . . no, that's not it.'

'Well, don't say I didn't warn you.'

'Oh, for God's sake,' Sam said, suddenly irritated. 'Can't you just be happy for me? I've met someone. He likes me. I like him. That's as far as it's got. I'm not about to run off and get married, you know.'

Paula was immediately contrite. 'No, of course not. I'm sorry . . . really, I am. I'm just being over-protective, that's all. I'm thrilled for you, honestly.'

'OK. Look, I've got to be up early . . . I'd better get some sleep. I'll call you tomorrow, OK?' Sam was suddenly over-whelmed by it all. She could feel her throat thickening and the last thing she wanted to do was burst into tears whilst Paula was on the line.

'Promise?' Paula's voice was anxious.

'Promise. Sleep tight.'

'You too.'

So here she was, unable to sleep, unable to believe what had happened to her in the short space of a few days, unable to turn her head to the meeting the following morning, unable to do anything, in other words, other than think about Nick Beasdale and the unbelievably exciting prospect of seeing him again. Paula was right. She did have it bad.

79

ABBY
Celle, Germany, 2009

The car tooted unexpectedly, nearly causing Abby to fall off. She wobbled for a second, righted herself and then flipped the driver the bird, cursing as she hurriedly mounted the pavement.

'Excuse me,' a pompous voice called out as the car swept past. 'That's no way to greet an officer.'

Abby nearly fell off for the second time. She pulled the brakes and wobbled to a halt. 'Ralph! Really . . . you nearly made me fall off,' she said crossly, putting both feet down on the ground. 'What are you doing home, anyway? It's not even lunchtime!'

'Sorry, darling.' Ralph had pulled the car over to the side and was now getting out of it. 'Couldn't resist.' He came over and placed a hand on her arm. There was someone behind him, in uniform. 'I was just taking Major Beasdale to his new home.'

Abby looked past him to where a man was getting out of the passenger seat. He stood up and walked towards her. Her eyes widened in surprise. Blue-grey eyes, tall, broad-shouldered, if anything a little heavier than when she'd seen him last. But *where* had she last seen him? It came to her in a flash. At the cemetery, in Cyprus. He'd stood to one side at the burial of that poor girl . . . what was her name? Magda. Magda Evgeni. She stood with her hands on the handlebars, unsure whether to say anything. Had he recognised her? If he had, his eyes made no sign of it.

'Major Beasdale, my wife.' Ralph made the introductions.

'Nice to meet you, Mrs Barclay,' he said, stepping forward. His handshake was brief and perfunctory.

'Oh, do call me Abby. I must say, you do look rather familiar,' she said, testing him. 'Were you in Belize or Cyprus perhaps?'

She'd scored a hit, she saw that immediately. He was good at concealing his emotions. Only the muscle next to his jaw gave him away. It twitched, a faint tremor across his face. 'Cyprus,' he confirmed. 'But I was only there for a couple of weeks. Got transferred almost straight away.'

What were you doing at Magda Evgeni's funeral? she wanted to ask, but couldn't. 'I must've bumped into you somewhere there, then,' Abby said, mostly for Ralph's benefit. 'Probably at the NAAFI.'

'Probably.' He had retreated back into himself.

'Right, well . . . we'd better get a move on,' Ralph said, stepping back and opening the car door again. 'He's going to be in the house on Kleingärtnersstrasse, along with Harding and MacKenzie.'

'Ah, the famous bachelor pad.' Abby smiled at him. 'No family, I take it?'

'Nope.'

'Well, do come round for dinner once you've settled in. We had Tom Astor and his wife round the other night.'

There it was again. The tremor. 'Thank you. Look forward to it.' He nodded at her and then turned and climbed back into the passenger seat. Abby gave them both a wave and then continued on her way. There was definitely something odd about Major Beasdale, but she couldn't work out what. His accent, for one . . . there was something in it . . . something not quite right. Was he English? And for another, there was his manner, a certain . . . she pondered over her choice of words . . . lack of feeling? Was that it? Those cold, steely eyes, and the way his face hid whatever he was really thinking. She was slightly unnerved by him. She liked being able to see into a person's eyes, to see what they were thinking and feeling. She was good at it. Growing up in a household where strict discipline was maintained at all times and at all costs had taught her to look beneath the surface of what was being said to get at the real meaning of events . . . she'd been doing it all her life. Now she'd come face to face with someone with whom she couldn't. Well, she thought to herself as she cycled up the short hill back to the house, if there was one thing she *was* sure of, it was that Nick Beasdale *did* have hidden depths; it was simply that he wouldn't allow her – or anyone else, she guessed – to see them.

Ralph came home late that evening, after having supper at the mess. She and Sadie had spent bedtime reading German fairy tales and Abby was exhausted. With a child's unerring ability to pick up whatever was said to her, Sadie's German was already nearly as good as Abby's. 'But what does that word *mean*, Mummy?' Sadie asked repeatedly. Abby's patience was wearing thin.

'Good evening, darling?' she asked, as Ralph came into the dining room. She was sorting out laundry.

'Not as good as yours, clearly,' Ralph murmured, hugging her from behind as she separated out the socks from the T-shirts and Ralph's boxer shorts.

'Stop it. I've got to get this done.' She slapped his hand lightly away from her breast.

'Ah. The laundry.'

'No, I'm serious. It's Heidi's day tomorrow and if I want her to do the ironing as well as—' Abby stopped herself just in time. The domestic details of the household were not Ralph's concern or interest. 'How about a drink?' she asked, turning away from the laundry. 'It's Friday, after all. Late start tomorrow.'

'Yeah, why not? Thanks.' Ralph moved past her and went into the lounge.

She took out a bottle of his favourite whisky and was back within minutes with ice and two crystal tumblers. 'Cheers,' she said, pouring them both a small measure. Neither she nor Ralph were particularly heavy drinkers.

'Cheers, darling.' He took a sip. 'Christ, what a day. I don't know how we're going to get this lot in shape before spring.'

'Is he any good?'

'Who?'

'Major Beasdale.'

'Oh, he's all right, I think. A bit of a plodder, as young Astor would say.'

'They knew each other, didn't they? Weren't they posted somewhere together?'

'Mmm. Massereene. County Antrim. That was a while ago, though. I believe he was married at the time.'

'Oh, he's divorced?' Abby was surprised. He didn't look like the marrying kind.

'Mmm. He's got a girlfriend, though. An entertainment lawyer, of all things. He was telling me about her this evening. He's quiet but with a couple of drinks in him, he opens up a bit. I like that, actually. Can't stand the types who spill everything out.'

Abby had to suppress a smile. Like Ian Harding, she wanted to say, but didn't. 'An entertainment lawyer? That's unusual. Where on earth did he meet her?'

Ralph shrugged. 'Don't know. Forgot to ask him.' He took another sip of whisky. 'She's coming over in about a fortnight, apparently, so you'll get to ask her all the questions you want.' He grinned at her. 'I know what you women are like.'

'No, you don't.' Abby smiled back at him. It was funny how easily the balance between them had been restored, she thought to herself as they both sipped their whiskies in comfortable silence. It was mostly down to Ralph, if she was honest about it. After all, he was the one who'd been wronged. She coughed suddenly.

'You all right?' Ralph looked up at her with a frown.

She nodded quickly. She could feel a blush stealing over her as it did whenever she thought about what had happened in Belize. Or him. She got up suddenly. She tried very hard not to think about it. One mistake, that was all. A silly, meaningless mistake

396

that had brought her very close to destroying everything she'd ever wanted. 'I . . . I think I'll go and get ready . . . for bed,' she said faintly. 'It's been a long day.'

'Be with you in a sec,' Ralph said, draining his own glass. 'Just need to sort out something for tomorrow. Don't go to sleep.'

'I . . . I won't.' Abby turned and fled the room before his eyes could detect anything further.

80

MEAGHAN
Celle, Germany, 2009

'Um, how much are these?' Meaghan held up a bunch of tight yellow roses, their curled, velvety petals still wrapped around each other so that the water drops trapped between them glinted like jewels in the sun. The stallholder released a torrent of incomprehensible sounds, followed by a frown. Meaghan's heart sank. She shook her head. 'I'm sorry, I don't speak German. English?' she asked hopefully. He shook his head again.

'*Wieviel sind die Blumen?*'

Meaghan spun round. Standing behind her, her hands resting jauntily on her bicycle handlebars, was Abby Barclay.

'*Fünf euros.*' The stallholder grinned at Abby; he was either relieved, or he knew her. Probably both.

'Five euros. Not bad. And they're fresh.' Abby's smile was quick and friendly.

Meaghan pulled a five-euro note from her wallet and handed it over. 'Thanks,' she said nervously. 'I really ought to learn. I'm so crap at other languages.'

'Oh, don't worry. By the time you leave you'll have picked up enough. I get most of mine from my daughter.'

'Oh, yes . . . I heard. She's in the German school, isn't she?'

Abby nodded. She rolled her eyes. 'Not really the done thing, I'm afraid. But I thought to myself, what's the point of moving around the world every two years if you don't at least pick up a couple of other languages whilst you're at it. Seems a bit of a wasted opportunity, if you ask me. And she'll thank me for it later on. No matter what top brass says.'

Meaghan didn't know what to say. There was something so light and easy about Abby Barclay – it was hard to grasp that she was the most senior army wife on the base. No one outranked her. Like her husband, she wore it lightly. 'Wish I could persuade Tom to send Alannah there,' she found herself saying. 'Not sure he'd like it, though.'

'But would you?' Abby asked, thanking the stallholder as he placed the wrapped parcel of roses on the counter.

'I . . . I don't know. I suppose so. For us . . . well, you know what Australians are like. We barely speak English.'

Abby laughed. 'That's not true. Kevin Rudd speaks Mandarin, you know.'

Meaghan was momentarily nonplussed. Kevin Rudd?

'Your prime minister,' Abby prompted gently.

'Oh, of course. *That* Kevin Rudd,' Meaghan stammered, blushing. Christ, the woman must think her a complete dolt. 'I . . . I just wasn't sure which . . .' She stopped herself. No need to be a liar as well as a dunce. 'Actually, I *do* know who Kevin Rudd is. I just wasn't expecting you to . . . dunno why. You're about the most intelligent woman I've ever met,' she said suddenly.

'That's incredibly kind of you,' Abby said, laughing. 'But I hardly think two A-levels and a certificate in typing makes me all that intelligent!'

Meaghan's eyes widened. A typist? It wasn't the image she'd formed of Abby Barclay. 'I . . . well, I don't even have those,' she said, smiling ruefully. 'Left school before I was sixteen.'

'Would you like to have a coffee?' Abby said suddenly. 'I've got about an hour to kill before I pick up Sadie. There's a very sweet little café just around the corner.'

'I'd love to,' Meaghan said, her heart lifting unexpectedly. 'Alannah's not back until three.'

'Well, shall we?' Abby stuck the packet of roses in the pannier of her bicycle and pushed it alongside. '*Kaffee und Küchen*. One of the best things about Germany.'

'How come you speak such good German?' Meaghan asked as they walked along.

'My dad was stationed here when I was a kid. I did the same as Sadie's doing . . . went to kindergarten and then the first year of primary school. I did German at school in England as well. It's a very precise language. I like that; I've no idea why.'

Meaghan didn't know what to say. As genuinely nice as Abby was, she was also clearly out of Meaghan's league. She'd heard Tom say only a dozen times that her father was one of the all-time army legends and that if there was anything on this planet like the perfect army wife, Abby Barclay was it. 'Oh,' she said, hoping the response would cover all bases.

Abby laughed. 'Don't mind me, I'm being pretentious. Look, here's the café. Nice, isn't it?'

Meaghan nodded, following her in. They ordered two cappuccinos and a slice of cheesecake to share. Not only was Abby Barclay clever, Meaghan noticed, she was enviably slim as well. She had a feeling she'd take one bite and she, Meaghan, would wolf down the rest.

'So . . . I hear you were with the new B Coy commander in Northern Ireland,' Abby said when their coffees had arrived. 'Major Beasdale.'

Meaghan nearly scalded her mouth. 'Er, yes. He . . . it was a long time ago. I . . . I don't remember him that well.'

Abby's eyes regarded hers frankly. 'Apparently he was in Cyprus when we were there, but only briefly. His girlfriend's coming over in a couple of weeks.'

'His girlfriend?' This time Meaghan really did scald her mouth. 'He's got a girlfriend?' It was a giveaway. 'I . . . I didn't know he had one. He . . . he was married when we knew him.'

'Divorced, I hear. Like so many others.' Abby gave a sigh. She took one forkful of cheesecake and pushed the plate across the table, just as Meaghan had feared. She couldn't stop herself –

she needed something to do with her hands. She took one mouthful, then another.

'So who's his new girlfriend?' she asked through a mouth of the most delicious cheesecake she'd ever tasted.

'I don't know. All Ralph said was that she's a lawyer. An entertainment lawyer.'

'A *lawyer*?' Meaghan couldn't stop herself from squeaking.

Abby smiled. 'Why? You sound surprised.'

Meaghan nodded, aware she was probably saying too much. 'His ex-wife was a barmaid,' she said, hoping she didn't sound too bitchy.

'Oh. Well. I suppose you've got more chance of meeting a barmaid than an entertainment lawyer if you're in the army,' Abby said after a moment. 'Would you like another coffee?'

Meaghan nodded. She needed something to get over the shock. What the hell was a *lawyer* doing with someone like Nick? 'When's she coming?' she asked.

'Ralph said something about a fortnight . . . probably just before the bank holiday. I'm assuming we'll meet her. I've no idea how long they've been together.' She smiled suddenly. 'Look at us. I used to hate it when my mother and her friends started gossiping about the other wives . . . and now here I am, doing the same.'

'Well, it's hardly gossiping. We haven't met her.'

'Mmm. I wonder if we will.'

81

'D'you think I ought to invite them round for dinner?' Abby asked Ralph later that evening. They were both sitting in her studio/study; she was at her easel, he was hunched over his laptop. 'Beasdale and his girlfriend. Or is that a bit too presumptuous?'

Ralph looked up from his screen. 'No, that'd be fine. I'll find out how long she's here for.'

'I had coffee with Meaghan Astor this morning. She's nice, you know.'

'Mmm.'

'She's a lot smarter than she lets on.'

'What d'you mean?'

'Oh, I don't know . . . she puts on a bit of a ditzy blonde act, but she's quite tough underneath. She used to be a beautician, back in Australia. Left school at sixteen.'

'Blimey.' Ralph's attention was only peripherally on her.

'I like her.'

'That's nice.' His comment signalled the end of his concentration. She turned back to her painting, slightly irritated but not willing to push him. It was almost halfway complete. She would try and finish it before the dinner party, she thought to herself. She particularly liked the way the colours of the fruit had come out – she'd chosen the right ones – yellows, reds, oranges, dark greens . . . but had added a touch of grey to each. *Chiaroscuro*. Light and dark. She remembered the term from school.

For a few minutes she was back there in the large, airy space overlooking the Hereford countryside where the art classes had taken place. She'd longed to go to art school. As soon as her O-levels were over and she returned to London she'd told her parents of her wish. She'd spent the whole of the upper fifth dreaming about it. The Slade School of Fine Art. She'd secretly applied for the prospectus and sat up in bed, night after night, poring over the courses on offer, dreaming of a life spent in a studio much like the one at school, wearing drainpipe blue jeans and splattered overalls, smoking Gitânes. The life of an artist. Of course it hadn't turned out like that. She'd gone to Lucie Clayton's and in the place of drainpipe jeans she'd worn a plaid skirt and a white blouse with a ruffle at the collar like everyone else. She'd never quite succumbed to a string of pearls – of that she was inordinately proud. But as for the rest . . . she'd gone along with her parents' wishes just like that.

Talking, however briefly, to Meaghan Astor that morning,

she'd suddenly had a glimpse of someone who hadn't – who'd said no, and voted with her feet. Abby had to admit to being shocked when she heard that as a girl she had left school before sixteen. She hadn't said much – to her credit, she wasn't the type to spill every single detail of her life to someone who, to all intents and purposes, was still a complete stranger but still . . . Abby was adept enough at reading between the lines. It couldn't have been easy. No wonder she'd married Tom Astor almost as soon as she clapped eyes on him. She would. Sixteen? God, practically the same age as Clara. At the thought of her eldest daughter stuffing a few clothes into an overnight bag and hitch-hiking some six hundred miles to the nearest big city, she was quite overcome with terror. She pushed her chair away from the easel and almost ran from the room. Luckily Ralph was too absorbed in whatever report he was writing to look up, never mind notice her fear. She walked quickly down the corridor to the bathroom and shut the door behind her. She splashed a handful of cool water on her burning cheeks. Funny how the past can sneak up behind you, she thought to herself as she patted her face dry. Just when you think you've forgotten it, too. She folded the towel neatly and switched off the light. Blast the past. Why couldn't it stay exactly where it belonged?

82

SAM
Celle, Germany, 2009

The plane began its slow, circular descent into Hanover. Sam, strapped into her seat with a G & T under her belt, felt her heart begin to accelerate. The flight was short – just over an hour – but actually getting to Stansted had taken twice as long. She'd walked out of court at three that afternoon, the case finally – *finally* – over. She jumped into her car and tore up Park Lane towards her flat, praying that today, of all days, wouldn't be the day she was caught speeding. She was in luck. She screeched to a halt in front of her flat, raced up the stairs and burst into her bedroom. There were already several outfits lying on the bed – jeans, a pair of black woollen trousers, a pair of tweed just-below-the-knee shorts . . . a selection of blouses and jumpers, as well as camisoles and, still in their candy-striped wrapping paper, a whole new wardrobe of underwear. She'd spent the most pleasurable afternoon she could recall in a long, long time on the third floor of Selfridges the previous weekend, trying and buying. Silk knickers in the most beautiful array of colours – burgundy, midnight blue, charcoal grey and ivory . . . with bras and demi-bras to match. She shuddered to think of just how much she'd spent that afternoon but she'd enjoyed it so much. Lying next to the brand-new orange leather weekend case from Tumi (basement, Selfridges) was her selection of shoes. Jimmy Choo, of course, and her favourite boots from Hobbs. Two pairs from L.K. Bennett and the brand-new loafers from Tod's, which she absolutely loved the minute she saw them in the window. Another expensive purchase but Christ, she hadn't been shopping like this in a while. What a pleasure it was to shop for clothes when there was someone there to admire them. What did Nick like? she wondered. In the three days they'd spent together, she'd only seen him in khaki cargo pants, a pair of jeans and those short-sleeved polo shirts that men always seemed to wear. At least they were colourful – pink, she recalled, and purple . . . and on the last day, light blue. Like his eyes. At the thought of him, her stomach gave another little lurch. It had been giving little lurches every few minutes since her arrival back in the UK.

She carefully stowed away her choices in the new suitcase, folding the more delicate items between sheets of tissue paper. Her shoes were the last to be slipped in – the red Jimmy Choos looked ever so stylish as she zipped up the case and stood it on its side. She took a quick shower, taking care not to wet her hair which had been cut and coloured two days earlier – she'd *begged* her stylist to stay open until eight. Body lotion, deodorant, perfume, and a light spray of body oil . . . she turned to face the mirror. She hadn't been to the gym in three days, dammit . . . not that you could tell. She stood in silent contemplation of her body for a second, marvelling at how much she'd changed. No one would ever have guessed that she would turn out this way. For a second, her mind drifted back to the sad, overweight teenager she'd been and to the night she'd stood outside Kate's room, listening to the sounds of Loïc Malaquais's laughter. As their whispers grew quieter and the moans grew louder, she'd crept along the corridor to her own room, blinded by tears of rage and jealousy . . . and what had she done? She'd hauled out her stash of chocolates and proceeded to eat her way through every single bar she could find. Well, not any more. She couldn't remember the last time she'd eaten a chocolate bar and as for the thought of Kate stealing her boyfriend . . . she almost laughed out loud.

'Ladies and gentlemen, this is your captain speaking.' The announcement interrupted her thoughts. They were a few minutes away from landing. She looked out of the window again, savouring every moment. Somewhere in the long, low building ahead of them, Nick was waiting. She suddenly found it hard to remember what he looked like. She could remember snatches – his eyes, and the texture of his hair . . . and that lovely, slow drawl of his that was both familiar and not. She tightened her seat belt against the butterflies in her stomach and closed her eyes. In less than half an hour, he would be there, in front of her . . . larger, in all senses, than life.

She sauntered through the sliding doors, trying not to look as though she was expecting to see anyone. There were several people standing there, all looking expectantly at each arrival as he or she came through the glass. But there was no Nick. She stood uncertainly for a moment, not sure what to do. She was so sure he'd be there . . . perhaps not with open arms and a bunch of flowers, but still . . . it was almost ten thirty at night and there was no sign of him. Disappointment felled her like a blow, followed almost immediately by fear. What if he'd changed his mind? What if he'd led her on, and had never intended to come? What if he didn't live in Celle at all . . . and wasn't even in the British Army? What if—?

'Sam.' She whirled round, all pretence of cool suddenly deserting her.

'Nick! I thought you'd—' She stopped herself just in time. 'There you are . . . was just wondering where you'd got to.'

'I can't believe it. I've been here since nine . . . just went to the loo.' He was smiling at her. That slow, wide smile she remembered from Morocco. Her knees suddenly went weak with relief.

'Since nine?' she echoed disbelievingly as he took her bag from her. 'Why on earth did you come so early?' She noticed he had a novel in his hand. She looked at the cover as discreetly as she could. J. M. Coetzee. *Disgrace*. He flew immediately upwards in her estimation. An army officer who read Coetzee?

'I . . . I was a bit nervous, to tell you the truth. Didn't know if you'd show up. And I couldn't bear sitting at home waiting, so I came early.'

Sam felt her heart do a slow somersault. He was nervous. Unsure. Like her. Oh, they were off to a good start. She could just *hear* Paula's voice in her head. *Just be careful, won't you?* Paula hadn't met him; that was the problem. If she had, she'd have realised immediately that her fears were completely unfounded. She followed him outside to the taxi rank, and within seconds they were in the back of the white Mercedes, speeding along a freeway towards Celle. Nick slid his arm around the back of her shoulders, pulling her close to him. She snuggled in, her skin tingling where he touched her. She couldn't wait to recount every single detail of the journey and her arrival to Paula when she got back. She still couldn't get over it. Four weeks ago she'd been single, returning home to an empty flat each night, staring down the prospect of another lonely weekend with no relief in sight. And now, here she was, sitting in the back of a cab in the middle of the German countryside with a man's hand on the bare nape of her neck, stroking it. She pushed herself closer into his embrace, breathing in his warm, vital scent, willing herself to remember every single detail, no matter how small. The song on the radio, the colour of the dashboard lights, the signs pointing to names she could barely pronounce, the darkly silhouetted trees as they rounded one forested bend after another. A sign leapt out at her from the darkness. *Bergen Belsen Konzentrationslager.* She blinked. Bergen Belsen Concentration Camp? 'Is that . . . isn't that—?'

'Bergen Belsen? Yeah, it's only about six kilometres away. We're close to Celle now.'

'I didn't know it was here,' she murmured. 'I always thought they were . . . I don't know . . . somewhere else?'

'No, it's just beyond the forest. I haven't been myself, mind you, but we do quite a lot of training exercises in those woods.'

'Oh.' Once again Sam was reminded of how far removed his world was from hers. Training exercises? What sort of exercises?

'Live ammunition,' he said, reading her mind. 'There's a firing range here and another one at Sennelager. Bit further south.'

She didn't quite know what to say. Luckily the taxi swept into the beginnings of a town and her attention was claimed by a sudden rash of neon signs. Most of them were for adult entertainment she noticed, blushing.

'Knocking shops.' Nick grinned against her hair. 'Goes with the territory. Wherever there's a bunch of squaddies . . . well, you can guess the rest.'

'And by that you mean brothels?' Sam asked, slightly embarrassed.

He gave a short laugh and was about to say something when the taxi driver interrupted them and asked what number. Nick gave a few directions in very halting German and a few minutes later they pulled up in front of a large, rather austere-looking house. 'This is it,' he said, opening the door. 'It's nothing special, I warn you. I only moved in a couple of weeks ago so don't expect anything fancy.'

'I won't.' Sam laughed, touched by his obvious nervousness.

'I'm a bachelor, remember?'

'How could I forget? Don't worry. I'm here to see you, not your flat.'

'Well, don't say I didn't warn you. Entrance is round the back. Come on.'

It certainly did belong to a bachelor, was Sam's first thought as she walked through the door. It had the stripped, pared-down look of a home that wasn't really a home, just a place to sleep, eat and occasionally watch TV. The walls were magnolia and none too clean and the carpet was a peculiar shade of green. What little furniture there was was uniformly dull and falling apart but there were two large green candles burning in the windowsill and a bunch of flowers on the dining room table. The hallway was pretty much taken up by three gigantic trunks of the sort she remembered friends taking to boarding school – black metal with red chevrons. She hurriedly suppressed a smile.

'Living room, dining room, couple of bedrooms . . . oh, the bathroom's down there and the kitchen's in here,' Nick said, throwing open a door. 'And this is my bedroom.'

She peered inside. A small room completely dominated by a large bed with a burgundy duvet, which had clearly been hastily smoothed, and three mismatched pillows. 'It looks . . . lovely,' she lied, thinking of her own, beautifully decorated flat back in London.

'No, it doesn't.' He grinned. 'But it's fine. It'll do for the time being. D'you want something to drink?' He came out of the kitchen already holding two wine glasses and a bottle by the neck.

'Er, sure. Why not?' It was nearly midnight but she could sense he didn't quite know what to do with his hands, his talk, himself. It touched her. They drank sitting on the couch, Sam half-lying against him. 'Why didn't you think I'd come?' she asked, savouring the feeling of having someone to talk to about herself, to see herself through someone else's eyes. She could feel him shrug as he took another mouthful of wine.

'Dunno. I just didn't.'

'But—'

'Here, we're wasting time.' He gave a light laugh and took her wine glass from her, setting it down carefully on the worn carpet. 'C'mere.' He stopped her from questioning any further by slipping a hand inside her shirt, expertly unfastening the buttons that hid her bra. His hand was warm and insistent and, in a millisecond, all thoughts of what he thought about her were banished by the tremendous need with which he sought her, and she responded. He almost tore the shirt from her back, freeing her hair from its clasp with a satisfied grunt. Both wine glasses were knocked over but he was beyond seeing, or caring. This was rougher and more urgent than it had been in Marrakech and, at first, Sam was a little unnerved by his haste.

'Hey, slow down,' she whispered, as his fingers tried to steady himself to enter her, barely a minute after they'd kissed. 'Slow down.'

'I . . . I can't,' he hissed against her mouth. 'Not now.'

She swallowed nervously. There was an undercurrent in his breathing and the way he pushed and pinched her flesh that genuinely unnerved her. She'd had so little experience of it but there was something strange about his thrusting in and out of her that made her cling on, not just to him but to the sides of the battered old couch, waiting for a storm of some unknown kind to rage through him. He was above her now; she was pinned beneath his considerable weight. She opened her eyes a fraction and the red, sweating face seemed to belong to someone else. The cords in his neck stood out and his cheeks blew in and out with some terrible effort he made, far below the surface of his expression. She closed her eyes again. It wasn't the welcome she'd been waiting for but she had so little idea of what to expect . . . perhaps it was best just to let him wear himself out? She tried to manoeuvre herself into a more comfortable position beneath him, but he was so heavy it was almost impossible. Her leg felt as though it were numb, pinned awkwardly by his knee. She could feel the buckle of his cargo pants cutting into her skin.

There'd be one hell of a bruise the following morning, she thought to herself, desperately trying to stay still, or calm . . . both. The jawing back and forth went on and on; Nick's hand was buried deep inside her hair, his mouth moved across her face, his other hand roamed across her stomach, stopping every now and then to grasp at her skin. Would it never end? Suddenly there was a great stiffening that seemed to come from deep within him. A groan – more like a growl, really – was ripped from his throat and with a great roar and a last, desperate thrust inside her, he came. It was nothing like Marrakech. The tenderness and the sensual teasing of her body and skin was gone. This was a rough, desperate race to some far-off end that seemed to have little to do with her.

He rolled away from her almost immediately, his whole body still spasming. Sam lay next to him, her heart thudding, almost too afraid to move. She glanced at him from underneath her lashes, unable to speak. His eyes were narrowed, almost closed and the reddish blush that stained his cheeks was slowly seeping towards his temples. After a moment, aware of her gaze, he turned his head a fraction and smiled. 'Sorry about that,' he whispered. 'I get like that if I haven't had sex in a while.'

Sam had no idea what to say, if a response was even required. *A while* – did that mean since the last time he'd seen her? But it was only three weeks . . . was that a long time? Or was it normal? She tried to stretch her rubbery legs. 'I . . . I'll just nip to the loo,' she mumbled, trying to sit upright.

'Sure.' He swung his legs aside and helped her up. 'You OK?'

She nodded, not trusting herself to speak. Her shirt was lying on the back of the sofa and her bra was nowhere to be seen. Her tweed pedal pushers had been pushed down to her ankles but both her boots were still on. She bent to pull her trousers up and try to arrange her clothing so that she looked and felt a little less ridiculous and vulnerable. She walked quickly to the bathroom that he'd pointed out when she came in and closed the door. Behind her she could hear the sound of the television being switched on. She looked at herself in the small, stained mirror above the sink. She blinked. There was an ugly red welt down the side of her face and her mascara was completely smudged. She looked as though she'd been crying. She put up a hand to touch her cheek – no pain, just a little tenderness. She bent down and drank water from the tap, cupping her hand to scoop it up. Then she turned on the hot tap and washed her face and between her legs, a conversation with herself beginning to develop as she cleaned herself up. She was fine; *it* was fine. He'd been so pleased to see her, that was all. He was a little rough around the edges, granted, but nothing she couldn't either handle or smooth out. He was a soldier – what did she expect? He'd been without the softening touches of a steady relationship for ages – she would have to give him time. She rinsed out the cloth and was just about to hang it back over the bathtub when her eye was caught by a plastic container next to the shower. It was full of brightly coloured condoms and half-empty bottles of lubricant. She stared at it, embarrassment and fear flooding her simultaneously. He hadn't used a condom; not then in Marrakech and not now. She'd been so taken aback by the sheer unexpectedness of the whole thing that it hadn't even occurred to her to ask. What if . . . ? She swallowed nervously. She was thirty-nine years old. The chances of her getting pregnant were slim, weren't they? And if he had a box full of condoms for his regular use – she stumbled over the word in her mind – well, that would mean the chances of catching something – she had no idea what – were equally slim. She ought to be relieved. She suddenly longed for Paula. Paula knew all about this stuff. How to behave, what to do, expect, demand, suspect. Paula would know what sorts of questions to ask, and more importantly, what the answers really meant.

'You OK?' Nick's voice suddenly sounded behind the closed door.

She gave a start. 'Yes, yes . . . just coming.' She turned on the tap again, splashed some cold water on her face and patted it dry. She opened the door. He was standing there with a bunch of red and pink roses, still wrapped in their brown paper with a covering of cellophane. He grinned at her sheepishly.

'Bought these for you this morning,' he said, looking down at them. 'Forgot to put them in a vase. Actually, that's a lie. I don't even possess a vase.' He stuck them out for her to take.

Sam was suddenly overcome with remorse. 'They're gorgeous,' she said, tears springing to her eyes. When was the last time anyone had bought her flowers? Even for her birthday? 'You shouldn't have.'

'And why not? You're gorgeous. You really are.' He pulled her to him, taking care not to squash the flowers, and kissed her on the forehead. 'Let's go to bed. It's way past midnight and we're going for a bike ride in the morning. I borrowed a bike from Ian . . . he's the bloke who lives upstairs. He's in the UK this weekend . . . persuaded him to visit his wife so we could have a bit of time to ourselves.'

Sam thought her heart would melt. He'd bought her flowers; he'd organised a bike for her; he wanted to spend time alone with her. The doubts she'd had in the bathroom fled, dissolving in the warmth that flowed through and around her. He *liked* her. He seemed to really like her. She was completely taken aback by the overwhelming feeling of gratitude that swept through her. Gratitude? Some distant part of her brain recognised it as such and was disdainful. *Gratitude?* Why on earth should she be *grateful* that he liked her? But Christ, she was.

83

ABBY
Celle, Germany, 2009

'They're here,' Ralph called out to Abby who was putting the last-minute touches to the lamb curry she'd spent the past two days making. The cheerful orange Le Creuset casserole pot was sitting on top of the stove; next to it, still simmering gently, was a pot of fragrant Thai rice. Good job Clara wasn't there, she thought to herself with a smile. She positively hated curry. 'It makes me feel *ill*,' she declared every time Abby made it. Sadie was spending the night at a friend's house, just up the road.

'Coming,' she answered. 'Would you get the door?'

'Astors are here too,' Ralph added as he passed on his way to the door. 'On time as always.'

She took a quick look around the kitchen; everything was under control. She peeled off her apron, checked the rice one last time, made sure her hair was in place and then stepped into the hallway.

She saw Nick Beasdale first. As usual, there was a second's shock recognition whenever she saw him, as though she would never be able to erase that first, unexplained glimpse of him, then the memory slid away. 'Hello, Nick,' she said, holding out a hand. 'Lovely to see you again.'

'Hi.' Nick was decidedly less formal than when she'd last seen him. He shook her hand warmly. Standing behind him, framed by the soft hallway light, was a woman. Blonde, tall, slim, elegant . . . Abby's mind took in the details. No, make that very blonde, very tall, very slim and very, very elegant. She gulped. She was wearing a black jersey dress with a large cowl-neck which draped itself elegantly over one shoulder, black fishnet tights which could just be seen at the knee and a pair of the softest, most gorgeous black leather boots Abby had ever set eyes on. Her hair was pulled back and set in a high chignon at the back of her head, held in place by a tortoiseshell comb and a couple of smaller, similar clasps. Silver hoop earrings and a large, mannish silver ring completed the outfit. No watch, no necklace, no bracelet. Just the earrings and the ring . . . and those damned boots. 'Mrs Barclay . . . this is, er, Sam,' he mumbled, clearly slightly embarrassed.

'Oh . . . I'm Abby. Do call me Abby,' Abby recovered enough poise to say smoothly, shaking the woman's hand. Her hand was firm.

'Lovely to meet you, Abby.' Her voice was low and beautifully modulated. Posh, but not too posh. Definitely middle class. Where the hell had Nick Beasdale found this woman?

'Meaghan . . . Tom . . . do come in.' Abby looked past them to where Meaghan was standing, open-mouthed. 'Let's get everyone into the living room, shall we? It's a bit more comfortable than standing in the hallway.' Abby smiled. She caught Meaghan's panicked expression. All three men were staring at Sam as if she'd landed on Halkettstrasse from another planet. 'Ralph?' Abby muttered as she walked past. 'Drinks?'

'Yes, of course.' He seemed to come to his senses. 'What can I get everyone?'

Ten minutes later they were all comfortably seated in the living room, glasses of wine and beer at hand. Meaghan was still looking dumbstruck, Abby noticed with a small tremor of sympathy. Among the rest of the wives on the base, Meaghan could just about hold her own. Her diffidence towards the social life that was on offer was as much to do with her own uncertainty about her place within it as any disdain she affected to feel. With her, it was different. Her status, not only as the CO's wife, but as her father's daughter, secured her a distance even before she arrived. She was aware of it, disliked it, but had lived long enough within the army's merciless hierarchy to know that fighting against it was pointless. Better to go with the flow, picking and choosing where and how to spend her time and, crucially, maintaining enough of a healthy distance not to allow the petty barbs and jibes that seemed part of the territory to pierce her. She'd had a lifetime's experience of it – Meaghan had not. The little comments – both said and unsaid – that accompanied her every time she stepped into their midst, hurt. She could see it; Meaghan, unlike the undeniably gorgeous and poised woman in front of them, wore her emotions right there on her sleeve.

'So, Nick tells us you're a lawyer.' Abby turned to Sam. It was another thing experience had taught her. Quickest way to draw someone in was to ask them something about themselves. Sam

413

nodded. Her smile was tentative, as if she wasn't quite sure of the source of Abby's curiosity.

'Yes, but of the totally commercial kind, I'm afraid.'

She had a deft sense of humour, Abby noted. Subtle, but nice. 'So what does that involve?'

'Corporate law. Well, entertainment law, actually. Boring. Money, mostly, and the desire to get more of it. My clients, not me,' she added with a laugh.

Abby warmed to her immediately. Smart, clearly, but not so smart she couldn't poke fun at herself. 'Oh, I don't know . . . sounds very glamorous to me.'

'And me,' Meaghan interjected.

The men looked on, clearly amused. They began to talk amongst themselves, as was usually the case, and the three women were left to size one another up.

'What a lovely painting,' Sam said, lifting her glass to point at the painting Abby had just put up that morning above the fireplace. 'Is it yours?'

Abby blushed. 'Yes, yes it is. How did you guess?' She was sure Ralph wouldn't have said to Nick that his wife was an amateur painter.

'I just noticed the others,' Sam said, looking around the room. 'Different subjects but the technique looks the same and some of the oil isn't quite dry. Just wondered if you were the artist.'

'No, you're absolutely right. I finished it this morning. It's just something I picked up—' She broke off suddenly, unused to her art being the subject of attention.

'They're beautiful.' Sam's compliment sounded sincere.

'I love your boots,' Meaghan interjected, looking at Sam's legs. 'London boots.'

Sam laughed. 'Ferragamo. Italian, actually, but yes, I bought them in London. I just love his shoes. They're strong, too. I'm quite tall and I weigh rather a lot so I've got to make sure the heels won't snap off.'

'They're lovely.' Ferragamo? Abby had never heard of him/ her/them. 'How did you two meet, if you don't mind me asking?

It's not every day that one of Ralph's men arrives with someone like you.' She was aware of the slight towards Meaghan, even as she said it, but hoped Meaghan wouldn't take it the wrong way.

'Oh, we met on holiday,' Sam said. 'In Morocco. It was completely unexpected . . . in my line of work you certainly don't meet army officers but, well, we met in the marketplace on my second day and he asked me to come and visit him on his new base. And so here I am.'

Abby frowned. 'You mean, you only just met?'

Sam nodded, a blush suddenly appearing on her face. 'Er, yes. About three weeks ago, actually.'

Abby was surprised. So was Meaghan. 'Oh, I was . . . I just thought . . . it seemed as though you'd been together for a while.'

Sam shook her head, her blush deepening even further. 'No. It's all very new.'

Abby wasn't quite sure what to say. Ralph had very clearly referred to Nick Beasdale's 'girlfriend' . . . but if they'd only just met? Perhaps it had been love at first sight? After all, that was what had happened with her and Ralph . . . it was possible.

'Well, you look great together,' Meaghan said, lifting her glass.

'I'll . . . I'll just check on the food,' Abby said, getting up. She left the room, slightly unnerved.

MEAGHAN
Celle, Germany, 2009

Meaghan tried not to stare at Sam. Everything about her reeked of class and taste and intelligence . . . qualities she would desperately like to possess, but felt, acutely, that she didn't. She was nice, too. She admired Meaghan's earrings and didn't for a second sound insincere. She asked about Alannah, and about moving from Australia to Europe and what it was like following

Tom all around the world. She could so easily have allowed the conversation to focus on her, Meaghan noticed . . . after all, it was clear everyone was completely enthralled. Even Tom couldn't keep his eyes off her and it seemed to have as little to do with her legs in those amazing boots as it did with her life and the things she did. 'You mean, you just went to Morocco on your own?' Tom asked, clearly impressed. 'Just like that?'

'Well, how else would I go?' Sam laughed, seemingly amused by the question. 'My PA found the hotel, organised the flight and the car to pick me up. It was brilliant. Easy as hell.'

'You should've seen her hotel,' Nick interjected. 'I'd never seen anything like it. Talk about luxury. I was scared to turn on the tap.'

'I can't believe you two have only just met,' Ralph said, shaking his head. 'It sounds like something out of those bloody magazines Abby's always reading.'

'Or a book. I mean, a novel,' Meaghan supplied. It was true. 'Your life sounds like a novel. Really glamorous.'

Sam laughed again. She shook her head. 'No, it's not, I promise you. I work fifteen hours a day; I go to the gym and then I collapse in front of the TV every night. That's it.'

'Well, it sounds as though it was meant to happen,' Ralph said. He turned to Nick and lifted his beer. 'You're punching way above your weight here, mate,' he said with a smile. 'But good on you.'

Meaghan noticed the tightening of Nick's jaw, even if Ralph didn't. She suddenly felt a little sick. Sam seemed like a genuinely nice, smart and clearly wealthy woman. Did she have any idea what she was getting into? A sudden image of Edie floated into view, blackened eyes, bleeding mouth, cracked lips . . . she swallowed. Perhaps Tom was right. She was being unfair. Perhaps Nick had changed? People changed, didn't they? Maybe he'd gone to counselling or whatever it was Edie was always talking about. Maybe he'd realised what he'd done and was determined not to make the same mistakes again. It was what she and Clive had talked about on her last trip home. He'd begged her to go back to the farm and make peace with the old man. He *was* an old man. 'He's changed, Meg. He *has*. He hasn't got the strength in him to fight any more.' But Meaghan just shook her head adamantly. There was no way she was going back; she didn't care how much he said he'd changed. She would not forgive him. What she couldn't say to Clive was that she couldn't. She wouldn't have put it in quite such articulate terms but she needed the energy she got from hating him. It was what drove her in moments when she was unsure, or afraid, or over-whelmed. She'd lived with the determination of hating him for so long she was unable to let go.

'Meg?' Tom was looking at her strangely. She looked up. Everyone was on their feet, moving towards the dining room. She got up hurriedly, almost spilling her drink.

'Sorry,' she muttered, embarrassed. As she followed them in, she looked ahead of them and caught Nick's eye. It had been nearly ten years since they'd last met. He looked straight through her, his face giving absolutely nothing away. It was as if they were complete strangers to one another. There was no indication that he even recognised her, much less as his ex-wife's closest friend, as if she hadn't been the one to patch Edie up, to pick her up after one fall too many and walk with her in the freezing Belfast fog to the clinic on the base where the nurses administered yet another local anaesthetic and some doctor stitched up her face. As if none of that had ever been. She was seated diagonally opposite him; as she sat down in her chair and glanced over at him and Sam, the thought suddenly came to her. He *hadn't* changed. Not one little bit. The bastard was just biding his time.

84

DANI
Freetown, Sierra Leone, 2009

'Just have a look at it. That's all . . . just one look. I'll pick you up at lunchtime and you'll be back at your desk in an hour, I promise.'

Dani hesitated. There was a part of her that was eager to please Sue. She was the most interesting, dynamic, generous and kind person she'd ever met, with the exception of Julian, of course, and there was something of him in her – but she had a veritable stack of reports to type up and file and Malin was counting on her to have them finished before the day was up. The generator had run out of petrol – no one quite knew where the man who'd been given the cans and the cash to fill it up had disappeared to – and the whole office was sweltering. The last thing she felt like doing was getting up and going down towards Foulah Town to see some ramshackle house that Sue's parents had left her. She'd had an idea, she said cryptically over the phone, but she wanted Dani to see the place first, before she divulged it. 'Oh, all right,' she said finally, giving in. 'But you've got to get me back here before one. Malin will have a fit if these aren't done by the time I go home tonight.'

'I promise. I'll pick you up just before twelve. I'll hoot outside, OK?'

'OK.' Dani put down the phone and looked at the clock on the wall. It was just after nine a.m. She had three hours to wade through thirty-odd reports. She'd better get cracking.

At noon on the dot a car horn sounded, its sharp blast marginally more insistent than the chorus of horns all around. Dani closed down the file she'd been working on – somehow the man had been found, petrol poured down the generator's greedy throat and power restored – and grabbed her handbag. She ran down the stairs and pushed open the front door. As always, the stench and noise of the street outside, held temporarily at bay by the door, rushed in to overwhelm her. Rubbish was piled up in an untidy heap a few metres ahead by the side of the road – gutter water and the local dogs had caused bits of it to drift away from the main heap and an incongruous trail of debris tracked its own path down the hill. Dani sighed. There'd been a time when the streets of Freetown had been cleaned every morning by an army of women dressed in blue overalls, wielding brooms. She hadn't seen those women in almost a decade and the streets were never clean.

'Come on! You're the one who's only got an hour,' Sue shouted at her through the open car window. She grinned at her as Dani clambered into the car, an ancient Peugeot 504, the likes of which Freetown hadn't seen for a decade, along with the street sweeping ladies.

'God, it's hot,' Dani said, fanning herself with a loose sheet of newspaper that was lying on the mat beneath her. 'The bloody air-conditioning's not working in the office, either.'

'Same here. I think the engineers are in cahoots with each other,' Sue agreed, releasing the clutch suddenly so that the car shot forwards into the thickening stream of traffic. 'We've used just about every outfit going and they all say the same damn thing. Time to buy a new one.'

'Could say that about the whole of Freetown,' Dani observed tartly as they inched their way down the hill. 'Time to buy a new city.'

Sue smiled. 'Ah, but wait until you see *this* place,' she said enigmatically.

'What's going on?' Dani asked, curious, in spite of her misgivings.

'Wait and see.'

Wait and see? She stood looking up at the house in barely disguised disappointment. From the way Sue had gone on about the place, she'd been expecting a palace – although why she should expect a palace in Foulah Town, of all places, was more to the point. But this . . . she looked around cautiously. The house was certainly *big*. Yes, it was big. And *old*. She could see it might once have been graceful, even stately, a little like her grandmother's, perhaps. But that was in a bygone era. *Now* was what mattered. And like most properties in Freetown, it was now on the verge of falling apart. Peeled paint, mottled, discoloured wood, crumbling plaster and plants that grew out of every crack . . . even the little front gate was falling off its hinges.

'Does anyone actually live here?' she asked, fearing the answer before it came. What the hell did Sue want with a place like this?

'Only the watchman. My parents had the foresight to make sure there was always someone here during the war. If not . . . well, it'd belong to anyone now and my brilliant idea would remain just that. A brilliant idea.'

'What *is* the idea?' Dani asked, half impatiently. 'What're you planning to do with this . . . this house?'

'OK. Here's what I've been thinking.' Sue took a deep breath. It touched Dani to see that she was actually nervous. 'You know we've been talking about doing something ourselves – as Sierra Leoneans?' Dani nodded. 'Well, here's our chance. I'm thinking we could turn this into a refuge – a proper refuge, run by us, for our own people. Girls. Pregnant girls, to be blunt. There are refuges like this all over the place in the UK. They're a sort of safe home, if you like. I used to work in one in Tower Hamlets, in London. Some of the girls there had absolutely nowhere to go . . . they were immigrants, or runaways, whatever. Hopewell was the absolute last resort. I want to make a Hopewell here, Dani. And I want you to do it with me. Come on, let's go inside. I'll show you what I mean.'

Speechless – for once in her life – Dani followed her in. The house was old and rotting but it was huge. There were rooms within rooms, corridors that led to hidden wings, four whole floors . . . she traipsed after Sue, listening to her excited voice. Finally they came back downstairs to the hallway where they'd started.

'There's easily enough space. If we turned the living room into a reception area and cleared out all the storerooms, there's enough space in here for fifteen, twenty rooms. I mean, I work with these girls, Dani . . . some of them . . . you can't imagine what they've been through. It'd be somewhere for them to come, have a child in safety if they choose to, or not . . . it'd be up to them, but at least they wouldn't have to make a decision out of desperation. What do you think? Say something.'

Dani was stunned. In a flash she was sixteen again, having to rely on the kindness of a man like Eric to get her out of the predicament Nick had left her in. She'd had nowhere to go and no one else to turn to. If she hadn't met Julian that night . . . there was no telling where or how she would have ended up . . . like Dixie, in all likelihood, whom she'd seen only the other day in the street, her pupils so dilated that her eyes appeared like sunken black holes in a face that was tight and closed with pain. High as a kite. It was the only way to survive what she had to endure. Or worse, like Desirée. She shuddered. She turned to Sue. 'It's a brilliant idea, Sue . . . just brilliant. But where will you get the money from? I mean, you and *I* can see it . . . but there's a fair bit of work to be done.'

'That's why I need you to do it with me, Dani. D'you remember that awful Danish man who came along with Malin to the UNHCR party?'

Dani nodded. He'd attached himself to her like a limpet – and he'd been sixty, if he were a day! Disgusting. 'Yeah, I remember him. Why?'

'He said something as you were leaving . . . something along the lines of lust being the best fundraiser ever. He thought you could raise money for anything. He's right. People like you, Dani . . . *I* like you and I'd give you money, especially if it was for a good cause. I don't know . . . there's something really honest about you. People trust you and you've got an amazing instinct for—'

'You're talking rubbish,' Dani said quickly, interrupting her. She couldn't help herself. No one since Julian had paid her a compliment and it was almost too painful to hear. 'But . . . OK, I get your point. We'd have to raise the money ourselves, somehow.' She was aware even as she was speaking that she'd begun to talk of 'we', not 'you'. She'd been sold. A small smile began to hover around the corners of her mouth . . . and Sue thought *she* was persuasive?

'You're smiling,' Sue said, her own face breaking into a grin. 'I've got you, haven't I?'

Dani began to laugh. Suddenly Hopewell seemed the most perfectly timed and logical thing to do. Of course she was in. Of course. She turned to look at Sue and her heart began to beat faster with excitement. It was as if the roads they'd both travelled, individually and together, had led to this one place and time. Sue was right; she would do the flirting and the persuading, Sue would do the rest. Between them, they would get the job done. She was wrong about one thing only. *You can't imagine what they've been through, Dani.* She could. She knew exactly what it was like. She was one of the lucky ones. She'd got out, largely because Julian had been there that night to lift her out of the mire. If there was one thing she knew with blinding certainty that she ought to do, it was honour the chance he'd taken on her. There was money in London; *now* was the time to write or call his mother and tell her, with justifiable pride, that she'd found something to do in Sierra Leone that was worthy of Julian's name.

There were tears in her eyes as she gripped Sue's forearm. 'Let's do it,' she said simply. There was nothing further to be said.

85

SAM
London, England, 2009

Sam and Paula sat opposite one another in Allegro's, their favourite restaurant on Hereford Road, just around the corner from Sam's flat. There was a half-empty bottle of Barolo on the table between them. They'd been talking for hours; every so often one or other of the waiters would stop by – some more wine? A little more cheese? Some coffee? They waved the distractions away. There was much more serious business at hand.

'You *can't* be serious,' Paula said. 'Has he asked you?'

'Not in so many words, no. But . . . the thing is . . . if this thing is going to work, I've got to be the one who's prepared to move. He can't. He can't leave the army.'

'Why ever not? What does he earn? Forty, fifty thousand? You must earn three times that, Sam. You can't just give up your job. What the hell would you do, anyway?'

Sam was quiet for a moment. At one level, Paula was right. She probably did out-earn Nick by a factor of three, especially when you took her annual bonus into account. She owned her own flat, her own car, a share of a house in France . . . if she liquidated even half of her assets she'd be able to continue living in more or less the same manner for at least another year or so. Nick, it seemed, owned nothing, aside from a bicycle. She wasn't sure what he did with his money – other than spend rather exorbitant sums on pieces of terrible 'African' art, which she privately hated but he seemed to love. He had the strangest collection of hideous-looking masks and statues, all of which he claimed were original but Sam had seen the tell-tale shoe-polish streaks. Still . . . if it made him happy to think so . . . who was she to argue? She reached for her wine glass, aware of Paula's eyes on her. 'I . . . I don't know. I've got ideas.'

'Like what?'

'Well, I've always wanted to . . . oh, you're going to laugh at this,' Sam faltered suddenly.

'No, I won't.'

'Well, I've always been interested in interiors and furniture design and . . . shit, Paula, you *promised* you wouldn't laugh.'

'A furniture designer? *You?*' Paula couldn't help herself. She put a hand to her mouth. 'Look, I'm sorry. I shouldn't laugh, I know. But Christ, I've known you most of your life, Sam . . .

I've never even heard you say the word "sofa" before. What on earth are you talking about?'

'That's not true!' Sam protested. 'When I bought my place – the first studio, in Fulham, don't you remember? I dragged you round all the second-hand furniture shops for weeks. Don't tell me you've forgotten. You used to complain about it all the bloody time!'

'Walking around second-hand furniture shops is a far cry from *designing* furniture, Sam. *I'm* a designer. I can barely rub two sticks together . . . it's not easy, you know.'

There was just the faintest edge to Paula's voice. Sam bit her lip. She knew she'd touched on a raw nerve. In all the years of their friendship, Sam had been the clever, brainy one, the sensible one, the one who earned grown-up money and knew how to spend and save it. Now, after all this time, she was attempting to muscle in on what Paula considered her territory. It would be too much to bear if Sam turned out to be good at that too. Paula was the creative one; Sam wasn't. If she was about to turn that little myth on its head, she had to do it carefully. 'Look, I *know* it's not going to be easy. And I'm not being silly, I promise. I don't know whether I'll be any good at it . . . all I know is that I *do* want to be with him, Paula, and that it's going to be up to me to move, that's all. I'm just thinking out loud about what I'd do if I did move, that's all.'

'But where would you move *to*? I mean, he's only going to be in Celle for a couple more months, right? Then where are they going? Cyprus?'

Sam's heart sank. It was sounding more and more ridiculous as the wine bottle emptied, a situation that usually worked in reverse. 'Well, yeah . . . but only for a few months. Then they go to Afghanistan.'

Paula's eyes widened. 'Don't tell me . . . you're going to open up a furniture store in Kandahar.'

Sam rolled her eyes. She knew Paula better than to take offence. 'No,' she said, glaring at her. 'I'd . . . I'd probably come back here whilst he's on tour—'

'Well, at least you've got the lingo right. On tour? He sounds like a bloody rock star.'

Sam ignored her. 'And then he says it'll be something a bit more regular. Maybe the Middle East . . . Dubai, or Qatar, or something.'

'Oh, yeah, très regular. Can't see *you* in a yashmak or whatever it is they wear out there, personally.'

'Burqa. And foreigners don't wear them.'

It was Paula's turn to glare at her. 'Well, if you've got it all sorted out, I don't know why you're asking *my* opinion,' she said huffily.

Sam sighed. Paula was upset; she could see beyond the tart sarcasm to something else . . . a fear of losing their friendship? Or could it possibly be more? Something deeper? Was it possible Paula was *jealous*? She shook herself immediately. *Don't be ridiculous. She's just concerned, that's all. I'd be exactly the same.* She took a deep breath. 'I'm asking you because you're my closest friend, Paula. You're the only person I trust to tell me the absolute truth and nothing but. Am I making a mistake?'

'Shit, Sam, don't ask *me*.' Suddenly the resentment had gone out of Paula's voice. 'I don't know. I've never even met him. All I hear from you is "Nick this, Nick that . . . Nick said this, Nick did that." It's like watching a ghost. No, that's not the right word but you know what I mean. I can't tell you whether you're doing the right thing or not. Why don't you invite him here for the weekend? Why didn't he come the last time, anyway?'

'He had work to do,' Sam said quickly. 'It's easier for me to travel.'

'You keep on saying that, but I *know* how hard you work. How can it be easier?'

Sam was silent. In the past three months she'd been to Celle six times. She'd invited Nick to London too many times to count. She'd even offered to pay for it, wondering if money were the reason he couldn't come, but he always turned it down. She didn't actually mind. She quite liked Celle with its quaint little streets and its weekend markets and cafés. She liked Abby

Barclay and Meaghan Astor and – perhaps more than anything – she liked being one half of something, a *couple*. She liked being known as Nick Beasdale's girlfriend, even though she was as surprised as everyone else to hear that he'd referred to her as such, practically from the day he'd met her. All her life she'd been simply Sam Maitland. Nothing else, other than Kate Maitland's twin sister, perhaps, but even that hadn't lasted long. Kate Maitland was now Kate Harvey and no one really remembered her as anything else. It was a tender surprise to Sam to hear herself being referred to as 'Nick's partner', or 'Beasdale's girlfriend'. She'd never heard anyone refer to her as 'my better half'. It still shocked her to think that he might actually believe it.

'Look,' she said eventually. 'I'm going to give it a try. I'll rent out my flat – I can find one of those agents to do me a short-term let or whatever they call it and I'll ask Peter for some unpaid leave. I'll stay in Germany until March, until he goes to Cyprus . . . and then we'll see. I've got nothing to lose, Paula.'

'You've got everything to lose,' Paula said darkly. 'But I can see that's not going to stop you. Has anyone else actually met him? *Your* friends, I mean.'

Sam shook her head. 'N-no, but that's just timing. You'll all meet him soon, I promise. It's not as if I'm going out with a *complete* stranger, you know. I'm friendly with a couple of the other army wives . . . they all seem to like him.' It wasn't *quite* true – Meaghan wasn't quite as forthcoming on the subject of Nick as Sam expected, but Nick thought it was probably because she and Edie, his ex-wife, had been good friends and her loyalties lay with Edie, not him. When she pressed him for more details, he withdrew and wouldn't say why. It was probably difficult for him, Sam reasoned. After all, she'd learned from the little snippets that Meaghan and Abby let drop that she'd run off with someone else and that the whole thing wasn't quite as amicable as Nick had made it sound. Which was fair enough, she thought to herself, on hearing a more complex version of the truth. If the same thing had happened to her, she too would be hesitant about spilling everything out on a first date. So she'd let the matter drop and she certainly hadn't told Paula.

Paula sighed. 'Well, get him to come over for the weekend. At least that way *I'll* be satisfied he's not just a figment of your imagination.' She took a large gulp of wine. 'I'm sorry I'm not being more enthusiastic about him,' she said, reaching across the table for Sam's hand. 'And it's not that I'm not happy for you. I am . . . it's just that the whole thing's happened so fast. I mean, one minute you're on holiday, the next you're moving to Afghanistan.'

'Qatar. And it might not even happen.'

'Protect yourself, Sam. That's all I'm saying. I know I'm a fine one to talk but you're so damn serious about everything. I just don't want to see you get hurt.'

'I won't get hurt,' Sam said, affecting a lightness she certainly didn't feel. 'And I am being careful, I promise.'

Paula said nothing but, as usual, her frank gaze spoke volumes. For a few seconds there was silence between them, then Sam lifted her glass almost defiantly. There was a tiny, niggling sense of doubt somewhere at the back of her mind . . . nothing she could reach for and pull out. Intuition, Paula would have called it. But Sam didn't operate on intuition, neither did she trust it. She'd spent her entire life suppressing it in favour of what she called the truth. And the truth of the matter was, at the age of thirty-nine, for the first time in her life, she was properly in love. With someone who loved *her*. The rest, as she was fond of saying at work, was just detail.

If she'd thought that telling Paula about her plans was hard, telling Peter Linman, her boss, was worse. Much worse. He looked at her as though she'd just announced her intention to fly to Mars. 'You're going to do *what*?' he asked, his eyes behind their lenses as wide as saucers. If it hadn't been so heart-wrenchingly, toe-curlingly embarrassing, she'd have laughed out loud. In all the years she'd worked with Peter, she'd only ever seen two emotions on display – cautious optimism tempered by dour pragmatism. 'Nothing's in the bag until your hand's closed over the neck,' was one of his favourite sayings, though no one was sure where it had come from, or precisely what it meant. No one had dared ask, either. Now he looked at her with those saucer-wide eyes and for once in all the time she'd known him, he seemed at a loss for words. 'Which guy? Where did you meet him?' he asked eventually.

'Er, on holiday. In Morocco,' Sam said, grimacing in embarrassment.

'In *Morocco*? I *knew* I shouldn't have let you go,' Peter said, hitting his palm against his forehead. 'I *knew* it was a bad idea!'

'Well, with all due respect—'

'Respect nothing!' Peter's voice rose alarmingly. He was practically shouting. 'You're the best damn lawyer I've got, Sam. I can't just let you walk out. We . . . we've got *plans* for you!'

Sam's heart sank a further few feet. Any more and it'd be seeping out of her Blahniks. 'I know . . . well, no, I *don't* know . . . but the thing is, I'm nearly forty, Peter. This . . .' She swallowed suddenly, unwilling to put into words what had been lying at the back of her mind for weeks. 'This may be my last chance.'

'To do *what*?'

She squirmed. Peter was married. He had three children whom a small army of staff looked after and a wife who ran his homes. 'To get married. Have children . . . you know, the stuff everyone else has.'

Peter sighed. His shoulders were already slumped. He held up his hands as if in defeat. 'OK, OK. I'm being unfair. Christ, Ruth Keneally would have my head on the block for this. Look, let me say this as a friend. Fine, you've met someone . . . wonderful. Frankly I'm surprised it hasn't happened already but there you are. How long ago was Morocco?'

'Two months,' Sam said, groaning inwardly.

'Two *months*? Well, far be it for me to say that there's no such thing as a *coup de foudre*, but two *months*? You can't decide to throw away your whole career on the strength of some squaddie you met on holiday after only two months.'

'He's an officer,' Sam said faintly.

'All the same. And what on earth are you going to do whilst you trot around the world after him?'

'I . . . it's not like that. I . . . there's other things I'd like to do—'

'Like what?'

Sam's heart hit the floor with a small thud. 'I haven't really th-thought it through yet,' she stammered. 'But I'm interested in lots of other things.'

Peter said nothing. He turned away from her and walked over to the window. He stood looking out over the park. There was silence in the room for a few minutes, then he turned back to her. His smile was rueful. 'I knew this would happen one day,' he said, shaking his head. 'But I rather thought you might come in and tell me you were taking a few months off to have a baby, something along those lines. But this . . . you're an excellent lawyer, Sam, one of the best I've seen in a very long time. You're diligent, you're thorough and you have such integrity . . . a rare commodity in our business. You'll go far. I know it's early days yet and perhaps entertainment law's a little, well, *light* for you in the long run, but the sky really is the limit where you're concerned. And that's why I'm concerned. If marriage and motherhood and the whole nine yards is what you *really* want, well . . . who am I to tell you otherwise? But I just want *you* to be sure you're doing this for the right reasons, not out of fear that it'll never happen. Now that's all I'm going to say today. Go away, have a think about it and at the end of the week, if it's still your decision, I'll accept your request. Now, leave before I throw one of these tomes at you.'

86

Freetown, Sierra Leone, 2009

The creeper, which had long enjoyed the absolute freedom to climb and curl as it pleased, was the last to go. Dani and Sue stood back, arms folded, as the group of young men whom the contractor had picked up off the side of the road at the start of the project, almost two months ago, hacked at it with their cutlasses. The flashing blades rose, glinting steel, fell and rose again. Like a wildly cavorting snake, it flailed and twisted as it was prised away from the supporting wall. Half an hour later, it was dead. They carted away its tangled carcass and the front of the house was bare. It would take the men a couple of days to patch and repair the plasterwork, another couple of days' worth of painting, and then it would finally – *finally!* – be finished. Hopewell would be one step further to opening.

'Looks good, doesn't it?' Sue murmured, watching as the last of the debris was hauled away. 'Can't believe it's the same place.'

Dani nodded. 'It's not the same place,' she said, watching one of the men attempt to lift one of the branches on his own. He shook his head in defeat and called a couple of his mates over. All three put their weight behind it and heaved the last of it into the back of the pick-up truck. Like most of the junk they'd carted out of the house, they would either sell it for firewood or drive a little way up the coast and dump it straight into the sea. She shuddered to think how many broken-down chairs and scraps of carpet had wound up in the Atlantic Ocean over the past few weeks. 'Come on, let's go inside. Final inspection.'

They walked up to the front door and opened it. The chemical smell of fresh paint lingered in the air. Dani breathed in great lungfuls, unpleasant as it was. It was better than the damp, rotting smell that had permeated the very floorboards for over a decade. Inside, the rooms were stripped completely, and painted white. They'd salvaged what they could of the wooden floor-boards and where they were too badly damaged, they'd patched them up and painted over them with thick, regulation-issue black floor-paint. After all, as Sue pointed out, Hopewell wasn't about to earn points for design. Clean and functional, lots of space and light . . . that was what mattered. Not whether the teak flooring was oiled or the light fittings were straight. They'd spent almost all the money that Dani had allocated out of the funds that had arrived from London, the money Julian's family had put in trust for her. Now, with the building almost done, it would actually be easier to raise more.

They wandered into the large room on the ground floor overlooking the garden – or what was left of it. Sue had wanted them to concrete over the entire thing. 'I don't want to have to employ a gardener just to keep the weeds at bay,' she'd complained, but Dani had managed to persuade her to gravel it instead in a rather striking combination of white and black, with a few circular beds left for plants. Sue had to admit it had been a good idea. It was infinitely more pleasant to look out onto a palm tree, however small, than a patch of bare concrete. 'I'll have my desk right here,' Sue said, pointing to a corner of the room. 'Where d'you want to go . . . by the window?'

Dani nodded. 'And we can put the receptionist next door. God, can you believe it's really going to happen?'

Sue nodded firmly. 'But I did have my doubts,' she said suddenly. 'Especially after that first week. I thought there'd be nothing left of the place by the time Fouad's guys finished clearing it out.'

'I know.' Dani giggled. 'When I saw them taking out the windows, I thought the walls would collapse.'

'Me too. Well, they didn't, hey?' She looked around and touched one of the walls as if to make sure. 'Solid as a rock.'

'Just don't punch too hard. OK . . . I'd better go. Malin's got a pile this high for me to go through before the weekend.' She hugged Sue briefly and made her way back through the empty house to the street. With any luck, in another six weeks' time, they would have completed the next stage of the project and be ready to start. Bella, Julian's sister, was planning to come to Freetown for the opening; just thinking about it brought a lump to her throat. They'd already had a substantial amount of pre-opening publicity – Sue had been right about one thing . . . the more photogenic the protagonists were, the easier the coverage. And the cameras *loved* Dani. She quickly flagged down a meandering cab and was on her way back to Oxfam.

It took them six and a half weeks, not six, but by the end of June, just before the rains came, they were ready. The last week was a flurry of constant activity. Dani had under-estimated – or plain didn't know – just how much still had to be covered. There were no phone lines – somehow, they'd forgotten to put in the application to the newly rejuvenated State Telephone Company but a quick call by Malin to one of her contacts in the Ministry of Communications got that little oversight taken care of. The phones were put in the next day, a miracle in Freetown if there ever was one. They had internet access – only just – and two not-quite-brand-new computers, but no software. Another phone call, another tense day of waiting and then a technician miraculously arrived and everything was installed. It was the same story with the generator. Sue and Dani flew around, their mobile phones attached permanently to their ears, pleading, shouting, cajoling, begging . . . and somehow, it all got done. No one wanted to be the one who refused these two young, dedicated and visionary Sierra Leonean girls – *homegirls, both of them!* – the help they needed. It became a matter of local pride. The radio stations were falling over themselves to secure interviews and by the end of the week, both BBC World and CNN had booked themselves a slot for the opening ceremony, scheduled for Saturday afternoon. When a reporter for Al Jazeera appeared at the front door on Friday night, just as Dani and Sue were walking around checking the place for last-minute piles of dirt or broken window panes ('leave nothing to chance or Joseph' –

their sad-eyed, hapless cleaner – was Sue's favourite phrase), they knew the opening at least was going to be a success.

Dani woke up early on the morning of the launch and lay in bed for a few minutes, the fan gusting over her face and body, stirring the sheet. On the bedside table was her speech, written out carefully by hand, words crossed out, scratched over, re-instated again . . . she would type it up that morning and have it, and everything else, ready by noon. The launch was scheduled for three. The Minister of Health had been invited and although she'd initially sent word that she wouldn't attend in person, Sue was sure she would turn up at the last minute, especially once it had got out that CNN would be there. 'Never misses an opportunity to show her face on the telly, that one,' was Sue's dry comment.

There was a strange, unfamiliar fluttering in the pit of her stomach. Nerves, she thought to herself, placing the palm of her hand on the flat, warm skin. Outside the heat of the day was slowly building. The clouds were low and grey, threatening the first of the rainy season storms. She pushed aside the damp sheet and went to stand by the window, looking out across the sea of corrugated tin roofs, reddened by rust, to where the sea rolled in oily, slow motion against the rocks and sand. The louvered slats were dusty, she noticed, running a finger slowly across one and inspecting it. Mary, the cleaner who came twice a week, was blind to dust. She cleaned only what *she* recognised as dirty – clothes, the floor, the cooker. Of all the tasks she'd been given, ironing was her favourite. Dani smiled faintly, remembering Julian's look of incredulity the first time she'd ironed a shirt. 'It'd cut a potato in half,' he'd laughed, showing her one of his sleeves. The crease appeared to have been sewn in. Dani had never seen anything quite so sharp or tight. Another one of the little idiosyncrasies of daily life. Would she ever have such a life again? she wondered. Someone like Julian to come home to, to talk to, share her failings – and her successes – with? What would he have made of Hopewell? He'd have been proud of her, she knew, but would his participation have changed it in any way?

She chewed her lip thoughtfully. In ways she didn't yet know how to express, his death had changed her. Under his gentle tutelage, she'd arrived at a deeper, more meaningful under-standing of what life might mean or offer. There was no ques-tion in her mind that he'd brought out a better self, not only in her, but in most of the people he met. What she hadn't reckoned with was her own unspoken ambition not to let what he'd taught her go to waste. She wasn't aware of having made choices, let alone the right ones . . . now, standing at the window looking down on the city, she realised slowly that she had. Going to work for Oxfam, meeting Sue, starting Hopewell . . . these were simply points of departure on a long journey towards something she couldn't yet grasp. She was filled with a sudden sense of wonder for the intricate, complex way of a world that was still unfolding in front of her. She had come into it, she was begin-ning to understand, without so many of the touchstones that made life both easy and graspable – a mother, a father, a family – in the sense that someone like Julian understood it. She'd spent her childhood perpetually on the outside – her fairer skin and yellowy eyes pointing to a heritage that everyone knew had fallen apart. At school she'd been the odd one out – the poor girl, the one whom others picked on for never having enough. She'd escaped it by flaunting the one thing she did have – a face and a body that men appeared to crave above all else. But her experience with Nick, however unpleasant, had taught her something she would never forget. *Attached herself to some man. Poor Dani.* She would never allow anyone to repeat those words. Never. It was luck that had delivered her, alone and pregnant, to Julian's door and fate, in a way, that had snatched him from her. She could see clearly now that a choice had been made at the moment of his death – walk backwards or forwards. It was Lorraine, unwittingly, who'd propelled her in the right direction and Sue, too, was keeping her on track. It was time to acknow-ledge the help she'd been given but it was also time to forge out the path herself. Hopewell, she suddenly saw with a clarity that astonished her, was simply another start. In time she would outgrow it, or it her . . . and then she would move on towards something else.

She turned away from the window and walked across the room. There was a dreamy vagueness to her movements, as though she wasn't quite in touch with the ground beneath her feet. She opened the wardrobe door. Her clothes – she didn't have many – were hanging neatly, Mary's creases standing sharp against the light. She pulled out a dress she'd had made for the occasion, a simple shift dress made of the wax print fabric from Ghana that she so liked. The vibrant colours – deep, almost iridescent blue, fresh lime green with splashes of warm yellow and white – suited her skin tone perfectly. She laid it on the bed and walked back to the wardrobe to fish out a pair of shoes. She bent down to choose which out of the five or six pairs she owned would go with the dress. There was a pair she hadn't worn for a while . . . white, with ankle straps. They would look nice, she thought, reaching into the back to grab them. She pulled the pair out; there was something sticking to the heel. She prised the small green card off and turned it over in her hands. *Al-Shalabi & Sons. Jewellers. Kendall Street, Freetown.* It was a receipt for a ring. Julian's name was scrawled across the back in an untidy hand. She frowned. She knew exactly where the jeweller's shop was – Kendall Street was close to her old school. She stood up and slipped it into her pocket. She would stop by some time in the coming week. Perhaps he'd taken something in for repair and forgotten it? She swallowed. It was a terrible, poignant reminder on the day she missed him the most.

87

SAM/ABBY/MEAGHAN
Celle, Germany, 2009

'Ohmigod . . . look at *this*!' Meaghan held aloft a pale lemon dress of the sheerest chiffon, gathered gently under the bust and floating to the ground in gossamer swathes of fabric. 'What is it? A dress?'

Sam looked up from her position on the ground where she knelt, putting shoes into clear plastic boxes and stowing them away in the wardrobe. 'Yes, it's a dress.' She laughed. 'I'd wear it with jeans, though.'

'And these?' Abby held up a pair of chunky rope-soled platforms. 'Jimmy Choo. I've heard of him,' she said conversationally.

'No, you haven't.' Sam grinned.

'OK. No, I haven't. Who is he?'

'Only the most famous shoe designer in the world,' Meaghan laughed, still holding the chiffon dress almost reverentially. 'Haven't you ever seen *Sex and the City*?'

Abby shook her head. 'I've heard of it,' she said, smiling ruefully. 'I've just never watched it.'

'Well, we'll have to remedy that,' Sam said, getting to her feet. 'I've got the box set at home in London. I'll bring it over when I go back to get the rest of my stuff. We can have a girls' night in.'

'I've never had one of those,' Abby remarked suddenly. 'A girls' night in. There aren't usually any girls on the base I'd want to go out with, never mind stay in.'

'Yeah, I know what you mean. Celle's different,' Meaghan agreed. 'Paderborn was just *awful*.'

'Nowhere near as bad as Shrivenham,' Abby said drily. 'You're going to think it's always like this . . . cafés and cakes by the river, girls' nights in. It's not, I promise you.'

'Oh, I know. Well, I can guess. But Nick says Cyprus'll be nice.'

Abby made a face. 'I didn't care for it much, I have to say. And then there was that terrible incident with that poor Ukrainian girl that really soured things for me. I've never wanted to go back.'

'What incident?'

'Oh, it was awful. It was in all the papers for about a week, then the whole thing was completely hushed up. She was a barmaid, I think . . . worked in Ayia Napa. She was murdered by three squaddies. They raped her and then bashed her head in and buried her in this half-open pit. It was just dreadful. The worst thing about it, though, was that she had no family. No one ever claimed her body, as far as I know. I went to her funeral . . . it was the saddest thing. No one else from the army went . . . just me and—' She stopped herself just in time. 'Just me and the priest.'

'Why did you go?' Meaghan asked curiously.

Abby shrugged. 'It just didn't seem right, no one going . . . I mean, *we* did it. The army. I just couldn't bear the thought of the poor girl being buried in some unmarked grave without a single person from our community being there to witness it.'

'What did Ralph say?'

Abby was quiet for a second. 'I didn't tell him,' she said finally. 'He wasn't allowed to go – no one from the base was. But I'm a civilian. The CO couldn't stop *me* from going.'

'That was brave of you,' Sam said quietly.

Abby blushed. 'No, not brave at all. Silly, perhaps, especially as I've sort of kept it a secret ever since. But I just kept thinking of her parents, wherever they were, or her brothers and sisters . . . *we* did it and we didn't even have enough respect for her to send a bunch of flowers.' She stopped suddenly. 'Sorry . . . I . . . it just made me angry, that's all.' There were two bright spots on her cheeks. She got up quickly and left the room.

'Toilet's down the hall,' Sam shouted after her. She looked at Meaghan doubtfully. 'Is she all right?'

437

Meaghan nodded slowly. 'I . . . I think so. She really *is* brave; it doesn't matter what she says. I know what the army's like to wives who step out of line.' Her own cheeks were red, Sam noticed. She'd probably done something to invoke the wrath of either her husband or his colleagues as well. She shook her head. It was all rather more *Stepford Wives* than she'd imagined. It was 2009, for crying out loud. Surely they didn't need to get permission from the army to do what they felt was right?

Just then Abby came back into the room, her face washed and calmer-looking. 'Sorry about that,' she said cheerfully. 'The whole thing just got to me. Anyway . . . where were we? *Sex and the City*? When you bring all your stuff over. Great. I can't wait. I've a feeling you're going to teach me a thing or two, Sam. I think I could probably use it!'

The story of the young girl stayed with her for the rest of the afternoon. Abby and Meaghan left just before lunchtime to collect their children from school. Abby seemed to be on every army wives' committee going – from the Wives' Club to the Rug Rats Football Team. She'd gathered some of it was expected of her as the CO's wife, but there was a part of Abby that Sam thought rather enjoyed it. She was one of the most practical, pragmatic people Sam had ever met – optimistic as all hell, too, which helped. Meaghan seemed less sure of herself, a little more fragile. From the little that Meaghan had told her, her childhood hadn't been much of one. There was clearly a toughness to her that had propelled her out of the small town where she'd grown up but there was also a slight nervousness to her that was more pronounced whenever Abby was around. Somewhat to Sam's surprise, Meaghan had let it slip once, on her third or fourth visit, that if it hadn't been for Sam, she wasn't sure she and Abby would ever have become friends.

'What d'you mean?' Sam was surprised. Abby and Meaghan seemed genuinely friendly towards one another.

'Oh, we like each other . . . no, don't get me wrong. It's not that . . . it's just that the army's so . . . so strict about rank and stuff. And, well, Abby's out of my league. I mean, her dad was the head of the SAS. My dad's an alcoholic.'

Sam pulled a face. 'Abby's one of the least stuck-up people I've ever met,' she said, protesting a little.

'*She* is, yeah . . . but the rest of them?' Meaghan tossed her hair back defiantly. 'Oh, I hear them . . . their snide little comments when I walk past them in the street. Some of the other company commanders' wives are real bitches. Tom just says not to pay them any attention but the funny thing is, now that you're here, and the three of us have sort of become friends, they're scared of me. I don't hear half the shit I used to and they don't dare look sideways at me any more.' Her chin was tilted defiantly as she said it but Sam could see through the posture to the hurt beneath.

'Yeah, I suppose army wives are the same as any other clique . . . the corporate world's not that much different, you know. I went to a party in the south of France a couple of years ago. One of my colleagues at work – it was his fortieth. He does – or he did – a lot of counsel for Goldman Sachs, the investment bankers. Anyhow, it was the first time I'd ever seen so many trophy wives in one place in my life. They kept coming up to me asking me if my husband was there, or where my kids were. When I said I didn't have either, you should've seen the looks I got! They kept their husbands away from me after *that*, I can tell you. Not that they had *anything* to worry about. They all looked like models.'

'Well, so do you.'

Sam gave a hoot. 'You've clearly been looking in the wrong magazines,' she said good-naturedly. 'But thanks.'

'I was talking to Abby and Meaghan this morning,' Sam said, deftly opening a wine bottle and placing it on the dining table to breathe. It was nearly eight o'clock; she'd spent the afternoon shopping for food and preparing dinner. 'She was telling me about an incident in Cyprus, when she and Ralph were there. Did you hear about it?'

Nick looked up from his laptop. 'What incident?'

'This young girl was murdered by three squaddies. They raped her and then beat her to death. And apparently nothing happened to them. I've been thinking about the poor thing all day.'

'Think there's a bit more to it than that,' Nick said, and his voice was suddenly cold.

'What d'you mean?'

He shrugged. 'She was a hooker.'

'So?'

'She took a risk. She went off with three men. Drunk, from what I re— hear. Look, we see these girls all the time, Sam. What did she expect?'

Sam was suddenly speechless. 'Not to be murdered, for a start,' she said, aware that her heart had started beating faster. 'So *what* if she was a prostitute? What difference does it make? It doesn't give anyone the right to take her life away.'

Nick shrugged again. 'Occupational hazard.'

Sam struggled to breathe, she was suddenly so angry. She stood there in the middle of the dining room, trying to bring her breathing back under control. It was the first time she'd ever been angry at him and she was shocked at the rage that swept over her. Occupational *hazard*? She'd never in all her life heard such ignorant, ill-informed rubbish. Nick must have sensed something; he raised his head from his laptop and looked at her coolly.

'Why are *you* so bothered about it? Thought you were an entertainment lawyer, not a human rights one.'

She stood there gaping at him, unable to think or speak. Very carefully, aware that anything she might say would only provoke the situation further, she put down the bottle and walked slowly out of the room. She opened the front door and stepped out into the warm summer night. The stars were out — she could see their hard, winking brightness all around her. She tilted her head back, mostly to allow the rush of anger that was like a blast of heat seep out of her. She had so little experience of the moods of others or how to handle them. How had she reached the age she was without the skills to know what, in a situation like this, was the best way to respond? This wasn't like the office where she was so utterly in command of things, not only of herself but of her grasp of the things that counted – the facts, figures, events and dates that, when combined in certain ways, gave her the interpretation she required in order to judge. After all, that was what she was paid to do and if there were some in the law firms she'd worked for who thought her a little too safe in her decisions than others, she'd always been reassured by the facts. She won her cases, time after time. Perhaps with a little less flair and panache than some, granted, but the point had always been to win. She was good at it. This – the sudden, bewildering rage that had blown up inside her, provoked by what she saw clearly as an intolerable bigotry – was different. It was Nick who'd voiced the opinion, not some random stranger or even client with whom she could disagree. She had no idea what to do next. The anger was slowly seeping out of her; in its wake came an agonising doubt.

She waited for a few more minutes, half-hoping he would come out into the passageway to look for her, but he did no such thing. After a while the sound of the television came to her; perhaps he'd decided the best thing to do was ignore it? She pushed open the door again and stepped back inside. She tried to recall what she'd seen her mother do whenever her parents argued but the truth of it was, they so rarely argued – at least not in front of her or Kate – that she couldn't actually remember. And Kate? What did Kate do? She almost smiled. Kate was so thoroughly domineering in her relationship with Grant that he was the one constantly falling over himself to appease her.

She walked into the living room, her heart beating faster than usual and was aware that her hands were clammy. Would he say anything? He did not. He was watching television, his concentration turned away from her entirely. He'd poured himself a glass of the wine and was sipping it slowly. She stood uncertainly in the middle of the room, then picked up her own glass. 'Bit more?' she asked, keeping her voice as light as she could make it. He shook his head, not taking his eyes off the screen. She swallowed nervously. She poured herself a generous glass and carried it through. He was sitting more or less in the middle of the couch but when she made a move to sit down beside him, he shifted himself to the edge. It was clear there was to be no comforting caress or squeeze of her hand, no kiss, no apology . . . not even an acknowledgement of her presence. She sat beside him in frozen, embarrassed silence and then when she couldn't stand it any longer, she got up and said she was ready for bed. Her announcement was met with a brief nod . . . and that was it. She was dismissed.

She walked into the bedroom, her throat aching with tears. She had no idea what to do. He hadn't shouted at her, or even raised his voice. There'd been no argument, no harsh words had been exchanged . . . nothing. Yes, she'd made it clear she didn't like his views . . . but that was normal, surely? Couples argued all the time. You couldn't expect to have the same opinions on everything. She stared at the door, wondering whether she ought to go back and apologise. But for what? She took her clothes off slowly, hanging them neatly on the back of the chair and stowing her shoes away in the wardrobe. The TV volume had been turned up; he was watching *The Simpsons*. She winced. He was in the living room, laughing at the humour she just couldn't get whilst she was in the bedroom, agonising over their relationship.

She peeled back the covers and got into bed. She closed her eyes tightly, not just against the light but against the wall of tears that had built up behind them and was threatening to break. She was floundering, her mind darting back and forth from one scenario to the next . . . by the time she fell into a patchy, troubled sleep, she could think of only one thing. How to make amends. It didn't seem to occur to her that she'd done nothing wrong.

88

Sam wasn't herself the following day, Abby noticed, when the two of them met for coffee at the little café on Zöllnerstrasse that had quickly become their favourite. The waitress brought over two tall glass mugs of steaming milk with a shot of espresso and two tiny cinnamon and raisin biscuits, tucked neatly to one side. Meaghan had gone to the library and the plan was to meet up with her afterwards and visit the local art museum – Sam's idea. Now, sitting opposite her, her normally bright, sunny face drawn and tired-looking, Abby gently enquired if everything was all right.

Sam nodded, hesitantly at first, then more firmly. 'Yes, I'm fine. I . . . I just didn't sleep very well,' she said, stirring her coffee. 'That story . . . about the girl from the Ukraine . . . it upset me, that's all.'

'Me too,' Abby said after a moment. 'But I like to think her family eventually got to hear of her . . . maybe even came for her. I suppose that's the bit that really got to me. Anyhow . . . it was a long time ago, now. We were all quite relieved to get out of Cyprus, to be honest. Too much bloody sunshine for me.' She smiled. 'Where did Nick go after that?'

'After what?'

'After Cyprus. We left quite soon afterwards and I never saw him again.'

'He was in Cyprus with you?' Sam sounded surprised.

'Um, yes . . . I . . . I think so. I might be mistaken, though . . . I never actually *met* him there. I just thought I'd seen him once . . . on the base. Probably not,' Abby said quickly, sensing she'd made Sam uncomfortable. She wondered why he hadn't mentioned he'd been in Cyprus. She'd never actually asked Ralph what Nick had been doing there or how long he'd stayed. 'I'm always getting things wrong,' she said with a smile. 'That's what happens when you move every

eighteen months; you keep recognising complete strangers . . .
Ralph's always teasing me about it.'

Sam smiled a little uncertainly. 'He never mentioned it . . .
I'll ask him, though. He's been to so many places, I don't know
how you all keep track.'

Abby smiled at her. 'Oh, you get used to it. One way or
another. I hear you're going down to Bournemouth to meet his
parents next month. That's exciting.'

Sam brightened visibly. 'I'm terrified, to be honest.'

'Why?'

She blushed. 'Well, meeting the parents and everything. It's
all a bit . . . new to me. I've never . . . well, this is my first
serious relationship, actually.'

Abby stared at her. 'What d'you mean?'

Sam's blush deepened. 'I've never really had a proper . . .
well, relationship before. I've been out with guys, of course, but
I've never really had a boyfriend.'

It was on the tip of Abby's tongue to say, 'You're joking,
aren't you?' but something stopped her. There was something so
earnestly painful about Sam's expression that she stopped herself
just in time. 'Gorgeous thing like you?' she said instead, turning
the question into something lighter.

Sam shook her head and looked down at her plate. 'That's
sweet of you,' she said, obviously uncomfortable with the compliment. 'But it just never seems to work; I don't know why.
I . . . it's hard to find the time . . .' Her voice trailed off.

'Well, better late than never,' Abby said cheerfully. 'And I'm
sure things will work out just fine. I hardly know him, to be
honest. It's a busy time for the battalion – I can't remember the
last time I saw Ralph work quite so hard.'

'What's it like . . . when they're away?' Sam asked suddenly.
'Are you ever afraid?'

Abby paused for a moment before replying. 'The standard
response is "no",' she said with a short laugh. 'That's what they
encourage old hands like me to tell all the new wives and

girlfriends. The WAGs,' she laughed suddenly. 'Except without the bling.' She took a sip of coffee. 'But the truth is, yes, I'm often scared. Sometimes I don't turn on the television at night, especially if I know they're on operations. It's never happened to anyone I know but there've been instances where the reporters get there before the army does . . . what a way to find out. But you learn to live with it. I know it sounds crazy, but you do. The fighting bit's their job – staying strong and supportive and in control is ours. That's what it's all about, to tell you the truth. If we do *our* job, it makes it easier for them to do theirs. Simple as that, really.'

'It sounds anything but simple,' Sam said with a shaky laugh. 'I suppose you do get used to it but it's a completely different world to the one I'm used to.'

'You're not exactly typical.' Abby laughed. 'There *are* a few wives who've got – or could have had – careers of their own, but they're the exception, not the rule. It's almost impossible if you're moving every few years. And if you have kids it's even harder. Do you want any?' she asked, hoping it wasn't an indelicate question.

Sam shrugged. 'I . . . I don't know. I never really thought about it. I mean, if you don't have a boyfriend or a partner . . . it just never seemed much of an issue, really.'

'Does Nick want children?'

Sam pulled a face. 'I don't really know. We . . . we've never really talked about it. It all happened so fast. I'm still sort of getting used to it.'

'It'll be fine,' Abby said suddenly, reaching across the table to touch her lightly on the forearm. Poor thing – she did look rather overwhelmed. She'd forgotten just how alienating the whole experience could be. She'd grown up in it, part of it . . . she'd never really known anything else. She tried to imagine what it would be like to step into Sam's shoes – her Jimmy Choos – for a day, and couldn't. From the little Sam had told her, her life seemed to be work, work, work and nothing but.

She went to the gym almost every day – there was one in the basement of the West End offices where she worked – but apart from that there didn't seem to be much room in it for anyone or anything else. She admired her; it was clear she'd worked hard to get where she was but it came as something of a surprise to realise that Sam wasn't quite the hard-bitten, determined career woman she'd assumed when they first met. She had all the material trappings – in her entire life, Abby had never met anyone with quite as extensive a wardrobe as Sam's, right down to all those lovely shoes. But deep down, beneath the successful exterior and all the gorgeous clothes, she'd caught a glimpse of someone who was essentially quite lonely. It made her suddenly long for her daughters and her husband. No, all the Choos and the Blahniks (she was slowly beginning to learn the difference) couldn't make up for what she, Abby, had. It touched her even more.

'Come on,' she said to Sam, signalling for the bill. 'Let's go and meet Meaghan. You look like you could do with a bit of fresh air or some art. And then a nice large drink. Don't worry, things have a way of working themselves out.' She picked up the tab, fought off Sam's attempts to pay it, and led her outside. She tucked her arm into Sam's and together they walked slowly down Zöllnerstrasse towards the Schloss.

The art museum – billed as the first twenty-four-hour museum in the world – was a delight. The collection was small, but beautifully chosen and there were some real gems in amongst the works strung across the four floors. Abby and Meaghan were clearly less impressed with the modern art than she was – Abby favoured the sorts of paintings she herself did – but her stint at Kenton Holman had instilled in her an appreciation for artworks that made some sort of comment on contemporary life, rather than simply trying to depict it. 'It's all bollocks to me,' Meaghan said cheerfully as they stood in front of two neon signs, one proclaiming 'LIFE' and the other 'DEATH', and no amount of explanation could persuade her otherwise, but the hour and a half they spent wandering around the galleries soothed Sam and restored something of her usual, sunnier disposition.

They left the museum and decided to have a quick glass of wine and a salad for lunch before they each went their separate ways. Meaghan and Abby had to pick up the girls and Sam wanted to go to the post office to collect a parcel of books. They sat down at one of the outside tables at the Café Müller, over-looking the Französischer Garten. It was a beautiful day; all along the many paths that criss-crossed the gardens people were strolling up and down in the early summer sunshine. Tables were set outside near the rose gardens: small, linen-covered islands round which people sat, getting up to greet and kiss one another, grasping forearms in the manner of those with some-thing to celebrate.

Sam sat with half an ear attuned to the chatter in German that flowed all around her. There was bread on the table with the salad. Every now and then she broke off a piece, dipped it in the salty olive oil and popped it in her mouth. An intense feeling of wellbeing and lassitude crept over her. It had been years since she'd sat outside in the sun in the middle of the week, gossiping, thinking, daydreaming. Her hand brushed idly at a pile of small postcards that had been left out for the tourists like her. She picked up one – it was an invitation to a public lecture and an exhibition at the municipal museum, just across the road from the art museum where they'd been. Her O-level German could just about manage that.

'What does that mean?' she asked Abby, pushing the postcard across the table. 'That word . . . there. *Jagd*. It means "hunt", doesn't it?'

'Celler Hasenjagd.' Abby frowned. 'Yes, the Celle Hare Hunt. I've no idea. Hang on a minute . . .' She frowned in concentration as she read on. 'Gosh, I'd never heard of it. It happened on the eighth of April, 1945.' She lowered her voice suddenly. 'It's something to do with the Bergen Belsen Con-centration Camp. It's only a few kilometres away from here.'

'When is it?' Sam asked. 'The lecture, I mean.'

447

'This afternoon. At two thirty.'

'It sounds interesting. I'd quite like to go.' Sam looked at them both enquiringly.

Meaghan bit her lip. 'I wouldn't mind but I've got to pick Alannah up at three. I don't know if I could get a babysitter in time.'

Abby shook her head. 'I've got one of those committee meetings in half an hour. No, I won't be able to come. But why don't you go? You can tell us about it at the weekend. You're coming to the dinner on Saturday night, aren't you?'

'Er, yes, I think so,' Sam said, trying to remember whether Nick had mentioned it or not. 'What's it in aid of again?'

'Hindustan Day. It's one of the regimental days,' Abby began.

'Sabroan, Hindustan, Talavera and Blenheim,' Meaghan finished up, laughing. 'I remember having to memorise all the names so I wouldn't congratulate the CO on the wrong one.'

'Oh.' Well, it would give her something to do with her mornings, Sam thought to herself with a wry smile. 'And what does one wear to Hindustan Day?'

'Evening dress. It's all quite formal but it's nice. The catering staff usually put on a good show.'

'Well, I suppose I'll see you on Saturday night,' Sam said, getting to her feet. She picked up her handbag, said her goodbyes and threaded her way through the tables until she reached the street. She glanced at her watch. It was just after two p.m. She had half an hour to kill until the lecture. An evening dress . . . she didn't really have anything suitable but the chances of finding something in Celle seemed rather remote. She'd seen only one shop in the whole town that she'd even consider. She quickly consulted her map. It was on the corner of Prinzengasse and Mauernstrasse . . . about five minutes away. She walked quickly down Südwall until she reached Heeringasse, then turned left. The little boutique was on the right-hand side. She pushed open the door and went in.

'*Guten Tag.*' The sales assistant looked up, a smile of welcome on her face.

Sam's schoolgirl German was beginning to improve. They chatted for a few minutes in a mixture of English and German about what she was looking for and then the woman led her to a rail of black and midnight-blue dresses at the rear of the shop. Sam fingered the labels appreciatively. Diane von Furstenberg, Mexx, Armani . . . she pulled out a long, black Armani number with a thin silver belt and a neckline decorated with tiny, silver studs. It was classical and edgy, exactly the sort of combination she liked. Within ten minutes she'd tried it on, examined herself from as many angles as she could and paid for it. With the stylish blue and silver bag swinging jauntily from one arm, she hurried back along the way she'd come.

She made it into the small auditorium just in time. There were only a handful of other guests: a woman with a pair of stern-looking glasses and the sort of short haircut seen on army recruits; an elderly couple holding hands, their faces turned towards one another in some kind of private, dreamy intuition; one or two young men who looked like university students the world over . . . and her. With her blue and silver bag. She took a seat towards the rear of the room and waited for the lights to go down. How long had it been since she'd been in an auditorium like this? she wondered. Not since her law school days, already nearly twenty years ago. She sank further down in her seat; she'd already forgotten the unpleasantness of the previous evening and was looking forward to telling Nick where she'd been, what she'd bought and what she'd heard. She just hoped her German would be good enough to follow what was being said. Suddenly a figure stepped out onto the stage. A young man, dressed in the corduroy jacket and jeans that announced him more clearly as a historian than anything else could. He introduced himself as Herr Doktor Martin Günzler. The lights dimmed and the projector illuminated the small space. She gave herself up to the talk.

It ended an hour and a half later. She sat back in her seat, too stunned to speak. Her poor German aside, his talk had been surprisingly easy to follow. The elderly couple who were sitting a few rows in front of her were quite clearly overcome with tears. She stole a quick look around her. The two young men had just asked a question and were waiting for the speaker's response. She suddenly felt short of air. She got up, aware that the proceedings hadn't quite finished, but she needed to be outside, amongst the crowds. She walked quickly back up the aisle, pushed open the doors as quietly as she could and escaped through the foyer. There were a couple of museum workers standing at the entrance; they saw her come out of the lecture hall and there was a strange, almost embarrassed look in their eyes as she passed. She thought she understood why.

It was almost nine by the time Nick finally came home that evening. Sam had cooked dinner but had been too upset to eat, and certainly not by herself. When she heard his key slide into the lock, she jumped up nervously. She had no idea what sort of mood he would be in. He'd left that morning with a quick brush on the cheek, saying nothing.

'Hey,' she said, coming up to him in the narrow corridor. She searched his face warily.

'Hey,' he said, giving her a hug. 'You smell nice.'

She felt the worry and tension she'd been carrying around all day suddenly slip from her. Relief flooded through her. 'Bad day?' she asked, her head going into the warm space between his own and his shoulder.

He nodded, his hand still holding her. Was it his way of saying sorry? she wondered, too relieved to speak. 'Crap day, actually. Had to dismiss one of the lads.'

'Tell me all about it,' she said softly. 'Hungry?'

He shook his head. 'We ate in the mess. Could use a beer, though.'

'Here, I'll bring you one.' Before he could argue, Sam propelled him towards the sitting room. She was peripherally aware of herself acting like a dutiful housewife but the truth was she was so happy to see his earlier, unexplained mood had disappeared that she'd have done anything to keep the peace. She quickly fetched a beer from the kitchen and poured herself a glass of wine. 'So . . . what did he do?' There followed a rather long and complicated story about one of the younger company members . . . a broken home, absent father, complete and utter lack of discipline.

'I don't know what they expect me to do with blokes like that. They're hopeless. Fucking hopeless. Anyway . . . enough. I've sent him home, that's all that counts.'

'Sounds tough.' Sam wasn't sure what else to say.

'Yeah, it can be. What have you been up to?'

She hesitated. Before she'd properly understood what the lecture was about, she couldn't wait to tell him about her day. Now, in light of last night's conversation, she wasn't so sure. 'Nothing much,' she said, as casually as she could. 'Met the girls for a coffee, then I went shopping for a dress. Look, I'll show you.' She got up quickly and went through to the bedroom. 'What d'you think?' she asked, holding it against her as she came back into the living room.

'Nice. What's it for?'

'The dinner on Saturday night. The Hindustan dinner, or whatever it's called.'

He looked up at her. 'Bloody hell . . . you *are* a quick learner,' he said with an appraising glance.

'Yeah, well, you're not going out with a housewife,' she retorted.

'No, that I'm not. Come here, gorgeous.' He reached up and grabbed hold of her arm.

'Careful, you'll wrinkle my dress,' she squealed.

'Yeah . . . that's what you all say.' He laughed. The tension of the previous night was gone, evaporated, as if it had never been. She'd overreacted, she thought to herself as his face came down on hers and she felt his lips touch her own. Her fault. As usual. She had to learn how to handle things, handle him. Once she'd done that, everything else would fall into place. Just as Abby said.

89

Freetown, Sierra Leone, 2009

Within a month of the opening, Dani found it hard to imagine she'd ever done anything else. Sue was an outright genius, she'd decided. She quickly established that the centre itself was one thing – a refuge, just as she'd envisioned, a place that girls could come to and either wait out the remainder of their term, or drop in on a daily basis, safe in the knowledge that someone would always be there with a cool drink and a smile, and that in the spacious living room there'd be other girls like her and in the same predicament. But with only twenty rooms, there was little they could do for the hundreds of girls living either in fear or on the streets who soon began to arrive on their doorstep. It was heartbreaking to have to turn them away. After one particularly terrified girl was led, weeping uncontrollably, from the front door by the gardener, Sue decided it was time to rethink Hope-well's central role. They needed to be part of a network, Sue told Dani one morning. A network of clinics, houses, hospitals and church-run establishments that could take girls from all over the country, not just the backstreets of Freetown. Hopewell operated on a first-come, first-served basis but who were they to say the girls' needs operated the same way?

'But we can't take them all in,' Dani said, trying to be practical. 'And they need different things. I mean, some of them *would* have an abortion if they had the funds, or knew of someplace safe to go. In a way, that's easy. We can raise money to help them to do that. Some of the others, though . . . they need counselling. Someone professional to talk to, someone to listen, that's all. The girl that came in yesterday, Carmen . . . if you believe her story – and I do – she was raped by the family priest.'

'He's no priest,' Sue interjected sharply. 'I heard from one of the other girls that he's a complete con-artist.'

'Yes, but it doesn't change the fact that she can't *talk* to anyone about it. No one will believe her, or so she says. She needs a psychologist, not an abortion clinic.'

'So what're you suggesting?'

'We need to hire a couple of counsellors, maybe do as you say and link up with some of the other aid agencies to see how they handle situations like this. Get some ideas. We can't come up with everything on our own. We've got to learn from others, too.'

Sue looked at her appraisingly. 'Yeah, you're right. Well, you go out and do what you do best . . . get us the money. I'll put my head down and try to come up with a list of people we might be able to partner up with.'

'I think we should write to Bella, Julian's sister. She was full of ideas at the launch.'

'Quick thinking, Batwoman,' Sue quipped, and got up. 'God, we're *really* doing this, Dani. It's really taking off.'

'Don't tell me *now* you thought it wouldn't.' Dani laughed. 'I gave up a perfectly good job.'

'And don't tell me that you'd rather still be there typing reports for Malin,' Sue shot back as she left the room.

Dani turned to her computer. It was nearly three o'clock in the afternoon on a Saturday. The city was preparing to shut down for the weekend. In her pocket she still had the small green receipt from Al-Shalabi Jewellers. She fingered it surreptitiously. She ought to go down to Kendall Street and see what it was he'd left there. She'd been meaning to do it for weeks, since the day of the opening, in fact, but she somehow had been putting it off. She had a quiet couple of hours ahead . . . the receptionist they'd hired was in the office next door and could take care of whatever came up. She stood up suddenly and picked up her bag. She might as well do it now. Now or never.

*

She pushed open the shop door; it gave way with a loud jangling bell. A rheumy-eyed old man looked up as she entered. Lebanese, the grandfather, no doubt. 'Can I help you?' he asked, coming round from the side of the counter to stand in front of it. He held onto an intricately carved walking stick for support.

She fished the receipt out of her pocket. 'I . . . I found this,' she said, holding it out. 'It was my husband's. He passed away some months ago . . . I've been meaning to come in and pick it up.'

The old man's eyes weren't up to the task. Peering at it, he shouted aside for someone. 'Fawaz! Nabil!' And then something in Arabic.

There was an answering yell from the back of the shop and the sound of the radio being switched off. A door opened and a young man walked up to them. His face had the distinctive pallor of mutton-fat, an almost jade tone to the skin and his hair was a shiny, black dollop atop his head. He wore a shirt unbuttoned almost to the navel; in the thick profusion of black chest hair, a gold chain slid in and out of view. 'Hi, can I help you?' he asked, a slight frown appearing between his eyes. 'Are you . . . aren't you . . . weren't you Julian's girlfriend?' he asked suddenly.

The words slid through Dani like a sharpened blade. 'Yes,' she nodded. Did she know him?

'We met a couple of times,' he said. His accent was identical to hers; he was probably one of the many sons of wealthy Lebanese traders who had come to West Africa in the 1920s and 30s, and stayed. 'At Mette's place. I used to go out with her. I'm Nabil. I'm sorry about what happened, man. I wanted to call you . . . just didn't have a number and didn't really know what to say.'

'Thanks,' Dani said, swallowing hard. She didn't remember him but there was something genuine about his honesty. So many people hadn't rung or stopped by, and wouldn't have the courage to say. 'I . . . I found the receipt in the back of the wardrobe . . . I just wondered if he'd brought in something for repair.'

Nabil's face registered some strange emotion. He brought his hand up to his cheek. 'He didn't . . . he didn't tell you?' he asked haltingly.

Dani shook her head. 'No . . . what?'

He hesitated then bent down under the counter. He drew out a small dark green velvet box. 'I found it in the back, on my father's workbench. I've been keeping it ever since, hoping you'd come in one day. He asked us to make it. My father was the one who did the inscription.' He handed it over.

Dani stared at it, her heart racing. Then she opened it. It was a simple gold band; no adornment, save two words etched in beautiful calligraphy along the inner rim. *Trust love*. It was a command, an exhortation. The image swelled and lurched; she snapped the box shut.

'Are . . . are you OK?' Nabil asked, his voice full of concern.

Dani nodded. She opened her mouth to speak but found she couldn't. 'I . . .'

'It's OK, it's OK.' Nabil was quick to reassure her. 'I know. It's hard.'

'*Al hamdu' lillah*.' The old man, sensing what had happened, gave his own blessing.

'Th-thanks,' she said shakily, putting the little box in her bag.

'No problem, no problem.'

'Is . . . do I need to settle anything?' she asked, just before she turned to go.

Nabil waved her concern before him as though swatting an irritating fly. 'No, no . . . nothing, *nothing*. Just . . . go well, you hear me? Look after yourself.'

She nodded again. Her fingers gripped the box in her pocket. She pulled the door towards her, heard again the loud jangle and then she was outside in the heat of the street. She stood for a moment in the shade of the awning above the shop entrance and then stepped out into the road. A taxi, sensing a fare, did an elaborate, slow-motion turn, narrowly missing a woman carrying a pyramid of oranges on a tray on top of her head. There was the usual exchange of curses, the honk of a horn and an answering blast before the woman continued on her way, her swathed and swaddled-in-cloth backside swaying insolently as she went. Dani was still holding onto the box in her pocket as she climbed into the back seat. Julian was suddenly, again, present. The car jerked forward; the moment was lost.

90

RALPH
Celle, Germany, 2009

Alone in his office for the first time that day, Ralph took off his cap, ran a hand through his short, cropped hair and kicked out his chair from under his desk. He sat down, sighing heavily, and pulled out a file from the pile of papers he'd been carrying all day. He laid the file on the desk and stared at it for a few moments. It was the report Personnel had been asking for for almost a fortnight. It wasn't like him to procrastinate but this report would be a tough one, no question. It wasn't the first time he'd been asked for his opinion – he'd done it more than once, he recalled, but this time, unlike others, he had a personal stake in its outcome. Something he rarely, if ever, allowed himself to think about, much less act upon.

He flicked the plastic cover away and withdrew the dossier. The cover sheet jumped out at him. *Name:* Nicholas Peter Beasdale. *Age:* 39. *Rank:* Major. He sighed again. He knew what was coming and what was expected of him. This was Beasdale's second attempt at promotion; he'd been a major for more than eight years. If he didn't make the grade this time, he'd join the ranks of 'passed over' majors, which effectively signalled the end of his army career. Ralph and Tom Astor had risen swiftly, both going through to Lt Col. on their first attempt. Beasdale was another case altogether. He opened the folder and began to read.

It was odd, he thought to himself half an hour later. There was nothing concrete against the man, nothing you could put your finger on or point to. He did his job, more or less within the parameters set out by the army code. Astor had once described him as a 'plodder', and to a certain extent it was true. He would never be the one to take the initiative or think outside the box, as Ralph would put it. Astor was quick and decisive and always kept faith with the bigger picture. Beasdale often failed to grasp the bigger picture, or when he did, Ralph had noticed it was generally a different image from the one everyone else saw. He was a complainer, too. If things didn't go according to plan, Beasdale would spend hours finding reasons why he shouldn't be blamed. It made for a kind of pettiness and churlishness that Ralph abhorred . . . but was it reason enough not to promote the man? It was extremely unlikely he'd ever take command of a battalion anyway. At the logistics level, he was operational, nothing more. He wrote reasonably detailed reports, handed them in on time and was more or less factually sound. The army was always in need of officers like that and the reason Beasdale's promotion chances were being looked at again was precisely because the command structure had to take a decision. Pass him over now, and therefore for ever, or take a chance on him?

But there was something else that bothered him and he found himself struggling to put it into words. He, like most COs, knew that listing every single standard to which an officer ought to adhere was a complex, often slippery task. He preferred to rely on a clear set of values, handed down over generations of army men – a soldier's behaviour should be lawful, appropriate and totally professional. Trust was the linchpin of the unit – putting the needs of others before your own, being honest at all times and supporting your individual team mates . . . those were the values he'd sworn to live by and he expected his men to do the same. The team was everything; without the trust he worked so hard to instil, everything could fall apart. In six months' time, the battalion would be deployed in Afghanistan to face an enemy that had defeated every single foreign invader since

Alexander the Great. Their chances of running a successful tour – and for him that meant the absolute minimal loss of life or injury to his men – were slim, at best. Who knew what would be thrown at them? The news coming out of Helmand was grim; could he depend on Beasdale to hold his own and, perhaps more importantly, to hold the company he'd been charged with together? He tapped the pencil against his teeth. The honest answer was 'no'. Beasdale wasn't a popular officer; he was sullen and withdrawn, despite his occasional flashes of charm. He was a loner; people assumed the sullenness stemmed largely from the messy affair with his wife, all those years ago in Massereene. Some, who had known him in his year-long training at Sandhurst, said he was a different fellow from the one who'd come out of Northern Ireland. Quiet, yes, but without the resentful despondency that sat below the surface of his skin like a bruise. But there'd been other rumours circling around at the time that hinted things weren't altogether rosy in the Beasdale household and the hint of physical violence was a stain that wouldn't go away. It didn't help that his ex-wife, Eithne, or whatever her name was, hadn't been popular, either. They were an odd pair. Both were originally from Kenya, or so he recalled someone saying. They'd been at school together. She'd got herself in financial trouble and Beasdale's own finances had come under both scrutiny and strain. When she ran off with another soldier, everyone more or less heaved a sigh of relief. Yeah, an odd pair.

But there were two other doubts that stubbornly refused to vanish. One in Cyprus, the other in Sierra Leone. Both involved the death of a young woman – barmaid, prostitute . . . it was never made clear. Beasdale had been on duty on both occasions and there was a worrying gap in the account of his whereabouts when the attacks had taken place. He grimaced. No accusations had been made and there was nothing to suggest that Beasdale had been involved in any way other than an inability to foresee trouble – and drunk soldiers on the rampage usually signalled nothing but trouble. But, more worryingly, Beasdale had never come forward, even privately, to suggest that his actions might have been found wanting. There was a reason the army demanded higher standards in certain types of behaviour than the rest of civil society – lowering the bar, as Ralph and every other officer knew, put everyone at risk. In those moments of danger out there on operations, wherever 'there' happened to be, he had to be able to count on the absolute loyalty and discipline of every single one of his men, officers more so than others. How could he count on a man whose instinct seemed to be to protect only himself?

The pencil was in his hand, hovering above the central question. Recommendation for promotion. Yes. No. He stared at the two little boxes which would determine the course of a man's life. His fingers twitched. There was one other thing worrying him, that he was ashamed to even admit thinking about. Beasdale's girlfriend. Soon to be his wife, if Abby was to be believed. She was clearly out of his league; he'd understood that the first evening they met. He'd never met a woman quite like her before. It was inconceivable to him that she could be fooled, in any way. He'd been slightly embarrassed by the way all three of them gaped at her that evening Beasdale had brought her round. How'd someone like *him* catch and hold someone like *her*? It was the question on everyone's lips. Beautiful, yes, but that in itself was nothing special. There were lots of beautiful wives on bases all over the world. Abby herself was no slouch. But Sam had something more . . . a beguiling sureness about her that made you want to talk to her – properly. Not about the weather and the children and what the last posting had been like and what the new one might turn out to be . . . the standard, meaningless chit-chat that was the staple of social life. Sam – he couldn't remember her last name – had opinions. Political, cultural, social . . . the last time they'd met he'd been coming over the bridge by the little Italian restaurant on the other side of the river. He'd forgotten something at home and took advantage of the early summer day to walk, rather than be driven. He'd seen her as soon as he reached the crest. She was sitting by herself on the terrace, a glass of wine in hand, reading a book. Her hair was golden in the sunlight. He'd stopped instinctively to watch her. She picked up her glass and with wonderful, easy slowness, lifted it to her lips. In that moment she saw him and waved. A light, friendly wave. It was, he realised, as his own hand went up, what he most liked about her. She had none of the wary, self-serving alertness of most army wives he'd met. They sized you up in terms of their husbands' prospects and launched into the acquaintance on the basis of that. Sam was outside it all. She spoke to him as an equal, nothing less. The army had no place between them. He'd hesitated for a moment, then turned back on himself and walked back along the bridge to join her. No wine for him – he was content to have a coffee and sit in the sunshine for a few minutes, that was all. He looked down at the book she was reading. *Down Under*. Bill Bryson. It was exactly the sort of book he'd have chosen himself on holiday. On holiday – he almost chuckled. When was the last time he'd been on holiday?

'How . . . how're you settling in?' he asked as he sat down next to her, aware even as he said it that it was the sort of mindless, standard question he despised.

She pulled a quick, culpable face. 'Fine. Although I can't honestly remember the last time I spent the afternoon sitting in the sun, reading. I keep thinking I'm going to wake up one morning and find out I've just lost a case.' She laughed. 'I ought to enjoy it, really. It won't last for ever.'

Again he was at a loss for words. Her life – insofar as he could even imagine it – was so far removed from his or Abby's that he didn't even know where to begin. 'Do you miss it? Work, I mean.'

She shook her head slowly. 'Not really. Not in the way I thought I would. I mean, I miss the structure of it . . . going to an office, travelling, taking on a new brief or a client . . . that sort of thing. It must be exactly the same for you, I imagine. Or Nick. But I suppose I'm also beginning to see things differently. There's a very big world out there . . . entertainment law is just one minuscule part of it. I rather like that, to be honest. Finding out that your world is so much smaller and less significant than you thought.' She gave another laugh. 'Don't listen to me. It's the wine.' She pointed to her half-empty glass.

Luigi, the elderly waiter who'd been at La Buca for a quarter of a century, came out towards them. He was beaming – another who'd fallen for Sam Maitland (Maitland – that was it!) and her sunny charm. He listened to them chatting in Italian for a few seconds. She apparently spoke a little – not much, she laughed, just enough to order a wine and say, '*Come va, Luigi*?' He clearly loved it.

Now, sitting in his office with Beasdale's report in front of him, the conversation and the warmth it had produced in him came back again. It wasn't that he *fancied* her – God, no. He was in love with his wife; always had been, always would be. It was that he found her *interesting*, which was more than he could say for ninety-nine per cent of the people with whom he came into contact. Abby liked her, enormously. She was the first person Abby had met in all their years of marriage with whom she could see herself becoming friends. Properly. The sort of close, female friendship she'd had in school but never again. He wanted Abby to be happy; he desperately needed it. What had happened in Belize could never happen again. He was aware it was partly – perhaps even largely – his fault. He'd left her on her own with the girls for such long periods of time. He'd neglected her, something he'd promised himself in the beginning he would never do. He wasn't sure he could stand the thought of it happening again. If Beasdale made the next step up the promotion ladder, it would mean Sam and Abby – and Tom's wife, too, though he was less interested in her – would be together in Cyprus and then in Kingston for the next two or three years.

He was sweating slightly, a damp, hot feeling on his skin. He picked up the pencil that he'd laid to one side and in a swift, almost unconscious movement ticked the box. *Yes.* He put the report back in its plastic folder and swiftly put it away from him.

That, he thought to himself, a sense of shame settling over him, is precisely how a decision *shouldn't* be made.

91

SAM
Celle, Germany, 2009

There was room for one more pair of shoes, a loose, crinkle-silk skirt and a little pouch containing her jewellery, and that was it. Her small suitcase couldn't possibly hold any more. She lifted it off the bed and let it fall to the ground with a thud. Bournemouth – or just outside it – for a month; she had no idea what to expect. She'd never been to Bournemouth in her life. His parents had only just moved there, so he said. He didn't say from where. She looked at her watch. It was nearly ten o'clock. Nick would be back in half an hour. His backpack – a messy khaki affair with straps and pouches hanging off every corner – was lying in the sitting room, waiting for his last-minute socks and T-shirts that Heidi had left, neatly ironed, on the couch. The taxi was scheduled for eleven. A forty-five-minute journey to the airport in Hanover and then the hour-long flight to London. They would take the train down from Paddington. She felt the sharp tug of excitement in her stomach. She was about to meet his parents; it was hugely significant, everyone said so. She knew next to nothing about them. He had surprisingly little to say about his family, other than the fact that his father hadn't worked in years and that his mother had more or less brought him up single-handedly. He was an only child. He was very close to his mother, she'd noticed. They spoke every other Sunday. He had a little ritual – first he would shave, make himself a mug of coffee and then go into his bedroom to ring home, closing the door behind him. She never heard what was said. The call would last about half an hour and then he'd emerge, whistling. He'd made one or two off-hand comments that indicated he'd at least

462

told them about her and that he'd be bringing her with him but other than that, he'd said very little about their reaction to the news. Oh, well . . . she'd meet them soon enough. She couldn't wait.

She heard his key in the lock and walked into the hallway to meet him, offering up her cheek for a kiss.

'You almost ready?' he asked, his eyes going past her to where the suitcase stood. 'You're not taking that, are you?'

'Yes. Why? What's wrong with it?'

'It's huge.'

'No, it's not.' She laughed. 'Don't worry, it's got wheels. I didn't know what to take so I took everything.'

'It's a cottage in the middle of nowhere, Sam. There's nothing to do.'

'Yeah, but we're not going to be there all the time, are we?'

'Pretty much, yeah. They've just moved in and there's a ton of stuff that needs doing. They've saved up all the odd jobs that Dad can't do any more. His health's not good. I don't plan on going anywhere else.'

'But what about me?' Sam started to protest. 'What'm I supposed to do whilst you're doing the odd jobs?'

He shrugged. 'I dunno. Take a couple of books along . . . you'll find something to do. You're good at that.'

Sam stared at him, disappointment flowing through her. She'd pictured something entirely different, she realised. The way he now spoke, *she* certainly wasn't the star attraction. In fact, she wasn't sure she was even an attraction at all. Did they even *know* she was coming?

The Three-Legged Cross. Verwood Road. Church Street. A cluster of small shops and houses and then they were out in the open countryside again. The taxi skirted the edges of the forest, then turned down a small country lane. Edmondsham Road. 'This it?' the taxi driver turned his head briefly.

Nick nodded, consulting the map. 'Yeah, about a mile down.

Just past the Dorset Heavy Horse. Yeah, we're on the right track.'

'Who the hell'd want to live out here?' the taxi driver mused, more to himself than either of them. In the back of the taxi, Sam stared wordlessly out. It was a typical English country scene – mile after mile of gently rounded hills, still in their thick summer coats. The forest was to their right, a dark, damply scented mass through which rows upon rows of freshly planted trees could be seen. She swallowed. It really was in the middle of nowhere. He hadn't been joking.

They bumped their way down a dirt track, the sun flashing and disappearing again as the clouds broke up, reformed and split apart, again and again. The car pulled up in front of a small, forlorn-looking bungalow that looked as though it belonged on one of the many housing estates that she remembered from her days at Bristol – dark brown brick, a yellow, incongruously cheerful front door, bay windows on either side and a brick chimney piece thrusting skywards. It was a child's drawing of a house. There were a few rose bushes in the small garden in front and to the side of the house there were apple trees. It ought to have looked bucolic; it somehow didn't. There was a faded, shut away and almost protective air to the place that she could sense, even at a distance.

'Have you got any pounds?' Nick asked her. 'I've only got euros.' She fished her purse out of her bag and handed it over. He took out the wad of twenty-pound notes that she'd taken from the cashpoint at Paddington. 'Great,' he said, peeling off a few. He tucked the rest in his breast pocket and murmured something about going to the bank later in the week. Sam said nothing. She was still too shocked at the sight of the house in which they were about to spend the next few weeks. Was there no one home? She opened the door and stepped out. The ground underfoot was hard and stony and she stumbled as she walked towards the front door. Nick was busy with their luggage. A wood pigeon suddenly swooped overhead, a soft, lulling call coming from it before it flitted away again. She could hear the taxi start up behind her and begin the laborious three-point turn to leave. The front door suddenly opened.

'Nick!' A woman stood in the doorway. She was tall – almost as tall as Nick – with the same stocky build. Her grey hair was pulled back from her face and she wore a pair of men's blue overalls. She looked past Sam to Nick. 'Nick!' she repeated, her face breaking out into a smile.

'Hi, Mum.' Nick came up the path and pushed past her. He gave his mother a clumsy hug. Sam stood still, feeling slightly out of place.

'Good to see you, son.' His mother held onto him tightly.

'Yeah . . . you too. Um, this is Sam.' He half-turned towards her.

His mother looked her up and down quickly, and stretched her face into something that resembled a smile, though not the kind she'd given her son minutes earlier. 'Hello, love. Sam? Isn't that a boy's name? Come in, come in. Don't let the flies in. It's that bloody neighbour . . . it's his horses. I *hate* them, don't you remember, love? That first farm we had, out near Kiambu? D'you remember the flies? Ugh, can't say I wasn't glad to see the back of that old dump. Mind you, the next one wasn't much better, was it, love? Gathanji. D'you remember? Not so many flies there, were there? But Christ, the *snakes*.'

Sam followed them in, bewildered. The woman kept up a running commentary on everything but what was she talking about? Snakes? Kiambu? Gathanji? Where the hell was Kiambu? She glanced quickly at Nick as they walked down the long corridor to a room at the end but he avoided her eyes. The ceiling was quite low; both Nick and his mother – she realised she didn't even know the woman's name – had to stoop a little. She pushed open the door at the end of the corridor. The living room was obviously at the rear of the property. It was small, like the rest of the bungalow, but at least it looked out onto a patchwork of fields and a small hill. 'Look who it is, love,' she called out as they trooped in. There was a man sitting beside the television. As he turned, Sam saw he was in a wheelchair. He manoeuvred it with some difficulty and slowly turned to face them. She recognised the tell-tale signs of an alcoholic immediately – the flushed, pink pallor, the slight tremble in the fingers, the bloodshot eyes.

'Hello, Dad,' Nick said, keeping his distance.

'Oh, it's you, is it?' His father looked across the room. 'And who's this?' He raised a stick and pointed it at Sam.

'That's Nick's girlfriend, love. What was your name again?' His mother turned to her briefly.

'Sam,' Sam managed to croak. 'Samantha.' She glanced at Nick again but his face was turned away. His father looked her up and down, almost exactly as his mother had done. 'Well, you're better-looking than the last one,' he said, leering up at her from his wheelchair. 'Didn't care for her much meself. Never liked those Asian types. Mind you, could've been worse. Could've been a munt, ay? Ay, Jane? What would you've said to *that*?'

Sam looked to Nick in astonishment but there was no response from him, not even a flicker of the eyes.

'Now, now,' Jane Beasdale said in the sort of tone one might use to admonish a wayward child. 'No need for that. None at all.'

'Yeah, well, I'm just saying . . .' His father's tone was petulant.

Nick turned away but not before Sam caught the look of thunderous, murderous rage on his face. Confusion broke out over her, like a light sweat. The image she had had of herself being introduced to his family slipped away from her and she was left standing in the middle of the room, acutely aware of her own disappointment rising hotly in her veins. She tried to keep her face composed but there was a painful prickling behind her eyes. There was an undercurrent to the place that she'd picked up almost as soon as she stepped through the door. It puzzled her. It was like a half-remembered song whose words she'd almost forgotten – just enough to catch it from one second to the next, then it was gone again. Something wasn't right. Who were these people? What the hell was a 'munt'? And who was the Asian girl he'd brought before her? She followed Jane back through the corridor to the small room at the end, which was clearly where they were to sleep. She and Nick were talking softly, their heads bent towards one another. She wasn't invited to take part. After a few seconds' worth of fussing – 'Is that bed comfy enough for you, Nick? D'you like the cover? D'you remember it? It was in the old house . . . yeah, we saved a bit of stuff. Not much. Didn't much fancy the idea of trailing all of that stuff around with us any more. God, not like the old days, ay? Half a dozen servants to do all the donkey work. Mind you, I don't miss it . . . not really. I mean, we couldn't be expected to stay on, could we? But I do miss the servants. Oh, that's him calling . . . we'd better see what he wants, ay?'

And without a word to her, mother and son left the room, leaving Sam alone. She sat down heavily on the bed, stunned by what she'd seen and heard in the ten minutes they'd been in the house. Her mind was whirling. Servants? The old days . . . what on earth was she talking about? Who were these people? she asked herself again. And, more importantly, who the hell was Nick?

92

ABBY/MEAGHAN
Celle, Germany, 2009

Sam had been gone a week before Abby bumped into Meaghan again. She was on her way out of Rossmann's supermarket and Meaghan was on her way in. There was a slightly embarrassed pause, as if each recognised in the other the failure to call or make plans to see one another in the week since Sam's departure.

'I should have rung,' Abby said, pulling a mock-guilty face. 'I kept meaning to.'

'I know. Same here. How are you?' There was no hint of resentment on Meaghan's face.

Abby smiled, relieved. It wasn't that she didn't like Meaghan – on the contrary – it was just that Sam's presence made the trio comfortable, and complete. Three's a crowd, her mother had always warned her at school, but somehow, with the three of them, it worked. Now that Sam was gone, a new balance had to be struck. 'All right, actually. Just busy . . . Ralph's hardly been home this past week. Well, suppose it's the same with Tom. Look, shall we have a quick coffee?' she asked, looking at her watch. 'I've got about an hour before I've got to pick Sadie up. D'you have time?'

Meaghan nodded. 'I'd love one. I've just got to get a couple of things . . . I'll meet you there in five. Won't be long.' She gave a quick wave and disappeared into the shop.

Ten minutes later, with their usual cappuccinos in front of them, they both leaned back and spoke at once.

'Wonder how she's getting on?'

'Have you heard from them?'

Meaghan smiled. 'You first.'

Abby laughed. 'Well, *have* you heard anything?'

'No. She said she wasn't sure if they'd have internet at his parents. I can't imagine her on a farm in the middle of the countryside, can you?' She stirred her coffee slowly. 'Or in the middle of anywhere, come to think of it. She's just a city girl.'

Abby shook her head. 'I wonder what they're like. His parents.'

Meaghan hesitated for a second. 'I was quite friendly with his ex-wife, Edie. We were together in Massereene for a while. She . . . she didn't get on with them. She said they were . . .' She stopped. 'I feel awful even saying this much—'

'What?' Abby asked, sensing her discomfort. 'You don't have to say anything,' she added quickly.

Meaghan shook her head. 'I should have said something to Sam, that's the thing. But I didn't know how to. I mean, the whole thing with his family and the divorce . . . in a way all of that's got nothing to do with her. But I do remember Edie saying his father was an absolute arsehole. A real coward. And he was always jealous of Nick. I don't remember exactly why – something to do with the way his life had turned out. They were from Kenya – white Kenyans. Edie always used to say it was like a curse, like bad blood. They didn't fit in anywhere. They both left when they were quite young, I think. His dad was a farmer – or a failed farmer, actually. Bit like my dad. He'd tried his hand at everything, apparently, but just couldn't make anything stick. He probably thought *he* should've been the one in the army, travelling round the world.'

Abby grimaced. 'Oh, dear. It doesn't sound like the most relaxing place to spend a month.'

Meaghan shook her head. 'No it's not, and believe me, I know what those little farms in the middle of nowhere are like. I grew up on one. Ran away as soon as I could.'

Abby looked at her, surprised. 'Ran away?'

Meaghan nodded slowly and looked down at her hands. 'My father was . . . well, let's just say it wasn't the happiest place to grow up.'

'Do you ever go back?'

Meaghan shook her head. 'I went back to Australia last year for the first time. But I didn't go and see *them*,' she said. 'I stayed with one of my brothers, Clive. *He* got out. We all did.'

Abby didn't know what to say. It was all so far removed from her own family and the stable, happy home life she'd known that any comment she might make would sound trite, even to her own ears. She felt a sudden rush of warmth for Meaghan. For the first time since they'd met, she found herself wondering what it must *really* be like for a girl from her background to find herself the wife of the 2/i/c. Officer culture, as Abby knew only too well, was unforgiving of differences of any sort – class, background, nationality, race . . . who'd been to what school, whose parents were whom. Oh, there were all the usual platitudes but she honestly couldn't remember the last time she'd met a senior officer's wife who wasn't in some way similar to all other senior officers' wives. Meaghan was different; it was only now, with the arrival of another woman who was also different, that those differences really stood out. 'I think you're incredibly brave,' Abby said after a moment. 'I don't suppose I ever gave it much thought but it must have been quite a culture shock for you . . . coming here.'

Meaghan smiled. 'Yeah, well . . . you get used to it. Sort of. That's why me and Edie were friendly, I suppose. We weren't all that different. She was a barmaid, I was a beautician. We sort of stood out.'

'What happened to her? Whilst she was married to Nick, I mean,' Abby asked hesitantly. 'I don't mean to pry, or anything . . . it's just that there's always been this sort of mystery surrounding Nick Beasdale. No one ever says anything outright . . . it's more what they *don't* say.'

Meaghan was quiet for a while. She seemed to be struggling with her own thoughts, not sure how to answer Abby's question. Finally, she lifted her eyes. 'He was a bully and a complete arsehole,' she said quietly. 'And Edie took the brunt of it.'

Abby felt a cold wave of shock and disgust break over her. 'What d'you mean?' she asked. 'Don't tell me . . . he used to *hit* her?'

'All the time. I can't tell you how often I used to take her down to the clinic on the base. Everyone knew. But no one wanted to say anything. And she wouldn't. She kept saying she'd fallen down the stairs, or off her bike . . . you know how it goes. And then she just ran off one day with someone else's husband. Everyone was so fed up by that stage they were just glad to get rid of them both. I think he went to Africa after that, or Iraq. I never heard from either of them again.'

'But surely we should say something? To Sam, I mean.'

Meaghan pulled a face. 'That's what I told Tom. But he says Sam's no fool and that Nick's changed. *I* don't think he has. Not for one moment.'

It was Abby's turn to be quiet. 'I suppose he's right,' she said slowly. 'I mean, you never really know what goes on behind the doors of someone else's marriage, do you? Who knows what really happened back then.'

'I know Edie wasn't always easy. She had her own problems and she knew how to really push his buttons. She used to enjoy it, in a bizarre kind of way. But Sam's completely different. I just don't know how he managed to catch someone like her. *She* wouldn't put up with his shit, not for a second. So I suppose Tom's right. It *is* different. What happened to Edie won't happen to Sam.'

'Thank God for that,' Abby said fervently. 'Poor Edie, though. Sounds awful.'

'It was.'

Abby waited until she'd poured them both a small glass of port that evening, then she opened her mouth. She couldn't not open it. The question had been gnawing at her ever since her conversation with Meaghan that morning. 'Darling,' she began hesitantly. 'Did you know Nick Beasdale used to beat his wife? I mean, *really* beat her. She was in hospital once. On the base in Belfast.'

Ralph looked up from his laptop. There was an expression on his face she didn't recognise. 'Who told you that?' he asked, and his voice was cold.

Abby's stomach gave a little lurch. Was he angry at her for gossiping? 'Meaghan,' she said. 'We've become quite close. We were just talking about Sam.'

'Well, you shouldn't. Sam's perfectly capable of looking after herself. She's the most intelligent woman I've ever met. She doesn't need you poking around in things that don't really concern you. Honestly, Abby, I'm surprised at you. What's the matter with you? Not enough to do?'

Abby was so stunned by his outburst that she couldn't think of a single thing to say in reply. He'd gone back to his report or whatever it was he was working on but she could tell from the dark flush that spread across his neck and face that he was angry.

She could feel her own anger building quickly inside her. She shoved the cork back onto the bottle of port and slammed it down on the sideboard. 'Don't you *ever* talk to me like that again,' she hissed, mindful of the fact that Sadie had only just gone to sleep. 'Who the *fuck* do you think you are?'

She saw his head jerk up in surprise but she was beyond caring. She turned on her heel and only just managed to prevent herself from slamming the door behind her. She locked herself in the bathroom, her hands shaking. In all their years of marriage, Ralph had never once spoken to her like that. *She's the most intelligent woman I've ever met.* His words reverberated around and around in her head.

93

SAM
Macheo Cottage, Bournemouth, 2009

The silence in the woods was thick and deep, so profound she felt as though she were walking into water, a medium that took hold of all her senses, sharpening each in turn. A thick plume of smoke rose from some neighbouring farm or cottage; she felt she could smell and taste the acrid smoke at the back of her throat. She walked on, enjoying for the moment the smell of pine and the sound of her own heartbeat, a loud, hollow echo in her ears. Behind her, hidden from view, was the house. Macheo Cottage. Sunrise Cottage. In Swahili. That was the mystery that was only now beginning to unfold. She still found it hard to comprehend how little she knew of Nick and his past. Or how he could have kept it so hidden. Finally, things were beginning to make sense. He was Kenyan, not English. That was the strange, flat quality she heard in his voice but had dismissed, thinking it a result of having moved around so much. It was there, much more pronounced, in his mother's voice. Jane Beasdale was properly Kenyan – *Keenyan*, as she pronounced it, signalling some clear

472

differentiation that Sam couldn't grasp. *Keenya*, not Kenya. His father, Dave, was originally English, but had gone 'out' to Kenya – *Keenya*, she corrected herself – in his thirties, hoping to make it as a farmer. He hadn't. He'd tried his hand at everything – tea, coffee, flowers – each time, he'd failed. When independence came he'd decided there was no future in the country for men like him. 'Couldn't bear the thought of being ruled over by a bunch of munts,' he said, over and over again. 'Rather be ruled by monkeys. Mind you, not far from the truth that, is it?' he smirked at his own joke.

By now, their third day, Sam was no longer shocked. It was simply in keeping with the man and his awful, ignorant views. Quite how or why they'd ended up in a tiny cottage on the edge of the New Forest was beyond her. They were a strange couple but after a few days, she began to see what it was that had seemed so familiar to her the moment she entered the house. The half-remembered song that had drifted by – she saw now that it was the song that had been playing throughout her own childhood. Nick was the one who'd got away, the traitor; the father had stayed behind, trapped. It was her and Kate all over again. Except here, it was the father who did the bullying, not the mother. That was what had confused her. In her own home, it was her father who more or less kept things intact when they should have fallen apart. As she sat at the dinner table with them, night after night, it was like stepping backwards in time. She saw, too, that her hopes of being welcomed into his family were hopelessly misguided. They could not have been less interested in her. She was a convenient sounding board and witness for the myriad dramas that fuelled their lives – the failure of the farms; the loss of a lifestyle that, in all honesty, had never really been theirs; their shame and discomfort at having to come back to England – in Dave's case, at least – not as the lords and masters of all they surveyed, or even as successful ex-colonials. No, they'd come back with their tails between their legs to find themselves no more special than the dustbin man or the milkman, notions of ordinariness that back home in *Keenya* would have been unthinkable. The colour of their skin meant nothing, here, at home. The slow, painful realisation that it was no more 'home' than Kiambu had been, or Gathanji. All that was left of that life was the pathetic little sign hanging rather crookedly on the front gate. Macheo Cottage. Sunset Cottage. Well, she'd been there three days and hadn't seen a sunset yet.

One morning, about a week and a half after their arrival, Sam woke in the early hours of the morning to feel the walls closing in on her. She lay in bed, listening to Nick's snores beside her and the just-beginning chorus of the dawn birds. There was a strange unreality to the coming morning, as though she'd stepped through the looking glass of her own dreams to find herself awake in someone else's life. She lay there in the growing light and thought of home. She traced the shape of the word with her mouth, silently. Home was London, less than three hours' drive away but on another planet altogether. Her flat, her possessions . . . the books, records, CDs, magazines, clothes that still hung in the closet, shoes in their plastic boxes, waiting for the right season and moment. She'd always been proud of the places she'd lived, her homes. From that first Bristol flat in her student days to her current flat in Notting Hill, they'd all been her own private refuge from the demands and disappointments of the world. She pictured the living room now with its high, arched windows that flooded the room with light, even on a grey day. Her dark grey Jasper Morrison couch that could seat her and Paula at either end, with room to spare. The oak dining table and benches from Habitat and the IKEA bookcases in glossy white. It was a calm, serene space, exactly what she needed after those long, gruelling days at work. Someone else was relaxing on the couch at that very moment; someone else was picking up the remote to the forty-two-inch plasma TV that Philip had persuaded her to buy. Or listening to CDs on the BOSE system and speakers that were another of his instructions to purchase. Someone else was enjoying the view over the tree tops to the park beyond. Was it only three months since her whole world had been turned upside down? Careful, a little voice inside her head began whispering. *You* wanted the change; you made it happen, no one else.

She lifted the cover gently and slid her legs out of bed. She needed some fresh air. There was something dark and menacingly oppressive about the place. Quietly, so as not to wake Nick, she pulled on her tracksuit bottoms and a thick sweater, tied her hair into a knot and opened the bedroom door. The house was silent; there was the faint hum of the refrigerator and the odd creak from the floorboards. She'd grown accustomed to the sounds, she realised. She opened the front door and stepped outside. A bluish pink stain lit up one corner of the sky, spreading fast; the day was slowly coming into shape. She walked around the side of the house, her feet making soft indentations in the dewy grass, intending to go up the hill behind the cottage. She walked quietly, careful not to make any noise that would disturb the sleeping household. There was a soft murmur in the air. It took her a second or two to work out that it was coming through one of the open windows; it was a voice. Two voices, in fact. She stopped and turned her head. It was his mother's voice. His parents were awake. She started to move off, when she heard his mother say her name.

'Sam's nice enough, I suppose. Better than the others, if you ask me. After what that Edie did to him, the poor love—'

'They all need their fucking heads examined.' It was his father's voice, unmistakably mean. 'And as for this one, Sam. What the hell's she doing with *him*? A girl like that? She could be with anyone. It's clear she's got money.'

'Oh, for goodness' sake! It's not always about money. She *loves* him. You can *see* she does. Follows him around everywhere. Takes him coffee in the morning, irons his shirts. That's more than I've ever done for *you*, you grumpy old sod.'

'She's as crazy as all the rest of 'em. Rotten to the core, he is.'

'Oh, stop it. You're always going on at him. Give it a rest, will you?'

'Christ, if he were *my* son—'

'Look, we're not going to go over that nonsense again, are we? Here, tell you what . . . I'll make us both a cup of tea and—'

Sam didn't wait to hear the rest. She turned and walked away as quickly and quietly as she could, leaving a trail of footprints in the moist, damp grass. Her heart was beating fast. *If he were my son.* Why hadn't Nick told her Dave wasn't his real father? Was it just another of the many things she didn't know about him, or perhaps – the thought clutched at her suddenly, worryingly – perhaps he didn't even know?

PART EIGHT

94
Two months later

SAM
London, England 2009

Sam had to hold the phone away from her ear. Her mother's voice had already begun to grate and she hadn't been on the line more than five seconds. 'What d'you mean you're thinking of getting *married*? We haven't even met him yet! You've only been going out with him for a couple of months. It's absurd! What your father's going to say about all this, I don't know, Sam . . . I just don't know. The whole thing sounds so *suspicious*. You meet this *complete* stranger on holiday in Mexico—'

'Morocco, Mum, not Mexico. And he's not a complete stranger. I've been living with him in Germany for the past two months. I've met his family. He's an officer in the British Army, for God's sake, not some random bloke I picked off the street. And you'll meet him on Sunday, anyway.'

'Well, I don't know,' her mother repeated huffily. 'The whole thing just sounds . . . *weird*. Plain weird. How old is he?'

'He's thirty-nine, Mum,' Sam said wearily. 'I already told you.'

'Thirty-*nine* and he's never been married? Ooh, I don't like the sound of *that*.'

'He *has* been married, I told you. He's divorced.'

'Divorced? Even worse. What on earth are you—'

Sam couldn't hear another word. She put down the phone on her mother's shrill protestations and didn't know whether to laugh out loud, or cry. Her entire family had done nothing over the past twenty years except bemoan – at every opportunity – her single status and now that she'd found someone, all her mother seemed able to do was pick faults. She stared at the phone, tears smarting behind her eyes. It was so typical. So fucking typical. It rang again a few seconds later but she didn't have the stomach to answer it. It went to her answering machine.

'Sam? You there? It's me, Paula . . . I've got—'

'Paula?' She grabbed the receiver like a drowning woman. 'Oh, thank God. I thought it was my mother.'

'Are you crying?' Paula asked suspiciously.

'No. Well, I was . . . but I'm not now.'

'Good. Look, the rings are ready. I was going to suggest you try them on . . . are you busy?'

'No, I'll come over.' Sam was already on her feet. 'I can't think of anything I'd like to do more,' she said, blowing her nose. 'I'll be there in ten.'

Paula's flat, as untidy and chaotic as hers was neat and serene, was immediately soothing. The front door was open; she walked quickly upstairs. She had the top half of a flat in an old, once-elegant period house on Elgin Avenue in Maida Vale. As soon as Sam walked into the large open-plan living room/bedroom/studio, she felt immediately better. Paula's chaos was an art form. She looked up as Sam entered.

'That was quick. Coffee?'

'Please.'

'So,' Paula said, carrying two steaming mugs over from the tiny kitchenette. 'What did she say?'

Sam waved her hand away from her face. 'Nothing. Everything. The usual.'

'Well, I suppose it is a little sudden,' Paula said hesitantly. 'For them, I mean,' she added quickly, seeing Sam's expression.

'*I* can't help it if she's never been the kind of mum I've wanted to share stuff with,' Sam said hotly. 'All she's ever done is go on about me not having a boyfriend. Now that I've got one . . . Christ. There's no pleasing them.'

'That's what you always used to say about me,' Paula said with a quick smile. 'Anyhow, you're getting married and that's all there is to it and here, my darling best friend, are your rings.' Paula held both of them out in her palm. 'Try them on.'

Sam looked at them and the tears that had been threatening ever since she'd picked up the phone and heard her mother's voice on the other end, spilled over. 'They're beautiful,' she whispered, swallowing hard.

'Here.' Paula handed her a tissue. 'How does it fit?' she asked anxiously as Sam tried on the first one, her engagement ring.

Sam nodded. Her throat was still too choked to speak. She looked down at her hand. A thick silver band, rounded in section so that it stood fractionally proud of her finger, with a single square diamond surrounded by ten tiny emeralds. It was both traditional and strikingly modern. 'It's perfect,' she said, holding out her hand.

'Not too tight? Not even here?' Paula touched the sides of the ring as it sat on her finger. 'It doesn't rub against your other fingers? That's the thing with this rounded section . . . it's a bit broader than traditional rings. No? Phew. OK. Now, try on the wedding ring. It'll go first . . . there, that's it.'

'Perfect,' Sam whispered again.

'Thank God for that.' Paula laughed shakily. 'It's a bit experimental, that shape. But it suits you . . . oh, I'm so pleased.'

'Thanks, Paula,' Sam said, smiling through a thin veil of tears. 'They're perfect, both of them.'

'Right. A glass of wine, methinks,' Paula said, walking back towards the kitchen. 'And a large one too, by the looks of things. Where's Nick, by the way? He's got to try on his.'

'He's on his way back to London now,' Sam said, looking at her watch. 'He had to go up to Leicester last night for some regimental dinner.'

'Why don't we have dinner together? Just the three of us. I hardly got a chance to talk to him the other night.'

Sam hesitated. 'Yeah, I suppose so . . . I'll . . . I'll call you when he's back.'

'Why don't you just text him now? He can meet us some-where round here.'

Sam hesitated again. 'Um, well . . . I don't . . . I already rang him once this morning.'

'So?' Paula looked puzzled. 'Just send him a quick text.'

'I . . . I don't like doing that,' Sam said, her face reddening.

Paula flashed her a quick, suspicious look. 'What are you talking about? Doing what? Sending him a text message?'

'He probably won't reply,' Sam said, feeling immediately defensive. 'He's always forgetting to switch his phone on and then I'll be worried that he's pissed off or—'

'Sam,' Paula's voice was suddenly serious. 'Stop it. You're not making sense.'

Sam looked at her, a guilty flush stealing over her face. 'It's just . . . he's a bit funny about texting and calls, that's all. He doesn't—'

'Sam. Listen to me. You're about to marry this man.' Paula's voice was quiet. 'I know the whole thing took you by surprise. Fuck, it took *us* by surprise. I've met him once and that was for half an hour. Fine, he had to go off to some army function . . . whatever. But if you think for one second that I'm going to sit here and listen to you telling me that you're afraid to text him, then you've got another think coming. What the hell's wrong with you?'

Sam looked at the floor. Paula just didn't understand. 'He's . . . he's busy. He doesn't like being disturbed, that's all.'

'It's a fucking text message!'

'It's . . . it's the same thing,' Sam faltered. There was a huge build-up of pressure behind her eyes and her chest suddenly felt tight. She was gripped with an overwhelming urge to tell Paula that she too thought it was strange, and wrong . . . but she couldn't. Admitting to Paula that there was even the tiniest of doubts about Nick, whom no one seemed to like, not even Abby and Meaghan, would be admitting to herself that she'd got it wrong. That the incredible, dizzying surges of joy she ex-perienced every time he touched her, or called her or went out of his way to do or say something that proved to her that he did love her, in his own, rather strange way, would be over. Gone. The past five months would be as if they'd never happened. She wasn't sure she would be able to bear it. She'd given everything up – her job, her flat, her home, her plans . . . everything. She couldn't even contemplate the possibility that it wouldn't work out, or that there was something really wrong. Nick was a little . . . funny, that was all. Everyone had their quirks. Everyone. Nick was no exception. His quirks were just a little . . . different. That was all. She slowly forced her breathing back to normal, struggling to calm herself down.

'Sam? Sam?' Paula's face was suddenly close to hers. 'Are you all right?'

Sam nodded, still feeling a little dazed. 'Yes, I'm . . . I'm fine.'

'I'm sorry, I shouldn't have shouted at you like that. You look awfully pale.'

'No, no . . . I'm fine,' Sam stammered. She suddenly felt faint. She hadn't realised quite how nervous she'd been about finally bringing Nick to London. It was different in Germany. There, she'd settled quickly into her own routine – mornings with Abby and Meaghan, afternoons spent reading or shopping, dinner in the evening, either with Nick, or alone . . . after so many years of living at the most frenetic pace imaginable, the months she'd spent in Celle had come as a pleasant and welcome respite. Her life there had an edge of unreality about it, as though it wasn't properly hers, or at least not yet. But after their return from visiting his parents where she'd been gripped by a mixture of tenderness and guilt, and Nick had surprised the life out of her by asking her to marry him, she hadn't hesitated, not for a second. It seemed the natural, logical thing to do . . . to marry him and move into the next stage of her life. The fact that this particular stage – marriage, possibly children – had occurred later than she or anyone else had planned seemed irrelevant. It had finally happened to her. She was like everyone else, no different and, most importantly, no worse.

'Here,' Paula said, handing her a glass of water. 'You sure you're OK? Look, we can do dinner another night, all right? There's no rush. Speak to Nick when he gets home and we'll make a plan. You're still here for another few days, right?'

Sam nodded, drinking thirstily. 'Yes, until Wednesday night.'

'That's fine. Get Sunday lunch with your parents out of the way, then we can talk. And take the rings now. Just don't wear both of them!' Paula tried to get her to smile.

'Th-thanks,' Sam said shakily, getting to her feet. 'I'll call you later.' She walked quickly back down the stairs before Paula could ask her anything further.

It was windy outside. September had brought with it gusts of colder, sharper air. In Germany the leaves were already turning. She walked back down Elgin Avenue towards Edgware Road, past a shivering pond and down avenues of trees whose leaves had begun to spiral downwards. She shoved her hands in her pockets, her boots scuffling the fallen leaves as she walked along. Her fingers kept going over the buttons of her mobile phone – Paula was right. It was just a text. *Hi, d'you fancy having dinner with Paula tonight?* Six or seven words, nothing demanding or unreasonable. Why couldn't she do it? She hesitated. Simple. A simple invitation. But she knew he wouldn't respond and she would be kept waiting for the rest of the evening in a state of nerves that he had induced. What was wrong with her? She ought to bring it up, talk about it . . . but she couldn't. As the weeks went by and she found herself falling deeper and deeper into the part-fairy tale, part-myth of a wonderful, happy relationship that she'd created, the fear that the slightest move on her part would upset it all grew disproportionately stronger. It was wrong; she *knew* it was wrong. The logical, rational side of her brain that had once guided her in everything she did recognised the idiocy of her thoughts. But the other side – the one that responded with a thrill to every gesture from Nick, no matter how small or insignificant – was too terrified to lose what little affection he gave her by taking a chance, having an argument and blowing it.

95

DANI
Freetown, Sierra Leone, 2009

She slipped her sunglasses on, glad of the chance to hide her eyes. The film of tears that had suddenly blinded her surprised her. Eric. The memory of the last time she'd seen him burned inside her. She'd half expected to hear from him in the weeks and months that followed but there was nothing; it was as if that part of her had simply ceased to exist . . . vanished, just the way Nick had. Seeing Eric again like that had brought it all rushing back. She was wise enough to recognise that Nick's betrayal was only the last in a long line of people who'd simply vanished, leaving her behind, but it did nothing to stop the swift, sharp stab of pain, a pain that was simply compounded by Julian's death. She'd watched a film the other night with Sue, *The English Patient*. There was a French actress in it – what was her name? – she'd said something that struck Dani right between the eyes. 'Everyone who loves me either leaves or dies. I'm in love with ghosts.' She felt the same way. And now, on the afternoon of what ought to have been one of the happiest days of her life, here was another ghost come to haunt her.

She walked quickly across the parking lot in front of State House and looked around for Sue. There would be a short press conference at one of the hotels, of course, and more photographs and questions. She'd been present at enough of these events over the past few years to know that they degenerated with the sinking of the sun. Expats, hustlers and local celebrities and their hangers-on would congregate in one or other of the international hotels, each seeking something from the other that couldn't be put into words, not at any price. Dani wanted none of it. Right now she wanted to wriggle out of the tight-fitting dress, ease off her high-heeled pumps and stand under a cold shower. She saw Sue waving frantically at her from across the parking lot. Not right now, then. Just as soon as she could escape. She reluctantly made her way over.

'*There* you are,' Sue exclaimed. 'I've been looking all over the place for you. I want you to meet someone,' she said, turning to draw in the person standing next to her. Dani looked up. He was very tall, with shoulder-length blond hair pulled back off his face into a loose ponytail, piercing green eyes, a five o'clock shadow of a beard . . . a foreigner. *Per Olafsson*. She quickly read the name badge. *Dagbladet Politiken*. 'This is Per,' Sue said, making the introductions. 'He's with one of the Danish newspapers. He wondered if—'

'I wondered if you would be kind enough to do an interview with us, for our weekend magazine. I'm here in Sierra Leone covering something else and just happened to hear from an American colleague about today's awards,' he interrupted gently, smiling down at them both. *Magasin*. His accent was similar to Malin's, she noticed. A soft, slurry 's' sound, disappearing into his throat. 'You would do us a great honour. It's not so often that we report on things that are going right, not wrong, in this part of the world.'

Sue was nodding at her vigorously. 'Er, yes, sure,' she found herself saying. 'Where would you like to talk?'

'So, do *you* think they can be rehabilitated?' Per asked, a few hours later. They were sitting in the bar at the Golden Tulip Hotel on Wilkinson Road, just across from the beach. Out there, in the darkness on the other side of the road, the sea rolled in and out of the bay in a dark, mimed yawn that couldn't penetrate the hotel's air-conditioning and sealed, floor-to-ceiling glass windows. The conversation – it was no longer an interview – had taken a deeper turn.

Dani picked up her glass of wine, her fingers playing a silent trill across the rim. 'I don't know,' she said finally. 'We just have to hope they *can* be, I suppose. It's a whole lost generation. D'you know how many of them there are, walking around, just part of normal life? They don't *look* any different from anyone else but they are. What they've seen and done . . . you can't even think about it. You'll wind up mad.'

'What made you start Hopewell? I mean, yes, I know Sue's parents had the house and everything but there must have been something . . . *something* that made you connect with their situation. After all, it's not as if Freetown is crawling with the same sort of initiatives. You strike me as quite a unique pair.'

Again Dani was quiet. There was something disconcerting about Per Olafsson. On the surface, he seemed utterly professional. A reporter, nothing more. He had all the tools and tricks of the trade – the notebook, page after page covered in neat, precise handwriting, most of it utterly illegible to her when she risked sneaking a glance. She'd never seen half the letters he used – ō, æ, ø – a foreign tongue. His questions were precise and thoughtful; he had a way of asking something that seemed innocuous, only to find it invariably led to a deeper, more personal question that she had a hard time wriggling out of. She'd been interviewed before – his was hardly the first set of questions she'd had to think about before answering – but there was something ungraspable about the way he cocked his head to one side, those still, calm and yet fiery green eyes watching hers, waiting for something . . . some sign, some tiny, escaped expression that would lead him further in. It was like sitting in front of a particularly beautiful but dangerous beast who, given the slightest chance, would reach out and idly claw her to death as was his nature, nothing to be done about it. She giggled suddenly.

'What's so funny?'

She put a hand to her mouth. It was almost nine o'clock and they'd been in the bar since six. She'd had three glasses of wine and nothing to eat since breakfast that morning. She was starving and the wine had gone straight to her head. 'Nothing,' she said, trying not to laugh. 'It was just . . . just a thought.'

'A funny thought, by the looks of it.' He considered her for a second. 'Look, I'm absolutely starving . . . I don't know about you but I could really use something to eat. Do you . . . would

487

you like to join me? We could eat here, but it looks a little bland. Like the sort of food you could find anywhere.'

Dani hesitated. She liked him, she decided. He was direct and clever and clearly worldly. He was Danish, but had lived in Oslo for almost twenty years. He was forty-three, divorced, with a daughter who lived with his ex-wife. He'd been the *Dagbladet Politiken* Africa correspondent for the past three years, had the use of a flat in Nairobi, another one in Lagos and spent the rest of his time in Johannesburg. He confused her; he was European, and yet he was not. A different type of European, then. He laughed when she mentioned it. 'Ah, yes . . . the Scandinavians. Well, we're not like the rest of Europe, it's true. We like to think of ourselves as *good* Europeans – in the moral sense, I mean. We weren't really involved in the slave trades, the scramble for Africa, the empires . . . small countries, relatively prosperous but without imperial ambition and all the shit that comes with it. But don't be fooled. We're just as avaricious as the rest of the world, just as hungry for power and influence . . . a little more polite, maybe, and with the disadvantage of language.'

'Language? Your English is perfect,' Dani said, shaking her head.

'That's what I mean. Who speaks Danish or Swedish except us? We *have* to learn English or French or Spanish. We have to get out of our comfortable little boxes with our high taxes and those amazing levels of public service that the rest of the world shakes its head at. When you come to a place like this . . .' He looked around at the hotel lobby and she understood immediately that his gaze had nothing to do with what was in front of them – the air-conditioned interior, potted plants and silent, flat-footed waiters whose sullen expressions were the only hint of what might lie beyond. 'That's when you see what a sham it all is, how precarious life *really* is. What people are capable of and what life is really all about. Not taxes and insurance and hedge funds and all the things we in the West do to prevent *this* from happening to us. It must happen to someone else, some*where* else. Preferably here. You ask me why I don't go back to my nice apartment in Oslo – and it really is nice, I can tell you! – well, this is why. Once you've understood *that*, you can't go back. At least *I* can't.'

She picked up her glass of white and took the last sip. 'Come on,' she said, making her mind up. 'I'll take you somewhere different. Nice, but different.'

He stood up. He was so tall she had to tip her head backwards just to see his face. He put his notebook and small recording device away and pulled a few bills out of his pocket. 'Lead the way, Mrs Kingsley-Safo. I'm all yours.'

She took him to Chez Tante Marie, one of the few restaurants in Freetown that served African food. Owned and run by a woman from Côte d'Ivoire, it had been one of Julian's favourite haunts. She hadn't been back to it since he died. It was just off Fourah Bay Road, in the dense warren of streets around the mosque. The taxi driver looked enquiringly at her as she gave the address but she ignored him. Per had to sit with his head half ducked for the twenty minutes it took to get there. 'I'm afraid I'm not made for the dimensions of this city,' he laughed as he got out and unfolded his long body. 'I'm staying in a friend's flat, up near Damba Road. I keep hitting my head on the door frame.'

Damba Road. The recognition flowed through her like a cold shock. She stumbled as she crossed the threshold into the restaurant. His hand was immediately at her elbow, sending another shock running up and down its length. 'You OK?'

'Yes, yes . . . just didn't see the step.'

'*Bonsoir . . . bienvenue.*' A large-bosomed woman in a long, patterned flowing robe was standing in the entrance, greeting customers as they came in. She smiled as Dani and Per approached, then her smile widened. 'Dani? *C'est toi?* Yes? Oh, *ma chérie* . . . it's a long, long time I no see you. How are you, *ma belle*? Oh, I'm so sad for what 'appen. Too much sad. How come you don' come no more? *Oui*, I understan'.' Her face rearranged itself into the appropriate expression of sympathy. 'Where you goin' sit, *ma petite*? I take you upstairs? It's cool upstairs. *Plus fraîche*.' She tucked her arm into Dani's and led the two of them up the rickety staircase to the terrace that hung rather precariously over the street. She was right; it was much cooler up there. Under the thatched roof there were large wooden ceiling fans that wafted air across the tables. The clientele, in direct contrast to the hotel, was almost entirely African.

Dani took her seat and looked around her with a mixture of pain and pleasure – she'd missed it. She and Julian used to come on a Friday night, arriving around eight p.m. but not leaving until three or four. Julian loved to get into discussions that broke apart, reformed as arguments, regrouped as laughter until the small hours, often with people he'd never met before who became part of his wider crowd of contacts and friends. The crowd who came to Tante Marie's were a mixture of local businessmen and women; glossy, well-fed Ghanaian bankers; slick, polished Nigerian oil men; tall, slender Senegalese artists; poets with goatees and impossibly French accents from Guinea and Benin, countries that were adjacent to Sierra Leone but might as well have been on the moon. Per was evidently impressed. He was the only white person in the place but he took his seat unselfconsciously, as at ease here as he'd been an hour earlier, among the potted plants and stiff white linen that were the more usual haunts of his kind.

'If it's not too personal a question,' he said as their drinks were brought to the table, 'what did happen to your husband?'

Dani was quiet for a second. 'A stray bullet, or that's what they said. He was coming up the road with the windows down. Just one of those things . . . wrong place, wrong time.'

'I'm sorry.'

'Thanks,' she said softly. 'We weren't actually legally married. Not in the British sense, I mean. But his family were fantastic to me. They provided the seed money for Hopewell . . . he was a doctor and I think it's been a kind of comfort to them that there's something here that carries on his work, in a way. His grandfather was educated at Fourah Bay College, not far from here, actually. There's a bit of a historical connection.'

'Ah, yes, of course. Kingsley-Safo. *Ethiopia Unbound.* I remember now. How did you meet, if you don't mind me asking?'

Dani shook her head. She had the feeling she could tell him anything. 'I had an abortion when I was sixteen. He . . . he was the doctor,' she said simply. 'He literally saved me.'

It was Per's turn to go silent. He looked at her, then pulled his lower lip into his mouth, his white, even teeth catching the soft pink flesh. It was a gesture of recognition . . . truth for truth, confidence for confidence . . . a promise of some sort, of something to come. He nodded slowly. 'You're young, Dani Kingsley-Safo, but I've the feeling you've lived. *Really* lived.'

She smiled faintly. 'I'm one of the lucky ones. I met Julian. He showed me . . . another way.'

'You'd have found your way, Julian or not. You're the type. You're too smart to let anything happen to you.'

Dani dropped her gaze. 'The place where you're staying . . . on Damba Road. Is it the tall block of flats?'

'Yes, yes it is. Why? D'you know someone who lives there? It's a beautiful building . . . the flat overlooks the sea.'

Dani nodded. 'The man I was with . . . before Julian. He lived there. On the sixth floor. An IMATT officer. I've never been back there.'

There was silence between them for a few seconds. Then Per lifted his glass. 'Then you must come. Not now, not tonight. But soon. When you feel it's right. But I must warn you, I'm a patient man. And I won't take "no" for an answer. Not where you're concerned.'

She looked up at him. There was a faint smile playing around the corners of his lips. She studied his face slowly. A beautifully proportioned face, the planes and angles and shadows forming a kind of calm, graceful symmetry that brought to mind leading men of a particular Hollywood era, the Cary Grants and James Deans of those black-and-white films she'd watched – somewhere, in someone's home – as a kid. His eyes were almost feline . . . a dark, emerald green, as unusual in his face as hers were in her own. She liked the way his hair fell across his forehead, a few long, wavy locks escaping the ponytail that rested casually across one shoulder. His five o'clock shadow had deepened and lengthened; the outline of a beard came up beneath the sun-ripened skin. She'd met one or two Scandinavians like him – blonde, blue- and green-eyed, fair people, but with the olive skin of more Mediterranean types. A beautiful man. Someone to get to know slowly, and, for the first time in her life, as an equal, not a saviour. She brought her glass carefully up to her lips. A memory resurfaced, breaking the tension between them. She was in England, a day or two after Julian's funeral. She'd gone to town with one of the sisters. She sat in the bus, staring blankly out of the window at the landscape drifting by. Here and there amongst the frost-covered branches and plants, tiny signs of life were beginning to show – next year's buds . . . unfamiliar to her. In Africa there are no seasons. She was suddenly afraid. Death had come and gone; soon life would start all over again. She was sitting amongst strangers who had not felt its touch, who were oblivious to the pain flowing in and around her. The bodies of strangers in the bus – full of life and vigour – were suddenly a threat. Now, seated opposite Per Olafsson, a man nearly twenty years her senior, full of experiences, landscapes, people that she could hardly imagine, she felt the tug of the renewal of life, just as she'd seen it that day. But the threat was gone; for the first time since Julian's death, she felt the stirrings of desire.

96

SAM
London, England, 2009

Her flat was quiet as she entered. Nick wasn't yet back. She closed the front door behind her and leaned against it for a few seconds, enjoying the view of the sitting room and the kitchen just beyond. The agents who'd let it out for her whilst she'd been in Germany had done a good job of finding the sort of tenants who came and went quietly, leaving practically no trace. A couple of bankers, a journalist. There was no reason to change things; it would be good to keep a London base, if not for their immediate use, for the future. She took off her coat and hung it on the back of the door. It was nearly four. Nick should be back any moment; perhaps once he was there, in front of her, she'd ask about dinner that evening. It was somehow easier to talk to him face to face. He was hopeless on the phone. Although he seemed to have no problem talking to his mother for hours . . . she'd rung the previous week and, to Sam's surprise, had asked to speak to her. They'd chatted for a few minutes, leaving Sam bemused but with a new warmth towards her. Perhaps it just took her a while to warm to other people . . . perhaps she'd misjudged her?

She walked into the living room. The cleaner had been in the previous day and everything was spotless. She looked around at her possessions, the furniture and pieces of art she'd bought and collected over the years. It was strange how good they made her feel − she felt stronger, calmer, somehow, amongst them. They carried *meaning* . . . in each piece there was a fragment of her own history which, when put together in a place and space that was hers, made up a tactile record of her life. Living in Nick's impersonal flat for the past few months had deprived her of something she was only now beginning to grasp. She went towards the kitchen to make herself a cup of tea. Her laptop was sitting open on the dining room table. Nick had been on it the previous day, finding train times to Leicester. She reached for the lid to shut it and found it was still powered on. He must have forgotten to switch it off. She clicked on the mouse . . . and froze. A ripple of fear swam instantly upwards through her body. Her hand trembled over the mouse. She blinked, unable to take in what she was seeing. The words on the screen leapt out at her, followed by girls in a flashing striptease.

The exotic beauty of Asian babes. These Far Eastern ladies have slender frames, olive complexions, glossy raven-coloured hair and a reputation for sweetness and submissiveness. Who can resist? Our Asian escorts are not only popular for their petite bodies and huge, innocent eyes, but their deference to their men and a willingness to please makes them a very exciting prospect for many discerning gentlemen. We have the slim, sweet little things that the reputation refers to, and we have wild babes with a personality that belies their tender frames. Our Asian escorts are available for in-call and out-call appointments and all are more than happy to spend time with you in your own home or hotel room. All major credit cards accepted. Call now to book your evening or night with one of our special girls. Satisfaction is guaranteed. Call now. You won't be disappointed.

She slammed the lid and sat down heavily, her legs giving way underneath her. It was a mistake, surely? Her heart was hammering so hard and fast she felt dizzy. He must have stumbled across the site by mistake. She stared at the closed lid of the computer. Then she opened it again. Her fingers were shaking as she scrolled back to the top of the browser. *History.* She clicked. Once. Twice. A waterfall of sites cascaded down. It was no mistake. She got up, ran to the bathroom and was violently sick.

Philip looked at her across the café table. He was distinctly uneasy but Sam, for once, didn't care. This wasn't something she could talk to Paula about. She had to talk to a man first.

'Well, no . . . I don't,' he said slowly. 'I've never used porn myself. I've just never seen the point, frankly. But Nick's a soldier, Sam. They're different. I guess. I don't know. I've never . . . no one's ever asked me anything like this before.' He ran a hand under his collar, clearly embarrassed. 'Why don't you just talk to him about it?'

Sam stared at her coffee cup. 'I don't know what to say,' she said at last. 'I mean, what do you say? Is it a problem?'

'Well, I suppose it depends on what he's looking at. Christ, Sam . . . couldn't you have found someone else to ask?' Philip's face was red.

'It's not just porn, though. There's other stuff . . . escort sites. Girls that'll come to your room. Prostitutes. He told me he was going to Leicester last night . . . he could've been anywhere.' Sam swallowed, close to tears.

'Look, I'm sure it's harmless stuff. Just because he looks up an escort site doesn't mean he actually, you know, goes there, or whatever. You've got to confront him if it bothers you that much.'

'You mean it wouldn't bother other people?' Sam was incredulous.

Philip shrugged. 'I don't know. Some women don't mind, I guess. Or they never find out . . . who knows? Like I said, it's not really my . . . er, cup of tea.'

Sam was quiet. She was already beginning the process of something she was only dimly aware of . . . she was beginning to rationalise Nick's behaviour. She was trying to put it into some kind of context that she could understand. That was why she hadn't gone to Paula with this. Paula, for all her hopelessness where men were concerned, was surprisingly clear. *If it doesn't work for me, I'm out.* She had no qualms, no second thoughts, no rationalisations of the sort that Sam was going through now, sitting in front of Philip. Paula would have picked up the laptop and cracked it over his head. And walked out. And that would have been that. Sam couldn't. 'Perhaps he was doing it for a friend,' she said at last. 'As a favour.'

Philip just looked at her. 'Perhaps,' he said quietly. The word fell like a stone between them.

97

She should have brought it up; she didn't. She left the computer exactly where it was. Nick got home around six. She'd just got back from her quick coffee with Philip when she heard his key in the lock. She went into the hallway to greet him, her eyes searching his face for some sign that he hadn't been in Leicester, that he'd been in a hotel room somewhere in central London, a dozen Asian escorts at his side. There was none. He was exactly the same as he'd been when he left. He kissed her, his arm going round her waist. The pressure was the same; he smelled, tasted, felt exactly the same. Nothing had changed. It would have been impossible to hide, she thought to herself wildly. No man could ring up a couple of prostitutes, spend the night with them and then return to his girlfriend the following day without some sign, some tiny, little giveaway sign . . . it would be marked on him in some way, identifiable only to her. It wasn't possible to hide. She clung to him weakly, happily. He'd done it for a friend; that was it. Someone had rung up and asked him to do them a favour, perhaps even one of the other officers . . . she began to fantasise wildly about who it could have been. By the time his suggestion of dinner with Paula was voiced, she was almost delirious with relief.

'With Paula?' she echoed. 'Funny, we were just thinking about dinner this afternoon. I went to pick up the rings . . . look. That's the engagement one.' She held out her hand.

He looked at it and gave a small smile. 'Looks good,' he said, shrugging off his jacket. 'I'm just going to take a shower. Crap journey. I hate going up to Leicester.' He disappeared into the bedroom. A second wave of relief broke over her. He'd been to Leicester, not Leicester Square. He'd said so.

They met at Churro Churro, a new Brazilian eatery just off Westbourne Grove. Nick looked good, Sam thought to herself with a stab of pride. She couldn't remember the last time she and Paula had been out with a man, together. She slipped her arm through Nick's as they walked down Hereford Road to meet her. 'You look nice,' Nick said suddenly, surprising her. 'I like that colour on you.' She looked down at her burnt orange dress that she'd worn over jeans . . . a pair of chunky, rubber-heeled boots from Nine West and a faux-fur trimmed gilet . . . it was nice of him to say so. She kept fingering her engagement ring with her thumb. She loved the way it sat on her finger, catching the light, the brilliance of the square-cut diamond offset by the emeralds surrounding it. She'd paid only for the stones – Paula wouldn't hear of charging her either for the workmanship or the platinum. 'It's my gift,' she said stubbornly. 'Don't expect a single thing else and if I could afford the stones, you know I'd throw them in.' Sam had paid for the stones immediately, expecting Nick to offer to pay her back, or at least split the cost, but he'd said nothing. Yes, she earned far more than he did but wasn't it tradition for the man to pay? By the looks of things, she'd be paying for the wedding, or most of it . . . perhaps she should bring it up? Yet another of the subjects she ought to broach . . . perhaps after they were married. There was still a tiny part of her that couldn't quite believe in it. Having a piece of paper would help.

Throughout the evening, Nick couldn't have been more charming, especially to Paula. She saw in him again the same man who'd apprehended a pickpocket in the streets of Marrakech on her behalf, and with whom she'd found herself lying shortly thereafter in bed. There was a tiny pinprick of jealousy as he talked to Paula about her jewellery, displaying a knowledge of stones and gems that she wasn't even aware he had but she quickly suppressed it. How could she be jealous of Paula?

'I've always really liked creative types,' he said, lifting his glass to Paula. 'Those rings are amazing. The colours are incredible. How'd you think of it?'

Paula flashed a quick glance at Sam. 'It was her idea, really,' she said loyally. 'She's got great taste.'

'Well, anyone can think of an idea,' he said loftily, 'but actually *designing* it . . . that's amazing.'

Sam could see Paula was about to object. 'No, you're right,' she interjected quickly, flashing a quick, imploring look at Paula. She could practically feel Paula's hackles begin to rise. 'Paula's the talent, not me.'

Paula opened her mouth to protest, but Sam cut her short. 'More wine, anyone? Did you choose this one, Nick? It's divine.'

She ignored Paula's look of incredulity and poured them all another glass.

'She's actually really nice,' Nick said as they made their way back home an hour or so later. 'I thought she was a bit stuck up the first time I met her.'

'Paula? Stuck up? God, no . . . she's the most down-to-earth person I know.' Sam was surprised by the comment.

'Yeah, well . . . she was a bit frosty that first night.'

'So were you,' Sam teased him a little. 'Philip nicknamed you the Ice Man.'

Nick stopped in the middle of the pavement. He moved his arm out of hers. 'What did he say?' he asked and his voice was suddenly cold.

'N-nothing,' Sam stammered. 'Just . . . he just said you were a little stiff, that's all.'

'You discussed me with him? With *them*?'

Sam stared at him, confusion breaking out all over her skin. 'Of course I did . . . they're my friends.'

'I don't care who they are. You have no right to talk about me behind my back.'

Sam gaped at him. Suddenly things had started to slide again; the ground had gone from under her feet. 'I wasn't talking about you behind your back,' she said quickly, wondering what was the best tactic here. 'They were saying how nice you were, and Philip just said you were a little frosty at first, but that you warmed up—'.

'Liar. I know when you're lying to me.'

'Nick . . . I'm not lying . . . that's exactly what he said! What . . . what's wrong with that?'

'You just don't get it, do you?'

'Get what?' Sam cried, bewildered by the turn of events. 'I don't understand. Look, it's nothing . . . we were just talking. They're my *friends*, Nick. They *care* about me and they don't want to see me making the wrong choice—'

'*You?* You wouldn't know a choice if it hit you,' Nick snarled at her contemptuously. 'Just who do you think you are?'

Sam stared at him in shock. The laughing, charming Nick who'd left the restaurant a few minutes earlier was gone, vanished. 'N-Nick?' she stammered, putting out a hand to touch his arm. 'Wh-what's got into you? What have I said?'

'Go fuck yourself, Sam!' He shouted suddenly, yanking his arm away from her hand. 'Go *fuck* yourself, d'you hear me? *Go fuck yourself!*'

Sam took a step backwards instinctively, and almost bumped into an elderly couple who were walking up the street. The woman's eyes met hers – there was a look of sympathy that passed between them which made Sam drop her own. When she looked up Nick was gone. She stood in the middle of the pavement, numb with shock, struggling to understand what had happened. The events of the day suddenly overwhelmed her. Everything – picking up the rings, talking to Paula, the shock waiting for her on her laptop and now this . . . she felt her legs giving way and she staggered to the nearest steps. She sat down heavily on the top one and buried her face in her arms. She began to cry, huge, heaving sobs that came from a place within her that was so deep and painful every breath seemed to cut through her. The following day they were due to have Sunday lunch with her parents and Kate and Grant. The thought of having to call and cancel it made her feel physically ill. She could practically hear her mother. I told you so. It'll all end in tears. And so it had. She struggled to breathe, trying to reconstruct the sequence of events so that they made sense – any kind of sense. What had she said? He was the one who'd made the comment about Paula . . . she'd simply echoed him. What was so wrong with that?

'Are you OK?' Someone spoke to her.

She looked up. A woman was standing over her, looking down on her with concern. She nodded, struggling to her feet. 'Yes, y-yes, I'm fine.' She grabbed her handbag with both hands and without waiting to hear another word she ran up the street, her bag banging awkwardly against her legs. She ran up the stairs to the flat, half-hoping, half-dreading to see Nick. She slid her key in the lock and pushed open the door. The flat was empty. She took off her coat and slid to the ground, hugging her knees against her chest. Nick was gone.

She had fallen into an uneasy, fitful sleep, punctuated by dreams that alternated from blissful to desperate, when she felt, rather than heard, someone enter the room. She struggled upright, groping for the light. It was Nick. He sat down heavily on the bed, breathing hard. She could smell the alcohol coming off him in waves. She hesitated, then let her hand drop. She didn't want him to see her face, reddened and blotchy with tears. He eased off his boots and lay back, his hand going out to touch hers. He turned towards her, burrowing under the duvet to pull her towards him. His face was in her hair; his hands pulling at her nightdress, roughly stroking her skin. 'Sorry,' he mumbled against her ear. 'Sorry.'

'It's OK,' she whispered, tears sliding down her face before she could put up a hand to stop them.

'Sorry. Dunno what happened there. You . . . it just . . . just reminded me. Of her.'

'Who?' Sam whispered, her heart beginning to race.

'Her. Edie. That bitch of a wife.'

It was the first admission on his part that things weren't quite as rosy as he'd made them out to be. A wave of relief rose up in her, mingling with the relief she'd felt as the bedroom door opened and he came back in. 'I'm not her,' she whispered. 'I'm *me*. Sam. I love you.'

'Love you too,' he mumbled. His hands were busy unbuttoning her nightdress so he could slip it off.

'If you'd just let me in, Nick,' she said softly, allowing him to undress her. 'You can't keep me locked out all the time. You've got to let me in.'

'You're already in,' he said, his tongue pushing its way into her mouth. 'Kiss me.'

She did as he asked, tasting the salt of her own tears on both their lips. He was in a hurry; he rolled over so that he was on top of her, pushing her legs apart with his knees. She wasn't ready for him, but he didn't seem to notice. In seconds he was inside her with a quick, painful thrust. She put her hands around his back, touching him gently, trying to slow him down but he was all urgency. He was hurting her, but she couldn't get him off. He began to saw in and out of her, his mouth grinding down on her teeth. She twisted her head to one side, forcing herself not to panic, to relax. His eyes were shut tightly, his face and chest sweaty with the effort of pushing himself deeper and deeper inside her, thrusting himself through to some other side that she couldn't see or feel. Her legs were beginning to ache; five minutes, ten minutes . . . fifteen. He was sweating; it ran in rivulets off his skin, pooling on her neck and breasts and stomach. Just when she thought she couldn't possibly stand it for a second longer, she felt his hands clutch her hair, his whole body stiffened and a strangled, inarticulate gasp was torn from his throat. She thought she would pass out from the violent spasm that gripped him as he gripped her legs and hips in turn. 'Fuck,' he panted, 'Fuck, fuck . . . oh, *fuck*!' His body shuddered, he jerked inside her once, twice, three times . . . then rolled off her immediately, his hands going up to his face. He was still shuddering, his breathing ragged and heavy. Was he crying? Sam opened one eye cautiously. His arm was flung across his face, hiding it. She couldn't tell. She lay next to him, as still as a mouse, too stunned to move. Minutes ticked past and neither said a word. The clock beside the bed glowed in the dark. 4.13 a.m. He'd been gone since ten. She forced herself to breathe easier, trying to calm her racing heart. It took her a few minutes to realise that he'd fallen asleep.

98

MEAGHAN
Celle, Germany, 2009

She turned the invitation over slowly in her hands. It was beautifully done; typical Sam. A heavy, cream-coloured card with an embossed rose on one side and the words 'Please join us in celebrating our marriage' on the other. A second, smaller card had the date and place. A registry office in Holland Park, London. The date was set for the following weekend.

'Look what just arrived in the post,' she said, walking into the kitchen where Tom was reading a last-minute story to Alannah before she walked to school. 'They're getting married. Next weekend.'

'Yeah, I saw Nick last night. He got back on Saturday, I think. She's staying in London until the wedding.'

'It's a bit short notice,' Meaghan said slowly. 'D'you think you'll be able to get the weekend off?'

Tom shook his head. 'Na, I'll stay behind. You go with Alannah. I imagine the CO'll be going . . . someone'll have to stay behind on the base.'

'You sure?' Meaghan was doubtful. 'Won't it look a bit funny?'

'What d'you mean?'

'Well, we're sort of their closest friends, aren't we?'

Tom shrugged. He was far less concerned about that sort of thing than she was. 'He'll get over it. The CO'll be there. I imagine that'll mean more to him than me being there,' he said cryptically. 'Go on, you go and enjoy yourself. I've been a bit of a grump lately. You could use the break.'

Meaghan smiled. It was true. 'You sure?' she asked again.

'Sure.' He looked up and winked at her. 'Go shopping. Get your hair done. Enjoy yourself. It'll be a while before you can do that again.'

She nodded slowly. In just under six weeks' time, the battalion would ship out to Cyprus, without the wives and children. She and Alannah would stay in Celle until the beginning of the summer recess, and then most of the families would return to the UK to wait out the next six months. She swallowed. She didn't want to think about it. Tom was right. A weekend in London would be one of the last chances to enjoy herself before the long period of waiting and worrying began. 'Well, if you're sure,' she said, yet again.

'I am. Now,' he said, turning back to Alannah. 'Where were we?'

Meaghan watched as Alannah's face lit up. The six-month absence would be hard on her, she knew. A daddy's girl, if there ever was one. She smiled and went back into the kitchen to make a second cup of coffee. She would take Alannah to school, then cycle over to Abby's. A weekend in London at Sam's wedding. She was excited, despite her misgivings about the relationship, which had never quite gone away.

'Lovely card,' Abby agreed, pulling hers out of her handbag. 'Very Sam.'

'What're you going to wear?' Meaghan asked anxiously.

'Not sure. I've got a lovely cashmere dress that I wore to an aunt's wedding a couple of years ago . . . it's cream, with one of those lovely big collars, comes to just above the knee. I'll have to get some shoes, I think. She said it's going to be a very simple ceremony. I don't think his parents are coming. His dad's in a wheelchair and it's a long journey, or so she said. And I don't think *he's* got many friends.'

'It's a pity Tom can't go. I've got to get us a hotel. I'll do it this afternoon.'

'A hotel? Whatever for? You'll stay with us. We've got a whole empty house in Chelsea.'

'Oh, no, we couldn't. We'll find a hotel. It's just me and Alannah.'

'Absolutely not. Don't be silly. It'll be lovely to have you with us. And Clara'll be down from school . . . the girls will all get on like a house on fire. No, I insist.'

Meaghan was touched. 'It's very kind of you,' she began hesitantly.

'Rubbish. It's nothing. It'll be fun. We can go shopping on Friday afternoon. My mum'll have the girls for the day and take them to the zoo or something on the Sunday. We've booked a table at Nobu for all of us on Saturday night after the reception – Ralph's gift to the happy couple.'

'Nobu? What's Nobu?'

Abby laughed. 'I don't know. It's some fancy restaurant . . . I read about it in *Vogue*. One of Sam's,' she added mischievously. 'I do hope they'll be happy together,' she said, her voice suddenly turning serious. 'Sam's no fool but I sometimes wonder . . .' She stopped, as if she were afraid to voice her thoughts.

'She'll be fine,' Meaghan said firmly. 'Like you said, she's no fool.'

'An army wife,' Abby mused. 'Who would've thought it?'

99

Judging by the comments floating around before and after the short ceremony, no one. Sam was right. The ceremony *was* simple. They met at the Westminster Register Office at ten o'clock on Saturday morning and the whole thing was over by eleven. Sam looked lovely. She wore a simple ivory silk dress with charcoal fishnet tights and dark grey and cream shoes with a square, chunky heel. Her hair was swept up into a smooth chignon and she had on a long, elegant string of pearls with matching studs in her ears. The hairdresser had done her make-up – again, it was simple and beautifully done. She and Nick did make a striking couple, Meaghan thought, watching them both bend to sign the register. Nick was wearing the regiment's formal dress . . . a dark, khaki colour that suited him. His hair was almost completely grey now, Meaghan noticed. He was quite different from the tall, rather gangly, dark-haired officer cadet she'd known nearly two decades ago. He'd filled out in almost every direction. Not fat, but broad, the sort of chest that made you want to lean into it. Only his eyes were the same. They flickered over her with the same cool, detached lack of interest that unnerved her, always had.

She turned her attention to Sam's family. Her parents and sister were absolutely nothing like her. She supposed it sometimes happened that way . . . look at her own family. Sam's mother was short and plump, forever fussing over her grandchildren, Sam's sister Kate's children. Kate couldn't have been more different from Sam if she'd tried. It was hard to believe they were sisters, let alone twins. Like the mother, she was short – at least a head shorter than Sam – and dumpy. She was dark-haired, like Sam's father, but it was the permanent scowl on her face that really stood out. Everything about her reeked of dissatisfaction, though quite what she had to be dissatisfied about was anyone's guess. From the few exchanges they'd had that morning, and from the little that Sam said, Kate was a doctor, married to a surgeon, with a thriving GP practice, a lovely home somewhere in south London and three children . . . what was there to be sour about? 'From what I gather, she's always been that way,' Abby whispered. 'Right old sourpuss. Bit like the mother, if you ask me. The dad's nice, though.' It was true. Sam's father was a tall, permanently stooped man with kindly eyes and a ready, gentle smile. It was clear he was henpecked half to death; barely a moment went by without his wife's eagle eyes upon him. Christ, Meaghan thought to herself . . . don't tell me we'll all be like that in twenty years' time. What would Alannah say about her parents at *her* wedding? She barely stifled a giggle.

'What's funny?' Abby whispered at her side.

Meaghan shook her head. 'I was just wondering what our kids'll say about us when *they* get married,' she whispered back.

'I mean, your parents seem wonderfully normal . . . but as for the rest of us . . .' She trailed off.

'Don't be fooled,' Abby said with a smile. 'Mine are as batty as everyone else's.'

'I doubt it,' Meaghan said drily. 'You want to see *mine*.'

They were interrupted by a loud clapping. The register had been signed. Sam looked out across the heads of everyone seated in front of them, caught Meaghan's eye and smiled. Her best friend, Paula, who'd designed the rings, suddenly burst into tears. There was a whoop from someone else – one of Sam's old colleagues – and then everyone got to their feet, cheering and clapping. It was over. Sam Maitland was now Sam Beasdale. An army wife.

100

SAM
Celle, Germany, 2009

Sam looked around the newly painted sitting room with pleasure. Much better. She'd replaced the standard magnolia with a warm mustard. The carpets had been lifted to reveal a rather nice, if worn, parquet floor, which she'd had sanded and sealed. Her own rugs now lay on the floor and most of the army furniture had been returned to stores and replaced with her own. She'd brought over a few pieces of artwork, her own pots and pans and plates, including a dozen fine wine glasses – always useful for a dinner party – and a beautiful, ornate glass lamp-shade now hung above the dining table. It was hard to believe it was the same flat she'd come to six months ago. All was transformed. She'd thoroughly enjoyed the process, too. The living room and dining room were done; the bedroom was in progress. The painters had assured her they'd be finished by the end of the week. She'd bought a new wardrobe and bed, new linen, re-upholstered an old ottoman that she'd found in a second-hand shop in town . . . soon it too was transformed. All that was left was the spare room at the end of the corridor, which she would turn into a study of her own, a little like Abby's studio. Nick just shrugged when she announced her plans. He, like Ralph and Tom, was working flat out in the months before the move to Cyprus. She'd gathered there'd been a bit of fuss about the high drop-out rate in Nick's company . . . in the past week alone two privates had asked to be released from the army and one had been sacked. It wasn't his fault, or so Meaghan and Abby reassured her. Just the way it was sometimes. Nick didn't seem to think so; he took it personally. Tom had made a joke about it the other night at dinner at La Buca and Nick had stormed out. It took her the better part of the night to calm him down.

She pushed open the door to the spare room and winced. Aside from the discarded, broken-down furniture that had somehow found its way in here, there were four giant plastic trunks that contained Nick's junk . . . paperwork, files, clothes, boots, CDs . . . you name it. All the stuff he'd collected over the years, he said, when she asked. 'Toss it if you like. I don't need any of it.' She looked at the furniture. She'd get WO Greaves from Housing to come in with a couple of lads and clear away the bed and what looked like two desks and a chest of drawers. That would be the first move. Then she'd get someone to take out the dryer that was rather incongruously kept in the room and re-install it in the kitchen. She looked at the trunks . . . she might as well get started on those herself. She'd pull everything out, arrange the stuff in piles and then check with him one last time before tossing it all out.

She lifted the lid on the one nearest her. Half a dozen photograph packets, plastic file folders and scores of negatives, old letters, tied together in bundles, a few paperback novels of the sort she knew he had never read . . . she pulled one out. A Mills & Boon-type novel . . . she opened the first page. *Edie Beasdale*. She shut it again. It must have belonged to his ex-wife. She picked up a couple of the photographs. Nick, in a variety of uniforms and landscapes . . . the sandy tones of the desert, the thick canopy of a jungle somewhere. She leafed through them, fascinated. He'd changed little over the years, she noticed. In each, he wore the same guarded, careful expression. There was one of him holding up an enormous fish . . . she hadn't known he liked to fish. Another showed him standing on the bridge of a speedboat, fishing tackle in hand. She wondered where they'd been taken . . . somewhere warm, by the looks of it. He was tanned, in shorts. She smiled. Nice, well-shaped, muscular legs. She'd always liked his legs. She picked up another photograph. Her heart gave a sudden lurch. It was him, with his arm round a girl . . . a very young girl. She had dark coffee-coloured skin and the most striking yellow-green eyes she'd ever seen. She was stunning. Her face was partially turned towards his – a row of pearly white teeth, full, dark lips parted in a smile, clouds of dark, curly hair that blew across her own face, falling over his arm. Nick wasn't smiling but there was something in the way he held her that denoted a kind of possession that was new to her, in him. She stared at the photograph for a few more minutes, searching for some sign that would reveal more than the image that was presented to her. Who was she? When was it taken? And, most importantly, who was she to him? She put it down, her fingers shaking slightly. Like so many other things about Nick, she was only able to grasp at part of the story. He was like a particularly complex jigsaw puzzle where the important pieces were always missing, or didn't quite fit. She found it hard to grasp the whole of him – there was always something, some little detail or event that didn't make sense. The girl in the photograph was just one more piece for which she had no home.

She got to her feet stiffly; she'd been kneeling for at least half an hour. She didn't feel like looking any further. She had no idea what she might find.

101

Sunlight poured in through the curtains in the bedroom; the room was suffused with light. Dani woke first. Per slept with his back to her, his blond hair spread across the pillow in a cascading fan of silky softness that tickled her nose when she moved her face towards him. She lay in the growing heat, the fan sending rhythmic wafts of cooler air as it moved towards them, then swung away, and then back again. It needed oiling, she noticed. There was a faint but discernible creak as it moved to and fro in a limited arc, stirring the papers that Per had laid on the bedside table the night before. She lay beside him in an intense physical silence that, curiously, was simply an extension of the surprising passion of the previous night and all that had gone on through it.

It had been a month since she'd met Per Olafsson in the car park opposite State House. Not very long; and yet it seemed for ever. She had never 'got to know' a man in this way before. He took his time, and hers . . . half-frustrating, half-fascinating her. Julian had so clearly stepped in to save her – Per had no such notion. She did not need saving. He came and went in that month with an ease that surprised and intrigued her. Two days in Freetown, a week in Lagos, punctuated by phone calls that lasted all night; a day and a half in Accra, then back to Freetown. He took her to dinner every night, regaled her with stories about stories that were about to break elsewhere on the continent, showed her pictures of Maja, his daughter who lived with his ex-wife somewhere in New England. His ex-wife was American, a peace corps volunteer whom he'd met in Malawi, years ago . . . it was part of the problem, he confessed. 'Americans . . .' A shrug of those impossibly broad shoulders. 'They're . . .

different.' She'd wanted to return, go home, be amongst her own kind.

'Maja's black,' she said, surprised.

'Adopted. She was three weeks old when we got her.'

She stared at the picture of the sixteen-year-old, cheekily self-possessed in a way that African children seldom are. 'She's pretty,' she said, not sure what else to say. There were no similarities between the blond, green-eyed man in front of her and the dark-skinned, dreadlocked teenager who stared cheekily out from beneath a fringe and a self-assured grin.

'Beautiful. Like the mother. She was our domestic worker.'

'Is it strange having a black child?' she asked.

He shook his head. 'It's a funny thing. After a while, you don't notice it any more. Everyone else does . . . but not me. Not us. She's Maja. That's all. Her mother – my ex-wife – struggled with her hair a bit, at first. It's not like yours . . .' He reached across the table to touch her curls. 'Yours is much softer.'

'That comes from my father,' Dani said with a small shrug. She could take no credit.

'Where was he from?'

'I don't know. I never knew him. He disappeared before I was born.'

'And your mother?'

Dani gave another shrug. 'I never really knew her. She left when I was still a baby.' She waited for him to make the sort of remark she'd heard foreigners make all her life. *Oh, that's a shame. Poor you. That must've been hard.*

He didn't. He raised his glass instead. 'Well, whoever did bring you up did a pretty good job,' he remarked quietly. 'It's the one thing that living in Africa for the past twenty years has taught me.'

'What's that?'

'Families, and what we mean by them, are infinitely more fluid than we think. People always say they have to be here in Africa, but I disagree. They like to pretend that it's because of politics, or wars, or famine . . . whatever excuse they can find to point to someone else and say, "there, at least we're not like that". But they miss the point. It's not because of wars that people here call each other "brother" and "sister" when they're not related.'

'What is it then?' She was aware of her heart beginning to accelerate. Per did that to her. She'd never talked to a man the way she found herself talking to him. He drew her in, at once, without preamble. His musings on the world were unlike any she'd ever heard. He seemed at once to be talking *about* her and *to* her simultaneously. Observations, in his mouth and mind, were really provocations, to be examined, discussed, overturned. He talked to her as an equal; he demanded no less. The almost twenty years between them seemed an irrelevance.

'It's a profound understanding of the complexity of life. Think about it, Dani. How many African languages have words for what we Europeans love to complicate? Stepmother, half-sister, father-in-law, second cousin, third cousin . . . all those . . . how do you call them? Declensions?' Dani shook her head in bewilderment. She had no idea. 'All this *measuring* . . . we make a fetish out of it and then we look around us and wonder what's gone wrong.'

'But . . . people need to know where they stand, surely?' Dani volunteered. She was groping her way towards an understanding of what he was trying to say.

'Yes, of course. But life gets in the way. Things happen. Shit happens. Your father left; your mother too. Here, there's always someone to step in, fill a missing pair of shoes, take on a role that wasn't always in the plan. There *is* no plan; there are only contingencies. In Europe we spend our lives hedging our bets against those very contingencies, not realising that that *is* life. That's just how it is. You cannot plan for everything.'

Dani was silent, yet again unsure what to say. There was a part of her that realised he was right – the fluidity he described *was* her life; she recognised it. But there was another part of her that resented it. When she met Julian's family, she immediately

grasped the shared interests and values that bound them together, across the divides of nationality and race – a bonding
that had eluded her own family. She was different; her father
had marked her out as such. Her grandmother simply wasn't in
possession of the tools that would smooth over her difference
and instead had paraded it as some mark of distinction. Her fair-
skinned, half-white granddaughter on whom all the money had
been lavished. Such as it was. There were times when she cursed
the semi-education she'd been given. There were so many gaps,
so many holes. When the war had closed down the school, most
of the really good teachers had fled. By the time they came
trickling back, she was gone but the gaps still remained. Julian
had filled in some of them; here, now, in front of her, was
someone else come to do the same. She couldn't have walked
away even if she'd tried.

'Awake?' She turned her head and bumped into his. His arms
were around her, despite the heat. They lay together in a damp,
sweaty embrace, neither wanting, it seemed, to break it.

'I've been awake for ages.'

'Liar.' His face burrowed into the hollow at the base of her
neck. She could feel his tongue darting there, collecting on its
tip the faint salt of her sweat. 'I was awake when you stopped
snoring.'

'I don't snore,' she protested in a giggle. 'But you do.'

'Yes, *min lille loppe*, I do.' The unfamiliar phrase struck her as
funny.

'What did you call me?'

'*Min lille loppe*. My little flea. It's a Danish expression.'

She giggled again. She couldn't remember the last time she'd
felt such a surge of happiness. '*Min lille loppe*.' She tested the
words on her tongue.

'Very good,' he said solemnly. 'I should speak to you only in
Danish.'

'Is it very cold?' she asked, miming a shiver. 'I was only cold
once. In England.'

'I'll take you there. Next month. It's my mother's eightieth birthday. We'll go together.'

She pulled her head back to look at him. 'D'you mean it?'

'I never say things I don't mean.'

'That's impossible,' Dani said, pushing her face back into the heat of his neck. 'This is how it works. Half of the time people don't say what they mean and the other half, they don't mean what they say.'

She could feel his laughter rumble deep in his belly. '*Min lille blomme*. My little flower. I don't think I've ever met anyone like you.'

He was as good as his word, she saw. He stayed with her for two more days and nights and then he was off, this time to Brazzaville. She listened to him reel off the places he was due to be in, and the people he was to meet, over the next few weeks – DR Congo; Chissano; Lumbumbashi; Kinshasa; Mbeki; Kumasi . . . they rolled easily off his tongue. He would fly down to Johannesburg, pick up some winter clothes and check on his flat and then he would meet her in Frankfurt in just over a month's time. For the second time in her life, she handed over her passport. He had a contact at the Danish Embassy in Lagos . . . they would sort it all out and return it to her with her ticket. No, no money required. None whatsoever. A birthday gift. It's not your birthday? OK, a Christmas gift, then.

102

NICK
Celle, Germany, 2009

He read the report a second and a third time, struggling to make sense of the words that kept leaping out at him. 'Hesitant under pressure'; 'lack of initiative'; 'uncooperative'; 'lack of leadership qualities that . . .' He pushed it away from him and brought his fingers to his temples, massaging them roughly. It was deathly quiet in his office; next door, the phones had stopped ringing, for once. His second-in-command, Chris Parks, was in the officers' mess where refreshments were being served for the visiting brass. Why had Barclay waited until now to hand it to him? He looked fearfully at the plain manila envelope that he'd found in his pigeonhole outside. Major N. P. Beasdale. He'd picked it up, turned it over, wondering what it could be. He'd brought it into his office, slid a finger under the flap and a piece of paper dropped out, separate to the three-page, neatly typed report. *Sorry about this. Argued as best I could in your favour. Rgds, Ralph.* He stared at it for a moment and laid it to one side. And then he read the report. He, Major N. P. Beasdale, would not be taking his company into Afghanistan. End of story.

An hour or two later – he couldn't tell, didn't care – he sat in the bar nursing his drink. It was his fifth or sixth of the afternoon. He couldn't remember. The interior of the bar swam before him in a watery, wavering light. In the corner, sitting with their backs to him, was a group of older men, the town alcoholics, muttering to themselves in that booze-sodden way that suddenly reminded him of his father. A surge of rage and shame swept through him. He struggled to push the memory aside but there it was, ready as ever, to mock him. He was six or seven and he'd been sent by his mother to 'collect' his father from the Coconut Grill, Thika's local pub/restaurant, half a mile down the highway from their home on Lord Delamere's estate. By then his father was no longer a farmer – he'd been reduced to working as a manager on the English lord's estate. He could remember the scene as if it were yesterday. He'd pushed his way into the bar, his heart already thumping in his chest at the thought of what he might find. It was the end of the month, payday, and an excuse to piss away most of what he'd earned. He'd have been in there since morning, his money long since run out. In those days Dave Beasdale had no shame and would do anything for a free pint or a dram or two, easy-going to the point of absurdity. He'd have almost nothing left of the man in him – a clown, a buffoon, swallowing insults and jeers, eager to make a fool of himself so long as a drink came attached. Nick remembered tugging at his trousers, his face hot with shame as the others looked on in a mixture of fascination and pity, including the flame-haired woman who ran the bar. 'Mum says to come home,' he said, hating the sound of his own voice, a thin, shamefaced whine.

'Gerroff, you little prick,' Dave Beasdale turned on him, cuffing him wherever he could. 'Gerroff!'

'Aw, leave him alone,' someone shouted. 'It's the missus wants you home, not 'im. Reckon 'e's just as happy to leave you here.' Sometimes a scuffle would follow, but not that time. A couple of the others shuffled over and helped Nick lift him off the bar stool. He was strong in those days, before the accident when the horse had thrown him, shattering his femur so that he never walked again. He could almost see their sidelong pitying glances. He wanted desperately to get his dad out of there and yet at the same time, he wished desperately that he would drop down dead, run off, get run over . . . anything to spare him the glances. They walked home in silence. In the dark a terrible rage came over his father. By the time they reached the bungalow at the edge of the estate, he was shouting, cuffing anything and everything within reach, including his mother. He yanked open the fridge, looking for a beer, then kicked the empty cupboards whilst his mother clung to him in fright, holding Nick in front of her like some kind of useless shield. There was a great roaring and a volley of curses and then he went off stomping down the short corridor and into the bedroom, slamming the door behind him. A few minutes later, calmer, he came out. 'Go on, Nick, there's a good boy. Nip down the road, will ya? Get us a couple of bottles. Quick now, before your bloody mother comes.'

'Get away from me,' Nick hissed, shoving him as hard as his young arms could push. His father lunged after him but Nick was too quick. He ran out into the darkness, the blood thundering in his heart and lungs, his whole body shaking with rage and fear and shame.

The memory of it came back to him like the rising tide, lapping over old wounds, opening them up once again to the stinging salt and pain. He looked up; the girl behind the bar was watching him. He lifted his glass – another one. She nodded and turned to fill it. Jack Daniel's on ice. A double. She set the new glass down in front of him, removing the old. He looked at her arm. She was an olive-skinned girl, Turkish. He didn't know her name but rumour had it that she swung 'both ways' – one of the squaddies had told the others in delight one night. How *he* knew was anyone's guess. He watched her as she walked back to the bar, turning in that way that only women do to squeeze her hips through the narrow opening between the edge of the counter and the raised flap. He was suddenly overcome with an unspecified, overwhelming desire. His body lifted and swelled inside his uniform. He knocked back the whisky in one smooth gulp, threw a handful of notes down on the counter and walked out into the late afternoon air.

It was very cold. It was early December but there had already been two or three light snowfalls, earlier than usual, everyone said. There were days when the wind seemed to blow down straight from Scandinavia, icy to the touch, turning your breath into a fire-breathing tongue in front of you. He shoved his hands into his pockets – he'd forgotten his coat and gloves in his office. He walked quickly down the road towards the city centre, cutting diagonally across the main square to reach Bahnhofstrasse. The club he was looking for was about halfway down. Judy's Kino Bar. A fifteen-minute walk.

The lady behind the counter looked up as he entered. If she recognised him, she gave absolutely no sign. It had been a couple of months since his last visit; he recognised her. He wrote out his name on the visitors' card. Only it wasn't his name. He knew better than that. He didn't even know why he did it. *Tom Astor*. It was the quickest name to mind. She didn't even look at it. Blonde, a wad of gum tucked into the pad of her cheek, a cigarette in one hand. She pushed the laminated card in front of him. Girls. Prices. Services. He quickly scanned the card.

'Black. Have you got any black girls?' he asked. Again he didn't know why he'd asked for one. Something to do with thinking about his father and Kenya and the shit holes he'd once called home. He felt a horrible, aching revulsion come over him; he needed something from back then . . . some*one*. The younger and darker the better.

'*Ja. Ein moment.*' She slipped off her stool and pushed open the door behind her. He saw a girl through the opening. She was quite pretty. Long, braided hair, slim . . . and yes, she was black. A bit older than he liked them, but still . . . it was four thirty on a Tuesday afternoon in the middle of Germany. It wasn't Sierra Leone and there wasn't the choice. He could see her looking back at him. She said something to the receptionist; he caught a glimpse of her shaking her head and then the receptionist came back out, closing the door behind her. 'Sorry. Not available,' she said, hopping back onto her stool.

'What d'you mean?' He frowned.

'She's busy with client.'

'No, she's not. I just saw her. Through there.' He pointed to the door. 'I just saw her.'

'She's busy.'

'All right, I'll wait.' A stubborn anger took hold of him. 'How long's she gonna be?'

The stupid woman shook her head, equally stubborn. 'She's not available.'

'Well, have you got any others?' he asked, his whole body beginning to shake with rage.

'Lots of girls.' She shoved the card back across the counter. She was looking back at him with those dull, cow eyes of the native girls on the farm that made his blood fucking boil. Some of his squaddies had the same look – a dull, coarse expression of placid, patient stupidity, better suited to animals.

'I don't *want* any of these fucking girls,' he said slowly, grinding the words out. 'I *told* you. I want a black girl.'

'*Keine schwarzen Mädchen,*' she repeated. 'No black girls.'

He hesitated. He had to keep his hands in his pocket for fear of reaching out and slapping her stupid face. He took a couple of deep breaths, steadying himself, then turned around and walked out. There was a bar on the other side of the road. He walked across and pushed open the door. It was quiet inside. He slipped into the nearest booth, aware that his hands were still shaking. A girl came up to him. '*Zum trinken?*'

'*Ein bier, bitte.*' It was about the extent of his German. She traipsed back to the bar and brought him a cold bottle of Budweiser. He cracked off the top and raised it to his mouth. Whisky and beer. There wasn't a combination like it in the whole fucking world for getting rid of stress.

If she hadn't stopped on the other side of the road to talk to someone, chances were he wouldn't have seen her. He was on his third bottle by then. He looked up, more to relieve his eyes of the gloomy interior than anything else . . . and saw her. She was talking to another girl, a blonde. They stood together for a few minutes, laughing. She was wearing a black coat and her hair was bundled up in a soft hat of some kind. They were standing under the yellow glow of the street light; that was how he saw her. They embraced and walked off in opposite directions. He got up, pulled out another handful of notes, and left the bar. He followed her back along Bahnhofstrasse on the opposite side, retracing his steps back into town. He was aware of his anger slowly returning, seeping through him as the beer had done, warming him from within. Why had she turned him down? They walked down Mühlerstrasse towards the town centre. She stopped at a chemist's; he hung around in the shadow of a shop awning on the other side of the road, only crossing to join her once she'd crossed into Marktpassage, taking the short cut towards the river. It was bitterly cold now, but he didn't feel it. He walked quietly after her, focusing only on the black coat and the blue-and-white striped hat. Her legs were thin and dark, he noticed. She was wearing boots, but no stockings, as far as he could tell. He didn't want to get too close. He wanted to wait until there were fewer people, then he'd stop her . . . ask her why. That was all. He just wanted to know *why*.

They must have been walking along for a good ten minutes before it dawned on him that they were in the woods beside the river, no longer in town. Where the hell was she going? He looked around him; there was nothing, not a sound, not a light. On the other side of the river, the street lights glowed weakly. Here, in the darkness of the trees, all was black. A light flurry of snow had begun to fall. She was just a few yards in front of him. There was a fork in the path up ahead – one path led to the housing estate on the other side of Wittingerstrasse . . . perhaps that was where she lived? She was mad. Granted, it was a short cut from the brothel where she worked but walking through the woods on a dark winter's evening wasn't for the faint-hearted. Suddenly the figure in front of him stopped. It was as if she'd read his mind. He stopped at once, moving backwards into the shadowy darkness of the woods. She turned her head slowly, like an animal, sniffing the air. He stood very still. She drew her handbag close towards her and then it all seemed to happen at once. He stepped back out onto the path, intending to follow her, but she whirled round, caught sight of him and suddenly broke into a run. Stupid girl. She ran down the wrong path, towards the river. He began to jog after her.

It was the way she did it that enraged him. She assumed automatically that he was going to hurt her, hit her. Why should she assume that? She put up her hands as soon as he grabbed hold of her coat. '*Bitte* . . .' she choked out, holding her head back and twisted away from him as if she couldn't bear to look at him. He stared at her, anger breaking over his body like sweat. There was something unbearably haughty about the way she looked down the length of her face at him, even though he was so much taller than her. Her nostrils, those wide, scrolled edges that he'd only ever seen on natives, her whiter-than-snow teeth and the dark, bottomless eyes that flickered over him in the same way Dani's had when she thought he wasn't looking. A mixture of some emotion – pity? – came over her face as he pulled her round to him. He grabbed hold of her hair – the thousand and one little braids that felt like rope in his hands – and twisted her round so that she was facing him. She looked up at him with those insufferably huge, dark eyes. And then she spat. Full on, straight in his face. A warm dollop of spit that hit him in the eye and cheek. He felt it slide, warm and wet, down the cold plane of his face. Everything went into slow motion.

'Cunt.' He felt the word shoot out of his mouth, compressed between his lips and teeth. 'You fucking *cunt.*'

She spat again. He slapped her. She said something in her own language, he had no idea what, but the sound of it assaulted him. He hit her again. There was no other sound on the path except for the gurgle of water rushing past a few yards from where they stood. She said it again. He drew back his hand, aiming for a punch. He felt her jaw underneath his fist as it made contact. A dull crack. It had been a while since he'd felt that particular combination of bone and skin underneath his own hand. A wave of nauseating anger rose in him like a thundering, crashing waterfall, drowning out everything but the sound of his own breath and the feeling of it surging through his veins. He was gripped with a mad, out-of-control lust. His whole body was swollen with tension and the desire to kick, punch, fuck, grab, squeeze . . . he kicked her again and again. She was on the ground now, heaving deep, frightened breaths. *Ah, you're not talking now, are you, you cunt?* He caught a glimpse of red underwear as her bare legs flailed upwards and there was a great roaring noise inside his head. He reached down and lifted her skirt, tearing it from her and tossing the scrap of material aside. He couldn't stop himself. He wanted to be inside her, stabbing her, literally, pushing himself through her to some other, cleaner, purer side. She wouldn't shut up, though. She weighed nothing but was surprisingly strong. Her legs came up to kick at him, catching him on the side of his chest, his ribs, his shins. He grabbed hold of her throat, as he'd been taught to do to incapacitate a would-be attacker. By cutting off the supply of oxygen to the brain, whoever he was struggling with would lose the ability to think, or to strategise. It worked. Her kicks subsided almost immediately. Her neck was paper-thin – he could circle it easily with one hand. With his other, he tore away the last of her resistance and guided himself in. Women were the same the world over. A vessel – hot and damp, no matter the circumstances. He began to thrust himself in and out, his whole body taken up with the effort of pushing himself in. She had stopped wriggling underneath him, stopped making any sort of movement, or sound. There was absolute silence. The only noise he could discern seemed to be coming from him. He felt a great roaring coming towards him from his own heavy pounding, like the breaking, tumbling rush of a waterfall. It all came rushing at him – his father, Edie's jeering face, Dani's sly looks of pity, Sam's incomprehension . . . the phrases, the report, the note . . . everything, all at once, the failures, the shame, the blame. He gave one last desperate shove. And then all was still.

103

ABBY
Celle, Germany, 2009

The phone was ringing as she came through the front door, a rather sleepy and exceedingly heavy Sadie in her arms. She put her down on the sofa, deposited her shopping bags and ran through to pick the phone up. Just as she reached it, it stopped. 'Fuck,' she said to herself, then looked guiltily around to see if Sadie had heard. She was forever telling the girls off about bad language. Sadie was fast asleep. She was just about to turn back to take the stuff to the kitchen when it began again. 'Hello? Abby Barclay speaking.'

'Abby?' It was Ralph. 'Abby?' He sounded agitated.

'Hello, darling. Yes, it's me. What's the matter?'

'Abby . . . I'm going to be home late tonight. Something's happened.'

'What?'

'I can't talk about it right now. I'll be home late . . . hopefully before midnight.'

'Ralph . . . what is it?'

'I can't talk. I'll fill you in later.' His voice was strained. He put down the phone before she could ask anything further. She looked at it for a second, then picked it up again and dialled Sam's mobile.

'Has Nick rung you?' she asked, hoping she wouldn't get into trouble with Ralph.

'No. Why? What's the matter?'

'I don't know. Ralph just rang . . . he said he probably wouldn't be back until midnight tonight. Something's happened but he wouldn't say what.'

'No idea. He was home late last night. Nick, I mean. And he left really early this morning. I was still asleep when he went.'

'Hmm. Wonder what it is. D'you want to come round for supper? I made a roast chicken but I don't really fancy eating on my own. I'll ring Meaghan. Maybe she's heard something. I'll call you back.'

'OK. I'll wait to hear from Nick. If he hasn't called by five, I'll come over.'

'Why don't you just ring him?'

'He . . . he doesn't like it when I ring him at work,' Sam said quickly. 'I'll . . . I'll just wait to hear from him.'

Abby shrugged. 'OK. Well, maybe see you later. I'm going to see if I can find out what's going on.' She put down the phone and dialled Meaghan's number. 'Have you heard anything?' she asked quickly.

'Tom just rang. Said he might not be back tonight. What happened?'

'No idea. Ralph said the same thing. He just said he couldn't talk.'

'D'you want to come over here for tea?' Meaghan asked.

'Well, I just asked Sam the same thing. I made a roast chicken. Bring Alannah over and she can sleep in Clara's room.'

'OK. I'll bring a bottle of wine. See you around six.'

Sadie and Alannah were delighted at the unexpected break from routine. They were put to bed at eight and could be heard enthusiastically discussing what each was getting for Christmas. '*My* mum said . . .'

Meaghan chuckled. 'She'll be lucky. Christ. Christmas already. Can't believe it, can you?'

Abby shook her head. Sam was sitting on the couch, a rather worried expression on her face. 'Don't worry, love. He'll phone soon.' Sam nodded but there was a faraway look in her eyes that Abby couldn't quite place. 'Some wine, girls? Now that they're finally in bed.'

'Yes, please.' Meaghan held out her hand for a glass. 'Oh, before I forget . . . I was thinking of going into Hanover tomorrow morning to do some Christmas shopping. Anyone feel like coming along? One of the ladies from the crèche is going to take the children ice-skating so it seems like a perfect time. Sam?'

'Oh, yes . . . maybe. I'll . . . I'll just check what Nick's doing.'

'What's the weather going to be like tomorrow?' Abby asked, picking up the remote. 'Did they say it would snow?'

'Don't ask me,' Meaghan said with a wry smile. 'We haven't got round to getting Sky so it's only the German channels . . . between me and Tom we can just about figure out what time *Lost* is on, but that's about it. It's the only one they don't dub.'

Abby smiled and flicked through the channels. Suddenly she stopped. She stood still in the middle of the living room, the remote still pointing at the screen, staring at it. The other two looked first at her, then at the screen. All three of them were rooted to the spot.

'That's . . . that's Trenchard Barracks,' Meaghan said incredulously. 'That's the officers' mess. What are they saying?' She turned to Abby, wide-eyed.

Abby's mouth was open. 'There's been an incident . . . someone's been killed, a girl. She was raped. They think it was a soldier who attacked her.' The image swung from the barracks to the river. 'There's the river. It happened by the river.'

'What are they saying?'

'She was a prostitute, worked at one of those bars by the station. They haven't named her yet. Someone in the bar where she worked called the police earlier this afternoon. Judy's Kino Bar. Look!' The picture swung again to the bar that they'd all passed on their way to and from the railway station at one point during their stay in Celle. 'I didn't know it was a brothel.' Abby struggled to keep up with the translation. The picture switched suddenly and another item of news came on. The three women were left staring at the screen, and each other.

Meaghan sat down heavily on the couch. 'Christ,' she said, taking a large gulp of wine. 'That's *all* they need right now. I just hope it wasn't anyone in . . . in any of *our* companies,' she said quickly, looking at the others.

'Not *again*,' Abby groaned. 'What's the matter with these squaddies? It's Cyprus all over again. The press'll have a field day. They already hate the fact that we're here. I just hope she wasn't a local girl.'

They stared at each other, not knowing what to say. Suddenly Sam got up from the couch. She put down her drink and walked to the door, not meeting anyone's eye. 'I . . . I've got to go,' she said, hurriedly pulling her coat off the rack. 'I . . . I'll see you tomorrow,' she mumbled, pulling her hat over her eyes. Before either Meaghan or Abby could say a word, she was gone.

104

SAM
Celle, Germany, 2009

She shoved her key in the lock with hands that were shaking so badly she couldn't hold the key properly. Knocking a fist against the doorway as she ran, she fell to her knees in front of the toilet, vomiting everything up – chicken, potatoes, wine . . . everything. She gasped between the spasms, tears of effort dripping from her eyes and nose. She laid her head on the rim, crouching over it, struggling for breath. As soon as the image had flashed up – Judy's Kino Bar – she knew where she'd seen it before. It wasn't on her way to and from the station. It was here, in the house. She got up, her whole being flooded with a desperate agitation. She pushed open the door to the spare room, wiping her nose with the back of her hand. She swept the magazines and papers off the top of the plastic box and prised open the lid. She burrowed through the photographs and paraphernalia until she came to the stack of cards, DVDs and leaflets she hadn't had the courage to face. One of them had caught her eye – a business card, a calling card. *Judy's Kino Bar. Your girl today was* _____. A scrawled, handwritten name that she couldn't read. *Cum again.* She stared at the card, tears blurring her sight. She clenched it in her hand, crumpling it, scrunching it to nothingness. She blew her nose, wiped her face and then knelt down next to the trunk. She began to take the DVDs out, one by one. She couldn't even bring herself to read the titles. Then the cards. One after the other. *Sauna. Massage. Escorts.* She stacked them to one side. Then the leaflets.

When she was done, she took everything through to the kitchen. She opened the door of the washing machine. She was breathing hard. There was a load inside. She'd started to take it out that afternoon but had stopped because of the snow. She hated the smell of damp laundry so she'd simply put it back in, thinking she'd put it in the dryer later. She took out the clothes, searching for Nick's load that she'd taken out that morning. She pulled out the trousers, cotton long-sleeved shirt and the camouflage jacket that she'd inspected earlier, puzzled by the tear marks and the traces of something brownish down one of the sleeves. She looked at the jacket again and closed her eyes. She sat back on her haunches, her mind racing over possibilities she'd never thought she would call upon. Then she got up and hurriedly fished out a plastic bag from under the kitchen sink. She stuffed everything in it – DVDs, cards, clothes – and got to her feet. The door slammed behind her; she was outside in the cold. Her bike was lying propped against the wall. She yanked it away, got on, her hands struggling to balance the handlebars with her bag banging awkwardly around her legs. She pedalled jerkily up the road, away from the houses towards the hospital. It was dark and the ground was frosty underneath her wheels. She cycled up the deserted street, light looming and fading as she passed the sodium street lamps under whose gentle glow small flakes of snow could be seen, falling, falling.

The hospital grounds were deserted. She flung the bicycle away from her, letting it land on the snow-covered grass, and ran towards the long bank of recycling and rubbish bins. Lifting the lid of the one closest to her, she tossed the bag inside and let it fall shut again. She stood there for a second, snow brushing past her cheeks. Then she turned and ran back to where she'd flung her bicycle, hopped awkwardly on and cycled away. The falling snow was beginning to thicken, covering her tracks.

Nick did not come home that night. Sam lay in the big double bed, the pillow pressed tightly against her head as if to ward off something – a dream, her own thoughts, fears, real or imagined? She slept a little, then woke, staring blankly into the darkness. As if an answer might be found there in the shadowy, half-familiar shapes of the things she'd brought to his flat in an attempt to make it a home. Dawn came up slowly; it had snowed almost all night. The sounds of the morning were muffled – a car starting somewhere down the road, the far-off church bells and the muted ripple of a dog barking over the voice of its owner. *Komm rein. Komm mal hier.* She lay in the cocoon of the new feather-filled duvet and blankets until the heat of her own body drove her out. She made the bed as she did every morning, plumping the pillows and smoothing down the sheets. In her dressing gown and slippers, she put the percolator on and then went through to the bathroom to shower and change.

She was in the dining room drinking her coffee and nibbling distractedly at a piece of toast when she heard the front door open. She put the cup down carefully, her heart suddenly beginning to beat faster. She could hear him in the bedroom; it was the first doorway on the left. She waited. There was almost no sound in the apartment; the radio was silent. She looked up. He was standing in the doorway. A strange, detached calm came over her. She pushed back her chair and got up. She walked over to him and touched him lightly on the arm. 'Coffee?' she asked, in a voice that was so normal and balanced it astonished her. From where had it come?

He nodded without saying anything. There was a moment when their eyes met as she passed – she looked up, unblinking, into the grey-blue pools of light that she had never been able to fathom. His eyelids were heavy. He lifted them thickly and slowly, looking down at her. She saw then that colour has to do with focus and that the particular feature of his outward gaze lacked it – *that* was the reason she could never decide, or decipher. Grey or blue? Light or dark? Seeing or blind? She felt the urge to say something, anything, rise in her throat but before she could open her mouth, it died down again, slipped away. She passed under his arm, not touching it, and went into the kitchen. Her movements were slow and precise – his favourite mug, coffee almost to the brim, no milk, one sugar. She stirred it carefully and brought the mug back through.

'I'll have to go back in again,' he said, taking it from her. 'Did the CO's wife ring you?'

The CO's wife. The 2/i/c's wife. The major's wife. Funny how they couldn't bring themselves to refer to each other's wives by their first names. 'Yes,' she nodded. 'We saw it on the news last night.' She wanted to say more, but couldn't. She waited for him to speak.

'A couple of lads've been taken in. There was a bit of a party in one of the bars in town, apparently.'

'Oh.'

'Anyhow, they'll get to the bottom of it.' He lifted his hand to scratch his head in an unconscious gesture of strain. 'I'd better take a shower.'

'I'll make breakfast.'

'Thanks.'

She sat for a long time at the dining table after he'd gone. She heard the snap and sigh of the back door opening and closing as the other inhabitants of the flats let themselves in and out. In the morning light and faint warmth, the snow had turned to rain. She could hear it slushing wetly against the window panes. She ought to get up, put on her coat, walk across the road and up Halkettstrasse to Abby's house to be amongst friends. She ought not to be alone. This was not the time to be alone. She got up slowly, levering herself up from the table with her hands. She felt heavy, absurdly heavy. She had a sudden longing to hear Paula's voice. Paula would tell her what was wrong. And how to right it.

105

ABBY
Celle, Germany, 2009

'I'll make you another cup,' Abby said, getting up from the table. 'A strong one. What time d'you have to be back?'

Ralph's shoulders were slumped with fatigue. He looked at

his watch. 'About half an hour. I'll get one of the lads to pick me up. I'm not sure I can drive. Not in this weather, anyway.'

'It's better when it's snowing,' Abby said distractedly as she passed into the kitchen. She put the little Italian stove-top on to boil. She stuck her head out of the door and looked down the corridor towards Sadie's room. She was still fast asleep. She and Meaghan had carried the sleeping Alannah out just before midnight; the disrupted night was reason enough to let her sleep in. Thank goodness it was a Saturday. She ought to ring Sam. Strange how she'd just rushed out like that, that funny look of anguish on her face. 'What's going to happen?' she asked, bringing him his third cup of coffee.

'I don't know. They've taken in two of B Coy's lads for questioning. No arrests yet . . . hopefully they'll get to the bottom of it by Monday. Christ, I need this like I need a hole in my head.'

'Ralph . . . a girl's dead,' Abby murmured automatically.

'I know. I'm being insensitive. But I can't afford any more distractions, especially not something like this. You know what it's like. Morale starts to slip, things start going wrong. I've lost enough men over the past couple of months as it is. The fact that they're Beasdale's men doesn't help either.'

'It's hardly his fault, though,' Abby said, buttering another piece of toast. There was a moment's hesitation. She looked up. Ralph was looking at her as though he wanted to say something. 'What?' she asked.

'Look, keep this to yourself, will you, Abs? I don't want this to get out. At least not now.'

'What is it?'

'It's been decided. Beasdale's not going to Cyprus and he's not taking B Coy into Afghanistan. We're replacing him.'

Abby stared at him. 'Why?'

'He's not up to it, Abs. I did my best . . . wrote him as clean a report as I could but the decision's out of my hands.'

'Does he know?'

Ralph nodded. 'Sent him a copy of the report on Thursday. Don't say anything, will you? Not to Sam.'

'I won't,' Abby said slowly. 'But what'll this mean for him?'

Ralph shrugged. 'Just another passed-over major. He'll either resign straight away or he'll stick it out for a couple more years until he's pensionable. You know what happens to men like that. We've seen it often enough.'

Abby was silent. She couldn't have cared less about Nick. It was Sam she was worried about. 'Poor Sam,' she said slowly. 'Bet she won't be expecting this.'

'Probably not. But she'll be fine,' Ralph said, getting up. 'She'll work it out. Smart girl.'

'So you keep saying.'

She had just come back from taking Sadie to the park when the phone rang again. She unwrapped her scarf and hurried to it, hoping it was Sam. She'd rung her a couple of times that morning already but she hadn't picked up the phone. 'Hello?' she said breathlessly. 'Sam?'

'No, it's me.' It was Ralph. 'Something else has come up,' he said, and his voice was strained. 'It'll be on the news shortly. Listen, I want you to ring Meaghan and get her to come round to ours with Alannah right away. Tell her to pack a few things, enough for a couple of nights. There may be reporters outside her door in an hour or so. Just make sure she's with you.'

'Ralph . . . what's going on?'

'I . . . I can't talk right now. I don't know when I'll be home. But just get Meaghan over to you.'

'Ralph . . . ?' But the line was dead. Her fingers shaking, she rang Meaghan straight away. 'I don't know,' she said, fielding Meaghan's questions as best she could. 'He wouldn't say. Have you heard from Tom?'

'No. And he's not picking up his mobile. It's not like him. What's going on?'

'I've no idea but Ralph said you're to get here as soon as you can. Bring a change of clothes – he said you might have to stay over for a couple of nights. Meg . . . don't worry, please. Just get here as soon as you can.'

'Have you heard from Sam?'

'No, she's not picking up her mobile either. As soon as you get here, I'll nip up the road and see if she's at home.' She put down the phone. Her hands were still shaking. Something was definitely wrong, but she didn't know what.

Meaghan was there in half an hour. There was a look of such bewildered fear in her eyes that Abby just held her for a few moments, stroking her hair. 'It'll be fine, whatever it is. Tom's probably had to go down to the police station, something like that. It might have been one or two of his men . . . who knows?'

'But he would've called me,' Meaghan said indistinctly. She was trying not to break down in front of the girls. Alannah looked on with the watchful, sceptical wariness that children sometimes display when they know they are being lied to.

'It's nothing, darling,' Abby said, bending down towards her. 'Nothing at all. Just something that happened at Daddy's work.'

'Where's my daddy?' Alannah asked and Abby saw, for all her self-assuredness, the beginnings of her own brand of childish fear.

'He'll be back this evening. Daddy will too,' she said to Sadie, who was looking fearfully on. 'Come on. Come into the kitchen. I've got some of those special Christmas biscuits.' She gave Meaghan a few moments to compose herself. 'Can you keep an eye on them for me?' she whispered as she passed. 'I'm just going to run up to Sam's.'

Meaghan nodded. She blew her nose, collected the two girls by the hand and led them in the direction of milk and biscuits. Abby pulled her coat and scarf from the back of the door and was gone before anyone would notice.

The flat seemed to be empty; Abby knocked loudly on the back door but there was no answer. She walked around the dustbins to the front and stepped carefully over the flowerbeds. She

531

peered in through the living room windows . . . there was no one. The place was eerily quiet.

'*Suchen Sie jemand?*' A voice behind her made her whirl round. It was an elderly man, holding onto a dog.

She clambered out of the flowerbeds, embarrassed. '*Meine Freundin,*' she stammered.

'Ah. *Sie ist heute morgen weg gefahren. Zum Flughaven.*'

Abby stared at him. She's gone to the airport? Yes, he confirmed. She left early that morning in a taxi. With a suitcase. He *presumed* it was the airport . . . she'd used the airport shuttle service. He seemed eager to talk. Was she British, perhaps? With the army? He'd heard all sorts of rumours in town that morning. Someone had been arrested, or so he'd been told. An officer, no less. Abby continued staring at him. Her heart was hammering against her ribcage. She finally came to her senses. Thanking him for the information, she extracted herself from the muddy, frozen ground as best she could and hurried off down the street. She practically ran all the way up Halkettstrasse and hurried round the back of the house.

Meaghan looked up as she came in. 'It's on the news,' she said quietly. Her nose was red with the effort of trying not to cry. 'I can't understand what they're saying but . . . but there's a picture of Tom. I had to switch it off.'

Abby nodded. 'I'll set up a jigsaw puzzle for the girls in Sadie's room,' she said quickly. 'I'll be back in a second. Come on, girls . . . let's find something for you to do.' She took them both by the hand. 'Sam's gone,' she said in a low voice as she passed. 'One of the neighbours said she'd taken the airport shuttle this morning.'

'Gone? Oh, Abby—'

'I'll be back in a sec.' She hustled the girls out of the room before Meaghan broke down completely.

Five minutes later she stood in the living room clutching the phone to her ear. Next to her Meaghan waited, her eyes soaked with fear.

'What did he say?' she asked, her voice breaking as she spoke.

'It's absurd . . . it's absolutely absurd. I can't *believe* it. Tom's been arrested.' She stared at the receiver that she'd just replaced. 'There's got to be some mistake. They've made a mistake. Ralph says we've all just to stay put. For now.' Abby was aware of herself beginning to babble. Next to her, Meaghan was absolutely silent. Tears were sliding down her face. Abby put out an arm and hugged her. 'Don't worry. It's a stupid mistake. They've got him mixed up with someone else . . . don't cry, please. It's unthinkable!' The phone rang again suddenly; both women sprang apart. Abby grabbed it, listened for a few seconds and then slammed it down again. Her face was white.

'Wh-who was it?' Meaghan asked shakily.

'No one. A wrong number,' Abby said shortly. She switched on the television. There was a woman reporter standing beside the river, talking rapidly into the microphone.

'What's she saying?' Meaghan couldn't hold back her tears.

Abby was frowning in concentration. 'Something about . . . something that happened sixty years ago. Wait, don't you remember? That morning we were all sitting at Café Müller. Sam asked me something . . . something about the Celler Hasenjagd. She went to a lecture that afternoon at the museum. I never asked her what it was about.'

'What's that got to do with this?'

'There was an inmate, a girl, on her way to the Bergen Belsen Concentration Camp. The trains carrying the prisoners derailed or something, just outside Celle. The locals apparently hunted them down . . . *that's* why it's called the Celle Hare Hunt. She was raped and murdered on the tow-path, in exactly the same spot, but it turned out it was a British officer who'd done it. Oh, Jesus . . . this is bad, Meaghan,' Abby whispered. 'This is really bad. The press are going crazy.'

As if on cue, there was a loud hammering at the front door. Both women looked at each other in fright. Meaghan's face was white. Abby swallowed. She had to get a grip on herself. There were two little girls in the bedroom; Meaghan was about to fall to pieces. 'I'll get it. Just stay here.'

The front door was on a chain. She opened it cautiously. Two uniformed soldiers and a woman she recognised from Army Welfare were standing outside. Behind them was an army jeep and behind that, a black, unmarked car with an antenna – the press.

'Morning, Mrs Barclay.' One of the soldiers identified himself. 'Staff Sergeant Kettering. I've been asked to escort Mrs Astor and her daughter to a hotel. CO thinks it'll be safer for them.'

Abby nodded. 'Just give me a moment,' she said and closed the door again. She took a couple of deep breaths. She needed to make sure Meaghan was strong enough to leave with Alannah and then she would go down to the barracks herself. She had to see Ralph. None of it made any sense. Ralph would know as well as she did that Tom Astor was about as capable of doing something like this as she herself was. It was simply unthinkable. But there was something else struggling to assert itself that she daren't even think about. Snatches of an argument she'd had with her father, years ago, were coming back to her now. She shut the lid tightly on the memory and walked into the kitchen. Right now her task was to get Meaghan and Abby safely into that jeep and into the hotel. Everything else could wait.

106

MEAGHAN
Celle, Germany, 2009

If it hadn't been for Abby's presence beside her, she would never have made it into the hotel room. She had the sensation of everything around her beginning to dissolve; it was as if she couldn't trust the ground in front of her to be flat, or solid. It was Abby who'd got Alannah's things together, holding her by the hand and telling her not to worry as they prepared to make a dash for it down the short garden path and into the back of the waiting jeep. She'd insisted on coming with them; the staff sergeant who'd been sent to pick them up wasn't about to argue with the CO's wife. Or Brigadier Hutton's daughter. She could pull out all the stops when she wanted. They scrambled into the back seat together, pushing the children in front of them, and then the soldiers jumped in. They took off with a screeching of tyres – a second later, three cars picked up pursuit. They went flying up the road, not stopping for the speed ramps, tearing down the main road towards the base. The base was off-limits to everyone else, including the press. Once they were inside, Sergeant Kettering shouted over the scream of the engine, they'd swap cars and exit out of the back. They'd be in their hotel room in less than an hour.

Meaghan nodded dumbly, unable to speak. Abby was holding onto her hand so tightly the circulation in her fingers was beginning to stop. Meaghan was trying not to think. The idea that Tom had done it – done *any*thing – was unthinkable. Abby was right – it was a horrible mistake. 'Don't you worry about a thing,' she'd whispered to Meaghan as they packed their belongings and prepared to leave the house. 'I'll speak to my dad this afternoon. This is absolutely ridiculous.' Meaghan couldn't speak. She and Tom were nobodies. Two young people from the outback who'd come to the UK seventeen years earlier with nothing and no one to fall back on except Tom's abilities as a soldier. She turned her head to one side so that Alannah wouldn't see her tears. Over and above the terrifying thought that something might actually happen to Tom over which neither of them had any control, there was something else she couldn't bring herself to admit to. When the news first came on and she'd seen Tom's face – his kind, dependable, handsome face – the thought had flashed through her mind before she could even stop it. *How well do we know anyone?* For one horrible, shameful second, the memory of his return from Kosovo came back to her. Tom had slept with someone else.

Fucked someone else. It wasn't an affair . . . of that she was one hundred per cent sure. Whoever he'd fucked had been someone he'd done it with once and never again. She'd forced herself not to think about it. He was a soldier. He'd been away. Things happen. Girls. Prostitutes. Hookers. She'd gone through the practised list of rationalisations until she'd managed to bury it, willing herself to believe it didn't matter. Whatever he'd done back there had no place in their marriage and certainly not in their home. But that morning, standing in front of the TV, the question had washed over her in a tidal wave of fear and shame. She'd clamped down on it immediately, trembling from head to toe. Now, sitting next to Abby, fear and panic forming, breaking up and reforming again in her throat, the thought kept surfacing again and again. *How well do we know anyone? Ever?*

107

SAM
London, England, 2009

All the way down Elgin Avenue, rolling her small weekend case behind her, Sam could only think about one thing. *Please let Paula be in. Please.* The entire day had been a series of steps; she'd been unable to think beyond each one. How to get from Celle to Hanover. How to get on the plane. How to get from Stansted to Liverpool Street, and then onto Maida Vale. She'd been unable to phone – what was to be said had to be done face to face. She couldn't have brought the words up and out of her chest and mouth, sending them spiralling down the line.

She turned into Randolph Avenue. It was the fourth house; third floor. She looked up. The lights were on. She tugged her case up the short flight of stairs and pressed the bell. There was an agonising wait of a few seconds, then she heard Paula's voice, breathing static. 'Hello?'

'Paula.' Her voice came out in a whisper. She tried again. 'Paula. It's me. Sam.'

'Sam? Sam . . . what are you . . . come up! It's freezing outside!'

The door buzzed and she pushed it open. She wasn't cold. She wasn't even aware it was winter. She heard Paula's door open; a second later, her face appeared three flights above her in the stairwell. There was a huge, surprised smile on her face. As soon as she saw Sam, it faded slowly.

'Sam? What's the matter? Are you all right?'

Sam opened her mouth but, again, nothing came out. She heard the pounding of feet. A second later, Paula was beside her in her stockinged feet. 'Sam? What's happened? Here, give me that. Are you all right? Sam! Talk to me. Say something!'

'I . . . I'm OK. I just got here. I didn't know . . . I didn't think . . . I couldn't call you, I'm sorry.'

'Sorry? For what . . . Jesus, Sam . . . your hands are *freezing*. Why haven't you got any gloves? Come in, come in.' She shut the door behind them both and turned to her. 'What's going on? Is . . . are you alone?'

Sam nodded. She suddenly needed to sit down. The room was beginning to sway. She allowed Paula to lead her to the sofa. She sat down heavily and buried her face in her hands. Paula was beside her; she felt her hand on her shoulder. The build-up of pressure in her chest was unbearable. There was a tidal wave of unspoken words and suppressed emotion waiting to break. She caught and held her breath . . . and then it all came rushing out, unstoppable and unchecked. Six months of things she'd been afraid to say or think, layer upon layer, painfully constricted and trapped somewhere deep within. One word followed another and the whole tight edifice came crashing down.

The radio was playing very softly in the background; Paula had been working when she arrived. She could hear the tinny, half-grasped snatch of some song she'd heard a hundred times before that autumn. There was an untouched cup of tea in front of her.

Paula stood up suddenly. She went to the kitchen without saying anything and fetched two glasses. She reached up to a shelf above the fridge and pulled down a bottle of brandy. 'Here,' she said, pouring a glass as she walked over. 'Get this down you. You've got to get some sleep. I'll sort out the tickets. You go to bed.'

'Tickets?' Sam looked up at her questioningly. Her throat ached with tears and her head was pounding.

'We're going back to Germany. First thing tomorrow morning. You and me. You're going to that rubbish dump, you're going to get that plastic bag out of there – if it hasn't been disposed of already – and then we're going straight to the police. Drink the rest of that and then let's get you to bed.'

'But—'

'But nothing. I never liked him. No one did. And none of us had the guts to say so.'

108

ABBY
Celle, Germany, 2009

It was past midnight when Ralph finally came home. He'd been gone for almost two days. Abby was sitting in the chair by the fireplace when she heard the car pull up outside. She sprang up and peered through the curtains. She had to put a hand to her mouth to stop herself crying out loud – though whether in relief or fear at what would happen next she couldn't say.

She was waiting on the other side of the door when he came in. He looked at her and in his face was all the tension and worry and strain of the previous two days. He buried his face in her shoulder, his hands going up to her hair. He loosened the knot that held it up and she felt it cascading over his arms.

'Darling,' she whispered. 'I'm so glad you're home.'

He nodded, but didn't say anything.

'What's happening . . . what have they said?'

He sighed, a long, drawn-out release that made her hair stand on end. 'He's with the military police . . . they're liaising with the Germans. I . . . I don't know what's going to happen. He'll be kept in the cell overnight and formally arraigned tomorrow. It's . . . it's *inconceivable*. Tom? It's just not possible.'

'Why do they think he did it?' Abby's voice was tight, echoing his disbelief.

'He gave the girl behind the desk his name, apparently. And he's got no alibi. That's the thing . . . everyone else is accounted for. He says he was in his office doing paperwork but there's no record of any activity on his computer and he made no phone calls during the time the girl left the bar and when she was found two and a half hours later. Everyone else has an alibi.'

'And Beasdale?' Abby's voice was quiet.

'He was in the gym. Two of his squaddies were with him. They've both sworn statements to that effect. I just can't believe it. I just can't believe it.'

'Sam's gone,' Abby said suddenly.

'What d'you mean, gone?' He looked at her sharply.

She lifted her shoulders and let them drop again. 'She left this morning, apparently. Took a shuttle to the airport. She's not picking up her mobile phone.'

'And Meaghan? How's she taking it?'

'They're in the hotel. I came back to the base with Kettering but I couldn't find you. They kept saying you were in with the army lawyers and that you couldn't be interrupted.'

'Well, they were right. Have you seen the news? I keep getting reports . . . haven't seen it myself. Not that I'd understand much. Have the UK got hold of it yet?'

Abby shook her head. 'Not that I've seen. But it'll only be a matter of time. That whole story about the girl in 1945 . . . it's awful, Ralph. It's like Cyprus all over again.'

Ralph was silent. 'At least she wasn't from round here,' he said slowly, his hand going up to feel the back of his neck.

'Who was she? Do they know? The media aren't saying.'

'She was black. An African girl. They think she's from Liberia.'

'Liberia? Wasn't . . . isn't that where Beasdale was before he was transferred here?'

Ralph shook his head. 'Sierra Leone. But that doesn't mean anything,' he sighed.

'There's something not quite right here,' Abby said. 'I mean, why would Sam take off like that? Without a word to anyone? And . . . and there's something else. Something I probably should have told you.'

Ralph looked at her quickly. 'What?'

Abby swallowed nervously. They were standing in the hall-way. Ralph hadn't even taken off his jacket yet. 'I know I should have told you . . . but . . . you remember the girl in Cyprus? The Ukrainian girl? Well, I did go to the funeral. I took the bus. I just couldn't bear the thought of no one being there. But there *was* someone else there, from our side, I mean. That was the first time I saw him.'

'Who?'

'Beasdale. He was the only other person at the service. We didn't speak . . . I'd never seen him before in my life. But I did remember his face and I caught a glimpse of his badge as the bus passed. That's why I was surprised he was here . . . he wasn't in Cyprus very long and I just wondered why.'

Ralph was looking at her with an expression she didn't recognise. He was quiet for a long time. Finally he reached out with one hand and pulled her towards him. He hugged her, hard. His mouth was somewhere close to her ear, his voice muffled by her hair. 'Don't say anything to anyone, Abs, promise?' he said quietly. 'Just . . . just stay out of this for the time being. And don't say anything to your father.'

'Why? What's going on?' she whispered back.

He shook his head. 'Just don't.'

She clung to him. Within the space of a couple of days, everything was turned upside down. Sam was gone; Tom had been arrested for something she would have sworn on her life he couldn't have done; Meaghan and Alannah were in a hotel on the other side of the river . . . and a girl was dead. It just didn't make sense. None of it made sense any more. Not even Ralph. *Don't say anything to your father.* The argument she'd had with her father, years earlier, which she'd done her best to forget, came back to her now, sending new ripples of anxiety crawling over the surface of her skin. Someone had, in her father's own words, 'been hung out to dry'. She no longer remembered the details, or even who it was. But she'd been at the dinner table one evening when the conversation turned to an officer who'd been arrested for something it was clear he hadn't done. Sacrifices have to be made, her father had said, tipping back the rest of his wine. She was fifteen or sixteen at the time. She'd spoken out of turn. Her mother had done her best to deflect the conversation from the unruly teenager but it was too late. She'd looked at them all . . . her father, his colleagues and friends, their wives . . . she'd shouted something. Something dramatic. 'You disgust me!' They'd smiled quietly, politely. 'Sometimes an injustice takes place that's for the greater good, Abigail.' Something along those lines. She'd flounced out of the room, her adolescent sense of outrage duly provoked. She could feel Ralph's heart thudding quietly underneath the scratchy fabric of his jacket. He too felt the fear. He had a battalion to keep together, men whose loyalty he had to secure. Was Tom Astor going to be sacrificed for the greater good? Dear God, surely not? Not Tom?

109

SAM
Celle, Germany, 2009

Her teeth chattering, and not just from the cold, she lifted up the lid of the bin. She remembered exactly which one. Paula was standing next to her, watching intently for anyone coming down the path. 'Quick,' she hissed. 'Is it there?'

'I can't see . . . there's a whole lot of stuff on top . . . the bin's full.'

'Well, that's a good sign. They probably haven't emptied them. Hurry!'

'I'm looking . . . yes, there it is.'

'Quick. Pull it out.'

Sam grabbed hold of the green M & S bag and yanked it out. A couple of loose cans, some orange peel and a few banana skins came with it. They both stared at it – the DVDs made an awkward angle on one side; the plastic had ripped a little and the corner of one of the boxes was poking out.

'Come on. Let's go before anyone sees us.' Paula was firm. They turned and walked back down the path to the main road, neither speaking. Sam's heart was hammering inside her chest. She couldn't believe she'd been gone only a day. She hadn't heard a word from Nick. She'd been too scared to go into the flat when they arrived and had checked into the Ibis hotel across the river instead. Neither of them intended to stay the night. Their plan was clear. They would retrieve the bag if they could, take it to Ralph and explain what she'd done. Then she and Paula would leave for the airport and military law would run its course. She couldn't think beyond that; getting the bag to Ralph was all she could manage.

They walked in silence back down Schlepergrellstrasse. She fished her mobile out of her pocket. There were at least a dozen missed calls from Abby. She drew in a deep breath and dialled. Abby picked up on the second ring. 'Sam? Oh, thank God . . . where are you? Where did you go?'

'Abby, I'll explain later. I'm back in Celle. I've got Paula with me. Are you at home?'

'Yes, but don't come here. There're reporters everywhere. I'll meet you at the base. Where are you exactly?'

'Schlepergrellstrasse. It'll take us about twenty minutes. But Abby . . . I don't want to see Nick.'

There was a sharp intake of breath. 'Fine. Meet me at the Officers' Wives Club. He'll never go there.'

She hung up and turned to Paula. 'Come on. Abby'll take the bag to him.'

'Sam . . . oh, *Sam!*' Abby was waiting in the hallway as they walked in. She rushed up to her, hugging her tightly. 'Christ . . . have you heard? Tom's been arrested. Meaghan and Alannah are in a hotel. The whole thing's gone haywire. What's this?'

Sam held up the plastic bag. 'It's all in here, Abby. Everything. Can you give it to Ralph? He'll know what to do with it.'

Abby looked at her questioningly. Her eyes widened. 'Wh . . . what are you talking about?'

'It's all there. He did it. Not Tom.' Sam's eyes were glassy with unshed tears. 'Give it to Ralph. Make sure he gets it, no one else.'

'Sam . . . where are you going?'

'Back to London. I can't stay here another second, Abby. I *can't.*'

'But . . . but what about your stuff? In the flat? What about Nick?'

'I don't care about any of it,' Sam said slowly, swallowing hard. 'I don't care what happens to it. I don't want any of it.'

Abby looked from her to Paula and back again. She nodded, holding tightly onto the bag. 'What d'you want me to tell him?' she asked. 'Ralph, I mean.'

Sam was quiet for a moment. Then she lifted her head. 'Tell him I should have brought it to him straight away and I didn't. And that I'm sorry. If I'd come to you as soon as I found it, Tom wouldn't be in jail right now.'

Abby bit her lip. She looked at the bag, then back at Sam. 'No, I'm the one who's sorry, Sam. I've no idea what this has cost you. Are you all right?'

Sam nodded slowly. 'Not right now. But I will be.'

'Get out of here,' Abby said, motioning them both towards the door. 'You're the lawyer . . . you know what to do. Get on that plane. I'll see you in London.'

Sam nodded. 'Will you tell Meaghan that I'm sorry?' she asked, a lump suddenly forming in her throat. 'I . . . I should never have let it happen.'

'It's not your fault. Now scram. Call me from London.' Abby was doing her best not to cry.

Sam's face was wet as she pushed her way through the double doors at the end of the corridor and she and Paula quickly made their way to the gate. She looked back at the austere façades of the barracks, dulled even further under the leaden sky. The trees were stripped bare; silhouetted against the fading light, they cast a ghostly, spider's web of branches onto the snow-covered ground. She pulled her woollen hat down over her forehead and tucked her scarf right up to her chin. She and Paula walked across the road in silence. At the end, she flagged down a passing cab. She didn't look back.

Epilogue

DANI
Frankfurt Airport, Germany, 2010

It was the headline that caught her eye. That, and the picture of a uniformed soldier. *Disgraced: British Army Brought into Disrepute.* She picked up the magazine curiously. Per had gone ahead and was waiting at the checkout with his habitual stack of newspapers and magazines, including his own. He looked back down the queue, glancing enquiringly at her – coming? She nodded, but waved him on. 'I'll catch up with you outside,' she mouthed. The queue was already forming in between them. He nodded, and turned away.

She flicked the magazine open. *The Girls, The Lies, The Major and His Wife. Page 26.* She turned the pages quickly: 22, 24, 26 . . . She stopped, frowning. It took her a few seconds to understand that the face of the man staring back out towards her was Nick. Older, heavier, yes . . . his hair was completely grey. His face was sallow; there were shadows under the eyes and the stubble beneath the mutton-fat pallor of his skin was almost a beard. But the eyes were the same, exactly the same. That peculiar combination of grey and blue that was neither, the gaze that held no focus save its own. There was a welling up of nausea in the pit of her stomach as she looked at him, saliva flooding her mouth. She swallowed and swallowed again. Her eyes skimmed over the article, coming to rest on the third paragraph. The girl was Liberian. There was a picture of her – pretty, wide-eyed and innocent-looking . . . the picture was one taken before she'd managed to make her way to Germany in all likelihood.

She was just twenty. Dani felt a prick of some deeply buried emotion behind her eyes as she read on. The charges laid against him had been reduced to manslaughter . . . some technicality she couldn't fathom. There was a mention of a wife. An English lawyer. No children. A reference to pornography, an unhappy childhood and the army's inability to weed out the rot. She swallowed again and put the magazine away from her, back on the rack, hiding it behind another.

She hoisted her bag on her shoulder and made her way past the queue to the café where Per was waiting. She slid into the seat next to him. She couldn't speak. Suddenly his hand was on hers, holding her by the wrist in the way of a doctor, measuring her heartbeat through her pulse. She began to cry. He held her wrist gently, steadying her. Slowly, since he was in charge of her pace, she began to quieten. *Min lille loppe.* He gestured towards the magazines that were spread on the table before them – his purchases. *I know.* He continued to hold her wrist, loosely, his strong, beautifully shaped fingers stroking out a pattern of comfort against the dark, delicate skin. *Yes, I know.* How *could* he have known? She had said very little about Nick but for all that, he knew. His curiosity was something she hadn't accounted for, she realised suddenly. He was a journalist, after all. It came to her slowly as she sat next to him, waiting for the storm of silent weeping to pass, that the quiet, determined way in which he unravelled the tightly held thread of her life and all the pain it contained was his most valuable gift yet. At the moment when she least expected it, Per had appeared. Without ever saying so, he let her know that the unmanageable misery she sometimes felt was simply part of something larger, shared by millions of other people in ways and forms she couldn't yet grasp or see and the knowledge of it would make it lighter, easier to bear.

She lifted a hand to her cheek, discreetly wiping away the snail's trail of tears. He glanced at her – everything OK? She nodded quickly, decisively. She felt a sudden lightening of her heart, as if she'd cast off something that had weighed her down for too long. She picked up the tiny cup of espresso he'd bought her and took a sip. The thick, bitter liquid flooded her mouth pleasurably. She tipped it back, feeling on her tongue the sudden rush of sweetness as the last drops of melted sugar slipped out. She put it down, settling it neatly into its saucer.

'Ready?' he asked, gathering the pile of newspapers and magazines into a more or less tidy bundle, save one which he left on the table. She glanced at it, nodded again and stood up. He tucked the bundle under one arm and offered her the other. She looked up at him, as if seeing him for the first time. With their arms linked, they walked slowly towards the gate.

The magazine lay open, its thin pages fluttering as passengers moved back and forth in a steady stream around the table-islands. Presently someone else parked his baggage trolley and took a seat. Idly, he pulled it towards him and began to read. Someone else's story. Someone else's life.